Selected Writings 1950-1990

BOOKS BY IRVING HOWE

The American Newness
Socialism in America
A Margin of Hope
Celebrations and Attacks
Leon Trotsky
World of Our Fathers
     (with the assistance of
     Kenneth Libo)
The Critical Point
Decline of the New
Steady Work: Essays in the Politics
     of Democratic Radicalism,
     1953–1966
Thomas Hardy: A Critical Study
A World More Attractive
The American Communist Party:
     A Critical History
     (with Lewis Coser)
Politics and the Novel
William Faulkner: A Critical
     Study
Sherwood Anderson: A Critical
     Biography
The U.A.W. and Walter Reuther
     (with B. J. Widick)

EDITED BY IRVING HOWE

The Penguin Book of Modern
     Yiddish Verse
     (with Ruth R. Wisse and
     Khone Shmeruk)
How We Lived
     (with Kenneth Libo)
The World of the Blue-Collar
     Worker
Essential Works of Socialism
The Seventies: Problems & Proposals
     (with Michael Harrington)
Jewish American Stories
Voices from the Yiddish
     (with Eliezer Greenberg)
A Treasury of Yiddish Poetry
     (with Eliezer Greenberg)
The Idea of the Modern
The Basic Writings of Trotsky
The Radical Imagination
Edith Wharton: A Critical
     Collection
The Radical Papers
A Treasury of Yiddish Stories
     (with Eliezer Greenberg)

IRVING HOWE

Selected Writings 1950–1990

HARCOURT BRACE JOVANOVICH, PUBLISHERS

San Diego   New York   London

Requests for permission to make copies
of any part of the work should be mailed to:
Permissions Department, Harcourt Brace Jovanovich, Publishers,
Orlando, Florida 32887.

Library of Congress Cataloging-in-Publication Data
Howe, Irving.
   [Essays, Selections]
   Selected writings 1950–1990/Irving Howe.—1st ed.
     p. cm.
   ISBN 0-15-180390-0
   I. Title.
  PS29.H68A5 1990
  814'.52—dc20   90-4318

Designed by Trina Stahl

Printed in the United States of America

First edition

A B C D E

To the Memory of Michael Harrington

Contents

Foreword   xiii

Preface   xvii

I THE FIFTIES

Céline: The Sod Beneath the Skin   3

Sholom Aleichem: Voice of Our Past   13

God, Man, and Stalin   19

This Age of Conformity   26

The Stories of Isaac Babel   50

Tomato or Cucumber?   56

The Snopes Saga   59

The Stories of Pirandello   67

II THE SIXTIES

T. E. Lawrence: The Problem of Heroism   77

Anarchy and Authority in American Literature   103

Black Boys and Native Sons   119

The Idea of the Modern   140

Dreiser: The Springs of Desire   167

Robert Frost: A Momentary Stay   179

Bourbon on the Rocks   189

New Styles in "Leftism"   193

Beliefs of the Masters   221

A Grave and Solitary Voice: An Appreciation of
      Edwin Arlington Robinson   229

The New York Intellectuals   240

III THE SEVENTIES

Zola: The Poetry of Naturalism   283

George Konrád's *The Case Worker*   296

The City in Literature   302

Delmore Schwartz: An Appreciation   318

Strangers   324

Lillian Helman and the McCarthy Years   340

George Eliot and Radical Evil   347

IV THE EIGHTIES

Oliver and Fagin   365

Absalom in Israel   374

Why Has Socialism Failed in America?   382

Reaganism: The Spirit of the Times   410

Writing and the Holocaust   424

Justice for Leskov   446

The Fate of Solzhenitsyn   459

Thinking about Socialism   464

Foreword

The first thing to notice about these essays is their range: they deal with literature, politics, and history; with American, Yiddish, French, and Russian writers; with movements, regimes, intellectual coteries, and "solitary voices." This much the table of contents will tell you. The second thing to notice is harder; you have to read the essays, not just the titles, and enter the world of their author. What Irving Howe writes on all his subjects is nourished and disciplined by a concrete, day-in, day-out political commitment. For as many years as he has been writing essays and reviews, he has been active in the organizations and gatherings of the democratic left, as editor, speaker, adviser, comrade. This commitment helps to explain the special qualities, the moral tone and timbre of his literary voice. It militates against the willful obscurity and theoretical high-mindedness of academic "criticism."

Howe has, no doubt, a sense for a language, a disdain for jargon, a stylistic elegance that he was probably born with. But he also has the sense of an audience, a public as much political as literary, a democratic public, waiting to read what he writes. This audience is made up of people whom he respects, people who might be his friends. Not intimates, not insiders or secret initiates of this or that sect or school, not professional adepts, not even graduate students, but men and women

with whom one might talk easily, who would resent fanciness and pre-
tension. I wish this were a larger and a growing audience. The conviction
that underlies Howe's essays is that it might be both; he aims to reach
an audience that is, in principle, as extensive as democracy itself.

Literature lies at the center of Howe's work, but it is rarely his sole
interest. Why have so many of our best writers about society and politics
been men and women of letters? Howe, himself a socialist intellectual,
stands in a larger tradition, European as well as Anglo-American, though
its leading European representatives have more often been novelists
(Silone, Orwell, Camus), its leading English and American representatives literary critics (Arnold, Leavis, Wilson, Trilling). Some time ago,
it seems, literature replaced religion and philosophy as the decisive genre
of confrontation with "real life." And so literary criticism can be a kind
of meditation on how we live and on how we think about how we live.
Philosophers and theologians still write about such matters, of course,
but mostly for their fellow professionals. Social scientists write about
them, but only indirectly, so as not to compromise their claims to scientific authority. Our self-understanding is most powerfully mediated
by literature, and our judgments about ourselves by criticism. The art
of the literary intellectual is to read the novel as a novel, the poem as
a poem, and still reach for a judgment that isn't narrowly literary—to
hear the moral or political resonance of plot and character, verse and
image. Howe provides a model of how this is done.

His essays over forty years constitute a sustained meditation on what
has been, mostly, a bad time. I can think of few writers who have seen
the badness so clearly and spoken about it so consistently. His criticism,
like his politics, is driven by a moral vision. The name of the vision is
socialism, and the principles in which it is best expressed are freedom
and equality. We are often told that these two are incompatible; we
must choose between them. But Howe's refusal to choose has served
him well. It accounts for his uncompromising opposition to totalitarian
regimes and movements (and to several generations of their apologists)
and, at the same time, for his refusal to make his peace with contemporary capitalism. A passion for individual autonomy that derives in
large part from American culture and a passion for equality and solidarity
that derives from European and Jewish immigrant experience come
together in these essays—and there seems no reason to argue for their
separation.

Howe has changed his mind over the years, but not his principles.
He speaks with a remarkably steady voice. There is nothing merely
fashionable in his writing; we sense instead an evident dislike for changing intellectual fashions and for what his friend Harold Rosenberg once

called "the herd of independent minds." Intellectuals have not distinguished themselves in the twentieth century. Too many of them have been fellow travelers of power or flatterers of the "people," serving the interests of the state or the party. In the East, the captive minds that Milosz described were soon replaced by dissident and rebellious minds. In the West, curiously, an uncoerced captivity lasted longer—lasts still. Irving Howe has been a critic of the critics, our own dissident, willing when necessary to stand alone. Readers of these essays will want, I think, to stand with him.

MICHAEL WALZER

Preface

Approaching threescore and ten, no small matter, I have decided to bring together a representative selection of my literary and political essays. Whether these are my "best" I cannot say, nor does it signify. What this selection does, I believe, is to give a reasonably fair picture of an intellectual career spanning four decades.

The essays are arranged in roughly chronological order, and within each group the literary and political ones are mixed, so as to show intertwining, sometimes conflicting, interests at work. Readers preferring a thematic arrangement can easily make up their own table of contents.

Some of the literary essays have been slightly changed—mainly to cut superfluous or clumsy language, rarely to modify an opinion. They remain essentially as written. One or two of my literary essays that once attained a slight notoriety now seem to me dated, and I have omitted them. As for the political and polemical pieces, these of course have not been changed with regard to substance or opinion, since it is obviously improper to grant oneself retrospective wisdom on such matters, unless it be clearly stated as retrospective. Dates of composition appear at the head of the political essays.

Several of the essays appearing in this book, especially those that deal with politics, reflect concerns and feelings specific to their moment—that, in part, is what they should do. Except for two instances, I have not added the sort of retrospective remarks, either by way of self-defense or self-correction, which are sometimes appended in such collections. For I assume my readers are quite capable of deciding on their own when I got things right and when I got them wrong.

The following essays appear for the first time in a book by me: "Absalom in Israel," "Reaganism: The Spirit of the Times," "George Eliot and Radical Evil," "Oliver and Fagin," "Writing and the Holocaust," "Justice for Leskov," "Konrád's *The Case Worker*," and "The Fate of Solzhenitsyn."

I hoped to give adequate representation to the various aspects of my work, but this was not always possible. For reasons of space I had to exclude any essay from *Politics and the Novel,* as well as from any of my book-length studies of individual authors. Nor was it possible to include a fair sample of my writings on Yiddish literature (available in several anthologies I have coedited). As for my political writings, a good portion of them have been journalistic, speaking to a moment, and I have included only a few of these pieces, mostly for the "flavor." But a few of my more ambitious political essays do appear in this book.

It is a book that may raise a question in the minds of some readers: What are we to make of a writer who divides his time and energy among several interests rather than confining himself to one? How does it affect a writer's work if he shuttles between literary and cultural criticism, on the one hand, and political comment, on the other? My belief is that it should be possible for a serious person to hold more than one interest, or one idea, at a time. How well I have done this is for my readers to judge.

I owe thanks in the making of this book to my friend David Bromwich, to my son, Nicholas Howe, to my wife, Ilana, and to my editor, Drenka Willen, all of whom made valuable suggestions and criticisms.

The dedication speaks for a relationship that, for more than forty years, enriched my life.

Selected Writings 1950-1990

I The Fifties

Céline: The Sod
Beneath the Skin

The underground man, as both literary figure and social type, first enters European awareness in the nineteenth century. As rebel against the previously secure Enlightenment, he rejects the claims of science, the ordered worldview of rationalists, the optimism of radicals. He speaks in the accents of romanticism, but a romanticism gone sour. He is tempted neither by knowledge, like Faust, nor by glory, like Julien Sorel; he is beyond temptation of any sort. The idea of ambition he regards as a derangement of ego, and idealism as the most absurd of vanities. He believes—it is the one thing he believes entirely—that the world is intent upon crushing him, and he takes a spiteful pleasure in delaying its victory. That in the end it will crush him, he never doubts.

A creature of the city, he has no fixed place among the social classes; he lives in crevices, burrowing beneath the visible structure of society. Elusive and paranoid, he plays a great many parts yet continues to be recognizable through his unwavering rejection of official humanity: the humanity of decorum, moderation, and reasonableness. Even while tormenting himself with reflections upon his own insignificance, the un-

From *A World More Attractive* (New York: Horizon Press, 1963).

derground man hates still more—hates more than his own hateful self—
the world above ground.

Meek and arrogant, dialectically resourceful and derisive of intellect,
starved for love and scornful of those who offer it, he lives in a chaos
of subterranean passions. Beneath each layer of his being there quivers
another, in radical conflict with the first. He can move in quick succession
from satanic pride to abject humility and then recognize, with mocking
self-approval, that the humility is no more than a curtain for his pride.
From a conviction of his inferiority he abases himself toward everyone—
toward everyone but the men of ordinary decent sentiments who seem
to have escaped the abyss of suffering and are therefore regarded by
him as objects of contempt. Yet to say this is also to notice his conviction
of superiority, for at heart he is gratified by the stigmata of his plight.
Gratified, he indulges in a vast self-pity; but this psychic quick-change
artist can also be mercilessly ironic about that self-pity. He is a master
of parody.

The assumption that man is rational, so important to Western society,
and the assumption that his character is definable, so important to Western literature, are both threatened when the underground man appears.
His emergence signifies the end of the belief that the human being can
be understood by means of a static psychology, and in accordance with
the modernist spirit, he is seen not as a person with a unique ensemble
of traits but as a history of experiences that are often impenetrable.

Brilliantly anticipated in Diderot's *Rameau's Nephew*, the underground man appears full face in Dostoevsky's novels. Here he assumes
his most exalted guise, as a whole man suffering the burdens of consciousness. In *Notes from the Underground* he scrutinizes his motives with
a kind of phenomenological venom; and then, as if to silence the moralists of both Christianity and humanism, he enters a few relationships
with other people, relationships that are commonplace yet utterly decisive in revealing the impossibility of escape from his poisoned self.

In the twentieth century the underground man comes into his own
and, like a rise of pus, breaks through the wrinkled skin of tradition.
He appears everywhere in modern literature, though seldom with the
intellectual resources that Dostoevsky accorded him. In France, during
the thirties, Louis-Ferdinand Céline published several novels in which
he expressed with exuberant completeness the underground man's revulsion from the modern world.

2

Céline was born in Paris in 1894. His life was shaped primarily by
his sufferings in World War I, during which he was severely wounded

and had to undergo several operations on his skull. Throughout his remaining years he was tormented by migraines. "My own trouble's lack of sleep," he once wrote, "I should never have written a line if I'd been able to sleep." Working as a doctor in a poor neighborhood of Paris, Céline wrote and published in 1932 his first novel, *Journey to the End of the Night (Voyage au bout de la nuit)*, in which he picked up the story of his life at the close of adolescence and carried it through his middle years. The book was an immediate critical success, with figures as various as André Gide, Ramon Fernandez, and Leon Trotsky saluting its irascible vitality.

Journey to the End of the Night is composed as a series of loosely related episodes, a string of surrealist burlesques, fables of horror and manic extravaganza, each following upon the other with energy and speed. While the sort of novel Céline wrote—a wandering first-person narrative, picaresque in structure and expressionist in manner—presupposes an intimate relationship between author and central character, he was describing less the actual events of his life than their hallucinatory echoes of sleepless nights. The material in these novels is frequently appalling, yet the voice of the narrator is not at all what we have come to expect in the literature of exposure. It is not a voice of cultivated sensibility, nor of moral anguish, and only on occasion does it rise to indignation. Céline writes in a tone of cheerful nausea, largely beyond bitterness or protest, as if he had decided to leave behind the metaphysics of Dostoevsky and the emotions of romanticism. Dostoevsky's underground man trembles in fright and despair before the possibility of nihilism; Céline's no longer regards a valueless existence as anything but a fact of life to be taken for granted.

Just as the hero of his novels is utterly unheroic ("I wasn't very wise myself but I'd grown sensible enough to be definitely a coward forever"), so is the style of these novels the opposite of literary. Fierce, sputtering, brawling, sometimes on the verge of hysteria, it is an "anti-style," a nose-thumbing at classical decorum. "To resensitize the language," Céline has written, "so that it pulses more than it reasons—that was my goal." Like most modern writers Céline does not hesitate to sacrifice composure to vividness, unity of effect to ferocity of expression. He neither cares about a fixed literary tradition nor worries about such tiresome souvenirs as formal tidiness. His aim is to launch the diatribe of a Parisian who is at one and the same time a miserable sod and an outraged man. Psychological refinements, introspective turns of self-analysis, romantic agonies—Céline will have none of these. The underground man who moves through his novels is beyond the Promethean gesture; he looks upon modern society as a blend of asylum and abattoir; so it is, so it must be; and meanwhile, with a jovial toughness, he acts out the slogan of the declassed and disabused: *Je m'en fiche.*

The "I" of the novel is something of a louse, indifferent to the cautions of morality, yet a man who can lay claim to one virtue: he dislikes lying to himself. Not that he is infatuated with notions about the sacredness of truth. It is simply that in weighing his own feelings he wants an honest measure: he intends to be sincere with himself, even if with no one else. In an infrequent moment of contemplativeness, he tells himself: "The greatest defeat, in anything, is to forget, and above all to forget what it is that has smashed you, and to let yourself be smashed without ever realizing how thoroughly devilish men can be. When our time is up, we people mustn't bear malice, but neither must we forget. . . ."

Sincerity is one of the few values to which Céline is genuinely—one almost says, sincerely—attached. It is a token of that "psychology of exposure" through which the nineteenth century unmasked itself and the twentieth shivers. The triumph of literary modernism is signaled by a turn from truth to sincerity, from the search for objective law to a desire for personal response. The first involves an effort to apprehend the nature of the universe, and can lead to metaphysics, suicide, revolution and God; the second involves an effort to discover our demons within, and makes no claim upon the world other than the right to publicize the aggressions of candor. Sincerity becomes the last-ditch defense for men without belief, and in its name absolutes can be toppled, morality dispersed, and intellectual systems dissolved. Sincerity of feeling and exact faithfulness of language—which now means a language of fragments, violence, and exasperation—becomes the ruling passion of Céline's narrator. In the terrible freedom it allows him, sincerity is a bomb shattering the hypocrisies of the Third Republic; in the lawlessness of its abandonment, a force of darkness and anti-intelligence.

The dominant motif of the book is undirected flight. From its opening pages, in which the narrator casually volunteers for the army (why not?), he is constantly running from the terrors and apparitions of his world. Céline, or as he calls himself in the novel, Bardamu, is trapped in World War I and unable to think about it; he refuses to take it seriously, even to the point of opposition. The pages describing the wartime experiences of Bardamu, in their reduction of official glory to nihilist farce, are among the most scathing ever composed on this theme. Bardamu prepares to go off to war; Poincaré, president of the Republic, prepares "to open a show of lapdogs"; *Vive la France!* Bardamu learns, soon enough, that bullets whistle and he must run. For a while he serves as runner to a senile, rose-loving general, and his reward—Bardamu's, not the general's—is that his feet smell. Running for the general, Bardamu comes to a major decision: if he is to survive he will have to stop running for generals and begin running from them. The Bardamus must exploit the resources of their cowardice.

And so he runs: from the army to the rear; from one hospital to another; from France to a fantastic trading post in a rotting African jungle; from the African jungle to the industrial jungle of America, first as a bum and then as a worker on the Detroit assembly lines; from America back to France, where, still running up and down stairs to earn a few francs, he becomes an indigent doctor. The one peaceful spot he finds is a post in an insane asylum. For ". . . when people are well, there is no way of getting away from it, they're rather frightening. . . . When they can stand up, they're thinking of killing you. Whereas when they're ill, there's no doubt about it, they're less dangerous."

Throughout the book Bardamu keeps looking for a strange character named Robinson, his down-at-the-heels double. Go to the edge of hopelessness and there you will find Robinson: in the front lines, where he proposes a scheme for desertion; in Africa, where he is getting ready to run off with the company's funds; in Detroit, where he provides tips on brothels. Repeated through the book as mock ritual, these meetings between underground man and shameless alter ego lead to nothing, for here all quests are futile. When Robinson dies, there is nothing more to look for, and the concluding words of the book are: "Let's hear no more of all of this."

Images of death streak the novel. The African episode is a journey to the death of archaic tribalism, the American a journey to the death of industrial civilization. Backward or forward, it's all the same, "a great heap of worm-eaten sods like me, bleary, shivering and lousy." Céline is obsessed not merely with the inexorability of death but even more with the vision of putrefaction: ". . . three feet below ground I . . . will be streaming with maggots, stinking more horribly than a heap of bank-holiday dung, all my disillusioned flesh absurdly rotting."

But is there in this wild and rasping novel perhaps something more, perhaps a flicker of positive vision? Doesn't the enormity of Céline's hatred indicate some hidden yearning for the good which he himself can hardly express? He too has his humanities, and can be lavish with bottom-dog compassion; some yearning for the good, one might suppose, is indispensable if he is to summon the energy needed for so vindictive an outburst against "man's viciousness." But the particular truth about this novel is less assuaging. A presumptive yearning for good is hard to discover, perhaps because it is buried beneath the debris of disillusion. Beneath that debris there may well be a misshapen core of moral sentiment, but it can seldom compete for attention with Céline's rich provisioning of disorder and disgust.

3

In *Death on the Installment Plan* (*Mort à crédit*) Céline returned to his childhood and adolescence in order to complete the record of his experience. An even grizzlier testimony than *Journey to the End of the Night*, Céline's second novel is written in a fitful and exuberant prose, and its tone is one of joyous loathing at having to turn back in memory to the miasma of youth. The misanthropy of the earlier novel ripens into outright paranoia: but with such bubbling energy, such a bilious and sizzling rhetoric, such a manic insistence upon dredging up the last recollection of filth! *Death on the Installment Plan* is a prolonged recital of cheating, venality, and betrayal: the child as victim. Still a boy, he learns to hate the whole social order: "It made me choke to think of it . . . of all the treachery of things! . . . all the swinishness! . . . the whole collection of ordures! Yes, God Almighty, I'd had my bellyful."

Two linked motifs control the book: the richest account of retching in modern literature (it is worthy of Smollett) and a profound yearning for solitude. Both are sequels to the running motif in *Journey to the End of the Night*: one runs from the filth and hopes to find a corner of quiet. When Céline describes retching, he is a virtuoso: "She brings up the lot . . . right into the wind . . . and I get it full in my face, the whole stinking stew that's been gurgling in her throat . . . I, who haven't so much as a crumb to bring up! Ah, now, yes, I find I have, after all . . . my stomach gives one more turn. . . ." Vomit links with Céline's fruitless effort to disgorge the whole of his experience, as he runs through the darkness of night. If only he could start afresh, with nothing on his stomach, and be rid of the rubbish of the past . . . but no, there is always one more crumb of recollection.

The yearning for solitude is poignantly developed in *Death on the Installment Plan*. All a paranoid ever wants is "to be let alone," a wish that to be satisfied would require nothing less than a reconstruction of the universe. In one section of the novel, he describes a stay in an English country-school, where he finds a happiness of sorts through taking long walks with a little idiot boy and an unobtrusive woman teacher, neither of whom troubles him by attempts at conversation. With the dumb and gentle he finds a paradise of muteness; here defenses can be lowered and nerves unraveled. And in this solitude it is also possible to enjoy the modest pleasures of masturbation. The adolescent hero of *Death on the Installment Plan* masturbates systematically, not with the excited curiosity of a youth but with the tameness of an old man. Pleasure can come only from himself, and only when alone with himself. And who knows, perhaps for the underground man this is an act of sincerity.

4

There are writers in whose work a literary theme can barely be kept apart from a personal obsession.

The Nose and the Mound. Céline depicts a severed universe: on one side, he himself, the big nose, and on the other, the world at large, an enormous mound of *merde*. Maestro of bad smells, Céline learns that his nose is the one organ he can trust implicitly: it is the organ of good faith, and by it one can know women, cities, nations, destinies. "It's by smells that people, places and things come to their end. A whiff up one's nostrils is all that remains of past experience." His journey to America is a prolonged exploit in olfactory revulsion, climaxed by a visit to an underground urinal in New York, where he is simply awestricken— Cortez before the Pacific!—by "its joyous communion of filth."

Forever exposing himself to the multiplicity of *merde*, Céline reacts not merely to the hideousness of our social arrangements but even more to the very conditions of existence itself, which dictate the stupidity of death and the prolonged stench of dying. In *Journey to the End of the Night* he declares himself "appalled by my realization of biological ignominy," the last two words breaking forth as the very source of Céline's inspiration. He flinches before the least offensive body, and every time he sees a man engaging in the physiological functions he seethes with rage. Lusting after Lola, the sweet American nurse with piquant buttocks, he shudders in his lust: worms will reign over that flesh too. Had Céline lived in the early Christian era, he would have found himself a Manichean sect and spat upon sensual appetite. Being a twentieth-century Parisian, he submits to the most humiliating debaucheries precisely from his fury at being unable to avoid decay. Sartre and Camus may be students in the metaphysic of nausea, but what, by comparison with Céline, do they know about its actual qualities? In the art of nausea they are theoretic specialists, while Céline is an empiric master.

Perhaps we can now understand somewhat better the running motif of *Journey to the End of the Night*. Céline is running not merely from society but from the sight of every living creature, and running, he trips over the knowledge that it is from himself he would flee, the self that is alone inescapable. In *Death on the Installment Plan* he often befouls himself as a child, an act which after a time comes to signify a recognition that even he is hopelessly implicated in the physicality against which he rages. One thinks of Swift, whose balked sense of purity melts into a fascination with filth, but there is a notable difference: Swift's writings almost always chart a descent from idea to matter, there is a wracking struggle of opposed life-principles, while in Céline rot is sovereign and flesh serves as argument for a gargantuan cosmic deception.

The Cheat of Language. Where finally can the compulsion to sincerity, to the last shameless self-revelation, lead but to silence? Céline writes: "I grow foul as soon as anyone talks to me; I hate it when they prattle." Or again: "The very idea made me howl with terror. Having to talk again—oh, Gawd." Anything beyond the reach of the nose is to be distrusted; all talk about human life is mere drivel unless it begins and ends with the breviary: "I am . . . thou art . . . all of us are despoilers, cheats, slobs." But once that has been said and said again and again, what remains?

Comedy and Nausea. Cut away from its context in the novels, Céline's outlook upon life is narrow-spirited and tiresome. What saves him as a writer is that because he so enjoys roaring his invective from the sewers, he makes his nausea into something deeply comic. In *Journey to the End of the Night* he solemnly observes that "horses are lucky. They go through the war, like us, but they're not asked to . . . seem to believe in it. In this business they are unfortunate but free." During his visit to Africa, after suffering the afflictions of the jungle, he remarks that he is especially misfortunate because, as it happens, he "does not like the country." In *Death on the Installment Plan* his boss, a bogus scientist, launches a typical Célinesque diatribe after having failed in a piece of chicanery: "I'll get them right this time. . . . Their bellies, Ferdinand! Not their heads, but their bellies. Their digestions shall be my customers. . . . I'm through with the spirit for keeps! We're onto the bowels now, Ferdinand, the grand alimentary canal."

It is this perspective of comic nausea that accounts for the vividness of Céline's novels. With noisy verbs and cascades of adjectives, he as-saults nose, ear, eye, creating a carnival of sensations. Yet precisely this vividness reveals Céline's limitation as a writer, for it tends to be monolithic and exhausting. Strictly speaking, Céline is not a satirist in the sense that Swift was, despite the energy of disgust the two writers share; Céline is neither intelligent nor discriminating enough to be a true satirist. His metier is a savage burlesque. The nausea that makes him recoil from experience is linked to the comedy that makes him relish the experience of recoil—beyond that he cannot go.

Philistine and Genius. Halfway, both of Céline's novels begin to lag, for they are really more like a vaudeville, a grab bag of skits, than coherently developed fictions. In terms of sheer *performance* they contain pages rivaling Dickens, yet once the climax of a skit is known there is seldom much point in waiting for either its conclusion or its repetition.

By its very nature, the skit cannot be sustained over a long period of time: it is essentially a virtuoso device and virtuosity holds one's attention largely through initial shock or brilliance. This is a technical difficulty, but the technical difficulty reflects a deeper problem in literary intelligence. The opening of a Céline novel is so seductively vigorous in manner and conclusive in meaning that little remains for further development. A mere accumulation of misfortunes, even when rendered with comic genius, becomes enervating unless the misfortunes are controlled by some idea of greater scope than the probability of further misfortune.

One comes at times to suspect that Céline writes from a total emptiness, that his show of energy hides a void. At such points his novels seem like charades in which the gestures of life are enacted but the content has been lost. Driven by his simplistic ethics and his raging indiscriminateness of feeling to always greater assertions of cynicism, he succumbs, predictably, to the opposite flaw of sentimentalism. Let a Detroit prostitute show him an ounce of kindness or an inch of thigh, and he moons like a schoolboy.

The ultimate limitation in Céline's work is a limitation of intelligence. He does not know what to do with his outpourings, except to multiply them; he cannot surmount his brilliant monomania. He is unable to distinguish among kinds of loathesomeness, between a speck of dust and a mound of filth. Irritation and outrage, triviality and betrayal grate on his nerves almost equally. There is something exasperating, at times even stupid, about a writer who roars with the same passion against nuisance and disaster. For all his gifts, Céline remains something of a philistine, a philistine blessed with genius but a philistine nonetheless.

5

Shortly after the appearance of *Journey to the End of the Night* there appeared a striking critical essay by Leon Trotsky praising the novel— "Céline walked into great literature as other men walk into their own homes"—and predicting that Céline "will not write a second book with such an aversion for the lie and such a disbelief in the truth. The dissonance must resolve itself. Either the artist will make his peace with the darkness or he will perceive the dawn."

Trotsky's timing was a little off, and what he meant by "the dawn" need not concern us here. Céline did manage to write a second novel with the same attitudes as those in *Journey to the End of the Night*, but essentially the prediction of Trotsky was correct. In 1936 Céline, by now a famous writer, took a trip to Russia and shortly thereafter wrote a little book called *Mea Culpa* in which, together with some shrewd observations about the Stalin dictatorship, he indulged himself in a wild harangue against the inherent bestiality of mankind. Apart from the humor and inventiveness of his novels, Céline's reflections served only to reveal his radical limitations of mind.

There now begins a visible disintegration of Céline as both writer and person. In 1938 he published a book entitled *Trifles for a Massacre* (*Bagatelles pour un massacre*), a dreary tract in which he blamed the Jews for everything from the defeat of Napoleon to the rise of surrealism. André Gide took it to be a satire on the assumption that it was impossible that a writer of Céline's gifts could mean what he said; but now it seems obvious that Céline did in fact mean what he said.

During World War II Céline played a dishonorable role, living at peace with the Nazi occupation forces and expressing admiration for the Vichy collaborators. After the war the French government accused Céline of having been a collaborator and he, self-exiled to Denmark, offered the sad reply that he had merely been an "abstentionist." Tried by the French authorities in absentia, he was convicted, sentenced, but not required to serve his time in prison. During the last decade of his life—he died in 1961—Céline was allowed to return to France, where he lived in semiretirement, a lonely and embittered man. Young readers in the late fifties and early sixties who have come to admire Beckett, Genet and Burroughs seem hardly to know that behind these writers, as predecessor and possible influence, stands Louis-Ferdinand Céline.

His career, like that of Ezra Pound, is a classical instance of how a writer suffers in his literary work when his powers of mind are unequal to his powers of imagination. From the depths of the underground man's soul Céline brought forth its effluvia, so that the world could see what was simmering there. His first two novels, in all their brilliant imperfection, seem likely to survive the sickness of their inspiration. But at the end, unable to transcend the foulness which was his authentic and entirely legitimate subject, he made "his peace with the darkness." And not he alone.

Sholom Aleichem: Voice of Our Past

Fifty or sixty years ago the Jewish intelligentsia, its head buzzing with Zionist, Socialist, and Yiddishist ideas, tended to look down upon Sholom Aleichem. His genius was acknowledged but his importance skimped. To the intellectual Jewish youth in both Warsaw and New York he seemed old-fashioned, lacking in complexity and rebelliousness—it is said he showed no appreciation of existentialism. Sh. Niger, the distinguished Yiddish critic, tried to explain this condescension by saying that laughter, the characteristic effect of Sholom Aleichem's stories, is for children and old people, not the young. Perhaps so. My own explanation would be that the Jewish intellectuals simply did not know what to make of Sholom Aleichem: they did not know how to respond to his moral poise and his invulnerability to ideological fashions.

It has been customary to say that Sholom Aleichem speaks for a whole people, but saying this we might remember that his people have not spoken very well for him. The conventional estimate—that Sholom Aleichem was a folksy humorist, a sort of jolly gleeman of the shtetl—is radically false. He needs to be rescued from his reputation, from the quavering sentimentality which keeps him at a safe distance.

From *A World More Attractive* (New York: Horizon Press, 1963).

When we say that Sholom Aleichem speaks for a whole culture, we can mean that in his work he represents all the significant levels of behavior and class in the shtetl world, thereby encompassing the style of life of the East European Jews in the nineteenth century. In that sense, however, it may be doubted that he does speak for the whole shtetl culture. For he does not command the range of a Balzac or even a Faulkner, and he does not present himself as the kind of writer who is primarily concerned with social representation. The ambition of literary "scope" leaves him untouched.

Nor can we mean, in saying that Sholom Aleichem speaks for a whole culture, that he advances its conscious program. Toward the dominant Jewish ideologies of his time Sholom Aleichem showed a mixture of sympathy and skepticism, and precisely this modesty enabled him to achieve a deeper relation to the *folksmassen* than any Jewish political leader. He never set himself up as cultural spokesman, in the style of Thomas Mann at his worst; he had no interest in boring people.

Sholom Aleichem speaks for the culture of the East European Jews because he embodies its essential values in the very accents of his speech, in the inflections of his voice and gestures of his hands, in the pauses between the words even more than the words themselves. To say that a writer represents a culture is to imply a certain distance between the two. But that is not at all the relationship between Sholom Aleichem and the culture of the East European Jews: it is something much more intimate, something for which, having so little experience of it, we can barely find a name. In Sholom Aleichem everything that is deepest in the ethos of the East European Jews is brought to fulfillment. He is, I think, the only modern writer who may truly be said to be a culture hero, a writer whose work releases those assumptions of his people, those tacit gestures of bias, which undercut opinion and go even deeper into communal life than values.

2

In his humorous yet often profoundly sad stories, Sholom Aleichem gave to the Jews what they instinctively felt was the right and true judgment of their experience: a judgment of love through the medium of irony. Sholom Aleichem is the poet of Jewish transcendence over the pomp of the world. For the Jews of Eastern Europe he was protector and advocate; he celebrated their communal tradition; he defended their style of life and constantly underlined their urge to dignity. But he was their judge as well: he ridiculed their pretensions, he mocked their vanity, and he constantly reiterated the central dilemma, that simultaneous tragedy and joke, of their existence—the irony of their claim to being a Chosen People, indeed, the irony of their existence at all.

Sholom Aleichem's Yiddish is one of the most extraordinary verbal achievements of modern literature, as important in its way as T. S. Eliot's revolution in the language of English verse or Bertolt Brecht's infusion of street language into the German lyric. Sholom Aleichem uses a sparse and highly controlled vocabulary; his medium is so drenched with irony that the material which comes through it is often twisted and elevated into direct tragic statement—irony multiplies upon itself to become a deep winding sadness. Many of his stories are monologues, still close to the oral folk tradition, full of verbal byplay, slow in pace, winding in direction, but always immediate and warm in tone. His imagery is based on an absolute mastery of the emotional rhythm of Jewish life. Describing the sadness of a wheezing old clock, he writes that it was "a sadness like that in the song of an old, worn-out cantor toward the end of Yom Kippur"—and how sad that is only someone who has heard such a cantor can really say.

The world of Sholom Aleichem is bounded by three major characters, each of whom has risen to the level of Jewish archetype: Tevye the dairyman; Menachem Mendel the *luftmensch*; and Mottel the cantor's son, who represents the spontaneous possibilities of Jewish childhood. Tevye remains rooted in his little town, delights in displaying his uncertain Biblical learning, and stays close to the sources of Jewish survival. Solid, slightly sardonic, fundamentally innocent, Tevye is the folk voice quarreling with itself, criticizing God from an abundance of love, and realizing in its own low-keyed way all that we mean, or should mean, by humaneness.

Tevye represents the generation of Jews that could no longer find complete deliverance in the traditional God yet could not conceive of abandoning Him. No choice remained but to celebrate the earthly condition: poverty and hope. For if you had become skeptical of deliverance from above and had never accepted the heresy of deliverance from below, what could you do with poverty but celebrate it? "In Kasrilevke," says Tevye, "there are experienced authorities on the subject of hunger, one might say specialists. On the darkest night, simply by hearing your voice, they can tell if you are hungry and would like a bite to eat, or if you are really starving." Tevye, like the people for whom he speaks, is constantly assaulted by outer forces. The world comes to him, most insidiously, in the form of undesired sons-in-law: one who is poverty-stricken but romantic; another who is a revolutionist and ends in Siberia; a third—could anything be worse?—who is a Gentile; and a fourth—this *is* worse—who is a Jew but rich, coarse, and unlearned.

Menachem Mendel, Tevye's opposite, personifies the element of restlessness and soaring, of speculation and fancy-free idealization, in Jewish character. He has a great many occupations: broker, insurance agent, matchmaker, coal dealer, and finally—it is inevitable—writer; but his fundamental principle is to keep moving. The love and longing he directs toward his unfound millions are the love and longing that later Jews direct toward programs and ideologies. He is the utopian principle of Jewish life; he is driven by the modern demon. Through Tevye and Menachem Mendel, flanked by little Mottel, Sholom Aleichem creates his vision of the Yiddish world.

There is a strong element of fantasy, even surrealism, in Sholom Aleichem. Strange things happen: a tailor becomes enchanted, a clock strikes thirteen, money disappears in the synagogue during Yom Kippur, a woman's corpse is dragged across the snow, a timid little Jew looks at himself in the mirror and sees the face of a czarist officer. Life is precarious, fearful, yet always bound by a sense of communal affection.

3

Sholom Aleichem came at a major turning point in the history of the East European Jews: between the unquestioned dominance of religious belief and the appearance of modern ideologies, between the past of traditional Judaism and the future of Jewish politics, between a totally integrated culture and a culture that by a leap of history would soon plunge into the midst of modern division and chaos. Yet it was the mark of Sholom Aleichem's greatness that, coming as he did at this point of transition, he betrayed no moral imbalance or uncertainty of tone. He remained unmoved by the fanaticisms of his time, those that were Jewish and those that were not; he lost himself to neither the delusions of the past nor the delusions of the future. His work is the fulfillment of that moment in the history of the Jews in which a people lives securely with itself, hardly aware of a distinction between the sacred and the secular.

In reading Sholom Aleichem one seldom thinks to wonder about his opinions. I doubt that there has ever been a reader naive enough to ask whether Sholom Aleichem *really* believed in God. For him it was not a living question, no more than it was for the people who read him. To say that he believed in God may be true, but it is also irrelevant. To say that he did not believe in God is probably false, but equally irrelevant. What Sholom Aleichem believed in was the Jews who lived with him and about him, most of them Jews still believing in God. Or perhaps he believed in those Jews who lived so completely in the orbit of their fathers—fathers who had surely believed in God—that there was no need to ask such questions. In Sholom Aleichem's stories God is there, not because He is God, not because there is any recognition or denial of His heavenly status, but simply because He figures in the life of the Jews. God becomes absorbed into the vital existence of the people, or to put it more drastically: God is there because Tevye is there.

But Tevye, does *he* believe in God? Another hopeless question. Tevye believes in something more important than believing in God; he believes in talking to God. And Tevye talks to God as to an old friend whom one need not flatter or assuage: Tevye, as we say in America, gives Him an earful.

Tevye, we may assume, makes God extremely uncomfortable— though also a little proud at the thought that, amid the countless failures of His world, He should at least have created a Tevye who can make Him so uncomfortable. And how does Tevye do this? By telling God the complete truth. It is not a pretty truth, and if God would care to dispute anything Tevye has told him, Tevye is entirely prepared to discuss it with Him further. But whatever other mistakes He may have made, God is too clever to get into an argument with Tevye. God knows that Tevye does not fear Him: a Jew is afraid of people, not of God. So perhaps you can see how absurd it is to ask whether Sholom Aleichem *really* believed in God—Sholom Aleichem who created a character to serve as the conscience of God.

4

Sholom Aleichem believed in Jews as they embodied the virtues of powerlessness and the healing resources of poverty, as they stood firm against the outrage of history, indeed, against the very idea of history itself. Whoever is unable to conceive of such an outlook, whoever cannot imagine the power of a messianism turned away from the apocalyptic future and inward toward a living people, cannot understand Sholom Aleichem or the moment in Jewish experience from which he stems.

It is here that the alien reader may go astray. He may fail to see that for someone like Tevye everything pertaining to Jewishness can be a curse and an affliction, a wretched joke, a source of mockery and despair, but that being a Jew is nevertheless something to be treasured. Treasured, because in the world of Tevye there was a true matrix of human sociability.

The stories Sholom Aleichem told his readers were often stories they already knew, but then, as the Hasidic saying goes, they cared not for the words but the melody. When Tevye talked to his horse, it was the same as if he were talking to his wife. When he talked to his wife, it was the same as if he were talking to God. And when he talked to God, it was the same as if he were talking to his horse. That, for Tevye, was what it meant to be a Jew.

Kierkegaard would never have understood it.

5

Between Sholom Aleichem and his readers there formed a community of outcasts: *edele kaptzunim*. Millions of words flowed back and forth, from writer to reader and reader to writer, for no people has ever talked so much in all recorded history; yet their companionship did not rest upon or even require words. Sholom Aleichem did not hesitate to thrust his barbs at his readers, and they were generous at reciprocating. Having love, they had no need for politeness. But the love of which I speak here is sharply different from that mindless ooze which the word suggests to Americans. It could be argumentative, fierce, bitter, violent; it could be ill-tempered and even vulgar; only one thing it could not be: lukewarm.

Jews never fooled Sholom Aleichem. With Sholom Aleichem, even as he was the defender of the Jews and their culture, there was always a sly wrinkle near his eyes which as soon as Jews saw it, they said to themselves: *Im ken men nisht upnaren*; him you cannot deceive. That is why, when you go through his stories, you find so little idealization, so little of that cozy self-indulgence and special pleading which is the curse of Jewish life.

Middleton Murry once said of Thomas Hardy that "the contagion of the world's slow stain has not touched him." This magnificent remark must have referred to something far more complex and valuable than innocence, for no one could take Hardy to be merely innocent; it must have referred to the artist's final power, the power to see the world as it is, to love it and yet not succumb to it; and that is the power one finds in Sholom Aleichem.

God, Man, and Stalin

1952

That Whittaker Chambers told the truth and Alger Hiss did not seems to me highly probable. Personal tragedy though their confrontation was, it had another, almost abstract, quality: the political course of the thirties made it inevitable that, quite apart from this well-groomed man and that unkempt one, there be a clash between two men, one a former Communist who repudiated his past and then, as his *Witness* testifies, swung to the politics of the far right, the other a "liberal" recruited from the idealistic wing of public service. If not these two, then two others; if not their shapes and accents, other shapes and accents. And that is why most of the journalistic speculation on their personalities proved so ephemeral: for what did it finally matter whether Hiss was a likable man or Chambers an overwrought one? what did it matter when at stake was the commitment of those popular-front liberals who had persisted in treating Stalinism as an accepted part of "the left"? and why should serious people have puzzled for long over the private motives

From *The Nation* 174 (May 24, 1952):21.

of Chambers or Hiss when Stalinism itself remained to be studied and analyzed?

Chambers has told his story and put down his ideas. *Witness* is a fascinating grab bag: autobiography, account of underground work, religious tract, attempt at an explanation of Stalinism. As confession, it has an almost classical stature: whatever opinions Chambers may now superimpose on his memory, the narrative itself demands the attention of anyone interested in modern politics. As autobiography, the book is embarrassing: Chambers' memoir of his family seems a needless act of masochism, while the portrait of his adult self suggests a man whose total sincerity is uncomplicated by humor, irony, or persuasive humility.

The most remarkable fact about *Witness* is that as a work of ideas it should be so ragged and patchy. In all its eight hundred pages there is hardly a sustained passage of, say, five thousand words devoted to a serious development of thought; everything breaks down into sermon, reminiscence, self-mortification, and self-justification. Service in the GPU is not, to be sure, the best training for the life of the mind; but there is something in Chambers' flair for intellectual melodrama that seems particular to our time and to the kind of personality always hungry for absolutes of faith. Writes Chambers: "I was not seeking ethics; I was seeking God. My need was to be a practising Christian in the same sense that I had been a practising Communist." A little time spent in "seeking ethics," or even a breather from "seeking" anything, might seem to have been in order.

The world, as Chambers sees it, is split between those who acknowledge the primacy of God and those who assert the primacy of man; from this fundamental division follows a struggle between morality and murder, with Communism merely the final version of the rationalist heresy; and the one hope for the world is a return to Christian virtue, the ethic of mercy. These views Chambers announces with an air of abject righteousness. Indifferent to the caution that the sin of pride takes no more extreme form than a belief in God as one's personal deus ex machina, he several times acknowledges a Mover at his elbow and declares the appointment of Thomas Murphy as government prosecutor in the Hiss case to be evidence that "it pleased God to have in readiness a man." From *Witness* an unsympathetic reader might, in fact, conclude that God spent several years as a special aide to the House Committee on Un-American Activities.

In reading this book one is nonplussed by the way its polemics violate its declared values. A few illustrations may suggest the quality of Chambers' thought:

Again and again he declares himself interested in presenting the facts. Without questioning his personal story, I must doubt his capacity as historian and social observer. It is not true that Trotsky "led in person" the Bolshevik troops that suppressed the Kronstadt rebellion. It is not true that "Lenin gave up listening to music because of the emotional havoc it played with him"; the man merely said, if Gorky's report of a casual remark be credited, that music made him want to stroke heads at a time when he felt it necessary to make revolutions. It is not true that "Communists are *invariably* as prurient as gutter urchins." It is an exaggeration to say that in the 1927 faction fight in the United States Communist Party, dirty as it was, each side "prompted scandalous whispering campaigns, in which embezzlement of party money, homosexuality, and stool pigeon were the preferred whispers." And it is a wild exaggeration to assert that the Communist agents in Washington, dangerous as they were, "if only in prompting the triumph of Communism in China, have *decisively* changed the history of Asia, of the United States, and therefore, of *the entire world*" (italics mine). Mao recruited his armies in the valley of Yenan, not the bars of Washington.

Chambers' extreme political turn has dizzied his historical sense. By noting that Alger Hiss was counsel for the Nye committee during the thirties, he tries to discredit its exposure of the munitions industry. "The penetration of the United States government by the Communist Party," adds Chambers, "coincided with a mood in the nation which lightheartedly baited the men who manufactured the armaments indispensable to its defense as 'Merchants of Death.'" But surely more was involved: the Nye committee revealed that some arms manufacturers had not hesitated to sell in bulk to Hitler, that their profits had been unconscionably high, that some had pressured both sides in the Chaco to buy their products and thus to prolong a war. The truth of these disclosures does not depend on whether Hiss was counsel for the committee that made them.

Chambers complains bitterly, and with justice, about the smears he has suffered from many Hiss supporters. Unfortunately, he is not himself above the use of similar methods. One of Hiss's attorneys was Harold Rosenwald, about whose face Chambers darkly pronounces: "I had seen dozens much like it in my time." The notion that people can be "placed" politically by the shape of their faces is both preposterous and, at least in this century, sinister.

In the course of breaking away from Stalinism, Chambers came to feel that "it is just as evil to kill the Czar and his family . . . as it is to starve two million peasants or slave laborers to death." What, if anything, does this highly charged statement mean? Coming from a pacifist, it would be perfectly clear, for it would suggest that killing is forbidden under any circumstances. We might then hope to hear as a sequel, "It is just as evil to kill 60,000 civilians in Hiroshima as it was to kill the Czar and his family." But Chambers is not a pacifist; he is willing to "struggle against [Communism] by all means, including arms." So the evil of killing the czar cannot for him be simply that it was a killing, but must be that it was an unjustified killing—which leaves him with the moral enormity "Several unjustified killings are just as evil as two million unjustified killings."

Throughout the book Chambers praises the Christian virtues of humility and meekness. Unfortunately, this credo does not prevent him from declaring "the left-wing intellectuals of almost every feather" to have been Hiss supporters and then from calling them "puffins, skimmers, skuas, and boobies." These delicate designations prompt one to remind Chambers that a good many "left-wing intellectuals" of one or another feather fought a minority battle against Stalinism at a time when *both* he and Hiss were at the service of Messrs. Yagoda and Yezhov.

Stalinism is evil, declares Chambers, a proposition neither disputable nor enlightening. Nowhere in his eight hundred pages does he attempt sustained definition or description, nowhere does he bound the shape of the evil. He seems unconcerned to examine the workings of Russian society, the social role of the Western Stalinist parties, the relation of the Asian parties to native nationalism. And with good reason. If you believe that the two great camps of the world prepare for battle under the banners Faith in Man and Faith in God, what is the point of close study and fine distinctions? You need only sound the trumpets.

Almost unwittingly, Chambers moves toward the view that the source of our troubles is the Enlightenment: "The crisis of the Western world exists to the degree in which it is indifferent to God." The French Revolution becomes the villain of history, its progeny every godless society of our time. Chambers accepts, of course, the common, crude identification of Stalin's totalitarianism with Lenin's revolutionary state; both seem to him forms of fascism; the New Deal was a social revolution which crippled "the power of business"; and the motto of "the welfare state" is best expressed by his former associate Colonel Bykov: "Who pays is boss, and who takes money must also give something." Everyone might thus be lumped together: Voltaire, Jefferson, Lenin, Roosevelt, Hitler, Stalin; not all equally evil, but all, apparently, "indifferent to God." A man who thinks in such patterns can hardly be expected to notice—or have much reason to care—that Stalinism and fascism, while symmetrical in their political devices, have different historical origins, class structures, political ideologies and social rationales. Or that the

Keynesian measures of the New Deal, far from constituting a revolution, proved a crutch for a stumbling capitalism.

Chambers' approach to history rests, finally, on no social theory at all; it is a return to Manichean demonology. Since for him everything depends on whether one takes God or man to be primary, he can write that "as Communists, Stalin and the Stalinists were absolutely justified in making the Purge. From a Communist point of view, Stalin could have taken no other course. . . . In that fact lay the evidence that Communism is absolutely evil. The human horror was not evil, it was the sad consequence of evil." The first two of these sentences are historically false; various Communists opposed the purges and proposed other courses of action, among them the removal of Stalin from power. The last sentence is shocking in its moral callousness. In effect, Chambers is saying that those of us who attack Stalinism for its inhumanity are sentimental, lacking in his austere disdain for what he calls "formless good will." Is it, however, more important to attack Stalin for disbelieving in the primacy of God than for killing millions of men? If the killing is to be regarded as a mere "consequence" of first principles, specific moral criticism of it can only seem superficial. But, in fact, the purges were the result of a decision by men in power, a decision for which they must be held responsible. A society is to be judged less by its philosophical premise about God and man, if it has any, than by its actual treatment of men; "the human horror" of the purges was evil, not merely "sad." What matters is not the devil's metaphysics, but his morals.

Chambers' major insight into the problem of Stalinism is his insistence that in this era of permanent crisis it provides a faith, a challenge, even an ideal. Feeding on crisis, Stalinism offers a vision. "The vision inspires. The crisis impels. The workingman is chiefly moved by the crisis. The educated man is chiefly moved by the vision." This is an important observation and a necessary corrective to vulgar theories which make of Stalinism mainly an atavistic drive for power. But Chambers, ignoring the fact that the vision of Stalinism is corrupt, treats it as if it were a legitimate form of socialism, and pays slight attention to the counterrevolution that occurred in Russia during the very years he was its underground agent.

Is this an academic matter? Not at all; for the essence of Stalinism, in its Russian form, is that it rests on a new kind of bureaucratic ruling class which engaged in "primitive accumulation" by destroying the revolutionary generation and appropriating to itself total economic and political power. Outside Russia, Stalinism utilizes the socialist tradition of Europe and the nationalist sentiment of Asia for its domestic class needs and international power maneuvers. Drawing on a unique blend of reactionary and pseudo-revolutionary appeals, Stalinism attracts, in this age of crisis, all those who feel the world must be changed but lack the understanding or energy to change it in a libertarian direction. Anticapitalist but not socialist, Stalinism causes, in the words of Marx, all the old crap to rise to the top; under its domination, the best impulses of modern man are directed toward the worst consequences. And the problem for the historian is to determine precisely the blend of seemingly contradictory elements that Stalinism comprises.

Chambers himself provides an anecdote which dramatically confirms these remarks. His boss in the underground, Colonel Bykov, was a perfect specimen of the new Stalinist man: coarse, obedient, unintellectual, brutal. To Bykov "the generation that had made the Revolution . . . seemed as alien and preposterous . . . as foreigners. They belonged to another species and he talked about them the way people talk about the beastly or amusing habits of cows or pigs." So disgusting was Bykov that Chambers felt, before introducing him to Hiss, that he would have to apologize for the Russian. Yet, after a brief conversation, Hiss found Bykov "impressive." Why? I would guess that it was the attraction of an extreme bureaucratic personality for a mild bureaucratic personality, of one man who instinctively scorned the masses of people for another who had been trained to think of them as objects for benevolent manipulation. If Hiss had possessed a trace of either revolutionary or liberal spirit, he would have been contemptuous of Bykov, he would have seen on Bykov's hands the blood of Bukharin and Tomsky and thousands upon thousands of others.

Where will Chambers go? His strength lies in a recognition that we live in an extreme situation; he agrees that "it is necessary to change the world." No longer a radical, scornful of liberals, convinced that "in the struggle against Communism the conservative is all but helpless," he accepts, formally, the position of those reactionaries manqués who edit William Buckley's National Review. But only formally; for unlike them, he is drenched with the consciousness of crisis, he has none of their complacence, he continues a disturbed and dissatisfied man. What remains? Only the fact that estranged personality and reactionary opinion form an explosive mixture.

In his final sentence Chambers hints that he believes a third world war both inevitable and necessary. Yet he yearns for some spiritual reformation, a turn to God. What likelihood there is that spiritual or any other desired values would survive in a worldwide atomic war, he does not discuss. Would there, in any case, be much point in reminding him that religious faith has rarely prevented despots from being despotic? that many of our most precious concepts of liberty are the work of skeptics? that Stalinism thrives in pious Rome as in worldly Paris? that it wins supporters in an Orient which has not known a loss of religious faith comparable to that of the West? that if Stalin is an atheist, Franco is a believer? that the priests in Russia pray for Stalin as in Germany they prayed for Hitler?

Very little point, I fear; little more than to have told him during the thirties that Stalinism was betraying the German workers to Hitler or by its trials and purges murdering thousands of innocent people. Those who abandon a father below are all too ready for a father above. But this shift of faith does not remove the gnawing problems which, if left unsolved, will drive still more people to Stalinism; it gives the opponents of the totalitarian state no strategy, no program with which to remake the world; it makes our situation appear even more desperate than it already is. For if Chambers is right in believing the major bulwark against Stalin to be faith in God, then it is time for men of conviction and courage to take to the hills.

This Age of Conformity

1954

Intellectuals have always been partial to grandiose ideas about them-selves, whether of a heroic or a masochistic kind, but surely no one has ever had a more grandiose idea about the destiny of modern intellectuals than the brilliant economist Joseph Schumpeter. Though he desired nothing so much as to be realistic and hard-boiled, Schumpeter had somehow absorbed all those romantic notions about the revolutionary potential and critical independence of the intellectuals which have now and again swept through the radical and bohemian worlds. Marx, said Schumpeter, was wrong in supposing that capitalism would break down from inherent economic contradictions; it would break down, instead, from an inability to claim people through ties of loyalty and value. "Unlike any other type of society, capitalism inevitably . . . creates, educates and subsidizes a vested interest in social unrest." The intel-lectuals, bristling with neurotic aspirations and deranged by fantasies of utopia made possible by the very society they would destroy, become agents of discontent who infect rich and poor, high and low. In drawing this picture Schumpeter hardly meant to praise the intellectuals, yet until a few years ago many of them would have accepted it as both truth and tribute, though a few of the more realistic ones might have smiled a doubt as to their capacity to do *all that*.

Schumpeter's picture of the intellectuals is not, of course, without historical validity, but at the moment it seems spectacularly, even comically wrong. And wrong for a reason that Schumpeter, with his elaborate sense of irony, would have appreciated: he who had insisted that capitalism is "a form or method of economic change and not only never is but never can be stationary" had failed sufficiently to consider those new developments in our society which have changed the whole position and status of the intellectuals. Far from creating and subsidizing unrest, capitalism in its most recent stage has found an honored place for the intellectuals; and the intellectuals, far from thinking of themselves as a desperate "opposition," have been enjoying a return to the bosom of the nation. Were Archibald MacLeish again tempted to play Cato and chastise the Irresponsibles, he could hardly find a victim. We have all, even the handful who still try to retain a glower of criticism, become responsible and moderate.

2

In 1932 not many American intellectuals saw any hope for the revival of capitalism. Few of them could support this feeling with any well-grounded theory of society; many held to a highly simplified idea of what capitalism was; and almost all were committed to a vision of the *crisis* of capitalism which was merely a vulgarized model of the class struggle in Europe. Suddenly, with the appearance of the New Deal, the intellectuals saw fresh hope: capitalism was not to be exhausted by the naive specifications they had assigned it, and consequently the "European" policies of the Roosevelt administration might help dissolve their "Europeanized" sense of crisis. So that the more American society became Europeanized, adopting measures that had been common practice on the Continent for decades, the more the American intellectuals began to believe in . . . American uniqueness. Somehow, the major capitalist power in the world would evade the troubles afflicting capitalism as a world economy.

The two central policies of the New Deal, social legislation and state intervention in economic life, were not unrelated, but they were separable as to time; in Europe they had not always appeared together. Here, in America, it was the simultaneous introduction of these two policies that aroused the enthusiasm, as it dulled the criticism, of the intellectuals. Had the drive toward bureaucratic state regulation of a

capitalist economy appeared by itself, so that one could see the state
becoming a major buyer and hence indirect controller of industry, and
industries on the verge of collapse being systematically subsidized by
the state, and the whole of economic life being rationalized according
to the long-run needs, if not the immediate tastes, of corporate economy—had all this appeared in isolation, the intellectuals would have
reacted critically, they would have recognized the trend toward "state
capitalism" as the danger it was. But their desire for the genuine social
reforms that came with this trend made them blind or indifferent to the
danger. Still, one may suppose that their enthusiasm would have mel-
lowed had not the New Deal been gradually transformed into a permanent war economy; for whatever the theoretical attractions of the
Keynesian formula for salvaging capitalism, it has thus far "worked" only
in times of war or preparation for war. And it was in the war economy,
itself closely related to the trend toward statification, that the intellectuals came into their own.

Statification, war economy, the growth of a mass society and mass
culture—all these are aspects of the same historical process. The kind
of society that has been emerging in the West, a society in which bureaucratic controls are imposed upon (but not fundamentally against)
an interplay of private interests, has need for intellectuals in a way the
earlier, "traditional" capitalism never did. It is a society in which ideology
plays an unprecedented part: as social relations become more abstract
and elusive, the human object is bound to the state with ideological
slogans and abstractions—and for this chore intellectuals are indispensable; no one else can do the job as well. Because industrialism
grants large quantities of leisure time without any creative sense of how
to employ it, there springs up a vast new industry that must be staffed
by intellectuals and quasi-intellectuals: the industry of mass culture. And
because the state subsidizes mass education and our uneasy prosperity
allows additional millions to gain a "higher" education, many new jobs
suddenly become available in the academy: some fall to intellectuals.
Bohemia gradually disappears as a setting for our intellectual life, and
what remains of it seems willed or fake. Looking upon the prosperous
ruins of Greenwich Village, one sometimes feels that a full-time bohemian career has become as arduous, if not as expensive, as acquiring
a Ph.D.

Bohemia, said Flaubert, was "the fatherland of my breed." If so, his
breed, at least in America, is becoming extinct. The most exciting periods
of American intellectual life tend to coincide with the rise of bohemia,
with the tragic yet liberating rhythm of the break from the small town
into the literary roominess of the city, or from the provincial immigrant

family into the centers of intellectual experiment. Given the nature of contemporary life, bohemia flourishes in the city—but that has not always been so. Concord too was a kind of bohemia, sedate, subversive, and transcendental all at once. Today, however, the idea of bohemia, which was a strategy for bringing artists and writers together in their struggle with and for the world—this idea has become disreputable, being rather nastily associated with kinds of exhibitionism that have only an incidental relationship to bohemia. Nonetheless, it is the disintegration of bohemia that is a major cause for the way intellectuals feel, as distinct from and far more important than what they say or think. Those feelings of loneliness one finds among so many American intellectuals, feelings of damp dispirited isolation which undercut the ideology of liberal optimism, are partly due to the breakup of bohemia. Where young writers would once face the world together, they now sink into suburbs, country homes, and college towns. And the price they pay for this rise in social status is to be measured in more than an increase in rent.

It is not my purpose to berate anyone, for the pressures of conformism are at work upon all of us, to say nothing of the need to earn one's bread; and all of us bend under the terrible weight of our time—though some take pleasure in learning to enjoy it. Nor do I wish to indulge in the sort of good-natured condescension with which Malcolm Cowley recently described the younger writers as lugubrious and timid longhairs huddling in chill academies and poring over the gnostic texts of Henry James—by contrast, no doubt, to Cowley's own career of risk-taking. Some intellectuals, to be sure, have "sold out" and we can all point to examples, probably the same examples. But far more prevalent and far more insidious is that slow attrition which destroys one's ability to stand firm and alone: the temptations of an improved standard of living combined with guilt over the historical tragedy that has made possible our prosperity; one's sense of being swamped by the rubbish of a reactionary period together with the loss of those earlier certainties that had the advantage, at least, of making resistance easy. Nor, in saying these things, do I look forward to any sort of material or intellectual asceticism. Our world is to be neither flatly accepted nor rejected: it must be engaged, resisted and—who knows, perhaps still—transformed.

All of life, my older friends often tell me, is a conspiracy against that ideal of independence with which a young intellectual begins; but if so, wisdom consists not in premature surrender but in learning when to evade, when to stave off, and when to oppose head-on. Conformity, as Arthur Koestler said some years ago, "is often a form of betrayal which can be carried out with a clear conscience." Gradually we make our peace with the world, and not by anything as exciting as a secret pact; nowadays Lucifer is a very patient and reasonable fellow with a gift for indulging one's most legitimate desires; and we learn, if we learn anything at all, that betrayal may consist in a chain of small compromises, even while we also learn that in this age one cannot survive without compromise. What is most alarming is not that a number of intellectuals have abandoned the posture of iconoclasm: let the zeitgeist give them a jog and they will again be radical, all too radical. What is most alarming is that the whole idea of the intellectual vocation—the idea of a life dedicated to values that cannot possibly be realized by a commercial civilization—has gradually lost its allure. And it is this, rather than the abandonment of a particular program, which constitutes our rout.

In a recent number of *Perspectives* Lionel Trilling addressed himself to some of these problems; his perspective is sharply different from mine. Trilling believes that "there is an unmistakable improvement in the American cultural situation of today over that of, say, thirty years ago," while to me it seems that any comparison between the buoyant free-spirited cultural life of 1923 with the dreariness of 1953, or between their literary achievements, must lead to the conclusion that Trilling is indulging in a pleasant fantasy. More important, however, is his analysis of how this "improvement" has occurred:

> In many civilizations there comes a point at which wealth shows a tendency to submit itself, in some degree, to the rule of mind and imagination, to apologize for its existence by a show of taste and sensitivity. In America the signs of this submission have for some time been visible. . . . Intellect has associated itself with power, perhaps as never before in history, and is now conceded to be in itself a kind of power.

Such stately terms as "wealth" and "intellect" hardly make for sharp distinctions, yet the drift of Trilling's remarks is clear enough—and, I think, disastrous.

It is perfectly true that in the government bureaucracy and institutional staff, in the mass-culture industries and the academy, intellectuals have been welcomed and absorbed as never before. It is true, again, that "wealth" has become far more indulgent in its treatment of intellectuals, and for good reasons: it needs them more than ever, they are tamer than ever, and its own position is more comfortable and expansive than it has been for a long time. But if "wealth" has made a mild bow toward "intellect" (sometimes while picking its pocket), then "intellect" has engaged in some undignified prostrations before "wealth." Thirty years ago "wealth" was on the defensive, and twenty years ago it was frightened, hesitant, apologetic. "Intellect" was self-confident, aggressive, secure in its belief or, if you wish, delusions. Today the ideology of American capitalism, with its claim to a unique and immaculate destiny, is trumpeted through every medium of communication: official propaganda, institutional advertising, and the scholarly writings of people who, until a few years ago, were its major opponents. Marx-baiting, that least risky of occupations, has become a favorite sport in the academic journals; a whining genteel chauvinism is widespread among intellectuals; and the bemoaning of their own fears and timidities a constant theme among professors. Is this to be taken as evidence that "wealth" has subordinated itself to "intellect"? Or is the evidence to be found in the careers of such writers as Max Eastman and James Burnham? To be sure, culture has acquired a more honorific status, as restrained ostentation has replaced conspicuous consumption: wealthy people collect more pictures or at least more modern ones, they endow foundations with large sums—but all this is possible because "intellect" no longer pretends to challenge "wealth."

What has actually been taking place is the absorption of large numbers of intellectuals, previously independent, into the world of government bureaucracy and public committees; into the constantly growing industries of pseudo culture; into the adult-education business, which subsists on regulated culture-anxiety. This process of bureaucratic absorption does not proceed without check: the Eisenhower administration has recently dismissed a good many intellectuals from government posts. Yet it seems likely that such stupidity will prove temporary and that one way or another, in one administration or another, the intellectuals will drift back into the government: they must, they are indispensable.

Some years ago C. Wright Mills wrote an article in which he labeled the intellectuals as "powerless people." He meant, of course, that they felt incapable of translating their ideas into action and that their consequent frustration had become a major motif in their behavior. His description was accurate enough; yet we might remember that the truly powerless people are those intellectuals—the new realists—who attach themselves to the seats of power, where they surrender their freedom of expression without gaining any significance as political figures. For it is crucial to the history of the American intellectuals in the past few decades—as well as to the relationship between "wealth" and "intellect"—that whenever they become absorbed into the accredited institutions of society they not only lose their traditional rebelliousness but to one extent or another *they cease to function as intellectuals*. The institutional world needs intellectuals *because* they are intellectuals but it does not want them *as* intellectuals. It beckons to them because of what they are but it will not allow them, at least within its sphere of articulation, to either remain or entirely cease being what they are. It needs them for their knowledge, their talent, their inclinations and passions; it insists that they retain a measure of these endowments, which it means to employ for its own ends, and without which the intellectuals would be of no use to it whatever. A simplified but useful equation suggests itself: the relation of the institutional world to the intellectuals is like the relation of middlebrow culture to serious culture. The one battens on the other, absorbs and raids it with increasing frequency and skill, subsidizes and encourages it enough to make further raids possible—at times the parasite will support its victim. Surely this relationship must be one reason for the high incidence of neurosis that is supposed to prevail among intellectuals. A total estrangement from the sources of power and prestige, even a blind unreasoning rejection of every aspect of our culture, would be far healthier, if only because it would permit a free discharge of aggression.

I do not mean to suggest that for intellectuals all institutions are equally dangerous or disadvantageous. Even during the New Deal, the life of those intellectuals who journeyed to Washington was far from happy. The independence possible to a professor of sociology is usually greater than that possible to a writer of television scripts, and a professor of English, since the world will not take his subject seriously, can generally enjoy more intellectual leeway than a professor of sociology. Philip Rieff, a sociologist, has caustically described a major tendency among his colleagues as a drift from "science" to "policy" in which "loyalty, not truth, provides the social condition by which the intellectual discovers his new environment." It is a drift "from the New School to the Rand Corporation."

There is, to be sure, a qualitative difference between the academy and the government bureau or the editorial staff. The university is still committed to the ideology of freedom, and many professors try hard and honestly to live by it. If the intellectual cannot subsist independently, off his work or his relatives, the academy is usually his best bet. But no one who has a live sense of what the literary life has been and might still be, in either Europe or this country, can accept the notion that the academy is the natural home of intellect. What seems so unfortunate is that the whole *idea* of independence is losing its traditional power. Scientists are bound with chains of official secrecy; sociologists compete for government research chores; foundations become indifferent to solitary writers and delight in "teams"; the possibility of living in decent poverty from moderately serious literary journalism becomes more and more remote. Compromises are no doubt necessary, but they had better be recognized for what they are.

Perhaps something should be said here about "alienation." Involved, primarily, is a matter of historical fact. During most of the bourgeois epoch, the European intellectuals grew increasingly alienated from the social community because the very ideals that had animated the bourgeois revolution were now being violated by bourgeois society; their "alienation" was prompted not by bohemian willfulness or socialist dogmatism but by a loyalty to Liberty, Fraternity, Equality, or to a vision of a preindustrial society that, by a trick of history, came pretty much to resemble Liberty, Fraternity, Equality. Just as it was the triumph of capitalism which largely caused this sense of estrangement, so it was the expansion of capitalism that allowed the intellectuals enough freedom to express it. As Philip Rahv has put it: "During the greater part of the bourgeois epoch . . . [writers] preferred alienation from the community to alienation from themselves." Precisely this choice made possible their strength and boldness, precisely this "lack of roots" gave them their speculative power. Almost always, the talk one hears these days about "the need for roots" veils a desire to compromise the tradition of intellectual independence, to seek in a nation or religion or party a substitute for the tenacity one should find in oneself. Isaac Rosenfeld's remark that "the ideal society . . . cannot afford to include many deeply rooted individuals" is not merely a clever mot but an important observation.

It may be that the issue is no longer relevant; that, with the partial submission of "wealth" to "intellect," the clash between a business civilization and the values of art is no longer as urgent as we once thought; but if so, we must discard a great deal, and mostly the best, of the literature, the criticism, and the speculative thought of the twentieth century. For to deny the historical fact of "alienation" (as if that would make it any the less real!) is to deny our heritage, both as burden and advantage, and also, I think, to deny our possible future as a community.

Much of what I have been describing here must be due to a feeling among intellectuals that the danger of Stalinism allows them little or no freedom in their relations with bourgeois society. This feeling seems to me only partly justified, and I do not suffer from any inclination to minimize the Stalinist threat. To be sure, it does limit our possibilities for action—if, that is, we still want to engage in any dissident politics—and sometimes it may force us into political alignments that are distasteful. But here a crucial distinction should be made: the danger of Stalinism may require temporary expedients in the area of *power* such as would have seemed compromising some years ago, but there is no reason, at least no good reason, why it should require compromise or conformity in the area of *ideas*, no reason why it should lead us to become partisans of bourgeois society, which is itself, we might remember, heavily responsible for the Stalinist victories.

3

"In the United States at this time liberalism is not only the dominant but even the sole intellectual tradition." This sentence of Lionel Trilling's contains a sharp insight into the political life of contemporary America. If I understand him correctly, he is saying that our society is at present so free from those pressures of conflicting classes and interests which make for sharply defined ideologies, that liberalism colors, or perhaps the word should be, bleaches all political tendencies. It becomes a loose shelter, a poncho rather than a program; to call oneself a liberal one doesn't really have to believe in anything. In such a moment of social slackness, the more extreme intellectual tendencies have a way, as soon as an effort is made to put them into practice, of sliding into and becoming barely distinguishable from the dominant liberalism. Both conservatism and radicalism can retain, at most, an intellectual recalcitrance, but neither is presently able to engage in a sustained practical politics of its own; which does not mean they will never be able to.

The point is enforced by looking at the recent effort to affirm a conservative ideology. Russell Kirk, who makes this effort with some earnestness, can hardly avoid the eccentricity of appealing to Providence as a putative force in American politics: an appeal that suggests both the intensity of his conservative desire and the desperation behind the intensity. Peter Viereck, a friskier sort of writer, calls himself a conservative, but surely this is nothing more than a mystifying pleasantry, for aside from the usual distinctions of temperament and talent it is hard to see how his conservatism differs from the liberalism of Arthur Schlesinger, Jr. For Viereck conservatism is a shuffling together of attractive formulas, without any effort to discover their relationship to deep *actual* clashes of interest: he fails, for example, even to consider that in America there is today neither opportunity nor need for conservatism (since the liberals do the necessary themselves) and that if an opportunity were to arise, conservatism could seize upon it only by acquiring a mass, perhaps reactionary dynamic, that is, by "going into the streets." And that, surely, Viereck doesn't want.

If conservatism is taken to mean, as in some "classical" sense it should be, a principled rejection of industrial economy and a yearning for an ordered, hierarchical society that is not centered on the city, then conservatism in America is best defended by a group of literary men whose seriousness is proportionate to their recognition that such a politics is now utterly hopeless and, in any but a utopian sense, meaningless. Such a conservatism, in America, goes back to Fenimore Cooper, who anticipates those implicit criticisms of our society which we honor in Faulkner; and in the hands of serious imaginative writers, but hardly in the hands of political writers obliged to deal with immediate relations of power, it can become a myth which, through abrasion, profoundly challenges modern experience. As for the "conservatism" of the late Senator Robert Taft, which consists of nothing but liberal economics and wounded nostalgia, it lacks intellectual content and, more important, when in power it merely continues those "statist" policies it had previously attacked.

This prevalance of liberalism yields, to be sure, some obvious and substantial benefits. It makes us properly skeptical of the excessive claims and fanaticisms that accompany ideologies. It makes implausible those "aristocratic" rantings against democracy which were fashionable in some literary circles a few years ago. And it allows for the hope that any revival of American radicalism will acknowledge not only its break from, but also its roots in, the liberal tradition.

At the same time, however, the dominance of liberalism contributes heavily to our intellectual conformity. Liberalism dominates, but without confidence or security; it knows that its victories at home are tied to disasters abroad; and for the élan it cannot summon, it substitutes a blend of complacence and anxiety. It makes for an atmosphere of blur in the realm of ideas, since it has a stake in seeing momentary concurrences as deep harmonies. In an age that suffers from incredible catastrophes it scoffs at theories of social apocalypse—as if any *more* evidence were needed; in an era convulsed by war, revolution and counter-revolution it discovers the virtues of "moderation." And when the dominant school of liberalism, the school of realpolitik, scores points in attacking "the ritualistic liberals," it also betrays a subterranean desire to retreat into the caves of bureaucratic caution. Liberalism as an ideology, as "the haunted air," has never been stronger in this country; but can as much be said of the appetite for freedom?

Sidney Hook discovers merit in the Smith Act: he was not for its passage but doubts the wisdom of its repeal.* Mary McCarthy, zooming to earth from never-never land, discovers in the American war economy

---

* The Smith Act, passed in 1940, was a loosely worded piece of legislation that made it unlawful to "conspire to advocate the overthrow of the government by force and violence."

no less than paradise: "Class barriers disappear or tend to become porous; the factory worker is an economic aristocrat in comparison to the
middle-class clerk. . . . The America . . . of vast inequalities and dramatic
contrasts is rapidly ceasing to exist." Daniel Boorstin—he cannot be
charged with the self-deceptions peculiar to idealism—discovers that
"the genius of American politics" consists not in the universal possibilities of democracy but in a uniquely fortunate geography which, obviously, cannot be exported. David Riesman is so disturbed by Veblen's
rebelliousness toward American society that he explains it as a projection
of father-hatred; and what complex is it, one wonders, which explains
a writer's assumption that Veblen's view of America is so inconceivable
as to require a home-brewed psychoanalysis? Irving Kristol writes an
article minimizing the threat to civil liberties and shortly thereafter is
chosen to be public spokesman for the American Committee for Cultural
Freedom. And in the committee itself, it is possible for serious intellectuals to debate—none is *for* Senator McCarthy—whether the public
activities of the Wisconsin hooligan constitute a serious menace to
freedom.

One likes to speculate: suppose Simone de Beauvoir and Bertrand
Russell didn't exist; would not many of the political writers for *Commentary* and the *New Leader* have to invent them? It is all very well, and
even necessary, to demonstrate that Russell's description of America as
subject to "a reign of terror" is malicious and ignorant, or that Beauvoir's
picture of America is a blend of Stalinist clichés and second-rate literary
fantasies; but this hardly disposes of the problem of civil liberties or of
the justified alarm many sober European intellectuals feel with regard
to America. Between the willfulness of those who see only terror and
the indifference of those who see only health, there is need for simple
truth: that intellectual freedom in the United States is under severe
attack and that the intellectuals have, by and large, shown a painful lack
of militancy in defending the rights which are a precondition of their
existence.*

It is in the pages of the influential magazine *Commentary* that liberalism is most skillfully and systematically advanced as a strategy for
adapting to the American status quo. Until the last few months, when
a shift in editorial temper seems to have occurred, the magazine was

---

* It must in honesty be noted that many of the intellectuals least alive to the problem of civil
liberties are former Stalinists or radicals; and this, more than the vast anti-Marxist literature
of recent years, constitutes a serious criticism of American radicalism. For the truth is that
the "old-fashioned liberals" like John Dewey and Alexander Meiklejohn, at whom it was once
so fashionable to sneer, have displayed a finer sensitivity to the need for defending domestic
freedoms than the more "sophisticated" intellectuals who leapt from Marx to Machiavelli.

more deeply preoccupied, or preoccupied at deeper levels, with the dangers to freedom stemming from people like Freda Kirchwey and Arthur Miller than the dangers from people like Senator McCarthy. In March 1952 Irving Kristol, then an editor of *Commentary*, could write that "there is one thing the American people know about Senator McCarthy: he, like them, is unequivocally anti-Communist. About the spokesmen for American liberalism, they feel they know no such thing. And with some justification." In September 1952, at the very moment when McCarthy had become a central issue in the presidential campaign, Elliot Cohen, the senior editor of *Commentary*, could write that McCarthy "remains in the popular mind an unreliable, second-string blowhard; his *only* support as a great national figure is from the fascinated fears of the intelligentsia" (emphasis mine). As if to blot out the memory of these performances, Nathan Glazer, still another editor, wrote an excellent analysis of McCarthy in the March 1953 issue; but at the end of his article, almost as if from another hand, there again appeared the magazine's earlier line: "All that Senator McCarthy can do on his own authority that someone equally unpleasant and not a Senator can't, is to haul people down to Washington for a grilling by his committee. It is a shame and an outrage that Senator McCarthy should remain in the Senate; yet I cannot see that it is an imminent danger to personal liberty in the United States." It is, I suppose, this sort of thing that is meant when people speak about the need for replacing the outworn formulas and clichés of liberalism and radicalism with *new ideas*.

4

To what does one conform? To institutions, obviously. To the dead images that rot in one's mind, unavoidably. And almost always, to the small grating necessities of day-to-day survival. In these senses it may be said that we are all conformists to one or another degree. When Sidney Hook writes, "I see no specific virtue in the attitude of conformity or non-conformity," he is right if he means that no human being can, or should, entirely accept or reject the moral and social modes of his time. And he is right in adding that there are occasions, such as the crisis of the Weimar republic, when the nonconformism of a Stefan George or an Oswald Spengler can have unhappy consequences.

But Professor Hook seems to me quite wrong in supposing that his remark applies significantly to present-day America. It would apply if we lived in a world where ideas could be weighed in free and delicate balance, without social pressures or contaminations, so that our choices would be made solely from a passion for truth. As it happens, however, there are tremendous pressures in America that make for intellectual conformism and consequently, in this tense and difficult age, there are very real virtues in preserving the attitude of critical skepticism and distance. Even some of the more extreme antics of the professional "bohemians" or literary anarchists take on a certain value which in cooler moments they might not have.*

What one conforms to most of all—despite and against one's intentions—is the zeitgeist, that vast insidious sum of pressures and fashions; one drifts along, anxious and compliant, upon the favored assumptions of the moment; and not a soul in the intellectual world can escape this. Only, some resist and some don't. Today the zeitgeist presses down upon us with a greater insistence than at any other moment of the century. In the 1930s many of those who hovered about the *New Masses* were mere camp followers of success; but the conformism of the party-line intellectual, at least before 1936, did sometimes bring him into conflict with established power: he had to risk something. Now, by contrast, established power and the dominant intellectual tendencies have come together in a harmony such as this country has not seen since the Gilded Age; and this, of course, makes the temptations of conformism all the more acute. The carrots, for once, are real.

Real even for literary men, who these days prefer to meditate upon symbolic vegetables. I would certainly not wish to suggest any direct correlation between our literary assumptions and the nature of our politics; but surely some of the recent literary trends and fashions owe something to the more general intellectual drift toward conformism. Not, of course, that liberalism dominates literary life, as it dominates the rest of the intellectual world. Whatever practical interest most literary men have in politics comes to little else than the usual liberalism, but their efforts at constructing literary ideologies—frequently as forced marches to discover values our society will not yield them—result in something quite different from liberalism. Through much of our writing, both creative and critical, there run a number of ideological motifs, the importance of which is hardly diminished by the failure of the men who employ them to be fully aware of their implications. Thus, a major charge that might be brought against some New Critics is not that they practice formal criticism but that they don't; not that they see the work of art as an object to be judged according to laws of its own realm but that, often unconsciously, they weave ideological assumptions into their writ-

---

* It may be asked whether a Stalinist's "nonconformism" is valuable. No, it isn't; the Stalinist is anything but a nonconformist; he has merely shifted the object of his worship, as later, when he abandons Stalinism, he usually shifts it again.

ings.* Listening last summer to Cleanth Brooks lecture on Faulkner, I was struck by the deep hold that the term "orthodox" has acquired on his critical imagination, and not, by the way, on his alone. But "orthodox" is not, properly speaking, a critical term at all; it pertains to matters of religious or other belief rather than to literary judgment; and a habitual use of such terms can only result in the kind of "slanted" criticism Mr. Brooks has been so quick, and right, to condemn.

Together with "orthodox" there goes a cluster of terms which, in their sum, reveal an implicit ideological bias. The word "traditional" is especially tricky here, since it has legitimate uses in both literary and moral-ideological contexts. What happens, however, in much contemporary criticism is that these two contexts are taken to either be one or to be organically related, so that it becomes possible to assume that a sense of literary tradition necessarily involves and sanctions a "traditional" view of morality. There is a powerful inclination here—it is the doing of the impish zeitgeist—to forget that literary tradition can be fruitfully seen as a series of revolts, literary but sometimes more than literary, of generation against generation, age against age. The emphasis on "tradition" has other contemporary implications: it is used as a not very courageous means of countering the experimental and the modern; it can enclose the academic assumption—and this is the curse of the Ph.D. system—that the whole of the literary past is at every point equally relevant to a modern intelligence; and it frequently includes the provincial American need to be more genteel than the gentry, more English than the English. Basically, it has served as a means of asserting conservative or reactionary moral-ideological views not, as they should be asserted, in their own terms, but through the refining medium of literary talk.

In general, there has been a tendency among critics to subsume literature under their own moral musings, which makes for a conspicuously humorless kind of criticism.† Morality is assumed to be a suffi-

* This may be true of all critics, but is most perilous to those who suppose themselves free of ideological coloring. In a review of my Faulkner book—rather favorable, so that no ego wounds prompt what follows—Robert Daniel writes that "Because of Mr. Howe's connections with . . . the *Partisan Review*, one might expect his literary judgments to be shaped by political and social preconceptions, but that does not happen often." Daniel is surprised that a critic whose politics happen to be radical should try to keep his literary views distinct from his nonliterary ones. To be sure, this is sometimes very difficult, and perhaps no one entirely succeeds. But the one sure way of not succeeding is to write, as Daniel does, from no very pressing awareness that it is a problem for critics who appear in the *Sewanee Review* quite as much as for those who appear in *Partisan Review*.

† Writing about *Wuthering Heights* Mark Schorer solemnly declares that "the theme of the moral magnificence of unmoral passion is an impossible theme to sustain, and the needs of her temperament to the contrary, all personal longing and reverie to the contrary, Emily Brontë teaches herself that this was indeed not at all what her material must mean as art." What is more, if Emily Brontë had lived a little longer she would have been offered a Chair in Moral Philosophy.

container for the floods of experience, and poems or novels that gain their richness from the complexity with which they dramatize the incommensurability between man's existence and his conceptualizing, are thinned, pruned, and allegorized into moral fables. Writers who spent— in both senses of the word—their lives wrestling with terrible private demons are elevated into literary dons and deacons. It is as if Stendhal had never come forth, with his subversive wit, to testify how often life and literature find the whole moral apparatus irrelevant or tedious, as if Lawrence had never written *The Man Who Died*, as if Nietzsche had never launched his great attack on the Christian impoverishment of the human psyche. One can only be relieved, therefore, at knowing a few critics personally: how pleasant the discrepancy between their writings and their lives!

But it is Original Sin that today commands the highest prestige in the literary world. Like nothing else, it allows literary men to enjoy a sense of profundity and depth—to relish a disenchantment which allows no further risk of becoming enchanted—as against the superficiality of *mere* rationalism. It allows them to appropriate to the "tradition" the greatest modern writers, precisely those whose values and allegiances are most ambiguous, complex and enigmatic, while at the same time generously leaving, as Leslie Fiedler once suggested, Dreiser and Farrell as the proper idols for that remnant benighted enough to maintain a naturalist philosophy. To hold, as Dickens remarks in *Bleak House*, "a loose belief that if the world go wrong, it was, in some off-hand manner, never meant to go right," this becomes the essence of wisdom. (Liberals too have learned to cast a warm eye on "man's fallen nature," so that one gets the high comedy of Arthur Schlesinger, Jr. interrupting his quite worldly political articles with uneasy bows in the direction of Kierkegaard.) And with this latest dispensation come, of course, many facile references to the ideas supposedly held by Rousseau* and Marx, that man is "perfectible" and that progress moves in a steady upward curve.

I say, facile references, because no one who has troubled to read Rousseau or Marx could write such things. Exactly what the "perfectibility of man" is supposed to mean, if anything at all, I cannot say; but it is not a phrase intrinsic to the *kind* of thought one finds in the mature Marx or, most of the time, in Rousseau. Marx did not base his argument for socialism on any view that one could isolate a constant called "human

---

* Randall Jarrell, who usually avoids fashionable cant: "Most of us know, now, that Rousseau was wrong; that man, when you knock his chains off, sets up the death camps." Which chains were knocked off in Germany to permit the setting up of death camps? And which chains must be put up again to prevent a repetition of the death camps?

nature"; he would certainly have agreed with Ortega that man has not a nature, but a history. Nor did he have a very rosy view of the human beings who were his contemporaries or recent predecessors: see in *Capital* the chapter on the Working Day, a grisly catalogue of human bestiality. Nor did he hold to a naive theory of progress: he wrote that the victories of progress "seem bought by the loss of character. At the same pace that mankind masters nature, man seems to become enslaved to other men or to his own infamy."

As for Rousseau, the use of even a finger's worth of historical imagination should suggest that the notion of "a state of nature" which modern literary people so enjoy attacking, was a political metaphor employed in a prerevolutionary situation, and not, therefore, to be understood outside its context. Rousseau explicitly declared that he did not suppose the "state of nature" to have existed in historical time; it was, he said, "a pure idea of reason" reached by abstraction from the observable state of society. As G. D. H. Cole remarks, "in political matters at any rate, the 'state of nature' is for [Rousseau] only a term of controversy . . . he means by 'nature' not the original state of a thing, nor even its reduction to the simplest terms; he is passing over to the conception of 'nature' as identical with the full development of [human] capacity. . . ." There are, to be sure, elements in Rousseau's thought which one may well find distasteful, but these are not the elements commonly referred to when he is used in literary talk as a straw man to be beaten with the cudgels of "orthodoxy."

What then is the significance of the turn to Original Sin among so many intellectuals? Surely not to inform us, at this late moment, that man is capable of evil. Or is it, as Cleanth Brooks writes, to suggest that man is a "limited" creature, limited in possibilities and capacities, and hence unable to achieve his salvation through social means? Yes, to be sure; but the problem of history is to determine, by action, how far those limits may go. Conservative critics like to say that "man's fallen nature" makes unrealistic the liberal-radical vision of the good society— apparently, when Eve bit the apple she predetermined, with one fatal crunch, that her progeny could work its way up to capitalism, and not a step further. But the liberal-radical vision of the good society does not depend upon a belief in the "unqualified goodness of man"; nor does it locate salvation in society: anyone in need of being saved had better engage in a private scrutiny. The liberal-radical claim is merely that the development of technology has now made possible—possible, not inevitable—a solution of those material problems that have burdened mankind for centuries. These problems solved, man is then on his own, to make of his self and his world what he can.

The literary prestige of Original Sin cannot be understood without reference to the current cultural situation; it cannot be understood except as a historical phenomenon reflecting, like the whole turn to religion and religiosity, the weariness of intellectuals in an age of defeat and their yearning to remove themselves from the bloodied arena of historical action and choice, which necessarily means, of secular action and choice. Much sarcasm and anger has been expended on the "failure of nerve" theory, usually by people who take it as a personal affront to be told that there is a connection between what happens in their minds and what happens in the world; but if one looks at the large-scale shifts among intellectuals during the past twenty-five years, it becomes impossible to put *all* of them down to a simultaneous, and thereby miraculous, discovery of Truth; some at least must be seen as a consequence of those historical pressures which make this an age of conformism. Like other efforts to explain major changes in belief, the "failure of nerve" theory does not tell us why certain people believed in the thirties what was only to become popular in the fifties and why others still believe in the fifties what was popular in the thirties; but it does tell us something more important: why a complex of beliefs is dominant at one time and subordinate at another.

5

I have tried to trace a rough pattern from social history through politics and finally into literary ideology, as a means of explaining the power of the conformist impulse in our time. But it is obvious that in each intellectual "world" there are impulses of this kind that cannot easily be shown to have their sources in social or historical pressures. Each intellectual world gives rise to its own patterns of obligation and preference. The literary world, being relatively free from the coarser kinds of social pressure, enjoys a considerable degree of detachment and autonomy. (Not as much as it likes to suppose, but a considerable degree.) That the general intellectual tendency is to acquiesce in what one no longer feels able to change or modify strongly encourages the internal patterns of conformism in the literary world and intensifies the yearning, common to all groups but especially to small and insecure groups, to draw together in a phalanx of solidarity. Then too, those groups that live by hostility to the dominant values of society—in this case, cultural values—find it extremely difficult to avoid an inner conservatism as a way of balancing their public role of opposition; anyone familiar with radical politics knows this phenomenon only too well. Finally, the literary world, while quite powerless in relation to, say, the worlds of business and politics, disposes of a measurable amount of power and patronage within its own domain; which makes, again, for predictable kinds of influence.

Whoever would examine the inner life of the literary world should turn first not to the magazines or the dignitaries or famous writers but to the graduate students, for like it or not the graduate school has become the main recruiting grounds for critics and sometimes even for writers. Here, in conversation with the depressed classes of the academy, one sees how the Ph.D. system—more powerful today than it has been for decades, since so few other choices are open to young literary men—grinds and batters personality into a mold of cautious routine. And what one finds among these young people, for all their intelligence and devotion and eagerness, is often appalling: a remarkable desire to be "critics," not as an accompaniment to the writing of poetry or the changing of the world or the study of man and God, but just critics—as if criticism were a *subject*, as if one could be a critic without having at least four nonliterary opinions, or as if criticism "in itself" could adequately engage an adult mind for more than a small part of its waking time. An equally astonishing indifference to the ideas that occupy the serious modern mind—Freud, Marx, Nietzsche, Frazer, Dewey are not great thinkers in their right, but reservoirs from which one dredges up "approaches to criticism"—together with a fabulous knowledge of what Ransom said about Winters with regard to what Winters had said about Eliot. And a curiously humble discipleship—but also arrogant to those beyond the circle—so that one meets not fresh minds in growth but apostles of Burke or Trilling or Winters or Leavis or Brooks or neo-Aristotle.

Very little of this is the fault of the graduate students themselves, for they, like the distinguished figures I have just listed, are the victims of an unhappy cultural moment. What we have today in the literary world is a gradual bureaucratization of opinion and taste; not a dictatorship, not a conspiracy, not a coup, not a Machiavellian plot to impose a mandatory "syllabus"; but the inevitable result of outer success and inner hardening. Fourth-rate exercises in exegesis are puffed in the magazines while so remarkable and provocative a work as Arnold Hauser's *Social History of Art* is hardly reviewed, its very title indicating the reason. Learned young critics who have never troubled to open a novel by Turgenev can rattle off reams of Kenneth Burke, which gives them, understandably, a sensation of having enlarged upon literature. Literature itself becomes a raw material which critics work up into schemes of structure and symbol; to suppose that it is concerned with anything so gauche as human experience or obsolete as human beings—"You mean," a student said to me, "that you're interested in the *characters* of novels!" Symbols clutter the literary landscape like the pots and pans a two-year-old strews over the kitchen floor; and what is wrong here is not merely the transparent absence of literary tact—the gift for saying when a pan is a pan and when a pan is a symbol—but far more important, a transparent lack of interest in represented experience. For Robert Wooster Stallman the fact that Stephen Crane looking at the sun felt moved to compare it to a wafer is not enough, the existence of suns and wafers and their possible conjunction is not sufficiently marvelous: both objects must be absorbed into Christian symbolism (an ancient theory of literature developed by the church fathers to prove that suns, moons, vulva, chairs, money, hair, pots, pans, and words are really crucifixes). Techniques for reading a novel that have at best a limited relevance are frozen into dogmas: one might suppose from glancing at the more imposing literary manuals that "point of view" is the crucial means of judging a novel. (Willa Cather, according to Caroline Gordon, was "astonishingly ignorant of her craft," for she refrained from "using a single consciousness as a prism of moral reflection." The very mistake Tolstoy made, too!) Criticism itself, far from being the reflection of a solitary mind upon a work of art and therefore, like the solitary mind, incomplete and subjective, comes increasingly to be regarded as a problem in mechanics, the tools, methods, and trade secrets of which can be picked up, usually during the summer, from the more experienced operatives. In the mind of Stanley Hyman, who serves the indispensable function of reducing fashionable literary notions, criticism seems to resemble Macy's on bargain day: *First floor, symbols; Second floor, myths (rituals to the rear on your right); Third floor, ambiguities and paradoxes; Fourth floor, word counting; Fifth floor, Miss Harrison's antiquities; Attic, Marxist remnants; Basement, Freud; Sub-basement, Jung. Watch your step, please.*

What is most disturbing, however, is that writing about literature and writers has become an industry. The preposterous academic requirement that professors write books they don't want to write and no one wants to read, together with the obtuse assumption that piling up more and more irrelevant information about an author's life helps us understand his work—this makes for a vast flood of books that have little to do with literature, criticism, or even scholarship. Would you care to know the contents of the cargo (including one elephant) carried by the vessel of which Hawthorne's father was captain in 1795? Robert Cantwell has an itemized list, no doubt as an aid to reading *The Scarlet Letter.* Jay Leyda knows what happened to Melville day by day and it is hardly his fault that most days nothing very much happened. Edgar Johnson does as much for Dickens and adds plot summaries too, no doubt because he is dealing with a little-read author. Another American scholar has published a full book on *Mardi*, which is astonishing not because he wrote the book but because he managed to finish reading *Mardi* at all.

I have obviously chosen extreme examples and it would be silly to contend that they adequately describe the American literary scene; but like the distorting mirrors in Coney Island they help bring into sharper contour the major features. Or as Donald Davie writes in the English journal, *Twentieth Century*:

> The professional poet has already disappeared from the literary scene, and the professional man of letters is following him into the grave. . . . It becomes more and more difficult, and will soon be impossible, for a man to make his living as a literary dilettante. . . . And instead of the professional man of letters we have the professional critic, the young don writing in the first place for other dons, and only incidentally for that supremely necessary fiction, the common reader. In other words, an even greater proportion of what is written about literature, and even of what literature is written, is "academic." . . . Literary standards are now in academic hands; for the free-lance man of letters, who once supplemented and corrected the don, is fast disappearing from the literary scene. . . .
>
> The pedant is as common as he ever was. And now that willy-nilly so much writing about literature is in academic hands, his activities are more dangerous than ever. But he has changed his habits. Twenty years ago he was to be heard asserting that his business was with hard facts, that questions of value and technique were not his affair, and that criticism could therefore be left to the impressionistic journalist. Now the pedant is proud to call himself a critic; he prides himself on evaluation and analysis; he aims to be penetrating, not informative. . . .
>
> The pedant is a very adaptable creature, and can be as comfortable with Mr. Eliot's "objective correlative," Mr. Empson's "ambiguities" and Dr. Leavis's "complexities" as in the older suit of critical clothes that he has now, for the most part, abandoned.

Davie has in mind the literary situation in England, but all one needs for applying his remarks to America is an ability to multiply.

6

All of the tendencies toward cultural conformism come to a head in the assumption that the avant-garde, as both concept and intellectual grouping, has become obsolete or irrelevant. Yet the future quality of American culture, I would maintain, largely depends on the survival, and the terms of survival, of precisely the kind of dedicated group that the avant-garde has been.

The avant-garde first appeared on the American scene some twenty-five or thirty years ago, as a response to the need for absorbing the meanings of the cultural revolution that had taken place in Europe during the first two decades of the century. The achievements of Joyce, Proust, Schoenberg, Bartók, Picasso, Matisse, to mention only the obvious figures, signified one of the major turnings in the cultural history of the West, a turning made all the more crucial by the fact that it came not during the vigor of a society but during its crisis. To counter the hostility which the work of such artists met among all the official spokesmen of culture, to discover formal terms and modes through which to secure these achievements, to insist upon the continuity between their work and the accepted, because dead, artists of the past—this became the task of the avant-garde. Somewhat later a section of the avant-garde also became politically active, and not by accident; for precisely those aroused sensibilities that had responded to the innovations of the modern masters now responded to the crisis of modern society. Thus, in the early years of a magazine like *Partisan Review*—roughly between 1936 and 1941— these two radical impulses came together in an uneasy but fruitful union; and it was in those years that the magazine seemed most exciting and vital as a link between art and experience, between the critical consciousness and the political conscience, between the avant-garde of letters and the independent left of politics.

That union has since been dissolved, and there is no likelihood that it will soon be re-established. American radicalism exists only as an idea, and that barely; the literary avant-garde—it has become a stock comment for reviewers to make—is rapidly disintegrating, without function or spirit, and held together only by an inert nostalgia.

Had the purpose of the avant-garde been to establish the currency of certain names, to make the reading of *The Waste Land* and *Ulysses* respectable in the universities, there would be no further need for its continuance. But clearly this was not the central purpose of the avant-garde; it was only an unavoidable fringe of snobbery and fashion. The struggle for Joyce mattered only as it was a struggle for literary standards; the defense of Joyce was a defense not merely of modern innovation but of that traditional culture which was the source of modern innovation. And at its best it was a defense against those spokesmen for the genteel, the respectable, and the academic who had established a stranglehold over traditional culture. At the most serious level, the avant-garde was trying to face the problem of the quality of our culture, and when all is said and done, it faced that problem with a courage and honesty that no other group in society could match.

If the history of the avant-garde is seen in this way, there is every reason for believing that its survival is as necessary today as it was twenty-five years ago. To be sure, our immediate prospect is not nearly so exciting as it must then have seemed: we face no battle on behalf of great and difficult artists who are scorned by the official voices of culture. Today, in a sense, the danger is that the serious artists are not scorned enough. Philistinism has become very shrewd: it does not attack its enemies as much as it disarms them through reasonable cautions and moderate amendments. But this hardly makes the defense of those standards that animated the avant-garde during its best days any the less a critical obligation.

It has been urged in some circles that only the pressure of habit keeps serious writers from making "raids" upon the middlebrow world, that it is now possible to win substantial outposts in that world if we are ready to take risks. Perhaps. But surely no one desires a policy of highbrow isolation, and no one could oppose raids, provided that is what they really are. The precondition for successful raids, however, is that the serious writers themselves have a sense—not of belonging to an exclusive club—but of representing those cultural values which alone can sustain them while making their raids. Thus far the incursions of serious writers into the middlebrow world have not been remarkably successful: for every short-story writer who has survived the *New Yorker* one could point to a dozen whose work became trivial and frozen after they had begun to write for it. Nor do I advocate, in saying this, a policy of evading temptations. I advocate overcoming them. Writers today have no choice, often enough, but to write for magazines like the *New Yorker*—and worse, far worse. But what matters is the terms upon which the writer enters into such relationships, his willingness to understand with whom he is dealing, his readiness not to deceive himself that an unpleasant necessity is a desirable virtue.

It seems to me beyond dispute that, thus far at least, in the encounter between high and middle culture, the latter has come off by far the better. Every current of the zeitgeist, every imprint of social power, every assumption of contemporary American life favors the safe and comforting patterns of middlebrow feeling. And then too the gloomier Christian writers may have a point when they tell us that it is easier for a soul to fall than to rise.*

---

* Thus Professor Gilbert Highet, the distinguished classicist, writing in *Harper's* finds André Gide "an abominably wicked man. His work seems to me to be either shallowly based symbolism, or else cheap cynicism made by inverting commonplaces or by grinning through them. . . . Gide had the curse of perpetual immaturity. But then I am always aware of the central fact about Gide—that he was a sexual pervert who kept proclaiming and justifying his perversion; and perhaps this blinds me to his merits . . . the garrulous, Pangloss-like, pimple-scratching, self-exposure of Gide." I don't mean to suggest that many fall so low, but then not many philistines are so well educated as Highet.

Precisely at the time that the highbrows seem inclined to abandon what is sometimes called their "proud isolation," the middlebrows have become more intransigent in their opposition to everything that is serious and creative in our culture (which does not, of course, prevent them from exploiting and contaminating, for purposes of mass gossip, everything that is serious and creative in our culture). What else is the meaning of the coarse attack launched by the *Saturday Review* against the highbrows, under the guise of discussing the Pound case? What, for that matter, is the meaning of the hostility with which the *Partisan Review* symposium on "Our Country and Our Culture" was received? It would take no straining of texts to see this symposium as a disconcerting sign of how far intellectuals have drifted in the direction of cultural adaptation, yet the middlebrows wrote of it with blunt enmity. And perhaps because they too sensed this drift in the symposium, the middlebrows, highly confident at the moment, became more aggressive, for they do not desire compromise, they know that none is possible. So genial a middlebrow as Elmer Davis, in a long review of the symposium, entitled with a characteristic smirk "The Care and Feeding of Intellectuals," ends up on a revealing note: "The highbrows seem to be getting around to recognizing what the middlebrows have known for the past thirty years. This is progress." It is also the best possible argument for the maintenance of the avant-garde, even if only as a kind of limited defense.

Much has been written about the improvement of cultural standards in America, though a major piece of evidence—the wide circulation of paperbound books—is still an unweighed and unanalyzed quantity. The basic relations of cultural power remain unchanged, however: the middlebrows continue to dominate. The most distinguished newspaper in this country retains as its music critic a mediocrity named Olin Downes; the literary critic for that newspaper is a philistine named Orville Prescott; the most widely read book reviewer in this country is a buffoon named Sterling North; the most powerful literary journal, read with admiration by many librarians and professors, remains the *Saturday Review*. Nothing here gives us cause for reassurance or relaxation; nothing gives us reason to dissolve that compact in behalf of critical intransigence known as the avant-garde.

No formal ideology or program is entirely adequate for coping with the problems that intellectuals face in the twentieth century. No easy certainties and no easy acceptance of uncertainty. All the forms of authority, the states and institutions and monster bureaucracies, that press in upon modern life—what have these shown us to warrant the surrender of independence?

The most glorious vision of the intellectual life is still that which is loosely called humanist: the idea of a mind committed yet dispassionate, ready to stand alone, curious, eager, skeptical. The banner of critical independence, ragged and torn though it may be, is still the best we have.

The Stories of Isaac Babel

The publication of Isaac Babel's collected stories is cause for happiness. Most of the stories have appeared in one or another English version, but now to have them in their proper order and thereby to receive their accumulative impact is to know that Babel is not merely, as Maxim Gorky claimed, the most gifted prose writer of postrevolutionary Russia, but one of the literary masters of our century.

Born in 1894, Babel was raised in a lower-middle-class Jewish family in Odessa, and during the prerevolutionary period, when he lived in Moscow as a literary bohemian, he became a protégé of Gorky. After five years of revolution and civil war, Babel returned to his writing and won immediate fame as the author of *Red Cavalry*, a book of breathtaking stories that drew from his experiences with a Cossack unit in Budenny's army. Later, as the Stalin dictatorship hardened its grip, Babel wrote less and less (he was not, in any case, very productive) and after a time he lapsed into silence.

In 1934 Babel made one of his rare public appearances, at the first Russian Writers' Congress, partly to join in the ritual of pledging loyalty to the regime, partly to explain his failure to publish. His performance

From *The New Republic* 133 (July 4, 1955):1, as "The Right to Write Badly."

was a remarkable political act. He practiced, said Babel, a new literary genre: he was "the master of the genre of silence." And in the midst of his praise for the regime and the party, he remarked, as if in passing, that they presumed to deprive writers of only one right, the right to write badly. "Comrades," he went on, "let us not fool ourselves: this is a very important right and to take it away from us is no small thing. . . . Let us give up this right, and may God help us. And if there is no God, let us help ourselves. . . ."

The right to write badly!—to write from one's own feelings, one's own mistakes. It would be hard to imagine a more courageous, and a more saddening, gesture on the part of a writer whose every impulse was for the spontaneity, the playfulness his society denied. Babel, who was protected by Gorky and for whom, it is rumored, even Number One had a soft spot, suffered no immediate punishment, other than the continued silence he had imposed on himself. But in 1937 he was arrested and two or three years later died in a concentration camp. Except for a memorial note on Gorky which appeared in 1938, Babel remained silent to the end, the master of his genre.

The stories in *Red Cavalry* impress in endless ways, but their primary impact is shock. Hard, terse, violent, gorgeously colored, they come upon one like disciplined explosions. Primitive Cossack ways jar against Babel's sophisticated consciousness; the random brutality that is the inheritance of centuries of blackness suddenly lifts itself to a selfless red heroism, and in the very moment of doing so helplessly corrupts the heroism; extremes of behavior, weaving into one another as if to spite all moralists, bewilder Babel as narrator and the reader as onlooker.

The stories turn upon Babel's struggle with a problem that cannot be understood unless it is seen both in the historical setting of the Russian Revolution and in the context of Babel's personal being as intellectual and Jew. Though he was not, so far as we know, concerned with politics as ideological definition or power strategy, Babel understood with absolute sureness the problem that has obsessed all modern novelists who deal with politics: the problem of action in both its heroic necessity and its ugly self-contamination, the "tragic flaw" that is at the heart of a historical action which by virtue of being historical must to some extent be conceived in violence and therefore as a distortion and coarsening of its "self." But it must be stressed that Babel sees this problem not as a mere exercise in metaphysics: for him it is at the very center of choice. And it is in this sense, despite the virtual absence of explicit politics, that the stories in *Red Cavalry* are profoundly revolutionary: under the red heat of Babel's passion, creation and contemplation melt into one.

The problem of historical action also absorbs André Malraux and Ignazio Silone in their best novels, and in Bertolt Brecht's poem "To Posterity" it receives its most exalted and most shameful expression, for here every word is bitterly true yet the poem itself is put to service as a rationale for Stalinism. For Babel, characteristically, the problem turns into one of personal assertion, his capacity to embrace and engage in, yet at some level of awareness to stand apart from, the most terrifying extremes of human conduct.

In his introduction to Babel's stories, Lionel Trilling has abstracted this problem into a kind of timeless moral dialectic. "In Babel's heart," he writes, "there was a kind of fighting—he was captivated by the vision of two ways of being, the way of violence and the way of peace, and he was torn between them." True as this is, I think it misses the center of Babel's concern, which was not so much the choice between "two ways of being" open to men in almost any circumstances, but, rather, the unbearable—unbearable because felt as entirely necessary—difficulties of being an artist committed to the fate of a desperate revolution. One very important side of Babel was a Bolshevik, or tried hard to be ("O regulations of the Russian Communist Party," begins one story, "you have laid headlong rails through the sour pastry of our Russian tales"), and precisely from this side of Babel came some of the energies and anxieties that give life to his work. Like it or not, we cannot blink this simple fact, nor the equally important fact that Babel, as a writer whose politics and aesthetics meet in an appetite for extremes, does not lend himself very easily to those more reasonable modes of feeling which Trilling has designated as the Liberal Imagination.

Some of the most terrible stories in *Red Cavalry* are directed against Babel himself, against his inability to kill other men and his tragicomic efforts to adapt himself to the ways of the Cossacks. The Jewish literary man, with spectacles on his nose and autumn in his heart, needs to prove to himself that, *given the historical necessity*, he can commit acts which for the Cossack are virtually second nature. But since he is also a writer of imaginative largesse, Babel in the course of "lending" himself to the Cossacks falls in love with their gracefulness of gesture and movement. Above all, Babel admires the Cossacks' sureness of manner, their unreflective absorption in inherited modes of life.

Yet he does not sentimentalize the Cossacks, nor use them, as a modern literary man might, to sanction his own repressed aggressiveness. He remains in awed puzzlement before the ancient mysteries of their ways, and even when he achieves occasional rapport with them he does not pretend to understand them. But he grants them every possible human claim, and he trembles beneath the lash of their simple criticism.

In a magnificent five-page story called "The Death of Doglushov,"
a wounded Cossack, his entrails hanging over his knees, begs Babel to
shoot him, but Babel, soft and scrupulous, funks it. A comrade of the
wounded man does the job and then turns furiously upon Babel: "You
guys in specs have about as much pity for chaps like us as a cat has for
a mouse." In another five-page masterpiece, "After the Battle," a Cossack curses Babel for having ridden into battle with an unloaded revolver
("You didn't put no cartridge in. . . . You worship God, you traitor!")
and Babel goes off "imploring fate to grant me the simplest of profi-
ciencies—the ability to kill my fellow-men." And at the end of *Red
Cavalry* another Cossack pronounces his primitive sentence upon Babel:
"You're trying to live without enemies. That's all you think about, not
having enemies."

As counterforce to the Cossacks Babel turns to the Polish Jews,
squatting in their villages while opposing armies trample back and forth,
passive and impervious to the clamor for blood. Even as he fights in the
Red Army, Babel listens, with the attentiveness of a child, to Gedali,
the Hasid who believes that "the Revolution means joy" and who wants
"an International of good people." "I would like every soul to be listed,"
says Gedali, "and given first-category rations. There, soul, please eat
and enjoy life's pleasures. Pan comrade, you don't know what the International is eaten with. . . ." "It is eaten with gun-powder," answers
Babel, "and spiced with best-quality blood."

The Jews of Poland, with their "long bony backs, their tragic yellow
beards," pierce through the taut objectivity of Babel's narrative and stir
in him a riot of memories ("O the rotted Talmuds of my childhood!")
He goes back and forth from the Cossacks, strange, cruel, and beautiful,
to the ghetto Jews, who "moved jerkily, in an uncontrolled and uncouth
way, but [whose] capacity for suffering was full of a sombre greatness.
. . ." If *Red Cavalry* is a paean, ambiguous but ardent, to the force of
revolution, it is also an elegy for "the Sabbath peace [which] rested
upon the crazy roofs of Zhitomer."

Even to mention Babel's style is to involve one's self in a tangle of
contradictions and frustrations. Gestures of bare violence turn abruptly,
without preparation, into states of reflective quietness. Objectivity
seems the dominant mode, yet few modern prose writers would dare
indulge in such lyrical apostrophes as fill Babel's pages. We have been
taught to value terseness and understatement; but in Babel terseness
has nothing whatever to do with understatement, since it is actually the
consequence of the boldest political and metaphysical generalizations.
Indeed, hardly another writer of our time has succeeded so well in

making the generalization, even the political slogan, so organically a part of his imagery. One moves in these stories with a dizzying speed from conceptual abstraction to primitive notation: Babel never permits the reader to rest in any mold of style or upon any level of perception; he always drives one from surprise to surprise. In some of the stories there is a surrender to sadness as complete as the urge to motion and violence. In other stories the event itself has been removed from sight, and the surface of the prose is devoted to a few wry ripples of talk and a few startling images of place and weather.

The best observation on Babel's style has been made by John Berryman, who has noted certain similarities to the style of Stephen Crane. In both writers there is an obsessive concern with compression and explosion, a kinesthetic ferocity of control, a readiness to wrench language in order to gain nervous immediacy. Both use language as if to inflict a wound. But the differences are also important. Babel is warm, while Crane is cold. And more important, Babel has a wider range of effects; by comparison, Crane seems a little stiff-jointed.

The two main literary sources upon which Babel seems to have drawn, Russian and Yiddish, flourished most in the fifty or seventy-five years directly before he began to write; he was one of those writers who spring up at the end of a creative period and absorb its energies as if they were still at their fullest. The Chekhov strain in Russian literature is strongly evident in Babel's miscellaneous stories; one quickly recognizes the pathos, the warm skepticism of the older writer. The Yiddish literary influence is less likely to be noticed by American critics. But surely no one who has read Sholom Aleichem can fail to see that in Babel's Odessa stories there is a remarkable parallel of effect: the comic grasp of social relationships, the sardonic arguing with God, the attraction to the undersides of history. Compare Babel's bitter wit with Sholom Aleichem's impudent reverence in writing about Jewish fate:

Babel: "But wasn't it a mistake on God's part to settle the Jews in Russia, where they've had to suffer the tortures of Hell? Would it be bad if the Jews lived in Switzerland, where they'd be surrounded by first-class lakes, mountain air and nothing but Frenchmen? Everybody makes mistakes, even God."

Sholom Aleichem: "Apparently if He wants it that way, that's the way it ought to be. Can't you see? If it should have been different it would have been. And yet, what would have been wrong to have it different?"

Sometimes the richness of emotion, and often the very phrasing of his idiom, is understandable only in terms of Babel's relationship to Yiddish literature. In a story called "In the Basement" the vulgar loving rebuke of a grandfather to a boy who tries to commit suicide ("My grandson . . . I'm taking a dose of castor oil, so as to have something to place on your grave") is given its true value and inflection only if one knows that in the Jewish mores suicide is taken to be not merely impious but shameful.

Lost as he often is in melancholia and sadness, perplexed and even a little betrayed as he sometimes is by violence, Babel—through his simple readiness to accept his own desires—makes upon life the most radical of demands: the demand for happiness. In his work one finds a straining toward a union of passion and tenderness, those two elements of feeling which Freud says have become dissociated in the life of modern man and which, because they are dissociated, tend to decline into aggressiveness and impotence. I do not say that Babel often achieves this union, only that he will not let anything, not even "the regulations of the Communist Party," distract him from straining toward it. In his work everything becomes eroticized, everything becomes animated: love and energy come closer.

There is a lovely little story by Babel in which he describes how a baby named Karl-Yankel (half Marxist-half Jew) is being fought over by the two sets of believers. Babel, watching the comic struggle, ends the story by telling himself, "It's not possible . . . it's not possible that you won't be happy, Karl-Yankel. It's not possible that you won't be happier than I."

Tomato or Cucumber?

Alain Robbe-Grillet's *The Voyeur* comes to us as an example of the "anti-novel novel," reinforced by an elaborate theoretical equipage. Robbe-Grillet writes that he wishes to dismiss "the old myth of 'depth,' " the assumption that a meaning is to be found in a depicted relationship between objects and/or events. *"Profundity,"* he writes in a sentence as shallow as it is sparkling, "has functioned like a trap in which the writer captures the universe to hand it over to society." What Robbe-Grillet wants is the chair and not the "signification" of the chair, for "the world is neither significant nor absurd. It *is*, quite simply." Quite simply!

Roland Barthes gives a more sustained explanation:

> Description for Robbe-Grillet is always "anthological"—a matter of presenting the object as if in a mirror, as if it were in itself a *spectacle*, permitting it to make demands on our attention without regard for its relation to the dialectic of the story. . . . The object has no being beyond *phenomenon*: it is not ambiguous or allegorical. . . . A slice of tomato in an automat sandwich, described according to this method, constitutes an object without heredity, without associations, and without references . . . and refusing with all the stubbornness of its *there*ness to involve the reader in an *elsewhere*. . . .

From *Celebrations and Attacks* (New York: Horizon Press, 1979).

As one might expect, these writers look for support in certain kinds of contemporary painting which seem also to represent the object in its thereness, without volunteering any value other than that which may reside in the visual moment.

But one is entitled to wonder: what principle of selection guides Robbe-Grillet in choosing one object for description rather than another? (An "anthological" description obviously implies selection.) Why a tomato rather than a cucumber? From certain points of view, this is by no means a trivial choice. And is not the act of choice necessarily dependent upon some bias of meaning, with its "heredity" and "associations," regardless of whether the writer is aware of this fact? Barthes's apparently casual reference to the position of the slice of tomato—that it lies within an *automat* sandwich—supplies it, actually, with a complex series of "depth" associations, indeed, with an entire historical aura.

For a painting it may be enough that the principle of selection be the visual satisfaction that can be had simply from looking at a created object, though here too one might wonder whether the object can exist on the plane of *thereness* without leading the observer to some *elsewhere*. But things seem to be quite different in literature, among other reasons because the verbal description of the object, no matter how effective, can seldom be as complete and self-contained an aesthetic unit as a painting can.

The reality of Robbe-Grillet's writing is quite different from the claims of his theory. The compulsive anthologizing of events and objects directs our attention not to the surface of things, not to mere phenomena, but—it seems almost perverse—to possible clues as to meaning, response, emotion; and the fewer clues we have, the more are we driven to hunt for them. Nor is this comic shifting of direction unique in modern literature. When we read Virginia Woolf's *The Waves*, we are so thoroughly immersed in the flow of psychic sensation and reflection that we soon find ourselves seeking desperately for guide-points of event; we wish to make whole again the universe she has split into a radical duality. Reading *The Waves*, as it keeps immersing us in depth, turns our attention to surfaces; reading *The Voyeur*, which confines itself to surfaces, turns our attention to depth.

The Voyeur, in any case, is not merely an "anthologized" string of described objects; it has a plot of sorts. And no sooner is plot in evidence than there must be a recourse to ideas, preconceptions, inflections of emotion. So that it is simply not true, as Barthes writes, that "the work of Robbe-Grillet is susceptible to no thematic index whatever." Robbe-Grillet might protest that we are thrusting upon him that very incubus of meaning which he seeks to discard; but short of inflicting lobotomies upon his readers, he will have to put up with the fact that in coming to his books they inevitably bring with them a heredity. Joyce demanded that his readers give him their future; Robbe-Grillet, more extravagant, demands their past.

The novel itself is more interesting than the theories that surround it. Robbe-Grillet is skillful at evoking moods of anxiety (as one might expect in a writer distrustful of "depth"). Incidents repeat themselves crazily in the way they do in some experimental films, creating an epistemological disturbance; the chaotic mental references of his protagonist are presented as if they were actual happenings or as if they were indistinguishable from actual happenings. Though severely limited by the writer's programmatic avoidance of emotion, the result is a novel with moments of considerable power—but a power that is primarily psychological. All of which suggests that reality—in this case, the spontaneous human striving for a unity of perception and comprehension—has a way of revenging itself upon those who go too far in violating it.

The Snopes Saga

The Snopeses have always been there. No sooner did Faulkner come upon his central subject—how the corruption of the homeland, staining its best sons, left them without standards or defense—than Snopesism followed inexorably. Almost anyone can detect the Snopeses, but describing them is hard. The usual reference to "amorality," while accurate, is not sufficiently distinctive and by itself does not allow us to place them, as they should be placed, in a historical moment. Perhaps the most important thing to be said about the Snopeses is that they are what comes afterward: the creatures that emerge from the devastation, with the slime upon their lips.

Let a world collapse, in the South or Russia, and there appear figures of coarse ambition driving their way up from beneath the social bottom, men to whom moral claims are not so much absurd as incomprehensible, sons of bushwhackers or muzhiks drifting in from nowhere and taking over through the sheer outrageousness of their monolithic force. They become presidents of banks and chairmen of party regional committees, and later, a trifle slicked up, they muscle their way into Congress or the Politburo.

From *The New Republic* 141 (December 7, 1959):23, as "Faulkner: End of a Road."

In a prefatory note to *The Mansion*, the novel which completes the Snopes trilogy, Faulkner says that he has been working on this clan since 1925. We can well believe it. The Snopeses have appeared in earlier books, *Sartoris* and *Sanctuary*, which contain snatches of portraiture or anecdote later to be worked up in *The Hamlet, The Town*, and *The Mansion*. One would speculate that by the mid-twenties, after Faulkner had returned to Mississippi from World War I, the originals of Snopes-ism, red-neck rascals and demagogues, had come to the social forefront. Perhaps it was some shock of perception, some encounter with an orig-inal of Flem or I. O. or Ike Snopes, which first prompted him to look back into the fate of the homeland, mulling over the collapse of the Sartorises and Compsons that left the field open for Flem Snopes and his plague of relatives.

The homeland drifted in poverty and xenophobia, without social direction or moral authority. Traditional relationships had decayed but there were no workable new ones. Into this vacuum, with a shattering energy, came the Snopeses. And insofar as they are both its sign and product, Faulkner's description of them in *The Hamlet* as "sourceless" is brilliant.

Most of *The Hamlet*, published in 1940, was written during the previous ten or twelve years, and together with *Go Down, Moses*, brings to a close Faulkner's great creative period. It is a comic extravaganza, half family chronicle and half tall tale, strung together in loosely related episodes that portray the swarming of the Snopeses upon Frenchman's Bend, a hamlet in a rich river bottom, "hill-cradled and remote," at the southern rim of Yoknapatawpha County. By the end of the book Flem Snopes, who had begun as a clerk in the village store, is ready to leave for Jefferson, the town where he will become a bank president and then owner of a splendid mansion.

Flem towers over the book, a figure with a marvelous energy for deceit, a Jonsonian monomania in pursuit of money. In Flem, Faulkner has embodied the commercial ethos with a grotesque purity, both as it represents the power of an undeviating will and as it appears in its ultimate flimsiness. This tour de force depends upon Faulkner's refusal to make Flem "human," his steadiness in holding Flem to an extreme conception which, violating verisimilitude, reaches truth. Though Flem stands for everything Faulkner despises and fears, he is treated in *The Hamlet* with a comic zest, a sheer amazement that such a monster could exist or even be imagined. The danger is real, but the battlefield still confined, and opposed to Flem there stands as a mature antagonist, if in the end a defeated one, the humane sewing-machine agent V. K. Ratliff. One of the few "positive" characters in Faulkner's novels who is utterly convincing and not a canting windbag, Ratliff provides an aura of security for the book. His presence makes possible a sustained comic perspective upon the Snopes invasion, and in its own right speaks for the possibilities of civilized existence. Seventeen years intervened between *The Hamlet* and *The Town*, years of a slowly mounting crisis in Faulkner's career. The more he kept reassuring us that man would "endure," the less assurance his own work showed. Though the novels he wrote in the forties and fifties contain many fine parts, they are on the whole forced, anxious and high-pitched, the work of a man, no longer driven, who now drives himself. *Intruder in the Dust* launches the marvelous Negro curmudgeon Lucas Beauchamp, but goes utterly dead with pages of barren Southern oratory. *Requiem for a Nun* contains some exquisite rhapsodic interludes, but in the central sections, so clearly meant to be dramatic, it falls into inert statement. *The Fable*, which may come to hold a place in Faulkner's work analogous to *Pierre* in Melville's, is a book noble in conception but incoherent in execution. What went wrong? In all these works there is a reliance upon a high-powered rhetoric which bears the outer marks of the earlier Faulkner, but is really a kind of self-imitation, a whipped-up fury pouring out in wanton excess. There is a tendency to fall back upon hi-jinks of plot, a flaunting arbitrariness and whimsicality of invention—as if Faulkner, wearied of telling stories and establishing characters, were now deliberately breaking his own spell. Consciously or not, he seems to be underscoring the incongruity between the overwrought, perhaps incommunicable seriousness of his intentions—his having reached a point where language seems no longer to suffice—and the triviality of the devices to which he turns.

There is, further, an apparent disengagement, perhaps even a disenchantment, with the Yoknapatawpha locale, which had fruitfully obsessed him in the past. Faulkner has now entered the familiar workaday world in which you and I live, at least one part of him has, the man you see in the photographs dressed in a natty gray topcoat; and no longer is it possible to imagine him, like Balzac, calling on his deathbed for a doctor—"get old Doc Peabody!"—from his own novels. His creative journey, begun with the nihilism of the twenties in *Soldier's Pay*, has led him, not as his conservative critics have maintained, to the strength of a traditionalist morality but to the more perilous edge of the nihilism of the fifties.

Faulkner has become our contemporary. He can no longer work within his established means; one senses a bewilderment and disorientation spreading through his pages, by which the subject of his earlier novels now becomes the force constraining his later ones. How else can one explain the frantic verbal outpourings of Gavin Stevens, the character so disastrously his alter ego? Anyone with a touch of feeling, to say nothing of respect, must respond to this new Faulkner who so evidently shares our hesitations and doubts. But in truth this is no longer the man who wrote *The Sound and the Fury*, not even the one who wrote *The Hamlet*.

By the time he turned back to the Snopeses, Faulkner could sustain neither his old fury nor his old humor. Both, to be sure, break out repeatedly in *The Town* and *The Mansion*; there are sections which, if torn out of context, read nearly as well as anything he has done in the past. But they have to be torn out of context. Nor is the difficulty to be found in the over-all design of the trilogy. That, on the contrary, is superb. Faulkner sees how Flem Snopes must assume the appearance of respectability, which in turn will rob him of a portion of his demonic powers and pinch him into ordinary helplessness. Faulkner also sees how Flem, though safe from attack by the "traditionalist" leaders of the county, must meet his destruction at the hands of a Nemesis from within his tribe: Mink Snopes, a pitiful terrier of a man who spends thirty-eight years in jail because, as he believes, Flem has failed him, and who knows that the meaning of his life is now to kill Flem.

Indeed, one can anticipate scores of critical essays which will trace the ways in which each incident in the trilogy contributes to the total scheme, and which thereby will create the false impression that a satisfying congruence exists between the conceptual design and the novels as they are. (This, I think, is the single greatest weakness of American criticism today: that, in its infatuation with the idea of literary structure as a system of thematic strands, it fails to consider performance as the decisive measure.) Yet, as regards *The Town* and *The Mansion*, such a congruence is not to be found, for only fitfully do these novels fulfill the needs of Faulkner's over-all design.

Let me cite an example. One of the Snopeses, Cla'ence, goes in for politics and in 1945, running for Congress, suddenly declares himself an opponent of the KKK. This shrewd maneuver, apparently made in response to the changing atmosphere of the South, greatly upsets Ratliff and Gavin Stevens, who fear that the minority of "liberal" Yoknapatawpha citizens will now be taken in. Ratliff then arranges that, at a picnic in Frenchman's Bend, a gang of dogs should mistake Cla'ence for a familiar thicket which they visit regularly each day—and this dampening of the candidate makes him so ridiculous that he must withdraw from the race. For as Uncle Billy Varner, the Croesus of Frenchman's Bend, says: "I ain't going to have Beat Two and Frenchman's Bend represented nowhere by nobody that ere a son-a-bitching dog that happens by cant tell from a fence post."

Simply as an anecdote, this comes off beautifully. Faulkner can tease this sort of joke along better than anyone else, just as he knows the mind of a grasping little demagogue like Cla'ence Snopes better than anyone else. But in the context of the trilogy the incident is damaging, since it suggests that the threat of Snopesism can easily be defeated by the country shrewdness of a Ratliff—an assumption which all the preceding matter has led us gravely to doubt and which, if we do credit it, must now persuade us that the danger embodied by the Snopeses need not be taken as seriously as the whole weight of the trilogy has seemed to argue. The incident is fine, and so is the over-all pattern; but their relationship is destructive.

There are more important difficulties. Through both *The Town* and *The Mansion* Flem Snopes moves steadily toward the center of Yoknapatawpha economic power. The meaning of this is fully registered, but Flem himself, as a represented figure, is not nearly so vivid in these novels as in *The Hamlet*. Partly this seems due to a flagging of creative gifts, so that, for the first time, one feels Faulkner is dutifully completing a cycle of novels rather than writing for the sheer pleasure of writing. Partly it is due to his propensity for avoiding the direct and dramatic, for straining the action through the blurred—and blurring—consciousness of the insufferable Stevens and the mediocre young Charles Mallison. Partly it is the result of a genuine literary problem: that Faulkner, having set up Flem with such a perfection of malevolence in *The Hamlet*, now faced the difficult task of finding ways to dispose of him, as a character, in the two later books. Apparently aware of this problem, Faulkner tries to outflank it in *The Mansion* by keeping Flem in the background as a figure whom we barely see, though his impact upon the other characters is always felt. That Flem Snopes, of all the memorable monsters in American literature, would end up seeming shadowy and vague—who could have anticipated this?

Faulkner has made the mistake of softening Flem; he verges at times on sociological and psychological explanations of Flem's behavior; and he even shows a few traces of sympathy for Flem, which is as unfortunate as if Ben Jonson broke into tears over Volpone. When the Flem we see—or, alas, more often hear about—is "the old fishblooded son of a bitch who had a vocabulary of two words, one being No and the other Foreclose," all is for the best in the best of Faulknerian worlds; but when it is a Flem who becomes still another item in the omnivorous musings of Gavin Stevens, then he suffers a fate worse than even he deserves. The greatest trouble, finally, with *The Mansion*, as with *The Town*, is that Faulkner feels obliged to give a large portion of his space to material that does not directly involve the Snopeses. Again, there is a conflict between the design of the trilogy and what Faulkner can bring off at the moment of composition. The trilogy requires that a new force of opposition to the Snopeses be found, since they have moved to the town, where, presumably, Ratliff can no longer operate with his accustomed assurance. In both *The Town* and *The Mansion* Ratliff suffers a sad constriction, all too often playing straight man to Gavin Stevens. For the new force of opposition to the Snopeses, as the Faulkner aficionado can sadly predict, now comes largely from Stevens, the district attorney with a degree from Heidelberg and a passion for rant.

The middle section of *The Mansion* deals with Stevens' relation to Linda Snopes, stepdaughter of Flem and daughter of Eula Varner Snopes, whom Gavin had worshipped in vain throughout *The Town*. Linda has left Jefferson; married a Jewish sculptor in New York; gone off to the Spanish Civil War, where she suffered a puncture of her eardrums; returned to Jefferson as a member of the Communist Party; and now loves Gavin (also in vain), "meddles" with the Negroes, and shares a home with Flem in cold silence, until her schemes lead to Mink being freed from jail, destroying Flem and thereby avenging the suicide of her mother. Gavin loves Linda too, but once more in vain. For reasons that two readings of the novel do not yield to me, they fail to marry or do anything else that might reasonably be expected from a man and a woman in love, except to purr sympathetically at each other.

In any case, this whole section is poorly managed. The New York locale, Linda's venture into Communism, the snooping of an FBI man— these are not matters that Faulkner can handle with authority. The relationship between Gavin and Linda, never allowed to settle into quiet clarity, elicits at most a mild pity, since Faulkner seems unable to face up to whatever remnants of Southern "chivalry," romantic ideology, or plain ordinary repression drive him to think of love as a grandiloquent "doom." The truth, I suspect, is that Faulkner cannot treat adult sexual experience with a forthright steadiness, despite the frequency with which sex appears in his earlier books as a symptom of disorder and violation. Only at the end of the novel, as Stevens and Linda kiss good-bye and he slides his hand down her back, "simply touching her . . . supporting her buttocks as you cup the innocent hipless bottom of a child," does Faulkner break into that candor for which this whole section cries out. If the Snopes trilogy, bringing together nearly the best and nearly the worst in Faulkner's career, is both imposing and seriously marred, *The Mansion* taken more modestly, as a novel in its own right, has some superb sections. Perhaps the reader who is not steeped in Faulkner's work and cares nothing about its relation to his previous books is in the best position to accept it with pleasure. For whenever Mink Snopes appears, the prose becomes hard, grave, vibrant, and Faulkner's capacity, as Malcolm Cowley has put it, for "telling stories about men or beasts who fulfilled their destiny," comes into full play. Like the convict in *The Wild Palms*, Mink drives steadily toward his end, without fear or hope.

Faulkner begins *The Mansion* by retelling a story told in *The Hamlet*, but with far greater depth of feeling. Mink Snopes, galled by the arrogance of his wealthy neighbor Houston and himself full of a bitter meanness as well as a bottom-dog dignity which draws the line beyond which humiliation is not to be borne, finally kills Houston and stands trial for murder. He expects Flem to rescue him, since for him, as for all the other Snopeses, Flem is the connection between their clan and the outer world. Flem, however, coldly abandons Mink, and Mink, sentenced to prison, lives only for the day he can destroy Flem. A stratagem of Flem's lures Mink into attempting an escape; his sentence is doubled; but he waits patiently, sweating out his blood over the state's cotton. At the age of sixty-three, his body as puny as a child's, he comes out a free man.

The portrait of Mink is beyond praise: a simple ignorant soul who sees existence as an unending struggle between Old Moster (God) and Them (the world), with Them forever and even rightly and naturally triumphant, always in control of events as they move along, yet with Old Moster standing in reserve, not to intervene or to help but to draw a line, like Mink himself, and say that beyond this line no creature, not even a wretched little Mink, dare be tried.

In the opening part of the novel, as well as in its brilliant final pages—where Mink goes to Memphis to buy a gun, gets caught up in a superbly rendered revivalist sect led by Marine Sergeant Goodyhay, mooches a quarter from a cop and supposes that this is one of those new dispensations he had dimly heard described as the "WP and A" and finally, as if in a pageant of fatality, returns to Jefferson to kill his cousin—in these pages Faulkner is writing at very close to the top of his bent. It all quivers with evocation, the language becomes taut, and Faulkner's sense of the power of life as it floods a man beyond his reason or knowledge, becomes overwhelming. Here is Mink reflecting:

> In 1948 he and Flem would both be old men and he even said aloud: "What a shame we cant both of us jest come out two old men setting peaceful in the sun or the shade, waiting to die together, not even thinking no more of hurt or harm or getting even, not even remembering no more

about hurt or harm or anguish or revenge,"—two old men not only incapable of further harm to anybody but even incapable of remembering hurt or harm. . . . But I reckon not, he thought, *Cant neither of us help nothing now. Cant neither one of us take nothing back.*

And here is Mink approaching Jefferson after thirty-eight years, as he rests on a truck:

He was quite comfortable. But mainly he was off the ground. That was the danger, what a man had to watch against: once you laid flat on the ground, right away the earth started in to draw you back down into it. The very moment you were born out of your mother's body, the power and drag of the earth was already at work on you . . . And you knew it too.

Reading such passages in the fullness of their context is like returning to a marvelous world that has gone a little dim, the world Faulkner made; and then all seems well.

The Stories of Pirandello

Luigi Pirandello is one of the honored names of European literature, but few Americans know anything about him. Literate persons are likely to be familiar with one or two of his titles: there is the play *Six Characters in Search of an Author* and then . . . well, there is the fact that he was a highly intellectual dramatist specializing in the interchange of appearance and reality. And usually that is about as far as it goes. For Pirandello has not shaped our feeling or bent our thought as Kafka or Lawrence or Proust has. Pirandello the writer is not warm or lovable or magnetic; he bears no theories of social renovation or psychic rebirth; he is not a culture hero promising, or threatening, to transform our lives.

Yet Pirandello is a major figure. Like Thomas Hardy, he managed in one lifetime (1867–1936) to complete two literary careers. He began as a writer of prose fiction, publishing several novels and hundreds of stories, and then he became a dramatist, composing over forty plays, several of them masterpieces. The plays and stories overlap in time of composition, but it is useful to regard them as products of two distinct careers.

Why then has he failed to capture the imagination of American

Introduction to *The Stories of Pirandello* (New York: Simon & Schuster, 1959).

readers and audiences? Some reasons are obvious: the early translations frequently muffled his brilliance, there has arisen a false notion that he is a mere juggler of a few ideas, and liberal intellectuals have been hostile to him because of his membership, more the result of opportunism than principle, in the Italian Fascist Party during the twenties.

There are other reasons, more elusive and important. Serious twentieth-century readers turn to literature not so much for the direct pleasure of seeing human experience represented fictionally or of sa- voring mastery of language and form. We expect more from literature: we expect that it discover norms of conduct, that it yield revelation as well as portray reality. Almost unwittingly we find ourselves insisting that the great modern writer be not merely a portraitist of life but also a self-affirmed prophet, a moral revolutionist, an agent of transcendence. The message of guidance that neither politics nor philosophy nor religion now seems able to provide, we look for in literature.

That message Pirandello refuses to give. He refuses on principle, for he does not believe there is such a message, and he does not believe the writer would have any business offering it even if it did exist. Pi- randello's best work is characterized by doubt, at times by an extreme relativism of perspective that can be said to approach epistemological panic. He searches for approximate truths rather than fixed salvation, and meanwhile he offers little solace. This skepticism, which in his writing often serves as an incitement to humaneness, is the only "sal- vation"—modest and depressing as it may be—that he would claim to offer. He never yields to, though he often deals with, rhetoric and apocalypse, vanity and program. The reader who comes to a Pirandello play or story with the usual complement of anxiety will leave without having been disburdened.

Pirandello is a writer strongly marked by the tone of his time, the tone of grayness that gradually suffuses the culture of Europe during the late nineteenth and early twentieth centuries. The energy of the immediate past, a moment of bourgeois confidence, has begun to wane; the energy of the immediate future, a moment of experimental daring, has not yet quite appeared. It is remarkable how widespread is this mood of twilight sadness, this psychic depression. Pirandello, Chekhov, Gissing, Hardy, the early Mann, and a bit later Martin du Gard—these writers, very different from one another, all reflect in their work the feeling that a great century of hope, work, and progress has come to an end and that a littleness of spirit has overtaken Europe.

Perhaps this feeling is due to the intensified crisis of bourgeois so- ciety, perhaps to the triumph of scientistic ideologies, perhaps to the decay of religious conviction, perhaps to the growth of modern cities.

For the moment it hardly matters. What does matter is that in writer after writer who comes to maturity at this time there is a weariness of spirit, a shared conviction, as the great German sociologist Max Weber put it, of being witness to "the disenchantment of the world." The forms of social existence harden. Energy seems to run down. The spirit of denial and cold rationalization takes command. And Freud's dictum that civilization is purchased through the suppression of instinct and pleasure must be regarded not merely as a speculation or personal statement but as the expression of attitudes common to many thoughtful men of the time.

Nowhere is this tone of things more seriously—or austerely—communicated than in Pirandello's stories and plays. The stories are filled with glimpses of lonely city streets, barren provincial towns, sluggish middle-class homes, stuffy Sundays, torn families. Pirandello is the poet of frustration, the kind that seems inevitable in civilized existence. Few writers have ever dealt more honestly with the tiresomeness of daily life, not as the emblem of some "deeper" metaphysical condition but simply as an irreducible fact. Finally, the vision of denial that dominates his work is more frightening than the visions of horror that would later appear in the work of the great twentieth-century modernists. To stay with Pirandello takes strong nerves.

Luigi Pirandello was born in Agrigento, Sicily, the son of a moderately well-to-do sulfur dealer. Sicily figured as the setting in a number of his early stories and one or two plays, mostly as a scene of social brutishness and provincial deprivation. It also proved important to his career in another way: the dominant literary influence upon his early work was the naturalism of the great Sicilian novelist Giovanni Verga.

As a youth Pirandello turned to philological studies, earning a degree at the University of Bonn and translating Goethe's *Roman Elegies* into Italian. He wrote some conventional verse, but his talent first came into evidence with *The Outcast*, a novel published in 1893. During this phase of his career Pirandello found life extremely difficult, at times insupportable. Because his family had lost its money, he had to turn to the drudgery of teaching at a girls school in Rome. His wife, an extremely jealous woman, finally collapsed into insanity, and Pirandello, with characteristic muted stoicism, nursed her at home, a virtual prisoner of her whims and delusions. In the twenty years between *The Outcast* and World War I he nevertheless managed to publish a great many stories and four full-length novels, including the very fine one entitled *The Late Mattia Pascal* (1904).

Only in 1916 did Pirandello begin to devote his major energy to writing plays. He had written one or two before, but there now occurred an outburst of creative speed: brilliant work composed in a few days or a week. In 1921 his famous play *Six Characters in Search of an Author* was produced, and the following year perhaps his greatest play, *Henry IV*. Pirandello now became an international literary figure, his work being performed in theaters throughout the world and the catchphrase "Pirandellian" applied, not always carefully, to a kind of cerebral drama that released the philosophical skepticism and the concern with personal identity that had been troubling serious minds in the West for some time. In 1925, partly through a subsidy from the Mussolini government, Pirandello started an art theater in Rome; later he took it on tour through the major capitals of Europe. Pirandello seems to have found little pleasure in his fame: he had suffered too intensely in the earlier years, his personality had, it seems, become too dry, and he had too keen a sense of the ridiculousness of success to remain anything but the isolated spectator he had always been. There is an amusing late play of his translated into English as *When Someone Is Somebody*, which portrays a great Italian writer, clearly a version of Pirandello himself, who has become so thoroughly a national institution he is not even named but merely designated as XXX. The great writer tries, through a clever trick, to establish for himself a new public identity, but the pressures upon him, not least of all the pressures from his decaying body, are too great. In a final scene XXX slowly turns into his own statue, a mere stone. Shortly before this happens he explains to his young admirers the reason for his loss of nerve: "You don't know what an atrocious thing happens to an old man, to see himself all of a sudden in a mirror, when the sorrow of seeing himself is greater than the astonishment of no longer remembering. You don't know the almost obscene shame of feeling a young and hot-blooded heart within an old body."

During the twenties Pirandello joined the Italian Fascist Party, not, so far as one can tell, out of enthusiasm for its chauvinist braggadocio, but simply because he preferred not to make difficulties for himself. Like most people, Pirandello seems to have had no strong political convictions; he took the easy way out; I suppose that his support of the Fascist regime had about the same sort of ritual expediency as the support certain Russian writers gave to the Communist regime. In any case there is no close or direct relationship between this Fascist membership and the content of his plays. Not only are the plays quite nonpolitical, but the very style of thought they display is at odds with the nationalist demagogy of the Fascists. In much of Pirandello's work there is a devotion to cerebral intensities, an anxious concern with reflection as a value in life, and this is in no way lessened by his having to conclude that human thought seems to him hopelessly rutted in subjectivity. Whatever the practical or personal reasons for his support of the Mussolini regime—and they are to be seen as reasons, not justifications—Pirandello's major plays are the work of a *European* writer, a "good European."

"Under Fascism," writes Eric Bentley, "Pirandello's playwriting entered a third and more problematic phase. . . . Pirandello withdraws into a strange, subjective world of his own . . . or, as he would probably prefer to say, tries to create myths." At the end of his career Pirandello was still an unsettled writer; he abandoned the philosophical comedy that marks his greatest achievement and turned to a semiallegorical, almost dreamlike mode of composition. Some of his late plays, such as *The Mountain Giants* and *The New Colony*—difficult but impressive—indicate that, far from yielding to the chiliastic vulgarities of totalitarianism, he remained a skeptic to the end. In *The New Colony* the skepticism is tempered by a strong humaneness, as Pirandello shows the effort of a group of smugglers and toughs to start a utopian community and its subsequent disintegration in petty disputes and failings. He writes with considerable sympathy for these colonists, and his critique of their utopian impulse is anything but scornful.

In the concluding gesture of his life Pirandello clearly dissociated himself from the secular and religious institutions of his world. "When I am dead," he gave instructions, "do not clothe me." (The Fascists would come to bury him in a black shirt, but be denied by his will.) "Wrap me naked in a sheet. No flowers on the bed and no lighted candle. A pauper's cart. Naked. And let no one accompany me, neither relatives nor friends. The cart, the horse, the coachman, *e basta*. Burn me . . ."

Pirandello's stories are in the main tradition of nineteenth-century European realism. Except for those set in Sicily, which have a distinctive regional flavor and something of the pained intensity that can be found in the work of a writer returning to the miseries of his homeland, they are stories that often seem close in manner and spirit to the writings of the French realists and naturalists. Ordinary social life forms their main setting. The weariness of middle-class routine, the sourings of domesticity, the familiar cruelty of city life provide their characteristic subjects. Like Flaubert, though with less fanatic insistence, Pirandello cuts himself out of his picture. He does not speak directly in his own voice; he allows the action to unfold according to its inner necessities. His prose is neither elevated nor familiar, for he cares very little about "fine" writing, and when he does engage in a rhetorical flight, it is usually for ironic effect or in behalf of the elliptical characterization required by the short story. He composes in a middle style, denotative, austere, and transparent, the style of an observer who achieves sympathy from a distance.

Far more than we have come to expect in the modern short story, Pirandello's stories depend upon their action, which sometimes contains enough matter to allow a great deal of expansion. It is not hard to see why some of the stories would later become the basis for plays: they read like compressed scenarios. It is also characteristic of Pirandello's stories that while one remembers the general tone and atmosphere of his "world," one rarely keeps in mind the features or voice of a particular character. In so masterful a story as "Such Is Life," it is the ambience of frustration and disappointment, the final sense of human entanglement, that stays in one's mind far more than the characters themselves.

There are rarely Joycean epiphanies of insight or Chekhovian revelations through a massing of atmosphere. Pirandello is more somber and subdued, more committed to the necessities of the ordinary. The function of his style is to serve as a glass with a minimum of refraction or distortion; and whatever we may conclude about his ultimate literary purpose must come, not from a fussing with details of metaphor, but from a response to the line of the action. In this respect Pirandello the story writer is not quite a "modern" writer.

There is still another way in which he is not quite a "modern" writer. Though in his plays he breaks with the psychology of nineteenth-century literary realism, abandoning the premises of a fixed individual character and of the knowability of human relationships, his stories do not go that far. The stories remained accessible to educated persons of his generation who had been brought up on rationalist assumptions. Such readers may have found them excessively bleak—one does not leave Pirandello in a mood to embrace the universe—but they had no difficulty in grasping their import, as later they would with the plays.

Pirandello himself has provided a valuable summary of his major themes: ". . . the deceit of mutual understanding, irremediably founded on the empty abstraction of words, the multiple personality of everyone (corresponding to the possibilities of being to be found in each of us), and finally the inherent tragic conflict between life (which is always moving and changing) and form (which fixes it, immutable)". Most of these are already visible in the stories, though the theme of "multiple personality" is fully realized only in the plays. But Pirandello's treatment in the stories is by and large a conventional one—he would save his experimentalism for the plays. The stories, that is, deal with the difficulties of communication among human beings, the radical isolation of the self as it confronts its public guises, the tragic absurdity of trying to fix the flow of existence in perceptual and behavioral schemes. Yet even as they deal with these matters, the stories do not threaten the reader with a vision of the human lot as beyond comprehension or as open to so many meanings that there must follow a paralysis of relativism.

Pirandello has a sharp eye for absurdities, but this is still far from the view that life is inherently absurd. There may be anticipations of existentialism in his stories, as there may be in many writers of his day who were oppressed by the loss of nineteenth-century convictions; but precisely the writers, like Pirandello, who do seem to have anticipated the existentialist stress upon the utter insecurity of life prove in the end to be the ones who resist its full display. And this, in turn, has some relation to the fact that they were raised in a culture where Christianity retained a portion of its historic power.

Fantasy, playfulness, sexual abandon, religious emotion, any sort of imaginative transcendence—these seldom break through in the stories. A full tragic release is rare. Much more characteristic are stories in which the final sadness arises from an acceptance by the characters that they will have to live on, performing their tasks without hope or joy. In a five-page masterpiece, "The Soft Touch of Grass," a bereaved and aging man is mistakenly suspected by a girl of having lewd intentions. Overcome by the hopeless confusion of things, he goes back to his room and turns "his face to the wall." The phrase could serve as Pirandello's literary signature.

In "Such Is Life," a work that would do honor to Chekhov, a hopeless marriage, long broken, is hopelessly resumed. This story, unrelieved by a single rebellious gesture, stays painfully close to experience. Its power depends upon Pirandello's decision not to allow his sympathies to interfere with what he sees. At the end the central figure is left with "an ever-present torment . . . for all things, all earthly creatures as she saw them in the infinite anguish of her love and pity, in that constant painful awareness—assuaged only by fleeting peaceful moments which brought relief and consolation—of the futility of living like this. . . ."

There are some humorous stories too, such as "The Examination," in which a good-tempered glutton is diverted from his studies by friends tempting him with shares of pleasure. One smiles at the end, for Pirandello manages it with suavity and tact, but it is a humor of sadness and it brings little gaiety or relief. About the pleasure of simply being alive Pirandello has little to say in his stories, certainly nothing to compare with his one marvelously lighthearted play, *Liolà*, in which youthful energies bubble without restraint or theory.

What I have been saying may seem to be contradicted by the brilliant long story "The Merry-Go-Round of Love." Traditional Italian humor, which delights in the undoing of a miserly schemer and in the longevity of an old man whose death everyone desires, seems to come alive once again in Pirandello's pages. (It is a humor somewhat similar to that of recent Italian films: a ridicule, both merciless and tender, of those who would live beyond their physical and psychic means.) Yet as the action unfolds there is a gradual darkening of tone, and the earlier comic absurdities give way to grotesque obsessions, so that finally the story comes to seem a revelation of the way energy itself, the very life-principle, can become a malicious affront to human life.

Only the stories set in Sicily have a certain buoyancy, not because Pirandello glosses over the misery of his homeland or indulges in peasant romanticism, but simply because here the human drama plays itself out with quick violence. Men rise, men fall; but they do not know the dribbling monotonies of an overrationalized mode of existence, as do so many characters in Pirandello's urban stories.

Behind Pirandello stands his master, the Sicilian novelist Giovanni Verga, from whom he learned to disdain Italianate grandeur and rhetoric. Reading Verga's stories one feels they are not so much "made-up" fictions as communal fables, the record of a people born to catastrophe. Reading Pirandello's stories one feels they have been wrought by a man increasingly estranged from a world he knows intimately. Pirandello does not achieve the virile spareness of Verga; no one does. In Verga everything is subordinated to the decisiveness of event; in Pirandello one must always be aware of psychological motives, even if these seldom appear on the surface of the story, and then mainly as a film of melancholy. Verga's happenings are more terrible than Pirandello's, yet are easier to take, since in Verga men howl as they suffer. Only a few decades separate the two writers, but the distance between them reflects a deep change in spiritual temper.

So quick an intelligence as that of Pirandello must have been aware of the difference in the literary possibilities open to Verga and himself, and he must have realized that most of the advantages lay with the older man. But no serious writer chooses his subject; he can only choose whether to face it.

II The Sixties

T. E. Lawrence:
The Problem of Heroism

Time has mercifully dulled the image he despised yet courted: T. E. Lawrence is no longer the idol of the twenties, no longer "Lawrence of Arabia." But for those to whom reflection upon human existence is need and pleasure, Lawrence seems still to matter. He continues to arouse sympathy, outrage, excitement.

During the early twenties, after his return from Arabia, Lawrence became a national hero, the adventurer through whom Englishmen could once more savor the sensations of war and rescue emotions of grandeur. What he had done in Arabia—more important, what he had experienced—was epic in its proportions, and even a glance at his life prompts one to speculate about the nature of heroism in our century. But transplanted from the desert to the lantern slides of the Albert Hall, where Lowell Thomas was conjuring for the English their stainless version of "Lawrence of Arabia," the whole wartime experience shrank to farce. Partly to salvage it from vulgarities he himself had condoned, Lawrence wrote *The Seven Pillars of Wisdom*, a bravura narrative packed with accounts of battle yet finally the record of his search for personal equilibrium and value. By then, however, his public image had acquired a

From *The Hudson Review* 15 (Autumn 1962):3.

being and momentum of its own. So the book too, though in some ways esoteric, became popular—and helped sustain the image it was meant to subvert.

This sad comedy was to continue to the end. In *The Seven Pillars of Wisdom* the ideal of a forthright manly heroism, which Lawrence had supposedly rescued for an unheroic age, was soon transformed into the burden of self-consciousness he was never to escape. The dynamiter of railroads and bridges turned out to be an intellectual harassed by ambition and guilt. The literary man who had read Malory between desert raids and later worried over the shape and rhythm of the sentences in his book made himself into a pseudonymous recruit tending the "shit-cart" of his camp. And these were but a few of his transfigurations.

Thomas Edward Lawrence was born in 1888, the second of five sons in a comfortable Victorian family. The father, a reserved gentleman, devoted himself to the domestic needs of his family and a number of mild sports. The mother, clearly of lower rank, was a strong-spirited Scotswoman, ambitious for her sons, eager to share in their growth, the psychic center of the family. Mrs. Lawrence raised her boys to be straightforward Christians—and the unambiguous piety with which two of them later met their death in France must command respect even from those who might prefer a touch of rebellion.

In his youth Lawrence shared the family devoutness, serving briefly as a Sunday-school teacher; but whatever mark his religious training left upon him, he refused all formal belief during his adult years. Almost all his biographers have noted strong religious traits in Lawrence, straining toward some absolute of value by which to brace his conduct. Fewer have remarked on the tacit assumption he shared with many serious persons of our century: that the religious sensibility could be nurtured only in a culture of radical skepticism. (His friend Eric Kennington has recorded a conversation in which the adult Lawrence, asked about religion, spoke of a "process without aim or end, creation followed by dissolution, rebirth, and then decay to wonder at and to love. But not a hint of a god and certainly none of the Christian God.")

"Lessons," wrote Mrs. Lawrence, "were never any trouble to Ned [Lawrence's boyhood name], he won prizes every year. . . . In the senior locals in 1906, he placed first in English language and literature. . . ." Like a good many of the achievements that would later be dredged up from Lawrence's boyhood, this is impressive, but hardly as remarkable as his admirers have wished to suggest. Ned Lawrence was a bright, lively, inquiring boy; not a prodigy.

One trait merits special notice. In a family where all the sons were encouraged to a modest independence of bearing, Ned Lawrence stood out for his nervous boldness, a readiness to risk himself. His escapades and feats of physical endurance, both as a boy and then as a student at Oxford, were in part the proofs of strength that a small-bodied person feels obliged to thrust at the world, in part symptoms of a vanity which took the form of needing always to seem original. But these escapades and feats can also be seen as anticipations of his adult view that life is a test through which the human will, to assert its mastery over contingency and pain, denies the flesh not only its desires but its needs.

At some point before entering Oxford in 1907 Lawrence discovered that he and his brothers, apparently the sons of a respectable Oxford gentleman, were actually of illegitimate birth. His father, an Anglo-Irish baronet named Sir Thomas Chapman, had left a wife and four daughters in Ireland to run off with a former governess, the woman who now figured both in public and at home as his wife. In letters written many years later to Mrs. Bernard Shaw, Lawrence would claim that he had known these facts before the age of ten. Like others of his stories, this seems implausible.

How deep a shock the discovery of illegitimate birth caused Lawrence, we do not really know. To what extent it was the source of his sense of "homelessness" during the later years and his need to keep asserting himself through a series of new identities—this question does not permit a firm conclusion. One may see in the boy's discovery a matrix for those dispositions to suffering which would mark the later Lawrence. One may see it as a blow to his self-esteem. But it is surely a vast simplification to claim, as does Richard Aldington in his venomous biography, that Lawrence received a wound that would leave him crippled for life. The bare facts—his gift for leadership, his success in winning the loyalty of distinguished men, his ability to complete a major literary work—all show that Lawrence was not permanently disabled by the effects of this adolescent trauma, if trauma it was. I add this last qualification because we must allow for the possibility that whatever pain the revelation caused him, Ned Lawrence, as an English boy raised on romantic notions and romantic books, might have felt it *interesting* to have a father capable of such unconventionality in behalf of love.

Large parts of the boy's experience were intellectually vital and traditionally wholesome. A fondness for history led him to take bicycle trips through the south of England and make rubbings of monumental brasses. On his bedroom walls were pasted life-size portraits of knights who had performed heroic deeds in the Crusades. He devoured the medieval romances of William Morris with a relish he would retain throughout his life. He attended lectures by Flinders Petrie that helped

spark his interest in antiquities. And he began spending time at the
Ashmolean Museum in Oxford, where he met the archaeologist D. G.
Hogarth, who would become his mentor, friend, protector—at critical
moments, a kind of father.

During the summers of 1906, 1907, 1908, on bicycle trips through
France, Ned Lawrence visited cathedrals and castles, made careful notes,
and wrote letters to his mother which, if too "composed," are still notable
for an exactness of observation beyond the usual capacity of an eighteen-
or nineteen-year-old boy. In the summer of 1909 he undertook a more
adventurous trip: a walking tour of Syria, the interior of which was
almost inaccessible to Europeans. His purpose was to prepare an Oxford
thesis on the Crusaders' castles. When he inquired about Syria from
C. M. Doughty, whose *Arabia Deserta* he loved, the older man sent back
a note advising that the journey would be risky if undertaken alone.
"Long daily marches," warned Doughty, "a prudent man who knows the
country would consider out of the question." But Lawrence went.

Suffering heat, fever, and a beating at the hands of a thief, Lawrence
tramped eleven hundred miles through Syria, an average of twenty a
day when on the move. He lived with Arab village families, ate *leben*,
the Syrian yogurt, and bread "almost leathery when fresh." He photo-
graphed some fifty castles and established to his satisfaction the main
point of his thesis.

Perhaps for the first time we come upon qualities in Lawrence that
may be considered remarkable: an intense fascination with the past, a
ruthless insistence upon seeing things for himself, a readiness to submit
to the customs of a strange people, an eagerness to pursue an idea or
action to its limits. And something else. In Syria Lawrence came to feel
the pull of an alien style of life, one that was almost the antipode of
Western civilization. Toward the Arabs he would now be drawn by ties
both stronger and less tender—certainly more abstract—than love. As
he wrote a few years later to a friend: "You guessed right that the Arab
appealed to my imagination. It is the old, old civilization which has
refined itself clear of household gods, and half the trappings which ours
hasten to assume."

By his twenty-first year Lawrence was beginning to think seriously
about a career in archaeology, though whether he thought seriously
about the close work required by archaeological scholarship is another
matter. Through the help of D. G. Hogarth, Lawrence became attached
in 1910 to a British Museum expedition that was to dig at Carchemish
on the banks of the Euphrates. For most of the next three years—the
happiest of his life, he called them—Lawrence worked as an assistant,

miscellaneous, nimble, and erratic, to the head of the expedition, first Hogarth and then Leonard Woolley.

At Carchemish Lawrence formed a close—and as it seems in retrospect, significant—friendship with Sheik Hamoudi, the foreman of the dig; and when he took another hike through Syria in the summer of 1911 which ended in bouts of fever and dysentery, it was Hamoudi who nursed him back to life. "He is our brother," the Arab would later say about Lawrence, "our friend and leader. He is one of us." *One of us:* a tribute that would have pleased Lawrence, amused him in its distance from truth, and finally disturbed him. For in stumbling upon Conrad's phrase, which for us evokes the whole tangle of fraternity and aloneness in human relationships, Hamoudi touched unwittingly upon the problem of bad faith that would torment Lawrence throughout his time in Arabia.

One fact more about the early Lawrence: In January 1914, as the world hurried toward war, he and Woolley went off on a trip through the area that runs south of Gaza and Beersheba and east of Akaba, ostensibly to retrace the routes of Biblical journeys for the Palestine Expeditionary Fund, actually to help provide the British army with maps of a zone under Turkish sovereignty. Had Lawrence been anything but a man of austere moral sensibilities, this would hardly be worth noticing. Had he justified it in the name of military need, criticism might be given pause. But what disturbs one is that there was a side of Lawrence—the eternal British undergraduate—that would regard such an incident as a lark. If the essential Lawrence was a man whose ordeal in Arabia burned every bit of pomp out of him, there was another Lawrence, a Kipling-esque schoolboy susceptible to romantic vanities about the mission of England, who was never quite to disappear. During the war years this other Lawrence would break out in a giggling superciliousness toward those military men he found dense and an equally callow adulation of those, like Allenby, he found enlightened.

In the spring of 1916 Sherif Hussein of the Hejaz, descendent of the Prophet and protector of the faith, launched a revolt against the Turks. For some time the British had been tempting him with promises of postwar independence; but this shrewd fanatic had played a cautious game, since he neither trusted the infidel British nor cared to risk the vengeance of the Turks.

At first the Arabs gained a few local victories, in their very success exposing a poverty of purpose and leadership. But having lost the advantage of surprise and unable, with their irregular bands, to do more than harass entrenched Turkish posts, they now faced the danger of being wiped out by counterattack. The Arabs were ignorant of modern warfare; they had no master plan and barely an idea of why one might be needed; their main advantage lay not in any capacities of their own but in the sluggishness of the Turks. To provide help and soothe Hussein, British headquarters in Cairo sent an experienced official, Ronald Storrs, as envoy to the Hejaz. With him went T. E. Lawrence, who until then had spent the war months as a quite undistinguished staff captain in Military Intelligence.

In *The Seven Pillars of Wisdom* Lawrence has left a brilliant description of his first exploratory visit from one Arab camp to another, studying Hussein's three elder sons, each of whom led a body of troops. Ali, Abdullah, Feisal: which of these princes could become the focal point of rebellion, the embodiment of Arab desire? The picture of Lawrence plunging into the chaos of the Arab world, measuring the worth of its leaders and quickly bringing order to its ranks—this picture is surely overdrawn if one considers the limited powers Lawrence actually enjoyed at the moment. Not until after his return to Cairo and his assignment as British liaison officer to the Arab troops in the winter of 1917 did he even begin to command such authority. Yet the picture is essentially faithful if one grants Lawrence the right—he won it in the desert and then through his book—to treat his own experience as a fable of heroism: the right, that is, to assign a scheme of purpose to hesitant improvisations which in the end did come to bear such a purpose.

It was Hussein's third son, Feisal, decided Lawrence, who could serve as the "armed prophet" of revolt: Feisal, "very tall and pillar-like," who displayed a posture of assurance and a patience for mediating tribal feuds. And, it had better be added, Feisal responsive to the cues of this darting little Englishman with his "kitchen Arabic," his love for flamboyant dress, his curious pleasure in bending to the ritual and guile of Arab politics.

The speed with which Lawrence now became a—not the—leader of the revolt is astonishing, yet not difficult to explain. Between the xenophobic suspicions of the Arabs, who saw infidels descending upon them, and the routine military outlook of the British, who saw inefficiency all about them, there arose in the Hejaz a vacuum of leadership. For the revolt to survive, the vacuum had to be filled. And it could be filled only by a man able to endow it with a coherent idea such as would appeal to both the caution and the fervor of the Arabs.

The idea Lawrence first brought to the Arab revolt was not primarily a military one; nor did it yet have in his private reflections those metaphysical bearings that would later absorb him. Lawrence began by approaching the revolt not as a partisan but as a strategist: what was needed to move these people into action and, given their notorious inconstancy, to keep them in action? what kind of an enterprise could they be expected to assume and complete? To ask such questions was to enter the realm of politics, not as a system of ideas but as a makeshift theory of national psychology.

The tribal Arabs with whom Lawrence had now to deal, unlike the city intelligentsia and middle class of Syria, had almost no tradition of nationalism; they knew at best glimmers of national feeling. The Arabs were not a nation at all; they were remnants and shards of what might once have been a nation; they contained perhaps the elements from which a nation might be forged. But Lawrence could not wait (nor could the Arabs) until they became one; he could only think of a course of action which, if they were enabled to pursue it with some freedom, would stir the Arabs into behaving *as if* they were a nation.

What might bring this about? Primarily the belief that they could or should be a nation; a burgeoning sense of their possibilities, such as they themselves could barely express; and a strategy of conflict that pressed them into momentary coherence without risking the full-scale warfare for which they were not prepared. Lawrence had to improvise a strategy of national politics for a cluster of tribes that neither was a nation nor had a politics. He had to find symbols and tactics for transforming their primitive antagonism to the Turks into a facsimile of a modern purpose: but a modern purpose that could retain its thrust only by drawing upon the primitive antagonism.

Such considerations were obviously beyond the reach of most British officers, who saw only the surface of Arab chaos and felt that the best policy would be to bring in a sizable body of disciplined European troops. The French mission in the Hejaz, understanding Lawrence better, feared him more. It knew that any mobilization of Arab consciousness, no matter how useful at the moment, would threaten the structure of Allied power in the Middle East. No wonder that Lawrence complained in *The Seven Pillars of Wisdom* about the "blindness of European advisors, who would not see that rebellion was not war: indeed, was more of the nature of peace—a national strike perhaps."

In so reconstructing his situation, I do not mean to imply that Lawrence fully grasped the workings of Arab society and religion, or the role of colonial rivalries among the great powers, or the general problem of nationalism in our century. Far from it. But what he grasped was that the revolt could succeed only if it wore the face of freedom, only if it became a cause. To become a cause, it would have to be fought mainly by the Arabs themselves and appear to be led mainly by the Arabs themselves. If they could not be trained to positional warfare in the style of the period, they would have to be directed to other varieties of combat in which the more experienced Turkish army could not destroy them. British troops, except for a few technical advisers, would have to be kept away from the desert, at least until the Arabs gained some sense of their own powers. Good light weapons and a steady flow of gold were indispensable. Upon the tribal rivalries, the greed, the religious particularism of the Arabs there would have to be grafted a façade of unity: from which, if skillful enough, there might yet come the reality of national existence.

Lawrence understood that the nationalism of colonial countries was often devious and venal; that today's oppressed might be tomorrow's oppressors; that once freedom was won there might follow a moral relapse which would make the whole effort seem a waste. But he also sensed that meanwhile there lay imbedded in this nationalism an unformed yearning for dignity. If, for a time, the Arabs could be brought to act by this yearning, the revolt might succeed. If not, it would fail.

Lawrence saw the revolt in its political wholeness and moral dynamism, as it might become, an ideal possibility. He possessed the vision which, historically, was the Arabs' privilege: that was cause for elation. He felt they could not sustain his vision: that was cause for despair. Balancing elation and despair Lawrence, while still under thirty, reached full knowledge of the burdens of leadership.

Am I here endowing Lawrence with a coherence he would later claim but never really possess? Or assigning to him perceptions he would reach, if at all, only after the event? The record of his work and writings must stand as answer, but consider at least this sequence of passages, written before, during, and immediately after the revolt:

1915
I want to pull them all [the "little powers" of Arabia] together, & to roll up Syria by way of the Hejaz in the name of the Sherif. You know how big his repute is in Syria . . . we can rush right up to Damascus, & biff the French out of all hope of Syria. It's a big game. . . . (From a letter to D. G. Hogarth)

1916
A difference in character between the Turkish and Arab armies is that the more you distribute the former the weaker they become, and the more you distribute the latter the stronger they become. (From *The Arab Bulletin*)

1917
The Arab movement is a curious thing. It is really very small and weak in its beginning, and anybody who had command of the sea could put an end

to it in three or four days. It has capacity for expansion however—in the same degree—over a very wide area. It is as though you imagine a nation or agitation that may be very wide, but never very deep, since all the Arab countries are agricultural or pastoral, and all poor today. . . .

On the other hand the Arab movement is shallow, not because the Arabs do not care, but because they are few—and in their smallness of numbers (which is imposed by their poverty of country) lies a good deal of their strength, for they are perhaps the most elusive enemy an army ever had. . . . (From a letter to his parents)

1920

. . . but suppose we were an influence (as we might be), an idea, a thing invulnerable, intangible, without front or back, drifting about like a gas? Armies were like plants, immobile as a whole, firm-rooted, nourished through long stems to the head. We might be a vapour, blowing where we listed. Our kingdoms lay in each man's mind, and as we wanted nothing material to live on, so perhaps we offered nothing material to the killing.

. . . The Turk . . . would believe that rebellion was absolute, like war, and deal with it on the analogy of absolute warfare. Analogy is fudge, anyway, and to make war upon rebellion is slow and messy, like eating soup with a knife.

. . . We had seldom to concern ourselves with what our men did, but much with what they thought. . . . We had won a province when we had taught the civilians in it to die for our ideal of freedom; the presence or absence of the enemy was a secondary matter. (From "The Evolution of a Revolt")

These passages chart Lawrence's growing mastery of statement, but, more important, a development of thought almost to the point of establishing him as a new person. First, the simpleminded scheme for "biffing" the French. In 1917 the notation of a newly seen complexity: a notation somewhat distant, neutral, but not unsympathetic. And finally the last statement, which Lawrence would work into *The Seven Pillars of Wisdom*, rising to a measured eloquence: the revolt as idea. Yet this pattern is surely too neat, for Lawrence did not shed his earlier views, he buried them beneath his later ones. And the further qualification must be added that if the last passage gives us the essence of what the revolt could still mean to Lawrence—for by 1920 it often turned to ashes in his mouth—the earlier passages provide evidence as to its less exalted realities.

In regard to so elusive a mind as Lawrence's, no simple distinction can be enforced between action and response, what "really" happened and what he made of it in memory. Lawrence neither was nor could be a detached observer; he was leader, follower, victim, all in one. He tells us that his first commanding view of the revolt came to him in March

1917 when, for ten days, he lay sick in the camp of Abdullah. Perhaps, in writing *The Seven Pillars of Wisdom*, Lawrence gave dramatic form to his memories by condensing a long experience of discovery into a moment of sudden realization. But this possibility should not be allowed to blur the fact that there was discovery.

It is possible that the innovations in military tactics claimed for Lawrence were neither so revolutionary nor so calculated as has been supposed—though by now only specialists and old friends will have strong opinions about Lawrence as commander. It is possible that a good many of his glamorous desert raids were of uncertain value—though in guerrilla warfare bold acts can have consequences beyond their immediate military effects. It is possible that without British gold Lawrence could not have held together the Arab chieftains, though one may wonder whether anyone else could have done it with twice as much gold. But one thing seems certain: it was Lawrence who grasped the inner logic of the revolt as a moral-political act and it was Lawrence who breathed into it a vibrancy of intention it had not previously known.

What his plunge into the desert meant to Lawrence he never fully said, perhaps because the main concern in his writings was to present his relations to the Arabs as a problem—a problem that could not be reduced to his private desires.* From fragments of evidence left by Lawrence and those who were close to him, one may cautiously reconstruct some of his responses.

Lawrence, the cocky young officer who had been disliked so fiercely by the military regulars in Cairo, saw the Arabian campaign as an adventure in the simplest, most *English* sense of the word. This Lawrence took eagerly to the whole ritual-pageant of the Arab camps and Arab ceremonies and Arab powwows. With a sharp eye for stylized effects, he continued in his own way the tradition of those English visitors to the Middle East who have managed to penetrate native life without ceasing to be immaculately English.

He loved to ride with Feisal at the head of a racing camel army. He loved to dress in spotless white robes, sometimes scarlet and white. He loved to sit in Feisal's tent, gravely listening and dropping an occasional word during negotiations with tribal chiefs who were edging toward the Arab cause. He loved to compete with Auda Abu Tayi, leading sheik

---

* Some private desires there surely were. *The Seven Pillars of Wisdom* bears a fervid dedication in verse to "S. A.," who is generally taken to be an Arab Lawrence knew before the war. It has also been surmised, from teasing hints dropped by Lawrence to his biographers, that one motive for wishing to undertake the campaign in the desert was to reach "S. A." But whether this person was, as Robert Graves insists, a woman Lawrence had met in Syria or whether it was the Arab boy Sheik Ahmoud, whom he had befriended at Carchemish, we do not know. The other possibilities are little more than guesses.

of the Howeitat, a warrior out of the barbaric past. And he took a special delight in acquiring for himself a bodyguard of dark-skinned Ageyl fighters, who formed a legion obedient to his command. An English officer, meeting Lawrence at Akaba in 1918, found him ". . . a small man dressed in extremely good and expensive Bedouin clothes, a richly braided and decorated goat's hair cloak over all, and on his head a wonderful silk kufaiyeh held in position by a gold agal. His feet were bare, and he had a gold Hejazi dagger in his belt. . . ."

But even to act out this operatic role, Lawrence had to pay so terrible a price that one comes to disregard the flash and histrionics. From his return to the Hejaz until the day the British and Arabs entered Damascus, Lawrence accepted an appalling quantity of hardship. He learned to walk barefoot on hot sands; to ride camels on lacerating marches; to go for days without food and then plunge his fingers into fatty stews; to show a contempt for pain which would win the respect of the most savage tribesman; to yield his body to exhaustion and then force it once again into war; to be on guard against those who might betray him for gold or wish him out of the way so they might pillage without check; to witness, often in necessary silence, repeated outbursts of cruelty (for the Arab's "sterile experience robbed him of compassion and perverted his human kindness to the image of the waste in which he hid").

Lawrence never wished to persuade the Arabs that he had become one of them. Not only would that have been ludicrous, but it would have threatened his mode of leadership. He did something more subtle and, in their eyes, impressive: he convinced the Arabs that in basic stoicism, outer bearing, and daily practice he could become remarkably like them. The dream of "going back," of stripping to a more primitive self, which has so often fascinated Western man, was an authentic motive in his Arabian experience; but it was also consciously used by Lawrence to further his public role.

For a man who was so deeply drawn to the idea and the experience of *overcoming*—particularly a self-overcoming in the sense foreshadowed by Nietzsche—the war in Arabia came to be a test through radical humiliation and pain.

As he immersed himself in the life of the desert, repeating again and again the cycle of exertion—a moment of high excitement, a plunge into activity, then sickness, self-scrutiny, the desire to escape, and finally a clenched return—Lawrence saw his experience as more than a romantic escapade or fearful discipline. Since in the bareness of the desert he had to remold his existence in order to meet a historical demand, he also found there the possibility of an action through which to carve out a chosen meaning for his life. From the trivia, the ugliness, the absurdity, the assured betrayal of events he would snatch a trophy of freedom.

In themselves courage and pain meant very little; men were being killed in France who also knew pain and showed courage. But most were mere dumb bodies led to slaughter. Lawrence, however, found himself in a situation where he might determine the character of his experience—or so it seemed to him in occasional moments of lucidity. To help make the Arabs into a free people was a task worthy of an ambitious man. To help steer the revolt past an enemy that would destroy it and allies that would disarm it was a challenge worthy of a serious man. The fighting, to be sure, brought moments when such visions seemed utterly fatuous. There were wretched little raids where he had to use all his strength just to keep his forces from disintegrating, since the Arabs, indifferent to consequences, took pillage as the natural fruit of victory. There was the despair following a discovery that Zeid, Feisal's younger brother, had squandered a large sum of money and imperiled the revolt. But through it all Lawrence kept hoping that he might do something fine in the desert, perhaps something extraordinary.

He seized upon the Arabian campaign as an occasion for heroism not merely or primarily because it meant courage and recklessness, but because it meant the possibility of stamping intelligence and value upon a segment of history. To leave behind the settled life of middle-class England, which seemed to offer little but comfort and destruction; to abandon the clutter of routine by which a man can fill his days, never knowing his capacity for sacrifice or courage; to break with the assumption that life consists merely of waiting for things to happen; to carve out an experience which, in the words of Georg Simmel, would "determine its beginning and end according to its own formative power"—these were the yearnings Lawrence discovered in the revolt.

Put aside the posturing and playacting, put aside the embroidered robes and gold daggers, and there still remains the possibility of that rare action by which a man, rising above the limitations of moment and place, reaches the heart of excellence—a possibility, as Lawrence knew, that comes but rarely and must be seized with total desire, if seized at all. In the words of the hero of Malraux's *The Royal Way*, he wished to "put a scar on the map."

It is also in this sense, so utterly unlike the one I noticed a page or two back, that Lawrence undertook the Arabian campaign as an adventure: the sense, in Simmel's words, that an adventure is like a work of art, "for the essence of the work of art is . . . that it cuts out a piece of endlessly continuous sequence of perceived experience, giving it a self-sufficient form as though defined and held together by an inner core.

... Indeed, it is an attribute of this form to make us feel that, in both the work of art and the adventure, the whole of life is somehow comprehended and consummated."

At one decisive point, however, Lawrence's career turns sharply from the pattern suggested by Simmel. "The adventurer of genius," writes Simmel, "lives, as if by mystic instinct, at the point where the course of the world and the individual fate have, so to speak, not yet been differentiated from one another." About Lawrence this was not true, and everything that led him to think of his experience in Arabia as an imposture shows it could not be true. Consider the qualities implied by Simmel when he evokes the hero or, as he prefers to call him, "the adventurer of genius." The hero is a man with a belief in his inner powers, a confidence that he moves in rhythm with natural and historic forces, a conviction that he has been chosen for his part and thereby lifted above personal circumstances. At moments Lawrence felt one or another of these, but surely not with classic fulfillment or ease.

Lawrence found it hard to believe in the very deeds he drove himself to perform. His fulfillment of the hero's traditional tasks was undercut at every point by a distrust and mockery of the idea of heroism. He could not yield himself to his own charisma; he was never certain of those secret gifts which for the hero ought to be an assured possession; he lived on the nerve's edge of consciousness, forever tyrannized by questions. At the end he abandoned his adventure with a feeling that inaction might be the most enviable of states and a desire to transform heroism into a discipline for the purging of self.

Is it fanciful to think that we have here a distinctly "modern" mode of heroism? So it seemed to Herbert Read when he reviewed *The Seven Pillars of Wisdom* in 1928.

> About the hero [wrote Read,] there is an essential undoubting directness . . . he is self-possessed, self-reliant, arrogant, unintelligent. Colonel Lawrence was none of these. . . . He was a lame duck in an age of lame ducks; a soldier spoilt by introspection and self-analysis; a man with a load on his mind. . . . [Lawrence's mind was] not great with thought, but tortured with some restless spirit that drives it out into the desert, to physical folly and self-immolation, a spirit that never triumphs over the body and never attains peace.

Except for the ungenerous phrase about "physical folly." Read was accurate and perceptive. By now it is almost impossible to accept as a model of the heroic the sort of divine ox that Read claimed to admire. For better or worse, the hero as he appears in modern life is a man struggling with a vision he can neither realize nor abandon, "a man with a load on his mind."

As Lawrence assumed greater burdens of responsibility in the desert campaign, his feeling that he had become a creature apart, isolated from both the Arabs and the English, kept steadily growing. So too did his need to subject himself to the cruelest accusations. Some of Lawrence's difficulties were of a personal character and would have troubled him, though perhaps less violently, even if he had never gone to Arabia; others followed from the very nature of warfare.

In the fall of 1917, during a scouting expedition into enemy territory, Lawrence was captured by the Turks at Deraa. Fortunately not recognized, he was taken to be a deserter and brought before the local commandant, "a bulky man [who] sat on the bed in a night gown, trembling and sweating as though with fever. . . ." There followed a scene in which physical torture and sexual violation merged in a blur of pain. Later, in *The Seven Pillars of Wisdom*, Lawrence would describe it with a cold, almost clinical hysteria:

> I remembered the corporal kicking with his nailed boot to get me up. . . .
> I remembered smiling at him, for a delicious warmth, probably sexual, was
> swelling through me: and then that he flung up his arm and hacked the full
> length of his whip into my groin. This doubled me half-over, screaming, or
> rather, trying impotently to scream, only shuddering through my open
> mouth. One giggled with amusement. A voice cried, "Shame, you killed
> him." Another slash followed. A roaring, and my eyes went black: while
> within me the core of life seemed to heave slowly up through the rending
> nerves. . . .

The two or three pages which recapture Lawrence's ordeal at Deraa anticipate a library of recollections by the victims of totalitarianism. Few are more terrible than Lawrence's, though even in this extreme self-exposure, so honest about that side of himself which sought after pain, he could not quite succeed in being candid about the extent of his violation. From it he never fully recovered; for years he would impress people as a man battling his nerves to maintain the appearance of control.

The incident at Deraa would have been enough to break stronger and more secure men, but one reason it so tortured Lawrence in memory has to do with his sexual life. Lawrence shied away from women unless they were notably maternal, and his repeated expressions of disgust concerning the sexual act go far beyond the bounds of timidity or fastidiousness. Whether Lawrence was a practicing homosexual it is not possible to say with any authority: the evidence of his friends ranges from genuine bewilderment to special pleading. There are passages in *The Seven Pillars of Wisdom* which show that Lawrence was drawn to the idea or image of homosexuality as it occurred with apparent simplicity and purity among the young Arab warriors. But if, as one suspects, his sexual impulses were usually passive and suppressed, that would have been all the more reason for suffering a poignant sense of isolation in the desert, where he was thrown into an exclusively male society and the habits of the Bedouins were accepted without fuss or judgment.

There were other, more public reasons for his despair. By the summer of 1917 he knew about the Sykes-Picot treaty, a secret arrangement among Britain, France, and Russia for perpetuating imperialism in the Middle East. This agreement made a farce of the promises of independence that had been given by Lawrence—though not by him alone—to the Arabs. Lawrence smarted under the knowledge that no matter what he would now say or do, he had no choice but to further this deceit. He had hoped, as he flamboyantly wrote in the suppressed preface for *The Seven Pillars of Wisdom*, "to restore a lost influence, to give 20 millions of Semites the foundations on which to build an inspired dream-palace of their national thoughts." The reality was "a homesickness [which] came over me stressing vividly my outcast life among the Arabs, while I exploited their highest ideals, and made their love of freedom one more tool to make England win." And when, at a moment of climax in the Arabian campaign, Lawrence delivered a "halting, half-coherent speech" to the Serahin tribe—

> There could be no rest-houses for revolt, no dividend of joy paid out. Its style was accretive, to endure as far as the senses would endure, and to use each such advance as base for further adventure, deeper privation, sharper pain. . . . To be of the desert was, as they knew, to wage unending battle with an enemy who was not of the world, nor life, nor anything but hope itself; and failure seemed God's freedom to mankind. . . . Death would seem best of all our works, the last free loyalty within our grasp, our final leisure. . . .

—he was speaking from the center of his new beliefs, assaulting his listeners at the point where he could make "their worldliness fade," but also, as he felt, enticing them into a net of deception.

Lawrence knew the Arabs had been selfish, narrow, treacherous all through the campaign but wondered whether, in the light of self-interest, they had not been justified. He knew Doughty had been right in saying the Arabs had "a presumptuous opinion of themselves, yet [also] a high indolent fantasy distempered with melancholy. . . ." Victory, wrote Lawrence, "always undid an Arab force." And in a sentence in *The Seven*

Pillars of Wisdom he brought together his complex feelings: "The Arab respected force a little: he respected craft more, and often had it in an enviable degree: but most of all he respected blunt sincerity of utterance, nearly the sole weapon God had excluded from his armament."

Had Lawrence been a principled anti-imperialist for whom sentiments of national pride were irrelevant, his problem might have been easier to bear. But he was not a principled anti-imperialist and he did retain sentiments of national pride. His shame and guilt derived precisely from a lingering belief in the British claim to fairness. Despite superb intuitions, he never reached a coherent view of the world political struggle in which finally he too was a pawn. There were moments when he saw, but he could not long bear the vision, that his whole adventure had been absorbed by a mere struggle for power. Lawrence was a man— hopeless, old-fashioned romantic!—who believed in excellence and honor; he came at the wrong time, in the wrong place.

On his thirtieth birthday, during a peaceful day shortly before the entry into Damascus, Lawrence tried to examine himself honestly, without delusion:

> Four years ago I had meant to be a general and knighted when thirty. Such temporal dignities (if I survived the next four weeks) were now in my grasp. . . . There was a craving to be famous; and a horror of being known to like being known. . . . The hearing other people praised made me despair jealously of myself. . . . I began to wonder if all established reputations were founded, like mine, on fraud. . . . I must have had some tendency, some aptitude, for deceit. Without that I should not have deceived men so well. . . .

When the British and Arabs marched into Damascus, the war came to an end for Lawrence. "In the black light of victory, we could scarcely identify ourselves."

Lawrence returned to England in October 1918, hoping, as he had written to his friend Vyvyan Richards, for "a long quiet like a purge and then a contemplation and decision of future roads." Nothing of the sort proved to be possible. The Versailles peace conference was a few months away; Feisal would be coming, ill-prepared and vulnerable; the Arab cause required pleading. Time and again Lawrence found himself wishing to shake off his responsibilities to the Arabs, who seemed far less admirable in peace than in war. It was not hard to surmise by now the order of civilization they would be bringing to the Middle East: the worst of several possible worlds. But having yielded himself to a historical action, Lawrence felt that as a matter of honor he had to see it through.

His mind was never more supple than during these months in which he prepared to sabotage French and then British ambitions. But in his writings of the period—the impression is strengthened by memoirs of his friends—one gains a sense of weariness beyond measure: as if he were trying to complete a necessary task and then lapse into silence.

In England Lawrence sent a memorandum to the Cabinet proposing the creation of several independent Arab states, with Hussein's sons as limited monarchs and with moderate guidance and help to come from the West. That the Arabs were not ready for independence Lawrence knew quite well; no long-suppressed people ever is, except as it breaks past the limits of its suppression. Lawrence reached the core of the problem in an article he published in 1920: "We have to be prepared to see [the Arabs] doing things by methods quite unlike our own, and less well; but on principle it is better that they half-do it than that we do it perfectly for them."

Lawrence realized that his proposal would be bitterly fought by the French, if only because it allowed independence to the Syrian coastal area which the Sykes-Picot treaty had reserved for France. He understood that the British, to gain any peace at all, would have to compromise with their main ally. What he did not foresee—and here one may charge him with political naiveté—was that strong voices in England would be eager to work out an arrangement giving Syria to the French and allowing Britain to dominate Iraq.

At the peace conference his status was ambiguous. Formally, he acted as adviser to the British delegation; actually, in the words of the Swedish writer Erik Lönnroth, he "functioned as representative of several Arab states which did not yet exist, and whose still vague contours he himself had greatly helped to form." The French, by now well briefed on his opinions and temper, treated him with frigid correctness. "If he comes as a British colonel, in an English uniform," read the instructions of the French foreign minister, "we will welcome him. But we will not accept him as an Arab. . . ." Yet it was precisely "as an Arab" that Lawrence did come.

As negotiations dragged into the summer of 1919, it became clear that the British had decided to let France take Syria; in the labyrinth of cynicism that would comprise the Versailles treaty, this was a small part of the bargain. The Arabs, sensing defeat, began to put up a show of truculence, notably in a popular congress held in Syria which proclaimed Feisal its head and independence its goal. The French, determined on a stern policy, were itching to drive Feisal's troops out of Damascus.

And Lawrence, alone and powerless, grew increasingly estranged from his countrymen.

In the spring he had taken an airplane flight to Cairo with the intention of collecting his notes for *The Seven Pillars of Wisdom*, and when the plane crashed near Rome, had suffered a broken collarbone and rib fractures. The painful accident, together with the recent death of his father and the crumbling of his hopes at Versailles, brought him close to nervous exhaustion. As his reputation grew, his capacities declined. When the French heard of the flight to Cairo, they set up a cry that he was returning to the Middle East to lead an Arab resistance; in reality, Lawrence was in no condition to lead anything. As he returned to Paris, all he could do was persist in a quixotic loyalty to the Arabs, a loyalty resting more on principle than affection. And this stubbornness—let us call it by its true name: this absolute unwillingness to sell out—began to strike his British colleagues as *unreasonable*, an embarrassment to their diplomacy.

On July 17 Lord Curzon telegraphed Balfour that Lawrence should not be allowed to work with Feisal any longer, since this would "cause us serious embarrassment with the French." An official of the British Foreign Office attached to the Paris delegation wrote in confidence: "While fully appreciating the value of Lawrence as a technical advisor on Arab affairs, we regard the prospect of his return to Paris in any capacity with grave misgivings."

Lawrence appealed to the Americans in the name of self-determination; wrote pleading notes to the English leaders; sent a letter to the London *Times* arguing the Arab case and declaring—though this the editor did not print—that he regretted his wartime actions since the British government clearly had no intention of living up to the promises it had authorized him to make the Arabs. But it was hopeless. "By the mandate swindle," as Lawrence later said, "England and France got the lot." What Lawrence now felt came to far more than personal disappointment; it was a rupture of those bonds of faith that had made him a good and, in some respects, characteristic Englishman of his day. Now he "looked at the West and its conventions with new eyes: they destroyed it all for me."

By the end of 1919 the strain had become too great. Lawrence told himself that he had failed, perhaps betrayed, the Arabs. He harassed himself mercilessly in the writing of *The Seven Pillars of Wisdom*. And then, at the very moment of failure, he was thrust into public notoriety through Lowell Thomas's illustrated lecture, "With Allenby in Palestine and Lawrence in Arabia," a spectacle that in London alone drew over a million adoring spectators. Lawrence became a popular legend—cheap and vulgar—through the devices of a journalist.

But also through his own connivance: a connivance in which vanity and masochism joined to betray him. "I'm a sublimated Aladdin, the thousand and second Knight, a Strand-Magazine strummer," moaned Lawrence in early 1920, for he was too intelligent not to see what Thomas was doing to him. Yet he failed to correct the numerous distortions, even after Hubert Young, his wartime companion, protested Thomas's statement that the British officers in Arabia had not accompanied Lawrence to the front. And he went to hear Thomas's lecture at least five times. When "spotted," reports Thomas, "he would turn crimson, laugh in confusion, and hurry away with a stammered word of apology."

How was this possible? Why did Lawrence permit and even encourage Thomas to continue? There is no single answer, only a complex of possible reasons. The vaudeville in which Lawrence was cast as prince of the desert, served as balm to feelings hurt at Versailles: there was pleasure of a kind in being recognized at the Albert Hall and stared at in the streets. His new public role appealed to his sense of the distance between hidden truth and outer parody. It stimulated a kind of self-mortification, a twisting of the knife of public shame into the wounds of his ego. But these explanations neither justify nor excuse. The truth is that it is hard to understand this episode, and harder still to accept it, unless of course we are prepared to show a little kindness toward a stricken man.

Yet not a hopelessly stricken man, for on one side of him Lawrence continued to behave like a tough and bouncy Irishman. Precisely during this period of heartsickness and notoriety Lawrence kept working away with an insatiable ambition, often for whole days and nights, at *The Seven Pillars of Wisdom*. Largely written in 1919, the manuscript was lost, completely and painfully redone, and in 1922 set up in proof at the Oxford *Times*. How ambitious he was Lawrence revealed in a letter to Edward Garnett: "Do you remember my telling you once that I collected a shelf of 'Titanic' books (those distinguished by greatness of spirit, 'sublimity,' as Longinus would call it): and that they were *The Karamazovs, Zarathustra* and *Moby Dick*. Well, my ambition was to make an English fourth. You will observe that modesty comes out more in the performance than the aim."

"An English fourth" Lawrence did not quite make. Still, the book is one of the few original works of English prose in our century, and if Lawrence's name lives past the next half-century it may well be for the book rather than the experience behind it.

As autobiography *The Seven Pillars of Wisdom* is veiled, ambiguous, misleading; less a direct revelation than a performance from which the truth can be wrenched. Nor can it be taken as formal history, since it focuses too subjectively, too obsessively, perhaps too passionately on its theme: which is the felt burden of history rather than history itself. Yet the book *as an act* has become part of the history of our politics.

Primarily the book is a work of art, the model for a genre that would become all too characteristic of the age: a personal narrative through which a terrible experience is relived, burned out, perhaps transcended. This genre, to be perfected by victims of totalitarianism, is a perilous one, succumbing too easily to verbal mannerism and tending to wash away the distinction between history and fable.

The Seven Pillars of Wisdom is a work of purgation and disgorgement. It is also, in order to resist the pressures of memory, a work of the most artful self-consciousness in which Lawrence is constantly "arranging words, so that the one I care for most is either repeated, or syllable-echoed, or put in a startling position." Robert Graves has said that "the nervous strain of its ideal of faultlessness is oppressive," and Lawrence himself found that the book is "written too hard. There are no flat places where a man can stand still for a moment. All ups and downs, engine full on or brakes hard on." The feverish state in which Lawrence composed the book, especially the early drafts—"I tie myself into knots trying to reenact everything, as I write it out. It's like writing in front of a looking-glass, and never looking at the paper, but always at the imaginary scene"—may help to explain why the book is "written too hard."

Its power depends upon a doubleness of perspective. It can be read as a narrative of high excitements and descriptive flourish. The scene is rendered with fierce, exotic particularity. Details are thrust out with brutal, even shocking intent; for in this kind of narrative the reader must not be allowed to settle into any comfort of expectation. The bleakness of the desert, the sudden killing of an Arab soldier, the horror of an assault upon helpless Turkish prisoners, the nomadic grandeur of a man like Auda, the nightmare detachment of the Deraa incident and then, at increasingly frequent intervals, the turnings toward aloneness, the merciless guerrilla raids Lawrence conducted against his self—these and a thousand other bits comprise the agitated surface of the book.

Yet at every crucial point the writing, through wrenchings of metaphor and perspective, pulls attention away from the surface. It turns toward something else, at first a mere scattering of sentiments and then the growing and molding "I" of the book: an "I" that is not at all the conventional first-person narrator but an approximation of a figure who comes into being, like Melville's Ishmael, through the writer's struggle to write his book. It is the emergence of this self which keeps *The Seven Pillars of Wisdom* from being a mere recital of excitements and horrors.

Because he tries to maintain an almost intolerable pitch of intensity, Lawrence seems repeatedly to fall into a state of exhaustion, and the book to crumble into a series of set pieces. By the nature of the set piece, these sections can be read as self-contained accounts of human exhaustion. Being detachable, they are so packed with nervous bravado and ambitious phrasing as to call attention to their life *as a form*, a series of compositional feats matching the feats of Lawrence's adventure. Yet through this accumulation of set pieces there recurs the struggle of a self in formation; and therein the book gains a kind of unity.

To an age that usually takes its prose plain, Lawrence's style is likely to seem mannered. Unquestionably there are passages that fail through a surplus of effort; passages that betray the hot breath of hysteria; passages that contain more sensibility than Lawrence could handle. But it is dangerous to dismiss such writing simply because we have been trained to suspect the grand. Lawrence was deliberately trying to achieve large-scale effects, a rhetoric of action and passion that may almost be called baroque: the style pursuing the thought. And while the reader has every reason to discriminate among these effects, it would be dull to condemn Lawrence merely for their presence.

Lawrence strives for a style of thrust and shock, and then, by way of balance, for passages of extreme sensibility. He often uses words with a deliberate obliqueness or off-meaning, so as to charge them with strangeness and potential life. The common meaning of these key words is neither fully respected nor wholly violated; but twisted, sometimes into freshness, sometimes into mere oddity. All of this followed from conscious planning: "I find that my fifth writing . . . of a sentence makes it more shapely, pithier, stranger than it was. Without that twist of strangeness no one would feel an individuality, a differentness, behind the phrase."

It is a coercive prose, as it is a coercive book, meant to shake the reader into a recognition of what is possible on this earth. No one can end it with emotions of repose or resolution; there is no pretense at conciliatory sublimation. The result, throughout, is a tensing of nerves, a series of broken reflections upon human incompleteness.

For Lawrence there was now to be one more significant entry into public life. Within a few months after the signing of the Versailles treaty, it became clear that he had been entirely right about the Middle East, and the massed heads of the French and British governments entirely

wrong. By 1920 the British were pouring millions of pounds into Iraq
in order to suppress Arab insurgents; the French were bombarding
Damascus and spreading hatred with each discharge of their cannon.
Soon the British decided they would have to modify their policy, which
had been neither effective nor economical, and when Winston Churchill
took over the Colonial Office in 1921 he offered Lawrence a post as
adviser on Middle East affairs.

Lawrence now joined in political conferences in Cairo and for a brief
time returned to the desert, where he helped work out a modus vivendi
between the British and the Arabs. A greater measure of autonomy was
granted the Arabs in Iraq; the British army but not the RAF withdrawn;
Feisal allowed to assume the throne; and peace momentarily restored.
Lawrence said that justice had finally been done, but the Arabs, wishing
complete independence, took a less sanguine view.

His labor in composing *The Seven Pillars of Wisdom* and then the
interval of service under Churchill had distracted Lawrence from himself. Now that both were done and nothing appeared to absorb or
consume him, there could be no evading the central fact of his postwar
years: *that, in his freedom, he no longer knew how or why to live.*

He was physically wearied, morally depleted, a man without the
strength of true conviction. He had run through life too fast, and now
had to face the cruel problem of how to continue living though his life
was done. The ordinary ways of middle-class England he could not settle
into; the literary world, which he admired to excess, made him wildly
uncomfortable; and politics seemed dirty, mean, a mug's game. Religion
as dogma or institution left him as cold as in the past, yet there burned
in him a desire for some enlarging selfless purpose he could neither find
nor name. Lord Halifax was surely right when he said that "some deep
religious impulse moved him . . . some craving for the perfect synthesis
of thought and action which alone could satisfy his test of ultimate truth
and his conception of life's purpose."

Perhaps Lawrence's trouble was simply that of a man who, at the
end of a great adventure, returns home and finds it impossible to slide
into quiet and routine. (Some years later he would choose to translate
the *Odyssey*, a book about a hero whose return is endlessly delayed.)
Whatever the reason, his life was painfully distraught. He would walk
the streets of London for nights on end. He ate poorly, carelessly. His
home in Oxford, palled by the death of two brothers in the war, was
unbearable. A mist of affection separated him from his mother. After
his return from Paris, she has remembered, he would sit motionless as
stone for entire mornings. In London he found new friends, many of
them famous men, to whom he could occasionally burst out in oblique

confession; but good will and understanding were not enough. "The worst thing about the war generation of introspects," he wrote several years later to the novelist Henry Williamson, "is that they can't keep off their blooming selves." Caught up as he was with his "blooming self," Lawrence would lapse into bouts of self-pity and puerile shows of vanity. It is easy enough to dislike the Lawrence of these days. But there were times when he expressed with a rare clarity the sense of drift he shared with so many of his contemporaries.

"What more?" he wrote to Eric Kennington in 1922. "Nothing. I'm bored stiff: and very tired, and a little ill, and sorry to see how mean some people I wanted to respect have grown." A year later, after he had joined the RAF, he wrote to Lionel Curtis: "It's terrible to hold myself voluntarily here: and yet I want to stay here till it no longer hurts me. . . . Do you think there have been many lay monks of my persuasion? One used to think that such frames of mind would have perished with the age of religion: and yet here they rise up, purely secular."

Somewhat later Lawrence wrote in a letter to Robert Graves: "You see, I know how false the praise is: how little the reality compared with the legend: how much luck: how little merit. Praise makes a man sick, if it is ignorant praise." And when Graves remarked that there were two selves in Lawrence, a Bedouin self "longing for the bareness, simplicity, harshness of the desert—that state of mind of which the desert is a symbol—and the over-civilized European self," Lawrence answered: "The two selves, you see, are mutually destructive. So I fall between them into the nihilism which cannot find, in being, even a false god in which to believe." Later still, in a note to an unknown correspondent, probably in 1929, Lawrence wrote: "I have done with politics, I have done with the Orient, and I have done with intellectuality. O, Lord, I am so tired! I want so much to lie down and sleep and die. Die is best because there is no reveille. I want to forget my sins and the world's weariness."

Taken from over a decade of Lawrence's life and grouped together in isolation, such passages unavoidably form a melodramatic picture. They omit the plateaus of ordinariness which fill the bulk of any life. They omit the moments of commonplace satisfaction. But that they are faithful to what Lawrence felt seems beyond doubt. Through these years Lawrence suffered from a loss of élan, a sense of the void. He suffered from a nihilism which revealed itself as a draining of those tacit impulsions, those root desires and values which make men continue to live.

This condition was by no means unique to Lawrence. When Hemingway wrote his stories, with their variations on the theme of *nada*; when Pirandello drove skepticism to intolerable extremes in his plays;

when so somber a figure as Max Weber could speak of the "disenchant-ment of the world"—they too were confronting the sense of the void, the sense that human life had entered a phase of prolonged crisis in which all of its sustaining norms had lost their authority. Lawrence reached these feelings in a unique way, through the desert of Arabia rather than the trenches of France. But once this strain of the exotic is put aside, there remains a shared dilemma.

It is this Lawrence—the hero who turns into a bewildered man suffering the aftermath of heroism—who now seems closest to us. Had Lawrence simply returned to the wholesome life of an English gentle-man, writing neither *The Seven Pillars of Wisdom* nor the remarkable letters to Lionel Curtis, he would still have been noteworthy. Such a man, however, could hardly have captured the imagination of reflective people as the actual Lawrence did. His wartime record was remarkable, the basis for all that was to come; without it he might have been just another young man afflicted with postwar malaise. But what finally draws one to Lawrence, making him seem not merely an exceptional figure but a representative man of our century, is his courage and vulnerability in bearing the burden of consciousness. "One used to think that such frames of mind would have perished with the age of religion: and yet here they rise up, purely secular."

In August 1922, as if to wipe out all he had once been, Lawrence joined the Royal Air Force as an ordinary recruit under the name John Hume Ross. In January 1923, when his identity became known, he was forced to leave but allowed to join the regular army. There he remained until 1925, when his pleas and the intervention of powerful friends persuaded Air Marshal Trenchard to accept him again, this time under the name T. E. Shaw. Until close to his death in 1935 Lawrence served the RAF as clerk and mechanic, in England and India.

Lawrence's decision to bury himself in the ranks was extraordinary; for a man who had fought all his life against the force of his own ambition, it was a climax of self-mortification, an act of symbolic suicide. No single explanation can account for thirteen years spent in a military whose spirit was at war with his passion for freedom, whose discipline chafed and humiliated him. All the explanations together are also unsatisfactory, except perhaps as they come to an absolute need to break from his old self, the heroic Lawrence and the helpless Lawrence both.

"Honestly," he wrote to Robert Graves, "it was a necessary step, forced on me by an inclination toward ground-level: by a despairing hope that I'd find myself on common ground with men . . . by an itch to make myself ordinary in a mob of likes: also I'm broke. . . . It's going to be a brain-sleep, and I'll come out of it less odd than I went in: or at least less odd in other men's eyes."

And in a preface that he wrote for the catalogue to Eric Kennington's exhibit of Arab portraits, there is a brief but perhaps deeper statement of motive: "Sometimes we wish for chains as a variety."

There were other, slightly different explanations. "Partly, I came here to eat dirt till its taste is normal to me. . . ." Less candidly, he told some people he had joined the RAF to insure himself a regular income. To Lionel Curtis, who brought out his metaphysical side, he wrote: "Free-will I've tried, and rejected: authority I've rejected (not obedience, for that is my present effort, to find equality only in subordination. It is domination whose taste I have been cloyed with): action I've rejected: and the intellectual life: and the receptive senses: and the battle of wits. . . ."

Somehow he managed to live through the torments of basic training, for which he was ten years and one war too old. He learned to claw his way past the obscenities that filled the barracks where he slept. He found odd sensations of pleasure and pain in breaking himself to obey men he knew to be unworthy of his obedience. And at times there was a rough companionship, a peace of sorts.

But again: why did he do it? To stamp forever upon his conscience the need for refusing power; to put himself beyond the possibility of taking power; to find some version of the monasticism he craved; to make up for the guilts that lingered from the war; to return to the commonest of common life; to test again his capacity for accepting pain; to distinguish himself in suffering—truth lies in all these but in none alone. We should not sentimentalize. Except for the months of basic training, Lawrence did not feel himself to be suffering acutely. He was happy or, if not happy, then peaceful for long stretches of time. Whether he was stationed in England or Karachi did not seem to matter much: he was the same in one place as another. Still, it would also be sentimental to forget that he had surrendered, had accepted his dispossession: "I was an Irish nobody. I did something. It was a failure. And I became an Irish nobody."

Throughout the years in service there were small pleasures, bits of compensation. Like a character in Conrad, he achieved a severe responsibility in his daily work, the "job-sense" that sees one through. ("One had but to watch him scrubbing a barrack-room table," recalled a corporal from the tank corps, "to realize that no table had been scrubbed just in that way before.") He found physical pleasure and a sense of freedom in racing his motorcycle across the narrow English roads. He made lasting friends in both the army and RAF, with whom he lived on terms of intermittent ease. He made friends, as well, with some of the great writers of the day: Bernard Shaw, E. M. Forster, Thomas Hardy. (Hardy he venerated with a filial emotion which is one of the most "human" of his qualities.) He tried his hand at critical essays, which are neither quite first-rate nor merely commonplace: a fine one on Landor, a respectable one on H. G. Wells. He turned the *Odyssey* into firm, often pungent English prose—some classicists have balked, but it is a living book. He finished *The Mint*, a severely chiseled picture of barrack life: Joycean in style, sometimes brilliant in evocation, structured as a series of set pieces, showing a decided advance in control over *The Seven Pillars of Wisdom*, but too markedly an exercise, a self-conscious effort to *write*.

His letters give a more faithful picture of the shifts and turns in Lawrence's life than do either his own books or the books written about him. They are not letters written systematically out of one impulse or idea. Some, like the early ones, are interesting because they show a typically intelligent English youth of a time we find increasingly hard to remember or imagine. Some, like the few from the war years, are valuable simply as a glass, transparencies upon action. Some, like those to Lionel Curtis, form a grave impersonal confession, not an unburdening of secrets, but the statement of a man in agony and quest. Others hold one by sudden bolts of power in expression.

In May 1935, to avoid two errand boys walking on a road, Lawrence crashed his motorcycle. He died a few days later, never having recovered consciousness. Like much of his life, his death was no completion; it failed to round off his problem. He left his name entangled with a cluster of unanswered questions, this prince of our disorder.

Anarchy and Authority
in American Literature

In the beginning was the wilderness. The earth, "almost pathless," writes Faulkner, was marked only "by the tracks of unalien shapes— bear and deer and panthers and bison and wolves and alligators and the myriad smaller beasts. And unalien men to name them too." America was paradise, the last paradise.

For Faulkner, as for many other American writers, there is a radical disjunction between social man and the natural world. The wilderness is primal, source and scene of mobility, freedom, innocence. Once society appears, it starts to hollow out these values. And not one or the other form of society, not a better or worse society, but the very idea of society itself comes to be regarded with skepticism and distaste.

This myth is lent credence by the hold of the frontier on our national life. A myth of space, it records the secret voice of a society regretting its existence, and recalls a time when men could measure their independence by their physical distance from one another, for "personal liberty and freedom were almost physical conditions like fire and flood."

Inescapably the settling of the wilderness was a violation. For a short time afterward, it was still possible to establish a precarious balance

From *University of Denver Quarterly*, Autumn, 1967, Vol. 2, No. 3.

between the natural and the social—a balance which might have preserved a margin of paradise. But the forest line recedes. In Faulkner's
"The Bear," set in the late nineteenth century, there can still be a return
to the wilderness, and within its narrowed precincts something of our
original freedom is recalled. By his "Delta Autumn," one must "drive
for hours to reach the woods. . . ." The wilderness is gone. Paradise has
been lost, again.

The Founding Fathers of the United States were hardheaded and
realistic men. They were sincere patriots, almost all of them, and
thoughtful students of government, some of them. They had a lively
sense of their own interests, and meant to create bulwarks for their
property; but they also wished to avoid tyranny. As they set about the
task of state-making, they grasped the need to reconcile all of those
conflicting interests and obligations in a society which, precisely because
it *was* a society, could yield only limited satisfactions.

At least some of the men who framed the Constitution believed
with John Calvin that evil and damnation are inherent in the human
condition. From Thomas Hobbes they took over the view that men are
contentious; that social struggle is endemic; that interest comes before
principle; and that the task of government is to control the beast in
mankind. Yet even as they absorbed these elements of English political
thought, they also inherited something of seventeenth-century English
republicanism, as well as the prescriptions of Locke for a limited con-
stitutional government. The Founding Fathers were strongly attached
to the idea of the United States as they were then creating it; but they
were naively romantic neither about the New World—for clearly they
found their principles of religion and state-making in the Old—nor about
the people—for clearly they believed that popular sovereignty should
be limited in behalf of liberty and property and in accordance with the
restraints of traditional wisdom. They worked into the Constitution a
series of balances which inhibit both the direct expression of the popular
will and tendencies toward autocratic usurpation. It is a system which
rests on the premise that the best way to ensure stable social conditions
and provide adequate protection of human rights is through a politics
of countervailing coalition. The philosophic premise behind this system
was stated by James Madison in *The Federalist*:

> Ambition must be made to counteract ambition. . . . It may be a reflection
> on human nature that such devices should be necessary to control the abuses
> of government. But what is government itself but the greatest of all re-
> flections on human nature? If men were angels, no government would be

necessary. . . . In framing a government which is to be administered by men over men, the great difficulty lies in this: you must first enable the government to control the governed; and in the next place oblige it to control itself.

With time there occurred a gradual democratization of American society, in part because Americans displayed in the nineteenth century what Louis Hartz has called "a genius for political participation"; in part because the structure created from Madison's model of limited government could be used advantageously by the agrarian interests for whom Thomas Jefferson spoke, and by the farmers and urban middle class who rallied behind Andrew Jackson; and in part because there continued to course through American life a profound feeling for a radical utopianism.

Now the question we must encounter is this: Could the principles upon which the American government was founded and the expectations that had arisen with the beginning of American settlement be at all reconciled? Can one bring together the worldly realism of *The Federalist* with the Edenic nostalgia coursing through American literature? That the conflict was a real one, and so regarded by the principal actors, may be seen in a caustic passage Alexander Hamilton wrote for *The Federalist*:

> Reflections of this kind [in behalf of a balance of power] may have trifling weight with men who hope to see realized in America the halcyon scenes of the poetic or fabulous age; but to those who believe we are likely to experience a common portion of vicissitudes and calamities which have fallen to the lot of other nations . . . [etc., etc.]*

Yet during the 1820s and 1830s, when the grip of Federalism had been loosened and the powers of capitalism not yet exerted, many Americans must have felt that a harmonious relation between social institutions and moral desires was indeed possible. Soon, everything changed. The issue of slavery provoked a crisis beyond compromise; the gradual development of commercial capitalism enforced a centralization of power greater than Hamilton could have imagined; and the Populistic hopes which would come to a climax in the late nineteenth and early twentieth centuries were largely fated to disappointment. With time, it became clear that America was trapped in a conflict between its guiding institutions (better though these might seem than any other within sight or memory) and its guiding myth (poignant as this would

* See, however, the brilliant essay by Cecelia M. Kenyon, "Alexander Hamilton: Rousseau of the Right" (*Political Science Quarterly*, June 1958), which argues that Hamilton was himself very much an ideologue. Perhaps the point to be stressed is that in the practical task of state-making the Founding Fathers had no choice but to put somewhat to the side their visionary preoccupations.

seem in its absolute unrealizability). And from this conflict there have
followed enormous consequences.

In the United States, a country with a passion for political spectacle,
the *idea* of politics—to say nothing of the figure of the politician—has
been held in ridicule and frequent disrepute. Along the margins of the
society there have arisen movements declaring themselves to be political
but actually dominated by Edenic and apocalyptic moods that make them
profoundly apolitical. Americans have often been tempted by the possibility of realizing through communities of salvation those ends which
other societies assign to politics—and conversely have often been
tempted by the idea of assigning to the arena of politics those ends
which other societies regard as proper to religion, philosophy, and morality. Yet the very conflicts which make for social impasse and human
frustration have served as the themes of our greatest and most poignant
literary works. The troubles of life are the convenience of literature.

2

Classical European literature often displays an extratemporal dimension—its urge to transcendence breaks past the crowded spaces of
an old world, to create itself anew in the guise of an ideal future, a
heavenly prospect sanctioned by Christianity and removed from the
paltriness of time. But at least until the idea of America takes hold of
the European imagination there is, for Europeans, no place else to go.
Locked into space, they can only transfer their hopes to a time beyond
time. Their escape is vertical.

In American literature the urge to break past the limits of the human
condition manifests itself through images of space. Our characteristic
fictions chart journeys not so much in order to get their heroes out of
America as to transport the idea of America into an undefiled space.
The urge to transcendence appears as stories of men who move away,
past frontiers and borders, into the "territory" or out to sea, in order
to preserve their images of possibility. For the enticements of space
offer the hope—perhaps only the delusion—of a new beginning: so that,
for a time, an individual hero can be seen as reenacting, within or beyond
the society, the myth upon which it rests but which it has not been able
to fulfill. In America this new start is seen not so much in terms of an
improvement or reordering of the social structure, but as a leap beyond
society—a wistful ballet of transcendence.

Now many critics have noticed these elements in our literature and
have discussed them in terms of an Adamic myth, a wish to return to
innocence, a nostalgia for a purity we never had. Or they have seen in
our writing a wish to escape the guilt brought on by the defilement of

the countryside; to put down the burdens of success, family, and women; and to be done with the whole idea of society and sink back into a state of primal fraternity: blood brothers on the raft, the hunting ground, the lonely river, all in common friendliness, black, red, and white.

Let us see what happens, however, if we somewhat shift the terms of this approach to nineteenth-century American literature. Let us see what happens if we acknowledge that many of our major poems and fictions release a hunger for a state of nature not yet soiled by history and commerce; if we further agree that troubled responses to sexuality and perhaps a wish to discard mature sexual life in behalf of a fellowship of innocents are tacitly expressed in these poems and fictions; and if we then look at them in political terms.

It is a special kind of politics that is here at stake: not the usual struggles for power among contending classes within a fixed society; nor the mechanics of power as employed by a stable ruling class; nor even the dynamics of party maneuvering; but, rather, a politics concerned with the *idea* of society itself, a politics that dares consider—wonderful question—whether society is good and—still more wonderful—whether society is necessary. The paradox of it all is that a literature which on any manifest level is not really political at all should nevertheless be precisely the literature to raise the most fundamental problem in political theory: What is the rationale for society, the justification for the state?

And if we agree for a moment so to regard nineteenth-century American literature, we discover running through it a strong if subterranean current of anarchism. Not anarchism as the political movement known to nineteenth-century Europe, a movement with an established ideology and a spectrum of emphases ranging from Populism to terrorism. That has meant very little in the United States. I have in mind something else: anarchism as a social vision arising spontaneously from the conditions of preindustrial American culture, anarchism as a bias of the American imagination releasing its deepest, which is to say its most frustrated, yearnings.

Anarchism here signifies a vision of a human community beyond the calculation of good and evil; beyond the need for the state as an apparatus of law and suppression; beyond the yardsticks of moral measurement; beyond the need, in fact, for the constraints of authority. It envisages a community of autonomous persons, each secure in his own being and aware of his own mind. It signifies a collective desire to refuse the contaminations of history, precisely at the point where the nation's history begins to seem oppressive and irreversible. The anarchist vision coursing through nineteenth-century American literature speaks for a wish to undo restrictions which violate the deepest myth of the very society that has suffered the necessity of establishing these restrictions. What is novel here is the assumption that because of our blessed locale, we could find space—a little beyond the border, farther past the shore— in which to return, backward and free, to a stateless fraternity, so that the very culture created on the premise of mankind's second chance would, in failing that chance, yet allow its people a series of miniature recurrences.

The oppressive system of laws, which Herman Melville would later call the "forms" in *Billy Budd*, gives way to the self-ordering discipline of persons in a fraternal relationship. While this relationship is enabled by, and perhaps only possible within, the arena of an unsullied nature, it is not so much the thought of pastoral which excites our major nineteenth-century writers as it is a vision of human comradeship being fulfilled within the setting of pastoral. And thereby the problem of authority, perhaps the most difficult that can be faced in political thought, is—at least on the imaginative plane—simply dissolved: a solution as inadequate as it is entrancing.

In my capsule description of this anarchist vision, the key word is "fraternal"—the notion of a society in which the sense of brotherhood replaces the rule of law, even the best law, since law by its very nature must be unjust insofar as it raises abstract standards above personal relations. The anarchist belief in the fraternal is a belief in the power of love as a mode of discipline, indeed, in an equable relationship which may even replace both love and discipline by something still more lovely: the composure of affection.

Both the theme of a relaxed anarchic community free from the constraints of law and the theme of a return to an unspoiled pastoral America call upon the same imaginative impulse. If the vision of a life without the regulations of the state seems impossible as a basis for a modern politics, it is no more impossible than the pastoral vision of a pansexual, unaggressive, and asocial fraternity in personal relations. To stress the political aspect, however, is a way of underscoring the dilemmas faced by the major nineteenth-century American writers.

The paradisal dream is lodged deeply in their imaginations, as in those of almost all sensitive Americans of the time. Yet they are living in a society Madison helped to form, Jackson to reform, and the expansion of American business to transform. The conviction that injustice and vulgarity grew stronger during the nineteenth century is shared by many of our writers—a conviction, finally, that an America is being created which frustrates both the dream of a new Eden and the idea of a democracy resting upon sturdy, independent citizens. Neither in practice nor in thought can our writers find a way of dealing with this sense of disenchantment, if only because the country with which they become disenchanted has itself been the object of enormous expectations. In their bitterness with the social reality and their tacit recognition that they cannot really affect its course, American writers seek to get around or to "transcend" the intractability of what they encounter. Whatever they cannot change head-on, they will now turn away from, clinging meanwhile to that anarchic vision which seems all the more poignant as it recedes into the distance of lost possibilities. And thereby they create an ideal place of the imagination—precarious, transient, unstained— which speaks far more eloquently to the inner desires of our collective life than it can represent, or cope with, its coarse actualities.

Have I not just worked out a paradigm of *Huckleberry Finn*, as Mark Twain turned from the torments of slavery to the idyll of Nigger Jim and Huck on the raft? If American literature in the nineteenth century seldom succeeds in depicting with any complexity or directness the rough textures of our social life, it nevertheless has an enormous relevance to our moral life: it speaks from the heart of a culture.

The idea of a utopian enclave is recurrent among nineteenth-century American intellectuals. What is Thoreau's Walden but a utopia for curmudgeons? Thoreau, who wrote that he would "rather keep a bachelor's hall in hell than go to board in heaven," was not exactly strong in sentiments of fraternity. The proper conclusion to Jefferson's motto, "that government is best which governs least," becomes for Thoreau, "that government is best which governs not at all." His conclusion is not logically binding, but it does indicate his commitment to an absolute selfhood which reflects hostility not only to the idea of government but also to the necessary consequences, the necessary inconveniences, of a democratic society. "Any man more right than his neighbors constitutes a majority of one already," said Thoreau, without troubling to say how that rightness is to be established. Thoreau drives to an extreme those implications of anarchic individualism which in the end must undercut both the fraternal vision and the democratic polity. It is as if Thoreau, temperamentally unable to share in the idea of fraternity which moved Melville and Twain so deeply, were tacitly accepting the skeptical theories of Madison and Hamilton concerning the limitations of man as a social animal and then settling for his own version of anarchy: an anarchy of one.

Lacking that sense of outgoing spaciousness—to say nothing of human trustingness—one finds in Melville and Twain, the New England writers tuck their utopian enclaves into the interstices of their tight little region. In Hawthorne's *The Blithedale Romance* the utopian community

is mourned with his characteristic irony and encircling skepticism—
though still mourned. Of all our major nineteenth-century writers Hawthorne was least susceptible to visions of paradise, yet as a nineteenth-
century American he could not entirely free himself from sentiments
that filled the air; and it is he, not Emerson, who joined Brook Farm.
The criticisms he made of this utopian community, a small-scale effort
to realize Eden through thrifty New England shareholding, are remarkably cogent. Hawthorne saw that, motives apart, the formation of an
isolated utopian community (whether in social actuality or imaginative
projection) is seldom a threat to established power; he understood that
no matter how unstained its inner morality, the utopian community
could not avoid becoming part of the materialistic world it detested—
a lesson, by the way, that even Huck and Nigger Jim must learn about
their life on the raft as it is related to everything beyond the raft. "I
very soon became sensible," writes the central character of *The Blithedale
Romance*, "that, as regarded society at large, we stood in a position of
new hostility, rather than new brotherhood. . . . Constituting so pitiful
a minority as now, we were inevitably estranged from the rest of mankind
in pretty fair proportion with the strictness of our mutual bond among
ourselves."

What Hawthorne is saying here is that the utopian community becomes a competitive unit in a competitive society and must therefore
be infected with its corruptions. The utopian who would cut himself off
from the ugly world must, to preserve his utopia, become a "practical
agriculturist"—which means to model his utopia on the society he rejects. This criticism, striking so hard a blow at the political fancies of
many nineteenth-century American intellectuals, is advanced by Hawthorne with a joyless and almost cruel insistence; but that does not make
it any the less true.

If Hawthorne criticizes the utopian impulse on the ground that it
does not really succeed in avoiding the evil of the great world, he also
implies that another trouble is that it does not bring its followers into
a sufficiently close relation with the evil of the great world. For the
utopian venture at Blithedale, with its transformation of political idealism into pastoral retreat, bears a thoroughly innocent air. It is an
innocence peculiar to many nineteenth-century American intellectuals,
who believed that politics, when not simply a vulgarity to be avoided,
could be undertaken through proclaiming a series of moral ultimates.
This innocence was mainly a revulsion from the hopelessly crude and
corrupt nature of our ordinary politics, and it showed itself in no more
endearing form than the assumption that ordinary politics could be

gotten away from or supplanted by the politics of pastoral retreat. America itself having gone astray, utopianism would remake it in the small.

3

But I have anticipated myself, for I should have begun by glancing at the anarchist vision in the work of our major writers.

It is in James Fenimore Cooper's fiction that this vision first appears with imaginative strength. Like Hawthorne, Cooper was deeply conservative in his thought; but together with this conscious bias there flows through Cooper's fiction a yearning for a state of social comeliness that he saw embodied in the life of the Indians and, more persuasively, in the habits of his culture-hero, Natty Bumppo.

Cooper's anarchist vision appears as a substratum of feeling, a cluster of wistful images, picturesque set pieces and mythic figures. It is a vision that breaks past his pompous style, as if meant to shatter his conservative opinions. Cooper's best fiction is set either at sea or in the forest, both areas which for him suggest psychic space, moral elbow room. I shall here look only at Cooper in the forest. He is not, of course, a realistic portraitist of the Indians; some of them, in his treatment, seem more sages than savages. But if we think of Cooper's treatment of the Indians as a way of projecting an image of an ideal America, then the material becomes remarkably interesting. In Cooper's fiction the Indian tribes are never burdened with government. Within the tribe, the essential unit of social life is the family, and in many respects a more powerful unit than the tribe itself. Military service is voluntary: when the braves go on the warpath they act out of their own free will. Disputes within the tribe always occur among individuals, so that factions are not formed—Madison's forebodings seem not to be borne out by Cooper's Indians. As Cooper portrays it—and historical accuracy need not concern us for a moment—the life of the Indians can be severely bound by tradition, rites, concepts of honor, and limitations of mind, but it is not subject to the institutional authority and the social regulation we associate with the state.

With Natty Bumppo, deer-slayer and pathfinder, Cooper's conservative and anarchist impulses achieve a true union. Natty brings together a version of civilized decorum and the purity of natural man—precisely the unlikelihood of this mixture makes him so poignant a figure. His ideal status depends pretty much on his social ineffectuality. Propertyless as a matter of principle and self-governing through ascetic training, Natty is a monk of the woods living in fraternal closeness with Chingachgook, his Indian companion. At ease with the natural world and apart from social crowding and hypocrisy, they neither tamper with their feelings nor reduce them to ideas. Natty is the American at once free from historical sophistication and primitivist degradation. In Natty self and society are at peace; or better yet, society becomes absorbed into self, in a truce of composure. Natty lives out the anarchist idyll of a life so beautifully attuned to its own inner needs and thereby so lucidly harmonious with the external world, there is need for neither rules nor restraints. In the experience of Natty and Chingachgook we have one of the few instances—imaginary, alas—where the Marxist prescription for the "withering away of the state" has been realized. With this proviso: that you have to keep moving steadily westward as the state keeps reaching farther and farther into the forest.

The serene power of Natty as mythic hero is heightened still further by a contrast Cooper provides in *The Prairie*. There, as Natty slides into advanced age, he meets Ishmael Bush, a vividly drawn squatter, who is also uneasy with civilized society but in whom are embodied the ugly potentialities of a crude individualism and a brutal clannishness. Ishmael is a distorting double of Natty, evidence of Cooper's shrewd insight that even the most profound of American visions may have its underside of ugliness. At the end of *The Prairie* Natty ascends to heaven in a virtual apotheosis, yet a shadow has already been cast by the figure of Ishmael, thrust to the forefront of the novel in order to call into question everything Natty stands for.

When Huck Finn and Nigger Jim are alone on that indispensable raft (itself so wonderful a symbol of the isolation, purity, and helplessness upon which the anarchist vision rests), they set up a communal order transcending in value the charms of their personal friendliness. They create a community of equals, because it is a community going beyond the mere *idea* of equality. The idea of equality must be enforced by a state and requires that fixed norms and regulations be imposed on persons of varying needs and powers. The community of equals is established by persons and involves a delicate adjustment, moment by moment, to the desires each perceives in the other.

The community of the raft is a community of friends, quietly competent at the tasks of self-preservation and self-ordering. The impulse embodied in the escape of Huck and Nigger Jim is toward a freedom that can neither be confined to nor adequately described in social terms. It comes into spontaneous existence, not as a matter of status, obligation, or right, but as a shared capacity for sympathetic identification with the natural world, seen as a resource which those with the proper sense of reverence can tap. Or it can be a sympathetic identification with other men, which is something to be learned, so that the learning becomes a way of moving past mere learning and received morality. Huck's education is an education of the emotions. And on the raft his emotions are freed because he knows that they—the people of the town, the figures of judgment, the men of authority, the agents of the state—are away. Huck Finn never reaches a conceptual grasp of the problem of slavery: what, as everyone quickly sees, would be so remarkable in his decision to help Nigger Jim gain freedom if he, Huck, concluded that it was the right thing to do? As a decent American boy, he would then have no choice but to help. But made in violation of norms he accepts, Huck's decision becomes a triumph of nature over culture, anarchic fraternity over registered authority. It is, for Huck, a matter of *friendliness*. And in a state of friendliness, men—at least in nineteenth-century American fiction—do not need society. Yet precisely because he does not understand practically the problem he has "surmounted" spiritually, Huck is also helpless before it: he may not want society but society wants him.

As long as Huck and Nigger Jim can float upon the raft there is no need for fixed measurements of right and wrong, good and evil. When Huck and Nigger Jim achieve their moments of fraternal union, we are transported to a muted rapture enabling them to rise beyond the fixed points of morality. One is reminded of the Hasidic legend which has it that if step by step you move upward on the ladder of morality you will in the end break loose and float away into a buoying space.

Yet Twain was too shrewd and troubled a writer to compose a mere idyll. The precarious community of friends established on the raft is threatened at almost every moment. It is invaded by alien figures, the King and the Duke, who are presented in comic terms but whose significance is steadily felt to be ominous. To the extent that Huck and Nigger Jim overcome them, and fend off assaults from enemies both on the river and on the shore, it is partly as a triumph of innocence, the innocence of friends, and partly as a triumph of shrewdness, Huck's shrewdness of social personality which upon need he quickly reestablishes.

Huck is a figure at once fixed and amorphous, recognizable and anonymous. On the raft he sheds his mask of personality: everything a human being absorbs from his society. The more comfortable he feels, the less individual he seems; for he blends into a state of passive receptivity, no longer a demarcated character but a current of experience. The self grows harmonious with its surroundings; it exists as awareness and caress rather than wariness and will. Between Huck and Jim there develops an I-Thou relationship, a sentience so keen that for a few moments we live in the America that might have been, our lost paradise of anarchy. On the river Huck's personality is always in process of dissolution, for there he can leave behind anxiety and shrewdness and ease himself into repose and contemplation. On the land Huck chooses the masquerades of personality, or more accurately, he knows he must choose them. He adopts a variety of names, sometimes passing himself off as Tom Sawyer, the commonplace American boy, and sometimes as the less-than-beatific riverside Huck Finn. Even on land he is an admirable moral figure. But on the raft he has no need for disguise, no burden of personality, no strategy of shrewdness. In the community of friends, lawless and stateless, there is storytelling, amiable philosophizing about Sollermun the King, eating, sleeping, and keeping loose.

It cannot last. For all the while Twain is making certain that we remember paradise consists of a few rickety boards nailed together as a raft; that the raft contains a runaway slave worth a sizable number of dollars; that violence threatens at every bend of the shore, and that the paradisal journey is a drift southward, deeper and deeper to slavery. The anarchic enclave must disintegrate under the pressures of the world and perhaps, in the end, contribute to a conservative resignation. Before the world itself, Huck and Nigger Jim are helpless. At one and the same time they represent the power of transcendence, of rising above the crippling grasp of society, and the pitiable vulnerability of a boy and a slave who try to evade the authority of that society. Between these two extremes is there not perhaps a causal relationship, one in which our most splendid yearnings derive from our utter impotence?

From *Huckleberry Finn* to Faulkner's "The Bear" there is a clear line of descent. In "The Bear" the enclave of utopia is seen far more modestly, since Faulkner is aware that it is merely an enclave, "a diminished thing." By now it has been reduced from a drift along the river to an arranged vacation in the woods. The trip to the woods is not a challenge to society, let alone a way of transcending it, but a mixture of refreshment and retreat. In both fictions there is a severe formal problem of finding a resolution for a historically conditioned narrative devoted to celebrating a timeless idyll; but the problem is easier for Faulkner than for Twain. Faulkner never allows the vision of paradise to get out of hand; he never allows it to be seen as anything more than an interval in the course of our usual occupations; and therefore he does not have to face the difficulties Twain encountered once he had yielded himself to the raft. For Twain allowed his vision to become too captivating, too beautiful, *too possible*—all in the face of the evidence he had accumulated to show it as anything but possible. Once you have been on a raft, no other place can matter. Huck will light out for "the territory," and no doubt become a responsible citizen; but he will now have to live, like the rest of us, within the clamps of social limitation.

The early writings of Herman Melville, up to and including *Moby-Dick*, are suffused with visions of anarchic bliss. How deeply the paradisal dream remained lodged, or buried, in Melville's imagination we can see from a little-known poem, "To Ned," which he published in 1888, three years before his death. Written in the style of most of his verse—at once gnarled and strong—"To Ned" addresses itself to Richard Tobias Greene, Melville's companion in the South Pacific adventures related in his first book, *Typee*. Its tone is nostalgic: "Where is the world we roved, Ned Bunn?" Melville sets up a contrast between "Authentic Edens in a Pagan sea" and their invasion by "Paul Pry . . . with Pelf and Trade." In the Marquesas Melville and Ned "breathed primeval balm / From Eden's eye yet overrun," but now, ends Melville rather sadly, he must marvel whether mortals can twice "Here and hereafter, touch a Paradise." One can only envy a man who supposed he had touched it once.

The picture of Taipa as a tempting if threatening Arcadia; the blood-brotherhood of Ishmael and Queequeg before they submit to Ahab's compulsive authoritarianism, one of the most beautiful enactments of plebeian fraternity in our literature—these are profoundly radical in stress, far more so than any mere expression of opinion.

They release Melville's distaste for those "forms," those arthritic regulations which in *Billy Budd* finally achieve their dubious victory. The young Melville is full of plebeian hope, utterly American in his democratic impatience with democratic constraints, pledged to a union of men that can surmount the cautions induced by Madison. Even in *Billy Budd* there is far more social irony—a protest muted, despairing, wary—than most critics acknowledge or readers notice. Billy himself is an archetype of innocence, as everyone remarks; but he is imaginable only as a creature of a utopian yearning so intense, so moving, and yet so untenable in the life we must lead that Melville's mature imagination has no choice but fondly to destroy him. And what is Captain Vere, that eminently sane and decent man, but an embodiment of the cruel justice which comprises the state? Captain Vere is a man who does his duty before and above all; and in our time we have learned what such men can be and do. Melville's great perception here is that the personal qualities of Vere, notable as these are, do not finally matter: so long as he acts out the impersonal violence of the state, his virtues as a man come to rather little and he has no choice but to be a judicial killer. Equally haunting is Melville's recognition that Billy in his innocence forgives Captain Vere, while the plebs who are his crew mates, men ground down in the harsh discipline of a state fearful of revolutionary upsurge, neither forgive nor know how to rebel against that which they cannot forgive.

Billy Budd is a work written from Melville's weary disenchantment with the radical utopianism, the gay anarchism of his youthful years, and thereby a work in which the vision of youth is embodied in a figure at once pure and helpless, angelic and speechless, loved and doomed. The power of the story rests in the fact that Melville does what Twain failed to do: he finds a literary resolution for a moral and social problem which, in its own terms, seems insoluble. Melville does not yield himself quite so easily as had Twain to the vision of anarchic bliss. But Melville takes the subject from a greater distance than Twain, which is why he presents it in its irreducible pain and complete outrage—as we see in the concluding three chapters, where Billy is dead but neither historical reports nor legends of the sea do his ordeal any justice whatever. By the time Melville came to write *Billy Budd* he could do no more than be the Abraham to his imaginary Isaac, sending to the sacrificial altar the boy who in gesture if not speech summoned the dreams of his youth, perhaps of his nation.

The clash between anarchic yearning and fixed authority leads both to the marvelously open and spacious quality of nineteenth-century American writing and to the choked misanthropy that so often follows. For writers caught up in the utopian vision it is peculiarly hard, as they grow older, to find the modulated resolutions available to the classical European writers. Our literature is schizoid, flaring to ecstasy and falling to misanthropy, but rarely pausing at the middle level of realism and social engagement. The American myth, of which the anarchic vision is one instance, exerts too great a hold upon our nineteenth-century masters; and then, as it shatters itself upon the shores of history, there follows a disenchantment beyond bearing. Where the traditional treatment of society in the English novel occurs through class adjustments, contained conflicts, even revolutions, all within the shared assumption of the inescapability of social authority and visible power, the American imagination, at its deepest level, keeps calling into question the idea of society itself. And as the nation moves into the modern world, what can that come to but despair?

4

There is no other Western culture of the past two centuries in which, to my knowledge, so many demands have been expressed for the "creation of values." When one comes to think of it, that is really an extraordinary fact. The literatures of Europe either sustain traditional values or enlarge upon revolutionary values; but both are seen as inseparable from the social order in which the writer writes and the reader reads. In our culture we have made the unprecedented demand upon writers that they "create values" quite apart from either tradition or insurgency. What we have often meant is that they establish a realm of values at a distance from the setting of actual life, thereby becoming priests of the possible in a world of shrinking possibilities. We ask them to discover, out of their desperate clarity, a vision we can cherish, and cherish perhaps in direct proportion to our knowledge that we will not—or cannot—live by it. The result is that every now and again we strike off a fiction of such transcendent powers it sends the world into enchantment, but also that we deny ourselves the possibilities of a hard realism in both our literature and our politics by means of which to transform or ease our condition. We are tempted to follow the path of Thoreau in a world utterly unlike that in which Thoreau lived, and we thereby succeed neither in honoring Thoreau nor in affecting our circumstances.

Yet, within our literature, the anarchic impulse—together with the accompanying moral ultimatism and apolitical politics—remains enormously powerful and even those who grow skeptical as to its social value must grant that it still has a notable imaginative thrust. If one looks, for example, at the writings of Norman Mailer, it becomes clear that behind all of them lies a fear of stasis, a dread of a future ruled by functional rationality. All of his recent writings seem to ask: Is it possible that "the smooth strifeless world" in which many cultivated Americans live will prove to be a model of tomorrow, a glass enclosure in which there will be a minimum of courage or failure, test or transcendence? For those of us marked, or marred, by the ethic of striving and dissatisfaction, this question seems endlessly haunting.

That Mailer's quest for a new energizing principle leads to gestures of desperation and then a self-mimicry of his own gestures, I need not demonstrate here. Yet despair, if it can remain genuine despair, is not the worst of emotions; it testifies, at least, to the earlier presence of desire. And in our world, the vision of a society of true friends living in composed fraternity is one that can only bring the writer to a ferocious impasse.

An endless dialectic in our life and our literature, this clash between anarchy and authority. Here a poet, Paul Goodman, cries out that he is

> still seeking
> on faces alive in this world
> ideal shapes of heaven,
> vengefully to wrest
> a stolen inheritance back . . .

and another poet, Robert Frost, writes in a poem significantly entitled "An Answer":

> But Islands of the Blessèd, bless you, son,
> I never came upon a blessèd one.

Black Boys
and Native Sons

James Baldwin first came to the notice of the American literary public not through his own fiction but as author of an impassioned criticism of the conventional Negro novel.* In 1949 he published an essay called "Everybody's Protest Novel," attacking the kind of fiction, from *Uncle Tom's Cabin* to *Native Son*, that had been written about the ordeal of the American Negroes; and two years later he printed "Many Thousands Gone," a tougher and more explicit polemic against Richard Wright and the school of naturalistic "protest" fiction that Wright represented. The protest novel, wrote Baldwin, is undertaken out of sympathy for the Negro, but through its need to present him merely as a social victim or a mythic agent of sexual prowess, it hastens to confine the Negro to the very tones of violence he has known all his life. Compulsively re-enacting and magnifying his trauma, the protest novel proves unable to transcend

From *Dissent* 9 (Autumn 1963):3.

* In the years since this essay was written, the issues it explores have undergone a complex, even torturous history—and so has some of the language associated with it. Upon rereading the essay I was tempted for a moment to change its language by substituting "black" or "African American" for "Negro," but then decided that would be a mistake. In 1963, when I wrote the essay, the courtesy term was "Negro," while "black" could even have been taken as a term of disparagement. Conventions of courtesy change, of course, and if I were writing today I would use one of the currently acceptable terms. But I think it right to remain faithful to the moment in which I wrote and therefore keep the original usage.

it. So choked with rage has this kind of writing become, it cannot show the Negro as a unique person or locate him as a member of a community with its own traditions and values, its own "unspoken recognition of shared experience which creates a way of life." The failure of the protest novel "lies in its insistence that it is [man's] categorization alone which is real and which cannot be transcended."

Like all attacks launched by young writers against their famous elders, Baldwin's essays were also a kind of announcement of his own intentions. He wrote admiringly about Wright's courage ("his work was an immense liberation and revelation for me"), but now, precisely because Wright had prepared the way for the Negro writers to come, he, Baldwin, would go further, transcending the sterile categories of "Negro-ness," whether those enforced by the white world or those defensively erected by the Negroes themselves. No longer mere victim or rebel, the Negro would stand free in a self-achieved humanity. As Baldwin put it some years later, he hoped "to prevent myself from becoming *merely* a Negro; or even, merely a Negro writer." The world "tends to trap and immobilize you in the role you play," and for the Negro writer, if he is to be a writer at all, it hardly matters whether the trap is sprung from motives of hatred or condescension.

Baldwin's rebellion against the older Negro novelist who had served him as a model and had helped launch his career was not, of course, an unprecedented event. The history of literature is full of such painful ruptures, and the issue Baldwin raised is one that keeps recurring, usually as an aftermath to a period of "socially engaged" writing. The novel is an inherently ambiguous genre: it strains toward formal autonomy and can seldom avoid being a public gesture. If it is true, as Baldwin said in "Everybody's Protest Novel," that "literature and sociology are not one and the same," it is equally true that such statements hardly begin to cope with the problem of how a writer's own experience affects his desire to represent human affairs in a work of fiction. Baldwin's formula evades, through rhetorical sweep, the genuinely difficult issue of the relationship between social experience and literature.

Yet in *Notes of a Native Son*, the book in which his remark appears, Baldwin could also say: "One writes out of one thing only—one's own experience." What, then, was the experience of a man with a black skin, what *could* it be in this country? How could a Negro put pen to paper, how could he so much as think or breathe, without some impulsion to protest, be it harsh or mild, political or private, released or buried? The "sociology" of his existence formed a constant pressure on his literary work, and not merely in the way this might be true for any writer, but with a pain and ferocity that nothing could remove.

James Baldwin's early essays are superbly eloquent, displaying virtually in full the gifts that would enable him to become one of the great American rhetoricians. But these essays, like some of the later ones, are marred by rifts in logic, so little noticed when one gets swept away by the brilliance of the language that it takes a special effort to attend their argument.

Later Baldwin would see the problems of the Negro writer with a greater charity and more mature doubt. Reviewing in 1959 a book of poems by Langston Hughes, he wrote: "Hughes is an American Negro poet and has no choice but to be acutely aware of it. He is not the first American Negro to find the war between his social and artistic responsibilities all but irreconcilable." All but irreconcilable: the phrase strikes a note sharply different from Baldwin's attack upon Wright in the early fifties. And it is not hard to surmise the reason for this change. In the intervening years Baldwin had been living through some of the experiences that had goaded Richard Wright into rage and driven him into exile; he too, like Wright, had been to hell and back, many times over.

2

"Gawd, Ah wish all them white folks was dead."

The day *Native Son* appeared, American culture was changed forever. No matter how much qualifying the book might later need, it made impossible a repetition of the old lies. In all its crudeness, melodrama, and claustrophobia of vision, Richard Wright's novel brought out into the open, as no one ever had before, the hatred, fear, and violence that have crippled and may yet destroy our culture.

A blow at the white man, the novel forced him to recognize himself as an oppressor. A blow at the black man, the novel forced him to recognize the cost of his submission. *Native Son* assaulted the most cherished of American vanities: the hope that the accumulated injustice of the past would bring with it no lasting penalties, the fantasy that in his humiliation the Negro somehow retained a sexual potency—or was it a childlike good nature?—that made it necessary to envy and still more to suppress him. Speaking from the black wrath of retribution, Wright insisted that history can be a punishment. He told us the one thing even the most liberal whites preferred not to hear: that Negroes were far from patient or forgiving, that they were scarred by fear, that they hated every moment of their suppression even when seeming most acquiescent, and that often enough they hated *us*, the decent and cultivated white men who from complicity or neglect shared in the responsibility for their plight. If such younger novelists as Baldwin and Ralph Ellison were to move beyond Wright's harsh naturalism and toward more supple modes of fiction, that was possible only because Wright had been there first, courageous enough to release the full weight of his anger.

In *Black Boy*, the autobiographical narrative he published several years later, Wright would tell of an experience while working as a bellboy in the South. Many times he had come into a hotel room carrying luggage or food and seen naked white whores lounging about, unmoved by shame at his presence, for "blacks were not considered human beings anyway . . . I was a non-man . . . I felt doubly cast out." With the publication of *Native Son*, however, Wright forced his readers to acknowledge his anger, and in that way, if none other, he wrested for himself a sense of dignity as a man. He forced his readers to confront the disease of our culture, and to one of its most terrifying symptoms he gave the name of Bigger Thomas.

Brutal and brutalized, lost forever to his unexpended hatred and his fear of the world, a numbed and illiterate black boy stumbling into a murder and never, not even at the edge of the electric chair, breaking through to an understanding of either his plight or himself, Bigger Thomas was a part of Richard Wright, a part even of the James Baldwin who stared with horror at Wright's Bigger, unable either to absorb him into his consciousness or eject him from it. Enormous courage, a discipline of self-conquest, was required to conceive Bigger Thomas, for this was no eloquent Negro spokesman, no admirable intellectual or formidable proletarian. Bigger was drawn—one would surmise, deliberately—from white fantasy and white contempt. Bigger was the worst of Negro life accepted, then rendered a trifle conscious and thrown back at those who had made him what he was. "No American Negro exists," Baldwin would later write, "who does not have his private Bigger Thomas living in the skull."

Wright drove his narrative to the very core of American phobia: sexual fright, sexual violation. He understood that the fantasy of rape is a consequence of guilt, what the whites suppose themselves to deserve. He understood that the white man's notion of uncontaminated Negro vitality, little as it had to do with the bitter realities of Negro life, reflected some ill-formed and buried feeling that our culture has run down, lost its blood, become febrile. And he grasped the way in which the sexual issue has been intertwined with social relationships, for even as the white people who hire Bigger as their chauffeur are decent and charitable, even as the girl he accidentally kills is a liberal of sorts, theirs is the power and the privilege. "We black and they white. They got things and we ain't. They do things and we can't."

The novel barely stops to provision a recognizable social world, often contenting itself with cartoon simplicities and yielding almost entirely to the nightmare incomprehension of Bigger Thomas. The mood is apocalyptic, the tone aggressive. Wright was an existentialist long before he heard the name, for he was committed to the literature of extreme situations both through the pressures of his rage and the gasping hope of an ultimate catharsis.

Wright confronts both the violence and the crippling limitations of Bigger Thomas. For Bigger the whites are not people at all, but something more, "a sort of great natural force, like a stormy sky looming overhead." And only through violence does he gather a little meaning in life, pitifully little: "He had murdered and created a new life for himself." Beyond that Bigger cannot go.

At first *Native Son* seems still another naturalistic novel: a novel of exposure and accumulation, charting the waste of the undersides of the American city. Behind the book one senses the molding influences of Theodore Dreiser, especially the Dreiser of *An American Tragedy*, who knows there are situations so oppressive that only violence can provide their victims with the hope of dignity. Like Dreiser, Wright wished to pummel his readers into awareness; like Dreiser, to overpower them with the sense of society as an enclosing force. Yet the comparison is finally of limited value, and for the disconcerting reason that Dreiser had a white skin and Wright a black one.

The usual naturalistic novel is written with detachment, as if by a scientist surveying a field of operations; it is a novel in which the writer withdraws from a detested world and coldly piles up the evidence for detesting it. *Native Son*, though preserving some of the devices of the naturalistic novel, deviates sharply from its characteristic tone: a tone Wright could not possibly have maintained and which, it may be, no Negro novelist can really hold for long. *Native Son* is a work of assault rather than withdrawal; the author yields himself in part to a vision of nightmare. Bigger's cowering perception of the world becomes the most vivid and authentic component of the book. Naturalism pushed to an extreme turns here into something other than itself, a kind of expressionist outburst, no longer a replica of the familiar social world but a self-contained realm of grotesque emblems.

That *Native Son* has grave faults anyone can see. The language is often coarse, flat in rhythm, syntactically overburdened, heavy with journalistic slag. Apart from Bigger, who seems more a brute energy than a particularized figure, the characters have little reality, the Negroes being mere stock accessories and the whites either "agit-prop" villains or heroic Communists whom Wright finds it easier to admire from a distance than establish from the inside. The long speech by Bigger's radical lawyer Max (again a device apparently borrowed from Dreiser) is ill-related to the book itself: Wright had not achieved Dreiser's capacity for absorbing everything, even the most recalcitrant philosophical passages, into a unified vision of things. Between Wright's feelings as a Negro and his beliefs as a Communist there is hardly a genuine fusion, and it is through this gap that a good part of the novel's unreality pours in.

Yet it should be said that the endlessly repeated criticism that Wright caps his melodrama with a party-line oration tends to oversimplify the novel, for Wright is too honest to allow the propagandistic message to constitute the last word. Indeed, the last word is given not to Max but to Bigger. For at the end Bigger remains at the mercy of his hatred and fear, the lawyer retreats helplessly, the projected union between political consciousness and raw revolt has not been achieved—as if Wright were persuaded that, all ideology apart, there is for each Negro an ultimate trial that he can bear only by himself.

Black Boy, which appeared five years after *Native Son*, is a slighter but more skillful piece of writing. Richard Wright came from a broken home, and as he moved from his helpless mother to a grandmother whose religious fanaticism (she was a Seventh-Day Adventist) proved utterly suffocating, he soon picked up a precocious knowledge of vice and a realistic awareness of social power. This autobiographical memoir, a small classic in the literature of self-discovery, is packed with harsh evocations of Negro adolescence in the South. The young Wright learns how wounding it is to wear the mask of a grinning nigger boy in order to keep a job. He examines the life of the Negroes and judges it without charity or idyllic compensation—for he already knows, in his heart and his bones, that to be oppressed means to lose out on human possibilities. By the time he is seventeen, preparing to leave for Chicago, where he will work on a WPA project, become a member of the Communist Party, and publish his first book of stories, *Uncle Tom's Children*, Wright has managed to achieve the beginnings of consciousness, through a slow and painful growth from the very bottom of deprivation to the threshold of artistic achievement and a glimpsed idea of freedom.

3

Baldwin's attack upon Wright had partly been anticipated by the more sophisticated American critics. Alfred Kazin, for example, had found in Wright a troubling obsession with violence: "If he chose to write the story of Bigger Thomas as a grotesque crime story, it is because his own indignation and the sickness of the age combined to make him dependent on violence and shock, to astonish the reader by torrential scenes of cruelty, hunger, rape, murder and flight, and then enlighten him by crude Stalinist homilies."

The last phrase apart, something quite similar could be said about the author of *Crime and Punishment*; it is disconcerting to reflect upon how few novelists, even the very greatest, could pass this kind of moral inspection. For the novel as a genre seems to have an inherent bias toward extreme effects, such as violence, cruelty, and the like. More important, Kazin's judgment rests on the assumption that a critic can readily distinguish between the genuine need of a writer to cope with ugly realities and the damaging effect these realities may have upon his moral and psychic life. But in regard to contemporary writers one finds it very hard to distinguish between a valid portrayal of violence and an obsessive involvement with it. A certain amount of obsession may be necessary for the valid portrayal—writers devoted to themes of desperation cannot keep themselves morally intact. And when we come to a writer like Richard Wright, who deals with the most degraded and inarticulate sector of the Negro world, the distinction between objective rendering and subjective immersion becomes still more difficult, perhaps even impossible. For a novelist who has lived through the searing experiences that Wright has there cannot be much possibility of approaching his subject with the "mature" poise recommended by high-minded critics. What is more, the very act of writing his novel, the effort to confront what Bigger Thomas means to him, is for such a writer a way of dredging up and then perhaps shedding the violence that society has pounded into him. Is Bigger an authentic projection of a social reality, or is he a symptom of Wright's "dependence on violence and shock"? Obviously both; and it could not be otherwise.

For the reality pressing upon all of Wright's work was a nightmare of remembrance, everything from which he had pulled himself out, with an effort and at a cost that is almost unimaginable. Without the terror of that nightmare it would have been impossible for Wright to summon the truth of the reality—not the only truth about American Negroes, perhaps not even the deepest one, but a primary and inescapable truth. Both truth and terror rested on a gross fact which Wright alone dared to confront: that violence is central in the life of the American Negro, defining and crippling him with a harshness few other Americans need suffer. "No American Negro exists who does not have his private Bigger Thomas living in the skull."

Now I think it would be well not to judge in the abstract, or with much haste, the violence that gathers in the Negro's heart as a response to the violence he encounters in society. It would be well to see this violence as part of a historical experience that is open to moral scrutiny but ought to be shielded from presumptuous moralizing. Bigger Thomas may be enslaved to a hunger for violence, but anyone reading *Native Son* with mere courtesy must observe the way in which Wright, even while yielding emotionally to Bigger's deprivation, also struggles to transcend it. That he did not fully succeed seems obvious; one may doubt that any Negro writer can.

More subtle and humane than either Kazin's or Baldwin's criticism is a remark made by Isaac Rosenfeld while reviewing *Black Boy*: "As with all Negroes and all men who are born to suffer social injustice, part of [Wright's] humanity found itself only in acquaintance with violence, and in hatred of the oppressor." Surely Rosenfeld was not here inviting an easy acquiescence in violence; he was trying to suggest the historical context, the psychological dynamics, which condition the attitudes all Negro writers take, or must take, toward violence. To say this is not to propose the condescension of exempting Negro writers from moral judgment, but to suggest the terms of understanding, and still more, the terms of hesitation for making a judgment.

There were times when Baldwin grasped this point better than anyone else. If he could speak of the "unrewarding rage" of *Native Son*, he also spoke of the book as "an immense liberation." Is it impudent to suggest that one reason he felt the book to be a liberation was precisely its rage, precisely the relief and pleasure that he, like so many other Negroes, must have felt upon seeing those long-suppressed emotions finally breaking through?

The kind of literary criticism Baldwin wrote was very fashionable in America during the postwar years. Mimicking the Freudian corrosion of motives and bristling with dialectical agility, this criticism approached all ideal claims—especially those made by radical and naturalist writers—with a weary skepticism, and proceeded to transfer the values such writers were attacking to the perspective from which they attacked. If Dreiser wrote about the power hunger and dream of success corrupting American society, that was because he was really infatuated with them. If James Farrell showed the meanness of life in the Chicago slums, that was because he could not really escape it. If Wright portrayed the violence gripping Negro life, that was because he was really obsessed with it. The word "really" or more sophisticated equivalents could do endless service in behalf of a generation of intellectuals soured on the tradition of protest but suspecting they might be pygmies in comparison to the writers who had protested. In reply, there was no way to "prove" that Dreiser, Farrell, and Wright were not contaminated by the false values they attacked; probably, since they were mere mortals living in the present society, they were contaminated; and so one had to keep insisting that such writers were nevertheless presenting actualities of modern experience, not merely phantoms of their neuroses.

If Bigger Thomas, as Baldwin said, "accepted a theology that denies him life," if in his Negro self-hatred he "*wants* to die because he glories in his hatred," this did not constitute a criticism of Wright unless one were prepared to assume what was simply preposterous: that Wright, for all his emotional involvement with Bigger, could not see beyond the limitations of the character he had created. This was a question Baldwin never seriously confronted in his early essays. He would describe accurately the limitations of Bigger Thomas and then, by one of those rhetorical leaps at which he is so gifted, would assume that these were also the limitations of Wright or his book.

Still another ground for Baldwin's attacks was his reluctance to accept the clenched militancy of Wright's posture as both novelist and man. In a remarkable sentence appearing in "Everybody's Protest Novel," Baldwin wrote, "Our humanity is our burden, our life; we need not battle for it; we need only to do what is infinitely more difficult—that is, accept it." What Baldwin was saying here was part of the outlook so many American intellectuals took during the years of a postwar liberalism not very different from conservatism. Ralph Ellison expressed this view in terms still more extreme: "Thus to see America with an awareness of its rich diversity and its almost magical fluidity and freedom, I was forced to conceive of a novel unburdened by the narrow naturalism which has led after so many triumphs to the final and unrelieved despair which marks so much of our current fiction." This note of willed affirmation—as if one could *decide* one's deepest and most authentic response to society!—was to be heard in many other works of the early fifties, most notably in Saul Bellow's *Adventures of Augie March*. Today it is likely to strike one as a note whistled in the dark. In response to Baldwin and Ellison, Wright would have said (I virtually quote the words he used in talking to me during the summer of 1958) that only through struggle could men with black skins, and for that matter, all the oppressed of the world, achieve their humanity. It was a lesson, said Wright with a touch of bitterness yet not without kindness, that the younger writers would have to learn in their own way and their own time. All that has happened since bears him out.

One criticism made by Baldwin in writing about *Native Son*, perhaps because it is the least ideological, remains important. He complained that in Wright's novel "a necessary dimension has been cut away; this dimension being the relationship that Negroes bear to one another, that depth of involvement and unspoken recognition of shared experience which creates a way of life." The climate of the book, "common to most Negro protest novels . . . has led us all to believe that in Negro life there exists no tradition, no field of manners, no possibility of ritual or intercourse, such as may, for example, sustain the Jew even after he has left his father's house." It could be urged, perhaps, that in composing a novel verging on expressionism Wright need not be expected to present the Negro world with fullness, balance, or nuance; but there can be little doubt that in this respect Baldwin did score a major point: the posture of militancy, no matter how great the need for it, exacts a heavy price from the writer, as indeed from everyone else. For "Even the hatred of squalor / Makes the brow grow stern / Even anger against injustice / Makes the voice grow harsh. . . ." All one can ask, by way of reply, is whether the refusal to struggle may not exact a still greater price. It is a question that would soon be tormenting James Baldwin, and almost against his will.

4

In his own novels Baldwin hoped to show the Negro world in its diversity and richness, not as a mere specter of protest; he wished to show it as a living culture of men and women who, even when deprived, share in the emotions and desires of common humanity. And he meant also to evoke something of the distinctiveness of Negro life in America, as evidence of its worth, moral tenacity, and right to self-acceptance. How can one not sympathize with such a program? And how, precisely as one does sympathize, can one avoid the conclusion that in this effort Baldwin has thus far failed to register a major success?

His first novel, *Go Tell It on the Mountain*, is an enticing but minor work: it traces the growing-up of a Negro boy in the atmosphere of a repressive Calvinism, a Christianity stripped of grace and brutal with fantasies of submission and vengeance. No other work of American fiction reveals so graphically the way in which an oppressed minority aggravates its own oppression through the torments of religious fanaticism. The novel is also striking as a modest *Bildungsroman*, the education of an imaginative Negro boy caught in the heart-struggle between his need to revolt, which would probably lead to his destruction in the jungles of New York, and the miserly consolations of black Calvinism, which would signify that he accepts the denial of his personal needs. But it would be a mistake to claim too much for this first novel, in which a rhetorical flair and a conspicuous sincerity often eat away at the integrity of event and the substance of character. The novel is intense, and the intensity is due to Baldwin's absorption in that religion of denial which leads the boy to become a preacher in his father's church, to scream out God's word from "a merciless resolve to kill my father rather than allow my father to kill me." Religion has of course played a central role in Negro life, yet one may doubt that the special kind of religious experience dominating *Go Tell It on the Mountain* is any more representative of that life, any more advantageous a theme for gathering in the qualities of Negro culture, than the violence and outrage of *Native Son*. Like Wright before him, Baldwin wrote from the intolerable pressures of his own experience; there was no alternative; each had to release his own agony before he could regard Negro life with the beginnings of objectivity.

Baldwin's second novel, *Giovanni's Room*, seems to me a flat failure. It abandons Negro life entirely (not in itself a cause for judgment) and focuses upon the distraught personal relations of several young Americans adrift in Paris. The problem of homosexuality, which is to recur in Baldwin's fiction, is confronted with a notable courage, but also with a disconcerting kind of sentimentalism, a quavering and sophisticated submission to the ideology of love. It is one thing to call for the treatment of character as integral and unique; but quite another for a writer with Baldwin's background and passions to succeed in bringing together his sensibility as a Negro and his sense of personal trouble.

Baldwin has not yet succeeded—the irony is a stringent one—in composing the kind of novel he counterpoised to the work of Richard Wright. He has written three essays, ranging in tone from disturbed affection to disturbing malice, in which he tries to break from his rebellious dependency upon Wright, but he remains tied to the memory of the older man. The Negro writer who has come closest to satisfying Baldwin's program is not Baldwin himself but Ralph Ellison, whose novel *Invisible Man* is a brilliant though flawed achievement, standing with *Native Son* as the major fiction thus far composed by American Negroes.

What astonishes one most about *Invisible Man* is the apparent freedom it displays from the ideological and emotional penalties suffered by Negroes in this country. I say "apparent" because the freedom is not quite so complete as the book's admirers like to suppose. Still, for long stretches *Invisible Man* does escape the formulas of protest, local color, genre quaintness, and jazz chatter. No white man could have written it, since no white man could know with such intimacy the life of the Negroes from the inside; yet Ellison writes with an ease and humor which are now and again simply miraculous.

Invisible Man is a record of a Negro's journey through contemporary America, from South to North, province to city, naive faith to disenchantment and perhaps beyond. There are clear allegorical intentions (Ellison is "literary" to a fault) but with a book so rich in talk and drama it would be a shame to neglect the fascinating surface for the mere depths. The beginning is both nightmare and farce. A timid Negro boy comes to a white smoker in a Southern town: he is to be awarded a scholarship. Together with several other Negro boys he is rushed to the front of the ballroom, where a sumptuous blonde tantalizes and frightens them by dancing in the nude. Blindfolded, the Negro boys stage a "battle royal," a free-for-all in which they pummel each other to the drunken shouts of the whites. Practical jokes, humiliations, terror—and then the boy delivers a prepared speech of gratitude to his white benefactors. At the end of this section, the boy dreams that he has opened the briefcase given him together with his scholarship to a Negro college and that he finds an inscription reading: "To Whom It May Concern: Keep This Nigger-Boy Running."

He keeps running. He goes to his college and is expelled for having innocently taken a white donor through a Negro gin mill that also happens to be a brothel. His whole experience is to follow this pattern. Strip down a pretense, whether by choice or accident, and you will suffer penalties, since the rickety structure of Negro respectability rests upon pretense and those who profit from it cannot bear to have the reality exposed (in this case, that the college is dependent upon the Northern white millionaire). The boy then leaves for New York, where he works in a white paint factory, becomes a soapboxer for the Harlem Communists, the darling of the fellow-traveling bohemia, and a big wheel in the Negro world. At the end, after witnessing a frenzied race riot in Harlem, he "finds himself" in some not entirely specified way, and his odyssey from submission to autonomy is complete.

Ellison has an abundance of that primary talent without which neither craft nor intelligence can save a novelist: he is richly, wildly inventive; his scenes rise and dip with tension, his people bleed, his language sings. No other writer has captured so much of the hidden gloom and surface gaiety of Negro life.

There is an abundance of superbly rendered speech: a West Indian woman inciting her men to resist an eviction, a Southern sharecropper calmly describing how he seduced his daughter, a Harlem street vender spinning jive. The rhythm of Ellison's prose is harsh and nervous, like a beat of harried alertness. The observation is expert: he knows exactly how zoot-suiters walk, making stylization their principle of life, and exactly how the antagonism between American and West Indian Negroes works itself out in speech and humor. He can accept his people as they are, in their blindness and hope: here, finally, the Negro world does exist, seemingly apart from plight or protest. And in the final scene

Ellison has created an unforgettable image: "Ras the Destroyer," a Negro nationalist, appears on a horse dressed in the costume of an Abyssinian chieftain, carrying spear and shield, and charging wildly into the police—a black Quixote, mad, absurd, unbearably pathetic.

But even Ellison cannot help being caught up with *the idea* of the Negro. To write simply about "Negro experience" with the aesthetic distance urged by the critics of the fifties is a moral and psychological impossibility, for plight and protest are inseparable from that experience, and even if less political than Wright and less prophetic than Baldwin, Ellison knows this quite as well as they do.

If *Native Son* is marred by the ideological delusions of the thirties, *Invisible Man* is marred, less grossly, by those of the fifties. The middle section of Ellison's novel, dealing with the Harlem Communists, does not ring quite true, in the way a good portion of the writings on this theme during the postwar years does not ring quite true. Ellison makes his Stalinist figures so vicious and stupid that one cannot understand how they could ever have attracted him or any other Negro. That the party leadership manipulated members with deliberate cynicism is beyond doubt, but this cynicism was surely more complex and guarded than Ellison shows it to be. No party leader would ever tell a prominent Negro Communist, as one of them does in *Invisible Man*: "You were not hired [as a functionary] to think"—even if that were what he felt. Such passages are almost as damaging as the propagandist outbursts in *Native Son*.

Still more troublesome, because it both breaks the coherence of the novel and reveals Ellison's dependence on the postwar zeitgeist, is the sudden, unprepared, and implausible assertion of unconditioned freedom with which the novel ends. As the hero abandons the Communist Party he wonders, "Could politics ever be an expression of love?" This question, more portentous than profound, cannot easily be reconciled to a character who has been presented mainly as a passive victim of his experience. Nor is one easily persuaded by the hero's discovery that "my world has become one of infinite possibilities," his refusal to be the "invisible man" whose body is manipulated by various social groups. Though the unqualified assertion of self-liberation was a favorite strategy among American literary people in the fifties, it is also vapid and insubstantial. It violates the reality of social life, the interplay between external conditions and personal will, quite as much as the determinism of the thirties. The unfortunate fact remains that to define one's individuality is to stumble upon social barriers which stand in the way, all too much in the way, of "infinite possibilities." Freedom can be fought for, but it cannot always be willed or asserted into existence. And it seems hardly an accident that even as Ellison's hero asserts the "infinite possibilities" he makes no attempt to specify them.

5

Throughout the fifties Richard Wright was struggling to find his place in a world he knew to be changing but could not grasp with the assurance he had felt in his earlier years. He had resigned with some bitterness from the Communist Party, though he tried to preserve an independent radical outlook, tinged occasionally with black nationalism. He became absorbed in the politics and literature of the rising African nations, but when visiting them he felt hurt at how great was the distance between an American Negro and an African. He found life in America intolerable, and he spent his last fourteen years in Paris, somewhat friendly with the intellectual group around Jean-Paul Sartre but finally a loner, a man who stood by the pride of his rootlessness. And he kept writing, steadily experimenting, partly, it may be, in response to the younger men who had taken his place in the limelight and partly because he was truly a dedicated writer.

These last years were difficult for Wright, since he neither made a true home in Paris nor kept in imaginative touch with the changing life of the United States. In the early fifties he published a very poor novel, *The Outsider*, full of existentialist jargon applied to, but not really absorbed in, the Negro theme. He was a writer in limbo, and his better fiction, such as the novelette "The Man Who Lived Underground," is a projection of that state.

In the late fifties Wright published another novel, *The Long Dream*, which is set in Mississippi and displays a considerable recovery of his powers. This book has been criticized for presenting Negro life in the South through "old-fashioned" images of violence, but one ought to hesitate before denying the relevance of such images or joining in the criticism of their use. For Wright was perhaps justified in not paying attention to the changes that have occurred in the South these past few decades. When Negro liberals write that despite the prevalence of bias there has been an improvement in the life of their people, such statements are reasonable and necessary. But what have these to do with the way Negroes feel, with the power of the memories they must surely retain? About this we know very little and would be well advised not to nourish preconceptions, for their feelings may be much closer to Wright's rasping outbursts than to the more modulated tones of some younger Negro novelists. *Wright remembered*, and what he remembered other Negroes must also have remembered. And in that way he kept faith with the experience of the boy who had fought his way out of the depths, to speak for those who remained there.

His most interesting fiction after *Native Son* is to be found in a posthumous collection of stories, *Eight Men*, written during the last twenty-five years of his life. Though they fail to yield any clear line of chronological development, these stories give evidence of Wright's literary restlessness, his often clumsy efforts to break out of the naturalism which was his first and, I think, necessary mode of expression. The unevenness of his writing is highly disturbing: one finds it hard to understand how the same man, from paragraph to paragraph, can be so brilliant and inept. Time after time the narrative texture is broken by a passage of sociological or psychological jargon; perhaps the later Wright tried too hard, read too much, failed to remain sufficiently loyal to the limits of his talent.

Some of the stories, such as "Big Black Good Man," are enlivened by Wright's sardonic humor, the humor of a man who has known and released the full measure of his despair but finds that neither knowledge nor release matters in a world of despair. In "The Man Who Lived Underground" Wright shows a sense of narrative rhythm which is superior to anything in his full-length novels and evidence of the seriousness with which he kept working.

The main literary problem that troubled Wright in recent years was that of rendering his naturalism a more terse and supple instrument. I think he went astray whenever he abandoned naturalism entirely: there are a few embarrassingly bad experiments with stories employing self-consciously Freudian symbolism. Wright needed the accumulated material of circumstance which naturalistic detail provided his fiction; it was as essential to his ultimate effect of shock and bruise as dialogue to Hemingway's ultimate effect of irony and loss. But Wright was correct in thinking that the problem of detail is the most vexing technical problem the naturalist writer must face, since the accumulation that makes for depth and solidity can also create a pall of tedium. In "The Man Who Lived Underground" Wright came close to solving this problem, for here the naturalistic detail is put at the service of a radical projective image—a Negro trapped in a sewer—and despite some flaws, the story is satisfying for both its tense surface and its elasticity of suggestion.

Richard Wright died at fifty-two, full of hopes and projects. Like many of us, he had somewhat lost his intellectual way, but he kept struggling toward the perfection of his craft and toward a comprehension of the strange world that in his last years was coming into birth. In the most fundamental sense, however, he had done his work: he had told his contemporaries a truth so bitter they paid him the tribute of trying to forget it.

6

Looking back to the early essays and fiction of James Baldwin, one wishes to see a little farther than they at first invite: to see past their brilliance of gesture, by which older writers could be dismissed, and past their aura of gravity, by which a generation of intellectuals could be enticed. What strikes one most of all is the sheer pathos of these early writings, the way they reveal the desire of a greatly talented young man to escape the scars—and why should he not have wished to escape them?—which he had found upon the faces of his elders and knew to be gratuitous and unlovely.

Chekhov once said that what the aristocratic Russian writers assumed as their birthright, the writers who came from the lower orders had to pay for with their youth. James Baldwin did not want to pay with his youth, as Richard Wright had paid so dearly. He wanted to move, as Wright had not been able to, beyond the burden or bravado of his stigma; he wanted to enter the world of freedom, grace, and self-creation. One would need a heart of stone, or be a brutal moralist, to feel anything but sympathy for this desire. But we do not make our circumstances; we can, at best, try to remake them. And all the recent writing of Baldwin indicates that the wishes of his youth could not be realized, not in *this* country. The sentiments of humanity which had made him rebel against Richard Wright have now driven him back to a position close to Wright's rebellion.

Baldwin's *Another Country* (1962) is a "protest novel" quite as much as *Native Son*, and anyone vindictive enough to make the effort could score against it the points Baldwin scored against Wright. No longer is Baldwin's prose so elegant or suave as it was once; in this book it is harsh, clumsy, heavy-breathing with the pant of suppressed bitterness. In about half of *Another Country*—the best half, I would judge—the material is handled in a manner somewhat reminiscent of Wright's naturalism: a piling on of the details of victimization, as the jazz musician Rufus Scott, a sophisticated distant cousin of Bigger Thomas, goes steadily down the path of self-destruction, worn out in the effort to survive in the white man's jungle and consumed by a rage too extreme to articulate, yet too amorphous to act upon. The narrative voice is a voice of anger, rasping and thrusting, not at all "literary" in the somewhat lacquered way the earlier Baldwin was able to achieve. And what that voice says, no longer held back by the proprieties of literature, is that the nightmare of the history we have made allows us no immediate escape. Even if all the visible tokens of injustice were erased, the Negroes would retain their hatred and the whites their fear and guilt. Forgiveness cannot be speedily willed, if willed at all, and before it can even be imagined there will have to be a fuller discharge of those violent feelings that have so long been suppressed. It is not a pretty thought, but neither is it a mere "unrewarding rage"; and it has the sad advantage of being true, first as Baldwin embodies it in the disintegration of Rufus, which he portrays with a ferocity quite new in his fiction, and then as he embodies it in the hard-driving ambition of Rufus's sister Ida, who means to climb up to success even if she has to bloody a good many people, whites preferably, in order to do it.

Another Country has within it another novel: a nagging portrayal of that entanglement of personal relationships—sterile, involuted, grindingly rehearsed, pursued with quasi-religious fervor, and cut off from any dense context of social life—which has come to be a standard element in contemporary fiction. The author of *this* novel is caught up with the problem of communication, the emptiness that seeps through the lives of many cultivated persons and in response to which he can only reiterate the saving value of true and lonely love. These portions of *Another Country* tend to be abstract, without the veined milieu, the filled-out world, a novel needs: as if Baldwin, once he moves away from the Negro theme, finds it quite as hard to lay hold of contemporary experience as do most other novelists. The two pulls upon his attention are difficult to reconcile, and Baldwin's future as a novelist is decidedly uncertain.

During the last few years James Baldwin has emerged as a national figure, the leading intellectual spokesman for the Negroes, whose recent essays, as in *The Fire Next Time*, reach heights of passionate exhortation unmatched in modern American writing. Whatever his ultimate success or failure as a novelist, Baldwin has already secured his place as one of the two or three greatest essayists this country has ever produced. He has brought a new luster to the essay as an art form, a form with possibilities for discursive reflection and concrete drama which make it a serious competitor to the novel, until recently almost unchallenged as the dominant literary genre in our time. Apparently drawing upon Baldwin's youthful experience as the son of a Negro preacher, the style of these essays is a remarkable instance of the way in which a grave and sustained eloquence—the rhythm of oratory, but that rhythm held firm and hard—can be employed in an age deeply suspicious of rhetorical prowess. And in pieces like the reports on Harlem and the account of his first visit south, Baldwin realizes far better than in his novels the goal he had set himself of presenting Negro life through an "unspoken recognition of shared experience." Yet it should also be recognized that these essays gain at least some of their resonance from the tone of unrelenting protest in which they are written, from the very anger, even the violence Baldwin had begun by rejecting.

Like Richard Wright before him, Baldwin has discovered that to assert his humanity he must release his rage. But if rage makes for power it does not always encourage clarity, and the truth is that Baldwin's most recent essays are shot through with intellectual confusions, torn by the conflict between his assumption that the Negro must find an honorable place in the life of American society and his apocalyptic sense, mostly fear but just a little hope, that this society is beyond salvation, doomed with the sickness of the West. And again like Wright, he gives way on occasion to the lure of black nationalism. Its formal creed does not interest him, for he knows it to be shoddy, but he is impressed by its capacity to evoke norms of discipline from followers at a time when the Negro community is threatened by a serious inner demoralization.

In his role as spokesman, Baldwin must pronounce with certainty and struggle with militancy; he has at the moment no other choice; yet whatever may have been the objective inadequacy of his polemic against Wright, there can be no question but that the refusal he then made of the role of protest reflected faithfully some of his deepest needs and desires. But we do not make our circumstances; we can, at best, try to remake them; and the arena of choice and action always proves to be a little narrower than we had supposed. One generation passes its dilemmas to the next, black boys on to native sons.

"It is in revolt that man goes beyond himself to discover other people, and from this point of view, human solidarity is a philosophical certainty." The words come from Camus: they might easily have been echoed by Richard Wright: and today one can imagine them being repeated, with a kind of rueful passion, by James Baldwin. No more important words could be spoken in our century, but it would be foolish, and impudent, not to recognize that for the men who must live by them the cost is heavy.

October 1969

Because "Black Boys and Native Sons" has a history of its own and, in some small way, has even entered recent literary history, I have resisted the temptation to modify a phrase here or there and have printed it as it first appeared in the Autumn 1963 *Dissent*. Shortly after its publication, Ralph Ellison, the distinguished novelist, wrote a long and sharp attack on this essay, which appeared in the *New Leader*, December 9, 1963. I then replied briefly in the same journal and Ellison rebutted in the February 3, 1964, issue. There the debate rests. It has never been published in its entirety.

It was Ellison's view that I had locked Negro writers into a narrow and asphyxiating box called "the protest novel" and thereby deprived them of those copious possibilities for creative work that white writers enjoyed. "Unrelieved suffering," charged Ellison, "is the only 'real' Negro experience" I credited. And, he continued, "To deny in the interest of revolutionary posture that such possibilities of human richness exist for others, even in Mississippi, is not only to deny us our humanity but to betray the critic's commitment to social reality." How accurate or valid Ellison's attack is I leave for others to judge.

What is, however, especially interesting is that in the years that have passed since we disagreed in print, the cultural atmosphere has changed radically. When our essays first appeared, the literary world was overwhelmingly sympathetic to Ellison: here, it would seem, was a Negro novelist defending creative autonomy against a radical critic who was said to insist that militancy and protest were the necessary, perhaps desirable, condition of the Negro writer. Every piety of the moment was prepared for enlistment.

By the late 1960s, however, all has changed. White literary intellectuals are often eager to declare an uncritical—which is, I think, a patronizing—acceptance of Black Power ideology. They jostle one another to join the New Left parade, if not as participants, then as its Adult Corps; and at least some of them, I imagine, would dismiss both Ellison and me as old-fashioned, irrelevant, and—most shattering of blows!—"mere liberal" advocates of "integration."

Among Negro writers the fashion has also changed. Instead of working, in the style of the early Baldwin, to break away from the naturalistic crudeness and racial anger of a Richard Wright and toward the novel of personal sensibility, most young black writers are now caught up in a separatist and nationalist ideology. They must surely be hostile, if also uneasily respectful, toward Ellison, and impatient, if not contemptuous, toward the distinctions of attitude that Ellison and I, each in his own way, were trying to make. Ellison's claim that he shares quite as much as any white writer in the heritage of Western culture, these black writers would dismiss as a token of inauthenticity, if not worse. My view that the Negro writer, while trapped in a historical situation that makes protest all but unavoidable, nevertheless seeks to find ways of mediating between the gross historical pressures that surround him and his needs and feelings as an individual would strike them as a token of equivocation, if not worse.

So it may be that, with the passage of only five or so years, the dispute between Ellison and me has taken on a new significance. The differences between us remain, and they matter; but both of us believe in the unity of experience and culture, both of us believe that the works of literature produced by black men should be judged by the same aesthetic criteria as those produced by white men, both of us resist attempts by whoever it may be to reinstitute a new version of social and cultural segregation, and both of us believe in the value of liberal discourse. That, in any case, is the way it now seems to me; how it seems to Ellison I cannot really say, though I should very much like to know.

January 1990

In the quarter-century since this essay was written there appeared the "black aesthetic" movement, claiming that works of literature by black writers adhere to a distinctive aesthetic and, in the more extreme versions of this outlook, that such works can be fully accessible only to black critics and readers. The adherents of this view would probably have dismissed me as an intruder and Ralph Ellison, because he insisted upon his ties to Western culture, as someone denying his heritage.

Now it is surely true that there has been a distinctive black experience. But this hardly warrants the claim for a distinctive black aesthetic—anymore than the fact of a distinctive Jewish experience would warrant a claim for a distinctive Jewish aesthetic. I think that an informed and sensitive critic should be able to write helpfully about literatures other than his own—as witness, the Russian critic Viktor Shklovsky on Laurence Sterne and the American critic Joseph Frank on Dostoevsky. I would be interested in anything Ralph Ellison wrote about white writers, and correspondingly there are surely some white critics who can write well about black writers.

By 1990 the "black aesthetic" movement seems to have faded, while the relationship between blacks and whites, though considerably changed and in some respects improved since 1963, continues to be difficult. The problems raised in both "Black Boys and Native Sons" and Ellison's attack upon it remain. I would now say that one of his main points has a certain validity: the charge that I underestimated the capacity of oppressed peoples like the American blacks to create a vital culture apart from social protest. But I also think that my original stress upon the inescapability of protest as a literary theme, both enabling and disabling black writers, is valid; it has been borne out by the writings of many younger black novelists. All of which brings to mind the remark of F. R. Leavis that in literary discussion the desired response is some version of "Yes, but . . ."

The Idea of the Modern

In the past hundred years we have had a special kind of literature. We call it modern and distinguish it from the merely contemporary; for where the contemporary refers to time, the modern refers to sensibility and style, and where the contemporary is a term of neutral reference, the modern is a term of critical placement. Modernist literature seems now to be coming to an end, though we can by no means be certain and there are critics who would argue that, given the nature of our society, it cannot come to an end.

The kind of literature called modern is almost always difficult: that is a sign of its modernity. To the established guardians of culture, the modern writer seems willfully inaccessible. He works with unfamiliar forms; he chooses subjects that disturb the audience and threaten its most cherished sentiments; he provokes traditionalist critics to such epithets as "unwholesome," "coterie," and "decadent."

The modern must be defined in terms of what it is not, the embodiment of a tacit polemic, an inclusive negative. Modern writers find that they begin to work at a moment when the culture is marked by a prevalent style of perception and feeling; and their modernity consists

From *Commentary* 44 (November 1967):5, as "The Culture of Modernism."

in a revolt against this prevalent style, an unyielding rage against the official order. But modernism does not establish a prevalent style of its own; or if it does, it denies itself, thereby ceasing to be modern. This presents it with a dilemma which in principle may be beyond solution but in practice leads to formal inventiveness and resourceful dialectic— *the dilemma that modernism must always struggle but never quite triumph, and then, after a time, must struggle in order not to triumph.* Modernism need never come to an end, or at least we do not really know, as yet, how it can or will reach its end. The history of previous literary periods is relevant but probably not decisive here, since modernism, despite the precursors one can find in the past, is, I think, a novelty in the development of Western culture. What we do know, however, is that modernism can fall upon days of exhaustion, when it appears to be marking time and waiting for new avenues of release.

At certain points in the development of a culture, usually points of dismay and restlessness, writers find themselves affronting their audience, and not from decision or whim but from some deep moral and psychological necessity. Such writers may not even be aware that they are challenging crucial assumptions of their day, yet their impact is revolutionary; and once this is recognized by sympathetic critics and a coterie audience, the avant-garde has begun to emerge as a self-conscious and combative group. Paul Goodman writes:

> . . . there are these works that are indignantly rejected, and called not genuine art, but insult, outrage, *blague, fumiste,* willfully incomprehensible. . . . And what is puzzling is not that they are isolated pieces, but some artists persistently produce such pieces and there are schools of such "not genuine" artists. What are they doing? In this case, the feeling of the audience is sound—it is always sound—there *is* insult, willful incomprehensibility, experiment; and yet the judgment of the audience is wrong—it is often wrong—for this is a genuine art.

Why does this clash arise? Because the modern writer can no longer accept the claims of the world. If he tries to acquiesce in the norms of the audience, he finds himself depressed and outraged. The usual morality seems counterfeit; taste, a genteel indulgence; tradition, a wearisome fetter. It becomes a condition of being a writer that he rebel, not merely and sometimes not at all against received opinions, but against the received ways of doing the writer's work.

A modernist culture soon learns to respect, even to cherish, signs of its division. It sees doubt as a form of health. It hunts for ethical norms through underground journeys, experiments with sensation, and a mocking suspension of accredited values. Upon the passport of the

Wisdom of the Ages, it stamps in bold red letters: *Not Transferable*. It cultivates, in Thomas Mann's phrase, "a sympathy for the abyss." It strips man of his systems of belief and his ideal claims, and then proposes the one uniquely modern style of salvation: a salvation by, of, and for the self. In modernist culture, the object perceived seems always on the verge of being swallowed up by the perceiving agent, and the act of perception in danger of being exalted to the substance of reality. *I see, therefore I am.*

Subjectivity becomes the typical condition of the modernist outlook. In its early stages, when it does not trouble to disguise its filial dependence on the Romantic poets, modernism declares itself as an inflation of the self, a transcendental and orgiastic aggrandizement of matter and event in behalf of personal vitality. In the middle stages, the self begins to recoil from externality and now devotes itself, almost as if it were the world's body, to a minute examination of its own inner dynamics: freedom, compulsion, caprice. In the late stages, there occurs an emptying-out of the self, a revulsion from the wearisomeness of both individuality and psychological gain. (Three writers as exemplars of these stages: Walt Whitman, Virginia Woolf, Samuel Beckett.) Modernism thereby keeps approaching—sometimes even penetrating—the limits of solipsism, the view expressed by Gottfried Benn when he writes that "there is no outer reality, there is only human consciousness, constantly building, modifying, rebuilding new worlds out of its own creativity."

Behind this extreme subjectivity lurks an equally extreme sense of historical impasse, the assumption that something about the experience of our age is unique, a catastrophe perhaps without precedent. The German novelist Hermann Hesse speaks about "a whole generation caught . . . between two ages, two modes of life, with the consequence that it loses all power to understand itself and has no standards, no security, no simple acquiescence." Above all, no simple acquiescence.

Whether all of this is true matters not nearly so much as the fact that modernist writers, artists, and composers—Joyce, Kafka, Picasso, Schoenberg—have apparently worked on the tacit assumption that it is true. The modernist sensibility posits a blockage, if not an end, of history: an apocalyptic cul-de-sac in which both teleological ends and secular progress are called into question, perhaps become obsolete. Man is mired—take your choice—in the mass, in the machine, in the city, in a loss of faith, in the hopelessness of a life without anterior intention or terminal value. By this late date, these disasters seem in our imaginations to have merged into one.

"On or about December 1910 human character changed." Through this vivid hyperbole Virginia Woolf meant to suggest that there is a frightening discontinuity between the traditional past and the shaken present; that the line of history has been bent, perhaps broken. Modernist literature goes on the tacit assumption that human character has indeed changed, probably a few decades before the date given by Mrs. Woolf; or, as Stephen Spender remarks, the circumstances under which we live, forever transformed by nature, have been so radically altered that people feel human nature to have changed and thereby behave as though it has. Commenting on this notion, Spender makes a keen distinction between the "Voltairean I" of earlier writers and the "I" of the moderns:

> The "Voltairean I" of Shaw, Wells, and others acts upon events. The "modern I" of Rimbaud, Joyce, Proust, Eliot's *Prufrock* is acted upon by events. . . . The faith of the Voltairean egoists is that they will direct the powers of the surrounding world from evil into better courses through the exercise of the superior social or cultural intelligence of the creative genius, the writer-prophet. The faith of the moderns is that by allowing their sensibility to be acted upon by the modern experience as suffering, they will produce, partly as the result of unconscious processes, and partly through the exercise of critical consciousness, the idioms and forms of new art.

The consequences are extreme: a break-up of the traditional unity and continuity of Western culture, so that the decorums of its past no longer count for very much in determining its present, and a loosening of those ties which, in one or another way, had bound it to the institutions of society over the centuries. Not their enemies but art and literature themselves assault the *Gemütlichkeit* of autonomy, the classical balances and resolutions of the past. Culture now goes to war against itself, partly in order to salvage its purpose, and the result is that it can no longer present itself with a Goethean serenity and wholeness. At one extreme there is a violent disparagement of culture (the late Rimbaud) and at the other, a quasi-religion of culture (the late Joyce).

In much modernist literature one finds a bitter impatience with the whole apparatus of cognition and the limiting assumption of rationality. Mind comes to be seen as an enemy of vital human powers. Culture becomes disenchanted with itself, sick over its endless refinements. There is a hunger to break past the bourgeois proprieties and self-containment of culture, toward a form of absolute personal speech, a literature deprived of ceremony and stripped to revelation. In the work of Thomas Mann both what is rejected and what is desired are put forward with a high, ironic consciousness: the abandoned ceremony and the corrosive revelation.

2

But if a major impulse in modernist literature is a choking nausea before the idea of culture, there is another in which the writer takes upon himself the enormous ambition not to remake the world (by now seen as hopelessly recalcitrant and alien) but to reinvent the terms of reality. I have already quoted Benn's remark that "there is only human consciousness . . . rebuilding new worlds out of its own creativity." In a similar vein, the painter Klee once said that his wish was "not to reflect the visible, but to make visible." And Baudelaire: "The whole visible universe is but an array of images and signs to which the imagination gives a place and relative value. . . ." At first glance this sentence reads like something an English Romantic poet or even a good American transcendentalist might have said; but in the context of Baudelaire's experience as a poet it comes to seem the report of a desire to create or perhaps re-create the very grounds of being, through a permanent revolution of sensibility and style, by means of which art could raise itself to the level of white or (more likely) black magic. Rationalistic psychoanalysts might regard this ambition as a substitute gratification of the most desperate kind, a grandiose mask for inner weakness; but for the great figures of literary modernism it is the very essence of their task.

We approach here another dilemma of modernism, which may also in principle be beyond solution but in practice leads to great inventiveness—that, as the Marxist critic Georg Lukács has charged, *modernism despairs of human history, abandons the idea of a linear historical development, falls back upon notions of a universal* condition humaine *or a rhythm of eternal recurrence, yet within its own realm is committed to ceaseless change, turmoil, and re-creation.* The more history comes to be seen as static (in the Marxist idiom: a locomotive stalled in the inescapable present), the more art must take on relentless dynamism.

It is quite as if Hegel's "cunning of reason," so long a motor force of progress in history, were now expelled from its exalted place and locked into the exile of culture. E. H. Gombrich speaks of philosophies of historical progress as containing "a strong Aristotelian ingredient in so far as they look upon progress as an evolution of inherent potentialities which will follow a predictable course and must reach a predictable summit." Modernist versions of literature do assign to themselves "an evolution of inherent potentialities": there is always the hope for still another breakthrough, always the necessary and prepared-for dialectical leap into still another innovation, always an immanent if by no means gradual progress in the life of a form. But these do not follow "a predictable course" nor can they reach "a predictable summit"—since the very idea of "predictable" or the very goal of "summit" violates the modernist faith in surprise, its belief in an endless spiral of revolution in sensibility and style. And if history is indeed stalled in the sluggishness of the mass and the imperiousness of the machine, then culture must all the more serve as the agent of a life-enhancing turmoil. The figure chosen to embody and advance this turmoil, remarks Gombrich, is the Genius, an early individualistic precursor of the avant-garde creative hero. If there is then "a conflict between a genius and his public," declares Hegel in a sentence which thousands of critics, writers, and publicists will echo through the years, "it must be the public that is to blame . . . the only obligation the artist can have is to follow truth and his genius." Close to Romantic theory at this point, modernism soon ceases to believe in the availability of "truth" or the disclosures of "genius." The dynamism to which it then commits itself—and here it breaks sharply from the Romantics—becomes not merely an absolute without end but sometimes an absolute without discernible ends.

It is a dynamism of asking and of learning not to reply. The past was devoted to answers, the modern period confines itself to questions. And after a certain point, the essence of modernism reveals itself in the persuasion that the true question, the one alone worth asking, cannot and need not be answered; it need only be asked over and over again, forever in new ways. It is as if the very idea of a question were redefined: no longer an interrogation but now a mode of axiomatic description. We present ourselves by the questions we allow to torment us. "All of Dostoevsky's heroes question themselves as to the meaning of life," writes Albert Camus. "In this they are modern: they do not fear ridicule. What distinguishes modern sensibility from classical sensibility is that the latter thrives on moral problems and the former on metaphysical problems."

A modernist culture sees the human lot as inescapably problematic. Problems, to be sure, have been noticed at all times, but in a modernist culture the problematic as a style of inquiry becomes imperious: men learn to find comfort in their wounds. Nietzsche says: "Truth has never yet hung on the arm of an absolute." The problematic is adhered to, not merely because we live in a time of uncertainty when traditional beliefs and absolute standards, having long disintegrated, give way to the makeshifts of relativism—that is by now an old story. The problematic is adhered to because it comes to be considered good, proper, and even beautiful that men should live in discomfort. Again Nietzsche: "Objection, evasion, joyous distrust, and love of irony are signs of health; everything absolute belongs to pathology."

One consequence of this devotion to the problematic, not always a happy consequence, is that in modernist literature there is a turn from truth to sincerity, from the search for objective law to a desire for authentic response. The first involves an effort to apprehend the nature of the universe, and can lead to metaphysics, suicide, revolution, and God; the second involves an effort to discover our demons within, and makes no claim upon the world other than the right to publicize the aggressions of candor. Sincerity becomes the last-ditch defense for men without belief, and in its name absolutes can be toppled, morality dispersed, and intellectual systems dissolved. But a special kind of sincerity: where for the Romantics it was often taken to be a rapid motion into truth, breaking past the cumbersomeness of intellect, now for the modernists it becomes a virtue in itself, regardless of whether it can lead to truth or whether truth can be found. Sincerity of feeling and exact faithfulness of language—which often means a language of fragments, violence, and exasperation—become a ruling passion. In the terrible freedom it allows the modernist writer, sincerity shatters the hypocrisies of bourgeois order; in the lawlessness of its abandonment, it can become a force of darkness and brutality.

Disdainful of certainties, disengaged from the eternal or any of its surrogates, fixated upon the minute particulars of subjective experience, the modernist writer regards settled assumptions as a mask of death. Restlessness becomes the sign of sentience, anxiety the premise of responsibility, peace the flag of surrender. Nowhere is this mode of sensibility expressed with greater energy than in an essay by the Russian novelist of the 1920s, Eugene Zamiatin. "On Literature, Revolution and Entropy" is a decisive manifesto of the modernist outlook:

> Revolution is everywhere and in all things: it is infinite, there is no final revolution, no end to the sequence of integers. Social revolution is only one in the infinite sequence of integers. The law of revolution is not a social law, it is immeasurably greater, it is a cosmic, universal law.

> Red, fiery, death-dealing is the law of revolution; but that death is the birth of a new life, of a new star. And cold, blue as ice, as the icy interplanetary infinities is the law of entropy. The flame turns from fiery red to an even, warm pink, no longer death-dealing but comfort-producing; the sun ages and becomes a planet suitable for highways, shops, beds, prostitutes, prisons: that is a law. And in order to make the planet young again, we must set it afire, we must thrust it off the smooth highway of evolution: that is a law.

> Explosions are not comfortable things. That is why the exploders, the heretics, are quite rightly annihilated by fire, by axes, and by words. Heretics are harmful to everybody today, to every evolution, to the difficult, slow,

useful, so very useful, constructive process of coral reef building; imprudently and foolishly they leap into today from tomorrow. They are romantics. It was right and proper that in 1797 Babeuf had his head cut off; he had leaped into 1797, skipping one hundred fifty years. It is equally right and proper that heretical literature that is damaging to dogma, should also have its head cut off: such literature is harmful.

But harmful literature is more useful than useful literature: because it is antientropic, militates against calcification, sclerosis, encrustedness, moss, peace. It is utopian and ridiculous. Like Babeuf, in 1797, it is right one hundred and fifty years later. . . .

The old, slow, soporific descriptions are no more. The order of the day is laconicism—but every word must be supercharged, high voltage. Into one second must be compressed what formerly went into a sixty-second minute. Syntax becomes elliptical, volatile; complicated pyramids of periods are dismantled and broken down into the single stones of independent clauses. In swift movement the canonical, the habitual eludes the eye: hence the unusual, often strange symbolism and choice of words. The image is sharp, synthetic, it contains only the one basic trait which one has time to seize upon from a moving automobile. . . . A new form is not intelligible to all; for many it is difficult. Maybe. The habitual, the banal is of course simpler, pleasanter, more comfortable. Euclid's world is very simple and Einstein's world is very difficult; nevertheless it is now impossible to return to Euclid's. No revolution, no heresy is comfortable and easy. Because it is a leap, it is a rupture, of the smooth evolutionary curve, and a rupture is a wound, a pain. But it is a necessary wound: most people suffer from hereditary sleeping sickness, and those who are sick with this ailment must not be allowed to sleep, or they will go to their last sleep, the sleep of death.

To follow the thrust of Zamiatin's language is to notice that he provides tacit answers to major questions: To what extent can modernism be seen as a phenomenon arising autonomously, as the outcome of an inner logic, from the development of earlier, especially Romantic literature? And to what extent can it be located in terms of a need or drive toward formal experimentation?

Zamiatin suggests, rightly I think, that the seeds of modernism lie deep within the Romantic movement, but that revolutionary events in the outer world must occur before those seeds will sprout. The Romantic poets break loose from classical-Christian tradition, but they do not surrender the wish to discover in the universe a network of spiritual meaning which, however precariously, can enclose their selves. They anticipate the preoccupation with psychic inwardness, by means of which the self is transformed into a cosmic center and mover, as this will later become characteristic of certain modernist writers; but they still seek to relate this preoccupation to transcendent values, if not sources. For them the universe is still alert, still the active transmitter of spiritual signs. Northrop Frye remarks that "the sense of identity with a larger power of creative energy meets us everywhere in Romantic culture," and Marius Bewley writes still more pointedly that "the desire to merge oneself with what is greater than oneself—to take one's place in a divine or transcendental continuum of some kind—is indeed the central fact for most of the Romantics." Now it seems to me impossible that anyone should use language of this sort in describing the work of Joyce or Kafka, Baudelaire or Brecht. For the modernist writer the universe is a speechless presence, neither hospitable nor hostile; and after a time he does not agonize, as did nineteenth-century writers like Hardy, over the dispossession of man in the cosmic scheme. He takes that dispossession for granted, and turns his anxieties toward the dispossession of meaning from inner life. Whatever spiritual signs he hears come from within his own imaginative resources and are accepted pragmatically as psychic events. Romanticism is, among other things, an effort to maintain a transcendent perspective precisely as or because the transcendent objects of worship are being withdrawn; modernism follows upon the breakdown of this effort. To be sure, a writer like Yeats tries in his famous "system" to take his place in a transcendental continuum of some kind, but the attempt remains eccentric, willful, and by no means organically related to his poetry. In his great lyrics Yeats shares in the premises and aftereffects of modernism.

To the second question posed in Zamiatin's manifesto he gives an answer that again seems correct. Formal experiment may frequently be a corollary or consequence of modernism, but its presence is not a sufficient condition for seeing a writer or a work as modernist. This suggests that the crucial factor in the style of a literary movement or period is some sort of inspiriting "vision," a new way of looking upon the world and man's existence; and while such a "vision" will no doubt entail radical innovations in form and language, there is by no means a direct or invariable correlation. In certain works of literature, such as Thomas Mann's stories, formal experiment is virtually absent, yet the spirit of modernism is extremely powerful, as a force of both liberation and mischief. Correspondingly, there are works in which the outer mannerisms and traits of the modern are faithfully echoed or mimicked but the animating spirit has disappeared—is that not a useful shorthand for describing some of the "advanced" writing of the years after World War II? A writer imbued with the spirit of modernism will be predisposed toward experiment, if only because he needs to make visibly dramatic his break from tradition; yet it is an error—and an error indulging the modernist desire to exempt itself from historical inquiry—to suppose that where one sees the tokens of experiment there must also be the vision of the modern.

3

At this point my essay will have to suffer from what Henry James called "a misplaced middle." For I should now speak at some length about the intellectual sources of modernism, especially those major figures in the nineteenth century who initiated the "psychology of exposure"—that corrosion of appearance in order to break into reality— by means of which old certainties were dislodged and new ones discouraged. I should speak about J. G. Frazer and his archetypal rhythms of human life, above all, the rhythm of the birth and rebirth of the gods, and the role of myth as a means for reestablishing ties with primal experience in a world deadened by "functional rationality." I should speak about Marx, who unmasked—they were all unmaskers, the great figures of the nineteenth century—Marx, who unmasked the fetishism of a commodity-producing society which "resolves personal worth into exchange value" and in which the worker's deed "becomes an alien power . . . forcing him to develop some specialized dexterity at the cost of a world of productive impulses." I should speak about Freud, who focuses upon the irremediable conflict between nature and culture, from which there followed the notorious "discontents of civilization," the damage done the life of instinct. I should speak, above all, about Nietzsche, a writer whose gnomic and paradoxical style embodies the very qualities of modernist sensibility. But there is no space, and perhaps by now these are familiar matters. Let me, therefore, turn to a few topics concerning the formal or distinctly literary attributes of modernism.

The historical development of a literature cannot, for any length of time, be hermetic. It has a history of its own, in which there occurs a constant transformation of forms, styles, and kinds of sensibility. At a given moment writers command an awareness of those past achievements which seem likely to serve them as models to draw upon or deviate from. That, surely, is part of what we mean by tradition: the shared assumptions among contemporaries as to which formal and thematic possibilities of the literary past are "available" to them. Tradition makes itself felt; tradition is steadily remade. Whether they know it or not, writers establish their personal lines of vision through a tacit acceptance or rejection of preceding masters. In that sense, then, one can speak of a literary history that is autonomous, with its own continuities of decorum, its own dialectic of strife, its own interweaving of traditions.

Yet over an extended period this literary history must be affected by the larger history of which it is part, the history of mankind. About

certain moments in the life of a literature—say, that of eighteenth-
century English poetry—one can say that the power of internal tradition
is so enormous that the historian's stress must properly be on the inner
logic of form and style: Dryden through Pope, a line of masters whose
innovations become tradition. About the eighteenth-century novel, by
contrast, it would be impossible to speak intelligently without noticing
the flanking pressures exerted by the society of the time.

In considering a major revolution in cultural style, it is very hard to
know precisely how much causal weight to assign to accumulating modulations in the career of a literary form and how much to the thrust of
external historical events as these bear down upon the writers employing
that form. I would venture the hypothesis—not a very novel one—that
while the internal evolution of a form can significantly affect its nature
and dress, there must also occur some overwhelming historical changes
for a major new cultural style to flourish. Retrospectively we can see
that the shift from Neoclassicism to Romanticism was anticipated by
certain late-eighteenth-century poets, but I doubt that a serious literary
historian would suppose that transition to be no more than the outcome
of an immanent development of literary forms.

In any case, it is when the inner dynamics of a literature and the
large-scale pressures of history cross that there follows a new cultural
style, in this case modernism. The results are to be observed in at least
three areas: modernist writers discard the formal procedures and decorums of their Romantic predecessors; they begin to feel that the very
idea of literary tradition is a nuisance, even a tyranny, to be shaken off;
and they question the Romantic faith in transcendence through individual ego or through its pantheistic merger with a God-filled universe,
as well as the belief held by some Romantics that the poet should actively
engage himself in behalf of a militant liberalism. And soon the new
writing is signaled by a dramatic change in the social place and posture
of the advanced writers.

Forming a permanent if unacknowledged and disorganized opposition, the modernist writers and artists constitute a special caste within
or at the margin of society, an avant-garde marked by aggressive de-
fensiveness, extreme self-consciousness, prophetic inclination, and the
stigmata of alienation. "Bohemia," writes Gustave Flaubert, "is my fatherland," bohemia both as an enclave within a hostile society and as a
place from which to launch guerrilla raids upon the bourgeois establishment, frequently upsetting but never quite threatening its security.
The avant-garde abandons the useful fiction of "the common reader";
it demands instead the devotions of a cult. The avant-garde abandons
the usual pieties toward received aesthetic assumptions; "no good po-

etry," writes Ezra Pound in what is almost a caricature of modernist dogma, "is ever written in a manner twenty years old." The avant-garde scorns notions of "responsibility" toward the audience; it raises the question of whether the audience exists—or should exist. The avant-garde proclaims its faith in the self-sufficiency, the necessary irresponsibility, and thereby the ultimate salvation of art.

As a device of exposition I write in the present tense; but it seems greatly open to doubt whether by now, a few decades after World War II, there can still be located in the West a coherent and self-assured avant-garde. Perhaps in some of the arts, but probably not in literature. (Only in the Communist countries is there beyond question a combative and beleaguered avant-garde, for there, as a rule, the state persecutes or seriously inconveniences modern writers and artists, forcing them into a self-protective withdrawal, sometimes an "internal emigration.")

In the war between modernist culture and bourgeois society, something has happened which no spokesman for the avant-garde quite anticipated. Bracing enmity has given way to wet embraces, the middle class has discovered that the fiercest attacks upon its values can be transposed into pleasing entertainments, and the avant-garde writer or artist must confront the one challenge for which he has not been prepared: the challenge of success. Contemporary society is endlessly assimilative, even if it vulgarizes what it has learned, sometimes foolishly, to praise. The avant-garde is thereby no longer allowed the integrity of opposition or the coziness of sectarianism; it must either watch helplessly its gradual absorption into the surrounding culture or try to preserve its distinctiveness by continually raising the ante of sensation and shock—itself a course leading, perversely, to a growing popularity with the bourgeois audience. There remains, to be sure, the option for the serious writer that he go his own way regardless of fashion or cult.

Still another reason should be noticed for the recent breakup of the avant-garde. It is very difficult to sustain the stance of a small, principled minority in opposition to established values and modes of composition, for it requires the most remarkable kind of heroism, the heroism of patience. Among the modernist heroes in literature, only James Joyce, I would say, was able to live by that heroism to the very end. For other writers, more activist in temper or less firm in character, there was always the temptation to veer off into one or another prophetic stance, often connected with an authoritarian politics; and apart from its intrinsic disasters, this temptation meant that the writer would sooner or later abandon the confinements of the avant-garde and try, however delusionally, to reenter the arena of history. Yeats and Pound, on the right; Brecht, Malraux, and Gide, on the left: all succumbed to the glamour of ideology or party machines, invariably with painful results. Fruitful as avant-garde intransigence was for literature itself and inescapable as it may have been historically, it did not encourage a rich play of humane feelings. On the contrary, in every important literature except the Yiddish, the modernist impulse was accompanied by a revulsion against traditional modes of nineteenth-century liberalism and by a repugnance for the commonplace materials of ordinary life (again with the exception of Joyce). Imperiousness of mind and impatience with flesh were attitudes shared by Yeats and Malraux, Eliot and Brecht. Disgust with urban trivialities and contempt for *l'homme moyen sensual* streak through a great many modernist poems and novels.

That modern literature apprehended with unrivaled power the decline of traditional liberalism is not to be questioned. But especially in Europe, where democracy has never been a common premise of political life to the extent that it has in the United States, this awareness of the liberal collapse frequently led to authoritarian adventures: the haughty authoritarianism of Yeats, with his fantasies of the proud peasant, and the haughty authoritarianism of Malraux, with his visions of the heroic revolutionist. It is by no means possible to pass an unambiguous judgment on the literary consequences, since major writing can be released through the prodding of distasteful doctrine. But once such writers turned to daily politics and tried to connect themselves with insurgent movements, they were well on the way to abandoning the avant-garde position. In retrospect, even those of us committed—however uneasily—to the need for "commitment" will probably have to grant that it would have been much better for both literature and society if the modernist writers had kept themselves aloof from politics. Only Joyce, the greatest and most humane among them, remained pure in his devotion to a kind of literary monasticism; and Beckett, the most gifted and faithful of his disciples, has remained pure in that devotion to this very day.

For brief moments, the avant-garde mobilized into groups and communities: Paris, Moscow, Rome, during the early twenties. Most of the time, however, these groups broke up almost as fast as they were formed, victims of polemic and schism, vanity and temperament. The metaphor lodged in the term avant-garde can be seriously misleading if it suggests a structured phalanx or implies that the modernist writers, while momentarily cut off from society at large, were trying to lead great numbers of people into a new aesthetic or social dispensation. Not at all. When we refer to the avant-garde we are really speaking of isolated figures who share the burdens of intransigence, estrangement, and dislocation;

writers and artists who are ready to pay the costs of their choices. And as both cause and effect of their marginal status, they tend to see the *activity* of literature as self-contained, as the true and exalted life in contrast to the life of contingency and mobs. (When now and again they make a foray into political life, it is mainly out of a feeling that society has destroyed the possibility of a high culture and that to achieve such a culture it is necessary to cleanse or bleed society.) Joyce demanded a reader who will devote a lifetime to his work; Wallace Stevens composed poems about the composition of poetry. These are not mere excesses or indulgences; they are, at one extreme, programs for creating quasi-religious orders of the aesthetic, and at the other extreme, ceremonies for the renewal of life—and then, in the boldest leap of all, for the improvisation of a realm of being which will simply dispense with the gross category of "life."

4

The crucial instance of the effort to make the literary work self-sufficient is Symbolist poetry. Symbolism moves toward an art severed from common experience—a goal perhaps unrealizable but valuable as a "limit" for striving and motion. The Symbolists, as Marcel Raymond remarks, "share with the Romantics a reliance upon the epiphany, the moment of intense revelation; but they differ sharply about its status in nature and its relation to art. Wordsworth's spiritual life is founded on moments of intense illumination, and his poetry describes these and relates them to the whole experience of an ordered lifetime." For the Symbolist poet—archetypal figure in modernism—there is no question, however, of *describing* such an experience; for him the moment of illumination occurs only through the action of the poem, only through its thrust and realization as a particular form. Nor is there any question of relating it to the experience of a lifetime, for it is unique, transient, available only in the matter—perhaps more important, only in the moment—of the poem. Not transmission but revelation is the poet's task. And thereby the Symbolist poet tends to become a Magus, calling his own reality into existence and making poetry into what Baudelaire called "suggestive magic."

Mallarmé, the Symbolist master, and Defoe, the specialist in verisimilitude, stand at opposite poles of the aesthetic spectrum, yet both share a desire to undo the premises and strategies of traditional art. Neither can bear the idea of the literary work as something distinct from, yet dependent upon, the external world. Defoe wishes to collapse his representation into the world, so that the reader will feel that the story of Moll Flanders *is* reality; Mallarmé wishes to purge his revelation of the contingent, so that the moment of union with his poem becomes the world. Both are adversaries of Aristotle.

Stretched to its theoretic limit, Symbolism proposes to disintegrate the traditional duality between the world and its representation. It finds intolerable the connection between art and flaws of experience; it finds intolerable the commonly accepted distance between subject and act of representation; it wishes to destroy the very program of representation, either as objective mimesis or subjective outcry. It is equally distant from realism and expressionism, faithfulness to the dimensions of the external and faithfulness to the distortions of the eye. Symbolism proposes to make the poem not merely autonomous but hermetic, and not merely hermetic but sometimes impenetrable. Freed from the dross of matter and time, poetry may then regain the aura, the power, of the mysterious. Passionately monistic, Symbolism wishes finally that *the symbol cease being symbolic* and become, instead, an act or object without "reference," sufficient in its own right. Like other extreme versions of modernism, Symbolism rebels against the preposition "about" in statements that begin "art is about. . . ." It yearns to shake off the burden of meaning, the alloy of idea, the tyranny and coarseness of opinion; it hopes for sacrament without faith. To fill up the spaces of boredom it would metamorphose itself into the purity of magic.

In his brilliant book *From Baudelaire to Surrealism* Marcel Raymond writes about the Symbolist vision:

> This state of happiness, "perfect and complete," ineffable as such, is also ephemeral. When it is gone, man is left with an even more acute awareness of his limitations and of the precariousness of his life. He will not rest until he has again forced the gates of Paradise, or if this is impossible, until he has profited from these revelations. . . . The soul engages in a kind of game, but aspires to an activity that is more elevated than any game—aspires to re-create its lost happiness by means of the *word*. And the function of these images, whose elements are borrowed from the dust of sensation, is not to describe external objects, but to prolong or revive the original ecstasy. . . . Words are no longer signs; they participate in the objects, in the psychic realities they evoke.

If, then, the poet becomes for a moment a kind of God, he finds that after six days of creation he cannot rest on the seventh: his work has crumbled into "the dust of sensation" and he must start again, shuffling the materials of omnipotence and helplessness, and forced to recognize once again the world he had hoped to transcend—perhaps had even managed to transcend—through the power of the word.

Here the crucial instance is Rimbaud, breaking with the conception of language as a way of conveying rational thought, returning to its most primitive quality as a means for arousing emotions, incantatory, magical, and automatistic. Rimbaud praised Baudelaire in terms of his own artistic ends: "To inspect the invisible and hear things unheard [is] entirely different from gathering up the spirit of dead things. . . ."

Heroic as this effort may have been, the Symbolist aesthetic is a severe reduction of the scope and traditional claims of literature, and beyond sustaining in practice for more than a few moments. It cannot survive in daylight or the flatness of time. Soon the world contaminates the poem and the poem slides back into the world.

As European civilization enters the period of social disorder and revolt that runs parallel to the life of literary modernism, there is really no possibility for maintaining a hermetic aestheticism. What follows from the impact of social crisis upon modernist literature is quite without that order and purity toward which Symbolism aspires—what follows is bewildering, plural, noisy. Into the vacuum of belief left by the collapse of Romanticism there race a number of competing world views, and these are beyond reconciling or even aligning. That is one reason it is quite impossible to sum up the central assumptions of modernism, as one perhaps can for Romanticism, by listing a sequence of beliefs and visions. Literary modernism is a battle of internal conflicts more than a coherent set of theories or values. It provides a vocabulary through which the most powerful imaginations of the time can act out a drama of doubt. Yet this commitment to the problematic is terribly hard to maintain, it requires nerves of iron; and even as the great figures of modernism sense that for them everything depends on keeping a firm grip on the idea of the problematic, many of them cannot resist completely the invading powers of ideology and system. It is at this point that there appears the famous, or but recently famous, problem of belief.

5

At a time when a number of competing world views impinge upon literature, radically in conflict with one another, there arise severe difficulties in trying to relate the tacit assumptions of the writer to those of the reader. The bonds of premise between the two are broken, and must now become a matter of inquiry, effort, conflict. We read the late novels of D. H. Lawrence or the cantos of Ezra Pound aware that these are works of enormously gifted writers yet steadily troubled by the outpouring of authoritarian and fascist ideas. We read Bertolt Brecht's "To Posterity," in which he offers an incomparable evocation of the travail of Europe in the period between wars yet also weaves in a justification of the Stalin dictatorship. How are we to respond to all this? The question is crucial in our experience of modernist literature. We may say that the doctrine is irrelevant, as many critics do say, and that would lead us to the impossible position that the commanding thought of a poem need not be seriously considered in forming a judgment of its value. Or we may say that the doctrine, being obnoxious, destroys our pleasure in the poem, as some critics do say, and that would lead us to the impossible position that our judgment of the work is determined by our opinion concerning the author's ideology. There is, I think, no satisfactory solution in the abstract, and we must learn to accept the fact that modernist literature is often—not in this way alone!—"unacceptable." It forces us into distance and dissociation; it denies us wholeness of response; it alienates us from its own powers of statement even when we feel that it is imaginatively transcending the malaise of alienation.

The problem of belief appears with great force in the early phases of modernism and is then intensely discussed for some decades later, most notably in the criticism of T. S. Eliot and I. A. Richards. Later there arises a new impulse to dissolve the whole problem and to see literature as beyond opinion or belief, a performance or game of surfaces. Weariness sets in, and not merely with this or the other belief, but with the whole idea of belief. Through the fervor of its straining, modernism begins to exhaust itself.

Yet no matter what impasse it encounters, modernism is ceaselessly active within its own realm, endlessly inventive in destruction and improvisation. Its main enemy is, in one sense, the culture of the past, even though it bears within itself a marvelously full evidence of that culture. Literature now thrives on assaulting the traditional rules, modes, and limits of literature; the idea of aesthetic order is abandoned or radically modified.

To condemn modernist literature for a failure to conform to traditional criteria of unity, order, and coherence is, however, quite to miss the point, since, to begin with, it either rejects these criteria or proposes radical new ways of embodying them. When Yvor Winters attacks the "fallacy of imitative form" (e.g., literary works dealing with the chaos of modern life themselves take on the appearance and sometimes the substance of chaos), he is in effect attacking modernist writing as such, since much of it cannot dispense with this "fallacy." In its assumption that the sense of the real has been lost in conventional realism, modernist writing yields to an imperative of distortion. A "law" could be advanced here: *Modernist literature replaces the traditional criteria of aesthetic unity with the new criterion of aesthetic expressiveness, or perhaps more accurately, it downgrades the value of aesthetic unity in behalf of a jagged and fragmented expressiveness.*

The expectation of formal unity implies an intellectual and emotional, indeed a philosophic composure; it assumes that the artist stands above his material, controlling it and aware of an impending resolution; it assumes that the artist has answers to his questions or that answers can be had. But for the modern writer none of these assumptions holds, or at least none of them can simply be taken for granted. He presents dilemmas; he cannot and soon does not wish to resolve them; he offers his *struggle* with them as the substance of his testimony; and whatever unity his work possesses, often not very much, comes from the emotional rhythm, the thrust toward completion, of that struggle. After Kafka it becomes hard to believe not only in answers but even in endings.

In modernist literature nature ceases to be a central subject and symbol. Beginning partly with Wordsworth, nature is transformed from an organic setting into a summoned or remembered *idea*, sometimes into a mere term of contrast. We remark upon the river Liffey, or the Mississippi woods, or the big two-hearted river, or the Abruzzi countryside, but mostly as tokens of deprivation and sometimes as willed signs of nostalgia. These places are elsewhere, not our home; nature ceases to be natural.

Perversity—which is to say: surprise, excitement, shock, terror, affront—becomes a dominant motif. I borrow from G. S. Fraser a charming contrast between a traditional poet:

> Love to Love calleth,
> Love unto Love replieth—
> From the ends of the earth, drawn by invisible bands,
> Over the dawning and darkening lands
> Love cometh to Love.
> To the heart by courage and might
> Escaped from hell,
> From the torment of raging fire,
> From the signs of the drowning main,
> From the shipwreck of fear and pain
> From the terror of night.

and a modern poet:

> I hate and love.
> You ask, how can that be?
> I do not know, but know it tortures me.

The traditional poet is Robert Bridges, who lived as far back as the early twentieth century; the modern poet is Catullus.

The modernist writer strives for sensations, in the serious sense of the term; his epigones, in the frivolous sense. The modernist writer thinks of subject matter not as something to be rehearsed or recaptured but, rather, to be conquered and enlarged. He has little use for wisdom; or if he does, he conceives of it not as something to be dug out of the mines of tradition, but to be won for himself through self-penetration, sometimes self-disintegration. He becomes entranced with depths—whichever you choose: the depths of the city, or the self, or the underground, or the slums, or the extremes of sensation induced by sex, liquor, drugs; or the shadowed half-people crawling through the interstices of society: *Lumpen*, criminals, hipsters; or the drives at the base of consciousness. Only Joyce, among the modernist writers, negotiates the full journey into and through these depths while yet emerging into the streets of the city and its ongoing commonplace life: which is, I think, one reason he is the greatest of the modernist writers, as also perhaps the one who points a way beyond the liberation of modernism.

The traditional values of decorum, in both the general ethical sense and the strictly literary sense, are overturned. Everything must now be explored to its outer and inner limits; but more, there may be no limits. And then, since learning seems often to be followed by ignorance, there come the demi-prophets who scorn the very thought of limits; so that they drive themselves into the corner of wishing always to go beyond while refusing to acknowledge a line beyond which to go.

A plenitude of sophistication narrowing into decadence—this means that primitivism will soon follow. The search for meaning through extreme states of being reveals a yearning for the primal: for surely man cannot have been bored even at the moment of his creation! I have already spoken of the disgust with culture, the rage against cultivation, that is so important a part of modernism: the turning in upon one's primary characteristics, the hatred of one's gifts, the contempt for intelligence, which cuts through the work of men as different as Rimbaud, Dostoevsky, and Hart Crane. For the modern sensibility is always haunted by the problem of succession: what, after such turnings and distensions of sensibility, can come next? One of the seemingly hopeful possibilities is a primitivism bringing a vision of health, blood consciousness, a relief from enervating rationality. A central text is D. H. Lawrence's story, "The Woman Who Rode Away"—that realistic fable, at once so impressive and ridiculous—in which a white woman seeks out an Indian tribe to surrender her "quivering nervous consciousness" to its stricken sun god and thereby "accomplish the sacrifice and achieve the power." But within the ambience of modernism there is another, more ambiguous and perhaps sinister kind of primitivism: the kind that draws us with the prospect not of health but of decay, the primitive as atavistic, an abandonment of civilization and thereby, perhaps, of its discontents. The central fiction expressing this theme is Conrad's *Heart of Darkness*, in which Marlow the narrator and *raisonneur* does not hesitate to acknowledge that the pull of the jungle for Kurtz and also, more ambiguously, for himself is not that it seems to him (I am quoting Lionel Trilling) "noble or charming or even free but . . . base and sordid—and for *that* reason compelling: he himself feels quite overtly its dreadful attraction." In this version of primitivism, which is perhaps inseparable from the ennui of decadence, the overwhelming desire is to shake off the burdens of social restraint, the disabling and wearisome moralities of civilized inhibition. The Greek poet C. P. Cavafy has a brilliant poem in which the inhabitants of a modern city wait for a threatened invasion by barbarians and then, at the end, suffer the exasperating disappointment that the barbarians may, after all, not come. The people of the city will have to continue living as in the past, and who can bear it?

> Why should this uneasiness begin all of a sudden,
> And confusion? How serious people's faces have become.
> Why are all the streets and squares emptying out so quickly,
> And everyone turning home again so full of thought?
> > Because night has fallen and the Barbarians have not come,
> > And some people have arrived from the frontier,
> > They said there are no Barbarians any more.
> And now what will become of us without Barbarians?
> > These people were some sort of solution.

6

If technical experiment and thematic surprise characterize modernist poetry, there are equivalent changes in the novel: a whole new sense of character, structure, and the role of its protagonist or hero. The problematic nature of experience tends to replace the experience of human nature as the dominant subject of the modern novel. Abandoning the assumption of a life that is knowable, the novelist turns to the problem of establishing a bridgehead into knowability as the precondition for portraying any life at all. His task becomes not so much depiction as the hypothesizing of a set of as-if terms, by means of which he may lend a temporary validation to his material.

Characters in a novel can no longer be assumed, as in the past, to be fixed and synthetic entities, with a set of traits available through

notations of conduct and reports of psychic condition. The famous remark of D. H. Lawrence—that he had lost interest in creating the "old
stable ego of character," but wished to posit "another ego, according to
whose action the individual is unrecognizable, and passes through, as it
were, allotropic states which it needs a deeper sense than any we've
been used to exercise, to discover are states of the same radically unchanged element"—this is not merely a statement of what he would try
to do in *The Rainbow* and *Women in Love*; it also reflects a general
intention among modern novelists. Character, for modernists like Joyce,
Virginia Woolf, and William Faulkner, is regarded not as a coherent,
definable, and well-structured entity, but as a psychic battlefield, or an
insoluble puzzle, or the occasion for a flow of perceptions and sensations.
This tendency to dissolve character into a stream of atomized experiences, a kind of novelistic *pointillisme*, gives way, perhaps through extreme reaction, to an opposite tendency (yet one equally opposed to
traditional concepts of novelistic character) in which character is severed
from psychology and confined to a sequence of severely objective
events.

Similar radical changes occur in the modernist treatment of plot.
The traditional eighteenth- or nineteenth-century novel depends upon
a plot which reveals a major destiny, such as Henchard's in Hardy's *The
Mayor of Casterbridge*. A plot consists here of an action purposefully
carved out of time, that is, provided with a beginning, sequence of
development, and climax, so that it will create the impression of completeness. Often this impression comes from the sense that the action
of a novel, as given shape by the plot, has exhausted its possibilities of
significant extension; the problems and premises with which it began
have reached an appropriate terminus. Thus, we can say that in the
traditional kind of novel it is usually the plot which carries or releases
a body of meanings: these can be profound or trivial, comic or tragic.
The Mayor of Casterbridge contains a plot which fulfills the potential for
self-destruction in the character of Henchard—but it is important to
notice that in this kind of novel we would have no knowledge of that
potential except as we can observe its effects through an action. Plot
here comes to seem inseparable from meaning, and meaning to inhere
in plot.

When a writer works out a plot, he tacitly assumes that there is a
rational structure in human conduct, that this structure can be ascer-
tained, and that in doing so he is enabled to provide his work with a
sequence of order. But in modernist literature these assumptions come
into question. In a work written on the premise that there is no secure
meaning in the portrayed action, or that while the action can hold our

attention and rouse our feelings, we cannot be certain, indeed must remain uncertain, as to the possibilities of meaning—in such a characteristically modern work what matters is not so much the plot but a series of *situations*, some of which can be portrayed statically, through tableaux, set pieces, depth psychology, and others dynamically, through linked episodes, stream of consciousness, and so on. Kafka's fiction, Joyce's novels, some of Faulkner's—these all contain situations rather than plot.

Still more striking are the enormous changes which the modern novel brings about in its treatment of the fictional hero.

The modern world has lost the belief in a collective destiny. Hence, the hero finds it hard to be certain that he possesses—or that anyone can possess—the kind of powers that might transform human existence. Men no longer feel themselves bound in a sacred or even, often enough, in a temporal kinship. Hence, the hero finds it hard to believe in himself as a chosen figure acting in behalf of a divine commandment or national will.

Since at least the beginnings of the bourgeois era, a central problem for reflective men has been the relation of the individual to the collectivity. In modern fiction this problem often appears as a clash between a figure of consciousness who embodies the potential of the human and a society moving in an impersonal rhythm that is hostile or, what is perhaps worse, indifferent to that potential. One likes to feel, by way of contrast, that in certain kinds of ancient or traditional heroes there was a union of value and power, the sense of the good and the capacity to act it out. But in modern literature, value and power are radically dissociated. In Ernest Hemingway's novels the price of honor is often a refusal of the world. In André Malraux's novels the necessity for action is crossed by a conviction of its absurdity. Between the apprehension and the deed falls a shadow of uncertainty.

D. H. Lawrence, not only a great novelist but himself a major hero of modern literature, embodies this duality. At one point he says: "Insofar as I am I, and only I am I, and I am only I, insofar as I am inevitably and eternally alone, it is my last blessedness to know it, and to accept it, and to live with this as the core of my self-knowledge." It is the self-knowledge of the Lawrentian hero, strong in pride, sick in strength. But there is another D. H. Lawrence: "What ails me is the absolute frustration of my primeval societal instinct. . . . I think societal instinct much deeper than sex instinct—and societal repression much more devastating. . . . I am weary even of my individuality, and simply nauseated by other people's." It is the yearning of the Lawrentian hero, eager for disciples, driven to repel those who approach him. This is a conflict which, in our time, cannot be resolved. The Lawrentian hero remains a man divided between the absolutism of his individuality and the frustration of his societal instinct.

Let me push ahead a bit farther, and list several traits of "the modern hero," though not in the delusion that any fictional character fulfills all or even most of them:

The modern hero is a man who believes in the necessity of action; he wishes, in the words of Malraux, to put "a scar on the map." Yet the moral impulsions that lead him to believe in action, also render him unfit for action. He becomes dubious about the value of inflicting scars and is not sure he can even locate the map.

He knows that traditionally the hero is required to act out the part of bravery, but he discovers that his predicament requires courage. Bravery signifies a mode of action, courage a mode of being. And since he finds it difficult to reconcile the needs of action with those of being, he must learn that to summon courage he will have to abandon bravery. His sense of the burden he must carry brings him close to the situation described by William James: "Heroism is always on a precipitous edge, and only keeps alive by running. Every moment is an escape."

He knows that the hero can act with full power only if he commands, for his followers and himself, an implicit belief in the meaningfulness of the human scheme. But the more he commits himself to the gestures of heroism, the more he is persuaded of the absurdity of existence. Gods do not speak to him, prophets do not buoy him.

The classical hero moved in a world charged with a sense of purpose. In the early bourgeois era, the belief in purpose gave way to a belief in progress. This the hero managed to survive, if only because he often saw through the joke of progress. But now his problem is to live in a world that has moved beyond the idea of progress; and that is hard.

The modern hero often begins with the expectation of changing the world. But after a time his central question becomes: Can I change myself?

If the modern hero decides the world is beyond changing, he may try, as in the novels of Hemingway, to create a little world of his own in which an unhappy few live by a self-willed code that makes possible—they tell themselves—struggle, renewal, and honorable defeat.

Still, the modern hero often continues to believe in the quest, and sometimes in the grail too; only he is no longer persuaded that quest is necessarily undertaken through public action and he is unsure as to where the grail can be found. If he happens to be an American named Jay Gatsby, he may even look for it on the shores of Long Island. There is reason to believe that this is a mistake.

The modern hero moves from the heroic deed to the heroism of consciousness, a heroism often available only in defeat. He comes as a conqueror and stays as a pilgrim. And in consciousness he seeks those moral ends which the hero is traditionally said to have found through the deed. He learns, in the words of Kyo Gisors in Malraux's *Man's Fate*, that "a man resembles his suffering."

The modern hero discovers that he cannot be a hero. Yet only through his readiness to face the consequences of this discovery can he salvage a portion of the heroic.

7

In its multiplicity and brilliant confusion, its commitment to an aesthetic of endless renewal—in its improvisation of "the tradition of the new," a paradox envisaging the limit of *limitlessness*—modernism is endlessly open to conflicting portraiture and analysis. For just as some of its greatest works strain toward a form freed from beginning or end, so modernism strains toward a life without fixity or conclusion. If, nevertheless, there is in literary modernism a dominant preoccupation which the writer must either subdue or by which he will surely be destroyed, that is the specter of nihilism.

A term not only wide-ranging in reference but heavily charged with historical emotion, nihilism signifies at least some of the following:

A specific doctrine, positivist in stress, of an all-embracing rebellion against traditional authority, which appeared in mid-nineteenth-century Russia;

A consciously affirmed and accepted loss of belief in transcendent imperatives and secular values as guides to moral conduct, together with a feeling that there is no meaning resident—or, at least, further resident—in human existence;

A loss of those tacit impulsions toward an active and striving existence which we do not even know to be at work in our consciousness until we have become aware of their decline.

In Western literature nihilism is first and most powerfully foreshadowed by Dostoevsky: there is nothing to believe in but the senses and the senses soon exhaust themselves. God is impossible but all is impossible without him. Dostoevsky is maliciously witty, maliciously inventive in his perception of the faces of nihilism. He sees it, first, as a social disorder without boundary or shame: Pyotr Verhovensky in an orgy of undoing, mocking the very idea of purpose, transforming the ethic of modernist experiment into an appeal for collective suicide, seizing upon the most exalted words in order to hollow them out through burlesque. "If there's no God, how can I be a captain then," asks an old army officer in *The Possessed,* and in the derision that follows one fancies that Dostoevsky joins, in half-contempt, half-enchantment. Nihilism appears in moral guise through the figures of Kirillov and Ivan Karamazov, the first a man of purity and the second a man of seriousness; that both are good men saves them not at all, for the demon of emptiness, says Dostoevsky, lodges most comfortably in the hearts of the disinterested. And in Stavrogin, that "subtle serpent" stricken with metaphysical despair and haunted by "the demon of irony," nihilism achieves an ultimate of representation: nothingness in flesh, flesh that would be nothing. "We are all nihilists," says Dostoevsky in the very course of his struggle to make himself into something else. His great achievement is to sense, as Nietzsche will state, the intrinsic connection between nihilism as doctrine and nihilism as experience of loss. Just as Jane Austen saw how trivial lapses in conduct can lead to moral disaster, so Dostoevsky insisted that casual concessions to boredom can drive men straight into the void.

Flaubert, though not concerned with the problem abstractly, writes: "Life is so horrible that one can only bear it by avoiding it. And that can be done by living in the world of Art." The idea of Art as a sanctuary from the emptying out of life is intrinsic to modernism: it is an idea strong in Nietzsche, for whom the death of God is neither novelty nor scandal but simply a given. The resulting disvaluation of values and the sense of bleakness which follows, Nietzsche calls nihilism. He sees it as connected with the assertion that God exists, which robs the world of ultimate significance, and with the assertion that God does not exist, which robs everything of significance.

Nihilism, then, comes to imply a loss of connection with the sources of life, so that both in experience and in literature it is always related to, while analytically distinguishable from, the blight of boredom.

Recognizing all this, Dostoevsky tries to frighten the atheist both within himself and within his contemporaries by saying that once God is denied, everything—everything terrible—has become possible. Nietzsche gives the opposite answer, declaring that from the moment man believes in neither God nor immortality, "he becomes responsible for everything alive, for everything that, born of suffering, is condemned to suffer from life." And thus for Nietzsche, as later for the existentialists, a confrontation with the nihilist void becomes the major premise of human recovery.

With remarkable powers of invention and variation, this theme makes its way through all of modernist literature. In Kafka's work negation and faith stand forever balanced on the tip of a question mark; there are no answers, there are no endings, and whether justice can be found at the trial, or truth in the castle, we never know for certain. The angel with whom Kafka wrestles heroically and without letup is the angel of nothingness. Proust constructs a social world marvelously thick and rich in texture, yet a shadow too, which a mere wind blows away; and the only hope we have that some meaning may be salvaged is through the power of art, that thin cloak between men and the beyond which nevertheless carries "the true last judgment." This very power of art is seen by Mann as a demon of nihilism trailing both himself and his surrogate figures from novel to novel, as a portent of disease in *Death in Venice* and as a creator-destroyer in *Doctor Faustus* who disintegrates everything through parody. Brecht leers at the familiar strumpet of city nihilism, vomits with disgust when she approaches too closely, and then kidnaps her for a marriage with the authoritarian idea: the result endears him to the contemporary world. But it is Joyce who engages in the most profound modern exploration of nihilism, for he sees it everywhere, in the newspaper office and the church, on the street and in bed, through the exalted and the routine. Exposing his characters to every version of nausea and self-disgust, bringing Stephen Dedalus to his outcry of *"Nothung"* in the brothel, Joyce emerges, as William Troy remarks, with "an energetic and still uncorrupted affirmation of life that is implicit in every movement of his writing." As for those who follow these masters, they seem to have relaxed in the death-struggle with the shapeless demon and some, among the more fashionable of the moment, even strike a pleasant truce with him.

Nihilism lies at the center of all that we mean by modernist literature, both as subject and symptom, a demon overcome and a demon victorious. For the terror which haunts the modern mind is that of meaningless and eternal death. The death of the gods would not trouble us if we, in discovering that they have died, did not have to die alongside them. Heroically the modern sensibility struggles with its passion for eternal renewal, even as it keeps searching for ways to secure its own end.

But no, it will not die, neither heroically nor quietly, in struggle or triumph. It will live on, beyond age, through vulgar reincarnation and parodic mimesis. The lean youth has grown heavy; chokes with the approval of the world he had dismissed; cannot find the pure air of neglect. Not the hostility of those who came before but the patronage of those who come later—that is the torment of modernism.

How, come to think of it, do great cultural movements reach their end? It is a problem our literary historians have not sufficiently examined, perhaps because they find beginnings more glamorous, and a problem that is now especially difficult because there has never been, I think, a cultural period in Western history quite like the one we call modern. But signs of a denouement begin to appear. A lonely gifted survivor, Beckett, remains to remind us of the glories modernism once brought. Meanwhile, the decor of yesterday is appropriated and slicked up; the noise of revolt, magnified in a frolic of emptiness; and what little remains of modernism, denied so much as the dignity of opposition.

Modernism will not come to an end; its war chants will be repeated through the decades. For what seems to await it is a more painful and certainly less dignified conclusion than that of earlier cultural movements: what awaits it is publicity and sensation, the kind of savage parody which may indeed be the only fate worse than death.

Dreiser: The Springs of Desire

Do I exaggerate in saying that Theodore Dreiser has dropped out of the awareness of cultivated Americans? If so, it is but a slight exaggeration. Few young writers now model themselves on his career, and not many readers think of him as one of those literary figures whose word can transform their experience. Dreiser has suffered the fate that often besets writers caught up in cultural dispute: their work comes to seem inseparable from what has been said about it.

Mention Dreiser to a bright student of literature, mention him to a literate older person, and only seldom will the response be a turning of memory to novels that have brought pleasure and illumination. Far more likely is a series of fixed associations: to a brooding, bearlike figure who dragged himself out of nineteenth-century poverty and provincialism, and in *Sister Carrie* composed a pioneering novel of sexual candor; or to a vague notion that the author of *The Financier* and *The Titan* turned out quantities of ill-tuned and turgid social documentation; or to a prepared judgment against a writer taken to be sluggish in thought and language, sluggishly accumulating data of destruction and failure, but

Afterword to *An American Tragedy* (New York: New American Library, 1964).

deaf to the refinements of consciousness, dull to the play of sensibility, and drab, utterly and hopelessly drab in the quality of his mind.

The decline of Dreiser's reputation has not been an isolated event. It has occurred in the context, and surely as a consequence, of the counterrevolution in American culture during the forties and fifties. For readers educated in these years, Dreiser became a symbol of everything a superior intelligence was supposed to avoid. For the New Critics, to whom the very possibility of a social novel seemed disagreeable; for literary students trained in the fine but narrow school of Jamesian sensibility; for liberals easing into a modest gentility and inclined to replace a belief in social commitment with a search for personal distinction; for intellectuals delighted with the values of ambiguity, irony, complexity and impatient with the pieties of radicalism—for all such persons Dreiser became an object of disdain. He stood for an earlier age of scientism, materialism, agnosticism: all of which were now seen as hostile to the claims of moral freedom and responsibility. He represented the boorishness of the Populist mentality, as it declined into anti-Semitism or veered toward a peculiarly thoughtless brand of Communism. He could not think: he could only fumble with the names of ideas. He could not write: he could only pile up words. He cared not for art as such, but only for the novel as a vehicle of social and "philosophical" ideas. He was uneducated, insensitive—the novelist as mastodon.

But now, when Dreiser's prejudices have begun to be forgotten and all that remains—all that need remain—are his three or four major novels, it is time for reconsideration. Dreiser's role in assaulting the taboos of gentility can no longer excite us as once it did his admirers. As for his faults, no great critical insight is required to identify them, since they glare out of every chapter, especially his solemnities as a cosmic voice and his habit of crushing the English language beneath a leaden embrace. Yet these faults are interwoven with large creative powers, and it can be argued that for the powers to be released there had first to be the triggering presence of the faults.

As a philosopher Dreiser can often be tiresome; yet his very lust for metaphysics, his stubborn insistence upon learning "what it's all about," helped to deepen the emotional resources from which he drew as a novelist. For he came to feel that our existence demands from us an endless contemplativeness, even if—perhaps because—we cannot think through our problems or solve our mysteries. In the frustrations he encountered when trying to extract some conceptual order from the confusion and trouble of existence, he grew more closely involved, more *at one*, with the characters he created, also confused and troubled. Somewhat like Hardy, he learned to stand back a little from the human spectacle and watch the endlessly repeated sequence of desire, effort, and disintegration; and from this distance—perhaps the sole reward of his philosophical gropings—he gained a sense of the shared helplessness of men, he learned how brutal and irrelevant the impulse to moral judgment can become, and he arrived at his inclusive compassion for the whole of human life.

In the first task of the novelist, which is to create an imaginary social landscape both credible and significant, Dreiser ranks among the very few American giants we have had. Reading *An American Tragedy* once again, I have found myself shaken by its repeated onslaughts of narrative, its profound immersion in human suffering, its dredging up of those shapeless desires which lie, as if in fever, just below the plane of consciousness. How much more vibrant and tender this book is than the usual accounts of it in recent criticism might lead one to suppose!

Dreiser published *An American Tragedy* in 1925. By then he was fifty-four years old, an established writer with his own fixed and hard-won ways, who had written three first-rate novels: *Sister Carrie, Jennie Gerhardt* and *The Financier*. These books are crowded with exact observation—observation worked closely into the grain of narrative—about the customs and class structure of American society in the phase of early finance capitalism. No other novelist has absorbed into his work as much knowledge as Dreiser had about American institutions: the mechanisms of business, the rhythms of the factory, the hierarchy of a large hotel, the chicaneries of city politics, the status arrangements of rulers and ruled. For the most part, Dreiser's characters are defined through their relationships to these institutions. They writhe and suffer to win a foothold in the slippery social world or to break out of the limits of established social norms. They exhaust themselves to gain success, they destroy themselves in acts of impulsive deviance. But whatever their individual lot, they all act out the drama of determinism—which, in Dreiser's handling, is not at all the sort of listless fatality that hostile critics would make it seem, but is, rather, a struggle by human beings to discover the harsh limits of what is possible to them and thereby perhaps slightly to enlarge those limits. That mostly they fail is the tribute Dreiser pays to reality.

This controlling pattern in Dreiser's novels has been well described by Bernard Rosenberg, a sociologist with a literary eye:

> Emile Durkheim had suggested in Dreiser's day that when men speak of a force external to themselves which they are powerless to control, their subject is not God but social organization. This is also Dreiser's theme, and

to it he brings a sense of religious awe and wonder. "So well defined," he writes, "is the sphere of social activity, that he who departs from it is doomed." . . . Durkheim identified social facts, i.e., the existence of norms, precisely as Dreiser did: by asking what would happen if they were violated. . . . Norms develop outside the individual consciousness and exist prior to it; we internalize them and are fully aware of their grip only when our behavior is deviant.

In Dreiser's early novels most of the central characters are harried by a desire for personal affirmation, a desire they can neither articulate nor suppress. They suffer from a need that their lives assume the dignity of dramatic form, and they suffer terribly, not so much because they cannot satisfy this need, but because they do not really understand it. Money, worldly success, sensual gratification are the only ends they can name, but none of these slakes their restlessness. They grapple desperately for money, they lacerate themselves climbing to success, yet they remain sullen and bewildered, always hoping for some unexpected sign by which to release their bitter craving for a state of grace or, at least, illumination. Dreiser's characters are romantics who behave as if the Absolute can be found, immaculately preserved, at the very summit of material power. Great energies can flow from this ingrained American delusion, both for the discharge of ambition and the aggressiveness of ego. And Dreiser too, because he had in his own experience shared these values and struggled, with varying effectiveness, to burn them out of his system—Dreiser too lived out, with an intense dramatic complicity, the longings of his characters.

There is usually present in his early novels a governing intelligence more copious and flexible than that of the characters. This governing intelligence is seldom revealed through direct statement. So thoroughly does Dreiser recognize the bond of vulnerability between a Carrie and himself, he never moralizes. So patiently does he join a Cowperwood and a Jennie through the course of their experience, he never condescends. Taking upon himself the perils and sharing in the miseries of his characters, he leaves the privilege of admonition to others. Yet there is never really a question as to what his novels "mean," nor any serious possibility that the characters will usurp control. Through the logic of the narrative, the working-out of its implications, we are enabled to grasp with an almost visceral intensity how shallow are the standards by which the characters live.

In these early novels society figures largely as a jungle; and with good reason—the capitalism of the early twentieth century resembled a jungle. The characters may begin with a hard struggle for survival, but quickly leave it behind them. Having emerged from the blunt innocence of their beginnings, they are now cursed with a fractional awareness. In their half-articulate way, Dreiser's characters are beset by the same yearnings that trouble the characters of Fitzgerald and many other American novelists: a need for some principle of value by which to overcome the meanness, the littleness of their lives. To know, however, that the goals to which one has pledged one's years are trivial, yet not to know in what their triviality consists—this is a suffering which overcomes Dreiser's characters again and again. In all its dumb misery, it is the price, or reward, of their slow crawl to awareness. One sometimes feels that in the novels of Dreiser there is being reenacted the whole progression of the race toward the idea of the human.

The prose in these early novels is often as wretched as unsympathetic critics have said. Dreiser had little feeling for the sentence as a rhythmic unit (though he had a strong intuitive grasp of the underlying rhythm of narrative as a system of controlled variation and incremental development). He had a poor ear for the inflections of common speech, or even for the colloquial play of language. And worst of all, he had a weakness, all too common among semieducated writers, for "elegant" diction. Yet, despite the many patches of gray and the occasional patches of purple prose, Dreiser manages to accumulate large masses of narrative tension; he pulls one, muttering and bruised, into the arena of his imagination; and finally one has no recourse but surrender to its plenitude, its coarse and encompassing reality.

Not even Dreiser's philosophical excursions—bringing together nativist American prejudice with the very latest ideas of 1900—can break the thrust of these narratives. Dreiser's thought has by now been analyzed, mauled, and ridiculed: his distortion of social life through metaphors of brute nature, his reduction of human motive to the malignant pressure of "chemisms," his toying with notions about "the superman" in the Cowperwood novels. But it hardly matters. One brushes all this aside, resigned to the malice of a fate that could yoke together such intellectual debris with so much creative power.

2

Though surely Dreiser's major achievement, *An American Tragedy* is not the work of a master who, at the approach of old age, decides upon a revolutionary break from the premises and patterns of his earlier writing. For that order of boldness Dreiser lacked a sufficient self-awareness and sophistication; he was cut off from too much of the tradition of Western, even of American, culture to do anything but continue with his version of naturalism. He was the kind of writer who must keep circling about the point of his beginnings, forever stirred by memories of early struggles. All such a writer can hope for—a very great deal—is to mine his talent to its very depth; and that Dreiser did in *An American Tragedy*. Still, there are some changes from the earlier novels, most of them to the good.

The prose, while quite as clotted and ungainly as in the past, is now more consistent in tone and less adorned with "literary" paste gems. Solecisms, pretentiousness, and gaucherie remain, but the prose has at least the negative virtue of calling less attention to itself than in some of the earlier books. And there are long sections packed with the kind of specification that in Dreiser makes for a happy self-forgetfulness, justifying Philip Rahv's remark that one finds here "a prosiness so primary in texture that if taken in bulk it affects us as a kind of poetry of the commonplace and ill-favored."

For the first and last time Dreiser is wholly in the grip of his vision of things, so that he feels little need for the buttress of comment or the decoration of philosophizing. Dreiser is hardly the writer whose name would immediately occur to one in connection with T. S. Eliot's famous epigram that Henry James had a mind so fine it could not be violated by ideas; yet if there is one Dreiser novel about which a version of Eliot's remark might apply, it is *An American Tragedy*. What Eliot said has sometimes been taken, quite absurdly, as if it were a recommendation for writers to keep themselves innocent of ideas; actually he was trying to suggest the way a novelist can be affected by ideas yet must not allow his work to become a mere illustration for them. And of all Dreiser's novels *An American Tragedy* is the one that seems least cluttered with unassimilated formulas and preconceptions.

Where the earlier novels dealt with somewhat limited aspects of American life, *An American Tragedy*, enormous in scope and ambition, requires to be judged not merely as an extended study of the American lower middle class during the first years of the twentieth century but also as a kind of parable of our national experience. Strip the story to its bare outline, and see how much of American desire it involves: an obscure youth, amiable but weak, is lifted by chance from poverty to the possibility of pleasure and wealth. To gain these ends he must abandon the pieties of his fundamentalist upbringing and sacrifice the tender young woman who has given him a taste of pure affection. All of society conspires to persuade him that his goals are admirable, perhaps even sacred; he notices that others, no better endowed than himself, enjoy the privileges of money as if it were in the very nature of things that they should; but the entanglements of his past now form a barrier to realizing his desires, and to break through this barrier he must resort to criminal means. As it happens, he does not commit the murder he had planned, but he might as well have, for he is trapped in the machinery of social punishment and destroyed. "So well defined is the sphere of social activity that he who departs from it is doomed."

Now this story depends upon one of the most deeply grounded fables in our culture. Clyde Griffiths, the figure in Dreiser's novel who acts it out, is not in any traditional sense either heroic or tragic. He has almost no assertive will, he lacks any large compelling idea, he reveals no special gift for the endurance of pain. His puny self is little more than a clouded reflection of the puny world about him. His significance lies in the fact that he represents not our potential greatness but our collective smallness. He is that part of ourselves in which we take no pride, but know to be a settled resident. And we cannot dismiss him as a special case or an extreme instance, for his weakness is the shoddiness of mortality. By a twist of circumstance he could be a junior executive, a country-club favorite; he almost does manage to remake himself to the cut of his fantasy; and he finds in his rich and arrogant cousin Gilbert an exasperating double, the young man he too might be. Clyde embodies the nothingness at the heart of our scheme of things, the nothingness of our social aspirations. If Flaubert could say, *Emma Bovary, c'est moi*, Dreiser could echo, Clyde Griffiths, he is us.

We have, then, in Clyde a powerful representation of our unacknowledged values, powerful especially since Dreiser keeps a majestic balance between sympathy and criticism. He sees Clyde as a characteristic reflex of "the vast skepticism and apathy of life," as a characteristic instance of the futility of misplaced desire in a society that offers little ennobling sense of human potentiality. Yet he manages to make the consequences of Clyde's mediocrity, if not the mediocrity itself, seem tragic. For in this youth there is concentrated the tragedy of human waste: energies, talents, affections all unused—and at least in our time the idea of human waste comprises an essential meaning of tragedy. It is an idea to which Dreiser kept returning in both his fiction and his essays:

> When one was dead one was dead for all time. Hence the reason for the heartbreak over failure here and now; the awful tragedy of a love lost, a youth never properly enjoyed. Think of living and yet not living in so thrashing a world as this, the best of one's hours passing unused or not properly used. Think of seeing this tinkling phantasmagoria of pain and pleasure, beauty and all its sweets, go by, and yet being compelled to be a bystander, a mere onlooker, enhungered and never satisfied.

The first half of *An American Tragedy* is given to the difficult yet, for Dreiser's purpose, essential task of persuading us that Clyde Griffiths, through his very lack of distinction, represents a major possibility in American experience. Toward this end Dreiser must accumulate a large sum of substantiating detail. He must show Clyde growing up in a family both materially and spiritually impoverished. He must show Clyde reaching out for the small pleasures, the trifles of desire, and learning from his environment how splendid are these induced wants. He must show Clyde, step by step, making his initiation into the world of sanctioned America, first through shabby and then luxury hotels, where he picks up the signals of status and sin. He must show Clyde as the very image and prisoner of our culture.

Yet all the while Dreiser is also preparing to lift Clyde's story from this mere typicality, for he wishes to go beyond the mania for the average which is a bane of naturalism. Everything in this story is ordinary, not least of all the hope of prosperity through marriage—everything but the fact that Clyde begins to act out, or is treated as if he had acted out, the commonplace fantasy of violently disposing of a used-up lover. This is the sole important departure from verisimilitude in the entire novel, and Dreiser must surely have known that it was. In the particular case upon which he drew for *An American Tragedy*, the young man did kill his pregnant girl; but Dreiser must nevertheless have realized that in the vast majority of such crises the young man dreams of killing and ends by marrying. Dreiser understood, however, that in fiction the effort to represent common experience requires, at one or two crucial points, an effect of heightening, an intense exaggeration. Clyde's situation may be representative, but his conduct must be extreme. And that is one way of establishing the dramatic: to drive a representative situation to its limits of possibility.

3

In *An American Tragedy* Dreiser solved a problem which vexes all naturalistic novelists: how to relate harmoniously a large panorama of realism with a sharply contoured form. Dreiser is endlessly faithful to common experience. No one, not even critics who have harshly attacked the novel, would deny the credibility of Clyde and Roberta Alden, the girl he betrays; most of the attacks on Dreiser contain a mute testimony to his achievement, for in order to complain about his view of life they begin by taking for granted the "reality" of his imagined world. Yet for all its packed detail, the novel is economically structured—though one must understand that the criterion of economy for this kind of novel is radically different from that for a James or Conrad novel. In saying all this, I do not mean anything so improbable as the claim that whatever is in the book belongs because it is there; certain sections, especially those which prepare for Clyde's trial, could be cut to advantage; but the over-all architecture has a rough and impressive craftsmanship.

The action of the novel moves like a series of waves, each surging forward to a peak of tension and then receding into quietness, and each, after the first one, reenacting in a more complex and perilous fashion the material of its predecessor. Clyde in Kansas City, Clyde in Chicago, Clyde alone with Roberta in Lycurgus, Clyde on the edge of the wealthy set in Lycurgus—these divisions form the novel until the point where Roberta is drowned, and each of them acts as a reflector on the others, so that there is a mounting series of anticipations and variations upon the central theme. Clyde's early flirtation with a Kansas City shopgirl anticipates, in its chill manipulativeness, the later and more important relationship with Sondra Finchley, the rich girl who seems to him the very emblem of his fantasy. Clyde's childhood of city poverty is paralleled by the fine section presenting the poverty of Roberta's farm family. The seduction and desertion of Clyde's unmarried sister anticipates Clyde's seduction and desertion of Roberta. Clyde receives his preliminary education in the hotels where he works as bellboy, and each of these serves as a microcosm of the social world he will later break into. Clyde's first tenderness with Roberta occurs as they float in a rowboat; the near-murder, also in a rowboat. The grasping Clyde is reflected through a series of minor hotel figures and then through the antithetic but complementary figures of his cousin Gilbert and Sondra; while the part of him that retains some spontaneous feeling is doubled by Roberta.

Reinforcing this narrative rhythm is Dreiser's frequent shifting of his distance from the characters. At some points he establishes an almost intolerable closeness to Clyde, so that we feel locked into the circle of his moods, while at other points he pulls back to convey the sense that Clyde is but another helpless creature among thousands of helpless creatures struggling to get through their time. In the chapters dealing with Clyde upon his arrival at Lycurgus, Dreiser virtually *becomes* his character, narrowing to a hairline the distance between Clyde and himself, in order to make utterly vivid Clyde's pleasure at finding a girl as yielding as Roberta. By contrast, there are sections in which Dreiser looks upon his story from a great height, especially in the chapters after Roberta's death, where his intent is to suggest how impersonal is the working of legal doom and how insignificant Clyde's fate in the larger motions of society. Through these shifts in perspective Dreiser can show Clyde in his double aspect, both as solitary figure and symbolic agent, confused sufferer and victim of fate.

In the first half of the novel Dreiser prepares us to believe that Clyde *could* commit the crime: which is to say, he prepares us to believe that a part of ourselves could commit the crime. At each point in the boy's development there occurs a meeting between his ill-formed self and the surrounding society. The impoverishment of his family life and the instinctual deprivation of his youth leave him a prey to the values of the streets and the hotels; yet it is a fine stroke on Dreiser's part that only through these tawdry values does Clyde nevertheless become aware of his deprivation. Yearning gives way to cheap desire and false gratification, and these in turn create new and still more incoherent yearnings. It is a vicious circle and the result is not, in any precise sense, a self at all, but, rather, the beginning of that poisonous fabrication which in America we call a "personality." The hotels are his college, and there he learns to be "insanely eager for all the pleasures which he saw swirling around him." The sterile moralism of his parents cannot provide him with the strength to resist his environment or a principle by which to overcome it. The first tips he receives at the Green-Davidson hotel seem to him "fantastic, Aladdinish really." When he tries to be romantic with his first girl, the images that spring to his mind are of the ornate furnishings in the hotel. Later, as he contemplates killing Roberta, the idea comes from casual reading of a newspaper. It would be hard to find in American literature another instance where the passivity and rootlessness of urban man is so authoritatively presented. For in one sense Clyde does not exist, but is merely a creature of his milieu. And just as in Dreiser's work the problem of human freedom becomes critically acute through a representation of its decline, so the problem of awareness is brought to the forefront through a portrait of its negation.

Even sexuality, which often moves through Dreiser's world like a thick fog, is here diminished and suppressed through the power of social will. Clyde discovers sex as a drugstore clerk, "never weary of observing the beauty, the daring, the self-sufficiency and the sweetness" of the girls who come to his counter. "The wonder of them!" All of these fantasies he then focuses on the commonplace figure of Sondra Finchley: Héloïse as a spoiled American girl. Apart from an interval with Roberta, in which he yields to her maternal solicitude, Clyde's sexuality never breaks out as an irresistible force; it is always at the service of his fears, his petty snobbism, his calculations.

What seems still more notable is Dreiser's related intuition that even in a crippled psyche there remain, eager and available, the capacities we associate with a life of awareness. False values stunt and deform these capacities, but in some pitiful way also express and release them. Clyde and Roberta are from the beginning locked in mutual delusion, yet the chapters in which they discover each other are extremely tender as an unfolding of youthful experience. That this can happen at all suggests how indestructible the life force is; that Dreiser can portray it in his novels is a reward of his compassion. He reckons human waste to the end; but at the same time he hovers over these lost and lonely figures, granting them every ounce of true feeling he possibly can, insisting that they too—clerk and shopgirl—can know "a kind of ecstasy all out of proportion to the fragile, gimcrack scene" of the Starlight Amusement Park.

Dreiser surrenders himself to the emotional life of his figures, not by passing over their delusions or failures but by casting all his energy into evoking their experience. And how large, finally, is the sense of the human that smolders in this book! How unwavering the feeling for "the sensitive and seeking individual in his pitiful struggle with nature— with his enormous urges and his pathetic equipment!" Dreiser's passion for detail is a passion for his subject; his passion for his subject, a passion for the suffering of men. As we are touched by Clyde's early affection for Roberta, so later we participate vicariously in his desperation to be rid of her. We share this desire with some shame, but unless we count ourselves among the hopelessly pure, we share it.

Other naturalists, when they show a character being destroyed by overwhelming forces, frequently leave us with a sense of littleness and helplessness, as if the world were collapsed. Of Dreiser that is not, in my own experience, true. For he is always on the watch for a glimmer of transcendence, always concerned with the possibility of magnitude. Clyde is pitiable, his life and fate are pitiable; yet at the end we feel a somber exaltation, for we know that *An American Tragedy* does not seek to persuade us that human existence need be without value or beauty.

No, for Dreiser life is something very different. What makes him so absorbing a novelist, despite all of his grave faults, is that he remains endlessly open to experience. This is something one cannot say easily about most modern writers, including those more subtle and gifted than Dreiser. The trend of modern literature has often been toward a recoil from experience, a nausea before its flow, a denial of its worth. Dreiser, to be sure, is unable to make the finer discriminations among varieties of experience; and there is no reason to expect these from him. But he is marvelous in his devotion to whatever portion of life a man can have; marvelous in his conviction that something sacred resides even in the transience of our days; marvelous in his feeling that the grimmest of lives retain the possibility of "a mystic something of beauty that perennially transfigures the world." Transfigures—that is the key word, and not the catchphrases of mechanistic determinism he furnishes his detractors.

In a lecture on Spinoza, Santayana speaks of "one of the most important and radical of religious perceptions":

> It has perceived that though it is living, it is powerless to live; that though it may die, it is powerless to die; and that altogether, at every instant and in every particular, it is in the hands of some alien and inscrutable power.
>
> Of this felt power I profess to know nothing further. To me, as yet, it is merely the counterpart of my impotence. I should not venture, for instance, to call this power almighty, since I have no means of knowing how much it can do: but I should not hesitate, if I may coin a word, to call it *omnificent*: it is to me, by definition, the doer of everything that is done. I am not asserting the physical validity of this sense of agency or cause: I am merely feeling the force, the friendliness, the hostility, the unfathomableness of the world.

The power of which Santayana speaks is the power that flows, in all its feverish vibrations, through *An American Tragedy*.

Robert Frost:
A Momentary Stay

The best of Robert Frost, like the best of most writers, is small in quantity and narrow in scope. There are a few dozen of his lyrics which register a completely personal voice, as to both subject and tone, and which it would be impossible to mistake for the work of anyone else. These lyrics mark Frost as a severe and unaccommodating writer: they are ironic, troubled, and ambiguous in some of the ways modernist poems are. Despite a lamentable gift for public impersonations, Frost has remained faithful to what Yeats calls "the modern mind in search of its own meanings."

This Frost seldom ventures upon major experiments in meter or diction, nor is he as difficult in reference and complex in structure as are the great poets of the twentieth century. But as he contemplates the thinning landscape of his world and repeatedly finds himself before closures of outlook and experience, he ends, almost against his will, in the company of the moderns. With their temperament and technique he has little in common; he shares with them only a vision of disturbance. This Frost is quite unlike the twinkling Sage who in his last years became the darling of the nation.

From *The New Republic* 148 (March 23, 1963):12.

Frost has also written a small number of memorable poems in another vein: dramatic monologues and dialogues set in northern New England, vignettes of social exhaustion. While neither as original or distinguished as the best of his lyrics, they often live in one's mind, somewhat as a harshly monochromatic picture might.

In his long poems, most of them uniting satire and didacticism, Frost is at his worst. An early long poem, "New Hampshire," foreshadows the sly folksiness that would later endear him to native moralists and middlebrows. The verse is limp; the manner coy; the thought a display of provincialism. In the least happy sense of the word, the poem is mannered: Frost catering to his own idiosyncrasies and minor virtuosities. Even when he is clever ("Lately in converse with a New York alec / About the new school of pseudo-phallic"), it is with the cleverness of a man holding fast to his limitations.

Some years ago Malcolm Cowley compared Frost to Hawthorne, Emerson, and Thoreau and shrewdly noticed the narrowing of sensibility Frost had come, at his worst, to represent: "Height, breadth and strength: he falls short in all these qualities of the great New Englanders. And the other quality for which he is often praised, his utter faithfulness to the New England spirit, is not one of the virtues they knowingly cultivated. They realized that the New England spirit, when it stands alone, is inclined to be narrow and arithmetical. It has reached its finest growth only when cross-fertilized with alien philosophies." Much of Frost's later work—"A Masque of Reason," "Build Soil," "A Masque of Mercy," and the bulk of "Steeple Bush"—illustrates the hardening of his public pose. It is a pose of crustiness and sometimes even heartlessness. In such writing he is the dealer in packaged whimsies, the homespun Horace scrutinizing man, God, and liberalism. Because political fashions changed during the last decades of his life, the aged Frost found himself being applauded for precisely the sententia which had previously, and with good reason, been attacked. In these poems conversational tone slips into garrulousness, conservatism declines into smallness of mind, public declamation ends as vanity of pronouncement. If this were all we had of Frost, there would be no choice but to accept the attack launched upon him some years ago by Yvor Winters. Frost, wrote Winters, had a way of "mistaking whimsical impulse for moral choice," a kind of irrational romanticism that left him a "spiritual drifter." Reading such passages as the one in "A Masque of Reason" where God declares—

> I'm going to tell Job why I tortured him,
> And trust it won't be adding to the torture.
> I was just showing off to the Devil, Job

—one is tempted to go along with Winters.

Frost the national favorite is a somewhat different figure. He is a writer of lyrics that often achieve a flawed distinction: the language clear, the picture sharp, the rhythm ingratiating. "Birches," "Mending Wall," "The Death of the Hired Man," "The Pasture"—such poems are not contemptible but neither are they first-rate. They lack the urge to move past easy facilities. They depend too much on the unconsidered respect good Americans feel obliged to show for "nature." They yield too readily to the common notion of poetic genius as an unaccountable afflatus:

> At least don't use your mind too hard,
> But trust my instinct—I'm a bard.

And they create a music too winsome and soothing:

> This saying good-by on the edge of the dark
> And the cold to an orchard so young in the bark
> Reminds me of all that can happen to harm
> An orchard away at the end of the farm.

The appeal of such poems rests upon Frost's use of what might be called false pastoral. Traditionally, pastoral poetry employs an idyllic setting with apparently simple characters in order to advance complex ideas and sentiments. The pastoral seems to turn away in disgust from sophisticated life and to celebrate the virtues of bucolic retreat; but it does not propose that we rest with either simple characters or simple virtues. It accepts the convention of simplicity in order to demonstrate the complexity of the real; and only in an inferior kind of poetry is the pretense of the pastoral taken at face value.

In his lesser poems Frost comes very close to doing precisely that. He falls back upon the rural setting as a means of endorsing the common American notion that a special wisdom is to be found, and found only, among tight-lipped farmers, village whittlers, and small-town eccentrics. Overwhelmingly urban, our society displays an unflagging nostalgia for the assumed benefits of country life. Millions of Americans like to fancy themselves as good rugged country folk, or suppose they would have a better life if they were. And the second-rank Frost is their poet.

He *becomes* his audience, mirroring its need for pastoral fancies. The more a magazine like the *New Yorker* influences the quality of sophisticated middle-class life, the more will many Americans feel a desire for some assuaging counter image—woodsy, wholesome, a bit melancholic—such as Frost can provide. As a writer who bends his gift to the sincere misapprehensions of his readers, he has become a figure deeply integral to our culture; and the middlebrows who adore him must in fairness be granted some right to claim him as their own.

Frost is so skillful a performer that some of his most popular poems, like "Acquainted With the Night," "After Apple-Picking," and "Stopping by Woods on a Snowy Evening" are also among his finest. It might be convenient, but is also a dangerous simplification, to draw a sharp line between his popular and superior poems. The two have a way of shading into one another, as has always been the case with major writers like Dickens, Mark Twain, and Sholom Aleichem, who managed to speak both to cultivated persons and to the mass audience. And part of what Frost's ordinary readers admire or look for in his poetry they are, I think, right in wanting: a renewal of primary experience, a relatedness to the physical world, a wisdom resting on moral health.

In his dramatic poems Frost seldom falls back upon ready-made pastoral. These are poems of rural realism: New England as a depressed landscape, country people who are poor and deprived, families torn apart by derangement. The best of this group, such as "Home Burial" and "Servant to Servants," are studies in frustration, often the frustration of women who can no longer bear the weight of suffering. There is no "community" behind these figures, no sustaining world. The men and women of Frost's poems are isolated; they are figures left over by a dead or dying culture; and the world they live in has begun turning into stone.

Powerful as some of these dramatic pieces are, they share a number of faults. Frost lacks the patience and the deep concern with moral nuance that are essential to a writer wishing to evoke human character. He tries to conform to the hard outlines of economical portraiture and to avoid the kind of detail that would be appropriate only to a novel, but the result is often that the poems rely too much on photographic anecdote. The events they depict are supposed to speak for themselves; events seldom do.

Precisely the shading one misses in Frost's dramatic poems are what distinguish the dramatic poems of his immediate New England predecessor, Edwin Arlington Robinson. Though not nearly so brilliant a virtuoso as Frost, Robinson writes from a fullness of experience and a tragic awareness that Frost cannot equal. Frost has a strong grasp on melodramatic extremes of behavior, usually extremes of loneliness and psychic exhaustion, but he lacks almost entirely Robinson's command of the middle range of experience. The life of Frost's poems is post-social, and the perspective from which it is seen a desperate one. Frost achieves a cleaner verbal surface and a purer diction, but Robinson is more abundant in moral detail and insight. Compared strictly on their performances as dramatic poets, Robinson seems a major poet and Frost a minor one. For while Frost can be a master of nuance, it is only, or almost only, when he speaks in his own voice.

And that he does when he bears down with full seriousness in a small number of distinguished lyrics. Here the archness and sentimentalism have been purged; he is writing for sheer life. To read these poems, as they confront basic human troubles and obliquely notice the special dislocations of our time, can be unnerving—they offer neither security nor solace. They set out to record tremors of being in their purity and isolation: as if through a critical encounter with the physical world one could move beyond the weariness of selfhood and into the repose of matter. But Frost, now supremely hard on himself, also knows that the very intensity with which these moments are felt makes certain their rapid dissolution, and that what then remains is the familiar self, once again its own prisoner. Approaching a condition in which the narrator strains to achieve a sense of oneness with the universe and thereby lose himself in the delight of merger, these lyrics return, chastened, with the necessity of shaped meaning. And in their somewhat rueful turning back to the discipline of consciousness, the effect is both painful and final. They conclude with the reflection that the central quandary of selfhood—that it must forever spiral back to its own starting point—cannot be dissolved. That Frost sees and struggles with this dilemma seems one reason for saying he inhabits the same intellectual climate as those modern writers whose presumed disorder is often compared unfavorably to his supposed health.

Frost's superior lyrics include: "Storm Fear," "An Old Man's Winter Night," "The Oven Bird," "Dust of Snow," "Stopping by Woods on a Snowy Evening," "Spring Pools," "Acquainted With the Night," "The Lovely Shall Be Choosers," "Neither Out Far Nor in Deep," "Provide, Provide," "Design," "Happiness Makes Up in Height for What It Lacks in Length," "The Most of It," "Never Again Would Bird's Song Be the Same," "The Silken Tent," and a few others.

These poems demand from the reader a sharp recognition of their brevity. They focus upon a moment of intense realization, a lighting-up of hope and a dimming-down to wisdom. They attempt not a full seizure of an event, but an attack upon it from the oblique. They present a scene in the natural world, sometimes one that is "purely" natural and apparently unmarred by a human observer, but more often one that brings the "I" of the poem starkly against a natural process, so that the stress falls upon a drama of encounter and withdrawal. The event or situation—how spring pools will be sucked dry by the absorptive power of trees, in "Spring Pools"; how an albino spider perched on a "white heal-all" forms a dumb show of purposeless terror, in "Design"; how the loneliness of a winter moment encompasses an observer unawares, in "Desert Places"; how a family caught in a fearful storm may not, unaided, be able to rescue itself, in "Storm Fear"—is rendered with a desire to make a picture that will seem complete in itself, but that will also, through the very perfection of completeness, carry an aura of suggestion beyond itself. Frost allows for the sensuous pleasure of apprehending a moment in nature, but he soon cuts it short, since the point is not to linger over scene or pleasure but to move beyond them, along a line of speculation. Perhaps that is what Frost meant when he said that poetry "begins in delight and ends in wisdom."

These lyrics can be placed on a spectrum ranging from a few that seem entirely focused upon a natural event to those which move past the event toward explicit statement. Despite the critical dogma which looks down upon statement in poetry, there is nothing inherently superior about the first of these kinds; Frost's greatest poems, as it happens, are those which end with a coda of reflection. "Spring Pools" is an example of a poem that seems, at first, merely a snapshot of the external world:

> These pools that, though in forests, still reflect
> The total sky almost without defect,
> And like the flowers beside them, chill and shiver,
> Will like the flowers beside them soon be gone,
> And yet not out by any brook or river,
> But up by roots to bring dark foliage on.
>
> The trees that have it in their pent-up buds
> To darken nature and be summer woods—
> Let them think twice before they use their powers
> To blot out and drink up and sweep away
> These flowery waters and these watery flowers
> From snow that melted only yesterday.

As a rendering of a natural event, the poem is precise and complete. Exactness of description can be very moving, and so it is in "Spring Pools"; but beyond that, the poem—partly through a play with prepositions in the tenth line—suggests how hard yet necessary it is that the brief loveliness of youth be sucked dry to form the strength of our prime. Where the poem moves beyond description is in its problematic use of a parallelism between natural event and human experience. An implied equivalence between nature and man quickly brings a writer to the edge of the sentimental; but Frost does not cross it, for the poem, in its descriptive self-sufficiency, leaves to the reader the problem of what symbolic import to infer and how much tact he can muster in defending the poem against his own inference. It is a poem about spring pools, the poignancy of youth, and problems of thinking, not in a hierarchy of value which dissolves everything into the "spiritual," but in a poised equality of perceiving.

Most of Frost's superior lyrics end with direct statement, and one measure of their success is his ability to make the statement seem an adequate climax to the descriptive writing that has preceded it. The problem is not one to be approached with a priori notions about the relationship between imagery and statement in verse. When Cleanth Brooks writes that "Frost does not *think* through his images; he requires statements," he is guilty of a modernist dogma if he means his remarks as an adverse criticism. Poetry has always been full of statement, even the poetry of modernist writers who are supposed to confine themselves to symbolic indirection; and the critical problem in regard to Frost, or any other writer, hinges on the extent to which the concluding statement is related, through logical fulfillment or irony, to the texture of the poem, and the extent to which the statement is in its own right serious in thought and notable in diction.

In "Desert Places" Frost starts with a description of a natural scene and then, in a very moving way, brings in the human observer:

> Snow falling and night falling fast, oh, fast
> In a field I looked into going past,
> And the ground almost covered smooth in snow,
> But a few weeds and stubble showing last.
>
> The woods around it have it—it is theirs.
> All animals are smothered in their lairs.
> I am too absent-spirited to count;
> The loneliness includes me unawares.
>
> And lonely as it is, that loneliness
> Will be more lonely ere it will be less—
> A blanker whiteness of benighted snow
> With no expression, nothing to express.

Thus far the poem is very fine, but there follows the concluding stanza—

> They cannot scare me with their empty spaces
> Between stars—on stars where no human race is.
> I have it in me so much nearer home
> To scare myself with my own desert places.

—in which Frost collapses into the kind of coyness one associates with his second-rank poems. Cut out the final stanza and "Desert Places" is a perfect small lyric; as it stands, the poem is a neat illustration of Frost's characteristic strengths and weaknesses; but the weakness of the last four lines is due not to the fact that Frost ventures a statement, but to the quality of the statement he ventures.

In most of the lyrics I have named Frost handles this problem with assurance. "The Oven Bird" presents a picture of a bird which in mid-summer sings loudly, as if in celebration of the lapsed spring:

> He says the early petal-fall is past,
> When pear and cherry bloom went down in showers
> On sunny days a moment overcast;
> And comes that other fall we name the fall.

The writing here, both vivid and witty, is satisfying enough, and the theme, though treated with greater toughness, resembles that of "Spring Pools." The bird is assigned, as a pleasing conceit, something of the poet's stoical resilience:

> The bird would cease and be as other birds
> But that he knows in singing not to sing.

Then come the concluding lines, in which Frost achieves a triumph of modulated rhetoric, a statement that can be regarded as an epitaph of his whole career:

> The question that he frames in all but words
> Is what to make of a diminished thing.

Many of Frost's first-rate lyrics unite with similar success a rapid passage of description and a powerful concluding statement. The familiar "Acquainted With the Night" owes a good part of its haunting quality not merely to Frost's evocation of a man walking the streets alone at night—

> I have stood still and stopped the sound of feet
> When far away an interrupted cry
> Came over houses from another street
>
> But not to call me back or say good-by;

—but also to the lines that immediately follow, lines of enigmatic statement indicating an ultimate dissociation between the natural world and human desire:

> And further still at an unearthly height
> One luminary clock against the sky
>
> Proclaimed the time was neither wrong nor right.
> I have been one acquainted with the night.

In discussing such poems it has become a commonplace to say, as W. H. Auden does, that Frost's style "approximates to ordinary speech" and that "the music is always that of the speaking voice, quiet and sensible." This does not seem an adequate way of describing Frost's lyrics. Try reading "Spring Pools" or "The Most of It" in a voice approximating to ordinary speech: it cannot be done, short of violating the rhythm of the poem. Quiet these lyrics may be, "sensible" they are not. They demand a rhythm of enticement and immersion, a hastening surrender to unreflective nature—which means a rising and tensing of the voice; and then a somewhat broken or subdued return to reflectiveness. They are poems that must be read with a restrained intoning, quite different from "ordinary speech," though milder than declamation.

It is a way of reading enforced by their structure and purpose: the structure and purpose of wisdom-poems. Frost's best lyrics aim at the kind of wisdom that is struck aslant and not to be settled into the comforts of an intellectual system. It is the wisdom of a mind confessing its nakedness. Frost writes as a modern poet who shares in the loss of firm assumptions and seeks, through a disciplined observation of the natural world and a related sequel of reflection, to provide some tentative basis for existence, some "momentary stay against confusion." The best of his poems are antipathetic to the notion that the universe is inherently good or delightful or hospitable to our needs. These lyrics speak of the hardness and recalcitrance of the natural world; of its absolute indifference to our needs and its refusal to lend itself to an allegory of affection; of the certainty of physical dissolution; but also of the refreshment that can be found through a brief submission to the alienness of nature, always provided one recognizes the need to move on, not stopping for rest but remaining locked in consciousness. The lyric that best illustrates these themes is "The Most of It," as it dramatizes our desire for cosmic solace and the consequence of discovering we cannot have it.

> He thought he kept the universe alone;
> For all the voice in answer he could wake
> Was but the mocking echo of his own. . . .

Bourbon on the Rocks

1964

In America we have become accustomed to thinking of the reactionary as a small-town primitive marked by the pathos of cultural obsolescence and moral fright. Historically, there is much to be said for this image. But in James Burnham we have something rather new, an American reactionary on the French style: the "aristocratic" intellectual who makes no pretense to humaneness, gladly proclaims his chauvinism, breathes a frigid contempt for the plebs, and indulges in public fantasies of imperial grandeur. It should be said in his behalf that Burnham's public career has been temperamentally consistent, even if ideologically distraught: he has always been a cold-blooded snob, first as a Trotskyist, then as herald of the "managerial revolution," and lately as geopolitical strategist in charge of World War III for the *National Review*. Though sophisticated enough to go through the motions of intellectual complexity, he is driven by an urge toward apocalyptic crudeness; and all those who will not plunge with him into preparations for atomic *fin du mondisme* he regards as "confused" or "muddled" or "weak" liberals,

From *New York Review of Books* 11 (May 14, 1964):7.

mere patsies for the oncoming Communist hordes, and more to be
despised than pitied. Whatever his ultimatistic obsession of the moment
(and there have been quite a few), he finds it hard to repress a well-
bred snarl for those men of humane doubts who refuse to go along with
him each time he discovers a new mission.

To whom, one wonders, is his strange book *Suicide of the West* addressed?—this rodomontade blending academic hauteur with fanatic
shrillness, which announces, as if it were a fact beyond dispute, that the
West has been seized by a lemminglike impulse toward collective suicide, for which liberalism provides the ideological rationale; that American foreign policy (perhaps because deprived of its bodily essences?)
is suspiciously soft on Communism; that the boundaries of "civilization"
are being steadily contracted under assault from barbarians; that the
welfare state corrodes American freedom and character; and that the
streets of our cities are menaced by dark-skinned hoodlums.

The conservative faithful have heard it all before, though hardly
from so cultivated a source; and surely the literate public is not likely
to respond to this odd yoking of Ortega y Gasset and General Jack D.
Ripper. But after a time I found an answer to my question: the book
will serve admirably as a tip sheet, a Barnes & Noble handbook, for
campus conservatives, those little-league Goldwaters looking for de-
bater's points with which to stun liberal professors. Here they can learn
that some liberals (those who do not wish to invade Cuba) shamefully
prefer peace to freedom, and that liberal theory is beset by an inherent
conflict between its devotion to popular sovereignty, which can sometimes lead to popular tyranny, and its devotion to minority rights, which
can sometimes lead to social immobility. (Hardly a problem for Burnham, however, who is not very infatuated with either term of this
dilemma.)

Most of the book is devoted to an agonizingly slow description of
liberalism, as if Burnham had been traumatized by too much exposure
to dim-witted students. You can learn here that the Americans for
Democratic Action is a liberal bulwark, that Arthur Schlesinger, Jr. and
Eleanor Roosevelt are representative liberals, that most liberals are internationalist in outlook—red-hot news that will just shake up everyone
at Bob Jones University. A curious result of this baby talk, however, is
that the American liberal emerging from Burnham's pages seems far
more principled, tough-spirited, and intellectually coherent than he is
likely in fact to have been these past few decades; for Burnham will
have nothing to do with the qualifications and modulations of political
reality, and as a result the fact that the distance between most American
liberals and most American conservatives has recently been lessening

never appears in his pages. He's a black-and-white man; and he stands for white.

The true qualities of his book come out in a sentence here, a passage there. In a section worthy of Dickens's Josiah Bounderby, he mocks those liberals who wish to erase such symptoms of social pathology as Skid Row, for "Skid Row is the end of the line; and there must be an end of the line somewhere." He deplores the "deterrence" strategy held by official United States opinion as "a gigantic bluff," for—believe me, I'm quoting accurately—"the purpose of the entire strategic nuclear force is not at all to be used." *(I don't say we wouldn't get our hair mussed up....)* He is troubled by the double standard of liberalism, its tendency to excuse methods employed by underdogs which it would condemn if used by oppressors. Writing about the treatment of Negroes by Southern cops, he remarks: "The truncheons of hard-pressed police struggling to preserve the minimum elements of public order against unloosed chaos become [for liberals] Satanic pitchforks. . . ." This concern for impartiality leads Burnham to notice that "There has never been a liberal protest against the outrages committed by the South African Negroes."

The author of *Suicide of the West* is a versatile, many-sided figure. Professor James Burnham, mellow sage of conservatism, notes that not all human troubles can be eradicated and that, sad as it may be, we had better reconcile ourselves to the likelihood that other peoples will continue to suffer hunger. Fighting Jim Burnham, last of the individualists, remarks that he has no objection to Social Security, but resents the welfare state's imposition of *automatic* Social Security and wishes it would allow citizens a choice of voluntary systems. (Whether he favors a similar voluntary arrangement in regard to the draft, he does not say.) Sir James, Leftenant-General in His Majesty's forces, bemoans the loss of those "splendid fighting men . . . the Gurkhas, Sikhs, Senegalese and Berbers . . . not the least of the grievous losses that the West has suffered from the triumph of decolonialization." Old African Pioneer Burnham, looking Voerward, decries independence in East Africa as "the occasion when native black men, who have neither spun nor reaped, can take for nothing or next to nothing many of those splendid farms and ranches that the knowledge, effort, foresight, administrative ability, and capital of Europe-sprung white men have slowly brought into being. . . ." And most spectacularly, behind a mountain of maps, Chief of Staff Burnham, fighting grimly to stiffen the jellied spine of the West, counts off the loss of our forts and our ports: "The great harbor of Trincomalee, commanding the western flank of the Bay of Bengal, southeast Asia and the Strait of Malacca, ceases to be a Western strategic base. Gone too are the mighty ports of Dakar and Casablanca, looming over the Atlantic passage. Of the guardian bases of the north African littoral, southern flank of Europe, only Mers-el-Kebir remains. . . ."

And yet, and yet, am I perhaps unjust? Is there not still another James Burnham, a good man with a kindly wink, a cheerful nod, for the lowest orders? Movingly he tells us about two Negroes—"cheerful, pleasant fellows" of course—whom he sees regularly in New York and who work at collecting piles of old paper-board boxes. Their IQs "were almost out of sight" (would a mere liberal bother to take the IQs of Negro peddlers?), but they "could handle the work they were doing." And then Mayor Robert Wagner, a "leading liberal politician," came along to demand that the state lift the minimum wage to $1.50 an hour. This "rise in the minimum wage," Burnham discovered, "would most certainly throw those two chaps out of their jobs." As it now is, "with their wives going out some as part-time maids and the older children running a few policy tickets," these Negroes can survive. But satisfy the liberals' "ideological abstraction," raise the minimum wage for those hundreds of thousands of New Yorkers living on a semistarvation level, and "my friends," Burnham sadly concludes, will become "bums and delinquents."

It is touchingly humane, this little story, and it leads me to another which Burnham in his modesty has failed to mention.

There are times—we all know them—when everything seems too much. The generals will not take advice on how to start atomic confrontations, Washington keeps knuckling under to the Reds, the welfare state won't let us set up a private Social Security system or buy TVA, and even some of those chaps at the *National Review* may not be so very bright. Wearied and harassed, our hero goes back to the Old Plantation, where order still prevails and, since it is an organic society, everyone knows his place. At the spacious entrance he is greeted by George, the grinning house-servant, who brings a mint julep and a happy smile: "We'z all glad to have you back, Marse James, moughty nice to have you back." You, reader, corrupted by "ideological abstractions" of liberalism, may suppose that George is unfree, a chattel slave. But the truth is that Marse James looks after George and speaks of him feelingly as "my friend." And you know—that George is a happy man. A happy man, suh.

New Styles in "Leftism"

1965

I propose to describe a political style or outlook before it has become hardened into an ideology or the property of an organization. This outlook is visible along limited portions of the political scene; for the sake of exposition I will make it seem more precise and structured than it really is.

There is a new radical mood in limited sectors of American society: on the campus, in sections of the civil rights movement. The number of people who express this mood is not very large, but that it should appear at all is cause for encouragement and satisfaction. Yet there is a segment or fringe among the newly blossoming young radicals that causes one disturbance—and not simply because they have ideas different from persons like me, who neither expect nor desire that younger generations of radicals should repeat our thoughts or our words. For this disturbing minority I have no simple name: sometimes it looks like kamikaze radicalism, sometimes like white Malcolmism, sometimes like black Maoism. But since none of these phrases will quite do, I have had

From *Dissent* 13 (Summer 1965):3.

to fall back upon the loose and not very accurate term "new leftists." Let me therefore stress as strongly as I can that I am not talking about all or the majority of the American young and not-so-young who have recently come to regard themselves as radicals.

The form I have felt obliged to use here—a composite portrait of the sort of "new leftist" who seems to me open to criticism—also creates some difficulties. It may seem to lump together problems, ideas, and moods that should be kept distinct. But my conviction is that this kind of "new leftism" is not a matter of organized political tendencies, at least not yet, and that there is no organization, certainly none of any importance, which expresses the kind of "new leftism" I am here discussing. So I would say that if some young radicals read this text and feel that much of it does not pertain to them, I will be delighted by such a response.

Some Background Conditions

A.   The society we live in fails to elicit the idealism of the more rebellious and generous young. Even among those who play the game and accept the social masks necessary for gaining success, there is a widespread disenchantment. Certainly there is very little ardor, very little of the joy that comes from a conviction that the values of a society are good, and that it is therefore good to live by them. The intelligent young know that if they keep out of trouble, accept academic drudgery, and preserve a respectable "image," they can hope for successful careers, even if not personal gratification. But the price they must pay for this choice is a considerable quantity of inner adaptation to the prevalent norms: there is a limit to the social duplicity that anyone can sustain.

The society not only undercuts the possibilities of constructive participation; it also makes very difficult a coherent and thought-out political opposition. The small minority that does rebel tends to adopt a stance that seems to be political, sometimes even ideological, but often turns out to be little more than an effort to assert a personal style.

Personal style: that seems to me a key. Most of whatever rebellion we have had up to—and even into—the civil rights movement takes the form of a decision on how to live individually within this society, rather than how to change it collectively. A recurrent stress among the young has been upon differentiation of speech, dress, and appearance, by means of which a small elite can signify its special status; or the stress has been upon moral self-regeneration, a kind of Emersonianism with shock treatment. All through the fifties and sixties disaffiliation was a central impulse, in the beatnik style or the more sedate J. D. Salinger way, but disaffiliation nevertheless, as both a signal of nausea and a tacit recognition of impotence.

I say "recognition of impotence" because movements that are powerful, groups that are self-confident, do not opt out of society: they live and work within society in order to transform it.

Now, to a notable extent, all this has changed since and through the civil rights movement—*but not changed as much as may seem*. Some of the people involved in that movement show an inclination to make of their radicalism not a politics of common action, which would require the inclusion of saints, sinners, and ordinary folk, but, rather, a gesture of moral rectitude. And the paradox is that they often sincerely regard themselves as committed to politics—but a politics that asserts so unmodulated and total a dismissal of society, while also departing from Marxist expectations of social revolution, that little is left to them but the glory or burden of maintaining a distinct personal style.

By contrast, the radicalism of an earlier generation, despite numerous faults, had at least this advantage: it did not have to start *as if* from scratch; there were available movements, parties, agencies, and patterns of thought through which one could act. The radicals of the thirties certainly had their share of bohemianism, but their politics were not nearly so interwoven with and dependent upon tokens of style as is today's radicalism.

The great value of the present rebelliousness is that it requires a personal decision, not merely as to what one shall do but also as to what one shall be. It requires authenticity, a challenge to the self, or, as some young people like to say, an "existential" decision. And it makes more difficult the moral double-bookkeeping of the thirties, whereby in the name of a sanctified movement or unquestioned ideology, scoundrels and fools could be exalted as "leaders" and detestable conduct exonerated.

This is a real and very impressive strength, but with it there goes a significant weakness: the lack of clear-cut ideas, sometimes even a feeling that it is wrong—or, worse, "middle-class"—to think systematically, and as a corollary, the absence of a social channel or agency through which to act. At first it seemed as if the civil rights movement would provide such a channel; and no person of moral awareness can fail to be profoundly moved by the outpouring of idealism and the readiness to face danger which characterizes the vanguard of this movement. Yet at a certain point it turns out that the civil rights movement, through the intensity of its work, seems to dramatize . . . its own insufficiency. Indeed, it acts as a training school for experienced, gifted, courageous people who have learned how to lead, how to sacrifice, how to work, but have no place in which to enlarge upon their gifts. There may in time appear a new kind of "dropout"—the "dropout" trained by and profoundly attached to the civil rights movement who yet feels that it does not, and by its very nature cannot, come to grips with the central problems of modern society; the "dropout" who has been trained to a fine edge of frustration and despair.

B. These problems are exacerbated by an educational system that often seems inherently schizoid. It appeals to the life of the mind, yet justifies that appeal through crass utilitarianism. It invokes the traditions of freedom, yet processes students to bureaucratic cut. It speaks for the spirit, yet increasingly becomes an appendage of a spirit-squashing system.

C. The "new leftism" appears at a moment when the intellectual and academic worlds—and not they alone—are experiencing an intense and largely justifiable revulsion against the immediate American past. Many people are sick unto death of the whole structure of feeling—that mixture of chauvinism, hysteria, and demagogy—which was created during the Cold War years. Like children subjected to forced feeding, they regurgitate almost automatically. Their response is an inevitable consequence of overorganizing the propaganda resources of a modern state; the same sort of nausea exists among the young in the Communist world.

Unfortunately, revulsion seldom encourages nuances of thought or precise discriminations of politics. You cannot stand the deceits of official anti-Communism? Then respond with a rejection equally blatant. You have been raised to give credit to every American power move, no matter how reactionary or cynical? Then respond by castigating everything American. You are weary of Sidney Hook's messages in the *New York Times Magazine?* Then respond as if talk about Communist totalitarianism were simply irrelevant or a bogey to frighten infants.

Yet we should be clear in our minds that such a response is not at all the same as a commitment to Communism, even though it may lend itself to obvious exploitation. It is, rather, a spewing out of distasteful matter—in the course of which other values, such as the possibility of learning from the traumas and tragedies of recent history, may also be spewed out.

D. Generational clashes are recurrent in our society, perhaps in any society. But the present rupture between the young and their elders seems especially deep. This is a social phenomenon that goes beyond our immediate subject, indeed, it cuts through the whole of society; what it signifies is the society's failure to transmit with sufficient force its values to the young, or, perhaps more accurately, that the best of the young take the proclaimed values of their elders with a seriousness which leads them to be appalled by their violation in practice.

In rejecting the older generations, however, the young sometimes betray the conditioning mark of the very American culture they are so quick to denounce: for ours is a culture that celebrates youthfulness as if it were a moral good in its own right. Like the regular Americans they wish so hard not to be, yet, through wishing, so very much are, they believe that the past is mere dust and ashes and that they can start afresh, immaculately.

There are, in addition, a few facts to be noted concerning the relationship between the radical young and those few older people who have remained radicals.

A generation is missing in the life of American radicalism, the generation that would now be in its mid-thirties, the generation that did not show up. The result is an inordinate difficulty in communication between the young radicals and those unfortunate enough to have reached—or, God help us, even gone beyond—the age of forty. Here, of course, our failure is very much in evidence too: a failure that should prompt us to speak with modesty, simply as people who have tried, and in their trying perhaps have learned something.

To the younger radicals it seems clear that a good many of the radicals of the thirties have grown tired, or dropped out, or, in some instances, sold out. They encounter teachers who, on ceremonial occasions, like to proclaim old socialist affiliations, but who really have little or no sympathy with any kind of rebelliousness today. They are quick—and quite right—to sense that announcements of old Young People's Socialist League ties can serve as a self-protective nostalgia or even as a cloak for acquiescence in the status quo. But it must also be said that there is a tendency among the "new leftists" toward much too quick a dismissal of those who may disagree with them—they are a little too fast on the draw with such terms as "fink" and "establishment."

All this may describe the conditions under which the new political outlook appears, but it does not yet tell us anything about the specific culture, so to say, in which it thrives. Let me therefore indicate some of the political and intellectual influences acting upon the "new leftism," by setting up two very rough categories.

Ideologues and Desperadoes

A. *Ideologues, White.* The disintegration of American radicalism these last few decades left a good many ideologues emotionally unemployed: people accustomed to grand theorizing who have had their theories shot out from under them; people still looking for some belated evidence that they were "right" all along; people with unexpended social energy and idealism of a sort, who desperately needed new arenas in which to function.

1. *The Remains of Stalinism.* The American Communist Party was broken first by McCarthyite and government persecution, and second by an inner crisis following Khrushchev's revelations and the Hungarian revolution. Those who left out of disillusionment were heartsick people, their convictions and sometimes their lives shattered. But those who left the party or its supporting organizations because they feared government attack were often people who kept, semiprivately, their earlier convictions. Many of them had a good deal of political experience; some remained significantly placed in the network of what might be called conscience organizations. Naturally enough, they continued to keep in touch with one another, forming a kind of reserve apparatus based on common opinions, feelings, memories. As soon as some ferment began in the civil rights movement and the peace groups, these people were present, ready and eager; they needed no directives from the Communist Party to which, in any case, they no longer (or may never have) belonged; they were quite capable of working on their own *as if they were working together*, through a variety of groups and periodicals like the *National Guardian*. Organizational Stalinism declined, but a good part of its heritage remained: people who could offer political advice, raise money, write leaflets, sit patiently at meetings, put up in a pleasant New York apartment visitors from a distant state, who, by chance, had been recommended by an old friend.

2. *True Believers.* On the far left there remains a scatter of groups still convinced that Marxism-Leninism, in one or another version, is "correct." What has failed them, however, is the historical motor provided by Marxist theory: the proletariat, which has not shown the "revolutionary potential" or fulfilled the "historical mission" to which it was assigned. Though the veteran Marxists cannot, for fear of shattering their whole structure of belief, give up the *idea* of the proletariat, they can hardly act, day by day, as if the American working class were indeed satisfying Marxist expectations or were the actual center of revolutionary ferment. Thus, in somewhat schizoid fashion, they have clung to their traditional faith in the proletariat as the revolutionary class, while in practice searching for a new embodiment of it which might provide the social energy they desire. And in the Negro movement they sometimes think to have found it.

That this movement, with great creative flair, has worked out an indigenous strategy of its own; that it has developed nonviolent resistance into an enormously powerful weapon; that the Negro clergy, in apparent disregard of Leninist formulas, plays a leading and often militant role—all this does not sit well with the old Marxists. They must therefore develop new theories, by means of which the Negroes become the vanguard of the working class or perhaps the "true" (not yet "bought-off") working class. And, clustering around the Negro movement, they contribute a mite of wisdom here and there: scoffing at nonviolence, employing the shibboleth of "militancy" as if it were a magical device for satisfying the needs of the Negro poor, and so forth. They are experienced in "deepening the struggle," usually other people's struggles: which means to scorn the leadership of Dr. Martin Luther King, Jr. without considering that the "revolutionary" course they propose for the Negro movement could, if adopted, lead it into a cul-de-sac of isolation, exhaustion, and heroic blood. Understandably, they find allies in Negro nationalists who want not so much to deepen as to divert the struggle, and among young militants who dislike the idea that Negroes might, if successful in their struggle, come to share some of the American affluence and thus become "middle class."

3. *Authoritarian Leftists.* In figures like Isaac Deutscher and Paul Sweezy we find the true intellectual progenitors of at least part of the "new leftism"; the influence they exert has been indirect, since they are not involved in immediate struggles, but it has nevertheless been there.

Sweezy's *Monthly Review* is the main spokesman in this country for the view that authoritarianism is inherent or necessary in the so-called socialist countries; that what makes them "socialist" is simply the nationalization of the means of production; that democracy, while perhaps desirable in some long-range calculation, is not crucial for judging the socialist character of a society; that the claim that workers must be in a position to exercise political power if the state can in any sense be called "theirs," is a utopian fallacy. At times this technological determinism, put to the service of brutal dictatorship, has been given a more subtle reading by Sweezy, namely, that when the conditions supposedly causing the Communist dictatorship—economic backwardness and international insecurity—have been overcome, the Soviet regime would in some unspecified way democratize itself. In November 1957, after the Khrushchev revelations, *Monthly Review* printed a notably frank editorial:

> The conditions which produced the [Soviet] dictatorship have been overcome. . . . Our theory is being put to the crucial test of practise. And so far—let us face it frankly—there is precious little evidence to confirm it. In all that has happened since Stalin's death we can find nothing to indicate that the Communist Party or any of its competing factions, has changed in

the slightest degree its view of the proper relation between the people and their leadership . . . there is apparently no thought that the Soviet people will ever grow up enough to decide for itself who knows best and hence who should make and administer the policies which determine its fate.

And finally from Sweezy: "Forty years is too long for a dictatorship to remain temporary"—surely the understatement of the Christian Era!

One might suppose that if "our theory is being put to the crucial test" and "there is precious little evidence to confirm it," honest men would proceed to look for another theory, provided, that is, they continued to believe that freedom is desirable.

A good number of years have passed since the above passage appeared in *Monthly Review*, the "precious little evidence" remains precious little, and Sweezy, once apparently dismayed over the lack of democracy in Russia, has moved not to Titoism or "revisionism." No, he has moved toward Maoist China, where presumably one does not have to worry about "the proper relation between the people and their leadership. . . ." Writing in December 1964 the *Monthly Review* editors declared with satisfaction that "there could be no question of the moral ascendency of Peking over Moscow in the underdeveloped world." They agreed with the Chinese that Khrushchev's fall was "a good thing" and they wrote further: "The Chinese possession of a nuclear potential does not increase the danger of nuclear war. Quite the contrary. The Chinese have solemnly pledged never to be the first to use nuclear weapons . . . and their revolutionary record of devotion to the cause of socialism and progress entitles them to full trust and confidence."

The logic is clear: begin with theoretical inquiry and concern over the perpetuation of dictatorship in Russia and end with "full trust and confidence" in China, where the dictatorship is more severe.

There is an aphorism by a recent Polish writer: "The dispensing of injustice is always in the right hands." And so is its defense.

B. *Ideologues, Negro.*

1. *Black Nationalism.* Here is a creed that speaks or appears to speak totally against compromise, against negotiating with "the white power structure," against the falsities of white liberals, indeed, against anything but an indulgence of verbal violence. Shortly before his tragic death Malcolm X spoke at a Trotskyist-sponsored meeting and listening to him I felt, as did others, that he was in a state of internal struggle, reaching out for an ideology he did not yet have. For the Negroes in his audience he offered the relief of articulating subterranean feelings of hatred, contempt, defiance, feelings that did not have to be held in

check because there was a tacit compact that the talk about violence would remain talk. For both the Negroes and whites in the audience there was an apparent feeling that Malcolm and Malcolm alone among the Negro spokesmen was authentic because . . . well, because finally he spoke for nothing but his rage, for no proposal, no plan, no program, just a sheer outpouring of anger and pain. And that they could understand. The formidable sterility of his speech, so impressive in its relation to a deep personal suffering, touched something in their hearts. For Malcolm, intransigent in words and nihilistic in reality, never invoked the possibility or temptations of immediate struggle; he never posed the problems, confusions, and risks of maneuver, compromise, retreat. Brilliantly Malcolm spoke for a rejection so complete it transformed him into an apolitical spectator, or in the language of his admirers, a "cop-out."

2. *Caricature.* If, nevertheless, there was something about Malcolm which commands our respect, that is because we know his life-struggle, his rise from the depths, his conquest of thought and speech. Leroi Jones, by contrast, stands as a burlesque double of whatever is significant in Malcolm.

In his success as both a New School lecturer and a prophet of "guerrilla warfare" in the United States; in his badgering of white liberal audiences; in his orgies of verbal violence committed, to be sure, not in Selma, Alabama, but Sheridan Square, New York; in his fantasies of an international race war in which the whites will be slaughtered, Jones speaks for a contemporary sensibility. But he speaks for it in a special way: as a distinctively American success, the pop-art guerrilla warrior.

He speaks at that center of revolutionary upsurge, the Village Vanguard. He explains that the murder of Negroes in the South does not arouse the kind of horror and indignation that the murder of white civil rights workers does. *He is absolutely right;* the point cannot be made too often. But Jones cannot stop there: it would be too sensible, too humane, and it would not yield pages in the *Village Voice.* Instead, responding to a question, "What about Goodman and Schwerner, the two white boys killed in Mississippi, don't you care about them?" Jones said, as quoted in the *Voice:* "Absolutely not. Those boys were just artifacts, artifacts, man. They weren't real. If they want to assuage their leaking consciences, that's their business. I won't mourn for them. I have my own dead to mourn for."

Is this not exactly the attitude Jones had a moment earlier condemned in regard to killings in the South, but the same attitude in reverse? And is it really impossible for the human heart to mourn for *both* Negro and white victims? *Not*, to be sure, for ordinary whites, since they, we all know, are "white devils"; but at least for those who have given their lives in the struggle?

The essential point about Jones's racist buffoonery has been made by George Dennison in a recent review of Jones's plays:

> Just as he mis-labels the victims *black*, he mis-labels the authority *white*. Certainly he knows, or should know, that the authority which in fact pertains is not the authority of race . . . but an authority of property and arms; and certainly he knows, or should know, that the life-destroying evil inheres in the nature of the authority, not in the color of those who wield it. But if Jones wanted change, he would speak change. He speaks, instead, for the greatest possible rejection, a rejection so absolute, so confined to fantasy, that it amounts to nothing more than hands-off-the-status-quo. . . . Point by point his is an upside down version of the most genteel, middle-class, liberal position. And I think that the liberals see him as one of their own, albeit a Dropout. He addresses every word to them and is confined to their systems of values because he is in the business of denying no other values but those. That spurious anger, so resonant with career, can be trusted not to upset the applecart.

C. Desperadoes, White.   In effect, I have already described this group, so let me here confine myself to a few remarks about one of its central battle cries, "alienation."

The trouble with the recurrent use of alienation as a mode of social analysis is that it includes almost everything, and thereby explains almost nothing. The term has become impossibly loose (like those other handy tags, "the establishment" and "the power structure"). As used by Marx, alienation had a rather precise reference: it pointed to the condition of the worker in the capitalist productive process, a condition in which "the worker's deed becomes an alien power . . . forcing him to develop some specialized dexterity at the cost of a world of productive impulses." This kind of analysis focuses upon the place of the proletarian within the social structure, and not upon the sediment of malaise among those outside it.

Since Marx wrote, the term has acquired an impossible load of signification. During most of the bourgeois era, the European intellectuals grew increasingly estranged from the social community because the very ideals that had animated the bourgeois revolution were now being violated by bourgeois society; their "alienation" was prompted not by bohemian willfulness but by a loyalty to Liberty, Fraternity, Equality, or to an induced vision of preindustrial society which, by a twist of history, came pretty much to resemble Liberty, Fraternity, Equality. Just as it was the triumph of capitalism which largely caused this sense of estrangement, so it was the expansion of capitalism which allowed the intellectuals enough freedom to release it. During the greater part of the bourgeois era, intellectuals preferred alienation from the community to alienation from themselves. Precisely this choice made possible their boldness and strength, precisely this "lack of roots" gave them their speculative power.

By now the term "alienation" frequently carries with it a curious reversal of moral and emotional stress. For where intellectuals had once used it as a banner of pride and self-assertion, today it tends to become a complaint, a token of self-pity, a rationale for a degree of estrangement from the society which connotes not an active rebellion against—nor even any active relation to—it, but, rather, a justification for marginality and withdrawal.

Somewhere amid the current talk about "alienation" an important reality *is* being touched upon or pointed to. There *is*, in our society, a profound estrangement from the sources of selfhood, the possibilities of human growth and social cohesion. But simply to proclaim this estrangement can be a way of preserving it. Alienation is not some metaphysical equivalent of the bubonic plague, which constitutes an irrevocable doom; it is the powerlessness deriving from human failure to act. It is neither a substitute for thought, nor a dissolvent of human will, nor even a roadblock in the way of useful work. To enter into the society which in part causes this estrangement and by establishing bonds with other men to transform the society is one way of partially overcoming alienation. Each time the civil rights movement brings previously mute Negroes into active political life, each time a trade union extends its power of decision within a factory, the boundaries of alienation are shrunk.

D. Desperadoes, Negro. A new kind of young Negro militant has appeared in the last few years, and he is a figure far more authentic and impressive than any of those I have thus far mentioned. He is fed up with white promises. He is proud to be estranged from white society. He has strong, if vague, "nationalist" inclinations. He is desperate—impatient with the tactics of gradualism, nonviolence, and passive resistance. He sees few, if any, allies upon whom he can count; few, if any, positive forces in society that might stir people into action. In effect, he decides that he must "go it alone," scornful of the white liberal and labor groups, as well as of those Negro leaders who choose to work with them. He seeks to substitute for a stagnant history his own desire and sacrifice.

Let me suggest a very limited comparison. This kind of young Negro militant, though not of course interested in any kind of individual terrorism, acts out of social and psychological motives somewhat like those of the late-nineteenth-century Russian terrorists, who also tried to substitute their intransigent will for the sluggishness of history. And the consequences will perhaps be similar: the best cadres exhausted in isolation and defeat.

Such a response may well be the inevitable result of an abrupt and painful coming-to-awareness on the part of young Negro militants who had previously suppressed their suffering simply in order to survive but now feel somewhat freer to release it. Their devotion is beyond doubt, as their heroism is beyond praise; yet what I'm here tempted to call kamikaze radicalism, or what Bayard Rustin calls the "no win" outlook, can become self-defeating in political life.

The "New Leftist"—a Sketch

We can now venture a portrait of the new leftist, not as one or another individual but as a composite type—with all the qualifications I stated at the outset.

A. *Cultural Style.* The "new leftist" appears, at times, as a figure embodying a style of speech, dress, work, and culture. Often, especially if white, the son of the middle class—and sometimes the son of middle-class parents nursing radical memories—he asserts his rebellion against the deceit and hollowness of American society. Very good; there is plenty to rebel against. But in the course of his rebellion he tends to reject not merely the middle-class ethos but a good many other things he too hastily associates with it: the intellectual heritage of the West, the tradition of liberalism at its most serious, the commitment to democracy as an indispensable part of civilized life. He tends to make style into the very substance of his revolt, and while he may, on one side of himself, engage in valuable activities in behalf of civil rights, student freedom, and so on, he nevertheless tacitly accepts the "givenness" of American society, has little hope or expectation of changing it, and thereby, in effect, settles for a mode of personal differentiation.

Primarily that means the wish to shock, the wish to assault the sensibilities of a world he cannot overcome. If he cannot change it, then at least he can outrage it. He searches in the limited repertoire of sensation and shock: for sick comics who will say "fuck" in nightclubs; for drugs that will vault him beyond the perimeters of the suburbs; for varieties, perversities, and publicities of sex so as perhaps to create an inner, private revolution that will accompany—or replace?—the outer, public revolution.

But the "new leftist" is frequently trapped in a symbiotic relationship with the very middle class he rejects, dependent upon it for his self-definition: quite as the professional anti-Communist of a few years ago was caught up with the Communist Party, which, had it not existed, he would have had to invent—as indeed at times he did invent. So that for all its humor and charm, the style of the "new leftist" tends to become a rigid antistyle, dependent for its survival on the enemy it is supposed to panic. *Épater le bourgeois*—in this case, perhaps *épater le père*—is to acquiesce in a basic assumption of at least the more sophisticated segments of the middle class: that values can be inferred from, or are resident in, the externals of dress, appearance, furnishings, and hairdos.

Shock as he will, disaffiliate as he may choose, the "new leftist" discovers after a while that nothing has greatly changed. The relations of power remain as before, the Man still hovers over the scene, the "power structure" is unshaken. A few old ladies in California may grow indignant, a DA occasionally arrest someone, a *Village Voice* reporter arrange an interview; but surely that is all small change. And soon the "new leftist" must recognize that even he has not been greatly transformed. For in his personal manner he is acting out the dilemmas of a utopian community, and just as Brook Farm had to remain subject to the laws of the market despite its internal ethic of cooperation, so must he remain subject to the impress of the dominant institutions despite his desire to be totally different.

Victimized by a lack of the historical sense, the "new leftist" does not realize that the desire to shock and create sensations has itself a long and largely disastrous history. The notion, as Meyer Schapiro has remarked, that opium is the revolution of the people has been luring powerless intellectuals and semi-intellectuals for a long time. But the damnable thing is that for an almost equally long time the more sophisticated and urban sectors of the middle class have refused to be shocked. They know the repertoire of sensationalism quite as well as the "new leftist"; and if he is to succeed in shocking them or even himself, he must keep raising the ante. The very rebel who believes himself devoted to an absolute of freedom and looks with contempt upon any mode of compromise, is thereby caught up in the compulsiveness of his escalation: a compulsiveness inherently bad enough, but rendered still more difficult, and sometimes pathetic, by the fact that, alas, each year he gets a year older.

Let me amend this somewhat. To say that the urban middle class has become jaded and can no longer be shocked is not quite correct. No; a kind of complicity is set up between the outraged and/or amused urban middle class and the rebels of sensation. Their mutual dependency requires that each shock, to provide the pleasures of indignation, must be a little stronger (like a larger dose) than the previous one. For the point is not so much that the urban middle class can no longer be shocked as that it positively yearns for and comes to depend upon the titillating assaults of its cultural enemies. So that when a new sensation (be it literary violence, sexual fashion, intellectual outrage, high-toned pornography, or sadistic denunciation) is provided by the shock troops of culture, the sophisticated middle class responds with outrage, resistance, and anger—*for upon these initial responses its pleasure depends*. But then, a little later, it rolls over like a happy puppy on its back, moaning, "Oh, baby, *épatez* me again, harder this time, tell me what a sterile impotent louse I am and how you are so tough and virile, how you're planning to murder me, *épatez* me again. . . ."

Thus a fire-eating character like LeRoi Jones becomes an adjunct of middle-class amusement and, to take an enormous leap upward in talent and seriousness, a writer like Norman Mailer becomes enmeshed with popular journalism and publicity.

The whole problem was anticipated many years ago by Trotsky when, writing about the Russian poet Esenin, he remarked that the poet thought to frighten the bourgeoisie by making scenes but as it turned out, the bourgeoisie was delighted, it adored scenes.

One thing alone will not delight the bourgeoisie: a decrease in income, a loss in social power, a threat to its property.

There is another sense in which cultural style dominates the behavior of the "new leftists." Some of them display a tendency to regard political—and perhaps all of—life as a Hemingwayesque contest in courage and rectitude. People are constantly being tested for endurance, bravery, resistance to temptation, and if found inadequate, are denounced for having "copped out." Personal endurance thus becomes the substance of, and perhaps even a replacement for, political ideas.

Now this can be a valid and serious way of looking at things, especially in extreme situations: which is, of course, what Hemingway had in mind. Among civil rights workers in the deep South such a vision of life reflects the ordeal they must constantly face; they *are* under extreme pressure and their courage *is* constantly being tested. Yet their situation cannot be taken as a model for the political life of the country as a whole. If one wants to do more than create a tiny group of the heroic, the tested, and the martyred, their style of work will not suffice. If one wants to build a movement in which not everyone need give "the whole of their lives," then the suspicion and hostility such an outlook is bound to engender toward the somewhat less active and somewhat less committed can only be damaging. For in effect, if not intent, it is a strategy of exclusion, leaving no place for anyone but the vanguard of the scarred.

It is, at times, a strategy of exclusion in a still more troubling sense: it reduces differences of opinion to grades of moral rectitude. If, for example, you think Martin Luther King or Bayard Rustin wrong in regard to certain tactical matters; if you disagree with what Rustin proposed at the Democratic national convention in 1964 and what King did in Selma, then you call into question their loyalty and commitment: you charge them with "copping out" or "fooling with the power structure." This approach makes it impossible to build a movement and, in the long run, even to maintain a sect.

B. Domestic Politics. A division of opinion, still incipient and confused, has appeared among people in the radical, student, and civil rights movements. There are those who, in effect, want to "go it alone," refusing to have anything to do with "the Establishment," and those who look forward to creating a loose coalition of Negro, labor, liberal, and church groups in order to stretch the limits of the welfare state. To an inexperienced eye, this may suggest a division between the more and less radical; but it is not. Radicalism is not a quantity.

The "go it alone" tendency in the civil rights movement starts from a recognition that the obstacles to success are enormous. It sees no forces within the society that could provide a new social dynamic. It shares with the liberals the questionable assumption that everyone in our society, except perhaps the bottom-dog poor, is bound to it by ties of material satisfaction. The labor movement is mired in its own fat; the ministers are Sunday allies; the liberals are two-faced, unreliable, perhaps cowards. What remains is a strategy of lonely assault, which must necessarily lead to shock tactics and desperation.

For if the above estimate of the American situation is valid, if there is so little possibility of a new social dynamism arising from or within its major social segments, then the outlook of the Black Muslims has to be acknowledged as persuasive. For obviously an estimate which sees major reforms as unlikely makes a traditional revolutionary overthrow seem still more unlikely; and the talk among irresponsibles about "guerrilla warfare in America" is mere self-indulgence since guerrilla warfare can succeed only when a large portion or a majority of the population is profoundly disaffected, something certainly not true in the United States. Consequently—the logic of this argument moves inexorably—there is nothing left for American Negroes but the separatism of the Muslims.

Unless, of course, one turns to the tactic of shock, inducing such misadventures as the 1964 stall-ins at the World's Fair or the Triborough Bridge fiasco. Neither of these demonstrations had a precise objective, neither had any way of measuring achievement, accumulating allies, registering victory. Such methods, born of desperation, could only cut off the dedicated minority of civil rights activists from their white allies and, more important, from the mass of Negroes.

Now it is not our business to give advice to the civil rights movement on tactical issues or to rush into taking positions about its inner disputes. It is not the business of anyone except those directly engaged. But about some larger aspects of its problem we can speak.

One issue has been posed simply but conveniently by a *Village Voice* reporter, Jack Newfield, who writes that Dr. King's "basic goal is integration, and SNCC's is a revolution." Earlier Newfield had described this revolution as being not against capitalist society but "against Brotherhood Weeks, factories called colleges, desperation called success, and sex twice a week."

What the people who talk about integration vs. revolution don't see is that to achieve integration, even in the limited terms presumably favored by Dr. King would indeed *be* a revolution, greater in consequence and impact than that effected by the rise of industrial unionism in the thirties.

Bayard Rustin puts the matter as follows:

> While most Negroes—in their hearts—unquestionably seek only to enjoy the fruits of American society as it now exists, their quest cannot objectively be satisfied within the framework of existing political and economic relations. The young Negro who would demonstrate his way into the labor market may be motivated by a thoroughly bourgeois ambition . . . but he will end up having to favor a great expansion of the public sector of the economy. . . .
> . . . the term revolutionary as I am using it, does not connote violence; it refers to the quantitative transformation of fundamental institutions, more or less rapidly, to the point where the social and economic structure . . . can no longer be said to be the same. . . . I fail to see how the [civil rights] movement can be victorious in the absence of radical programs for full employment, abolition of slums, the reconstruction of our educational system, new definitions of work and leisure. Adding up the cost of such programs, we can only conclude that we are talking about a refashioning of our political economy.

To this lucid analysis I would add only a word concerning the desire of Negroes "to enjoy the fruits of American society as it now exists." Certain intellectuals bemoan this desire because they don't want the Negro poor integrated into a "rotten middle-class society" and thereby end up with two cars, barbecue pits, and ulcers. Even more than wrong, these intellectuals seem to me snobbish. For Negroes should have just as much *right* to suburban pleasures as anyone else; they should be in a position just as much as the whites to choose the middle-class style of life. We need not approve, we can argue against that choice, but we are obliged to support their right to make it. And why not? I don't notice James Baldwin or LeRoi Jones taking vows of poverty. Nor should they. There is something a bit manipulative in the view that Negroes should be preserved from the temptations that, presumably, all the rest of us are entitled to. What's more, the Negroes themselves are far too experienced in the ways of the world to allow themselves to be cast in the role of sacrificial ascetic.

But let us return to "integration vs. revolution" and for the sake of the argument accept this formulation. Naturally enough—it's an old habit—we then opt for revolution; there remains only the little detail of who is going to make it.

Clearly, the vast majority of whites are in the grip of the Establishment. The liberals? Establishment. The churches? Establishment. The unions? Establishment. Intellectuals? Establishment.

But not only the whites, also the Negroes. Wilkins, Young, Powell, King, Farmer? The black Establishment. Rustin? He sold out to it.

Where then does that leave us? Well, some students . . . but can we be so sure of *them*? May they not in time decide to go back to graduate school, perhaps after discovering that "the people," in refusing to heed the revolutionary missions from the campus, are a rather hopeless quantity? What is left, then, is a handful . . . and where that handful must end is in despair, exhaustion, burning themselves out in the all-too-characteristic rhythm of American radicalism, which too often has tried to compensate for its powerlessness in reality by ferocity in words.

At this point I hear a voice crying out: "No, not just a vanguard of the desperate! We are going to organize the poor, the millions beneath the floor of society, those who have been mute and unrepresented for too long . . . and it is they who will form the basis of a new movement, beyond the pale of Establishment politics."

Good. The poor need to be organized, and more power to those who try. Every such effort, big or small, deserves the approval and support of socialists and liberals. But some problems remain. I leave aside the fact that twentieth-century history indicates a high rate of failure in previous efforts of this kind; that the unstructured, atomized, and often demoralized "underclass" has been the most resistant to organization. History need not always repeat itself, and perhaps this time the effort will succeed. No, the questions I would raise have to do not with failure but with success.

Imagine a campaign to organize the poor in a large city, undertaken by young people who will have no truck with the Establishment. Through hard work and devotion, they build up a group of, let's say, 150 people in a slum of mixed racial composition—a notable achievement. What happens next? The municipal "power structure" begins to pay some attention and decides either to smash the group as a dangerous nuisance or to lure away some of its leading members. If the local organization of the poor must now face attack, it would seem to have no choice but quickly to find some allies—in the unions, among churchmen, perhaps even in the American Jewish Congress, "establishmentarian" as all of these may seem. Suppose, however, the "power structure" decides to offer various inducements—jobs, improved housing—to some of the Negro members, and various other organizations, like the reform wing of the Democrats and certain trade unions, also enter the picture. What will the uncompromising, anti-Establishment leaders of the poor do now? Does not the reality of the situation require them to enter ne-gotiations, formally or informally, and thereby become involved in the socioeconomic life of the city? Can they remain exempt from it? And if so, how long do you suppose their followers will stay with them? For that matter, why should they? The goods and services that, with enough pressure, the "power structure" can be made to provide, the poor need, want, and deserve. Can one seriously suppose they will be exempt from such "temptations"? There is only one way to be certain the poor will remain beyond the temptations of our society, and that is to keep them hopelessly poor.

Nor is this quite a new problem. It was faced, in somewhat different form, years ago when revolutionists led trade unions and discovered that they had to sign agreements which in practice signified acquiescence in the bargaining arrangements between capital and labor within the confines of the status quo. Had these revolutionists, in the name of principle, refused to sign such agreements with the employers, they would have been sabotaging the functions of the union and would soon, deservedly, cease to be leaders.

The idea of coalition or realignment politics as advanced by socialists is not a rigid formula, or a plot to deliver our souls into the hands of the Establishment. It is meant as a strategy for energizing all those forces within the society that want to move forward toward an extension of the welfare state. In some places, such a loose coalition might take the form of politics outside the established institutions, like the Freedom Democratic Party of Mississippi—though that movement, if it is to suc-ceed, must begin to find allies within the white community. In other places, as in Texas, there is a coalition of labor, liberal, intellectual, and minority groups (Negro, Mexican) within the Democratic Party—and by all accounts a pretty good coalition. Can one say, as if all wisdom were bunched into our fists, that such a development should not be supported simply because it grows up within the framework of a major party?

If we are serious in our wish to affect American political life, we must learn to see the reality as it is. We have to seek out and prod the forces that exist. And I think it is a gross error—the kind of deep-seated conservatism that often alloys ultraradicalism—to say that everything in the major sectors of American society is static, sated, "Establishment." Who, twenty-five or thirty years ago, could have foreseen that Catholic priests and nuns would be marching into Montgomery? Who could have foreseen the thoroughgoing ferment in the American churches of which this incident is merely a symptom? Instead of scoffing at such people as civil rights "tourists," we ought to be seeking them out and trying to get them to move a little further, up north too.

And a word about the labor movement. Its failures, ills, and decline have been documented in great detail by American socialists—perhaps because we ourselves have not quite understood what its nature and possibilities are, preferring instead to nag away when it did not conform to our preconceptions. Right now, to be sure, the unions look pretty sluggish and drab. Still, two leaders, named David MacDonald and James Carey, have recently been toppled by membership votes (and when something like that happens to a trade-union leader in Russia, China, Cuba, North Vietnam, or Zanzibar, please let me know).

Bayard Rustin says: "The labor movement, despite its obvious faults, has been the largest single organized force in this country pushing for progressive social legislation." That is true, but not enough. What seems the static quality of the trade unions may be a phase of rest between the enormous achievements of the past forty years and possible achievements of the future. If the civil rights movement succeeds, may it not also enter such a phase? And do you suppose that the struggles a few decades ago to organize unions were any the less difficult, bloody, and heroic than those in the South today? And if it's a revolution in the quality of American life that you want, then have not the industrial unions come closer to achieving that for millions of people than any other force in the country?

We are speaking here partly of speculations, partly of hopes. None of us has any certain answer or magic formula by which to overcome the painful isolation of the radical movement: if there were such a thing, someone would by now have discovered it. We are all groping to find a way out of our difficulties. I don't wish to draw a hard-and-fast line between "realigners" and "go-it-aloners." There is room for both disagreement and cooperation. You want to organize the poor? Splendid. We propose certain sorts of coalitions? An essential part of such a coalition ought to be drawn from the poor you propose to organize. And in turn, if you're to keep them organized, you will have to engage in coalitions. Right now—let's be candid—you don't have very many of the poor and we don't have much of a coalition. Disagreements of this kind are fraternal, and can be tested patiently in experience.

The true line of division between democratic socialists and left authoritarians concerns not tactics, but basic commitments, values, the vision of what a good society should be. It concerns:

C. Politics and Freedom. The "new leftists" feel little attachment to Russia. Precisely as it has turned away from the more extreme and terroristic version of totalitarianism, so have they begun to find it unsatisfactory as a model: too Victorian, even "bourgeois." Nor are they interested in distinguishing among kinds of anti-Communism, whether of the right or the left.

When they turn to politics, they have little concern for precise or complex thought. A few years ago the "new leftists" were likely to be drawn to Communist China, which then seemed bolder than Khrushchev's Russia. But though the Mao regime has kept the loyalty of a small group of students, most of the "new leftists" seem to find it too grim and repressive. They tend to look for their new heroes and models among the leaders of underdeveloped countries. Figures like Lumumba, Nasser, Sukarno, Babu, and above all Castro attract them, suggesting the possibility of a politics not yet bureaucratized and rationalized. But meanwhile they neglect to notice, or do not care, that totalitarian and authoritarian dictatorship can set in even before a society has become fully modernized. They have been drawn to charismatic figures like Lumumba and Castro out of a distaste for the mania of industrial production which the Soviet Union shares with the United States; but they fail to see that such leaders of the underdeveloped countries, who in their eyes represent spontaneity and anarchic freedom, are themselves—perhaps unavoidably—infused with the same mania for industrial production.

Let me specify a few more of the characteristic attitudes among the "new leftists":

1. An extreme, sometimes unwarranted, hostility toward liberalism. They see liberalism only in its current version, institutional, corporate, and debased; but avoiding history, they know very little about the elements of the liberal tradition, which should remain valuable for any democratic socialist. For the "new leftists," as I have here delimited them, liberalism means Clark Kerr, not John Dewey; Max Lerner, not John Stuart Mill; Pat Brown, not George Norris. And thereby they would cut off the resurgent American radicalism from what is or should be, one of its sustaining sources: the tradition that has yielded us a heritage of civil freedoms, disinterested speculation, humane tolerance.

2. *An impatience with the problems that concerned an older generation of radicals.* Here the generational conflict breaks out with strong feelings on both sides, the older people feeling threatened in whatever they have been able to salvage from past experiences, the younger people feeling the need to shake off dogma and create their own terms of action.

Perhaps if we all try to restrain—not deny—our emotions, we can agree upon certain essentials. There are traditional radical topics which no one, except the historically minded, need trouble with. To be unconcerned with the dispute in the late twenties over the Anglo-Russian Trade Union Committee or the differences between Lenin and Rosa Luxemburg on the "national question"—well and good. These are not quite burning problems of the moment. But *some* of the issues hotly debated in the thirties do remain burning problems: in fact, it should be said for the anti-Stalinist left of the past several decades that it anticipated, in its own somewhat constricted way, a number of the problems (especially, the nature of Stalinism) which have since been widely debated by political scientists, sociologists, indeed, by all people concerned with politics. The nature of Stalinism and of post-Stalinist Communism is not an abstract or esoteric matter; the views one holds concerning these questions determine a large part of one's political conduct: and what is still more important, *they reflect one's fundamental moral values.*

No sensible radical over the age of thirty (something of a cutoff point, I'm told) wants young people merely to rehearse his ideas, or mimic her vocabulary, or look back upon his dusty old articles. On the contrary, what we find disturbing in some of the "new leftists" is that, while barely knowing it, they tend to repeat somewhat too casually the tags of the very past they believe themselves to be transcending. But we do insist that in regard to a few crucial issues, above all, those regarding totalitarian movements and societies, there should be no ambiguity, no evasiveness.

So that if some "new leftists" say that all the older radicals are equally acceptable or equally distasteful or equally inconsequential in their eyes; if they see no significant difference between, say, Norman Thomas and Paul Sweezy such as would require them to regard Thomas as a comrade and Sweezy as an opponent—then the sad truth is that they have not at all left behind them the old disputes, but, on the contrary, are still completely in their grip, though perhaps without being quite aware of what is happening to them. The issue of totalitarianism is neither academic nor merely historical; no one can seriously engage in politics without clearly and publicly defining an attitude toward it. I deliberately say "attitude" rather than "analysis," for while there can be a great many legitimate differences of analytic stress and nuance in discussing totalitarian society, morally there should be only a candid and sustained opposition to it.

3. *A vicarious indulgence in violence, often merely theoretic and thereby all the more irresponsible.* Not being a pacifist, I believe there may be times when violence is unavoidable; being a man of the twentieth century, I believe that a recognition of its necessity must come only after the most prolonged consideration, as an utterly last resort. To "advise" the Negro movement to adopt a policy encouraging or sanctioning violence, to sneer at Martin Luther King for his principled refusal of violence, is to take upon oneself a heavy responsibility—and if, as usually happens, taken lightly, it becomes sheer irresponsibility.

It is to be insensitive to the fact that the nonviolent strategy has arisen from Negro experience. It is to ignore the notable achievements that strategy has already brought. It is to evade the hard truth expressed by the Reverend Abernathy: "The whites have the guns." And it is to dismiss the striking moral advantage that nonviolence has yielded the Negro movement, as well as the turmoil, anxiety, and pain—perhaps even fundamental reconsideration—it has caused among whites in the North and the South.

There are situations in which Negroes will choose to defend themselves by arms against terrorist assault, as in the Louisiana towns where they have formed a club of "Elders" which patrols the streets peaceably but with the clear intent of retaliation in case of attack. The Negroes there seem to know what they are doing, and I would not fault them. Yet as a matter of general policy and upon a nationwide level, the Negro movement has chosen nonviolence: rightly, wisely, and heroically.

There are "revolutionaries" who deride this choice. They show a greater interest in ideological preconceptions than in the experience and needs of a living movement; and sometimes they are profoundly irresponsible, in that their true interest is not in helping to reach the goals chosen by the American Negroes, but is, rather, a social conflagration which would satisfy their apocalyptic yearnings even if meanwhile the Negroes were drowned in blood. The immediate consequence of such talk is a withdrawal from the ongoing struggles. And another consequence is to manufacture a cult out of figures like Malcolm X, who neither led nor won nor taught, and Robert Williams, the Negro leader who declared for violence and ended not with the Negroes in Selma, or at their strike in the hospitals of Westchester County, or on the picket line before the Atlanta Scripto plant (places where the kind of coalition we desire between Negro and labor was being foreshadowed), but by delivering shortwave broadcasts from Cuba.

4. *An unconsidered enmity toward something vaguely called the Establishment.* As the term "Establishment" was first used in England, it had the value of describing—which is to say, delimiting—a precise social group; as it has come to be used in the United States, it tends to be an all-purpose put-down. In England it refers to a caste of intellectuals with an Oxbridge education, closely related in values to the ruling class, and setting the cultural standards which largely dominate both the London literary world and the two leading universities.

Is there an Establishment in this, or any cognate, sense in the United States? Perhaps. There may now be in the process of formation, for the first time, such an intellectual caste; but if so, precise discriminations of analysis and clear boundaries of specification would be required as to what it signifies and how it operates. As the term is currently employed, however, it is difficult to know who, besides those merrily using it as a thunderbolt of opprobrium, is *not* in the Establishment. And a reference that includes almost everyone tells us almost nothing.

5. *An equally unreflective belief in "the decline of the West"*—apparently without the knowledge that, more seriously held, this belief has itself been deeply ingrained in Western thought, frequently in the thought of reactionaries opposed to modern rationality, democracy, and sensibility.

The notion is so loose and baggy, it means little. Can it, however, be broken down? If war is a symptom of this decline, then it holds for the East as well. If totalitarianism is a sign, then it is not confined to the West. If economics is a criterion, then we must acknowledge, Marxist predictions aside, that there has been an astonishing recovery in Western Europe. If we turn to culture, then we must recognize that in the West there has just come to an end one of the greatest periods in human culture—that period of "modernism" represented by figures like Joyce, Stravinsky, Picasso. If improving the life of the workers is to count, then the West can say something in its own behalf. And if personal freedom matters, then, for all its grave imperfections, the West remains virtually alone as a place of hope. There remains, not least of all, the matter of racial prejudice, and here no judgment of the West can be too harsh—so long as we remember that even this blight is by no means confined to the West, and that the very judgments we make draw upon values nurtured by the West.

But is it not really childish to talk about "the West" as if it were some indivisible whole we must either accept or reject without amendment? There are innumerable strands in the Western tradition, and our task is to nourish those which encourage dignity and freedom. But to envisage some global apocalypse that will end in the destruction of the West is a sad fantasy, a token of surrender before the struggles of the moment.

6. *A crude, unqualified anti-Americanism, drawing from every possible source, even if one contradicts another: the aristocratic bias of Eliot and Ortega, Communist propaganda, the speculations of Tocqueville, the* ressentiment *of postwar Europe, and so on.*

7. *An increasing identification with that sector of the "third world" in which "radical" nationalism and Communist authoritarianism merge.* Consider this remarkable fact: In the past decade there have occurred major changes in the Communist world, and many of the intellectuals in Russia and Eastern Europe have reexamined their assumptions, often coming to the conclusion, masked only by the need for caution, that democratic values are primary in any serious effort at socialist reconstruction. Yet at the very same time most of the "new leftists" have identified not with the "revisionists" in Poland or dissident Milovan Djilas in Yugoslavia— or even Tito. They identify with the harder, more violent, more dictatorial segments of the Communist world. And they carry this authoritarian bias into their consideration of the "third world," where they praise those rulers who choke off whatever weak impulses there may be toward democratic life.

About the problems of the underdeveloped countries, among the most thorny of our time, it is impossible to speak with any fullness here. Nor do I mean to suggest that an attack upon authoritarianism and a defense of democracy exhausts consideration of those problems; on the contrary, it is the merest beginning. But what matters in this context is not so much the problems themselves as the attitudes, reflecting a deeper political-moral bias, which the "new leftists" take toward such countries.

• Between the suppression of democratic rights and the justification or excuse the "new leftists" offer for such suppression there is often a very large distance, sometimes a complete lack of connection. Consider Cuba. It may well be true that United States policy became unjustifiably hostile toward the Castro regime at an early point in its history; but how is this supposed to have occasioned, or how is it supposed to justify, the suppression of democratic rights (including, and especially, those of all other left-wing tendencies) in Cuba? The apologists for Castro have an obligation to show what I think cannot be shown: the alleged close causal relation between United States pressure and the destruction of freedom in Cuba. Frequently, behind such rationales there is a tacit assumption that in times of national stress a people can be rallied more effectively by a dictatorship than by a democratic regime. But this notion—it was used to justify the suppression of political freedoms during the early Bolshevik years—is at the very least called into question by the experience of England and the United States during World War II. Furthermore, if Castro does indeed have the degree of mass support that his friends claim, one would think that the preservation of democratic liberties in Cuba would have been an enormously powerful symbol of self-confidence; would have won him greater support at home and certainly in other Latin-American countries; and would have significantly disarmed his opponents in the United States.

• We are all familiar with the "social context" argument: that for democracy to flourish there has first to be a certain level of economic development, a quantity of infrastructure, and a coherent national culture. As usually put forward in academic and certain authoritarian-left circles, it is a crudely deterministic notion, which I do not believe to be valid: for one thing, it fails to show how the suppression of even very limited political-social rights contributes, or is *in fact* caused by a wish, to solve these problems. (Who is prepared to maintain that Sukarno's suppression of the Indonesian Socialists and other dissident parties helped solve that country's economic or growth problems?) But for the sake of argument let us accept a version of this theory: let us grant what is certainly a bit more plausible, that a full or stable democratic society cannot be established in a country ridden by economic primitivism, illiteracy, disease, cultural disunion, and so on. The crucial question then becomes: can at least some measure of democratic rights be won or granted?—say, the right of workers to form unions or the right of dissidents within a single-party state to form factions and express their views? For if a richer socioeconomic development is a prerequisite of democracy, it must also be remembered that such democratic rights, as they enable the emergence of autonomous social groups, are also needed for socioeconomic development.

• Let us go even further and grant, again for the sake of argument, that in some underdeveloped countries authoritarian regimes may be necessary for a time. But even if this is true, which I do not believe it is, then it must be acknowledged as an unpleasant necessity, a price we are paying for historical crimes and mistakes of the past. In that case, radicals can hardly find their models in, and should certainly not become an uncritical cheering squad for, authoritarian dictators whose presence is a supposed unavoidability.

The "new leftists," searching for an ideology by which to rationalize their sentiments, can now find exactly what they need in a remarkable book recently translated from the French, *The Wretched of the Earth*. Its author, Frantz Fanon, is a Negro from Martinique who became active in the Algerian revolution. He articulates with notable power the views of those nationalist revolutionaries in the underdeveloped countries who are contemptuous of their native bourgeois leadership, who see their revolution being pushed beyond national limits and into their own social structure, who do not wish to merge with or become subservient to the Communists yet have no strong objection in principle to Communist methods and values.

Fanon tries to locate a new source of revolutionary energy: the peasants who, he says, "have nothing to lose and everything to gain." He deprecates the working class: in the Western countries it has been bought off, and in the underdeveloped nations it constitutes a tiny "aristocracy." What emerges is a curious version of Trotsky's theory of permanent revolution concerning national revolts in the backward countries which, to fulfill themselves, must become social revolutions. But with one major difference: Fanon assigns to the peasants and the urban declassed poor the vanguard role Trotsky had assigned to the workers.

What, however, has really happened in countries like Algeria? The peasantry contributes men and blood for an anticolonial war. Once the war is won, it tends to disperse, relapsing into local interests and seeking individual small-scale ownership of the land. It is too poor, too weak, too diffuse to remain or become the leading social force in a newly liberated country. The bourgeoisie, what there was of it, having been shattered and the working class pushed aside, what remains? Primarily the party of nationalism, led by men who are dedicated, uprooted, semieducated, and ruthless. The party rules, increasingly an independent force perched upon and above the weakened classes.

But Fanon is not taken in by his own propaganda. He recognizes the dangers of a preening dictator. He proposes, instead, that "the party should be the direct expression of the masses," and adds, "Only those underdeveloped countries led by revolutionary elites who have come up from the people can today *allow* the entry of the masses upon the scene of history" (emphasis added).

Fanon wants the masses to participate, yet throughout his book the single-party state remains an unquestioned assumption. But what if the masses do not wish to "participate"? And what if they are hostile to "the"—always "the"—party? Participation without choice is a burlesque of democracy; indeed, it is an essential element of a totalitarian or authoritarian society, for it means that the masses of people act out a charade of involvement but are denied the reality of decision.

The authoritarians find political tendencies and representative men with whom to identify in the Communist world; so do we. We identify with the people who have died for freedom, like Imre Nagy, or who rot in prison, like Djilas. We identify with the "revisionists," those political *marranos* who, forced to employ Communist jargon, yet spoke out for a socialism democratic in character and distinct from both Communism and capitalism. As it happens, our friends in the Communist world are not in power; but since when has that mattered to socialists?

In 1957, at the height of the Polish ferment, the young philosopher Leszek Kolakowski wrote a brief article entitled "What Is Socialism?" It consisted of a series of epigrammatic sentences describing what socialism is not (at the moment perhaps the more immediate concern), but tacitly indicating as well what socialism should be. The article was banned by the Gomulka regime but copies reached Western periodicals. Here are a few sentences.

Socialism is not

A society in which a person who has committed no crime sits at home waiting for the police.

A society in which one person is unhappy because he says what he thinks, and another happy because he does not say what is in his mind.

A society in which a person lives better because he does not think at all.

A state whose neighbors curse geography.

A state which wants all its citizens to have the same opinions in philosophy, foreign policy, economics, literature, and ethics.

A state whose government defines its citizens' rights, but whose citizens do not define the government's rights.

A state in which there is private ownership of the means of production.

A state which considers itself solidly socialist because it has liquidated private ownership of the means of production.

A state which always knows the will of the people before it asks them.

A state in which the philosophers and writers always say the same as the generals and ministers, but always after them.

A state in which the returns of parliamentary elections are always predictable.

A state which does not like to see its citizens read back numbers of newspapers.

These negatives imply a positive, and that positive is a central lesson of contemporary history: the unity of socialism and democracy. To preserve democracy as a political mode without extending it into every crevice of social and economic life is to allow it to become increasingly sterile, formal, ceremonial. To nationalize an economy without enlarging democratic freedoms is to create a new kind of social exploitation. Radicals and liberals may properly and fraternally disagree about many other things; but upon this single axiom concerning the value of democracy, this conviction wrung from the tragedy of our age, politics must rest.

Beliefs of the Masters

In the fifties, perhaps even the early sixties, John Harrison's study of the politics of the great modern writers (*The Reactionaries*, 1967) would have raised a storm of debate among those concerned with literary criticism. Writers like Eliot, Yeats, and Lawrence were accredited culture heroes of the literary young, and attacks upon or even analyses of their political views were likely to be dismissed as gross, Marxistic or, most damning of all, "unliterary." When evidence was marshaled to show that these writers had flirted with authoritarian outlooks and movements, there would usually be two kinds of reply: first, that it didn't really matter since the political views of the great modernist writers were of small importance (an estimate not shared by these writers themselves), and second, that the political statements of poets and novelists had to be accorded a reading that avoids the sin of the literal and in which the usual criteria for judging an argument are relaxed in behalf of "the imagination." In the literary discussions of the 1950s, "the imagination" was allotted an absolute sovereignty, beyond challenge and sometimes beyond specification.

By now, all this has changed. Young people interested in literature

From *The New Republic* 157 (September 16, 1967):12.

have, so far as I can tell, no special concern for Eliot, Yeats, and Pound, though a few still celebrate Lawrence. They tend to look upon the literary "modernism" of the last seventy-five or one hundred years as a period tucked away in a dim past. Feeling no particular kinship with the masters of literary modernism, they experience little distress at learning that Pound was a propagandist for fascism, Yeats harbored authoritarian visions, and Eliot several times verged on or crossed into anti-Semitism.

For readers of my generation, however, such facts were painful. We looked upon "The Waste Land" as the voice of our age: it was more than a poem, more even than a great poem; it spoke for us in a profoundly intimate and authoritative way. How then could we reconcile ourselves to Eliot's nastiness about "Bleistein with a cigar" or his proclaimed admiration for Charles Maurras, the French theorist of authoritarianism? Dilemmas of this kind forced many critics into convolutions and ingenuities concerning "the problem of belief"—by which was meant, among other things, the problem of maintaining a separation, in analysis if not always in response, between the literary work itself and offensive doctrines that might animate or course through it.

Mr. Harrison's book comes, therefore, as a sharp reminder of unfinished business. The "problem of belief," like most intellectual difficulties, was never really resolved, nor could it be; what happened was that both writers and readers grew weary of it. Yet such questions have a way of lodging themselves in a corner of one's mind and breaking out again with renewed force. No sooner did *The Reactionaries* appear than several distinguished literary men—Philip Rahv, Stephen Spender, Denis Donoghue—wrote extended reviews in which they turned back to the politics of the modern masters. And reading Mr. Harrison's book has also brought me back to the passions of a decade or two ago.

What Mr. Harrison has done is to bring together material more or less familiar, material drawn from both the literary works and the public statements of Eliot, Yeats, Lawrence, Pound, and Wyndham Lewis, and then to offer speculations as to what drove writers of such eminence to opinions so appalling and inhumane. *The Reactionaries* is a civilized book, not a rant or a philippic; but finally it is not the book it ought to be. Mr. Harrison writes in that bluff and low-keyed manner which has recently been affected by English writers who consider themselves admirers of George Orwell, enemies of Establishment gentility, and stalwarts of hygienic provincialism. Since, however, Mr. Harrison has chosen to tackle a subject that is often beyond the reach of red-brick common sense, the result is a book inadequate to the problems it casts out. Nevertheless I am glad to have it, if only because it does raise questions which both the formalist critics of yesterday and the literary swingers of today prefer to avoid.

Yeats yearned for an aristocracy of spirit and perhaps blood, which would return Ireland to the dignity he associated with an age (not clearly located) of nobles and peasants united in mutual responsibility. He hated the commercial spirit:

> A levelling, rancorous, rational sort of mind
> That never looked out of the eyes of a saint
> Or out of a drunkard's eye.
>   All's Whiggery now,
> But we old men are massed against the world.

Yeats was never at ease with common humanity and his peasants were mostly creatures of fantasy. What stirred him was contempt for the petty egotism of the middle class, its calculations and lack of heroic temper. He was impatient with the patience of humanity, and like many other European intellectuals, he had no use for the sluggishness of flesh. For the creaky apparatus of the modern state he snapped out his distaste:

> A statesman is an easy man,
> He tells his lies by rote;
> A journalist makes up his lies
> And takes you by the throat;
> So stay at home and drink your beer
> And let the neighbors vote.

Yeats mourned the loss of "the old religion of the Irish with its magical view of nature, its unbounded sorrow at the universal victory of old age and decay, the ultimate rejection of nature by the lonely spirit of man." Hoping for an ordered hierarchical state that would be ruled by a natural aristocracy, he turned in 1932–33, not in action but sentiment, to the Blueshirts of O'Duffy, the leader of Irish fascism. "A fascist opposition is forming behind the scenes," he wrote. "There is so little in our stocking that we are ready at any moment to turn it inside out, and how can we not feel emulous when we see Hitler juggling with his sausage of stocking. Our chosen color is blue, and blue shirts are marching about all over the country."

The case of Eliot is more complicated. Possessed of a literary culture both more learned and more deracinated than that of Yeats, Eliot could not satisfy himself with the particularities, or the eccentricities, of a national tradition. In his most serious intellectual phase, Eliot wanted a return to the classical culture of Christian Europe; but he also understood, at least as well as his secular critics, that such a return was highly improbable. He was not nearly so ideological as Pound and he clung to fewer historical fantasies than Yeats; a more contemplative man than either, he had no interest in organized movements, with or without shirts. Yet his despair over the quality of the civilization in which he lived, his conviction that without religion all modern cultures must end in sterility and nihilism, and his own difficulties in establishing a firm grip upon the faith to which he aspired—all these led to outbreaks of what might be called "apocalyptic irritation," as for example in the disgraceful passage about the Jews in *After Strange Gods*. Whatever his other virtues—and they were notable—Eliot found it hard to ease his soul into Christian charity toward the slobs, sensualists, and slackminded agnostics he saw populating the modern world.

Intellectually, however, Eliot was far more serious than Yeats or Pound, a Midwestern provincial let loose in the inferno of Europe. Eliot had a better sense of the historical dynamics of mass society; he understood that the aspects of modern industrialism and urbanism he detested were probably irrevocable; and he therefore thought in terms not of mass movements or anointed leaders but of a saving remnant, a devoted semimonastic minority which would hold fast to the Christian word. Given the desperation of this project, it is hardly any wonder that Eliot lapsed into rhetorical excesses and occasional nastiness.

The other writers discussed by Mr. Harrison are, politically, less interesting. Pound was free of the snobbism and aristocratic pretensions of Eliot and Yeats, but except in regard to literary matters, he simply could not think. And Lawrence is also somewhat special: not really political at all. Much of what he cried forth—his blood cult, his bullying contempt for the weak, his painful effort to establish himself as a prophetic hero—seems to me intolerable. But while all this has its obvious political implications, Lawrence was so idiosyncratic a figure, and as a writer often so vibrantly attuned to human needs and depths, that it will not do simply to pin him with a political label.

What was it that drove many writers in the modernist era toward one or another form of authoritarianism? Mr. Harrison provides a clue when he suggests that they "were really interested in society only in so far as it would allow the arts to flourish." Eliot would largely have to be exempted from this charge, but in the main Mr. Harrison seems right. The "reactionaries" hoped that an authoritarian state would restore an earlier cultural grandeur, real or imaginary; they yearned for style in life and art, distinction in bearing, honor in relationships, decorum in conduct—all the versions of order modern society conspicuously lacks. They knew little about what fascism would mean, any more than most left-wing writers knew what Stalinism would mean; and with the exception of Pound they neither supported nor were actively involved with fascism once it came to power. To that extent, their records are somewhat better than those of certain writers who continued to defend Stalinism long after its criminal brutality had become obvious.

What can, however, be charged against the "reactionaries" is intellectual dilettantism, arrogance, and irresponsibility. Yeats would never have dared talk about metrics with the ignorance he showed in talking about politics, nor Pound about diction with the ignorance he showed about economics. They assumed that because they were eminent writers they had special qualifications for speaking on social topics. They said things that would have been laughed away if coming from anyone but famous writers. They arrogated to themselves an authority they had not earned. They played with fire and did not even know it. The detachment of a Joyce, even in the years when political choices were desperately needed, seems by comparison a stance of honor and humaneness. Years earlier Yeats had written:

> I think it better that in times like these
> A poet's mouth be silent, for in truth
> We have no gift to set a statesman right

But he did not remember or heed his own words.

Yet, this is by no means the whole story: the defense is still to be heard. In a formidable attack on Mr. Harrison's book in *Commentary* (August 1967), Denis Donoghue writes:

> Mr. Harrison cannot conceive of a profound case that might be directed against the kind of mass society which we have today, or the kind of democracy which determined English life between the wars. He does not understand the sense in which liberal democratic life is, as Pound called it, "a mess of mush." Or the forces which drove Yeats to write "Lapis Lazuli," or anyone at all to conceive "a sympathy with the abyss."

Fair enough. Mr. Harrison does not sufficiently grasp, and having been born in 1937 perhaps he cannot grasp, the justified revulsion which almost all the writers of the modernist generation felt toward bourgeois Europe. Surely this was a major source of their imaginative energy: Eliot's nightmare of the wasteland, Lawrence's horror before the English mining town, Yeats's contempt for an age that must "engender in the ditch."

These were the shared perceptions of the time: shared by writers of both left and right, by writers without politics, and even by such old-fashioned liberals as E. M. Forster. Insofar as the reaction of the modernist writers took a cultural form, it was extremely valuable for their criticism of bourgeois civilization. They enjoyed the vantage point of criticism from the rear, in the name of tried verities and proven glories; they had at their command the sediments of tradition; and they spoke for a sense of community which, no matter how illusory it may now seem, enabled them to dramatize the moral shoddiness of Europe. All of this hardly constitutes an adequate politics, and could easily lead, as in fact it did, to political delusion and adventurism, most notably through the assumption that the categories of the literary imagination could readily be transferred to political analysis. But for the "reactionary" writers simply as writers, the stance they took often brought critical strength and sharpness of perspective.

Still more can be said in their behalf. Mr. Harrison operates mostly with abstract ideas or details of a literary text; and he is ingenuous enough to claim that he can demonstrate "the relationship between the 'tendency' of these five writers and their literary style, also their literary principles." Were he in fact able to do this, he would become at one stroke the greatest critic of our time; but of course he cannot. Style is at once too impersonal, the consequence of a received tradition, and too personal, the signature of an individual, to permit any decisive correlation with political "tendency." There is, however, in the work of novelists and poets an intermediary area, between overarching ideology and local style, which has to do with their deepest sense of human existence: their biases, insights, emotions, barely articulated values. In trying to locate this area we speak, awkwardly but perhaps unavoidably, of a writer's vision, that quality of his work for the description of which ideological pattern is too gross and stylistic detail too fine. Precisely here did Eliot, Yeats, and Lawrence manifest their greatness as writers, in the sense of human dilemma and possibility embodied in their best work. What emerges in their poems and novels is often in conflict with their abstract statements, and almost always to the benefit of the poems and novels.

Having gone this far with Mr. Donoghue, I want to go a step farther and turn his argument against him. In the decade between the Paris Commune and World War II both right- and left-wing intellectuals were gravely mistaken—and morally at fault—in their contemptuous dismissal of liberalism. That the society which they saw as the tangible embodiment of bourgeois liberalism required the most scathing criticism, I do not for a moment question. But they failed utterly to estimate the limits of what was historically possible or relevant in their time, as they failed—more important—to consider what the consequences might be of their intemperate attacks upon liberalism. These attacks could never restore ancient glories, but they might help usher in modern barbarism. It was all very well to denounce bourgeois liberalism as a "mess of mush," for so it often was, and worse too; but to assault the vulnerable foundations of democracy meant to bring into play social forces repressive in a way the writers could not—or at least did not—foresee. There were, as it turned out, far worse things in the world than a "mess of mush."

Nor am I indulging in mere retrospective wisdom. Writers as vastly different as E. M. Forster and Bertrand Russell (in his *Theory and Practice of Bolshevism*) warned of the frightful consequences of that apocalyptic nihilism—that brutal haste to destroy democratic institutions and values but recently created and inherently precarious—which was shared by writers of both the far right and far left.

The society of bourgeois Europe, as everyone sensed, was overripe for social change. But the assumptions that such change required a trampling on liberal values in the name of hierarchical order or proletarian dictatorship and that liberal values were inseparable from cultural decadence and capitalist economy—these proved a disaster beyond reckoning. Beyond reckoning! In the joy and brutality of their verbal violence, the intellectuals did not realize how profound a stake they had in preserving the norms of liberalism. They felt free to sneer at liberalism because, in a sense, they remained within its psychological orbit: they could not really imagine its destruction and took for granted that they would continue to enjoy its shelter. Even the most authoritarian among them, on both right and left, could not foresee a situation in which *their* freedom as writers would be destroyed. Dreaming of natural aristocrats, they helped pave the way for maniac lumpen. They had inherited and then grotesquely magnified the critique of liberalism which had been a major intellectual activity of the nineteenth century; they joined to it a hostility toward "the mob," a disdain for the masses stifling and bored in the cities; but they failed utterly to consider that the assault upon liberalism might lead to unwished-for consequences, since this assault would sweep away both scruples and hopes in the tide of totalitarianism. There are times when the price of fecklessness runs high.

But is it not too much to ask that in an age of chaos and disintegration, writers honor the kind of distinctions I have here suggested? No, it is not too much.

Precisely their extreme awareness of the depths of crisis to which liberal bourgeois society had sunk should have led the "reactionaries"— and the radicals also—to see the absolute value of liberal norms and procedures, those norms and procedures which transcend and should survive any particular form of society. And in fact there were writers who remained true to the heritage of Western humanism, while they strove for a re-creation of Western society. Even so nonpolitical a man as Joyce grasped intuitively the need to reject the smelly little ortho-doxies of authoritarianism; he had no use for all those bullying leaders and movements. He remarked sardonically in 1934, "I am afraid poor Mr. Hitler will soon have few friends in Europe apart from my nephews, Masters W. Lewis and E. Pound"; and throughout his career he never lost his connection, however complicated and ironic, with ordinary hu-man existence. That is why, among all the modernist writers, he now seems the most humane and the most durable. Carrying experiment further than anyone, he could also break past the rigid liberations of experiment. Wyndham Lewis, that snarling authoritarian, attacked *Ulys-ses* for "plain-manism" and few words of praise count as much as this damnation.

I know that what I have been saying in these last few paragraphs goes against the dominant notions of the fifties and sixties, the new conservatism and the new leftism, both of which—for opposite but symmetrical reasons—refuse to make the essential distinction between transient bourgeois institutions and abiding values of liberal freedom. But I do not claim that what I have said is novel or exciting; I claim only that it is true.

A Grave and Solitary Voice:
An Appreciation of
Edwin Arlington Robinson

The centennial of Edwin Arlington Robinson passed—he was born on December 22, 1869—with barely a murmur of public notice. There were a few academic volumes of varying merit, but no recognition in our larger journals and reviews, for Robinson seems the kind of poet who is likely to remain permanently out of fashion. At first, thinking about this neglect, I felt anger, since Robinson seems to me one of the best poets we have had in this country. But then I came to see that perhaps it doesn't matter whether the writers we most care about receive their "due." Writers like Robinson survive in their work, appreciated by readers who aren't afraid to be left alone with an old book.

Robinson himself would hardly have expected any other fate, for he was not the sort of man to make demands on either this world or the next. Shy of all literary mobs, just managing to keep afloat through a mixture of stoicism and alcohol, he lived entirely for his poetry. Most of the time he was poor, a withdrawn and silent bachelor. He wrote "too much," and his *Collected Poems*, coming almost to fifteen hundred crowded pages, has a great deal of failed work. But a small portion is very fine, and a group of fifteen or twenty poems unquestionably great.

From *Harper's Magazine* 240, no. 1441 (June 1970).

This, to be sure, is not the received critical judgment—though a few critics, notably Conrad Aiken in some fine reviews of the 1920s and Yvor Winters in a splendid little book published in 1946, have recognized his worth. The public acclaim of a Robert Frost, however, Robinson could never hope to match; the approval of the avant-garde, when it came at all, came in lukewarm portions, since T. S. Eliot had declared his work to be "negligible" and that, for a time, was that. Robinson stood apart from the cultural movements of his day, so much so that he didn't even bother to *oppose* literary modernism: he simply followed his own convictions. He was one of those New England solitaries—great-grandsons of the Puritans, nephews of the Emersonians—whose lives seem pinched but who leave, in their stolid devotion to a task, something precious to the world.

The trouble in Robinson's life was mostly interior. Some force of repression, not exactly unknown to New England character, had locked up his powers for living by, or articulating openly, the feelings his poems show him to have had. Even in the poems themselves a direct release of passion or desire is infrequent; they "contain," or emerge out of, enormous depths of feeling, but it is a feeling pressed into oblique irony or disciplined into austere reflection. He was not the man to yield himself to what Henry James called "promiscuous revelation."

Among his obsessive subjects are solitude and failure, both drawn from his immediate experience and treated with a richness of complication that is unequaled in American poetry. For the insights Robinson offered on these grim topics, in poems such as "The Wandering Jew" and "Eros Turannos," he no doubt paid a heavy price in his own experience. But we should remember that, finally, such preoccupations are neither a regional morbidity nor a personal neurosis: they are among the inescapable themes of literature. In his own dry and insular way, Robinson shared in the tragic vision that has dominated the imagination of the West since the Greek playwrights. By the time he began to write, it had perhaps become impossible for a serious poet to compose a tragedy on the classical scale, and as a result his sense of the tragic, unable to reach embodiment in a large action, had to emerge—one almost says, leak through—as a melancholy contemplativeness.

At the age of twenty-two, Robinson could already write, half in wisdom and half in self-defense, sentences forming an epigraph to his whole career: "Solitude . . . tends to magnify one's ideas of individuality; it sharpens his sympathy for failure where fate has been abused and self demoralized; it renders a man suspicious of the whole natural plan, and leads him to wonder whether the invisible powers are a fortuitous issue of unguided cosmos. . . ."

Like Hawthorne and Melville before him, Robinson came from a family that had suffered both a fall in circumstances and a collapse of psychic confidence. To read the reliable biography by Herman Hagedorn is gradually to be drawn into a graying orbit of family nightmare, an atmosphere similar to that of a late O'Neill play. Tight-lipped quarrels, heavy drinking, failing investments, ventures into quack spiritualism and drugs—these were the matter of his youth. Hagedorn describes the few months before the death of the poet's father: The elder Robinson's "interest in spiritualism had deepened and, in the slow disintegration of his organism, detached and eerie energies seemed to be released. There were table rappings and once the table came off the floor, 'cutting my universe . . . clean in half'. . . . Of these last months with his father, he told a friend, 'They were a living hell.' "

Not much better were Robinson's early years in New York, where he slept in a hall bedroom and worked as a subway clerk. He kept writing and won some recognition, including help from President Theodore Roosevelt, who was impressed by one of Robinson's (inferior) poems but had the honesty to admit he didn't understand it. Toward the end of his career Robinson scored his one commercial success with *Tristram*, the least interesting of his three lengthy Arthurian poems. This success did not much affect his life or, for that matter, his view of life. He died in 1935, a victim of cancer. It is said that as Robinson lay dying one of his hangers-on approached him for a small loan: life, as usual, trying to imitate art.

2

The imprint of New England on Robinson's sensibility is strong, but it is not precise. By the time he was growing up in the river-town of Gardiner, Maine (the Tilbury Town of his poems), Puritanism was no longer a coherent religious force. It had become at best an ingrained and hardened way of life surviving beyond its original moment of strength. Yet to writers like Hawthorne and Robinson, the New England tradition left a rich inheritance: the assumption that human existence, caught in a constant inner struggle between good and evil, is inherently dramatic. It also left the habit of intensive scrutiny, at once proud and dust-humble, into human motives. Writers like Hawthorne and Robinson were no longer believers but since they still responded to what they had rejected, they found themselves in a fruitful dilemma. They did not wish entirely to shake off the strict moralism of the New England past; yet they were fascinated by the psychological study of behavior that would come to dominate twentieth-century literature and, meanwhile, was both a borrowing from nineteenth-century European Romanticism and a distillation of Puritan habits of mind. The best of the New England writers tried to yoke these two ways of regarding the human enterprise, and if their attempt is dubious in principle, it yielded in practice a remarkable subtlety in the investigation of motives. As for Emersonianism, by the time Robinson was beginning to think for himself it was far gone in decay, a mist of genteel idealism.

Robinson borrowed from both traditions. His weaker poems reveal an Emersonian yearning toward godhead and transcendence, which is an experience somewhat different from believing in God. His stronger poems share with the Puritans a cast of mind that is intensely serious, convinced of the irreducibility of moral problems, and devoted to nuance of motive with the scrupulosity his grandfathers had applied to nuance of theology. Even in an early, unimpressive sonnet like "Credo," which begins in a dispirited tone characteristic of much late-nineteenth-century writing,

> I cannot find my way: there is no star
> In all the shrouded heavens anywhere

Robinson still felt obliged to end with an Emersonian piety:

> I know the far-sent message of the years,
> I feel the coming glory of the Light.

Whenever that "Light" begins to flicker, so tenuous a symbol for the idea of transcendence, it is a sure sign of trouble in Robinson's poems. A straining toward an optimism in which he has no real conviction, it would soon be overshadowed, however, by Robinson's darkening fear, as he later wrote in a long poem called *King Jasper*, that

> No God,
> No Law, no Purpose, could have hatched for sport
> Out of warm water and slime, a war for life
> That was unnecessary, and far better
> Never had been—if man, as we behold him,
> Is all it means.

Such lines suggest that Robinson's gift was not for philosophizing in verse; he was eminently capable of thinking as a poet, but mainly through his arrangement of dramatic particulars and casual reflections he wove in among them. What makes Robinson's concern with God and the cosmos important is not its doctrinal content, quite as vague and dispirited as that of other sensitive people of his time, but the way in which he would employ it as the groundwork for his miniature dramas.

It is an advantage for a writer to have come into relation with a great tradition of thought, even if only in its stages of decay, and it can be a still greater advantage to struggle with the problem of salvaging elements of wisdom from that decayed tradition. For while a culture in decomposition may limit the scope of its writers and keep them from the highest achievement, it offers special opportunities for moral drama to those who can maintain their bearing. The traps of such a moment are obvious: nostalgia, at one extreme, and sensationalism, at the other. Most of the time Robinson was strong enough to resist these temptations, a portion of the old New England steel persisting in his soul; or perhaps he could resist them simply because he was so entirely absorbed in his own sense of the human situation and therefore didn't even trouble about the cultural innovations of his time. He made doubt into a discipline, and failure into an opening toward compassion.

3

Many of Robinson's shorter poems—lyrics, ballads, sonnets, dramatic narratives—are set in Tilbury Town, his down-east locale where idlers dream away their lives in harmless fantasy, mild rebels suffer the resistance of a community gone stiff, and the tragedy of personal isolation seems to acquire a universal character. Other nineteenth-century writers had of course employed a recurrent setting in their work, and later, Faulkner would do the same with Yoknapatawpha County. Yet Robinson's use of Tilbury Town is rather different from what these writers do: he makes no attempt to fill out its social world, he cares little about details of place and moment, he seems hardly to strive for historical depth. Tilbury Town is more an atmosphere than a setting, it is barely provisioned, and it serves to suggest less a community than a lack of historical continuity. The foreground figures in these poems are drawn with two or three synoptic strokes, but Tilbury Town itself is shadowy, no longer able to bind its people. Robinson eyes it obliquely, half in and half out of its boundaries, a secret sharer taking snapshots of decline. He seems always to be signaling a persuasion that nothing can be known with certainty and the very thought of direct assertion is a falsehood in the making.

Some of these Tilbury pieces, as Robinson once remarked, have been "pickled in anthological brine." Almost "everybody" knows "Miniver Cheevy" and "Richard Corey," sardonic vignettes of small-town character, Yankee dropouts whose pitiable condition is contrasted—in quirky lines and comic rhymes—with their weak fantasies. These are far from Robinson's best poems, but neither are they contemptible. In the sketch of poor Miniver, who "loved the days of old," there are flashes of cleverness:

> Miniver mourned the ripe renown
> That made so many a name so fragrant;
> He mourned Romance, now on the town,
> And Art, a vagrant.

Such pieces lead to better ones of their kind, such as the tautly written sonnets about Reuben Bright, the butcher who tears down his slaughterhouse when told his wife must die, and Aaron Stark, a miser with "eyes like little dollars in the dark." My experience in teaching these poems is that students trained to flounder in *The Waste Land* will at first condescend, but when asked to read the poems again, will be unsettled by the depths of moral understanding within them.

The finest of Robinson's sonnets of character is "The Clerks." Describing a return to Tilbury Town, the poet meets old friends, figures of "a shopworn brotherhood," who now work as clerks in stores. The opening octet quietly evokes this scene, and then in the closing sestet Robinson widens the range of his observation with a powerful statement about the weariness of slow defeat:

> And you that ache so much to be sublime,
> And you that feed yourselves with your descent,
> What comes of all your visions and your fears?
> Poets and kings are but the clerks of Time,
> Tiering the same dull webs of discontent,
> Clipping the same sad alnage of the years.

Without pretending to close analysis, I would like to glance at a few of the verbal refinements in these six lines. The opening "ache . . . to be sublime" has its workaday irony that prepares for the remarkable line which follows: to "feed" with "your descent" is a characteristic Robinsonian turn, which in addition to the idea of consuming oneself through age suggests more obliquely that indulgence in vanity which claims distinction for one's decline. Poets and kings who are "clerks of Time" are helplessly aligned with the Tilbury clerks, yet Robinson sees that even in the democracy of our common decay we cling to our trifle of status. For in the "dull webs of discontent" which form the fragile substance of our lives, we still insist on "tiering" ourselves. Coming in the penultimate line, the word "tiering" has ironic thrust: how long can a tier survive as a web? And in the concluding line Robinson ventures one of his few deviations from standard English, in the use of "alnage," a rare term meaning a measure of cloth, that is both appropriate to the atmosphere of waste built up at the end and overwhelming as it turns us back to the "shop-worn" clerks who are Robinson's original donnée.

Now for readers brought up in the modernist tradition of Eliot and Stevens, these short poems of Robinson's will not yield much excitement. They see in such poems neither tangle nor agony, brilliance nor innovation. But they are wrong, for the Tilbury sonnets and lyrics do, in their own way, represent a significant innovation: Robinson was the first American poet of stature to bring commonplace people and commonplace experience into our poetry. Whitman had invoked such people and even rhapsodized over them, but as individuals with warm blood they are not really to be found in his pages. Robinson understood that "even the happy mortals we term ordinary or commonplace act their own mental tragedies and live a far deeper and wider life than we are inclined to believe possible. . . ."

The point bears stressing because most critics hail poets like Eliot and Stevens for their innovations in metrics and language while condescending toward Robinson as merely traditional. Even if that were true, it would not, of course, be a sufficient reason for judgments either favorable or hostile; but it is not true. Robinson never thought of himself as a poetic revolutionary, but like all important poets, he helped enlarge for those who came after him the possibilities of composition.

His dramatic miniatures in verse—spiritual dossiers of American experience, as someone has nicely called them—remind one a little of Hawthorne, in their ironic undercurrents and cool explorations of vanity, and a little of James, in their peeling away of psychic pretense and their bias that human relationships are inherently a trap. Yet it would be unjust to say that Robinson was a short-story writer who happened to write verse, for it is precisely through traditional forms—precisely through his disciplined stanzas, regular meters, and obbligatos of rhyme—that he released his vision. Robinson's language seldom achieves the high radiance of Frost, and few of his short poems are as beautifully complexioned as Frost's "Spring Pools" or "The Most of It." But in Robinson there are sudden plunges into depths of experiences and then stretches of earned contemplativeness that Frost can rarely equal. Here, for example, is the octet of a Robinson sonnet, "The Pity of the Leaves," that deals with an experience—an old man alone at night with his foreboding of death—which in "An Old Man's Winter Night" Frost also treated memorably but not, I think, as well:

Vengeful across the cold November moors,
Loud with ancestral shame there came the bleak
Sad wind that shrieked and answered with a shriek,
Reverberant through lonely corridors.
The old man heard it; and he heard, perforce,
Words out of lips that were no more to speak—
Words of the past that shook the old man's cheek
Like dead remembered footsteps on old floors.

It is always to "the slow tragedy of haunted men" that Robinson keeps returning. One of his greatest lyrics on this theme, the kind of hypnotic incantation that *happens* to a poet once or twice if he is lucky, is "Luke Havergal": a grieving man hears the voice of his dead love and it draws him like an appetite for death, quiet and enclosing.

The greatest of these Tilbury poems, and one of the greatest poems about the tragedy of love in our language, is "Eros Turannos." Yvor Winters aptly calls it "a universal tragedy in a Maine setting." It deals with a genteel and sensitive woman, advancing in years and never, apparently, a startling beauty, who has married or otherwise engaged herself to a charming wastrel with a taste for the finer things of life:

She fears him, and will always ask
    What fated her to choose him;
She meets in his engaging mask
    All reasons to refuse him. . . .

With a fierce concentration of phrase, the poem proceeds to specify the entanglements in which these people trap themselves, the moral confusions and psychic fears. The concluding stanza reaches a wisdom about the human lot such as marks Robinson's poetry at its best. Those, he writes, who with the god of love have striven,

Not hearing much of what we say,
    Take what the god has given;
Though like waves breaking it may be,
Or like a changed familiar tree,
Or like a stairway to the sea
    Where down the blind are driven.

Thinking of such poems and trying to understand how it is that in their plainness they can yet seem magnificent, one finds oneself falling back on terms like "sincerity" and "honesty." They are terms notoriously inadequate and tricky, yet inescapable in discussing poets like Robinson and Thomas Hardy. It is not, after all, as if one wants to say about more brilliant poets like Eliot and Yeats that they are insincere or lacking in honesty; of course not. What one does want to suggest is that in poems like Robinson's "Eros Turannos" and "Hillcrest," as in Hardy's "The Going" and "At Castle Boterel," there is an abandonment of all pretense and pose, all protectiveness and persona. At such moments the poet seems beyond decoration and defense; he leaves himself vulnerable, open to the pain of his self; he cares nothing for consolation; he looks at defeat and does not blink.

4

Robinson was also a master of a certain genre poem, Wordsworthian in tone and perhaps source, which Frost also wrote but not, in my judgment, as well. These are poems about lost and aging country people, mostly in New England: "Isaac and Archibald," "Aunt Imogen," and "The Poor Relation." The very titles are likely to displease readers whose hearts tremble before titles like "Leda and the Swan," "The Idea of Order at Key West," and "The Bridge."

"Isaac and Archibald" is the masterpiece of this group, a summer idyll tinged with shadows of death, told by a mature man remembering himself as a boy who spent an afternoon with two old farmers, lifelong friends, each of whom now frets that the other is showing signs of decay. The verse is exquisite:

> So I lay dreaming of what things I would,
> Calm and incorrigibly satisfied
> With apples and romance and ignorance,
> And the still smoke from Archibald's clay pipe.
> There was a stillness over everything,
> As if the spirit of heat had laid its hand
> Upon the world and hushed it; and I felt
> Within the mightiness of the white sun
> That smote the land around us and wrought out
> A fragrance from the trees, a vital warmth
> And fulness for the time that was to come,
> And a glory for the world beyond the forest.
> The present and the future and the past,
> Isaac and Archibald, the burning bush,
> The Trojans and the walls of Jericho,
> Were beautifully fused; and all went well

Till Archibald began to fret for Isaac
And said it was a master day for sunstroke.

Another kind of poem at which Robinson showed his mastery, one
that has rarely been written in this country, is the dramatic monologue
of medium length. "Rembrandt to Rembrandt," "The Three Taverns"
(St. Paul approaching Rome), and "John Brown" are the best examples.
The pitfalls of this genre are notorious: an effort to capture the historic
inflections of the speaker's voice, so that both conciseness of speech
and poetic force are sacrificed to some idea of verisimilitude; a tendency
toward linguistic exhibitionism, blank verse as a mode of preening; and
a lack of clear focusing of intent, so that the immediate experience of
the speaker fails to take on larger resonance. Robinson mostly transcends
these difficulties. He chooses figures at moments of high crisis, Rembrandt as he plunges into dark painting, St. Paul as he ruminates upon
his forthcoming capture, and John Brown as he readies himself for
hanging. The result is serious in moral perception, leading always to the
idea of abandonment of the self, and dignified in tone, for Robinson
had little gift for colloquial speech and was shrewd enough to maintain
a level of formal diction.

It is Frost who is mainly honored for this kind of dramatic poem,
but a sustained comparison would show, I think, the superiority of
Robinson's work. Though not nearly so brilliant a virtuoso as Frost,
Robinson writes from a fullness of experience and a tragic awareness
that Frost cannot equal. Frost achieves a cleaner verbal surface, but
Robinson is more abundant in moral detail and insight.

There remains finally a word to be said about Robinson's Arthurian
poems, *Merlin, Lancelot,* and *Tristram,* the first two of which are very
considerable productions. I am aware of straining my readers' credulity
in saying that *Merlin* and *Lancelot,* set in the court of King Arthur and
dealing with the loves and intrigues of his knights, are profound explorations of human suffering.

Tennyson's *Idylls of the King,* dealing with the same materials, is
mainly a pictorial representation of waxen figures, beautiful in the way
a tapestry might be but not gripping as drama. Robinson's Guinevere
and Lancelot, however, are errant human beings separated from us only
by costume and time; his Merlin is an aging man of worldly power and
some wisdom who finds himself drawn to the temptations of private
life. Long poems are bound to have flaws, in this case excessive talk and
a spun-thin moral theorizing that can become tedious. And any effort
at sustained blank verse will, by now, lead to padding and looseness of
language. Still, these are poems for mature men and women who know

that in the end we are all as we are, vulnerable and mortal. Here Merlin speaks at the close of his career, remembering his love:

> Let her love
> What man she may, no other love than mine
> Shall be an index of her memories.
> I fear no man who may come after me,
> And I see none. I see her, still in green,
> Beside the fountain. I shall not go back . . .
> If I come not,
> The lady Vivian will remember me,
> And say: 'I knew him when his heart was young,
> Though I have lost him now. Time called him home,
> And that was as it was; for much is lost
> Between Broceliande and Camelot.'

In my own experience Robinson is a poet who grows through re-reading, or perhaps it would be better to say, one grows into being able to reread him. He will never please the crowds, neither the large ones nor the small ones. All that need be said about Robinson he said himself in a sonnet about George Crabbe, the eighteenth-century English poet who also wrote about commonplace people in obscure corners of the earth:

> Whether or not we read him, we can feel
> From time to time the vigor of his name
> Against us like a finger for the shame
> And emptiness of what our souls reveal
> In books that are as altars where we kneel
> To consecrate the flicker, not the flame.

The New York Intellectuals

1969

The social roots of the New York writers are not hard to trace. With a few delightful exceptions—a tendril from Yale, a vine from Seattle—they stem from the world of the immigrant Jews, either workers or petty bourgeois.* They come at a moment in the development of immigrant Jewish culture when there is a strong drive not only to break out of the ghetto but also to leave behind the bonds of Jewishness entirely. Earlier generations had known such feelings, and through many works of fiction, especially those by Henry Roth, Michael Gold, and Daniel Fuchs, one

From *Commentary* 46 (October 1968):4.

* In placing this emphasis on the Jewish origins of the New York intellectuals, I am guilty of a certain—perhaps unavoidable—compression of realities. Were I writing a book rather than an essay, I would have to describe in some detail the relationship between the intellectuals who came on the scene in the thirties and those of earlier periods. There were significant ties between *Partisan Review* and the *Dial, Politics* and the *Masses*. But I choose here to bypass this historical connection because I wish to stress what has been distinctive.

A similar qualification has to be made concerning intellectuals associated with this milieu but not Jewish. I am working on the premise that in background and style there was something decidedly Jewish about the intellectuals who began to cohere as a group around *Partisan Review* in the late thirties—and one of the things that was "decidedly Jewish" was that most were of Jewish birth! Perhaps it ought to be said, then, that my use of the phrase "New York intellectuals" is simply a designation of convenience, a shorthand for what might awkwardly be spelled out as "the intellectuals of New York who began to appear in the thirties, most of whom were Jewish."

can return to the classic pattern of a fierce attachment to the provincialism of origins as it becomes entangled with a fierce eagerness to
plunge into the Gentile world of success, manners, freedom.

The New York intellectuals were the first group of Jewish writers
to come out of the immigrant milieu who did not define themselves
through a relationship, nostalgic or hostile, to memories of Jewishness.
They were the first generation of Jewish writers for whom the recall of
an immigrant childhood does not seem to have been completely overwhelming. That this severance from Jewish immigrant sources would
later come to seem a little suspect is another matter. All I wish to stress
here is that, precisely at the point in the thirties when the New York
intellectuals began to form themselves into a loose cultural-political
tendency, Jewishness as idea and sentiment played no significant role
in their expectations—apart, to be sure, from a bitter awareness that no
matter what their political or cultural desires, the sheer fact of their
recent emergence had still to be regarded as an event within Jewish
American life.

For decades the life of the East European Jews, in both the old
country and the new, might be compared to a tightly gathered spring,
trembling with unused force, which had been held in check until the
climactic moment of settlement in America. Then the energies of generations came bursting out, with an ambition that would range from
pure to coarse, and indeed would mix all these together, but finally—
this ambition—would count for more as an absolute release than in any
of its local manifestations. What made Sammy run was partly that his
father and his father's father had been bound hand and foot. And in all
the New York intellectuals there was a fraction of Sammy.

The youthful experiences described by Alfred Kazin in his autobiography are, apart from his distinctive outcroppings of temperament,
more or less typical of the experiences of many New York intellectuals—
except for the handful who involved themselves deeply in the radical
movement. It is my impression, however, that Kazin's affectionate stress
on the Jewish sources of his experience is mainly a feeling of retrospect,
mainly a recognition that no matter how you might try to shake off your
past, it would still cling to your speech, gestures, skin, and nose; it would
still shape, with a thousand subtle movements, the way you did your
work and raised your children. In the thirties, however, it was precisely
the idea of discarding the past, breaking away from families, traditions,
and memories which excited intellectuals.

The Jewish immigrant world branded upon its sons and daughters
marks of separateness even while encouraging them to dreams of universalism. This subculture may have been formed to preserve ethnic

continuity, but it was a continuity that would reach its triumph in self-disintegration. It taught its children both to conquer the Gentile world and to be conquered by it, both to leave an intellectual impress and to accept the dominant social norms. By the twenties and thirties the values dominating Jewish immigrant life were often secular, radical, and universalist, and if these were conveyed through a parochial vocabulary, they nonetheless carried some remnants of European culture. Even as they were moving out of a constricted immigrant milieu, the New York intellectuals were being prepared by it for the tasks they would set themselves. They were being prepared for the intellectual vocation as one of assertiveness, speculation, and freewheeling; for the strategic maneuvers of a vanguard, at this point almost a vanguard in the abstract, with no ranks following in the rear; and for the union of politics and culture, with the politics radical and the culture cosmopolitan. What made this goal all the more attractive was that the best living American critic, Edmund Wilson, had triumphantly reached it. The author of both *The Triple Thinkers* and *To the Finland Station*, he gave this view of the intellectual life a special authority.

That the literary avant-garde and the political left were not really comfortable partners would become clear with the passage of time; in Europe it already had. But during the years the New York intellectuals began to appear as writers and critics there was a feeling in the air that a union of *the advanced*—critical consciousness and political conscience—could be forged.

Throughout the thirties the New York intellectuals believed, somewhat naively, that this union was not only a desirable possibility but also a tie both natural and appropriate. Except, however, for the surrealists in Paris—and it is not clear how seriously this instance should be taken—the paths of political radicalism and cultural modernism have seldom met.

The history of the West in the last century offers many instances in which Jewish intellectuals played an important role in the development of political radicalism; but almost always this occurred when there were sizable movements, with the intellectuals serving as propagandists and functionaries of a party. In New York, by contrast, the intellectuals had no choice but to begin with a dissociation from the only significant radical movement in this country, the Communist Party. What for European writers like Koestler, Silone, and Malraux would be the end of the road was here a beginning. In a fairly short time, the New York writers found that the meeting of political and cultural ideas which had stirred them to excitement could also leave them stranded. Radicalism, in both its daily practice and ethical biases, proved inhospitable to certain aspects of modernism—and not always, I now think, mistakenly. Literary modernism often had a way of cavalierly dismissing the world of daily existence, a world that remained intensely absorbing to the New York writers. Literary modernism could sometimes align itself with reactionary movements, an embarrassing fact that required either tortuous explanations or complex dissociations. The New York writers discovered, as well, that their relationship to modernism as a purely literary phenomenon was less authoritative and more ambiguous than they had wished to feel. The great battles for Joyce, Eliot, and Proust had been fought in the twenties and mostly won; and now, while clashes with entrenched philistinism might still take place, they were mostly skirmishes or mopping-up operations (as in the polemics against the transfigured Van Wyck Brooks). The New York writers came at the end of the modernist experience, just as they came at what may yet have to be judged the end of the radical experience, and as they certainly came at the end of the immigrant Jewish experience. One shorthand way of describing their situation, a cause of both their feverish intensity and their recurrent instability, is to say that *they came late.*

During the thirties and forties their radicalism was anxious, problematic, and beginning to decay at the very moment it was adopted. They had no choice: the crisis of socialism was worldwide, profound, with no end in sight, and the only way to avoid that crisis was to bury oneself, as a few did, in left-wing sects. Some of the New York writers had gone through the "political school" of Stalinism, a training in coarseness from which not all recovered; some had even spent a short time in the organizational coils of the Communist Party. By 1936, when the anti-Stalinist *Partisan Review* was conceived, the central figures of that moment—Philip Rahv, William Phillips, Sidney Hook—had shed whatever sympathies they once felt for Stalinism, but the hope that they could find another ideological system, some cleansed version of Marxism associated perhaps with Trotsky or Rosa Luxemburg, was doomed to failure. Some gravitated for a year or two toward the Trotskyist group, but apart from admiration for Trotsky's personal qualities and dialectical prowess, they found little satisfaction there; no version of orthodox Marxism could retain a hold on intellectuals who had gone through the trauma of abandoning the Leninist weltanschauung and had experienced the depth to which the politics of this century, notably the rise of totalitarianism, called into question Marxist categories. From now on, the comforts of system would have to be relinquished.

Though sometimes brilliant in expression and often a stimulus to cultural speculation, the radicalism of the New York intellectuals during the thirties was not a deeply grounded experience. It lacked roots in a popular movement which might bring them into relationship with the complexities of power and stringencies of organization. From a doctrine it became a style, and from a style a memory. It was symptomatic that the *Marxist Quarterly*, started in 1937 and probably the most distinguished Marxist journal ever published in this country, could survive no more than a year. The differences among its founders, some like James Burnham holding to a revolutionary Marxist line and others like Sidney Hook and Lewis Corey moving toward versions of liberalism and social democracy, proved too severe for collaboration. And even the radicalism of the *Partisan Review* editors and writers during its vivid early years—how deeply did it cut, except as a tool enabling them to break away from Marxism?

2

Yet if the radicalism of the New York intellectuals seems to have been without much political foundation or ideological strength, it certainly played an important role in their own development. For the New York writers, and even, I suspect, those among them who would later turn sour on the whole idea of radicalism (including the few who in the mid-sixties would try to erase the memory of having turned sour), the thirties represented a time of intensity and fervor, a reality or illusion of engagement, a youth tensed with conviction: so that even Dwight Macdonald, who at each point in his life made a specialty out of mocking his previous beliefs, could not help displaying tender feelings upon remembering his years, God help us, as a "revolutionist." The radicalism of the thirties gave the New York intellectuals their distinctive style: a flair for polemic, a taste for the grand generalization, an impatience with what they regarded (often parochially) as parochial scholarship, an internationalist perspective, and a tacit belief in the unity—even if a unity beyond immediate reach—of intellectual work.

By comparison with competing schools of thought, the radicalism of the anti-Stalinist left, as it was then being advanced in *Partisan Review*, seemed cogent, fertile, alive: it could stir good minds to argument, it could gain the attention of writers abroad, it seemed to offer a combination of system and independence. With time the anti-Stalinist intellectuals came to enjoy advantages somewhat like those which have enabled old radicals to flourish in the trade unions: they could talk faster than anyone else, they were quicker on their feet.

Yet in fairness I should add that this radicalism did achieve something of substantial value in the history of American culture. It helped destroy Stalinism as a force in our intellectual life, and also those varieties of populist sentimentality which the Communist movement of the late thirties exploited with notable skill. If certain sorts of manipulative softheadedness have been all but banished from serious American writing, and the kinds of rhetoric once associated with Archibald MacLeish and Van Wyck Brooks cast into permanent disrepute, at least some credit for this ought to go to the New York writers.

It has recently become fashionable, especially in the pages of the *New York Review of Books,* to sneer at the achievements of the anti-Stalinist left by muttering darkly about "the Cold War." But we ought to have enough respect for the past to avoid telescoping several decades. The major battle against Stalinism as a force within intellectual life, and in truth a powerful force, occurred before anyone heard of the Cold War; it occurred in the late thirties and early forties. In our own moment we see "the old crap," as Marx once called it, rise to the surface with unnerving ease; there is something dizzying in an encounter with Stalin's theory of "social Fascism," particularly when it comes from the lips of young people who may not even be quite sure when Stalin lived. Still, I think there will not and probably cannot be repeated in our intellectual life the ghastly large-scale infatuation with a totalitarian regime which disgraced the thirties.

A little credit is due. Whatever judgments one may have about Sidney Hook's later political writings, and mine have been very critical, it is a matter of decency to recall the liberating role he played in the thirties as spokesman for a democratic radicalism and a fierce opponent of all the rationalizations for totalitarianism a good many intellectuals allowed themselves. One reason people have recently felt free to look down their noses at "anti-Communism" as if it were a mass voodoo infecting everyone from far right to democratic left is precisely the toughness with which the New York intellectuals fought against Stalinism. Neither they nor anybody else could reestablish socialism as a viable politics in the United States; but for a time they did help to salvage the honor of the socialist idea—which meant primarily to place it in the sharpest opposition to all totalitarian systems. What many intellectuals now say they take for granted had first to be won through bitter and exhausting struggle.

I should not like to give the impression that Stalinism was the beginning and end of whatever was detestable in American intellectual life during the thirties. Like the decades to come, perhaps like all decades, this was a "low dishonest" time. No one who grew up in, or lived through, these years should wish for a replay of their ideological melodramas. Nostalgia for the thirties is a sentiment possible only to the very young or the very old, those who have not known and those who no longer remember. Whatever distinction can be assigned to the New York intellectuals during those years lies mainly in their persistence as a small minority, in its readiness to defend unpopular positions against apologists for the Moscow trials and Popular-Front culture. Some historians, with the selectivity of retrospect, have recently begun to place the New York intellectuals at the center of cultural life in the thirties—but this is both a comic misapprehension and a soiling honor. On the contrary; their best hours were spent on the margin, in opposition.

Later, in the forties and fifties, most of the New York intellectuals would abandon the effort to find a renewed basis for a socialist politics—to their serious discredit, I believe. Some would vulgarize anti-Stalinism into a politics barely distinguishable from reaction. Yet for almost all New York intellectuals the radical years proved a decisive moment in their lives. And for a very few, the decisive moment.

I have been speaking here as if the New York intellectuals were mainly political people, but in reality this was true for only a few of them, writers like Hook, Macdonald, and perhaps Rahv. Most were literary men with no experience in any political movement; they had come to radical politics through the pressures of conscience and a flair for the dramatic; and even in later years, when they abandoned any direct political involvement, they would in some sense remain "political." They would respond with eagerness to historical changes, even if these promised renewed favor for the very ideas they had largely discarded. They would continue to structure their cultural responses through a sharp, perhaps excessively sharp, kind of categorization, in itself a sign that political styles and habits persisted. But for the most part, the contributions of the New York intellectuals were not to political thought. Given the brief span of time during which they fancied themselves agents of a renewed Marxism, there was little they could have done. Sidney Hook wrote one or two excellent books on the sources of Marxism, Harold Rosenberg one or two penetrating essays on the dramatics of Marxism; and not much more. The real contribution of the New York writers was toward creating a new, and for this country almost exotic, style of work. They thought of themselves as cultural radicals even after they had begun to wonder whether there was much point in remaining political radicals. But what could this mean? Cultural radicalism was a notion extremely hard to define and perhaps impossible to defend, as Richard Chase would discover in the late fifties when against the main drift of New York opinion he put forward the idea of a radicalism without immediate political ends but oriented toward criticism of a meretricious culture.

Chase was seriously trying to preserve a major impetus of New York intellectual life: the exploration and defense of literary modernism. He failed to see, however, that this was a task largely fulfilled and, in any case, taking on a far more ambiguous and less militant character in the fifties than it would have had twenty or thirty years earlier. The New York writers had done useful work in behalf of modernist literature. Without fully realizing it, they were continuing a cultural movement that had begun in the United States during the mid-nineteenth century: the return to Europe, not as provincials knocking humbly at the doors of the great, but as equals in an enterprise which by its very nature had to be international. We see this at work in Howells's reception of Ibsen and Tolstoy; in Van Wyck Brooks's use of European models to assault the timidities of American literature; in the responsiveness of the *Little Review* and the *Dial* to European experiments and, somewhat paradoxically, in the later fixation of the New Critics, despite an ideology of cultural provincialism, on modernist writing from abroad.

3

The New York critics helped complete this process of internationalizing American culture (also, by the way, Americanizing international culture). They gave a touch of glamour to that style which the Russians and Poles now call "cosmopolitan." *Partisan Review* was the first journal in which it was not merely respectable but a matter of pride to print one of Eliot's *Four Quartets* side by side with Marxist criticism. And not only did the magazine break down the polar rigidities of the hard-line Marxists and the hard-line nativists; it also sanctioned the idea, perhaps the most powerful cultural idea of the last half-century, that there existed an all but incomparable generation of modern masters, some of them still alive, who in this terrible age represented the highest possibilities of the imagination. On a more restricted scale, *Partisan Review* helped win attention and respect for a generation of European writers—Silone, Orwell, Malraux, Koestler, Victor Serge—who were not quite of the first rank as novelists but had suffered the failure of socialism.

If the *Partisan* critics came too late for a direct encounter with new work from the modern masters, they did serve the valuable end of placing that work in a cultural context more vital and urgent than could be provided by any other school of American criticism. For young people up to and through World War II, the *Partisan* critics helped to mold a new sensibility, a mixture of rootless radicalism and a desanctified admiration for writers like Joyce, Eliot, and Kafka. I can recall that even in my orthodox Marxist phase I felt that the central literary expression of the time was a poem by a St. Louis writer called "The Waste Land."

In truth, however, the New York critics were then performing no more than an auxiliary service. They were following upon the work of earlier, more fortunate critics. And even in the task of cultural consolidation, which soon had the unhappy result of overconsolidating the modern masters in the academy, the New York critics found important allies among their occasional opponents in the New Criticism. As it turned out, the commitment to literary modernism proved insufficient either as a binding literary purpose or as a theme that might inform the writings of the New York critics. By now modernism was entering its period of decline; the old excitements had paled and the old achievements been registered. Modernism had become successful; it was no longer a literature of opposition, and thereby had begun a metamorphosis signifying ultimate death. The problem was no longer to fight for modernism; the problem was now to consider why the fight had so easily ended in triumph. And as time went on, modernism surfaced an increasing portion of its limitations and ambiguities, so that among some critics earlier passions of advocacy gave way to increasing anxieties of judgment. Yet the moment had certainly not come when a cool and objective reconsideration could be undertaken of works that had formed the sensibility of our time. The New York critics, like many others, were trapped in a dilemma from which no escape could be found, but which lent itself to brilliant improvisation: it was too late for unobstructed enthusiasm, it was too soon for unobstructed valuation, and meanwhile the literary work that was being published, though sometimes distinguished, was composed in the heavy shadows of the modernists. At almost every point this work betrayed the marks of *having come after*.

Except for Harold Rosenberg, who would make "the tradition of the new" a signature of his criticism, the New York writers slowly began to release those sentiments of uneasiness they had been harboring about the modernist poets and novelists. One instance was the notorious Pound case,* in which literary and moral values, if not jammed into a head-on collision, were certainly entangled beyond easy separation. Essays on writers like D. H. Lawrence—what to make of his call for "blood consciousness," what one's true response might be to his notions of the leader cult—began to appear. A book by John Harrison, *The Reactionaries*, which contains a full-scale attack on the politics of several modernist writers, is mostly a compilation of views that had already been gathering force over the last few decades. And then, as modernism

---

* In 1948 Ezra Pound, who had spent the war years as a propagandist for Mussolini and whose writings contained strongly anti-Semitic passages, was awarded the prestigious Bollingen Prize. The committee voting for this award contained a number of ranking American poets. After the award was announced, there occurred a harsh dispute as to its appropriateness.

stumbled into its late period, those recent years in which its early energies evidently reached a point of exhaustion, the New York critics
became still more discomfited. There was a notable essay by Lionel
Trilling in which he acknowledged mixed feelings toward the modernist
writers he had long praised and taught. There was a cutting attack by
Philip Rahv on Jean Genet, that perverse genius in whose fiction the
compositional resources of modernism seem all but severed from its
moral—one might even say, its human—interests.

For the New York intellectuals in the thirties and forties there was
still another focus of interest, never quite as strong as radical politics
or literary modernism but seeming, for a brief time, to promise a valuable
new line of discussion. In the essays of writers like Clement Greenberg
and Dwight Macdonald, more or less influenced by the German neo-
Marxist school of Adorno-Horkheimer, there were beginnings at a theory of "mass culture," that mass-produced pseudo-art characteristic of
industrialized urban society, together with its paralyzed audiences, its
inaccessible sources, its parasitic relation to high culture. More insight
than system, this slender body of work was nevertheless a contribution
to the study of that hazy area where culture and society meet. It was
attacked by writers like Edward Shils as being haughtily elitist, on the
ground that it assumed a condescension to the tastes and experiences
of the masses. It was attacked by writers like Harold Rosenberg, who
charged that only people taking a surreptitious pleasure in dipping their
noses into trash would study the "content" (he had no objection to
sociological investigations) of mass culture. Even at its most penetrating,
the criticism of mass culture was beset by uncertainty and improvisation;
perhaps all necessary for a beginning.

Then, almost as if by common decision, the whole subject was
dropped. For years hardly a word could be found in the advanced journals about what a little earlier had been called a crucial problem of the
modern era. One reason was that the theory advanced by Greenberg
and Macdonald turned out to be static: it could be stated but apparently
not developed. It suffered from weaknesses parallel to those of Hannah
Arendt's theory of totalitarianism: by positing a cul-de-sac, a virtual end
of days, for twentieth-century man and his culture, it proposed a suffocating relationship between high or minority culture and the ever-
multiplying mass culture.

In the absence of more complex speculations, there was little point
in continuing to write about mass culture. Besides, hostility toward the
commercial pseudo-arts was hard to maintain with unyielding intensity,
mostly because it was hard to remain all that *interested* in them—only

in Macdonald's essays did both hostility and interest survive intact. Some felt that the whole matter had been inflated and that writers should stick to their business, which was literature, and intellectuals to theirs, which was ideas. Others felt that the movies and TV were beginning to show more ingenuity and resourcefulness than the severe notions advanced by Greenberg and Macdonald allowed for, though no one could have anticipated that glorious infatuation with trash which Marshall McLuhan would make acceptable. And still others felt that the multiplication of insights, even if pleasing as an exercise, failed to yield significant results: a critic who contributes a nuance to Dostoevsky criticism is working within a structured tradition, while one who throws off a clever observation about Little Orphan Annie is simply showing that he can do what he has done.

There was another and more political reason for the collapse of mass-culture criticism. One incentive toward this kind of writing was the feeling that industrial society had reached a point of affluent stasis where major events could now be registered much more vividly in culture than in economics. While aware of the dangers of reductionism here, I think the criticism of mass culture did serve, as some of its critics charged, conveniently to replace the criticism of bourgeois society. If you couldn't stir the proletariat to action, you could denounce Madison Avenue in comfort. Once, however, it began to be felt among intellectuals in the fifties that there was no longer so overwhelming a need for political criticism, and once it began to seem in the sixties that there were new openings for political criticism, the appetite for cultural surrogates became less keen.

Greenberg now said little more about mass culture; Macdonald made no serious effort to extend his theory or test it against new events; and in recent years, younger writers have seemed to feel that the whole approach of these men was heavy and humorless. Susan Sontag has proposed a cheerfully eclectic view which undercuts just about everything written from the Greenberg-Macdonald position. Now everyone is to do "his thing," high, middle, or low; the old puritan habit of interpretation and judgment, so inimical to sensuousness, gives way to a programmed receptivity; and we are enlightened by lengthy studies of the Beatles.

By the end of World War II, the New York writers had reached a point of severe intellectual crisis, though they themselves often felt they were entering a phase of enlarged influence. Perhaps there was a relation between inner crisis and external influence. Everything that had kept them going—the idea of socialism, the advocacy of literary modernism, the assault on mass culture, a special brand of literary criticism—was judged to be irrelevant to the postwar years. But as a group, just at the time their internal disintegration had seriously begun, the New York writers could be readily identified. The leading critics were Rahv, Phillips, Trilling, Rosenberg, Lionel Abel, and Kazin. The main political theorist was Hook. Writers of poetry and fiction related to the New York milieu were Delmore Schwartz, Saul Bellow, Paul Goodman, and Isaac Rosenfeld. And the recognized scholar, and also inspiring moral force, was Meyer Schapiro.

4

A sharp turn occurs, or is completed, soon after World War II. The intellectuals now go racing or stumbling from idea to idea, notion to notion, hope to hope, fashion to fashion. This instability often derives from a genuine eagerness to capture all that seems new—or threatening—in experience, sometimes from a mere desire to please a bitch goddess named Novelty. The abandonment of ideology can be liberating: a number of talents, thrown back on their own resources, begin to grow. The surrender of "commitment" can be damaging: some writers find themselves rattling about in a gray freedom. The culture opens up, with both temptation and generosity, and together with intellectual anxieties there are public rewards, often deserved. A period of dispersion; extreme oscillations in thought; and a turn in politics toward an increasingly conservative kind of liberalism—reflective, subtle, acquiescent.

The postwar years were marked by a sustained discussion of the new political and intellectual problems raised by the totalitarian state. Nothing in received political systems, neither Marxist nor liberal, adequately prepared one for the frightful mixture of terror and ideology, the capacity to sweep along the plebeian masses and organize a warfare state, and above all the readiness to destroy entire peoples, which characterized totalitarianism. Still less was anyone prepared—who had heeded the warning voices of the Russian socialist Julian Martov or the English liberal Bertrand Russell?—for the transformation of the revolutionary Bolshevik state, through either a "necessary" degeneration or an internal counterrevolution, into one of the major totalitarian powers. Marxist theories of fascism—the "last stage" of capitalism, with the economy stratified to organize a permanent war machine and mass terror employed to put down rebellious workers—came to seem, if not entirely mistaken, then certainly insufficient. The quasi- or pseudo-Leninist notion that "bourgeois democracy" was merely a veiled form of capitalist domination, little different in principle from its open dictatorship, proved to be a moral and political disaster. The assumption that socialism was an ordained "next step," or that nationalization of industry constituted a sufficient basis for working-class rule, was as great a disaster. No wonder intellectual certainties were shattered and these years marked by frenetic improvisation. At every point, with the growth of Communist power in Europe and with the manufacture of the Bomb at home, apocalypse seemed the fate of tomorrow.

So much foolishness has been written about the New York intellectuals and their anti-Communism, either by those who have signed a separate peace with the authoritarian idea or those who lack the courage to defend what *is* defensible in their own past, that I want here to be both blunt and unyielding.

Given the enormous growth of Russian power after the war and the real possibility of a Communist takeover in Europe, the intellectuals— and not they alone—had to reconsider their political responses.* An old-style Marxist declaration of rectitude, a plague repeated on both their houses? Or the difficult position of making foreign-policy proposals for the United States, while maintaining criticism of its social order, so as to block totalitarian expansion without resort to war? Most intellectuals decided they had to choose the second course, and they were right.

Like anticapitalism, anti-Communism was a tricky politics, all too open to easy distortion. Like anticapitalism, anti-Communism could be put to the service of ideological racketeering and reaction. Just as ideologues of the fanatic right insisted that by some ineluctable logic anticapitalism led to a Stalinist terror, so ideologues of the authoritarian left, commandeering the same logic, declared that anti-Communism led to the politics of Dulles and Rusk. But there is no "anticapitalism" or "anti-Communism" in the abstract; these take on political flesh only when linked with a larger body of programs and values, so that it becomes clear what *kind* of "anticapitalism" or "anti-Communism" we are dealing with. It is absurd, and indeed disreputable, for intellectuals in the sixties to write as if there were a unified "anti-Communism" which can be used to enclose the views of everyone from William Buckley to Michael Harrington.

There were difficulties. A position could be worked out for conditional support of the West when it defended Berlin or introduced the Marshall Plan or provided economic help to underdeveloped countries;

---

* Some recent historians, under New Left inspiration, have argued that in countries like France and Italy the possibility of a Communist seizure of power was really quite small. Perhaps; counterfactuals are hard to dispose of. What matters is the political consequences these historians would retrospectively have us draw, if they were at all specific on this point. Was it erroneous, or reactionary, to believe that resistance had to be created in Europe against further Communist expansion? What attitude, for example, would they have had intellectuals, or anyone else, take during the Berlin crisis? Should the city, in the name of peace, have been yielded to the East Germans? Did the possibility of Communist victories in Western Europe require an extraordinary politics? And to what extent are later reconsiderations of Communist power in postwar Europe made possible by the fact that it was, in fact, successfully contained?

but in the course of daily politics, in the effort to influence the foreign policy of what remained a capitalist power, intellectuals could lose their independence and slip into vulgarities of analysis and speech.

Painful choices had to be faced. When the Hungarian revolution broke out in 1956, most intellectuals sympathized strongly with the rebels, yet feared that active intervention by the West might provoke a world war. For a rational and humane mind, anti-Communism could not be the sole motive—it could be only one of several—in political behavior and policy; and even those intellectuals who had by now swung a considerable distance to the right did not advocate military intervention in Hungary. There was simply no way out—as there was none in Czechoslovakia.

It became clear, furthermore, that United States military intervention in underdeveloped countries could help local reactionaries in the short run, and the Communists in the long run. These difficulties were inherent in postwar politics, and they ruled out—though for that very reason, also made tempting—a simplistic moralism. These difficulties were also exacerbated by the spread among intellectuals of a crude sort of anti-Communism, often ready to justify whatever the United States might do at home and abroad. For a hard-line group within the American Committee for Cultural Freedom, all that seemed to matter in any strongly felt way was a sour hatred of the Stalinists, historically justifiable but more and more a political liability even in the fight against Stalinism. The dangers in such a politics now seem all too obvious, but I should note, for whatever we may mean by the record, that in the early fifties they were already being pointed out by a mostly unheeded minority of intellectuals around *Dissent*. Yet, with all these qualifications registered, the criticism to be launched against the New York intellectuals in the postwar years is not that they were strongly anti-Communist but, rather, that many of them, through disorientation or insensibility, allowed their anti-Communism to become something cheap and illiberal.

Nor is the main point of *moral* criticism that the intellectuals abandoned socialism. We have no reason to suppose that the declaration of a socialist opinion induces a greater humaneness than does acquiescence in liberalism. It could be argued (I would) that in the ease with which ideas of socialism were now brushed aside there was something shabby. It was undignified, at the very least, for people who had made so much of their Marxist credentials now to put to rest so impatiently the radicalism of their youth. Still, it might be said by some of the New York writers that reality itself had forced them to conclude socialism was no longer viable or had become irrelevant to the American scene, and that while this conclusion might be open to political argument, it was not to moral attack.

Let us grant that for a moment. What cannot be granted is that the shift in ideologies required or warranted the surrender of critical independence which was prevalent during the fifties. In the trauma—or relief—of ideological ricochet, all too many intellectuals joined the American celebration. It was possible, to cite but one of many instances, for Mary McCarthy to write: "Class barriers disappear or tend to become porous [in the U.S.]; the factory worker is an economic aristocrat in comparison with the middle-class clerk. . . . *The America . . . of vast inequalities and dramatic contrasts is rapidly ceasing to exist*" (Emphasis added.) Because the New York writers all but surrendered their critical perspective on American society—*that* is why they were open to attack.

It was the growth of McCarthyism which brought most sharply into question the role of the intellectuals. Here, presumably, all men of good will could agree; here the interests of the intellectuals were beyond dispute and directly at stake. The record is not glorious. In New York circles it was often said that Bertrand Russell exaggerated wildly in describing the United States as "subject to a reign of terror" and that Simone de Beauvoir retailed Stalinist clichés in her reportage from America. Yet it should not be forgotten that, if not "a reign of terror," McCarthyism was frightful and disgusting, and that a number of Communists and fellow-travelers, not always carefully specified, suffered serious harm.

A magazine like *Partisan Review* was of course opposed to McCarthy's campaign, but it failed to take the lead on the issue of freedom which might once again have imbued the intellectuals with fighting spirit. Unlike some of its New York counterparts, it did print sharp attacks on the drift toward conservatism, and it did not try to minimize the badness of the situation in the name of anti-Communism. But the magazine failed to speak out with enough force and persistence, or to break past the hedgings of those intellectuals who led the American Committee for Cultural Freedom.

Commentary, under Elliot Cohen's editorship, was still more inclined to minimize the threat of McCarthyism. In September 1952, at the very moment McCarthy became a central issue in the presidential campaign, Cohen could write: "McCarthy remains in the popular mind an unreliable, second-string blowhard; his only support as a great national figure is from the fascinated fears of the intelligentsia"—a mode of argument all too close to that of the anti-anti-Communists who kept repeating that Communism was a serious problem only in the minds of anti-Communists.

In the American Committee for Cultural Freedom the increasingly conformist and conservative impulses of the New York intellectuals, or at least of a good number of them, found formal expression. I quote at length from Michael Harrington in a 1955 issue of *Dissent*, because it says precisely what needs to be said:

> In practice the ACCF has fallen behind Sidney Hook's views on civil liberties. Without implying any "conspiracy" theory of history . . . one may safely say that it is Hook who has molded the decisive ACCF policies. His *Heresy Yes, Conspiracy No* articles were widely circulated by the Committee, which meant that in effect it endorsed his systematic, explicit efforts to minimize the threat to civil liberties and to attack those European intellectuals who, whatever their own political or intellectual deficiencies, took a dim view of American developments. Under the guidance of Hook and the leadership of Irving Kristol . . . the American Committee cast its weight not so much in defense of those civil liberties which were steadily being nibbled away, but rather against those few remaining fellow-travelers who tried to exploit the civil-liberties issue.
>
> At times this had an almost comic aspect. When Irving Kristol was executive secretary of the ACCF, one learned to expect from him silence on those issues that were agitating the whole intellectual and academic world, and enraged communiqués on the outrages performed by people like Arthur Miller and Bertrand Russell in exaggerating the dangers to civil liberties in the U.S.
>
> Inevitably this led to more serious problems. In an article by Kristol, which first appeared in *Commentary* and was later circulated under the ACCF imprimatur, one could read such astonishing and appalling statements as "there is one thing the American people know about Senator McCarthy; he, like them, is unequivocally anti-Communist. About the spokesmen for American liberalism, they feel they know no such thing. And with some justification." This in the name of defending cultural freedom!

Harrington then proceeded to list several instances in which the ACCF had "acted within the United States in defense of freedom." But

> these activities do not absorb the main attention or interest of the Committee; its leadership is too jaded, too imbued with the sourness of indiscriminate anti-Stalinism to give itself to an active struggle against the dominant trend of contemporary intellectual life in America. What it *really* cares about is a struggle against fellow-travelers and "neutralists"—that is, against many European intellectuals. . . .
>
> One of the crippling assumptions of the Committee has been that it would not intervene in cases where Stalinists or accused Stalinists were involved. It has rested this position on the academic argument . . . that Stalinists, being enemies of democracy, have no "right" to democratic privileges. . . . But the actual problem is not the metaphysical one of whether enemies of democracy (as the Stalinists clearly are) have a "right" to dem-

ocratic privileges. What matters is that the drive against cultural freedom and civil liberties takes on the guise of anti-Stalinism.

Years later came the revelations that the Congress for Cultural Freedom, which had its headquarters in Paris and with which the American Committee was for a time affiliated, had received secret funds from the CIA. Some of the people, it turned out, with whom one had sincerely disagreed were not free men at all; they were accomplices of an intelligence service. What a sad denouement! And yet not the heart of the matter, as the malicious *Ramparts* journalists have tried to make out. Most of the intellectuals who belonged to the ACCF seem not to have had any knowledge of the CIA connection—on this, as on anything else, I would completely accept the word of Dwight Macdonald. It is also true, however, that these intellectuals seem not to have inquired very closely into the Congress's sources of support. That a few, deceiving their closest associates, established connections with the CIA was not nearly so important, however, as that a majority within the Committee acquiesced in a politics of acquiescence. We Americans have a strong taste for conspiracy theories, supposing that if you scratch a trouble you'll find a villain. But history is far more complicated; and squalid as the CIA tie was, it should not be used to smear honest people who had nothing to do with secret services even as they remain open to criticism for what they did say and do.

At the same time, the retrospective defenses offered by some New York intellectuals strike me as decidedly lame. Meetings and magazines sponsored by the Congress, Daniel Bell has said, kept their intellectual freedom and contained criticism of U.S. policy—true but hardly to the point, since the issue at stake is not the opinions the Congress tolerated but the larger problem of good faith in intellectual life. The leadership of the Congress did not give its own supporters the opportunity to choose whether they wished to belong to a CIA-financed group. Another defense, this one offered by Sidney Hook, is that private backing was hard to find during the years it was essential to publish journals like *Preuves* and *Encounter* in Europe. Simply as a matter of fact, I do not believe this. For the Congress to have raised its funds openly, from nongovernmental sources, would have meant discomfort, scrounging, penny-pinching: all the irksome things editors of little magazines have always had to do. By the postwar years, however, leading figures of both the Congress and the Committee no longer thought or behaved in that tradition.

Dwight Macdonald did. His magazine *Politics* was the one significant effort during the late forties to return to radicalism. Enlivened by Macdonald's ingratiating personality and his table-hopping mind, *Politics* brought together sophisticated muckraking with tortuous revaluations of Marxist ideology. Macdonald could not long keep in balance the competing interests which finally tore apart his magazine: lively commentary on current affairs and unavoidable if depressing retrospects on the failure of the left. As always with Macdonald, honesty won out (one almost adds, alas) and the "inside" political discussion reached its climax with his essay "The Root Is Man," in which he arrived at a kind of anarcho-pacifism based on an absolutist morality. This essay was in many ways the most poignant and authentic expression of the plight of those few intellectuals—Nicola Chiaromonte, Paul Goodman, Macdonald— who wished to dissociate themselves from the postwar turn to realpolitik but could not find ways of transforming sentiments of rectitude and visions of utopia into a workable politics. It was also a perfect leftist rationale for a kind of internal emigration of spirit and mind, with some odd shadings of similarity to the Salinger cult of the late fifties.*

The overwhelming intellectual drift, however, was toward the right. Arthur Schlesinger, Jr., with moony glances at Kierkegaard, wrote essays in which he maintained that American society had all but taken care of its economic problems and could now concentrate on raising its cultural level. The "end of ideology" became a favorite shield for intellectuals in retreat, though it was never entirely clear whether this phrase meant the end of "our" ideology (partly true) or that all ideologies were soon to disintegrate (not true) or that the time had come to abandon the nostalgia for ideology (at least debatable). And in the mid-fifties, as if to codify things, there appeared in *Partisan Review* a symposium, "Our Country and Our Culture," in which all but three or four of the thirty participants clearly moved away from their earlier radical views. The rapprochement with "America the Beautiful," as Mary McCarthy now called it in a tone not wholly ironic, seemed almost complete.

5

In these years there also began that series of gyrations in opinion, interest, and outlook—so frenetic, so unserious—which would mark our intellectual life. In place of the avant-garde idea we now had the *style of fashion*, though to suggest a mere replacement may be too simple,

---

* It is not clear whether Macdonald still adheres to "The Root Is Man." In a BBC broadcast he said about the student uprising at Columbia: "I don't approve of their methods, but Columbia will be a better place afterwards." Perhaps it will, perhaps it won't; but I don't see how the author of "The Root Is Man" could say this, since the one thing he kept insisting was that means could not be separated from ends, as the Marxists too readily separated them. He would surely have felt that if the means used by the students were objectionable, then their ends would be contaminated as well—and thereby the consequences of their action. But in the swinging sixties not many people troubled to remember their own lessons.

since fashion has often shadowed the avant-garde as a kind of dandified double. Some intellectuals turned to a weekend of religion, some to a semester of existentialism, some to a holiday of Jewishness without faith or knowledge, some to a season of genteel conservatism. Leslie Fiedler, no doubt by design, seemed to go through more of such episodes than anyone else: even his admirers could not always be certain whether he was davenning or doing a rain dance.

These twists and turns were lively, and they could all seem harmless if only one could learn to look upon intellectual life as a variety of play, like potsy or king of the hill. What struck one as troubling, however, was not this or that fashion (tomorrow morning would bring another), but the dynamic of fashion itself, the ruthlessness with which, to remain in fashion, fashion had to keep devouring itself.

It would be unfair to give the impression that the fifteen years after the war were without significant growth or achievement among the New York writers. The attempt of recent New Left ideologues to present the forties and fifties as if they were no more than a time of intellectual sterility and reaction is an oversimplification. Together with the turn toward conservative acquiescence, there were serious and valuable achievements. Hannah Arendt's book on totalitarianism may now seem open to many criticisms, but it certainly must rank as a major piece of work which, at the very least, made impossible—I mean, implausible— those theories of totalitarianism which, before and after she wrote, tended to reduce fascism and Stalinism to a matter of class rule or economic interest. Daniel Bell's writing contributed to the rightward turn of these years, but some of it, such as his excellent little book *Work and Its Discontents*, constitutes a permanent contribution, and one that is valuable for radicals too. The stress upon complexity of thought which characterized intellectual life during these years could be used as a rationale for conservatism, and perhaps even arose from the turn toward conservatism; but in truth, the lapsed radicalism of earlier years *had* proved to be simplistic, the world of late capitalism *was* perplexing, and for serious people complexity *is* a positive value. Even the few intel- lectuals who resisted the dominant temper of the fifties underwent dur- ing these years significant changes in their political outlooks and styles of thought: e.g., those around *Dissent* who cut whatever ties of sentiment still held them to the Bolshevik tradition and made the indissoluble connection between democracy and socialism a crux of their thought. Much that happened during these years is to be deplored and dismissed, but not all was waste; the increasing sophistication and complication of mind was a genuine gain, and it would be absurd, at this late date, to forgo it.

In literary criticism there were equivalent achievements. The very instability that might make a shambles out of political thought could have the effect of magnifying the powers required for criticism. Floundering in life and uncertainty in thought could make for an increased responsiveness to art. In the criticism of men like Trilling, Rahv, Richard Chase, and F. W. Dupee there was now a more authoritative relation to the literary text and a richer awareness of the cultural past than was likely to be found in their earlier work. And a useful tension was also set up between the New York critics, whose instinctive response to literature was through a social-moral contextualism, and the New Critics, whose formalism proved of great value to those who opposed it.

Meanwhile, the world seemed to be opening up, with all its charms, seductions, and falsities. In the thirties the life of the New York writers had been confined: the little magazine as island, the radical sect as cave. Partly they were recapitulating the pattern of immigrant Jewish experience: an ingathering of the flock in order to break out into the world and taste the Gentile fruits of status and success. Once it became clear that waiting for the revolution might turn out to be steady work and that the United States would neither veer to fascism nor sink into depression, the intellectuals had little choice but to live within (which didn't necessarily mean, become partisans of) the existing society.

There was money to be had from publishers, no great amounts, but more than in the past. There were jobs in the universities, even for those without degrees. Some writers began to discover that publishing a story in the *New Yorker* or *Esquire* was not a sure ticket to Satan; others to see that the academy, while perhaps less exciting than the Village, wasn't invariably a graveyard for intellect and might even provide the only harbor in which serious people could do their own writing and perform honorable work. This dispersion involved losses, but usually there was nothing sinister about it. Writers ought to know something about the world; they ought to test their notions against the reality of the country in which they live. Worldly involvements would, of course, bring risks, and one of these was power, really a very trifling kind of power, but still enough to raise the fear of corruption. That power corrupts everyone knows by now, but we ought also to recognize that powerlessness, if not corrupting, can be damaging—as in the case of Paul Goodman, a courageous writer who stuck to his anarchist beliefs through years in which he was mocked and all but excluded from the New York journals, yet who could also come to seem an example of asphyxiating righteousness.

What brought about these changes? Partly ideological adaptation, a feeling that capitalist society was here to stay and there wasn't much point in maintaining a radical position. Partly the sly workings of prosperity. But also a loosening of the society itself, the start of that process which only now is in full swing—I mean the remarkable absorptiveness of modern society, its readiness to abandon traditional precepts for a moment of excitement, its growing permissiveness toward social criticism, perhaps out of indifference, or security, or even tolerance.

In the sixties well-placed young professors and radical students would denounce the "success," sometimes the "sellout," of the New York writers. Their attitude reminds one a little of George Orwell's remark about wartime France: only a Pétain could afford the luxury of asceticism, ordinary people had to live by the necessities of materialism. But really, when you come to think of it, what did this "success" of the intellectuals amount to? A decent or a good job, a chance to earn extra money by working hard, and in the case of a few, like Trilling and Kazin, some fame beyond New York—rewards most European intellectuals would take for granted, so paltry would they seem. For the New York writers who lived through the thirties expecting never to have a job at all, a regular paycheck might be remarkable; but in the American scale of things it was very modest indeed. And what the "leftist" prigs of the sixties, sons of psychiatrists and manufacturers, failed to understand— or perhaps understood only too well—was that the "success" with which they kept scaring themselves was simply one of the possibilities of adult life, a possibility, like failure, heavy with moral risks and disappointment. Could they imagine that they too might have to face the common lot? I mean the whole business: debts, overwork, varicose veins, alimony, drinking, quarrels, hemorrhoids, depletion, the recognition that one might prove not to be another T. S. Eliot, but also some good things, some lessons learned, some "rags of time" salvaged and precious.

Here and there you could find petty greed or huckstering, now and again a drop into opportunism; but to make much of this would be foolish. Common clay, the New York writers had their share of common ambition. What drove them, and sometimes drove them crazy, was not, however, the quest for money, nor even a chance to "mix" with White House residents; it was finally a gnawing ambition to write something, even three pages, that might live.

The intellectuals should have regarded their entry into the outer world as utterly commonplace, at least if they kept faith with the warning of Stendhal and Balzac that one must always hold a portion of the self forever beyond the world's reach. Few of the New York intellectuals made much money on books and articles. Few reached audiences beyond the little magazines. Few approached any centers of power, and precisely the buzz of gossip attending the one or two sometimes invited to a party beyond the well-surveyed limits of the West Side showed how confined their life still was. What seems most remarkable in retrospect is the innocence behind the assumption, sometimes held by the New York writers themselves with a nervous mixture of guilt and glee, that whatever recognition they won was cause for either preening or embarrassment. For all their gloss of sophistication, they had not really moved very far into the world. The immigrant milk was still on their lips.

6

In their published work during these years, the New York intellectuals developed a characteristic style of exposition and polemic. With some admiration and a bit of irony, let us call it the style of brilliance. The kind of essay they wrote was likely to be wide-ranging in reference, melding notions about literature and politics, sometimes announcing itself as a study of a writer or literary group but usually taut with a pressure to "go beyond" its subject, toward some encompassing moral or social observation. It is a kind of writing highly self-conscious in mode, with an unashamed vibration of bravura. Nervous, strewn with knotty or flashy phrases, impatient with transitions and other concessions to dullness, calling attention to itself as a form or at least an outcry, fond of rapid twists, taking pleasure in dispute, dialectic, dazzle—such, at its best or most noticeable, was the essay cultivated by the New York writers. Until recently its strategy of exposition was likely to be impersonal (the writer did not speak much as an "I") but its tone and bearing were likely to be intensely personal (the audience was to be made aware that the aim of the piece was not judiciousness, but, rather, a strong impress of attitude, a blow of novelty, a wrenching of accepted opinion, sometimes a mere indulgence of vanity).

In some of these essays there was a sense of *tournament*, the writer as gymnast with one eye on other rings, or as skilled infighter juggling knives of dialectic. Polemics were harsh, often rude. And audiences nurtured, or spoiled, on this kind of performance, learned not to form settled judgments about a dispute until all sides had registered their blows: surprise was always a possible reward.

This style may have brought new life to the American essay, but among contemporary readers it often evoked a strong distaste, even fear. "Ordinary" readers could be left with the fretful sense that they were not "in," the beauties of polemic racing past their sluggish eye. Old-line academics, quite as if they had just crawled out of *The Dunciad*, enjoyed dismissing the New York critics as "unsound." And for some younger souls, the cliffs of dialectic seemed too steep. Seymour Krim has left a poignant account of his disablement before "the overcerebral, Europeanish, sterilely citified, pretentiously alienated" New York intellectuals. Resentful at the fate which drove them to compare themselves with "the overcerebral, etc., etc.," Krim writes that he and his friends "were often tortured and unappeasably bitter about being the offspring of this unhappily unique-ingrown-screwed-up breed." Similar complaints could be heard from other writers who felt that New York intellectualism threatened their vital powers.

At its best the style of brilliance reflected a certain view of the intellectual life: free-lance dash, peacock strut, daring hypothesis, knockabout synthesis. For better or worse it was radically different from the accepted modes of scholarly publishing and middlebrow journalism. It celebrated the idea of the intellectual as antispecialist, or as a writer whose speciality was the lack of a speciality: the writer as dilettante-connoisseur, *Luftmensch* of the mind, roamer among theories. But it was a style which also lent itself with peculiar ease to a stifling mimicry and decadence. Sometimes it seemed—no doubt mistakenly—as if any sophomore, indeed any parrot, could learn to write one of those scintillating *Partisan* reviews, so thoroughly could manner consume matter. In the fifties the cult of brilliance became a sign that writers were offering not their work or ideas but their persona as content; and this was but a step or two away from the exhibitionism of the sixties. Brilliance could become a sign of intellect unmoored: the less assurance, the more pyrotechnics.

If to the minor genre of the essay the New York writers made a major contribution, to the major genres of fiction and poetry they made only a minor contribution. As a literary group, they will seem less important than, say, the New Critics, who did set in motion a whole school of poetry. A few poets—John Berryman, Robert Lowell, Randall Jarrell, perhaps Stanley Kunitz—have been influenced by the New York intellectuals, though in ways hardly comprising a major pressure on their work: all were finished writers by the time they brushed against the New York milieu. For one or two poets, the influence of New York meant becoming aware of the cultural pathos resident in the idea of the Jew (not always distinguished from the idea of Delmore Schwartz). But the main literary contribution of the New York milieu has been to legitimate a subject and tone we must uneasily call American Jewish writing. The fiction of urban malaise, second-generation complaint, Talmudic dazzle, woeful alienation, and dialectical irony, all found its earliest expression in the pages of *Commentary* and *Partisan Review*—fiction in which the Jewish world is not merely regained in memory as a point of beginnings, an archetypal Lower East Side of spirit and place, but is also treated as a portentous metaphor of man's homelessness and wandering.

Such distinguished short fictions as Bellow's *Seize the Day*, Schwartz's "In Dreams Begin Responsibility," Mailer's "The Man Who Studied Yoga," and Malamud's "The Magic Barrel" seem likely to survive the cultural moment in which they were written. And even if one concludes that these and similar pieces are not enough to warrant speaking of a major literary group, they certainly form a notable addition—a new tone, a new sensibility—to American writing. In time, these writers may be regarded as the last "regional" group in American literature, parallel to recent Southern writers in both sophistication of craft and a thematic dissociation from the values of American society. Nor is it important that during the last few decades both of these literary tendencies, the Southern and the Jewish, have been overvalued. The distance of but a few years has already made it clear that except for Faulkner Southern writing consists of a scatter of talented minor poets and novelists; and in a decade or so a similar judgment may be commonly accepted about most of the Jewish writers.

What is clear from both Southern and Jewish writing is that in a society increasingly disturbed about its lack of self-definition, the recall of regional and traditional details can be intensely absorbing in its own right, as well as suggestive of larger themes transcending the region. (For the Jewish writers New York was not merely a place, it was a symbol, a burden, a stamp of history.) Yet the writers of neither school have thus far managed to move from their particular milieu to a grasp of the entire culture; the very strengths of their localism define their limitations; and especially is this true for the Jewish writers, in whose behalf critics have recently overreached themselves.

Whatever the hopeful future of individual writers, the "school" of American Jewish writing is by now in an advanced state of decomposition: how else explain the attention it has lately enjoyed? Or the appearance of a generation of younger Jewish writers who, without authentic experience or memory to draw upon, manufacture fantasies about the lives of their grandfathers? Or the popularity of Isaac Bashevis Singer, who, coming to the American literary scene precisely at the moment when writers composing in English had begun to exhaust the Jewish subject, could, by dazzling contrast, extend it endlessly backward in time and deeper in historical imagination?

Just as there appear today young Jewish intellectuals who no longer know what it is that as Jews they do not know, so in fiction the fading immigrant world offers a thinner and thinner yield to writers of fiction. It no longer presses on memory, people can now *choose* whether to care about it. We are almost at the end of a historic experience, and it now seems unlikely that there will have arisen in New York a literary school comparable to the best this country has had. Insofar as the New York intellectual atmosphere has affected writers like Schwartz, Rosenfeld, Bellow, Malamud, Mailer, Goodman, and Philip Roth, it seems to have been too brittle, too contentious, too insecure for major creative work. What cannot yet be estimated is the extent to which the styles and values of the New York world may have left a mark on the work of American writers who never came directly under its influence.

Thinking back upon intellectual life in the forties and fifties, and especially the air of malaise that hung over it, I find myself turning to a theme as difficult to clarify as it is impossible to evade. And here, for a few paragraphs, let me drop the porous shield of impersonality and speak openly in the first person.

7

We were living directly after the holocaust of the European Jews. We might scorn our origins; we might crush America with discoveries of ardor; we might change our names. But we knew that but for an accident of geography we might also now be bars of soap. At least some of us could not help feeling that in our earlier claims to have shaken off all ethnic distinctiveness there had been something false, something shaming. Our Jewishness might have no clear religious or national content, it might be helpless before the criticism of believers; but Jews we were, like it or not, and liked or not.

To recognize that we were living after one of the greatest catastrophes of human history, and one for which we could not claim to have adequately prepared ourselves either as intellectuals or as human beings, brought a new rush of feelings, mostly unarticulated and hidden behind the scrim of consciousness. It brought a low-charged but nagging guilt, a quiet remorse. Sartre's brilliant essay on authentic and inauthentic Jews left a strong mark. Hannah Arendt's book on totalitarianism had an equally strong impact, mostly because it offered a coherent theory, or at least a coherent picture of the concentration-camp universe. We could no longer escape the conviction that, blessing or curse, Jewishness was an integral part of our life, even if—and perhaps just because—there was nothing we could do or say about it. Despite a few simulated seders and literary raids on Hasidism, we could not turn back to the synagogue; we could only express our irritation with "the community" which kept nagging us like disappointed mothers; and sometimes we tried, through imagination and recall, to put together a few bits and pieces of the world of our fathers. I cannot prove a connection between the holocaust and the turn to Jewish themes in American fiction, at first urgent and quizzical, later fashionable and manipulative. I cannot prove that my own turn to Yiddish literature during the fifties was due to the shock following the war years. But it would be foolish to scant the possibility.

The violent dispute which broke out among the New York intellectuals when Hannah Arendt published her book on Eichmann had as one of its causes a sense of guilt concerning the Jewish tragedy—a guilt pervasive, unmanageable, yet seldom declared. In the quarrel between those attacking and those defending *Eichmann in Jerusalem* there were polemical excesses on both sides, since both were acting out of unacknowledged passions. Yet even in the debris of this quarrel there was, I think, something good. At least everyone was acknowledging emotions that had long gone unused. Nowhere else in American academic and intellectual life was there such ferocity of concern with the problems raised by Hannah Arendt. If left to the rest of the American intellectual world, her book would have been praised as "stimulating" and "thoughtful," and then everyone would have gone back to sleep. Nowhere else in the country could there have been the kind of public forum sponsored on this subject by *Dissent*: a debate sometimes ugly and outrageous, yet also urgent and afire—evidence that in behalf of ideas we were still ready to risk personal relationships. After all, it had never been dignity that we could claim as our strong point.

Nothing about the New York writers is more remarkable than the sheer fact of their survival. In a country where tastes in culture change more rapidly than lengths of skirts, they have succeeded in maintaining a degree of influence, as well as a distinctive milieu, for more than thirty years. Apart from reasons intrinsic to the intellectual life, let me note a few that are somewhat more worldly in nature.

There is something, perhaps a quasireligious dynamism, about an ideology, even a lapsed ideology that everyone says has reached its end, which yields force and coherence to those who have closely experienced it. A lapsed Catholic has tactical advantages in his apostasy which a lifelong skeptic does not have. And just as Christianity kept many nineteenth-century writers going long after they had discarded religion, so Marxism gave bite and edge to the work of twentieth-century writers long after they had turned from socialism.

The years in which the New York writers gained some prominence were those in which the style at which they had arrived—irony, ambiguity, complexity, the problematic as mode of knowledge—took on a magnified appeal for the American educated classes. In the fifties the cultivation of private sensibility and personal responsibility were values enormously popular among reflective people, to whom the very thought of public life smacked of betrayal and vulgarity.

An intelligentsia flourishes in a capital: Paris, St. Petersburg, Berlin. The influence of the New York writers grew at the time New York itself, for better or worse, became the cultural center of the country. And thereby the New York writers slowly shed the characteristics of an intelligentsia and transformed themselves into—

An Establishment?

Perhaps. But what precisely *is* an Establishment? Vaguely sinister in its overtones, the term is used these days with gay abandon on the American campus; but except as a spread-eagle put-down it has no discernible meaning, and if accepted as a put-down, the problem then becomes to discover who, if anyone, is not in the Establishment. In England the term has had a certain clarity of usage, referring to an intellectual elite which derives from the same upper and middle classes as the men who wield political power and which shares with these men Oxbridge education and Bloomsbury culture. But except in F. R. Leavis's angrier tirades, "Establishment" does not bear the conspiratorial over-tones we are inclined to credit in this country. What it does in England is to locate the social-cultural stratum guiding the tastes of the classes in power and thereby crucially affecting the tastes of the country as a whole.

In this sense, neither the New York writers nor any other group can be said to comprise an American Establishment, simply because no one in this country has ever commanded an equivalent amount of cultural power. The New York writers have few, if any, connections with a stable class of upper-rank civil servants or with a significant segment of the rich. They are without connections in Washington. They do not shape official or dominant tastes. And they cannot exert the kind of control over cultural opinion that the London Establishment is said to have maintained until recently. Critics like Trilling and Kazin are listened to by people in publishing, Rosenberg and Greenberg by people in the art world; but this hardly constitutes anything so formidable as an Es-tablishment. Indeed, at the very time mutterings have been heard about a New York literary Establishment, there has occurred a rapid disin-tegration of whatever group ties may still have remained among the New York writers. They lack—and it is just as well—the first require-ment for an Establishment: that firm sense of internal discipline which enables it to impose its taste on a large public.

During the last few years the talk about a New York Establishment has taken an unpleasant turn. Whoever does a bit of lecturing about the country is likely to encounter, after a few drinks, literary academics who inquire enviously, sometimes spitefully, about "what's new in New York." Such people seem to feel that exile in outlying regions means they are missing something remarkable (and so they are: the Balanchine company). The cause of their cultural envy is, I think, a notion that has become prevalent in our English departments that scholarship is somehow unworthy and the "real" literary life is to be found in the periodical journalism of New York. Intrinsically this is a dubious notion, and for the future of American education a disastrous one; when directed against the New York writers it leads to some painful situations. As polite needling questions are asked about the cultural life of New York, a rise of sweat comes to one's brow, for everyone knows what no one says: New York means Jews.*

Whatever the duration or extent of the influence enjoyed by the New York intellectuals, it is now reaching an end. There are signs of internal disarray: unhealed wounds, a dispersal of interests, the damage of time. More important, however, is the appearance these last few years of a new and powerful challenge to the New York writers. And here I shall have to go off on what may appear to be a long digression, since one cannot understand the present situation of the New York writers without taking into account the cultural-political scene of America in the late sixties.

8

There is a rising younger generation of intellectuals: ambitious, self-assured, at ease with prosperity while conspicuously alienated, unmarred by the traumas of the totalitarian age, bored with memories of defeat, and attracted to the idea of power. This generation matters, thus far, not so much for its leading figures and their meager accomplishments, but for the political-cultural style—what I shall call the "new sensibility"—it thrusts into absolute opposition against both the New York writers and other groups. It claims not to seek penetration into, or accommodation with, our cultural and academic institutions; it fancies the prospect of a harsh generational fight; and given the premise with which it begins—that everything touched by older writers reeks of betrayal—its claims and fancies have a sort of propriety. It proposes a revolution—I would call it a counterrevolution—in sensibility. Though linked to New Left politics, it goes beyond any politics, making itself felt, like a spreading blot of anti-intellectualism, in every area of intel-

* Not quite no one. In an attack on the New York writers (*Hudson Review*, Autumn 1965) Richard Kostelanetz speaks about "Jewish group-aggrandizement" and "the Jewish American push." One notices the delicacy of his phrasing.

lectual life. Not yet fully cohered, this new cultural group cannot yet be fully defined, nor is it possible fully to describe its projected sensibility, since it declares itself through a refusal of both coherence and definition.

There is no need to discuss once more the strengths and weaknesses of the New Left, its moral energies and intellectual muddles. Nor need we be concerned with the tactical issues separating New Left politics from that of older left-wing intellectuals. Were nothing else at stake than, say, "coalition politics," the differences would be both temporary and tolerable. But in reality a deeper divergence of outlook has begun to show itself. The new intellectual style, insofar as it approximates a politics, mixes sentiments of anarchism with apologies for authoritarianism; bubbling hopes for "participatory democracy" with manipulative elitism; unqualified populist majoritarianism with the reign of the cadres.

A confrontation of intellectual outlooks is unavoidable. And a central issue is certain to be the problem of liberalism, not liberalism as one or another version of current politics, nor even as a theory of power, but liberalism as a cast of mind, a structure of norms by means of which to humanize public life. For those of us who have lived through the age of totalitarianism and experienced the debacle of socialism, this conflict over liberal values is extremely painful. We have paid heavily for the lesson that democracy, even "bourgeois democracy," is a precious human achievement, one that, far from being simply a mode of mass manipulation, has been wrested through decades of struggle by the labor, socialist, and liberal movements. To protect the values of liberal democracy, often against those who call themselves liberals, is an elementary task for intellectuals as a social group.

Yet what I have just been saying has in the last few years aroused opposition, skepticism, open contempt among professors, students, and intellectuals. On the very crudest, though by no means unpopular level, we find a vulgarization of an already vulgar Marxism. The notion that we live in a society that can be described as "liberal fascism" (a theoretic contribution from certain leaders of the Students for a Democratic Society) isn't one to be taken seriously; but the fact that it is circulated in the academic community signifies a counterrevolution of the mind: a refusal of nuance and observation, a willed return to the kind of political primitivism which used to declare the distinctions of bourgeois rule— democratic, authoritarian, totalitarian—as slight in importance.

For the talk about "liberal fascism" men like Norman Mailer must bear a heavy responsibility, insofar as they have recklessly employed the term "totalitarian" as a descriptive for present-day American society.

Having lived through the ghastliness of the Stalinist theory of "Social Fascism" (the granddaddy of "liberal fascism") I cannot suppose any literate person really accepts this kind of nonsense, yet I know that people can find it politically expedient to pretend that they do.

There are sophisticated equivalents. One of these points to the failings and crises of democracy, concluding that the content of decision has been increasingly separated from the forms of decision-making. Another emphasizes the manipulation of the masses by communication media and declares them brainwashed victims incapable of rational choice and acquiescing in their own subjugation. A third decries the bureaucratic entanglements of the political process and favors some version, usually more sentiment than scheme, for direct plebiscitary rule. With varying intelligence, all point to acknowledged problems of democratic society; and there could be no urgent objection were these criticisms not linked with the premise that the troubles of democracy can be overcome by undercutting or bypassing representative institutions. Thus, it is quite true that the masses are manipulated, but to make that the crux of a political analysis is to lead into the notion that elections are mere "formalities" and majorities mere tokens of the inauthentic; what is needed, instead, is Herbert Marcuse's "educational dictatorship" (in which, I hope, at least some of the New York intellectuals would require the most prolonged reeducation). And in a similar vein, all proposals for obligatory or pressured "participation," apart from violating the democratic right not to participate, have a way of discounting those representative institutions and limitations upon power which can alone provide a degree of safeguard for liberal norms.

Perhaps the most sophisticated and currently popular of antidemocratic notions is that advanced by Marcuse: his contempt for tolerance on the ground that it is a rationale for maintaining the status quo, and his consequent readiness to suppress "regressive" elements of the population lest they impede social "liberation." About these theories, which succeed in salvaging the worst of Leninism, Henry David Aiken has neatly remarked: "Whether garden-variety liberties can survive the ministrations of such 'liberating tolerance' is not a question that greatly interests Marcuse." Indeed not.

Such theories are no mere academic indulgence or sectarian irrelevance; they have been put to significant use on the American campus as rationalizations for breaking up meetings of political opponents and as the justification for imaginary coups d'état by tiny minorities of enraged intellectuals. How depressing that "men of the left," themselves so often victims of repression, should attack the values of tolerance and freedom.*

These differences concerning liberal norms run very deep and are certain to affect American intellectual life in the coming years; yet they do not quite get to the core of the matter. In the Kulturkampf now emerging there are issues more consequential than the political ones, issues that have to do with the nature of human life.

One of these has been with us for a long time, and trying now to put it into simple language, I feel a measure of uneasiness, as if it were bad form to violate the tradition of antinomianism in which we have all been raised.

What, for "emancipated" people, is the surviving role of moral imperatives, or at least moral recommendations? Do these retain for us a shred of sanctity or at least of coercive value? The question to which I am moving is not, of course, whether the moral life is desirable or men should try to live it; no, the question has to do with the provenance and defining conditions of the moral life. Do moral principles continue to signify insofar as and if they come into conflict with spontaneous impulses, and more urgently still, can we conceive of moral principles retaining some validity if they do come into conflict with spontaneous impulses? Are we still to give credit to the idea, one of the few meeting points between traditional Christianity and modern Freudianism, that there occurs and must occur a deep-seated clash between instinct and civilization, or can we now, with a great sigh of collective relief, dismiss this as still another hang-up, perhaps the supreme hang-up, of Western civilization?

For more than one hundred and fifty years there has been a line of Western thought, as also of sentiment in modern literature, which calls into question not one or another moral commandment or regulation, but the very idea of commandment and regulation; which insists that the ethic of control, like the ethic of work, should be regarded as

---

* That Marcuse chooses not to apply his theories to the area of society in which he himself functions is a tribute to his personal realism, or perhaps merely a sign of a lack of intellectual seriousness. In a recent public discussion, recorded by the *New York Times Magazine* (May 26, 1968), there occurred the following exchange:

Hentoff: We've been talking about new institutions, new structures, as the only way to get fundamental change. What would that mean to you, Mr. Marcuse, in terms of the university, in terms of Columbia?

Marcuse: I was afraid of that because I now finally reveal myself as a fink. I have never suggested or advocated or supported destroying the established universities and building new anti-institutions instead. I have always said that no matter how radical the demands of the students and no matter how justified, they should be pressed within the existing universities. . . . I believe—and this is where the finkdom comes in—that American universities, at least quite a few of them, today are still enclaves of relatively critical thought and relatively free thought.

spurious, a token of a centuries-long heritage of repression. Sometimes this view comes to us as a faint residue of Christian heresy, more recently as the blare of Nietzschean prophecy, and in our own day as a psychoanalytic gift.

Now even those of us raised on the premise of revolt against the whole system of bourgeois values, did not—I suppose it had better be said outright—imagine ourselves to be exempt from the irksome necessity of regulation, even if we had managed to escape the reach of the commandments. Neither primitive Christians nor romantic naifs, we did not suppose that we could entrust ourselves entirely to the beneficence of nature, or the signals of our bodies, as a sufficient guide to conduct. (My very use of the word "conduct," freighted as it is with normative associations, puts the brand of time on what I am saying.)

By contrast, the emerging new sensibility rests on a vision of innocence: an innocence through lapse or will or recovery, an innocence through a refusal of our and perhaps any other culture, an innocence not even to be preceded by the withering away of the state, since in this view of things the state could wither away only if men learned so to be at ease with their desires that all need for regulation would fade. This is a vision of life beyond good and evil, not because these experiences or possibilities of experience have been confronted and transcended, but because the categories by which we try to designate them have been dismissed. There is no need to taste the apple: the apple brings health to those who know how to bite it: and look more closely: there is no apple at all; it exists only in your sickened imagination.

The new sensibility posits a theory that might be called *the psychology of unobstructed need:* men should satisfy those needs which are theirs, organic to their bodies and psyches, and to do this they must learn to discard or destroy all those obstructions, mostly the result of cultural neurosis, which keep them from satisfying their needs. This does not mean that the moral life is denied; it only means that in the moral economy costs need not be entered as a significant item. In the current vocabulary it becomes a matter of everyone doing "his own thing," and once everyone is allowed to do "his own thing," a prospect of easing harmony unfolds. Sexuality is the ground of being, and vital sexuality the assurance of the moral life.

Whether this outlook is compatible with a high order of culture or a complex civilization I shall not discuss here; Freud thought they were not compatible, though that does not foreclose the matter. More immediately, and on a less exalted plane, one is troubled by the following problem: what if the needs and impulses of human beings clash, as they seem to do, and what if the transfer of energies from sexuality to sociality does not proceed with the anticipated abundance and smoothness? The new sensibility, as displayed in the writings of Norman Brown and Norman Mailer, falls back upon a curious analogue to laissez-faire economics: Adam Smith's invisible hand, by means of which innumerable units in conflict with one another achieve a resultant of cooperation. Is there, however, much reason to suppose that this will prove more satisfactory in the economy of moral conduct than it has in the morality of economic relations?

Suppose that, after reading Mailer's "The White Negro," my "thing" happens to be that, to "dare the unknown" (as Mailer puts it), I want to beat in the brains of an aging candy-store keeper; or after reading LeRoi Jones, I should like to cut up a few Jews, whether or not they keep stores—how is anyone going to argue against the outpouring of my need? Who will declare himself its barrier? Against me, against my ideas it is possible to argue, but how, according to this new dispensation, can anyone argue against my *need*? Acting through violence I will at least have realized myself, for I will have entered (to quote Mailer again) "a new relation with the police" and introduced "a dangerous element" into my life; thereby too I will have escaped the cellblock of regulation which keeps me from the free air of self-determination. And if you now object that this very escape may lead to brutality, you reveal yourself as hopelessly linked to imperfection and original sin. For why should anyone truly heeding his nature wish to kill or wound or do anything but love and make love? That certain spokesmen of the new sensibility seem to be boiling over with fantasies of blood, or at least suppose that a verbal indulgence in such fantasies is a therapy for the boredom in their souls, is a problem for dialecticians. And as for skeptics, what have they to offer but evidence from history, that European contamination?

When it is transposed to a cultural setting, this psychology—in earlier times it would have been called a moral psychology—provokes a series of disputes over "complexity" in literature. Certain older critics find much recent writing distasteful and tiresome because it fails to reach or grasp for that complexity which they regard as intrinsic to the human enterprise. More indulgent critics, not always younger, find the same kind of writing forceful, healthy, untangled. At first this seems a mere problem in taste, a pardonable difference between those who like their poems and novels knotty and those who like them smooth; but soon it becomes clear that this clash arises from a meeting of incompatible world outlooks. For if the psychology of unobstructed need is taken as a sufficient guide to life, it all but eliminates any place for complexity— or, rather, the need for complexity comes to be seen as a mode of false consciousness, an evasion of true feelings, a psychic bureaucratism in which to trap the pure and the strong. If good sex signifies good feeling; good feeling, good being; good being, good action; and good action, a healthy polity, then we have come the long way round, past the Reichian way or the Lawrentian way, to an Emersonian romanticism minus Emerson's complicatedness of vision. The world snaps back into a system of burgeoning potentialities, waiting for free spirits to attach themselves to the richness of natural object and symbol—except that now the orgasmic blackout is to replace the Oversoul as the current through which pure transcendent energies will flow.

9

We are confronting, then, a new phase in our culture, which in motive and spring represents a wish to shake off the bleeding heritage of modernism and reinstate one of those periods of the collective naif which seem endemic to American experience. The new sensibility is impatient with ideas. It is impatient with literary structures of complexity and coherence, only yesterday the catchwords of our criticism. It wants instead works of literature—though literature may be the wrong word—that will be as absolute as the sun, as unarguable as orgasm, and as delicious as a lollipop. It schemes to throw off the weight of nuance and ambiguity, legacies of high consciousness and tired blood. It is weary of the habit of reflection, the making of distinctions, the squareness of dialectic, the tarnished gold of inherited wisdom. It cares nothing for the haunted memories of old Jews. It has no taste for the ethical nail-biting of those writers of the left who suffered defeat and could never again accept the narcotic of certainty. It is sick of those magnifications of irony that Mann gave us, sick of those visions of entrapment to which Kafka led us, sick of those shufflings of daily horror and grace that Joyce left us. It breathes contempt for rationality, impatience with mind, and a hostility to the artifices and decorums of high culture. It despises liberal values, liberal cautions, liberal virtues. It is bored with the past: for the past is a fink.

Where Marx and Freud were diggers of intellect, mining deeper and deeper into society and the psyche, and forever determined to strengthen the dominion of reason, today the favored direction of search is not inward but sideways, an "expansion of consciousness" through the kick of drugs. The new sensibility is drawn to images of sickness, but not, as with the modernist masters, out of dialectical canniness or religious blasphemy; it takes their denials literally and does not even know the complex desperations that led them to deny. It seeks to charge itself into dazzling sentience through chemicals and the rhetoric of violence. It gropes for sensations: the innocence of blue, the ejaculations of red. It *ordains* life's simplicity. It chooses surfaces as against relationships, the skim of texture rather than the weaving of pattern. Haunted by boredom, it transforms art into a sequence of shocks which, steadily magnified, yield fewer and fewer thrills, so that simply to maintain a modest frisson requires mounting exertions. It proposes an art as disposable as a paper dress, to which one need give nothing but a flicker of notice. Especially in the theater it resurrects tattered heresies, trying to collapse aesthetic distance in behalf of touch and frenzy. (But if illusion is now worn out, what remains but staging the realities of rape, fellatio, and murder?) Cutting itself off from a knowledge of what happened before the moment of its birth, it repeats with a delighted innocence much of what did in fact happen: expressionist drama reduced to skit, agitprop tumbled to farce, Melvillean anguish slackened to black humor. It devalues the word, which is soaked up with too much past history, and favors monochromatic cartoons, companionate grunts, and glimpses of the ineffable in popular ditties. It has humor, but not much wit. Of the tragic it knows next to nothing. Where Dostoevsky made nihilism seem sinister by painting it in jolly colors, the new American sensibility does something no other culture could have aspired to: it makes nihilism seem casual, good-natured, even innocent. No longer burdened by the idea of the problematic, it arms itself with the paraphernalia of postindustrial technique and crash-dives into a Typee of neoprimitivism.

Its high priests are Norman Brown, Herbert Marcuse, and Marshall McLuhan,* all writers with a deeply conservative bias: all committed to a stasis of the given: the stasis of unmoving instinct, the stasis of unmovable society, the stasis of endlessly moving technology. Classics of the latest thing, these three figures lend the new sensibility an aura of profundity. Their prestige can be employed to suggest an organic link between cultural modernism and the new sensibility, though in reality their relation to modernism is no more than biographical.

Perhaps because it is new, some of the new style has its charms—mainly along the margins of social life, in dress, music, and slang. In that it captures the yearnings of a younger generation, the new style has

---

* John Simon has some cogent things to say about Brown and McLuhan, the pop poppas of the new: ". . . like McLuhan, Brown fulfills the four requirements for our prophets: (1) to span and reconcile, however grotesquely, various disciplines to the relief of a multitude of specialists; (2) to affirm something, even if it is something negative, retrogressive, mad; (3) to justify something vulgar or sick or indefensible in us, whether it be television-addiction (McLuhan) or schizophrenia (Brown); (4) to abolish the need for discrimination, difficult choices, balancing mind and appetite, and so reduce the complex orchestration of life to the easy strumming of a monochord. Brown and McLuhan have nicely apportioned the world between them: the inward madness for the one, the outward manias for the other."

more than charm: a vibration of moral desire, a desire for goodness of heart. Still, we had better not deceive ourselves. Some of those shiny-cheeked darlings adorned with flowers and tokens of love can also be campus *enragés* screaming "Up Against the Wall, Motherfuckers, This Is a Stickup" (a slogan that does not strike one as a notable improvement over "Workers of the World, Unite").

That finally there should appear an impulse to shake off the burdens and entanglements of modernism need come as no surprise. After all the virtuosos of torment and enigma we have known, it would be fine to have a period in Western culture devoted to relaxed pleasures and surface hedonism. But so far this does not seem possible. What strikes one about a great deal of the new writing and theater is its grindingly ideological tone, even if now the claim is for an ideology of pleasure. And what strikes one even more is the air of pulsing *ressentiment* which pervades this work, an often unearned and seemingly inexplicable hostility. If one went by the cues of a critic like Susan Sontag, one might suppose that the ethical torments of Kamenetz Podolsk and the moral repressiveness of Salem, Massachusetts, had finally been put to rest, in favor of creamy delights in texture, color, and sensation. But nothing of the sort is true, at least not yet; it is only advertised.

Keen on tactics, the spokesmen for the new sensibility proclaim it to be still another turn in the endless gyrations of modernism, still another revolt in the permanent revolution of twentieth-century sensibility. This approach is very shrewd, since it can disarm in advance those older New York (and other) critics who still respond with enthusiasm to modernism. But several objections or qualifications need to be registered:

Modernism, by its very nature, is uncompromisingly a minority culture, creating and defining itself through opposition to a dominant culture. Today, however, nothing of the sort is true. Floodlights glaring and tills overflowing, the new sensibility is a success from the very start. The middle-class public, eager for thrills and humiliations, welcomes it; so do the mass media, always on the alert for exploitable sensations; and naturally there appear intellectuals with handy theories. The new sensibility is both embodied and celebrated in the actions of Mailer, whose condition as a swinger in America is not quite comparable with that of Joyce in Trieste or Kafka in Prague or Lawrence anywhere; it is reinforced with critical exegesis by Susan Sontag, a publicist able to make brilliant quilts from grandmother's patches. And on a far lower level, it has even found its Smerdyakov in LeRoi Jones, that parodist of apocalypse who rallies enlightened Jewish audiences with calls for

Jewish blood. Whatever one may think of this situation, it is surely very different from the classical picture of a besieged modernism.

By now the search for the "new," often reduced to a trivializing of form and matter, has become the predictable old. To suppose that we keep moving from cultural breakthrough to breakthrough requires a collective wish to forget what happened yesterday and even the day before: ignorance always being a great spur to claims for originality. Alienation has been transformed from a serious revolutionary concept into a motif of mass culture, and the content of modernism into the decor of kitsch. As Harold Rosenberg has pungently remarked:

> The sentiment of the diminution of personality is an historical hypothesis upon which writers have constructed a set of literary conventions by this time richly equipped with theatrical machinery and symbolic allusions. . . . The individual's emptiness and inability to act have become an irrefrangible cliché, untiringly supported by an immense, voluntary phalanx of latecomers to modernism. In this manifestation, the notion of the void has lost its critical edge and is thoroughly reactionary.

The effort to assimilate new cultural styles to the modernist tradition brushes aside problems of value, quality, judgment. It rests upon a philistine version of the theory of progress in the arts: all must keep changing, and change signifies a realization of progress. Yet even if an illicit filiation can be shown, there is a vast difference in accomplishment between the modernism of some decades ago and what we have now. The great literary modernists put at the center of their work a confrontation and struggle with the demons of nihilism; the literary swingers of the sixties, facing a nihilist violation, cheerfully remove the threat by what Fielding once called "a timely compliance." Just as in the verse of Swinburne echoes of Romanticism sag through the stanzas, so in much current writing there is indeed a continuity with modernism, but a continuity of grotesque and parody, through the doubles of fashion.

Still, it would be foolish to deny that in this kulturkampf, the New York intellectuals are at a severe disadvantage. Some have simply gone over to the other camp. A critic like Susan Sontag employs the dialectical skills and accumulated knowledge of intellectual life in order to bless the new sensibility as a dispensation of pleasure, beyond the grubby reach of interpretation and thereby, it would seem, beyond the tight voice of judgment. That her theories are skillfully rebuilt versions of aesthetic notions long familiar and discarded; that in her own critical writing she interprets like mad and casts an image anything but hedonistic, relaxed, or sensuous—none of this need bother her admirers, for a highly literate spokesman is very sustaining to those who have discarded or not acquired intellectual literacy. Second only to Sontag in trumpeting the new sensibility is Leslie Fiedler, a critic with an amiable weakness for thrusting himself at the head of parades marching into sight.*

But for those New York (or any other) writers not quite enchanted with the current scene there are serious difficulties.

They cannot be quite *sure*. Having fought in the later battles for modernism, they must acknowledge to themselves the possibility that, now grown older, they have lost their capacity to appreciate innovation. Why, they ask themselves with some irony, should "their" cultural revolution have been the last one, or the last good one? From the publicists of the new sensibility they hear the very slogans, catchwords, and stirring appeals which a few decades ago they were hurling against such diehards as Van Wyck Brooks and Bernard de Voto. And given the notorious difficulties in making judgments about contemporary works of art, how can they be certain that Kafka is a master of despair and Burroughs a symptom of disintegration, Pollock a pioneer of innovation and Warhol a triviality of pop? The capacity for self-doubt, the habit of self-irony which is the reward of decades of experience, renders them susceptible to the simplistic cries of the new.

Well, the answer is that there can be no certainty: we should neither want nor need it. One must speak out of one's taste and conviction, and let history make whatever judgments it will care to. But this is not an easy stand to take, for it means that after all these years one may have to face intellectual isolation, and there are moments when it must seem as if the best course is to be promiscuously "receptive," swinging along with a grin of resignation.

---

* Fiedler's essay "The New Mutants" (*Partisan Review*, Fall 1965) is a sympathetic charting of the new sensibility, with discussions of "pornoesthetics," the effort among young people to abandon habits and symbols of masculinity in favor of a feminized receptiveness, "the aspiration to take the final evolutionary leap and cast off adulthood completely," and above all, the role of drugs as "the crux of the futurist revolt."

With uncharacteristic forbearance, Fiedler denies himself any sustained or explicit judgments of this "futurist revolt," so that the rhetorical thrust of his essay is somewhere between acclaim and resignation. He cannot completely suppress his mind, perhaps because he has been using it too long, and so we find this acute passage concerning the responses of older writers to "the most obscene forays of the young":

". . . after a while, there will be no more Philip Rahvs and Stanley Edgar Hymans left to shock—antilanguage becoming mere language with repeated use and in the face of acceptance; so that all sense of exhilaration will be lost along with the possibility of offense. What to do then except to choose silence, since raising the ante of violence is ultimately self-defeating; and the way of obscenity in any case leads as naturally to silence as to further excess?"

About drugs Fiedler betrays no equivalent skepticism, so that it is hard to disagree with Lionel Abel's judgment that, "while I do not want to charge Mr. Fiedler with recommending the taking of drugs, I think his whole essay is a confession that he cannot call upon one value in whose name he could oppose it."

10

In the face of this challenge, surely the most serious of the last twenty-five years, the New York intellectuals have not been able to mount a coherent response, certainly not a judgment sufficiently inclusive and severe. There have been a few efforts, some intellectual polemics by Lionel Abel and literary pieces by Philip Rahv; but no more. Yet if ever there was a moment when our culture needed an austere and sharp criticism—the one talent the New York writers supposedly find it death to hide—it is today. One could imagine a journal with the standards, if not the parochialism, of *Scrutiny*. One could imagine a journal like *Partisan Review* stripping the pretensions of the current scene with the vigor it showed in opposing the Popular Front and neoconservative cultures. But these are fantasies. In its often accomplished pages *Partisan Review* betrays a hopeless clash between its editors' capacity to apply serious standards and their yearnings to embrace the moment. Predictably, the result leaves everyone dissatisfied.

One example of the failure of the New York writers to engage in criticism is their relation to Mailer. He is not an easy man to come to grips with, for he is "our genius," probably the only one, and in more than a merely personal way he is a man of enormous charm. Yet Mailer has been the central and certainly most dramatic presence in the new sensibility, even if in reflective moments he makes clear his ability to brush aside its incantations.* Mailer as thaumaturgist of orgasm; as metaphysician of the gut; as psychic herb-doctor; as advance man for literary violence;† as dialectician of unreason; and above all, as a novelist who has laid waste his own formidable talent—these masks of brilliant, nutty restlessness, these papery dikes against squalls of boredom—all require sharp analysis and criticism. Were Mailer to read these lines he would surely grin and exclaim that, whatever else, his books have suffered plenty of denunciation. My point, however, is not that he has failed to receive adverse reviews, including some from such New York critics as

---

* Two examples: "Tom Hayden began to discuss revolution with Mailer. 'I'm for Kennedy,' said Mailer, 'because I'm not so sure I want a revolution. Some of those kids are awfully dumb.' Hayden the Revolutionary said a vote for George Wallace would further his objective more than a vote for RFK." (*Village Voice*, May 30, 1968—and by the way, some Revolutionary!) "If he still took a toke of marijuana from time to time for Auld Lang Syne, or in recognition of the probability that good sex had to be awfully good before it was better than on pot, yet, still!—Mailer was not in approval of any drug, he was virtually conservative about it, having demanded of his eighteen-year-old daughter . . . that she not take marijuana, and never LSD, until she completed her education, a mean promise to extract in these apocalyptic times." (*The Armies of the Night*.)

† In this regard the editor of *Dissent* bears a heavy responsibility. When he first received the manuscript of "The White Negro," he should have expressed in print, if he chose to publish the essay, his objections to the passage in which Mailer discusses the morality of beating up a fifty-year-old storekeeper. That he could not bring himself to risk loosing a scoop is no excuse whatever.

Norman Podhoretz, Elizabeth Hardwick, and Philip Rahv; perhaps he has even had too many adverse reviews, given the scope and brightness of his talent. My point is that the New York writers have failed to confront Mailer seriously as an intellectual spokesman, and instead have found it easier to regard him as a hostage to the temper of our times. What has not been forthcoming is a recognition, surely a painful one, that in his major public roles he has come to represent values in deep opposition to liberal humaneness and rational discourse. That the New York critics have refused him this confrontation is both a disservice to Mailer and a sign that, whatever it may once have been, the New York intellectual community no longer exists as a significant force.

An equally telling sign is the recent growth in popularity and influence of the *New York Review of Books*. Emerging at least in part from the New York intellectual milieu, this journal has steadily moved away from the styles and premises with which it began. Its early dependence on those New York writers who lent their names to it and helped establish it seems all but over. The Jewish imprint has been blotted out; the *New York Review*, for all its sharp attacks on current political policies, is thoroughly at home in the worlds of American culture, publishing, and society. It features a strong Anglophile slant in its literary pieces, perhaps in accord with the *New Statesman* formula of blending leftish (and at one time, fellow-traveling) politics with Bloomsbury culture. More precisely, what the *New York Review* has managed to achieve—I find it quite fascinating as a portent of things to come—is a link between campus "leftism" and East Side stylishness, the worlds of Tom Hayden and George Plimpton. Opposition to Communist politics and ideology is frequently presented in the pages of the *New York Review* as if it were an obsolete, indeed a pathetic, hangover from a discredited past or, worse yet, a dark sign of the CIA. A snappish and crude anti-Americanism has swept over much of its political writing—and to avoid misunderstanding, let me say that by this I do not mean anything so necessary as attacks on the ghastly Vietnam war or on our failures in the cities. And in the hands of writers like Andrew Kopkind (author of the immortal phrase "morality . . . starts at the barrel of a gun"), liberal values and norms are treated with something very close to contempt.

Though itself too sophisticated to indulge in the more preposterous New Left notions, such as "liberal fascism" and "confrontationism," the *New York Review* has done the New Left the considerable service of providing it with a link of intellectual respectability to the academic world. In the materials it has published by Kopkind, Hayden, Rahv, Edgar Z. Friedenberg, Jason Epstein, and others, one finds not an acceptance of the fashionable talk about "revolution" which has become a sport on the American campus, but a kind of rhetorical violence, a verbal "radicalism," which gives moral and intellectual encouragement to precisely such fashionable (self-defeating) talk.

This is by no means the only kind of political material to have appeared in the *New York Review*; at least in my own experience I have found its editors prepared to print articles of a sharply different kind; and in recent years it has published serious political criticism by George Lichtheim, Theodore Draper, and Walter Laqueur. And because it is concerned with maintaining a certain level of sophistication and accomplishment, the *New York Review* has not simply taken over the new sensibility. No, at stake here is the dominant tone of this skillfully edited paper, an editorial keenness in responding to the current academic and intellectual temper—as for instance in that memorable issue with a cover featuring, no doubt for the benefit of its university readers, a diagram explaining how to make a Molotov cocktail. The genius of the *New York Review*, and it has been a genius of sorts, is not, in either politics or culture, for swimming against the stream.

Perhaps it is too late. Perhaps there is no longer available among the New York writers enough energy and coherence to make possible a sustained confrontation with the new sensibility. Still, one would imagine that their undimmed sense of the zeitgeist would prod them to sharp responses, precise statements, polemical assaults.

Having been formed by, and through opposition to, the New York intellectual experience, I cannot look with joy at the prospect of its ending. But not with dismay either. Such breakups are inevitable, and out of them come new voices and energies. Yet precisely at this moment of dispersion, might not some of the New York writers achieve renewed strength if they were to struggle once again for whatever has been salvaged from these last few decades? For the values of liberalism, for the politics of a democratic radicalism, for the norms of rationality and intelligence, for the standards of literary seriousness, for the life of the mind as a humane dedication—for all this it should again be worth finding themselves in a minority, even a beleaguered minority, and not with fantasies of martyrdom but with a quiet recognition that for the intellectual this is likely to be his usual condition.

III The Seventies

Zola: The Poetry of Naturalism

Each generation fashions its own blinkers and then insists that they allow unimpeded vision. My generation grew up with a mild scorn for the writers of naturalistic fiction who flourished in the late nineteenth and early twentieth centuries. Some of them we took to be estimable and others talented: we did not mean to be unfair. Many naturalists had a strong feeling for social justice, and if irrelevant to their stature as writers, this seemed to their credit as men. Zola's great cry during the Dreyfus Affair could still rouse admiration. His great cry could stir even those of us who had reached the peak of sophistication where Flaubert was judged superior to Balzac, Stendhal to Flaubert, and all three, it need hardly be said, to Zola—for Zola was tendentious, Zola was rhetorical, Zola was coarse.

Everyone had of course read Zola earlier, in those years of adolescence when all that matters in our encounter with a novel is to soak up its experience. Then *Germinal* had stirred us to the bone. But later we learned that literary judgment must not be defiled by political ideas, and Zola, that clumsy bear of a novelist, became an object of condescension.

Introduction to *Germinal* (New York: New American Library, 1970).

It was wrong, hopelessly wrong—like those literary fashions of our own moment which two or three decades from now will also seem wrong. Reading *Germinal* again, I have been overwhelmed by its magnitude of structure and fertility of imagination.

Still, it should be admitted that if we were once unjust to Zola, some of the blame must fall on his own shoulders. He pontificated too much about Literature and Science. We are accustomed in America to bemoaning the dumbness that overcomes many of our writers, and behind this complaint there is often a naive assumption that European writers have commonly possessed the range of culture we associate with, say, a Thomas Mann. It is not true, of course. What had Dickens or Balzac to say about the art of the novel? As for Zola, there can hardly have been a modern writer so confused about the work he was doing. Consider the mechanical scientism to which he clung with the credulousness of a peasant; the ill-conceived effort to show forces of heredity determining the lives of his characters; the willful absurdity of such declarations as "the same determinism should regulate paving-stones and human brains"; the turgid mimicry with which Zola transposed the physiological theories of Claude Bernard into his *Le Roman expérimental*.

Yet we ought not to be too hasty in dismissing Zola's intellectual claims. His physiological determinism may now seem crude, but his sense of the crushing weight which the world can lower upon men remains only too faithful to modern experience, perhaps to all experience. If his theories about the naturalistic novel now seem mainly of historical interest, this does not mean that the naturalistic novel itself can be brushed aside. What remains vital in the naturalistic novel as Zola wrote it in France and Dreiser in America is not the groping toward an assured causality; what remains vital is the massed detail of the fictional worlds they establish, the patience—itself a form of artistic scruple—with which they record the suffering of their time.

In looking back upon the philosophical improvisations of those late nineteenth-century writers who were driven by conscience to surrender the Christian faith and then to improvise versions of rigid mechanism and spiritualized secularism, we like to suppose that their "ideas" were little more than impediments they had to put aside. You ignore Dreiser's pronouncements about "chemisms"; you agree with Huysmans' remark about Zola: "Thank God he has not carried out in his novels the theories of his articles, which extol the infusion of positivism in art." There is something to be said for this view of the matter, but less than we commonly suppose, for the announced ideas behind a novel ought not to be confused with the actual play of its author's intelligence. We may judge these announced ideas as tiresome or a mere reflex of fashion;

we may be irritated by their occasional appearance, like a mound of fossil, along the path of the narrative; yet in the novel itself the writer can be engaged in a play of intelligence far more supple than his formal claims lead us to suppose. A reductive determinism is what Zola flaunts, as when he places Taine's not very brilliant remark, "Vice and virtue are products like sugar and vitriol," on the title page of *Thérèse Raquin*; but a reductive determinism is by no means what controls *Germinal* and *L'Assommoir*. When we say that a work of literature "takes on a life of its own," we mean that the process of composition has brought fundamental shifts in perspective which could not have been foreseen by studying the author's original intention.

Even among ideas we regard as mistaken, sharp discriminations must be made when trying to judge their literary consequences. A writer infatuated with one or another kind of psychic charlatanism is hard to take seriously. A writer drawn to the brutalities of fascism rouses a hostility that no aesthetic detachment can keep from spilling over into our feelings about his work. But when writers like Zola, Hardy, and Dreiser were attracted to the thought of Darwin and Huxley, they were struggling with serious problems. They may have succumbed too easily to the "advanced ideas" of the moment—precisely the kind that date most quickly. Still, they were grappling with questions that gave them no rest, just as a half-century later Sartre and Camus would be grappling with the questions raised by existentialism, a school of philosophy that may not last much longer than deterministic scientism but which has nevertheless helped to liberate creative powers.

One large tendency in nineteenth-century literature is an impulse to spiritualize the world, to distribute the godhead among numberless grains of matter, so that in a new if less tidy way, purpose can be restored to the cosmos and the sequence of creation and re-creation be made to replace the promise of immortality. Toward the end of the nineteenth century men like Zola could no longer accept transcendental or pantheist derivatives from Christianity, yet they wanted some principle of order by means of which to locate themselves in the universe; whereupon they proceeded to shift the mystery of the creation onto the lawfulness of the determined. What then frightened reflective people was something that we, in our benumbed age, seem to accept rather easily: the thought of a world without intrinsic plan or point.

Zola went still further than those writers who transferred the dynamic of faith into a fixity of law. Like Balzac before him, he yielded to the brilliant impiety of transforming himself into a kind of god, a god of tireless fecundity creating his universe over and over again. The nineteenth-century novelist—Dickens or Balzac, Hardy or Zola—enacts in his own career the vitalism about which the thought of his age drives him to a growing skepticism. Zola's three or four great novels are anything but inert or foredoomed. He may start with notions of inevitability, but his narrative boils with energy and novelty. *Germinal* ends with the gloom of defeat, but not a gloom predestined. There is simply too much appetite for experience in Zola, too much solidarity with the struggles by which men try to declare themselves, too much hope for the generations always on the horizon and promising to undo the wrongs of the past, for *Germinal* to become a mere reflex of a system of causality. Zola's gropings into the philosophy of determinism freed him to become a writer of energy, rebellion, and creation.

2

Germinal releases one of the central myths of the modern era: the story of how the dumb acquire speech. All those at the bottom of history, for centuries objects of control, begin to transform themselves into active subjects, determined to create their own history.

Now we cannot say that this myth has gained universal acceptance in our culture, nor that those of us who register its moral claims can do so with the unquestioning credence and mounting awe we suppose characteristic of men in ancient cultures. Still, we might remember that insofar as we know Greek myth through Greek drama, we know it mediated by individual artists, and with the passage of time, mediated in directions increasingly skeptical. The myth in *Germinal*—if we agree, however hesitantly, to call it a myth—is one that takes its formative energies from the French Revolution. It is the myth of the people and more particularly the proletariat. They who had merely suffered and at times erupted into blind rebellion; they who had been prey to but not part of society; they who had found no voice in the past—they now emerge from the sleep of history and begin the task of collective self-formation. This, of course, is a schematized version of historical reality, or at least a perspective on historical reality. Where traditional myths appear to us as transhistorical, a frieze of symbolic representation, our own take their very substance from the materials of history, magnifying and rendering heroic the actions of men in time. Some idea of this kind may have led Thomas Mann to write that "in Zola's epic," made up as it is of events taken from everyday life, "the characters themselves are raised up to a plane above that of everyday life."

The myth of *Germinal* as I have been sketching it is close to the Marxist view of the dynamics of capitalism, but to yield ourselves to Zola's story is not necessarily to accept the Marxist system. Zola himself does not accept it. At crucial points he remains a skeptic about the myth that forms the soul of his action. His skepticism is not really about the recuperative powers of the miners, for it is his instinctive way of looking at things that he should see the generations crowding one another, pushing for life space, thrusting their clamor onto the world. His skepticism runs deeper. Zola sees the possibility that in the very emergence of solidarity—that great and terrible word for which so many have gone smiling to their death!—there would be formed, by a ghastly dialectic of history, new rulers and oppressors: the Rasseneurs, the Plucharts, and even the Lantiers of tomorrow, raised to the status of leaders and bureaucrats, who would impose their will on the proletariat. Zola does not insist that this must happen, for he is a novelist, not a political theoretician. What he does is to show in the experience of the Montsou workers the germ of such a possibility. As it celebrates the greatest event of modern history, the myth of emergence contains within itself the negation of that greatness.

At the center of the novel is the mine. Dramatic embodiment of exploitation, the mine nevertheless makes possible the discipline through which to overcome exploitation. But for the moment, man's nature still bows to his history, personal need to the workings of the market. The mine has a "natural" awesomeness, with its crevices and alleys, depths and darkness: its symbolic power arises organically, spontaneously, and not as a willed imposition of the writer. And then, in a stroke that does bear the mark of will, Zola creates an astonishing parallel to the miners. The mine-horses share the misery of the men, but without the potential for motivated rebellion; the mine-horses represent, with an expressionist grossness that defeats critical scruples, what the men may yet accept or sink to.

The mine is voracious and unappeasable, a physical emblem of the impersonality of commodity production. It "seemed evil-looking, a hungry beast crouched and ready to devour the world." It "kept devouring men . . . always ravenous, its giant bowels capable of digesting an entire nation." But this suggestion of a force bursting out of the control of its creators gains its strength not merely from the intrinsic properties of the mine. Here Zola does come close to the Marxist notion that men must beware of fetishizing their predicaments; they must recognize that not in mines or factories lie the sources of their troubles but in the historically determined relations between contending classes. And here surely historical associations come into play, associations which even the least literate reader is likely to have with mining—a major industry of early industrialism, notorious for its high rate of exhaustion and accident. As always in *Germinal*, the mythic and symbolic are of the very substance of the historical. And thereby Zola can fill out his myth with the evidence of circumstantiality. The more he piles up descriptions of the mine's tunnels, shafts, timbering, airlessness, and dampness, the more are we prepared to see it as the setting for the apocalypse with which the book reaches its climax.

In a fine piece some years ago William Troy remarked that the great scene in which Etienne and Catherine are trapped in the mine

> . . . brings us back to an atmosphere and a meaning at least as old as the story of Orpheus and Eurydice. For what is the mine itself but a reintegration of the Hades-Hell symbol? The immediate and particular social situation is contained within the larger pattern of a universal recrudescence. . . . Etienne emerges from his journey underground to *la vita nuova* of his own and of social experience.

The Orpheus-Eurydice motif is there, Etienne experiences a recrudescence, though of a somewhat ambiguous kind, and the mine is surely the symbolic center of the book. Yet we should be clear as to how Zola achieves these effects. Zola controls his narrative with one overriding end in mind, and that is to show not the way men are swallowed by their work (surely not new) nor how a hero can emerge healed from the depths (also not new) but the gradual formation of *a collective consciousness*. When Maheu, that superbly drawn worker, begins to speak to the manager, "the words were coming of themselves, and at moments he listened to himself in surprise, as though some stranger within him were speaking." The stranger is his long-buried self, and this transfiguration of Maheu is at least as morally significant as that of the individual protagonist gaining access to self-knowledge in the earlier nineteenth-century novel.

Etienne reads, Maheu speaks, La Maheude cries out: everything is changed. Gathering their strength and for a time delirious with fantasies of freedom, almost childlike in the pleasures of their assertiveness, the workers become what Marx called a class for itself. And then, with his uncanny gift for achieving mass effects through individual strokes, Zola begins to individualize his characters. He does this not to approximate that fragmented psychology we associate with nineteenth-century fiction but toward the end of preparing the characters for their new roles: Etienne in the pride and exposure of leadership, Maheu in the conquest of manhood, La Maheude as the voice of ancient grievance, and even the children, led by the devilish Jeanlin, who in their debauchery release the spontaneous zest that the overdisciplined life of the miners has suppressed.

The strike becomes the central action. The workers are shown in their rise to a noble solidarity and their fall to a brutal mob—better yet, in the ways the two, under intolerable stress, become all but indistinguishable. ("Do not flatter the working class nor blacken it," Zola told himself in notes for *L'Assommoir*.) And nothing is more brilliant than Zola's intuition—it speaks for his powers of insinuating himself beneath the skin of the miners—that after the horrible riot with which Part Five closes, he sees the men continuing their strike, digging in with a mute fatalism, "a great somber peacefulness," which rests far less on expectations of victory than on a common yielding to the pathos of standing and starving together. Defeat comes, and demoralization too, but only after Zola has charted the rhythms of struggle, rhythms as intrinsically absorbing for the novelist (and at least as difficult to apprehend) as those of the individual psyche in turmoil.

Again, it should be stressed that the myth Zola employs is not the vulgar-Marxist notion of an inevitable victory or of a victory-in-defeat ending with resolves for the future. True, he shows as no other European novelist before him, the emergence of a new historical force, and he reveals the conflict that must follow; but its outcome remains uncertain, shadowy, ambiguous.

3

A work of modern literature may employ a myth and perhaps even create one, as I think *Germinal* does, but it cannot satisfy its audience with a composed recapitulation of a known, archetypal story. With theme it must offer richness of variation, often of a radical kind, so as slyly to bring into question the theme itself. The hieratic does not seem a mode easily accessible to modern literature. We want, perversely, our myths to have a stamp of the individual, our eternal stories to bear a quiver of nervous temporality.

The picture Zola draws of Montsou as a whole, and of Montsou as a microcosm of industrial society, depends for its effectiveness mainly on the authority with which he depicts the position of the miners. Just as the novel is a genre that gains its most solid effects through accumulation and narrative development, so the action of Zola's book depends on his command of an arc of modern history. If he can persuade us that he sees this experience with coherence and depth, then we will not be excessively troubled by whatever intellectual disagreements we may have with him or by our judgment that in particular sections of the novel he fails through heavy exaggeration and lapses of taste. Two lines out of tune in a sonnet can spoil our pleasure; but in a novel whole episodes can be out of tune without necessarily spoiling our pleasure, since an extended prose fiction depends mainly on such large-scale effects as narrative thrust and character development.

Again we reach an interpenetration of commanding myth and historical material—what I take to be Zola's great achievement in *Germinal*. A stranger arrives, slightly removed from the workers because of superior intellect, yet required to enter their lives and ready to share their troubles. So far, the pattern of the story is not very different from that of much fiction composed earlier in the nineteenth century. But then comes a radical shift; the stranger, now on the way to being a leader, remains at the center of the book, but his desires and reflections do not constitute its central matter. What engages us primarily is the collective experience of the miners, the myth of their emergence. In Part Five of *Germinal*, the most original and exciting portion, this entry into consciousness is shown with a complexity of tone that unites passionate involvement and dispassionate removal. In his notes for the book Zola understood that he must remain faithful to his story as archetype:

> To get a broad effect I must have my two sides as clearly contrasted as possible and carried to the very extreme of intensity. So that I must start with all the woes and fatalities which weigh down the miners. Facts, not emotional pleas. The miner must be shown crushed, starving, a victim of ignorance, suffering with his children in a hell on earth—but not persecuted, for the bosses are not deliberately vindictive—*he is simply overwehelmed by the social situation as it exists.* On the contrary I must make the bosses humane so long as their direct interests are not threatened; no point in foolish tub-thumping. The worker is the victim of the facts of existence— capital, competition, industrial crises.

For this perception to be transformed into a dramatic action, Zola relies mainly on the narrative increment that follows from his myth of the speechless and the symbolic suggestiveness of the mine. In saying this I don't mean to imply that everything which occurs in the novel is necessary or appropriate. The narrative is frequently flawed by lurid effects. Zola, as someone has remarked, had an overwhelming imagination but only an uncertain—and sometimes a corrupted—taste. That the riot of the miners should be a terrifying event seems entirely right; that it should end with the ghastly frisson invented by Zola is a sign of his weakness for sensationalism. Zola tries hard to present his middle-class characters, the Hennebeaus and Grégoires, with some objectivity and even sympathy, but he usually fails. Not, I think, for the reason William Troy gives: ". . . the inherent unsuitability of naturalism, a system of causality based on quasi-scientific principles, to the practice of literature." I doubt that local failures in a novel are ever to be traced so directly to philosophical conceptions. Zola fails because in this novel he is not interested in such people at all. They are there because his over-all scheme demands it, to "fill out the picture." Sensing as much, we read these inferior portions with a certain tolerance, assuaged by the likelihood that further great scenes with the miners lie ahead. The mediocre intervals come to serve as "rests" helping Zola regather suspense. M. Hennebeau, the mine manager, is a partial exception, if only because he is a figure of power and power is always fascinating for Zola. Still, the subplot of Hennebeau's personal unhappiness and his envy of what he takes to be the miners' unsoiled virility is obviously weak—just how weak one can see by comparing it to D. H. Lawrence's treatment of similar material. And again, the immersion of Etienne and Catherine in the mine, once the strike has been lost, is both a scene of considerable power and a scene marred by Zola's lack of discipline when he has the body of Chaval, the girl's former lover, float horribly up to them in the darkness. Zola does not know when to stop.

To notice such flaws can be damaging, and to write as if *Germinal* were no more than the sum of local incidents could be a strategy for dismissing the book entirely. But this seems a poor way of dealing with a novel. *Germinal* depends upon effects that are larger, more gross, and less open to isolated inspection than picking out scenes of weakness would suggest; it depends upon the large-muscled rhythms of the narrative as a whole. We are dealing here with a writer of genius who, in both the quality of his imagination and the occasional wantonness of his prose, can sometimes be described as decadent. One remembers T. S. Eliot's remark that Dickens was "a decadent genius," a remark accurate enough if the noun is stressed at least as much as the modifier. The decadence of Zola, which has points of similarity to that of Dickens, comes through in the excesses of local episodes, the vulgarities of particular paragraphs, the flushed rhetoric with which Zola seeks to "reinforce" material that has already been presented with enough dramatic vitality. The genius comes through in the mythic-historical sweep of the narrative as a whole.

If what I have been saying has validity, it follows that there will also be frequent episodes of brilliance—else how could the novelist achieve his large rhythms of narration? And there are, of course, such episodes. Two kinds may be distinguished: those persuading us of Zola's authority as imaginative historian (substantiating detail) and those persuading us of his psychological penetration into a given moment of the action (illuminating detail).

The first kind is to be found mainly in his treatment of the miners

at the peak of crisis. Etienne reading a Belgian socialist weekly, hastily
and poorly absorbing its contents, seeking to make up for years of waste
as he is "gripped by the uneducated man's methodless passion for study"
and then overcome by "the dull dread that he had shown himself unequal
to the task"—all this bears the thick circumstantiality of the actual. Zola
knew the kind of men who were drawn to socialist politics: not merely
learned bourgeois intellectuals like Marx and Kautsky, but self-educated
workers like Bebel, straining with ambition and stumbling into knowledge. This command of his material is shown even more subtly in the
portrayal of the inner relationships among his three radicals: Rasseneur,
the most cautious and experienced, clearly on the way to becoming a
classical social democrat; Souvarine, also a classical figure, though of the
anarchist-terrorist kind who declares the need "to destroy everything
. . . no more nations, no more governments, no more property, no more
God or religion" and then to return to "the primitive and formless
community," and Etienne, the sincere unformed worker, open to a wide
range of possibilities but determined—his aspiring intellectuality prods
his ambition—to make a place for himself on the stage of history.

The second kind of detail shows Zola's imagination at work somewhat more freely, releasing incidents which do not depend directly on
the over-all design of the novel. On the simplest level there is the pathos
of the mine girl Mouquette, hopelessly generous with all she has (her
body to the men, her affection to almost anyone, her bared bottom to
the strikebreakers), who offers Etienne a dozen cold potatoes to still
the hunger of the Maheu household. It is a trifle, but from such trifles
novels are made. On a level hard to apprehend in strictly rational terms,
there is Etienne finding himself a place to hide, after the riot, in one of
the hated mines. But the greatest of such imaginative strokes concerns
the strange old Bonnemort, introduced at the outset as a ghost of a man
embodying the workers' exhaustion. He has nothing to say, he is barely
alive, until at the strike meeting, amid the predictably rousing speeches

> . . . everybody was surprised to see old Bonnemort standing on the tree
> trunk and trying to make himself heard. . . . No doubt he was giving way
> to one of those sudden fits of babbling that would sometimes stir up the
> past so violently that old memories would rise from his depths and flow
> from his lips for hours. It had become very quiet, and everybody listened
> to the old man, so ghostly pale in the moonlight; as he was talking about
> things that had no obvious connection with the discussion, long stories that
> nobody could understand, their astonishment increased. He spoke of his
> youth, told of his two uncles who had been crushed to death at Le Voreux,
> then went on to the pneumonia that had carried off his wife. Through it

all, however, he never lost hold of his one idea: things had never been right and they never would be right.

Without rhetorical strain, this passage summons the whole unreckoned waste that forms our history. The mode is grotesque, but for readers with a measure of historical imagination, Zola achieves something far beyond the limits of what that descriptive usually suggests.

4

Zola's style aspires toward a rich and heavy impasto rather than toward a lucid line drawing, and it is often marred by excess. In *Germinal* the writing is nevertheless effective at two points: first, the passages describing the mine with that wary respect for the power of the actual a novelist must have, and second, the episodes in which he evokes the surge of conflict and the passions of enraged men. In these episodes the prose can be extremely effective, combining mass and speed—as long as Zola stays with his central purpose, which is to depict the sensations of men who have thrown off the discipline of society but not yet discovered the discipline of self. Nor need we succumb to any version of "the imitative fallacy"—that in its internal qualities a style must reflect the matter it is trying to convey—in order to recognize at least some correspondences as proper to the relation between style and subject. One does not write about the collapse of a mine in the style of Henry James.

Zola achieves the effect of speed, but not the light or nervous speed of a Stephen Crane or an Isaac Babel. Especially in Part Five of the novel, his style is that of a rumbling and heavy speed—a leaden speed. The writing is rarely nimble or graceful; the sentences are weighted with qualifiers and prepositional phrases, as well as with accumulating clauses which repeat and magnify the matter of their predecessors. Admittedly, this prose is highly rhetorical: it employs organic metaphors of anger, release, and cataclysm ("Nature," says Zola, "is associated with our griefs"), and it depends heavily on Zola's hoarse and rasping voice. For what he is trying to do seems decidedly risky, even from the vantage point of years later: he is giving dramatic embodiment to a collective as it disintegrates into a mob, and since he must keep his attention mainly on the group, which has of course no individuality of consciousness or will, he finds himself forced to speak in his own voice. That, in the actuality of composition, is the paradox the novelist must face when he tries to dramatize the conduct of a group. His effort to create an action of objectivity, a plot of collective behavior, leads the novelist to a style of subjectivity in which he finds himself driven to "impersonate" the group. At its worst, this kind of writing can seem willed—an effort to do for the action through rhetoric what filmmakers try to do for their stories through music. At its best, the writing has a coarse strength and even splendor—what might be called the poetry of naturalism.

Still, it would be foolish to claim for Zola that his prose yields the kind of sentence-by-sentence pleasure that can be had from the prose of a James or Flaubert. Zola is often careless as a stylist, sometimes wanton, occasionally cheap. His trouble, however, is not that his prose lacks nicety of phrasing or epigrammatic neatness; it is that he does not content himself with plainness but must reach out for the ornamental and exalted, seeking through rhetorical fancywork to establish his credentials as a literary man.

His style, like almost everything else in *Germinal*, is interesting mainly when considered in the large. One then encounters a phenomenon which seems an essential mystery of literature. For long portions of the novel Zola yields himself entirely to the passions of the miners, and his prose becomes strongly, even exorbitantly, passionate. We are swept along by the surge of men in revolt; the language heaves and breaks, sweeping across us with torrents of rhetoric. Rhetoric, yes; but a rhetoric which accompanies and sustains a remarkably strong evocation. The passion Zola pours out finds its match, its justification, in the incidents he imagines. Yet, as we read into the depths of the book, we grow aware that there is another Zola, one who draws back a little, seeing the whole tragedy as part of an eternal rhythm of struggle and decision. This Zola is finally dispassionate, withdrawn from his own commitments, and capable of a measure of irony toward the whole human enterprise. Zola the partisan and Zola the artist: for those who like their "commitment" straight such ambivalence is detestable. But I take it to be a sign of Zola's achievement. If there has ever been a novel concerning which one might forgive a writer his unmodulated passions it is *Germinal*; yet precisely here Zola's "scientism" proves to be an unexpected advantage, enabling him to achieve an aesthetic distance that gives the book its ultimate austerity.

There is still another doubleness of response in *Germinal*. Hardly a Zola critic has failed to note the frequency with which images of fecundity occur in the book—repeated scenes in which, along and beyond the margin of his central narrative, Zola displays the unplanned and purposeless creativity of existence. Henry James, in his essay on Zola, remarks: "To make his characters swarm, and to make the great central thing they swarm about 'as large as life,' portentously, heroically big, that was the task he set himself very nearly from the first."

Now for many nineteenth-century novelists, this "swarming" can be a source not merely of narrative energy but also of a pseudoreligious sentimentalism. Everyone has encountered it as a special kind of fictional cant: the generations come, the generations go, and so on. Asserted without irony, such declamations often constitute a kind of psychic swindle, convenient enough for novelists who fear the depressing logic of their own work or who need some unearned lilt in their final pages. That Zola does approach this kind of sentimentalism seems beyond doubt, but again and again he draws back into a baffled stoicism, evading the trap his romantic heritage has set for him. "A black avenging army" is "germinating in the furrows"; "soon this germination would sunder the earth." But even as such sentiments fill Zola's final pages there is no simple assurance—indeed, no assurance of any kind. Despite the sense of a swarming procreation which keeps the race alive, Zola ends on a note of anguish; he does not propose an easy harmony between the replenishments of nature and the desires of men. Etienne, clumsily balancing idealism and ambition, goes out into the world. To one reader at least, he enters upon neither personal triumph nor the "final conflict" promised by the dialectic of history, but upon a journey into those treacherous regions of the unknown where sooner or later we all find ourselves.

George Konrád's
The Case Worker

George Konrád's *The Case Worker* is a fiction that takes us into the underlife of the city and the inner life of a man who is its creature.

Beneath the lowest rungs of the social order live the hopeless and speechless, the broken and deformed, the flotsam and lumpens, all those who have signed a separate peace with reality (what the narrator calls "the faulty nature of things") and now need not confront rules, skills, or responsibilities. The hierarchy of class weighs upon them, yet they are not part of it. They form the waste of modern life, the sweepings of the city, and they are kept going, sometimes kept down, by those agents of the state we call social workers.

Modern literature has noticed them not as "cases" but as figures. They appear as tragic buffoons in Dostoevsky, rasping comic voices in Céline, sad grotesques in Nathanael West, stumps of life in Hubert Selby's *Last Exit to Brooklyn*. But rarely, if ever, have they been rendered with such intimate, even professional, authority as in *The Case Worker*, the book by which, in the early 1970s, George Konrád first became known in Europe and America.

Earlier writers had glimpsed and even portrayed these figures, but

Introduction to the Penguin Book edition, based on a review in the *New York Times Book Review*, January 27, 1974.

Konrád was perhaps the first to place them in a distinctive contemporary setting, as the "clients" of a social welfare system that is overwhelmed by their needs and clamor, and proceeds to slot them into categories, hospitals, files, and clinics, attempting through society's benevolence or callousness to cope with the gratuitous cruelties of nature.

I remember that, when first reading *The Case Worker*, I found myself struggling, as one always does with original works, to "place" it, that is, to find terms of description drawn from other works of literature that might evoke its special qualities. The claustrophobic atmosphere of welfare bureaucracy and torpid streets, as Konrád wrote about his city of Budapest—a faint echo of Kafka? The bizarre gaieties of the deformed—perhaps like Grass? A fixation upon physical detail and sensory assault—reminds one of Smollett? Such comparisons, if they had any use at all, would come to mind only to be put aside, in the hope that they would lead from the familiar to the fresh.

Konrád's narrator speaks as a case worker, which is what Konrád himself was during his younger years in Budapest. This case worker, as we soon come to know him, is a fairly decent and competent bureaucrat whose job it is to record the pleas, the lies, the confessions of his "clients," and then to send them to some home or office, or back to the street from which they came. The case worker is also a policeman, he tells himself, regulating "the traffic of suffering." Who can cope with the battalions of misfits, the hordes of victims? "My interrogations make me think of a surgeon who sews up his incision without removing the tumor." For something lies embedded in the nature of things that is radically terrible, not so much evil in purpose as gratuitously malformed. The case worker does his job in Communist Budapest, but except for the apparent absence of drugs, it seems very much like capitalist Manhattan.

Making no accusations and placing no blame, the narrator speaks in a rhetoric of dispassionate grief. He is not indignant. Who can imagine these shattered "clients" being stirred to revolt? He is not sentimental. Who can suppose them to be models of innocence? They stink, they cheat, they lie—quite like successful people. Thrust into the web of their troubles, the case worker is shaken, implicated, drawn to their fumbling, stained by their need.

The book is constructed as a chain of vignettes, as if the case worker were thumbing through his files and stopping at an especially vivid or wretched case. There is the old man "standing on a chair with his pants down, he is blowing kisses out of the window"; mistaken for a common exhibitionist, he is freed on the case worker's recommendation and the next day strangles a runaway child. There is the senile couple: "both of them have false teeth, and after depositing them in glasses of water for the night, they shout lisped insults at each other." There is the room of another client: "A black lace brassiere hung from the window fastening; in a corner two stringless tennis racquets, on a shelf an alcohol stove, an illustrated horoscope, some old lottery tickets with a rubber band around them, and a cheese bell with two white mice inside." These glimpses of physical dislocation signal psyches of dislocation, beyond remedy or perhaps help.

Immediately after its translation from the Hungarian into English, *The Case Worker* was greeted with quick and all-but-universal praise for its brilliance, though exactly what that brilliance consisted of still remains to be considered. *The Case Worker* is, of course, a novel, the term we use these days to name any sort of prose fiction. It has a plot, though a very thin one; much of the "action" of the book, actually a skein of reverie and grieving, can easily be separated from the movement of the plot. It has characters, rapidly thrust to the forefront and as rapidly whisked away, but only one of them, the narrator, is allowed to emerge with any fullness. He comes to us as a cross section, so to say, of consciousness, through a staccato depiction of speech and thought, but not through the eyes of any other characters, which might allow us to check his statements or escape the confinement of his meditations. There is also in *The Case Worker* a climax of sorts, when the central figure recognizes that he must give up the deformed child he has been sheltering; but I don't suppose anyone would claim that this climax bears very keenly on our feelings or our nerves, since long before we reach it Konrád has prepared us to surmise what it will be and why it must be so.

If only for lack of another familiar term, we may still call *The Case Worker* a novel, but it really does seem different from the traditional social novel, with its interplay of characters and its interweaving strands of plot. Different also from the modernist novel—though in rereading the book I have been struck by the extent to which, in its own obsessive way, it draws upon strategies and styles of European modernism, such as its free mixture of genres and its distension and displacement of plot.

The Case Worker, I'd say, is not so much a novel as it is a grotesque-lyrical rumination, twisting in its self-enclosed space, like the mind it reveals. This mind becomes obsessed with the hardness of nature's dispensations and the consequent harshness of the human condition. Apart from all else, Konrád forces a deep entry into a mind's suffering, the pain of a quite ordinary person, and therefore, in the economy of modern life, a pain all the more consequential. It is a suffering that draws upon reserves of conscience: Nothing in the case worker's situation requires him to care for the deformed child except those fragments of sensibility we like to think of as distinctively human.

As the book presses us to engage with pointless suffering, unaccountable wastes, cruel malformations, it allows no compensating rationale, either political or religious, for this state of affairs. The reflective mind stands bewildered and helpless before the sheer wantonness of life. Konrád undercuts the notion that all human problems can be solved through social management, and this must have set loose a certain nervousness in the upper echelons of Budapest, which at least formally come close to accepting this notion—even if in practice they often fail to cope even with those problems that can be solved, or at least eased, through social management.

Yet Konrád's narrator—I see little reason to separate him from Konrád himself—does not fall into a fashionable collapse of spirit. He does not yield to the despair that, making his rounds, he finds everywhere about him. To say that he "transcends" that despair would be fatuous. What he does is both less exalted and more impressive: He reaches a standoff with despair, engaging the demons of negation in a battle he cannot win and will not cease. There is a very fine passage along these lines in which the case worker thinks to himself:

> One of the lodgers has gonorrhea, another plays the trumpet, the third sits for hours in the communal toilet, the fourth collects stray cats or rags, or dry crusts or bones for glue or broken glass or rancid butter, the fifth is a voyeur, the sixth a police informer, the seventh explains the Gospels, the eighth throws knives, the ninth exhibits his boils, and the tenth cadges a bowl of soup, but the eleventh washes the paralytic old woman and helps her drink her milk. The twelfth sits in the doorway and blows soap bubbles for the children, the thirteenth makes fireman's outfits with brass buttons for raffia dolls, the fourteenth agrees with everyone, the fifteenth brings the dying man stewed pears and tells him jokes, the sixteenth lets prurient adolescents into her bed in return for a few buckets of coal, the seventeenth climbs up on the roof to catch an escaped parrot, the eighteenth feeds the neighbor's baby, the nineteenth tells the paralytic girl's fortune and predicts a husband with a car, the twentieth always says hello first, even to the feebleminded.

Still, the odds are not very favorable for the case worker. His decision to take on the malformed child has no visible social purpose, since Konrád never yields to the sentimentalism of suggesting that somehow this will bring good therapeutic consequences. It is an act that, if good, is good in its own right, without any need or perhaps even possibility of justification. Taking into his care the hopeless child might, with a bit of stretching, be seen as a civilized man's expression of discontent with civilized existence, not only its failures, which he adds up every day, but also those necessary compromises of decency that he himself will soon have to accept. (Accept but not approve.) Perhaps, without being too grandiose, we could say that the case worker has been gripped by a metaphysical vision, a persuasion concerning the interchangeability of men. "I search for my fellow man, always certain that the chosen one, my brother, is the one who happens to be coming toward me." The hope that one can find some firm grounding in a sentiment of unconditional fraternity fails. Perhaps it must fail. When the case worker says that the child "has become my fate," we may see his remark as poignant but also as a statement of intention he will not be able to sustain over any length of time.

At the end, with no very glorious future awaiting him, he is again a case worker, almost adjusted, forced back to the ruts of the ordinary, regulating "the traffic of suffering." He repudiates "the high priests of individual salvation, and the sob sisters of altruism, who exchange commonplace partial responsibility for the aesthetic transports of cosmohistorical guilt or the gratuitous slogans of universal love. . . . My highest aspiration is that a medium-rank, utterly insignificant civil servant should, as far as possible, live with his eyes open." The key phrase here is "commonplace partial responsibility," by no means a small morality.

What sustains *The Case Worker* in its agitated movement is less its plot or characters than a free surge of language, as it carries the protagonist's seeings and imaginings. The book asks to be read as a kind of prose poem, fertile both in its objective, precise notations of place and atmosphere, and in its thickly matted imagery. The imagery is directed mainly toward creating an effect of constriction, a fierce moral airlessness, such as might afflict a man who has seen too much. Konrád has mastered here what might be called a rhetoric of claustrophobia, which yields the oppressive, beaten-down feeling of city life.

The risks in this method of composition are considerable, and what keeps *The Case Worker* from becoming monotonous or clotted is that Konrád recurrently inserts a quick vignette, encapsulating the book's theme and opening up, as it were, its language. A further help is the occasional dash of humor, usually grotesque or sardonic, like the passage where, lost in a Budapest crowd with the deformed child, the case worker feels like

the aging clerk who, after smiling at his companions and greeting his superiors in the front ranks, is just about to slip away from the May Day parade, when someone thrusts a heavy banner into his hands. Now he can't leave. . . . He looks around for someone to take it, but nobody does; and so, grimly bidding good-bye to the hoped-for day of rest, he trudges onward on swollen ankles, the heroic banner waving over his thinning hair.

Necessarily, there are losses in this kind of fiction, and the very success of Konrád's book helps to define them. The vignette, the prose snapshot, the virtuoso passage cannot yield us that experience of a sustained narrative that Lionel Trilling has described as "being held spellbound, momentarily forgetful of onself. . . ." No; in reading *The Case Worker* we are not held spellbound, nor are we forgetful of ourselves. The author is trying for other effects—the effects of a kind of ratiocinative blow, almost a cringing, before the extreme possibilities of existence. But what saves the book from mere shock is that Konrád writes out of an overwhelming belief in the moral significance of other people's experience, out of a conviction that the world, no matter how terrible, is still the substance of our days.

The City in Literature

Simplicity, at least in literature, is a complex idea. Pastoral poetry, which has been written for more than two thousand years and may therefore be supposed to have some permanent appeal, takes as its aim to make simplicity complex. With this aim goes a convention: universal truths can be uttered by plebeian figures located in a stylized countryside. In traditional or sophisticated pastoral these plebeian figures are shepherds. In naive pastoral they can be dropouts huddling in a commune. Traditional pastoral is composed by self-conscious artists in a high culture, and its premise, as also its charm, lies in the very "artificiality" untrained readers dislike, forgetting or not knowing that in literature the natural can be a category of artifice. As urban men who can no more retreat to the country than could shepherds read the poems celebrating their virtues, we are invited by pastoral to a game of the imagination in which every move is serious.

With time there occurs a decline from sophisticated to romantic pastoral, in which the conventions of the genre are begun to be taken literally, and then to naive pastoral, in which they *are* taken literally. Yet in all these versions of pastoral there resides some structure of

From *Commentary* 51 (May 1971):5.

feeling that seems to satisfy deep psychic needs. Through its artifice of convention, the pastoral toys with, yet speaks to, a nagging doubt concerning the artifice called society. It asks a question men need not hurry to answer: Could we not have knowledge without expulsion, civilization without conditions?

Now between such questions and pastoral as a genre there is often a considerable distance. We can have the genre without the questions, the questions without the genre. We can also assume that pastoral at its best represents a special, indeed a highly sophisticated version of a tradition of feeling in Western society that goes very far back and very deep down. The suspicion of artifice and cultivation, the belief in the superior moral and therapeutic uses of the "natural," the fear that corruption must follow upon a high civilization—such motifs appear to be strongly ingrained in Western civilization. There are Sodom and Gomorrah. There is the whore of Babylon. There is the story of Joseph and his brothers, charmingly anticipating a central motif within modern fiction: Joseph, who must leave the pastoral setting of his family because he is too smart to spend his life with sheep, prepares for a series of tests, ventures into the court of Egypt, and then, beyond temptation, returns to his fathers. And there is the story of Jesus, shepherd of his flock.

Western culture bears, then, a deeply grounded tradition that sees the city as a place both inimical and threatening. It bears, also, another tradition, both linked and opposed, sacred and secular: we need only remember St. Augustine's City of God or Aristotle's view that "Men come together in the city in order to live, they remain there in order to live the good life." For my present purpose, however, the stress must fall on the tradition, all but coextensive with culture itself, which looks upon the city as inherently suspect. It is a way of looking at the city for which, God and men surely know, there is plenty of warrant. No one can fail to be haunted by terrible stories about the collapse of ancient cities; no one does not at some point recognize the refreshment to be gained from rural life; no one can look at our civilization without at moments wishing it could be wiped out with the sweep of a phrase.

2

Our modern disgust with the city is foreshadowed in the eighteenth-century novelists. Smollett, connoisseur of sewage, has his Matthew Bramble cry out upon the suppurations of Bath: "Imagine to yourself a high exalted essence of mingled odors, arising from putrid gums, imposthumated lungs, sour flatulencies, rank arm-pits, sweating feet, running sores." In London Bramble feels himself lost in "an immense wilderness

. . . the grand source of luxury and corruption." Foreshadowing the late
Dickens, Smollett is also a literary grand-uncle of Louis-Ferdinand Céline, impresario of Parisian *pissoirs* and New York subway toilets.

Smollett helps create the tradition of disgust, but Fielding, a greater
writer, helps set in motion the dominant literary pattern of discovery and
withdrawal in regard to the city. It is the pattern of *Tom Jones* and later, in
more complicated ways, of those nineteenth-century novels recording
the travels of the Young Man from the Provinces: the youth leaving the
wholesomeness of the country and then, on the road and in the city, experiencing pleasures, adventures, and lessons to last a lifetime. Fielding
has little interest in blunt oppositions between mountain air and pestilent
streets such as Smollett indulges. Smollett's city is more vivid than Fielding's, but Smollett rarely moves from obsessed image to controlled idea:
the city, for him, is an item in that accumulation of annoyance which is
about as close as he comes to a vision of evil. And thereby, oddly, Smollett is closer to many twentieth-century writers than is Fielding. A man of
coherence, Fielding knows that the city cannot be merely excoriated, it
must be imaginatively transformed. Just as Tom Jones's journey is a shaping into spiral pattern of the picaro's linear journey, so the city of the
picaresque novel—that setting of pratfalls, horrors, and what the Elizabe-
than writer Robert Greene had called "pleasant tales of foist"—becomes
in Fielding an emblem of moral vision. The picaro learns the rules of the
city, Fielding's hero the rules of civilized existence. In Fielding the city is
a necessary stopping point for the education of the emotions, to be encountered, overcome, and left behind.

It is customary to say that the third foreshadower of the eighteenth
century, Daniel Defoe, was a writer sharing the later, nineteenth-century
vision of the city, but only in limited ways is this true. For Defoe's
London is bodiless and featureless. Populated with usable foils, it provides less the substance than the schema of a city; finally, it is a place
where you can safely get lost. The rationality of calculation Max Weber
assigns to capitalism becomes in *Moll Flanders* an expert acquaintance
with geographic maze. Moll acts out her escapade in a city functional
and abstract, mapped for venture and escape. Defoe anticipates the
design of the city, insofar as it is cause and token of his heroine's spiritual
destitution, just as Kafka will later dismiss from his fiction all but the
design of the city, an equivalent to his dismissal of character psychology
in behalf of metaphysical estrangement.

3

The modern city first appears full-face—as physical concreteness,
emblem of excitement, social specter, and locus of myth—in Dickens

and Gogol. Nostalgic archaism clashes with the shock of urban horror, and from this clash follows the myth of the modern city. Contributing to, though not quite the main component of this myth, is the distaste of Romanticism for the machine, the calculation, the city.

"The images of the Just City," writes W. H. Auden in his brilliant study of Romantic iconography, "which look at us from so many Italian paintings . . . are lacking in Romantic literature because the Romantic writers no longer believe in their existence. What exists is the Trivial Unhappy Unjust City, the desert of the average from which the only escape is to the wild, lonely, but still vital sea."

Not all Romantics go to sea; almost all bemoan the desert. Wordsworth complains about London in *The Prelude*:

> The slaves unrespited of low pursuits,
> Living amid the same perpetual flow
> Of trivial objects, melted and reduced
> To one identity, by differences
> That have no law, no meaning, and no end.

This Romantic assault upon the city continues far into our century. Melville's Pierre says, "Never yet have I entered the city by night, but, somehow, it made me feel both bitter and sad." "I always feel doomed when the train is running into London," adds Rupert Birkin in *Women in Love*. Such sentences recur endlessly in modern writing, after a time becoming its very stock in trade. And the assault they direct against the modern city consists of more than sentimentalism, or archaism, or *Gemeinschaft*-nostalgia. The Romantic attack upon the city derives from a fear that the very growth of civilization must lead to a violation of traditional balances between man and his cosmos, a Faustian presumption by a sorcerer who has forgotten that on all but his own scales he remains an apprentice. Nothing that has happened during this past century allows us easily to dismiss this indictment.

Darkened and fragmented, it is an indictment that comes to the fore in Dickens's later novels. In the earlier ones there is still a responsiveness to the youthfulness of the world, an eager pleasure in the discoveries of streets. Almost every *idea* about the city tempts us to forget what the young Dickens never forgot: the city is a place of virtuosity, where men perform with freedom and abandonment. And it is Dickens's greatness that he displays London as theater, circus, vaudeville: the glass enlarging upon Micawber, Sarry Gamp, Sam Weller. If the city is indeed pesthole and madhouse, it is also the greatest show on earth, continuous performances and endlessly changing cast. George Gissing notes that

Dickens seemed "to make more allusions throughout his work to the *Arabian Nights* than to any other book," a "circumstance illustrative of that habit of mind which led him to discover infinite romance in the obscurer life of London." Continues Gissing: "London as a place of squalid mystery and terror, of the grimly grotesque, of labyrinthine obscurity and lurid fascination, is Dickens's own; he taught people a certain way of regarding the huge city."

In Dickens's early novels there are already ominous chords and frightening overtones. The London of *Oliver Twist* is a place of terror from which its young hero must be rescued through a country convalescence, and the London of *The Old Curiosity Shop*, as Donald Fanger remarks, "impels its victims . . . to flee to the quasi-divine purity of the country . . . repeatedly identified with the remote springs of childhood, innocence and peace."* Yet throughout Dickens's novels London remains a place of fascination: he is simply too keen a writer to allow theory to block perception.

In his earlier novels sentimental pastoral jostles simple pleasure in color and sound; and the pattern toward and away from the city, as classically set forth by Fielding, is used in a somewhat casual way until it receives a definitive rendering in *Great Expectations*. But it is in his three late novels—*Bleak House, Little Dorrit,* and *Our Mutual Friend,* with their commanding images of fog, prison, dustheap—that Dickens works out that vision of our existence which has so brilliantly and oppressively influenced later writing. Here the by now worn notions of our culture—alienation, depersonalization, forlornness—are dramatized with an innocence of genius. That in cities men become functions of their function; go crazy with the dullness of their work; transform eccentricities into psychic paralysis; soon come to look as if they themselves *were* bureaucracies; and die without a ripple of sound—all this Dickens represents with a zest he had not yet learned to regard as illbecoming. He enlarges his earlier comic gifts into the ferocious splendor of the Smallweeds, the Guppys, the Snagsbys, so that even as the city remains a theater, the play is now of a hardening into death.

Not only, as Edmund Wilson remarks, does Dickens develop the novel of the social group; but he becomes the first to write the novel of the city as some enormous, spreading creature that has gotten out of control, an Other apart from the men living within it. By the time he writes his last complete novel, the savage and underrated *Our Mutual Friend,* Dickens sees London as "a hopeless city, with no rent in the

* Let me here record my debt to the brilliant writings on the theme of the city and literature by Donald Fanger and John Raleigh.

leaden canopy of its sky . . . a heap of vapour charged with muffled sounds of wheels and enfolding a muffled catarrh."

We have learned to speak lightly of "society" as something pressing and enclosing us, but imagine the terror men must have felt upon first encountering this sensation! Reading these late novels of Dickens we seem to be watching a process like that of the earth being buried beneath layers of ice: a process we now can name as the triumph of the Collective. And to this process Dickens's most intimate response is a bewilderment he projects onto an alienated space, in that chaos where Mr. Krook, double of the Lord High Chancellor, reigns and the dustheap becomes a symbol of the derangements of exchange value. The indeterminacy of urban life, for Dostoevsky a frightening idea, is for Dickens a frightening experience.

As if in echo, one of Gogol's clerks cries out, "There is no place for me." Not in Petersburg there isn't, nor in the grotesque emblem of Petersburg Gogol created. Meek spiritual cripples, his clerks lure us for a moment into sympathy with the smallness of their desires. But perhaps out of that awe at the endlessness of suffering which leads Faulkner and Leskov into harshness, Gogol treats pathos not as pathetic but as the material for comedies of irreducible disorder. The grander the city, the more wormlike its creatures. Socially fixed, the clerks are personally erased. Reduced to clerkness, one of them takes home documents to copy for pleasure—this zero reveling in his zeroness recalls another zero, Peretz's Bontche Shveig, who when asked in heaven to name his ultimate desire, requests merely a hot roll with butter each morning.

How can one bear such a world, this Gogol-city of innumerable petty humiliations? By a gesture signifying the retribution of arbitrariness. In "The Overcoat" Akaky Akakievich (in Russian a name with cloacal associations) affirms himself only after death, when Petersburg is haunted by an Akakyish specter: an excremental cloud hanging over this excremental city. In "The Nose" a character finds that his nose has simply quit his face, with a sauciness he would not himself dare. But how can a nose quit a face? (As well ask Kafka how a man can turn into a cockroach.) When the weight of the determined becomes intolerable, the arbitrary gesture may come to seem a token of freedom. The nose leaves the face because Gogol *tells* it to.

The figures and atmospheres of Dickens and Gogol are appropriated by Dostoevsky, but in his novels men appear as conscious beings, their alienated grotesqueness elevated to psychological plenitude. The life of man in the city becomes a metaphysical question, so that in those airless boardinghouses into which Dostoevsky crams his characters there is enacted the fate of civilization. Raskolnikov's ordeal relates to Petersburg and Christianity: Can man live in this world; is there a reason why he should? *Crime and Punishment* offers a wide repertoire of city sensations, not as a catalogue of display but as a vibrant correlative to Raskolnikov's spiritual disorder. God and the Devil still live in this city, the former as idiot or buffoon, the latter as sleazy good-natured petit bourgeois. That is why in Dostoevsky the city of filth retains a potential for becoming the city of purity. The city brings out Raskolnikov's delusions: it is the locale of the modern fever for mounting sensations, for the modern enchantment with the sordid as a back alley to beatitude. The city is also the emblem of Raskolnikov's possible redemption: it is the locale of men who share a community of suffering and may yet reach the ear of Christ. Never does Dostoevsky allow the attractions of nihilism to deprive him of the vision of transcendence. In "Notes from Underground" the city bears a similar relation, what might be called a dialectical intimacy, with the narrator: each of his intellectual disasters is publicly reenacted as a burlesque in the streets.

4

Let us turn from what literature may tell about the city to what the city does in and to literature.

The city as presence brings major changes in narrative patterns. Abandoning the inclusive tourism of the picaresque, the nineteenth-century novel often employs a spiral-like pattern; first a pull toward the city, then a disheartened retreat to some point of origin (the blacksmith shop in *Great Expectations*, the chestnut tree in *The Charterhouse of Parma*). Elements of pastoral seem still attached to this narrative configuration, for one of its tacit ends is to retain in the novel clusters of feeling that flourished best in earlier genres. Lionel Trilling describes this kind of narrative: ". . . equipped with poverty, pride and intelligence, the Young Man from the Provinces stands outside life and seeks to enter. . . . It is his fate to move from an obscure position into one of considerable eminence in Paris or London or St. Petersburg, to touch the life of the rulers of the earth. He understands everything to be 'a test.' "

And then? Always the same denouement: the Young Man's defeat or disillusion, and his retreat to the countryside, where he can bind his wounds, cauterize his pride, struggle for moral renewal. Even more striking than its presence in novels as explicitly hostile to the city as *Great Expectations* and *Sentimental Education* is the way this pattern dominates novels in which the author seems consciously to intend a celebration of the city. For Balzac Paris is a place of "gold and pleasure," and the central portion of *Lost Illusions* evokes a stormy metropolis of excitement. Yet even this most cosmopolitan of novels follows the pattern of attraction and withdrawal, taking its hero, Lucien, back to the countryside in bewilderment and thereby offering a distant nod to pastoral. At the end, to be sure, Balzac's cynicism triumphs (one almost adds, thank God) and Lucien is seen in the tow of the Devil, who will take him to the city, where life, naturally, is more *interesting*: the city, as Balzac said, that "is corrupt *because* it is eminently civilized."

If the pattern of nineteenth-century fiction forms a spiral to and away from the city, it is in the sharpest contrast to later novels in which the city becomes a maze beyond escape. In *Ulysses* and *The Trial* the traditional journeys of the hero are replaced by a compulsive backtracking: there is no place else to go, and the protagonist's motions within the city stand for his need, also through backtracking, to find a center within the self.

The city allows for a more complex system of social relationships than any other locale. Sociologists keep repeating that the city impels men into relationships lacking in warmth, often purely functional and abstract; and from this once-revolutionary perception they slide into nostalgia for an "organic community" located at notoriously imprecise points in the past. For the novelist, however, the city's proliferation of casual and secondary relationships offers new possibilities: the drama of the group and the comedy of the impersonal. The experiences of Ulysses for which Homer had to arrange complicated journeys, Joyce can pack into a day's wandering through a single city. There follows the possibility of fictions constructed along the lines that the Soviet critic M. M. Bakhtin calls a "polyphonic" structure, in which social loss may yield literary advance. Dostoevsky's novels, writes Bakhtin, "caught intact a variety of social worlds and groups which had not [yet] . . . begun to lose their distinctive apartness" and thereby "the objective preconditions were created for the essential multilevel and multivoice structure of the polyphonic novel."

To which I would add: The rise of the city is a blessing for minor characters who might otherwise never see the light of day; and the inclination of some novelists to employ a multiplicity of narrative points of view is conditional upon the rise of the city.

As the city becomes a major locale in literature, there occur major changes in regard to permissible subjects, settings, and characters. The idea of literary decorum is radically transformed, perhaps destroyed. Literature gains a new freedom; everything, which may be too much, is now possible. Out of the dogmas of anticonvention, new conventions arise. The city enables the birth of new genres: who could imagine surrealism without Paris?

In the novel of the city, a visit to a slum can serve as shorthand for a descent into hell, as in *Bleak House* or *Redburn*. An address, a neighborhood, an accent—these identify the condition of a man, or the nature of an act, quite as much as social rank or notations of manners once did. So powerful, at first liberating and then constricting, do these new conventions become that in *The Waste Land* their rapid evocation permits a summary vision of an entire culture. The typist's life as a familiar barrenness, the dialogue in the bar as a characteristic plebeian mindlessness, the conversation between upper-class husband and wife as a recognizable sterility—these serve as the terms of spiritual assessment.

As the city breaks down traditional rankings, there emerges the plebeian writer or the writer of fallen circumstances. The city erases family boundaries, in one direction toward those rootless wanderers of the streets first imagined by Edgar Allan Poe, and in the other direction toward the extended families pictured by Dostoevsky. The city yields stunning juxtapositions: "In Paris," gloats Balzac, "vice is perpetually joining the rich man to the poor, and the great to the humble."

The city thereby offers endless possibilities of symbolic extension. In Gissing's *New Grub Street* it becomes a place of paralyzing fatigue, a grayness of spirit that finds its extension in the grayness of a London winter. To Flaubert in *Sentimental Education*, as if to anticipate Max Weber's fear that we are entering "a long polar night of icy darkness and hardness," Paris comes to represent a collective yielding to acedia and nihilism, and as we read we have the sensation of watching men turn slowly into stone.

The city affects literature in still another way: it provides a range of vocabularies, from the coarse eloquence of Balzac's Parisians to the mixture of racy street-Jewishness and intellectual extravaganza of Bellow. The city also encourages that flavorless language of sawdust we associate with naturalism, as if the denial of will must be reflected in the death of words; yet the city also yields to writers like Dickens and Gogol new resources for grotesquerie and mockery. Language can be reduced to bureaucratic posture, as in Guppy's proposal to Esther Summerson in *Bleak House*, employing the terms of a brief for a small-claims court. Or it can be used by Gogol in a style the Russians call *skaz*, described by Yevgeny Zamyatin as "The free, spontaneous language of speech, digressions . . . coinages of the street variety, which cannot be found in any dictionary . . . [and in which] the author's comments are given in a language close to that of the milieu depicted."

One of the great temptations for the writer dealing with city life is to think of it as a "creature" or "being" independent from and looming over the people who live in it. Apostrophes to London and Paris are frequent in Dickens and Balzac, but these are only feeble rhetorical intimations of what they are struggling to apprehend. The sense that somehow a city has "a life of its own" is so common, it must have some basis in reality; but precisely what we mean by such statements is hard to say. For Dickens and Gogol, as for Melville, such metaphors become ways of expressing the sense of littleness among people forming the anonymous masses. For other writers, such as Zola, Andrey Biely, and Dos Passos, these metaphors prepare the way for an effort to embody the life of the group in its own right, to see the collective as an autonomous and imperious organization.

The city as presence in modern literature gives rise to a whole series of new character types, and these come to be formidable conventions in subsequent writing. A few of them:

The clerk, soon taken to represent the passivity, smallness, and pathos of life in the city: Gogol, Melville, Dickens, Kafka.

The Jew, bearer of the sour fruits of self-definition: Joyce, Proust, Mann.

The cultivated woman, a triumph of modern writing, inconceivable anywhere but in the city, a woman of intelligence, seductiveness and awareness, traditional refinement and modern possibilities: Tolstoy's Anna, James's Madame Vionnet, Colette's Julie.

The underground man, a creature of the city, without fixed rank or place, burrowing beneath the visible structure of society, hater of all that flourishes aboveground, meek and arrogant, buried in a chaos of subterranean passions yet gratified by the stigmata of his plight: Dostoevsky and Céline.

"The psychological basis of the metropolitan type of individual," writes Georg Simmel in his essay "The Metropolis and Mental Life," "consists in the intensification of nervous stimulation which results from the swift and uninterrupted change of outer and inner stimuli. . . . Lasting impressions . . . use up, so to speak, less consciousness than does the rapid crowding of changing images, the sharp discontinuity in the grasp of a single phrase, and the unexpectedness of onrushing impressions."

Dostoevsky and Joyce best capture this experience in the novel, Baudelaire and Hart Crane in verse.

In *Crime and Punishment*, Raskolnikov is assaulted by repeated impressions during his dazed wanderings through Petersburg. He walks along the street and sees a coachman beating his horse with gratuitous brutality. He watches a street entertainer grinding out a tune on a barrel organ, tries to strike up a nervous conversation with a stranger and frightens the man away. Another man approaches him and without warning mutters, "You are a murderer." At still another moment he notices a woman in front of him, "at first reluctantly and, as it were, with annoyance, and then more and more intently"; he supposes her a victim of a seduction; the terribleness of the city seems flaringly vivid to him. Each of these apparently stray incidents becomes a tonal equivalent to Raskolnikov's condition.

5

Together with what I have called the myth of the modern city— enemy of man: pesthole, madhouse, prison—there appear in modern literature at least two other significant visions of urban life. The first is benign, fairly frequent among American writers who have grown up in a culture devoted to the virtues of the countryside. For Henry James the city serves as a token of high civilization. The Paris of *The Ambassadors* is a mixture of Balzac's Paris (without Balzac's greasepaint, vulgarity, and financial delirium) and an American dream of a European City of Beauty. Paris becomes the shining gloss of man's history, the greatness of the past realized in monuments and manners. Paris stands for the Jamesian vision of a culture far gone in sophistication yet strangely pure, as if no dollar were exchanged there or loyalty betrayed. James was not a naif, he knew he was summoning a city of his desire; and in an earlier novel, *The American*, he had shown himself capable of presenting a Paris sinister and shabby. But now Paris has become the home of civilization, with the splendor of its history yielding a myth of idealization.

Quite as benign is Whitman's vision of New York. His poems do not capture the terrible newness of the industrial city, for that he does not really know. Whitman's city flourishes in harmony with surrounding forests and green; it figures modestly in the drama of democracy; there is still psychic and social roominess, so that this bohemian singing of the masses can easily knock about in the streets, a New World flaneur, without feeling crowded or oppressed. Between the noisy groping city and Whitman's persona as the Fraternal Stranger there are still large spaces, and this very spaciousness allows him to celebrate the good nature and easy style of his "camerados" in New York. Not many nineteenth-century writers can share that comfort.

The second and by far more influential vision of the city proceeds in a cultural line from Baudelaire through Eliot and then through Eliot's many followers. In the smudge of our time, this vision of the city has come to seem indistinguishable from the one I have attributed to the nineteenth-century masters; but it is distinguishable. There is in Baudelaire little of that recoil from the city about which I have spoken and little, if any, pastoral indulgence. He accepts the city as the proper stage for his being; he apprehends, better than anyone, the nervous currents that make cosmopolitan life exciting and destructive; he writes in the *Tableaux Parisiens* not only of ugliness and debauchery but also, in Proust's words, of "suffering, death, and humble fraternity." A famous passage celebrates the public concerts, "rich in brass," that "pour some heroism into the hearts of town dwellers."

Walter Benjamin notes that "Baudelaire placed the shock experience at the very center of his artistic work," and he remarks also on the relation between that "shock experience" and Baudelaire's "contact with the metropolitan masses . . . the amorphous crowd of passers-by" with whom he "becomes an accomplice even as he dissociates himself from them." In Baudelaire's poems shock serves more than a social end; it has to do with his struggle for a scheme of moral order, a struggle conducted, in extremis, through images of disorder. Baudelaire's fear is not, as others had already said before him, that the city is hell: his fear is that it is *not* hell, not even hell. His strategy of shock comes to seem a modernist terror-raid in behalf of classical resolution—not always so, of course, since poets can become secret sharers of the devils they grapple with. It hardly matters whether Baudelaire is seen as a figure of urban satanism or inverted Christianity; he moves in the orbits of both, emanating, in Mallarmé's wonderful line, "a protective poison that we must go on breathing even if we die of it." For Baudelaire, Paris embodies the fear of a life reduced from evil to the merely sordid, a life sinking into the triviality of nihilism.

This is the side of Baudelaire that Eliot appropriates the *The Waste Land*: "Unreal City . . . I had not thought death had undone so many." Eliot lacks Baudelaire's capacity for surrendering himself to the quotidian pleasures of a great city, but he narrows the Baudelairean vision into something of enormous power. Eliot's idea of the city has become assimilated to that of the great nineteenth-century writers, though it is imperative to insist on the difference between madhouse and wasteland, even prison and wasteland. Eliot's vision is then taken up, more and more slackly, by the writers of the last half-century, charting, mourning, and then—it is unavoidable—delectating in the wasteland. Life in the city is shackled to images of sickness and sterility, with a repugnance authentic or adorned; and what seems finally at the base of this tradition is a world view we might designate as *remorse over civilization*. "When one has a sense of guilt after having committed a misdeed," says Freud gloomily, "the feeling should . . . be called remorse." Our guilt, almost casual in its collective sedimentation, proceeds from the feeling that the whole work of civilization—and where but in cities?—is a gigantic mistake. This remorse appears first as a powerful release of sensibility, in imaginative works of supreme value, and then as kitsch, Madison Avenue modernism. The strength of the masters remains overwhelming, from Baudelaire to Eliot to Auden, as they fill their poems with forebodings of the collapse of cities, the crumbling of all man's works. Auden writes in "The Fall of Rome":

> Private rites of magic send
> The temple prostitutes to sleep;
> All the literati keep
> An imaginary friend.
>
> Caesar's double-bed is warm
> As an unimportant clerk
> Writes I DO NOT LIKE MY WORK
> On a pink official form.

And the Greek poet Cavafy writes about a city waiting, with impatient weariness, for the barbarians to take over:

> What does this sudden uneasiness mean,
> And this confusion? (How grave the faces have become!)
> Why are the streets and squares rapidly emptying,
> and why is everyone going back
> home lost in thought?
>
> Because it is night and the barbarians have not come,
> and some men have arrived from the frontiers
> and they say there are no barbarians any more
> and now, what will become of us without barbarians?
> These people were a kind of solution.

6

The suspicion of the city and all it represents seems to run so deep in our culture that it would be impossible to eradicate it, even if anyone were naive enough to wish to. In its sophisticated variants it is a suspicion necessary for sanity. And perhaps, for all we know, it is a suspicion emblematic of some ineradicable tragedy in the human condition: the knowledge that makes us cherish innocence makes innocence unattainable.

In traditional pastoral, suspicion of the city is frequently contained through a discipline of irony proceeding through a sequence something like this: game of the shepherds, seriousness of the game, recognition of how limited are the uses of that seriousness. In modern literature, which can have but little interest in shepherds, there is a violence of response to the city which breaks past the discipline of irony—our experience demands that. But then, just as traditional pastoral suffers the corruptions of literalism, so must the modernist assault upon the city. How, we ask ourselves, can we bring together, in some complex balance of attitude, our commitment to the imaginative truth in what the modern writers show us about the city and our awareness that it may no longer be quite sufficient?

We are the children, or stepchildren, of modernism. We learned our ABCs lisping "alienation, bourgeoisie, catastrophe." As against those who brushed aside the twentieth century, we were right in believing our age to be especially cursed, on the rim of apocalypse. But today loyalty to the tradition of modernism may require a rejection of its academic and marketplace heirs, and far more important, a questioning of its premises and values.

To deride the epigones of modernism who have reduced it from a vision to a fashion is no great intellectual risk. We should go farther and ask whether the masters must, in some sense, be held responsible for their corrupted followers, if only insofar as the corruption may point back to some little-noticed flaw in the worldview of the masters. Our problem then becomes to ask whether the visions of the great modernist writers can retain for us the moral urgency and emotional command they so powerfully exerted only a few decades ago.

Clearly this is not a question to be answered in a few paragraphs. What matters, in behalf of a serious confrontation with our dominant literary heritage, is to move past (which is not to say abandon) both the authentic pieties we retain from an earlier moment and the false ones that have followed them.

I propose a hypothesis: We have reached the point in our cultural history where it seems both possible and useful to remove ourselves from the partisanship that cultural modernism evoked throughout the past century. Modernism is no longer threatened, nor in question. Its achievements are solid and lasting, its influence is incalculable. It is

beginning to take a place in the development of Western culture somewhat like that which Romanticism can be said to have taken by the last
two or three decades of the nineteenth century. *Modernism has become
part of history*, and thereby a complex of styles and values we can accept
through the mediation of its classical works. Modernism can now enter
our moral experience complicated by that awareness of historical distance which is a mark of a cultivated sensibility, and thereby it remains
a crucial part of our experience, as Romanticism does too. But if we
ask ourselves questions as to the truth of the vision of a Lawrence or
an Eliot or a Yeats—and I have some awareness of how tricky such
questions can be—we are no longer likely, and younger people are
certainly no longer likely, to answer them with an unbroken passion,
that total assent or denial elicited by a cultural movement both contemporary and embattled.

If we lose much by no longer seeing modernism as a contemporary
cultural presence, we may gain something too. We may gain a certain
detached perspective upon its achievements, as in recent decades,
through discovery, polemic, and reassessment, we have been gaining
such a perspective upon Romanticism. And if we do approach modernism in this way, then we may discover that a good many of our earlier
enthusiasms will have to be qualified. Not repudiated; qualified. The
famous "revolutionary" aspect of modernism may come to have for us
an ambiguous value: in part an authentic response to the terribleness of
the age and in part a nostalgia for a historically unlocatable and morally
dubious "organic past"; in part a profound engagement with the inner
nerves of city life and in part a snobbism of the fastidious embraced by
those who look down upon the commonplace desires of commonplace
mankind; in part an assault upon the calculation that lies at the heart of
the bourgeois ethic and in part a cruel dismissal of those fragmented
solutions and moderate comforts which it has become easy to dismiss
as bourgeois. And we may then have to conclude that the now established hostility to the idea of the city, which is one portion of the
modernist legacy, will no longer serve as well as in the past. The vision
of the city we inherit from Eliot and Baudelaire, Céline and Brecht—
with its ready nausea, packaged revulsion, fixed estrangement—will have
to be modulated and itself seen as a historical datum.

To remain faithful to its tradition means to call it sharply into question. Can we not, for example, say, yes, the city remains the pesthole
and madhouse, the prison and setting of spiritual void that you have
shown it to be; nevertheless we can no longer be satisfied with this
perception alone.

Nor is it as if we lack an inspiring model from within literacy mod-

ernism itself. No writer has portrayed the city with such severity as
James Joyce. Every assault that the modernist literary tradition can make
upon the city appears in *Ulysses*, magnified in scope and feverish with
intensity. Yet that assault is also, in *Ulysses*, transcended through a skeptical humaneness, a tolerance beyond tolerance, a recognition that man
was not put on this earth to scratch his eyes out. Of all the writers who
render the modern city, it is Joyce who engages in the most profound
struggle with nihilism, for he sees it everywhere, in the newspaper office
and the church, on the street and in the bed, through the exalted and
the routine. Joyce, says Richard Ellmann, shows that "the world of cigars
is devoid of heroism only to those who don't understand that Ulysses'
spear was merely a sharpened stick . . . and that Bloom can demonstrate
the qualities of man by word of mouth as effectively as Ulysses by thrust
of spear." The theme of *Ulysses*, says Ellmann, is simply that "casual
kindness overcomes unconscionable power." Does it? In reality? In
Joyce's book? I hardly know but cherish Ellmann's sentence, as I believe
Joyce would have too.

We may destroy our civilization, but we cannot escape it. There is
no turning back: our only way is a radical struggle for the City of the
Just. The City of the Just . . . the phrase rings a little hollow right now,
so far do we seem to be from it. Still, we shall create genuine cities,
which means vital civilizations, or we shall perish. Assault upon the city
is now to be valued only when understood as the complex play of men
who live in cities and would live nowhere else. It is too late for tents
and sheep and lutes, or whatever surrogates we may invent. "Perhaps
the best definition of the city in its higher aspects," says Lewis Mumford,
"is that it is a place designed to offer the widest facilities for significant
conversation."
So we must turn again, to build the Just City, where men can be
decent and humane and at ease, that ease Wallace Stevens speaks of:

> One's grand flights, one's Sunday baths,
> One's tootings at the wedding of the soul
> Occur as they occur. . . .

And what will we do in the city? Take our Sunday baths, toot at
"the wedding of the soul," read Colette, marvel at Balanchine, and with
proper modulations of irony, realize the claims of pastoral, that indestructible artifice of the urban imagination. More than four hundred
years ago Barnaby Googe understood it all: "God sends me Vittayles
for my nede, and I synge Care awaye."

Delmore Schwartz: An Appreciation

Delmore Schwartz's most famous story, "In Dreams Begin Responsibilities," came out in 1937, as the leading piece of fiction in the first issue of the new *Partisan Review*. Those of us who read it at the time really did experience a shock of recognition. The intellectual heavyweights of the *PR* group had been mobilized for this opening issue, and they performed in high style. Young readers like me who looked forward to the magazine as a spokesman for "our" views on culture and politics—that is, the views of the anti-Stalinist left—were probably more interested in the polemics than the fiction. Still, we did read Schwartz's story, if only because the editors had put it at the top of their table of contents; and we were stunned. Many people I know have remembered the story long after forgetting everything else in that first issue.

We were charmed by the story's invention, though this could hardly explain the intensity of our response, since you didn't have to be a New Yorker—you could as well live in London or Singapore—in order to admire Schwartz's technical bravura. Still, it was the invention—the sheer cleverness of it—that we noticed first. A movie theater becomes the site of dreams; the screen, a reflector of old events we know will

Introduction to *In Dreams Begin Responsibilities* (New York: New Directions, 1978).

soon be turning sour. The narrator watches father propose to mother at a Coney Island restaurant. Already, during the delights of courtship, they become entangled in the vanities and deceptions that will embitter their later years. But what can the audience do about it? The past revived must obey its own unfolding, true to the law of mistakes. The reel must run its course: it cannot be cut, it cannot be edited.

When I first read the story, at the age of seventeen or eighteen, I felt my blood rise at the point where the narrator cries out to his parents on the screen: "Don't do it. It's not too late to change your minds, both of you. Nothing good will come of it, only remorse, hatred, scandal, and two children whose characters are monstrous." The hopelessness, and as it seemed then, the rightness of the son's lament appealed to my deepest feelings as another son slipping into estrangement. Naturally, this struck me as the high point of the story, the cry against the mistakes of the past.

Only later, when I now and again reread the story, did I come to see what I could not yet see in 1937: that its tragic force depends not so much on the impassioned protest of the young narrator as on the moment in the last paragraph when an usher hurries down the aisle of the theater and says to him: "What are *you* doing? Don't you know that you can't do whatever you want to do?" This voice of remonstrance, as it speaks for inexorability, fulfills the story on both the plane of invention (the business in the movie house) and the plane of implication (how presumptuous yet inevitable that we should want to unwind the reel of our lives!). Once you see that the usher's statement has to be given a central place in the story, then you also realize that the narrator's outcry, whatever our sympathy for it, is not so much a protest against mistakes, but a protest against life itself, inconceivable without mistakes.

There is still one thing more, and it comes in the last line of the story, a phrase that would serve almost as Schwartz's literary signature: the young narrator wakes up on a bleak winter morning from his dream of a movie depicting the past of his parents, and outside, on the windowsill, he sees "a lip of snow." It is a haunting phrase—the plenitude and renewal of nature become through metaphor a human shape, soon to melt, but still, the shape of that part of our body with which we speak and love. Through all the wretchedness of Schwartz's later years as man and writer, he would now and again invoke such images of snow as an enchanting presence, the downpour, as if through God's or nature's generosity, of purity, beauty, evanescence.

The tone of "In Dreams Begin Responsibilities"—flat, gray, a little sluggish, but with sudden spinnings of eloquence and literary self-consciousness—is distinctively urban. It speaks of Brooklyn, Coney Island, and Jewish immigrants fumbling their way into the New World, but also of their son, proudly moving toward the culture of America and finding there a language for his parents' grief. This sense that Schwartz had found both voice and metaphor for our own claustral but intense experience—this, more than any objective judgment of his technical skill—must have been the source of our strong response. We heard a voice that seemed our own, though it had never quite existed until Schwartz invented it: a voice at home with the speech of people not quite at home with English speech.

For a decade there followed story after story in which Schwartz wrote about his characteristic themes: the pathos and comic hopelessness of the conflict between immigrant Jewish families and their intellectual children, the occasional recognition by those children that they had left behind not only a ghetto parochialism but also a culture of value, and the quasi-bohemian life of New York intellectuals in the 1930s and 1940s, with its frantic mixture of idealism and ambition, high seriousness and mere sententiousness. These wry, depressed, and insidiously clever stories—"America, America," "The World Is a Wedding," "The Child Is the Meaning of This Life"—were put together in a form that Schwartz was making his own: longer than the story but shorter than the novelette, with little visible plot but much entanglement of relationship among characters, stylized dialogue replacing action or drama, and a major dependence on passages of commentary, ironic tags, deflated epigrams, and skittish ventures into moral rhetoric.

The risks of this kind of story were very considerable. To an unsympathetic reader, Schwartz's stories could seem ill-fitted, self-conscious, excessively parochial in reference and scope. Some of the inferior ones are precisely that: manner becoming mannered, an adept mimicry of itself. But this hardly counts, since a writer must be judged by his strengths, not the necessary failures.

One charge frequently made against Schwartz's work, however, merits a closer look. The "tougher" literary people of his time—and it was then very much the fashion to be "strict" and "severe" in judgment—often said that Schwartz's work suffered from self-pity. They were sometimes right, but in the main they lacked the patience to see that in stories about the kinds of people Schwartz was describing self-pity is a necessary theme—how else can you write about young intellectuals at once lost in the coldness of the world and subsisting on dreams of later glory? Schwartz had the rare honesty to struggle with this out in the open, struggle with it as not merely a literary theme but also a personal temptation, so that in his best work he could control or even transcend it. A good many other, less honest writers learned to mask their self-pity as comic heartiness or clipped stoicism. But no one reading "America, America" or "The Child Is the Meaning of This Life" is likely, I think, to suppose that the self-pity which plagues some of the characters is unresistantly shared by the author.

The stories Schwartz wrote in the years between "In Dreams Begin Responsibilities" and *The World Is a Wedding* (1948), capture the quality of New York life in the thirties and forties with a fine comic intensity—not, of course, the whole of New York life but that interesting point where intellectual children of immigrant Jews are finding their way into the larger world while casting rueful glances over their backs. These were stories that helped one reach an emotional truce with the world of our fathers, for the very distance they established from their subject allowed some detachment and thereby, in turn, a little self-criticism and compassion. (Not too much, by the way.) Sliding past the twin dangers of hate and sentimentalism, Schwartz's best work brought one to the very edge of the absurd, I mean to that comic extremity in which the characters of, say, "New Year's Eve" and "The World Is a Wedding" were wrenched almost to caricature even as it remained easy to identify their "originals." It was as if ironic distancing, even ironic disdain were a prerequisite for affection, and thereby one could gain through these stories a certain half-peace in contemplating the time of one's youth. The mockery Schwartz expended upon the New York intellectuals and would-be intellectuals can be caustic, even bitter and, to be honest, sometimes pretty nasty; but it is not dismissive, it does not exclude anyone, it does not relegate to the limbo of the nonhuman. Schwartz's voice is sad and almost caressing, as if overcome by the waste of things.

What is more, this comedian of alienation also showed a gift for acceptance, a somewhat ambiguous reconcilement with the demands and depletions of common experience. Schwartz's work gained its fragile air of distinction partly from the fact that he avoided the pieties of both fathers and sons, established communities and floundering intellectuals. I am not speaking here about Schwartz the person. As a writer he came to see, especially in "America, America" and "The Child Is the Meaning of This Life," with the eyes of both fathers and sons, or perhaps from a distance greater than either could manage, as if he were somehow a detached student of the arts of misunderstanding.

In the early stories (more disturbingly in the later ones) there was also a strong awareness of the sheer foolishness of existence, the radical ineptitude of the human creature, such as reminds one a trifle of Dostoevsky's use of buffoonery in order to discharge aggressiveness against both readers and characters. The persona of buffoonery, which goes perfectly well with a sophisticated intelligence, brings with it some notable dangers, but at its occasional best it enabled Schwartz to catch his audience off guard, poking beneath the belt of its dignity, enforcing the shared ridiculousness of . . . I guess, everything.

By the time Schwartz published *The World Is a Wedding*, he had developed his own style. Some years ago I tried to describe this style, and since I can't now do any better I beg the reader's pardon for quoting myself: "it seemed to be composed of several speech-layers: the sing-song, slightly pompous intonations of Jewish immigrants educated in night schools, the self-conscious affectionate mockery of that speech by American-born sons, its abstraction into the jargon of city intellectuals, and finally the whole body of this language flattened into a prose of uneasiness, an antirhetoric."

An antirhetoric is of course a rhetoric. But more important, in his stories dealing with immigrant Jewish families Schwartz may have begun by using language as an affectionate and deliberate mimicry of immigrant speech, but very soon, I think, he yields himself to it almost entirely. Yielding himself, *he simply writes that way*. It becomes his language. The world is a wedding? Then turn back shyly, ambivalently to the past—though not quite yet with ceremonies of marriage.

It is in "America, America," as the "young writer of promise," listens to his mother, Mrs. Fish, tell the story about the neighbors, the Baumanns, that all of Schwartz's themes come to fulfillment and his literary voice strikes its characteristic note. Hearing his mother, recognizing the intuitive wisdom and depths of experience out of which she speaks, Shenandoah Fish experiences a revelation of how smug he has been in his judgment of the Baumanns and all the people like them, how unearned has been "the irony and contempt" he has shown them. It is this humane readiness to see both links and breaks between the generations that helps to make this story so rich a portrait of immigrant life.

> He reflected on his separation from these people [the immigrant Jews], and he reflected that in every sense he was removed from them by thousands of miles, or by a generation. . . . Whatever he wrote as an author did not enter the lives of these people, who should have been his genuine relatives and friends, for he had been surrounded by their lives since the day of his birth, and in an important sense, even before then. . . . The lower middle-class of Shenandoah's parents had engendered perversions of its own nature, children full of contempt for everything important in their parents. . . .

> Shenandoah had thought of this guilt and perversion before, and he had shrugged away his unease by assuring himself that this separation had nothing to do with the important thing, which was [his] work itself. But now . . . he began to feel that he was wrong to suppose that the separation, the contempt, and the gulf had nothing to do with his work; perhaps, on the

contrary, it was the center; or perhaps it was the starting-point and compelled the innermost motion of the work to be flight, or criticism, or denial,
or rejection.

Of dismay and disintegration, chaos and ugliness, waste and malaise
there was more than enough in the life, sometimes the work, of Delmore
Schwartz. Yet there is something else in his poems and stories, so rare
in our time and so vulnerable to misuse that I hesitate to name it. What
enriches Schwartz's comedy is, I think, a reaching out toward nobility,
a shy and aspiring spirituality, a moment or two of achieved purity of
feeling.

Strangers

Being an American, we have been told repeatedly, is a complex fate, and being an American writer still more so: traditions ruptured, loyalties disheveled. Yet consider how much more complex, indeed, how utterly aggravating, it could have been to grow up in an American subculture, one of those immigrant enclaves driving itself wild with the clashing hopes that it would receive the New World's blessing and yet maintain a moment of identity neither quite European nor quite American. The rise and fall of such subcultures is said to be intrinsic to the American experience, and no doubt it is. But when one looks into conventional accounts of our literature, it is hard to find much evidence that our writers ever felt themselves to be strangers in the land—though about their estrangement from the cosmos everyone speaks. It is hard to find evidence of that deep, rending struggle which marked those writers who had to make, rather than merely assume, America as their native ground.

The whole of our literary history for the past century might be reworked so as to encourage a richer sense of what cultural influence really signifies—a sense, for example, that it is not enough simply to trace lines of continuity, since these lines are blocked, distorted, and

From *Yale Review* 66 (Summer 1977):4.

even obliterated by recurrent outcroppings of transported Europe. Toward such a history I would here offer a few words, based not on hard evidence, of which we have little, but on recollections of the experiences shared by a generation of American Jewish writers. I will use the first person plural, though with much uneasiness, since I am aware that those for whom I claim to speak are likely to repudiate that claim and wish to provide their own fables of factuality. Here, in any case, is mine.

Lines of connection from writer to writer are never as neat or as "literary" as historians like to make out. Between master and disciple there intervene history, popular culture, vulgarization, organized forgetting, decades of muck and complication. Still, if only to ease my argument, we may agree that for writers like Robinson and Frost, Ralph Waldo Emerson towered as an ancestor imposing and authoritative, sometimes crippling, and that he figured for them not merely through the books they picked up at home or had to read in school, but through the very air, the encompassing atmosphere, of their culture. How much of "transcendentalism" remains in their writing everyone can estimate on his own, since no one has yet found a scale for weighing weightlessness; but that the pressures of this weightlessness are at work upon their writing seems beyond dispute. Despite inner clashes and discontinuities, American culture moves from the generation of Emerson to that of Robinson and Frost, as a bit later, that of Crane and Stevens, with a more or less "natural" or spontaneous rhythm. There is a passing on of the word.

But for young would-be writers growing up in a Jewish slum in New York or Chicago during the twenties and thirties, the main figures of American literature, as well as the main legends and myths carried through their fictions and stories, were not immediately available. What could Emerson mean to a boy or girl on Rivington Street in 1929, hungry for books, reading voraciously, hearing Yiddish at home, yet learning to read, write, and think in English? What could the tradition of American romanticism, surely our main tradition, mean to them?

Together with the poems of Browning and Tennyson, such young people took in the quasi- or pseudo-Emersonian homilies their Irish teachers fed them at school. They took in the American legends of an unspoiled land, heroic beginnings, pioneer aloneness, and individualist success. All of these had a strong, if sometimes delayed, impact. In the course of this migration of myth from lady teachers to immigrant children there had, however, to occur twistings, misapprehensions. Besides, we immigrant children did not come as empty vessels. We had *other stories*. We had stories about legendary endurance in the Old World;

stories about the outwitting of cruel priests; stories about Biblical figures still felt to be contemporaries though by now largely ripped out of their religious setting; stories about endless martyrs through the ages (while America seemed to have only one martyr and he, in beard and shawl, had a decidedly Jewish look).

These stories of ours were the very material out of which cultures are made, and even as we learned to abandon them with hurried shame and to feign respect for some frigid general who foolishly had never told a lie, or to some philosopher of freedom who kept slaves, we felt a strong residue of attachment to our own stories. We might be preparing to abandon them, but they would not abandon us. And what, after all, could rival in beauty and cleverness the stories of Isaac and Ishmael, Jacob and the angel, Joseph and his brothers?

Raised to a high inclusiveness, a story becomes a myth. It charts the possibilities and limits for the experience of a people, dramatizing its relations with the universe. We are speaking here of *possession*: that which we know, or remember, or remember that we have been forgetting. We are speaking about those tacit gestures, unseen shrugs, filaments of persuasion which form part of subverbal knowledge.

For a time, then, we tried to reconcile our stories with the American stories. The two of them would coexist in our minds, awkwardly but fruitfully, and we would give to the one our deep if fading credence and to the other our willed if unsure allegiance.

With American literature itself, we were uneasy. It spoke in tones that seemed strange and discordant. Its romanticism was of a kind we could not really find the key to, for while there were figures of the Jewish past who had striking points of kinship with the voices of Concord, we had partly been deprived of the Jewish past. (When the comparison was first made between Whitman's poetry and the teachings of Hasidism, it came from a Danish critic, Frederick Schyberg; but most of us, who ought to have noticed this immediately, knew little or nothing about Hasidism, except perhaps that it was a remnant of "superstition" from which our fathers had struggled to free themselves.)

Romanticism came to us not so much through the "American Renaissance" as through the eager appropriations that East European Jewish culture had made in the late nineteenth century from Turgenev and Chernyshevsky, Tolstoy and Chekhov. The dominant outlook of the immigrant Jewish culture was probably a shy, idealistic, ethicized, "Russian" romanticism, a romanticism directed more toward social justice than personal fulfillment. The sons and daughters of this immigrant milieu were insulated from American romanticism by their own inherited romanticism, with the differences magnified and the similarities, for a time, all but suppressed.

American romanticism was more likely to reach us through the streets than the schools, through the enticements of popular songs than the austere demands of sacred texts. We absorbed, to be sure, fragments of Emerson, but an Emerson denatured and turned into a spiritual godfather of Herbert Hoover. This American sage seemed frigid and bland, distant in his New England village—and how could we, of all generations, give our hearts to a writer who had lived all his life "in the country"? Getting in touch with the real Emerson, whoever *that* might be—say, with the Emerson radiant with a sense of universal human possibility yet aware enough, in his notebooks, of everything that might thwart and deny—this was not for us a natural process of discovering an ancestor or even removing the crusts of misconstruction which had been piled up by the generations. It was a task of rediscovering what we had never really discovered and then of getting past the barriers of sensibility that separated Concord, Massachusetts from the immigrant streets of New York.

These were real barriers. What could we make of all the talk, both from and about Emerson, which elevated individualism to a credo of life? Nothing in our tradition, little in our experience, prepared us for this, and if we were growing up in the thirties, when it seemed appropriate to feel estranged from whatever was "officially" American, we could hardly take that credo with much seriousness. The whole complex of Emersonian individualism seemed either a device of the Christians to lure us into a gentility that could only leave us helpless in the worldly struggles ahead, or a bit later, when we entered the phase of Marxism, it seemed a mere reflex of bourgeois ideology, especially that distinctive American form which posited an "exceptionalist" destiny for the New World.

Perhaps a more fundamental way of getting at these matters is to say that we found it hard to decipher American culture because the East European Jews had almost never encountered the kind of Christianity that flourished in America. The Christianity our fathers had known was Catholic, in Poland, or Orthodox, in Russia, and there was no reason to expect that they would grasp the ways or the extent to which Protestantism differed. We knew little, for instance, about the strand of Hebraism running through Puritan culture—I recall as a college student feeling distinct skepticism upon hearing that the Puritan divines had Hebrew. (If they had Hebrew, how could they be Gentiles?) It was only after reading Perry Miller in later years that this aspect of American

Protestant culture came alive for me. All that was distinctive in Protestant culture, making it, for better or worse, a radically different force in confrontation from Catholicism or Eastern Orthodoxy, we really could not grasp for a long time. We read the words but were largely deaf to the melody.

2

For most of us, individualism seemed a luxury or deception of the Gentile world. Immigrant Jewish culture had been rich in eccentrics, cranks, and individualist display; even the synagogue accepted prayer at personal tempos. But the idea of an individual covenant with God, each man responsible for his own salvation; the claim that each man is captain of his soul (picture those immigrant kids, in white middy blouses, bawling out, "O Captain, My Captain"); the notion that you not only have one but more than one chance in life, which constitutes the American version of grace; and the belief that you rise or fall in accord with your own merits rather than the will of alien despots—these residues of Emersonianism seemed not only strange but sometimes even a version of that brutality which our parents had warned was intrinsic to Gentile life. Perhaps our exposure to this warmed-over Emersonianism prompted us to become socialists, as if thereby to make clear our distaste for these American delusions and to affirm, instead, a heritage of communal affections and responsibilities.

Then, too, Jewish would-be writers found the classical Americans, especially Emerson and Thoreau, a little wan and frail, deficient in those historical entanglements we felt to be essential to literature because inescapable in life. If we did not yet know we surely would have agreed with Henry James's judgment that Emerson leaves "a singular impression of paleness" and lacks "personal avidity." Born, as we liked to flatter ourselves, with the bruises of history livid on our souls, and soon to be in the clutch of New World "avidities" that would make us seem distasteful or at least comic to other, more secure, Americans, we wanted a literature in which experience overflowed. So we abandoned Emerson even before encountering him, and in later years some of us would never draw closer than to establish amiable diplomatic relations.

Hardest of all to take at face value was the Emersonian celebration of nature. Nature was something about which poets wrote and therefore it merited esteem, but we could not really suppose it was as estimable as reality—the reality we knew to be social. Americans were said to love Nature, though there wasn't much evidence of this that our eyes could take in. Our own tradition, long rutted in shtetl mud and urban smoke, made little allowance for nature as presence or refreshment. Yiddish literature has a few pieces, such as Mendele's "The Calf," that wistfully suggest it might be good for Jewish children to get out of the heder (school) and into the sun; but this seems more a hygienic recommendation than a metaphysical commitment. If the talk about nature seemed a little unreal, it became still more so when capitalized as Nature; and once we reached college age and heard that Nature was an opening to God, perhaps even his phenomenal mask, it seemed quite as farfetched as the Christian mystification about three gods collapsed into one. Nothing in our upbringing could prepare us to take seriously the view that God made his home in the woods. By now we rather doubted that He was to be found anywhere, but we felt pretty certain that wherever He might keep himself, it was not in a tree, or even leaves of grass.

What linked man and God in our tradition was not nature but the commandment. Once some of us no longer cared to make such a linkage, because we doubted either the presence of God or the capacity of man, we still clung to the commandment, or at least to the shadow of its severities, for even in our defilements it lay heavily upon us.

I think it ought to be said that most of us were decidedly this-worldly, in that sardonic Yiddish style which, through the genius of a Sholom Aleichem or occasionally a Peretz, can create its own darkly soothing glow. Our appetites for transcendence had been secularized, and our messianic hungers brought into the noisy streets, so that often we found it hard to respond to, even to hear, the vocabulary of philosophical idealism which dominates American literature. Sometimes this earth-boundedness of ours was a source of strength, the strength of a Delmore Schwartz or a Daniel Fuchs handling the grit of their experience. Sometimes it could sour into mere candy-store realism or sadden into park-bench resignation. If the imagination soared in the immigrant slums, it was rarely to a Protestant heaven.

I am, of course, making all this seem too explicit, a matter of words. It went deeper than words. We had grown up, for instance, with the sovereign persuasion, which soon came to seem our most stringent imprisonment, that the family was an institution unbreakable and inviolable. Here, though we might not yet have known it, we were closer to the Southern than to the New England writers. For where, if you come to think of it, is the family in Emerson, or Thoreau, or Whitman? Even in Melville the family is a shadowy presence from which his heroes have fled before their stories begin. And where is the family in Hemingway or Fitzgerald? With Faulkner, despite all his rhetoric about honor, we might feel at home because the clamp of family which chafed his characters was like the clamp that chafed us. When we read Tolstoy we were witness to the supremacy of family life; when we read Turgenev we saw in Bazarov's parents a not-too-distant version of our own. But in American literature there were all these strange and homeless solitaries, motherless and fatherless creatures like Natty and Huck and Ishmael. Didn't they know where life came from and returned to?

Glance at any significant piece of fiction by an American Jewish writer—Schwartz's "America, America," Malamud's "The Magic Barrel," Bellow's "The Old System"—and you will see that the family serves as its organizing principle, just as in Jewish life it had become the last bulwark of defenselessness. Even in the stories of Philip Roth, which herald and perhaps celebrate the breakup of immigrant culture, there is finally a crabbed sort of admiration for the family. The Jewish imagination could not so much as conceive a fiction without paying tribute, in both senses of the word, to the family.

We had, to be sure, other and more positive reasons for keeping an uneasy distance from American literature. We felt that together with the old bedclothes, pots and pans that our folks had brought across the ocean, they had also kept a special claim on Russian culture. Tolstoy, Turgenev, Chekhov—though not the sensationalist and anti-Semite Dostoevsky—were very close to us. They had been liberally translated into Yiddish and read by the more advanced Jewish youth of Eastern Europe. Breathing moral idealism, they spoke for humanity at large; they told us to make life better and, as it seemed to us then, what better word could literature tell? The works of these masters revealed a generosity of spirit at the very moment that the spirit of the East European Jews was straining for secular generosity. In the devotion of the Yiddish-speaking intelligentsia to Tolstoy, Turgenev, and Chekhov it almost came to seem as if these were *Jewish* writers! Tolstoy presented some problems—perhaps we regarded him as a Jew for Jesus. But the other two, they were ours! I remember Isaac Rosenfeld, the most winning of all American Jewish writers, once explaining to me with comic solemnity that Chekhov had really written in Yiddish but Constance Garnett, trying to render him respectable, had falsified the record. Anyone with half an ear, said Rosenfeld, could catch the tunes of Yiddish sadness, absurdity, and humanism in Chekhov's prose—and for a happy moment it almost seemed true.

Coming as strangers who possessed, so to say, the Russian masters, we could afford to be a little cool toward the American ones. What was Dreiser to Tolstoy, Anderson to Turgenev, and the sum of all American short stories to one by Chekhov? These Russians formed a moral dike guarding the immigrant Jewish intelligentsia and then their children from the waves of American sensibility and myth. Like the Yiddish culture from which we had emerged, we were internationalist in our sentiment before we were part of *any* nation, living in the exalted atmospheres of European letters even as we might be afraid, at home, to wander a few streets away.

The situation was further complicated by the fact that the young would-be Jewish writers were themselves only tenuously connected with the Jewish culture from which they had emerged. They were stamped and pounded by the immigrant experience, but that was something rather different from the Jewish tradition. Brilliant and vital as the immigrant experience may seem to us now, it was nevertheless a thinned-out residue of the complex religious culture that had been built up over the centuries by the East European Jews. A process of loss was being enacted here—first, the immigrant culture was estranged from its Old World sources, and second, we were estranged from the immigrant culture. Especially were we estranged from—in fact, often ignorant of—those elements of religious mysticism and enthusiasm, ranging from the Cabalists to Hasidism, which had wound their way, as a prickly dissidence, through East European Jewish life. It was, for many of us, not until our late teens that we so much as heard of Sabbatai Zevi or Jacob Frank, the false messiahs who had torn apart the life of the East European Jews in the seventeenth and eighteenth centuries. Even as the fierce self-will of the immigrant culture kept us at a certain distance from American literature, so did it also screen out "reactionary" elements of the Jewish past.

I sometimes think that respectful Gentile readers have been badly gulled by the American Jewish writers into believing that they, the writers, possess a richer Jewish culture than in fact they do. The truth is that most of the American Jewish writers are painfully ignorant of the Jewish tradition. When they venture to use a Yiddish phrase they are liable to absurd mistakes. There is a delicious bit revealing this condition in a story by Irvin Faust about a Brooklyn boy who has gone for a season to Vermont and is asked by the farmer's daughter, "Myron, talk Jew to me." He has to scramble in his memories to find a phrase: "Ish leeba Dick."

"Oh," Rita Ann moaned softly, "say that again."
"Ish . . . leeba . . . Dick."
"Oooh. What's it mean?"
This I remembered, at least to a point. "I love you . . . Dick."

The work of the American Jewish writers represented an end, not a beginning—or perhaps more accurately, its end was in its beginning. It was a sign of the breakup of Jewish community and the crumbling of

Jewish identity; it spoke with the voice of return, nostalgia, retrospection, loss. And even if we chose to confine our sense of Jewish experience to the immigrant milieu, something that would already constitute a major contraction, many of these writers didn't even command that milieu in a deep, authentic way. Abraham Cahan, Henry Roth, and Daniel Fuchs did command it, with their very bones; Delmore Schwartz and Michael Seide made wry poetry out of their boyhood recollections; Saul Bellow re-created the immigrant world through ironic scaffoldings and improvisations; Bernard Malamud, by some miracle of transmutation, summoned in English an occasional true replica of the Yiddish story. But the work of many American Jewish writers is filled not only with cultural and linguistic errors; more important, it also suffers from a gross sentimentalism, a self-comforting softness, with regard to the world they suppose themselves to be representing or reconstructing. Especially is this true of those younger writers who are, so to say, exhausting the credit of their grandfathers' imaginations, making of the East Side a sort of black-humored cartoon, half-Chagall, half-Disney. By now it is clear that the world of our fathers, in its brief flare of secular passion, gave the American Jewish writers just enough material to see them through a handful of novels and stories. The advantages of remembered place soon gave way to the trouble of having lost their place. Which is why so many of the American Jewish writers seem to enter the second half of their careers as displaced persons: the old streets, the old songs, have slipped away, but the mainstream of American life, whatever that may be, continues to elude their reach. America, it turns out, is very large, very slippery, very recalcitrant.

For the American Jewish poets, whom I have largely ignored here, things may yet turn out more favorably. Once milieu and memory are exhausted, Jewishness can take on the strangeness of a fresh myth, or at least myth rediscovered; that myth need have no precise location, no street name or number; and the Bible may lose its tyranny of closeness and become a site to be ransacked. Something of the sort has happened in the last few decades among Yiddish writers, the novelists and storytellers among them finding it more and more difficult to locate their fictions in a recognizable place, while precisely an awareness of this dilemma has yielded the poets a rich subject.

3

But now I must retrace my steps and make things a little more complicated. For if I've been talking about the pressures that kept us at a certain distance from American literature, it must surely be remembered that there were other pressures driving us, sometimes feverishly, toward it.

With time we discovered something strange about the writing of Americans: that even as we came to it feeling ourselves to be strangers, a number of the most notable writers, especially Whitman and Melville, had also regarded themselves as strangers, though not quite in the blunt and deprived way that we did. Whitman saw himself as a poet-prophet who necessarily had to keep a certain distance from his culture—a stranger in the sense proposed by Georg Simmel, that is, a potential wanderer who "has not quite lost the freedom of coming and going," so that even when "fixed within a particular spatial group . . . his position in this group is determined, essentially, by the fact that he has not belonged to it from the beginning, that he imports qualities into it. . . ." The Whitman who has often been seen as "furtive," the wanderer of the streets who comes into touch with everyone but remains close to no one, is a stranger, making of that condition the metaphysical coloring of his persona.

In the early years of the immigrant culture, Whitman was the most popular American writer (except perhaps Poe) among Yiddish readers and writers; there are odes addressed to him in Yiddish and some rough translations of his shorter poems. One reason for this affection was that to the Yiddish-speaking immigrant intelligentsia Whitman seemed really to *mean* it when he invited everyone to make himself at home in the New World. They detected in Whitman an innocence of soul which touched their own innocence; they heard in his voice strains of loneliness which linked with their own loneliness; they saw him as the American who was what Americans ought to be, rather than what they usually turned out to be. They may have been misreading him, but, for their purposes, very usefully.

By the time our turn came—I mean, those of us who would be writing in English—Whitman had lost some of his charm and come to seem portentous, airy, without roots in the griefs of the city, not really a "modern" sensibility. In 1936 "Crossing Brooklyn Ferry" might not speak very strongly to a boy in the slums, even one who had often crossed on the Staten Island ferry on Saturday nights; it would take several decades before the poem could reveal itself in its grandeur, this time to the aging man that boy had become. But probably not until the late thirties or early forties did there come into our awareness another American writer who seemed to speak to us as comrade to comrade, stranger to stranger. Herman Melville was a "thicker" writer than Whitman, "thicker" with the pain of existence and the outrage of society, a cousin across the boundaries of nationality and religion who seemed the archetypal young man confronting a world entirely prepared to do him in. Had we known *Redburn* in time, we might have seen Melville as the tenderfoot only a step or two away from the greenhorn, and we would have been enchanted by the great rhetorical outpouring in that book where Melville welcomes immigrants, all peoples, to the American fraternity. We would have seen the young Melville as a fellow who had to work in a ship—I was about to say, in a shop—where he was hooted at because he wanted to keep some of the signs of his delicate youth. And we would have seen him as a writer who bore the hopes, or illusions, that we were bearing about the redemptive possibilities of "the people."

But the Melville book that we knew was, of course, *Moby-Dick*, quite enough to convince us of a true kinship. Melville was a man who had worked—perhaps the only authentic proletarian writer this country has ever known—and who had identified himself consciously with the down-trodden plebs. Melville was a writer who took Whitman's democratic affirmations and made them into a wonderfully concrete and fraternal poetry. If he had been willing to welcome Indians, South Sea cannibals, Africans, and Parsees (we were not quite sure who Parsees were!), he might have been prepared to admit a Jew or two onto the *Pequod* if he had happened to think of it.

The closeness one felt toward Melville I can only suggest by saying that when he begins with those utterly thrilling words, "Call me Ishmael," we knew immediately that this meant he was not Ishmael, he was really Isaac. He was the son who had taken the blessing and then, in order to set out for the forbidden world, had also taken his brother's unblessed name. We knew that this Isaac-cum-Ishmael was a mama's boy trying to slide or swagger into the world of power; that he took the job because he had to earn a living, because he wanted to fraternize with workers, and because he needed to prove himself in the chill of the world. When he had told mother Sarah that he was leaving, oh, what a tearful scene that was! "Isaac," she had said, "Isaac, be careful," and so careful did he turn out to be that in order to pass in the Gentile world he said, "Call me Ishmael." And we too would ask the world to call us Ishmael, both the political world and the literary world, in whose chill we also wanted to prove ourselves while expecting that finally we would still be recognized as Isaacs.

The stranger who wore Redburn's hunting jacket and subjected himself to trials of initiation on Ahab's ship, this stranger seemed "one of us," as we could never quite suppose the heroes of Cooper or Twain or Hawthorne were "one of us." These remained alien writers, wonderful but distant, while Melville was our brother, a loose-fish as we were loose-fish.

To be a loose-fish seemed admirable. Alienation was a badge we carried with pride, and our partial deracination—roots loosened in Jewish soil but still not torn out, roots lowered into American soil but still not fixed—gave us a range of possibilities. Some we seized. The American Jewish writers began developing styles that were new to American literature. That we should regard ourselves as partisans of modernism, defenders of the European experimentalists against middlebrow sluggards and know-nothing nativists—this followed a pattern already established in America. Decades earlier the first struggling painters to escape from the immigrant Jewish milieu, figures like Abraham Walkowitz and Max Weber, had leapt across their worthy American contemporaries in order to become pupils at the School of Paris. That, simultaneously, we should respond with pleasure and draw upon the styles of the popular Jewish entertainers, from Fanny Brice to the Marx Brothers, from Willie and Eugene Howard to S. J. Perelman—this too was made possible by the freedom of our partial deracination.

Not fixed into a coherent style, we could imitate many. Not bound by an enclosing tradition, we could draw upon many. It was a remarkable feat for Alfred Kazin, still under thirty and living in Brooklyn, to write a book called *On Native Grounds*, in which he commandeered the whole of American prose fiction. It was a canny self-insight for Paul Goodman to declare his cousinship with Emerson and his American patriotism as a sign of anarchist desire, even though most of his friends, including me, were not quite sure what he was up to. And it was a display of sheer virtuosity, the virtuosity of a savored freedom, for Saul Bellow to write in *Henderson the Rain King* a pure Emersonian fiction, quite as if he had finally wrenched loose from Napoleon Street and the Hotel Ansonia.

Imitation could not always be distinguished from improvisation. If I ask myself, where did the style of the *Partisan Review* essay come from, I think I know a few of the sources. The early Van Wyck Brooks may be one, Edmund Wilson another, and some Continental writers too. But I want also to add that *we made it up*, or, rather, the writers of a decade earlier, those who started out in the middle thirties, dreamed it out of their visions or fantasies of what a cosmopolitan style should be. They drew upon Eliot and Trotsky, perhaps also Baudelaire and Valéry, but finally they made it up: a pastiche, brilliant, aggressive, unstable.

It remains, then, an interesting question why it was that while the first literary passions of the American Jewish intellectuals were directed toward modernism, there was rather little modernist experimentation among the American Jewish writers of fiction. I have a few simple answers. In their imaginations these writers were drawn to Eliot and Joyce, Kafka and Brecht, but the stories most of them composed had little to do with the styles or methods of modernism. Modernism had come to America a decade earlier, in the twenties, with Hemingway and Faulkner, Eliot and Stevens, Crane and Williams. By the thirties, when the generation of Schwartz and Bellow began to write, experimentalism no longer seemed so very experimental; it was something one rushed to defend but also, perhaps, with some inner uneasiness. To the revolution of modernism we were latecomers.

But more. Reaching American literature with heads full of European writing yet also still held by the narrowness of experience in the cities, the American Jewish writers turned inevitably and compulsively to their own past, or to that feverish turf of the imagination they declared to be their past. It was the one area of American life they knew closely and could handle authoritatively, no more able to abandon it in memory than bear it in actuality. The sense of place is as overpowering in their work as, say, in the stories of Eudora Welty and Flannery O'Connor; it soon becomes a sense of fate: hovering, lowering, confining, lingering, utterly imperious.

In the end, as we like to say, it was upon language that the American Jewish writers left their mark. Just as the blacks left theirs upon the vocabulary of American music, so the Jews brought to the language of fiction turnings of voice, feats of irony, and tempos of delivery that helped create a new American style—probably a short-lived style and brought to fulfillment in the work of a mere handful of writers, but a new style nonetheless. Style speaks of sensibility, slant, vision; speaks here of a certain high excitability, a rich pumping of blood, which the Jews brought with their baggage, a grating mixture of the sardonic and sentimental, a mishmash of gutter wisdom and graduate-school learning. I think it no exaggeration to say that since Faulkner and Hemingway the one major innovation in American prose style has been the yoking of street raciness and high-culture mandarin which we associate with American Jewish writers.

Not, to be sure, all of them. There really is no single style that is shared by these writers, and some—Delmore Schwartz in the artifice of his antirhetoric, Michael Seide in the mild purity of his diction, Tillie Olson in her own passionate idiom—clearly challenge the generalizations I shall nevertheless make. For what I want to assert is that the dominant American Jewish style is the one brought to a pitch by Saul Bellow and imitated and modified by a good many others.

In the growth of this style one can see reenacted a pattern through which our nineteenth-century writers created the major American styles. Cooper and Hawthorne, though fresh in their matter, still employed versions of formal Augustan prose; even as they were doing so, however, a language of native storytellers and folkloristic colloquialism was being forged by the humorists of the Old Southwest and the Western frontier; and then, to complete a much-too-neat triad, Twain and Melville blended formal prose with native speech, the heritage from England with the improvisations of American regions, into a style that in Twain might be called "purified demotic" and in Melville "democratic extravagance."

A similar development, on a much smaller scale, has been at work in the fiction of the American Jewish writers. The first collection of stories by Abraham Cahan, *Yekl,* is written in a baneful dialect so naturalistically faithful, or intent upon being faithful, to the immigrant moment that it now seems about as exotic and inaccessible as the argot of Sut Lovingood. Cahan's major novel, *The Rise of David Levinsky,* employs, by contrast, a flavorless standard English, the prose of an earnest but somewhat tone-deaf student worried about proper usage. More interesting for its mythic narrative line than for verbal detail, this novel shows Cahan to be not quite in possession of *any* language, either English or Yiddish, a condition that was common enough among the immigrants, and in the case of their occasionally talented sons would become the shifting ground upon which to build a shifty new style. The problem foreshadowed in Cahan's work is: How can the Yiddishisms of East Side street talk and an ill-absorbed "correct" prose painfully acquired in night school be fused into some higher stylistic enterprise?

One answer, still the most brilliant, came in Henry Roth's *Call It Sleep,* a major novel blending a Joyce roughened to the tonalities of New York and deprived of his Irish lilt with a Yiddish oddly transposed into a pure and lyrical English but with its rhythms slightly askew, as if to reveal immigrant origins. In Roth's novel the children speak a ghastly mutilated sort of English, whereas the main adult characters talk in Yiddish, which Roth renders as a high poetic, somewhat offbeat, English. Thus, the mother tells her little boy: "Aren't you just a pair of eyes and ears! You see, you hear, you remember, but when will you know? . . . And no kisses? . . . There! Savory, thrifty lips!" The last phrase may seem a bit too "poetic" in English speech, but if you translate it into Yiddish—*Na! geshmake, karge lipelakh!*—it rings exactly right, beautifully idiomatic. Roth is here continuing the tradition of Jewish bilingualism, in the past a coexistence of Hebrew as sacred and Yiddish or Ladino as demotic language; but he does this in an oddly surreptitious way, by making of English, in effect, two languages, or by writing portions of this book in one language and expecting that some readers will be able to hear it in another.

Yet, so far as I can tell, Roth has not been a major stylistic influence upon later American Jewish writers, perhaps because his work seems so self-contained there is nothing much to do with it except admire. Perhaps a more useful precursor is Daniel Fuchs, a lovely and neglected writer, especially in his second novel, *Homage to Blenholt*, where one begins to hear a new music, a new tempo, as if to echo the beat of the slums.

This American Jewish style, which comes to fulfillment and perhaps terminus with Bellow, I would describe in a few desperate phrases:

A forced yoking of opposites: gutter vividness and university refinement, street energy and high-culture rhetoric.

A strong infusion of Yiddish, not so much through the occasional use of a phrase or word as through an importation of ironic twistings that transform the whole of language, so to say, into a corkscrew of questions.

A rapid, nervous, breathless tempo, like the hurry of a garment salesman trying to con a buyer or a highbrow lecturer trying to dazzle an audience.

A deliberate loosening of syntax, as if to mock those niceties of Correct English which Gore Vidal and other untainted Americans hold dear, so that in consequence there is much greater weight upon transitory patches of color than upon sentences in repose or paragraphs in composure.

A deliberate play with the phrasings of plebeian speech, but often the kind that vibrates with cultural ambition, seeking to zoom into the regions of higher thought.

In short, the linguistic tokens of writers who must hurry into articulateness if they are to be heard at all, indeed, who must scrape together a language. This style reflects a demotic upsurge, the effort to give literary scale to the speech of immigrant streets, or put another way, to create a "third language," richer and less stuffy, out of the fusion of English and Yiddish that had already occurred spontaneously in those streets. Our writers did not, of course, create a new language, and in the encounter between English and Yiddish, the first has survived far better than the second; but still, *we* have left our scar, tiny though it be, on *their* map.

The other day a gentile friend of mine remarked that in getting from City College in uptown Manhattan to the City University's Graduate Center at Forty-Second Street she had had a long *shlep*. She used this word without a trace of self-consciousness, and she was right, for what she had experienced was not quite an inconvenience nor even a drag; it was a *shlep*. The word in Yiddish bears a multitude of burdens, as if to take a New York subway comes, as indeed it does, to taking on the weight of the world. *Shlep* is becoming part of the American language and in the hard days ahead it can only help.

But there is more. There is the *shlepper*, in whom the qualities of *shlepping* have become a condition of character. There is a *shleppenish*, an experience that exhausts the spirit and wearies the body. And as virtual apotheosis there is *shlepperei*, which raises the burdens of *shlepping* into a statement about the nature of the world. Starbuck unable to resist Ahab was a bit of a *shlepper*; Prufrock afraid to eat his peach made his life into a *shleppenish*; Herzog ground down by his impossible women transformed all of existence into sheer *shlepperei*.

Of such uncouth elements is the American language made and re-made. Upon such renewals does the American experience thrive. And if indeed our dream of a New World paradise is ever to be realized, this time beyond mere innocence, how can we ever expect to get there except through the clubfoot certainties of *shlepping*?

Lillian Hellman and the McCarthy Years

There are writers with so enticing a style that, in their own behalf, they must stop themselves and ask: "Is what I am saying true? Charming yes, persuasive also; but *true?*" This has, or should, become a problem for Lillian Hellman. Her three recent memoirs recalling her life with Dashiell Hammett and, in *Scoundrel Time*, her 1952 clash with the House Un-American Activities Committee (HUAC), all make attractive reading. By the same token, however, Miss Hellman has reached a point where she risks mythologizing her own life, transfiguring the story of a taciturn Dash and the peppery Lillian into a popular literary romance.

But let that pass, and let us turn to the claim of Miss Hellman and her admirers that in her latest book she provides an accurate and balanced record of the McCarthy years. My contention is that she does not. What she provides is half the story, a vivid and useful half, but no more.

Nothing, to be sure, in her book is as false and certainly nothing as vulgar as the Introduction Garry Wills has written for it. Yet, nuance and sensibility apart, Miss Hellman and Wills hold pretty much the same view of the early 1950s. Quickly summarized, it is this: The U.S. was

From *Dissent* 23 (Fall 1976):4.

seized in those years by an ideological fever, whipped up by Cold War reactionaries. America, says Wills, had fallen "in love with total war"; American intellectuals, says Miss Hellman, grew fearful that the spread of Communism might bring to an end "their pleasant way of life." Now that the Nazis were smashed, a new scapegoat was needed and for this the Communists were ready at hand. The dirty work was done by congressional inquisitors, the intellectual support given by anti-Communist liberals and radicals. Americans for Democratic Action (ADA), sneers Wills, did "the Committee's [HUAC's] kind of work in a more sophisticated way."

This view of the McCarthy years is simple, self-serving, and untrue. It starts from a premise always dear to those who would deny the reality of Communism as problem or threat: the premise that there is a single, undifferentiated, and necessarily reactionary "anti-Communism." Thus, writes Miss Hellman, the anti-Stalinist intellectuals have not yet found it "a part of conscience to admit that their Cold War anti-Communism was perverted, possibly against their wishes, into the Vietnam War and then into the reign of Nixon, their unwanted but inevitable leader." It is an astonishing sentence, with gaps in the argument through which battalions of historical complications could march.

• It assumes the existence of a unified body of intellectuals, all holding the same views about Communism, McCarthyism, and so on. But even within the ranks of the New York intellectuals, whom Miss Hellman seems mostly to have in mind, this was untrue.

• It is preposterous as history. Complicated chains of events, as well as unforeseeable accidents, intervened between the McCarthy years and the Vietnam War; events and accidents that could more plausibly be assigned as causes of that war than could the McCarthyite inquisition. Equally preposterous is the claim that Nixon as leader was "inevitable." What about the many intellectuals who did *not* follow Nixon, either evitably or inevitably? What about the possibility that the events of the late 1960s created a backlash from which Nixon profited? Suppose that in a few crucial states, like California, voters inclined toward the New Left had voted for Humphrey—might not Nixon have been defeated and not become our "inevitable" leader? Miss Hellman has wandered into a swamp of determinism/freedom that more experienced historians know it is wise to avoid.

• The shoddiness, in any case, of Miss Hellman's argument can be revealed by proposing an equivalent: "The uncritical support given Stalinist Russia by people like Dashiell Hammett and other literary people led, possibly against their wishes, to a whitewash of Gulag Archipelago and the murder of millions, and for this the fellow-traveling intellectuals must inevitably be held responsible." I imagine Miss Hellman would be outraged by such an argument, insisting we must make discriminations as to kinds of support, degrees of involvement, and the nature of motives. Well, let her try to imagine as much for others.

Except as a rhetorical device for dull-witted reactionaries, on the one hand, and bashful fellow-travelers on the other, there was no such thing as a monolithic "anti-Communism." Opposition to Communism by demagogues like McCarthy rested on reactionary opinions and a fear that privileges might be lost; opposition to Communism by liberals and radicals rested on libertarian opinions and a fear that freedoms might be lost. In political methods and outlook, Joe McCarthy was a lot closer to the Communist Khrushchev than to the anti-Communist Norman Thomas.

That "anti-Communism" was exploited by the McCarthy hooligans does not mean there was no reason for serious people to worry about Communism as a threat to freedom. The Soviet Union had just gobbled up Eastern Europe—but Garry Wills sees only the "aggressive" foreign policy of Harry Truman. If Miss Hellman and Wills want to provide a balanced picture of this historical period, they must point not only to the failures of American policy, real and grave as these were, but also to the reasons that led many of us to fear that the Communist movement in Europe had gathered a dynamic of expansion threatening political freedom.

At the least, a few simple facts! Though Wills carries on at length about foolishness spewed by Ayn Rand before HUAC in order to ridicule the very idea that there was any ground for concern about Communism, he says nothing, nor does Miss Hellman, about the discussions then being carried on throughout the world on this matter by such people as Ignazio Silone, George Orwell, Nicola Chiaromonte, Willy Brandt, Norman Thomas, and many others. Really, to think you can dispose of any point of view by invoking Ayn Rand!

Still more—and here we come to a *feat*—both Wills and Miss Hellman talk about the early fifties without so much as mentioning the event that sent shivers through the hearts of intellectuals, and not theirs alone. Imagine writing about this period, imagine discussing the response of intellectuals to Communism, McCarthyism, and all the rest, without even mentioning the 1948 Communist coup in Czechoslovakia. It would be like writing a study of the upheavals in the late 1960s without mentioning the Vietnam War! For it was the coup in Czechoslovakia that persuaded many people that there could be no lasting truce with the Communist world. I don't know whether Garry Wills is old enough to remember that event, or has troubled to read anything about it, but Lillian Hellman must remember it.

There were, to be sure, intellectuals who buckled under the Mc-Carthyite assault (it was not, by the way, a "terror": people could speak, write, agitate against it without fearing a knock on their doors at 4:00 in the morning). Other intellectuals allowed their hatred of Communism to deflect them from an adequate resistance to McCarthy. As instances of the latter, Miss Hellman cites *Partisan Review* and *Commentary*. She is largely unfair about the first, largely right about the second. *Partisan Review*, as she notes, printed in 1954 a violently anti-McCarthy and free-swinging attack by me on conformist intellectuals; the piece was written at the suggestion of Philip Rahv, then its leading editor; and it could hardly have gotten into the pages of *PR* behind the backs of the editors. What seems to me true is that the magazine didn't take a sufficiently bold lead in rallying intellectuals against McCarthyism; but that is something very different from what Miss Hellman says. As for *Commentary*, it was then controlled by intellectuals hurrying rightward (a fate that seems to befall that journal periodically) and its record on McCarthyism was, let us say, shabby. Two of its leading editors, Elliot Cohen and Irving Kristol, while not giving their approval to McCarthy, went to some lengths to dismiss the idea that the Wisconsin demagogue constituted a serious threat to American liberties.

Surely Miss Hellman must remember, as Wills might have troubled to find out, that there were old-fashioned liberals like Henry Steele Commager and Roger Baldwin and old-fashioned Socialists like Norman Thomas who combined a principle opposition to Communism with an utter rejection of McCarthyism. Thomas fought for the liberties of the very Stalinists who had supported the prosecution of Trotskyists in Minneapolis under the notorious Smith Act. In the early issues of *Dissent* there were attacks on McCarthy and all he stood for, as well as criticism of the *Commentary* people for their waffling.

The same holds for the liberal Americans for Democratic Action. Perhaps some people in that group had bad records in the early 1950s. There were cowards everywhere in scoundrel time. But as it happens, a hero of Miss Hellman's book is Joe Rauh, the lawyer who represented her before HUAC. Everyone who knows ADA also knows that Rauh has been one of its two or three central figures from the moment of its birth. If Garry Wills is so intent upon pillorying ADA, shouldn't he at least ask how he can reconcile the charge that ADA did "the work" of HUAC with the fact that this leading ADA figure emerges in the Hellman book as a staunch defender of liberties? Didn't Wills read Hellman or Hellman Wills?

Wills is equally feckless in writing about the once-famous Waldorf Conference in 1949, of which Miss Hellman was a prominent sponsor. In the name of peace, this gathering was organized by "the Cultural and Scientific Conference for World Peace," a group Wills neglects, somehow, to characterize politically. In fact, it was dominated by Communists and their friends, and represented the last hurrah of the fellow-traveling intellectuals in the United States. Its overwhelming stress was to blame the developing Cold War on the United States.

Wills tells us that U.S. footpads and intellectual auxiliaries joined at this conference to harass lovers of peace. "Guardians of liberalism" like Mary McCarthy and Dwight Macdonald went to the sessions "in order to disrupt them." The composer Shostakovich, who was one of the Russian delegates, "was, in the name of freedom, publicly insulted for not being free."

False, every word. In 1949 Mary McCarthy and Dwight Macdonald were anti-Stalinist, independent radicals—to speak of them as "guardians of liberalism" is gratuitously patronizing. Nor did they disrupt the conference. McCarthy, Macdonald, and Robert Lowell asked questions of Shostakovich (who looked as if he wanted to be anywhere but where he was) and of the Russian culture commissar, Alexander Fedayev (who looked as if he'd like to get these American wiseguys back home; he'd teach them to ask questions!). The questions concerned the fate of Russian writers persecuted by the regime and, in the case of Lowell, the sufferings of conscientious objectors in the Soviet Union.

Now to someone trained in a GPU school all this might have seemed "disruptive." But to Garry Wills, so severe in his judgments about standing up for freedom?

In her own essay Miss Hellman is more charming and certainly writes better than Wills. She has earned the right to be proud of her record in defying the HUAC bums, though her explanation of why some of her friends, like Clifford Odets, lost their nerve and gave names to the committee is very disturbing. "The children of timid immigrants [Jewish immigrants?] are often remarkable people: energetic, intelligent, hardworking; and often they make it so good that they are determined to keep it at any cost." Are we to infer that the children of bourgeois German Jews or starchy Protestant Americans have proven themselves to be rocks of fortitude in resisting tyrannical authority? And as for that remark about "timid immigrants," Miss Hellman ought to look at a recent book called *World of Our Fathers*, where she can learn just how "timid" many of those immigrants were.

Miss Hellman's main target is finally the intellectuals, those—mostly unnamed—who failed to stand up or stand up strongly enough to

McCarthy. "Up to the late 1940s," she had believed that "the educated, the intellectual lived by what they claimed to believe: freedom of thought and speech, the right of each man to his own convictions." Well, as I've indicated, a number of American intellectuals did just that. Yet before Miss Hellman grows so furious with the others, those who caved in and those who wobbled, oughtn't she to be asking the same *kind* of questions about the people with whom she collaborated politically over the years, signing statements, organizing the Waldorf Conference, sponsoring the Progressive party? How can it be that someone who believed in such splendid things didn't trouble to ask friends and collaborators whether *they* lived by "freedom of thought and speech, the right of each man to his own convictions"?

Miss Hellman doesn't ask such questions; she isn't inclined to make things hard for herself. She is riding high these days—and no one, really, should begrudge Lillian Hellman her success, for she is a gifted writer. Still, I find myself disturbed by the way she clings to fragments of old dogmas that, at other and more lucid moments, she knows she should have given up long ago. "Most of the Communists I had met," she writes, "seemed to me people who wanted to make a better world; many of them were silly people and a few of them were genuine nuts, but that doesn't make for denunciations. . . ."

No individual should be harassed or persecuted, or denounced to the cops, for holding even the most obnoxious opinions. But what about judgments of the opinions themselves and of the public consequences of holding them?

Most of the Communists Miss Hellman met may have wanted a better world, but the better world they wanted came down to a soul-destroying and body-tormenting prison: the Moscow trials, the Stalin dictatorship, the destruction of millions during the forced collectivization, and a systematic denial of the slave camps in Siberia. (Do you really think we didn't know about Gulag Archipelago until Solzhenitsyn published his remarkable book? He offered new material, but the essential facts were known as far back as the late 1930s—and were violently denied by many of the people with whom Miss Hellman worked at the Waldorf Conference and in the Progressive party.)

A final point and we are done. On her next-to-last page Miss Hellman writes that the intellectuals whom she has attacked have a right to criticize her for "taking too long to see what was going on in the Soviet Union. But whatever our mistakes, I do not believe we did our country any harm."

Lillian Hellman could not be more mistaken! Those who supported Stalinism and its political enterprises, either here or abroad, helped befoul the cultural atmosphere, helped bring totalitarian methods into trade unions, helped perpetuate one of the great lies of our century, helped destroy whatever possibilities there might have been for a resurgence of serious radicalism in America. Isn't that harm enough?

Scoundrels there were in the 1950s, as in all other times, and Lillian Hellman has pointed to some of them accurately. But she would have done both her readers and herself a greater service if she had been more precise—and more comprehensive—in her pointing.

George Eliot
and Radical Evil

Toward the end of their careers, great writers are sometimes roused to a new energy by thoughts of risk. Some final stab at an area of human experience they had neglected or at a theme only recently become urgent: this excites their imaginations. They leave behind assured achievement, all they have done well and could still do better, and start clambering up the slopes of uncertainty. Watching them as they slide, slip, and start up again can be very moving—it can also make one very nervous.

Jane Austen, triumphant in *Emma*, edges toward a shy romanticism in *Persuasion*. Dickens, triumphant in *Little Dorrit*, grapples with *ressentiment* in the Bradley Headstone segment of *Our Mutual Friend*: quite as if he were "becoming" Dostoevsky. George Eliot, seldom regarded as an innovator in the art of fiction, brushes past the serene equilibrium and symmetrical ironies of *Middlemarch* in order to test new perceptions in her final novel, *Daniel Deronda*. What moves these writers is some inner restlessness to go beyond the known and the finished, to undertake work that will probably turn out to be only partly fulfilled. With George

Introduction to *Daniel Deronda* (New York: New American Library, 1979).

Eliot, it is a movement into ways of writing about the world that partly anticipate the modernism of twentieth-century fiction.

Now this is by no means the usual account of her concluding years and work. By the time she published *Middlemarch*, in 1873, she was commonly regarded as the leading English novelist of her day, indeed, as a cultural sage of gravity and truthfulness. When she came to publish *Daniel Deronda*, in 1876, there was a cooling of public response. By now anything from her pen was certain to be treated respectfully, but this was not a book most English readers could feel easy with. Beneath the critical acclaim could be heard sighs of perplexity: Why was she taxing them with so ponderous, so *un-English* a theme as the proto-Zionism to which the hero of the novel commits himself? Why does it contain so many passages of "heavy" reflection? And why could she not restrain that ardent, nervous idealism of hers, perhaps forgivable in youth but unseemly in a woman of mature years?

In the standard accounts of English literature *Daniel Deronda* was for many years regarded as, at best, a worthy embarrassment, and only with F. R. Leavis's *The Great Tradition* (1947) did there occur a decisive shift in critical opinion. Leavis, while dismissing "the Jewish part" as a flat failure, insisted that in "the Gwendolen Harleth part" Eliot had done her most brilliant work. He toyed with the notion that the two segments of the book might be ripped apart, so that a new novel to be called *Gwendolen Harleth* would emerge, though on a later occasion he admitted that this was an utterly impractical idea since the two strands are, for better or worse, inseparable. With Leavis's over-all judgment one isn't disposed to quarrel, only to offer a few complicating amendments. (There are, after all, significant gradations of literary realization in "the Jewish part" of the book; it is not simply to be dismissed.) But even Leavis, probably the best Eliot critic of our time, didn't trouble to ask what it was that Eliot was trying to do in this book, how it might relate to her lifelong moral and intellectual concerns, and to what extent it signified a change in her attitudes toward English society. Answer these questions, and you are in a position to measure the extraordinary *interest* of this novel, an undertaking more valuable than simply laying out its strengths and weaknesses.

The last part of *Middlemarch* appeared in December 1873; the first part of *Daniel Deronda* in February 1876. Between these two dates, and no doubt somewhat before the earlier one, there was intense activity in George Eliot's creative life.

So great a book as *Middlemarch* can hardly be reduced to one or two concerns, but for my present purpose let me stress these: It is a novel that portrays the difficulties encountered by serious people, those who would live beyond mere appetite or ego, as they try to survive in the society of nineteenth-century England (perhaps any society). If they are to make their way in the world without surrendering their values, such people need a sizable moral and intellectual armament—they cannot permit themselves relaxation or slackness. Not that the society of *Middlemarch* is merely despicable; not at all. It contains elements of benign feeling and remnants of religious faith, but essentially it is a philistine society, sluggish in its provincialism, hostile to the uses of mind, and streaked with that complacent egoism Eliot regards as the most damaging of human failings—an egoism, it may be suggested with just a bit of overstatement, that flourishes in the life of the middle class. Characters like the serious young doctor Lydgate and the earnest but drifting young woman Dorothea, who set themselves a little apart from the standards of this world, seeking vocations of purpose and lives graced by consciousness, have to measure very soberly the odds against them. They have to know that their struggle, while not doomed, will be difficult. They have to be alert to those subtle corruptions with which the world would stain them (those "spots of commonness," as Eliot calls Lydgate's patronizing view of women).

To be personally distinguished in the world of Jane Austen is to experience some inconvenience; one has to set oneself at a certain distance, yet by no means wholly apart, from the bulk of ordinary, dull people. Somewhat more than half a century later, in the world of George Eliot, the problem has become far more severe. To engage in a serious vocation, whether as artist or scientist or political thinker, or to live by disinterested moral ends that don't necessarily require a particular vocation, is now to face a harsh struggle with the powers that dominate society. It may still be possible to reach a truce allowing a margin of survival, but only by commanding large gifts of self-knowledge and strategy. As George Eliot sees it, this is not a political struggle; she does not often think in such categories. The Lydgates and Dorotheas need a patient, clearheaded strength in order to hold their ground, defend their standards, and, above all, do the work they really want to. Flaws of character can lead to defeat in the enterprise of defining one's life. When a Lydgate suffers the humiliation of worldly "success," it is mostly because he has not understood what his dedication as a scientist demands from him as citizen and man. It is not possible, suggests George Eliot, simultaneously to defy the standards of the community and drift painlessly in its commonplace ways of life.

At the end of *Middlemarch* the problem remains mostly unresolved: how can intelligent and sensitive people carve out a portion of autonomy in their lives? And because no certain answer emerges, Eliot's preoccupation with the problem of vocation seems, so to say, a problem remaining beyond the last page of the book. It will become more urgent still—indeed, all but obsessional—in *Daniel Deronda*. One might even say that she is here bringing to bear an essentially religious vision, that hunger for spiritual consecration which is the heritage of the Christianity she abandoned in her earlier years. A contemporary spoke of Eliot as "the first great *godless* writer of fiction that has appeared in England," and this is keen provided one adds that precisely her "godlessness," forlorn and serious, kept prompting her to search for equivalents to belief that would give moral weight to human existence.

In the time between *Middlemarch* and *Daniel Deronda* George Eliot plunged into the study of Jewish history, custom, lore. More, one suspects, than her usual conscientiousness led her to so thorough an investigation. Some years earlier she had gotten to know a Jewish scholar, Emanuel Deutsch, who became head of a "Back to Palestine" group foreshadowing Zionism. Deutsch, from whom George Eliot took lessons in Hebrew, would serve as a model for Mordecai, the prophetic figure in *Daniel Deronda* who speaks at times in the accents of religious mysticism, at times as a modern rationalist, but always in behalf of a Jewish national revival. In 1873, during a continental journey, George Eliot visited synagogues in Frankfurt and Mainz. (Deronda visits one in Frankfurt too.) All the while she was reading avidly in Jewish history: the works of Graetz, Zunz, Geiger, and Steinschneider among Jewish historians, and such Gentile students of Jewish life and language as Milman and Renan. From the historians she learned about a long-standing dispute regarding the condition of Jews in Europe: had they sunk irrevocably into "cultural degeneracy," becoming, as the twentieth-century historian Toynbee would say, a mere "historical fossil," or were they at the brink of a national renaissance? These disputes, in simplified but affecting form, are echoed in the discussions at the "Hand and Banner" workingmen's club which Daniel Deronda visits with Mordecai (in turn a possible model for Hyacinth Robinson's visit to the "Sun and Moon" café in James's *The Princess Casamassima*). From this range of sources, then—from books, conversations, and visits—George Eliot came to know something about Jewish life in Europe and to respond to it with that warmth which is her signature.

She knew perfectly well, as she noted in her journal, that the Jewish part of the novel seemed "likely to satisfy nobody," but she stubbornly insisted on the unity of her book—at least, unity of intention and design. Shortly after its publication she wrote to a friend, objecting to "readers who cut the book into scraps and talk of nothing in it but Gwendolen. I meant everything in the book to be related to everything else there." With so self-conscious a writer as George Eliot, this last sentence merits serious attention. Whether, nonetheless, everything in the book is related to everything else is another matter.

Daniel Deronda tried the tolerance of the English public, even its most cultivated segment. The fate of the Jews, scattered and in some cases demoralized, was a subject too distant—perhaps it even seemed a little "unsavory"—for a literary public largely fixed in the self-regarding premises of Victorian England. One might favor religious liberty, even deplore persecution in far-off places, but that was hardly a reason to have the Jews thrust upon one, page after page. The public had adored *Adam Bede* and *The Mill on the Floss*, Eliot's earlier fictions about English country life; such books were familiar, delightful. The public respected, or was trained to respect, the solidity of *Middlemarch*. But Jews, especially loquacious ones prophesying miracles in Palestine, were too much.

Why was George Eliot drawn to the Jews at all? What made her suppose them a usable novelistic subject—or, if not usable, then necessary? Not, apparently, any special feelings of personal attachment: she had to "work up" this subject. Something more entangled must have been at stake, and though we cannot know for certain, since we are speculating about the inner life of a great writer, I want to put down a few suppositions.

She saw in the usual contempt for the Jews a gross instance of that English xenophobia, that English smugness of feeling which she had come increasingly to deplore. As she wrote to Harriet Beecher Stowe: "Precisely because I felt that the usual attitude of Christians toward Jews is—I hardly know whether to say more impious or more stupid when viewed in the light of their professed principles. I therefore felt urged to treat Jews with such sympathy and understanding as my nature and knowledge could attain to."

Anti-Semitism she proceeded to locate as an example of "a spirit of arrogance and contemptuous dictatorialness . . . which has become a national disgrace." Estimable these sentiments are, but they can hardly be supposed fully to explain why she gave the Jews so large a role in her book, why she *turned* to them late in her career.

She found herself going back, through channels of yearning, to something like her youthful religious enthusiasms. The fervor of the young Evangelical, Marian Evans (her family name), who almost forty years earlier had thrilled to the word of Christianity, would now reappear, far more complex and problematic, in the speeches of Mordecai and the quest of Deronda. "Toward the Hebrews," she wrote to Harriet Beecher Stowe, "we western people who have been reared in Christianity, have a peculiar debt and, whether we acknowledge it or not, a peculiar thoroughness of fellowship in religious and moral sentiment." The phrase "a peculiar thoroughness of fellowship" refers to the linkage Daniel Deronda is meant to embody between the two great religions of "East" and "West," Judaism and Christianity, neither given literal credence by Eliot in her mature years but both seen as repositories of moral wisdom. None of this, to be sure, is made very explicit in a novel that probably makes too many other things explicit; but it is suggested irresistibly by the scheme, the organizing fable, of the book—which in one part is the transfiguration of a fine young Protestant apparently of upper-class English birth into an eager young Jew of dubious yet blessed birth, with the first Deronda in search of some ennobling purpose, whether transcendent or not, and the second presumably having found it.

She saw in the barely dawning movement of the Jews toward national regroupment something that might arouse the imagination of cultivated people—was not that movement somewhat like the other resurgences of oppressed Europeans in the nineteenth century? She saw in the Jews a usable symbol for the search, recurrent in her work, for modes of action through which to realize moral ideals.

Now among sophisticated critics—there is of course no other kind— it has become customary to patronize George Eliot a little for this sudden turn of interest toward the Jews. That there are major flaws in her treatment of Jewish experience, almost everyone agrees. But to see that is by no means the same as simply to dismiss "the Jewish part" as lacking in interest. Such a response blurs a notable moment in the growth of human consciousness. For we should remember that the most vivid Jewish character in nineteenth-century English fiction is, alas, Fagin, the thief and mentor of thieves, drawn in brilliant accord with the dominant myth of the Jewish villain, a corrupting agent of Satan let loose to defile Christian society. To deny the power of this myth would be foolish; to deny the fearful strength with which Dickens embodied it, still more foolish. *Daniel Deronda*, as Lionel Trilling remarked in a youthful essay, "enshrined the Jew" in a "counter-myth": he is now benevolent, wise, pure-spirited. But if neither myth nor counter-myth allows a fully shaded characterization of Jews, still, the counter-myth is a step toward that end. Grappling with the "counter-myth," and thereby coming to see the Jews—some of them—as a possible counter-force to the English society depicted in the novel, George Eliot undertook a task that can only be called heroic. Anyone with a grain of historical imagination ought to feel admiration even for those parts of *Daniel Deronda* that obviously fail, the failures of great writers often being more valuable than the successes of lesser ones.

This much said, we can turn to the novel itself.

2

On its strong side *Daniel Deronda* is the most penetrating scrutiny in nineteenth-century English fiction, perhaps in all English fiction, of human beings caught up in a web of inhuman relations. Only *Little Dorrit* offers perhaps as mordant and relentless a criticism of English (but of course, more than English) society: its devaluation of love and friendship through the exercise of power, its subordination of human affections to the cash nexus, its bone-chilling social elitism.

One doesn't usually think of George Eliot as a social critic, and her liberalism seems more a quality of tone and temper—the tone of generosity, the temper of humaneness—than of any militant desire for social change. But what she shows here of the relationship between Gwendolen and Henleigh Grandcourt, the suavely perverse aristocrat who becomes her husband, is not just the anatomy of a bad marriage, nor even the terror felt by a young woman trapped by an overmastering husband. It is *a system of dehumanized personal relations*, and thereby more than personal relations; it is the barbarism that civilization lightly coats and readily becomes. Except perhaps for Henry James's study of Isabel Archer's subjugation in *Portrait of a Lady* there is nothing else in our language quite like this.

In its strength, then, *Daniel Deronda* is a novel about the crushing weight of power, the power of those who rule over other human beings and take it to be proper that they should rule. Social rulers, personal rulers: there is of course an important difference, but a still more important affinity. A long-entrenched aristocracy can exert its power with so complete a sense of assurance that its members feel its domination to be "natural," ordained by the order of the universe. Grandcourt is hardly a typical aristocrat, but he drives to an ugly extreme a good many aristocratic values. What makes him so fearful is his assumption that lording it over other people is his right, simply by virtue of the place he occupies in the structure of English society. No chink of doubt or streak of shame mars this belief. He is all of a piece, monolithic in arrogance, and intelligent in maneuver.

No sooner are Gwendolen and Grandcourt married than he sets out quietly to break her will. He rarely lifts his voice, never his hand. As a civilized man—and surely George Eliot meant him to be so regarded—he wants to rule over his wife not by cracking a whip, which would be both vulgar and bothersome, but by creating an atmosphere of wordless mastery so complete there will be no need for cracking a whip. (Theorists of totalitarianism call this terror-in-reserve.) In Grandcourt's behavior there are elements of sadistic perversity, a personal psychopathology, but there is also a strong component of class feeling which covers the perversity. It is not a casual insight, it is a stroke of genius, that Eliot should say of Grandcourt: "If this white-handed man with the perpendicular profile had been sent to govern a difficult colony, he might have won reputation among his contemporaries. He had certainly ability, would have understood that it was safer to exterminate than to cajole superseded proprietors, and would not have flinched from making things safe in that way." (The magnitude of Eliot's work can sometimes lead one to pass by such small but brilliant touches as "this white-handed man," utterly evocative of Grandcourt's nature, status, and style.) Nor does he flinch with Gwendolen. Mastery of person over person, sex over sex, class over class (we steadily hear the clink of money) is shown in an accumulating discipline of incidents. And, as I say, this is a mastery of and within civilization, well-mannered and well-spoken, in refined English style: Grandcourt is a gentleman. This gentleman who would not hesitate to slaughter the brutes in some "difficult colony" knows exactly how to break his wife at home, with a glance of scorn, a muttered phrase. The connoisseur of domination finds his pleasure in *playing* with power.

Gwendolen is a creature whose entire upbringing, false and corrupt, prepares her for the role of victim. Her suffering is extreme, prolonged, without any certain end, and it is remarkable that George Eliot should make us care so strongly about the fate of a young woman in many ways distasteful, even deplorable. This happens not, as foolish critics say, because George Eliot is "didactic" and rubs in "the lesson," but because she has grasped her characters to their bone, their blood, because she shapes their confrontations into fierce dramatic scenes. Gwendolen has entangled herself in a web of bad faith—it is this, of course, which keeps her from rebelling against Grandcourt's tyranny, or it is this partly. Knowing before her marriage that Grandcourt keeps another woman and children to whom she will do harm if she marries him, Gwendolen still cannot back off. She cannot forgo the pride of place this marriage will bring, she cannot face the social humiliation that good faith would entail. All this, the weakness and the shame, makes her suffering more credible, closer to our own knowledge of how suffering is compounded by weakness and shame.

In the brilliant opening scene everything is prepared, foreshadowed: Gwendolen plays feverishly at the gaming table, as later she will enter the greater gamble of marriage, and Deronda watches from a distance, as he must always watch. A spoiled creature, Gwendolen is ill-prepared for any useful work or purpose; she is vain with the untouchable vanity of youthful beauty; she is snobbish in a small provincial way, out of ignorance of the world. Beneath her lively manner there hover a good many fears—she fears being touched, she fears poverty, she fears strong emotions, she fears unspecified terrors. There is an incident in Chapter 5, clearly meant to bear symbolic weight, where Gwendolen becomes hysterical before a customarily hidden picture of a dead person: "She [Gwendolen] looked like a statue into which a soul of Fear had entered." A bit later Eliot remarks on Gwendolen's "susceptibility to terror," though without trying to detail its nature. (Toward the end of the novel, there is a parallel, though of a far more serious kind, when Gwendolen cannot shake from her mind's eye the picture of Grandcourt as he is drowning.) The incident suggests Gwendolen's fear of, distance from, her own inner being, all that lies hidden in memory and below routine consciousness, all that cannot readily be controlled by will. She is a person who has been trained to avoid self-scrutiny—innerness is a threat to her scheme of life. Adored by those near her, assuming that comforts are a birthright, she relishes the prospect of future distinction but has no clear picture of what it might be: "she did not wish to lead the same sort of life as ordinary young ladies did; but what she was not clear upon was, how she should set about leading any other. . . ." A seepage of boredom has begun, as it must with anyone lacking strong self or belief, and this too prepares her for becoming Grandcourt's victim, since he at least seems likely to provide some diversions from boredom.

All the while, in this creature formed unsystematically upon a system of false values, there is a quickness of life, attractive, keen, touching. Her wit is lively, her mind agile. Somewhere within her a "root of conscience" can invite pain, enough to spoil the pleasures she wants. "Pleasures" may not be the exact word here: she is not free enough for pleasures; it is a breed of vanities that drives her. Finally, Gwendolen is innocent. She is innocent of the world, of its hardness, of her own self. As Henry James puts it: "The universe forcing itself with a slow, inexorable pressure into a narrow, complacent, and yet after all extremely sensitive mind, and making it ache with the pain of the process—that is Gwendolen's story."

Her innocence comes out as both damaging and touching when she seeks advice from the musician Klesmer. The family investments having gone bad, she fancies becoming a singer or actress who will assume a distinguished position in the arts because she is . . . well, herself. The enlightenment to which Klesmer subjects her is painful. He stresses the hard work such a career demands; he is honest about the likelihood of failure, or a mediocrity not much better, as the outcome even of hard work. "You have not said to yourself, 'I must know this exactly,' 'I must understand this exactly,' 'I must do this exactly.' . . . You have not yet conceived what excellence is; you must unlearn your mistaken admirations. . . ."

Klesmer is the first of the positive voices—there are not many—to be heard in the novel: he speaks for the calling of art and he speaks as an outsider, a German Jew, who has already been seen in a bristling encounter with the amiable philistinism of the English politician, Mr. Bult. Gwendolen has the brains to recognize that Klesmer is telling her the truth, and the sensitivity to blush at the presumptuousness he has been gentle enough not to name. She concludes that there is no alternative to marrying Grandcourt.

Elegant, gliding with the slow movements of a "lizard," preceding each sentence with an authoritative pause, this Grandcourt is one of the supreme inventions of English fiction. He is not larger than life, as a Lovelace or Heathcliff is sometimes felt to be; he is scaled to social ordinariness, and the demonic principle to his ordinary flesh. He is not torn, as Gwendolen can be, by divisions of the will, for he is the pure double of her "lower self," bringing to completion all within her that thrills to the demands of status, rank, money, power. Everything about him is realized with a remarkable vividness, as if derived from an enmity so deep as to dispense with rancor.

George Eliot is not often given credit for employing the novelistic techniques usually associated with later, supposedly more sophisticated writers like James and Conrad, but she does so with complete authority in her treatment of Gwendolen and Grandcourt. The girl she depicts through a hum of analysis, a kind of psychological paraphrase that dramatizes impulse, whim, feeling, inhibition. It is Eliot who speaks, her voice that we hear, but she is so close, in both sympathy and irony, to Gwendolen that we can easily suppose we are "in" Gwendolen's consciousness. We come to know Gwendolen as a history of reflection and confusion; we are privy to the evasions of her self, the maneuvers of her will. Grandcourt, however, is done mainly from a distance, through the pressure of his behavior on those near him. George Eliot is careful not to pretend to have tapped his inner being, for she knows it is important to preserve a margin of opacity—if you wish, of mystery. The important task of the novelist in creating a figure like Grandcourt is not so much to explain him as to validate him: let the reader then puzzle over what he signifies, so long as there can be no doubt that he is *there*. (Deronda, by contrast, is transparent, since in the scheme of the book he

serves mostly as a convenience, or inconvenience.) We know that Grandcourt is arrogant, bored, intelligent—extremely intelligent; but we are
not likely to make the mistake of thinking we fully understand him.

Spider and fly meet: they must. At a country party, with Chinese
lanterns lighting up a conservatory, Grandcourt "languidly" asks Gwendolen, "Do you like this sort of thing?" The next few sentences strike
a note to be repeated throughout the book: "If the situation had been
described to Gwendolen half an hour before, she would have laughed
heartily at it, and could only have imagined herself returning a playful,
satirical answer. But for some mysterious reason—it was a mystery of
which she had a faint wondering consciousness—she dared not be satirical: she had begun to feel a wand over her that made her afraid of
offending Grandcourt."

That "faint wondering consciousness" and the "mystery" behind it
will grow into Gwendolen's terror before her husband, the vibration of
an inescapable submissiveness. George Eliot explores this "mystery" but
is too much the novelist simply to clear it up. Later in their courtship,
when it seems as if Gwendolen might refuse his offer, we enter more
deeply into Grandcourt's psychology: "At the moment his strongest wish
was to be completely master of this creature—this piquant combination
of maidenliness and mischief: that she knew things which made her start
away from him, spurred him to triumph over that repugnance. . . ."

And a few pages later the full measure of Grandcourt's sadism is
taken, in its perverse silkiness. Is there another writer in English capable
of this passage?

> From the very first there had been an exasperating fascination in the
> tricksiness with which she had—not met his advances, but—wheeled away
> from them. She had been brought to accept them in spite of everything—
> brought to kneel down like a horse under training for the arena, though
> she might have an objection all the while. On the whole, Grandcourt got
> more pleasure out of this notion than he could have done out of winning
> a girl of whom he was sure that she had a strong inclination for him per-
> sonally. And yet this pleasure in mastering reluctance flourished along with
> the habitual persuasion that no woman whom he favored could be quite
> indifferent to his personal influence; and it seemed to him not unlikely that
> by-and-by Gwendolen might be more enamored of him than he of her. In
> any case, she would have to submit; and he enjoyed thinking of her as his
> future wife, whose pride and spirit were suited to command everyone but
> himself. He had no taste for a woman who was all tenderness to him, full
> of petitioning solicitude and willing obedience. He meant to be master of
> a woman who would have liked to master him, and who perhaps would
> have been capable of mastering another man.

To stress the social dimension in Eliot's portrait of Grandcourt isn't of course to imply that he "stands for" the English aristocracy or anything else so absurd. It is to suggest that in Grandcourt, George Eliot brought to a point of completeness all those elements in the psychology of aristocratic rulers (also, in part, nonaristocratic ones) that destroy human affections, spontaneities of feeling, and mutual respect. Henry James says of Grandcourt that he is "the most detestable kind of Englishman— the Englishman who thinks it low to articulate," and this keenly links Grandcourt to ideas of class power: for to think it "low to articulate" is to believe that others must be trained to obey without so much as the need to assert dominion. Grandcourt is here not just an aberrant psychological "case," nor a male monster conjured up by a feminine imagination hungry for revenge. His historical plausibility once acknowledged, we can then, however, give credit to Eliot's treatment of all that is personal or idiosyncratic in his makeup. "The power of tyranny in him," she writes in a dazzling sentence, "seemed a power of living in the presence of any wish that he should die." No wonder the marriage is described as an "empire of Fear," a phrase that comes shortly before the observation that Grandcourt would make an able governor for a "difficult colony."

If we now turn to one of the greatest chapters in the novel, Chapter 48, we find on its very first page a brilliant juxtaposition, but also a joining, of the social and personal components of Grandcourt's character. Here, in ironic voice and with obvious public references, is the first paragraph:

> Grandcourt's importance as a subject of this realm was of the grandly passive kind which consists in the inheritance of land. Political and social movements touched him only through the wire of his rental, and his most careful biographer need not have read up on Schleswig-Holstein, the policy of Bismark, trade unions, household suffrage, or even the last commercial panic. He glanced over the best newspaper columns on these topics, and his views on them can hardly be said to have wanted breadth, since he embraced all Germans, all commercial men, and all voters liable to use the wrong kind of soap, under the general epithet of "brutes"; but he took no action on these much agitated questions beyond looking from under his eyelids at any man who mentioned them, and retaining a silence which served to shake the opinions of timid thinkers.

Now the third paragraph, personal in reference:

> No movement of Gwendolen in relation to Deronda escaped him. He would have denied that he was jealous; because jealousy would have implied some doubt of his power to hinder what he had determined against. That

his wife should have more inclination to another man's society than to his own would not pain him; what he required was that she should be as fully aware as she would have been of a locked hand-cuff, that her inclination was helpless to decide anything in contradiction to his resolve. . . . He had not repented of his marriage; it had really brought more of aim into his life, new objects to exert his will upon; and he had not repented of his choice. His taste was fastidious, and Gwendolen satisfied it; he would not have liked a wife who had not received some elevation of rank from him; nor one who did not command admiration by her mien and her beauty; nor one whose nails were not of the right shape; nor one the lobe of whose ear was at all too large and red; nor one who, even if her nails and ears were right, was at the same time a ninny, unable to make spirited answers.

And here is the brief second paragraph indicating Eliot's intention to link "the subject of this realm," whose importance was "of the grandly passive kind," with the husband who found in marriage "new objects to exert his will upon":

But Grandcourt within his own sphere of interest showed some of the qualities which have entered into triumphal diplomacy of the widest continental sort.

The marriage then is the dramatized realization of modes of life, systems of value, social relationships that George Eliot had come to despise. No explicit political or social intent is at work here: George Eliot was not an ideological novelist. But that she wrote with a strong awareness of what her vision of society implied, there is no reason to doubt.

A glance at some of the subsidiary characters should reinforce this opinion. Lush, Grandcourt's minion, the pleasure-loving dog he takes pleasure in kicking, has not the slightest illusion about Grandcourt's ways; he acquiesces in them to keep his creature comforts, as in other circumstances he might bow to a party committee or a corporate board. Sir Hugo Mallinger, Deronda's foster father, is a good-natured, slack-minded man whose "worldliness" consists in seeing much of the world's ugliness for what it is, yet not at all discommoding himself in behalf of a remedy. He forms no opposition to Grandcourt's values. And Gascoigne, the rector who is Gwendolen's uncle, is a man of decency, but so conventional in his judgments, so acquiescent to the powers that be, that he comes in effect to serve as an enabler of the wretched marriage. He thinks of it

as a sort of public affair; perhaps there were ways in which it might even strengthen the Establishment. To the Rector, whose father (nobody would have suspected it, and nobody was told) had risen to be a provincial corn-dealer, aristocratic heirship resembled regal heirship in excepting its pos-sessor from the ordinary standard of moral judgments. Grandcourt, the almost certain baronet, the probable peer, was to be ranged with public personages, and was a match to be accepted on broad general grounds national and ecclesiastical.

The English side of *Daniel Deronda* projects a sweeping moral-social criticism. The world of Grandcourt, to which Gwendolen submits herself and to which her friends and relatives urge her to submit herself, is "an empire of Fear," where the spirit is crushed by the urge to power. The novel seems to me one of the great imaginative criticisms of modern society, its works and its ways.

3

It should now be clear why George Eliot had to place so intolerable a burden on the shoulders of poor Deronda. A writer for whom the idea of purpose, the claims of moral idealism, the "larger life" form the premise of her work, indeed, of her very being, now finds herself at the climax of her career with a vision of society astonishingly caustic, still more astonishingly deficient in positive figures or voices. Eliot's unused aspirations, the values now so difficult to locate in any English class or group, she thrusts upon Deronda. The precepts he declaims so sententiously betray depths of uneasiness on the part of his creator. They are unexceptionable: a call for "sympathy" as the balm for our afflictions, a hope of moving past the shallow appetites of ego toward a concern for the suffering of the world, everything, in short, we have come to know as Eliot's "religion of humanity." But the possibility of embodying very much of this in the world depicted in *Daniel Deronda* is decidedly meager. Through a good part of the novel, Deronda is a young man of affirmed high-mindedness who hasn't the vaguest idea of what to do with it. He is given the further assignment of enabling Gwendolen to grasp the significance of her plight and thereby to see beyond it; this would be hard enough in the best of circumstances, the role of mentor seldom allowing for much novelistic spontaneity, but here it becomes impossibly stiff in light of the fact that Deronda does so little except stand about, morally impeccable, and talk.

There are moments when Eliot recognizes, apparently, that in the friendship between Gwendolen and Deronda, mostly snatched bits of conversation, she has set in motion a relationship that leads to or into a liaison. The girl's vibrations are quick enough, but Deronda, perhaps because he must be preserved for the Jewish cause, backs away from the beauty, the pathos of Gwendolen. It is no small feat for a young man to do that, and at times we're reminded uncomfortably of Joseph Andrews retreating from Lady Booby. . . . The truth is, George Eliot simply cannot manage what she has begun, perhaps because this is an instance in which Victorian conventions do exact a price, perhaps because the conflicting roles assigned to Deronda cannot easily be reconciled—the young man who responds sympathetically to Gwendolen's condition, the poised moral figure waiting for his "election and calling."

George Eliot needs to find a locus for those moral aspirations that had always illuminated her novels, sometimes unsettled them. She must now, in her last work, move past her familiar world, toward some wished-for "beyond." The need for a crux of meaning by which to justify and sustain the human struggle—this need she tries to satisfy through turning to the Jewish tradition and the new hunger for a Jewish renaissance. Some residue of her youthful self must have responded warmly to the thought that in the Jewish tradition might be found the moral grounding of all religious life; some part of her adult mind must have responded as warmly to the secular universalism of the incipient Jewish movement. Deronda is to be the carrier of this new light—but not in England, only toward distant Palestine. Abundantly virtuous but only intermittently alive, he must bear the weight of the ideals which George Eliot finds increasingly difficult to authenticate in her own world. No wonder he comes to seem a mere figment of will or idea, a speechmaker without blood, a mere accessory to the prophetic Mordecai, the dying spokesman of Jewish rebirth. At some level George Eliot seems to have understood that as a novelist she had made for herself enormous difficulties of specification, concreteness, dramatization. She tried to ease them a little by insuring that at least a few of the Jewish characters, like the shopkeeper Cohen and his family, be stereotypically commonplace. She clearly wanted to avoid the vaporousness of excessive idealization—she wanted this as a novelist, but the pressures of the moral sage, the spokesman for "the religion of humanity," overcame her. To be sure, there are bits and pieces in the Jewish part of the book that have their anecdotal or representative interest, where the novelist triumphs over recalcitrant materials. And there have in recent years been some shrewd efforts at justifying, or at least placing, the Jewish part of the book, by denying that it should be seen as novelistic at all. It must, so this argument runs, be regarded as an instance of another genre, say, the visionary romance, which makes demands upon narrative, character, and plausibility of action quite different from those of the novel. Perhaps so; but to say this is only to transfer the difficulty to another plane, for the juxtaposition of two genres of prose fiction, novel and visionary romance, is here as disconcerting as the usual judgment about the varying merits of the two sides of the book conceived simply as a novel.

The difficulties George Eliot encountered in her last novel arose from the greatness of her achievement in *Daniel Deronda* itself—against that darkly luminous picture of systematic debasement, what invoked positives could survive?

Neither Eliot's dilemma nor her strategy for coping with it is unique. One thinks of Mark Twain in *The Adventures of Huckleberry Finn* as he turns toward the black slaves for some point of moral authority that will contrast with the violence and falsity pervading life along the Mississippi. It is a strategy that works for Twain, but not for Eliot.

One wonders why. An answer that comes to mind is that Twain knew the blacks intimately, they were a familiar part of his culture, he did not have to go to books in order to learn about them, whereas George Eliot was turning here to a portion of European experience she did not know intimately, the Jews were far from a familiar part of her culture, and she did have to go to books in order to learn about them. But surely there is more to it. Writing *Huck Finn* only a few years before Eliot's last novel came out, Twain could draw upon the warmly remembered and still-vibrant tradition of plebeian fraternity in America. He could not, to be sure, find a satisfactory way of ending his book, but in yielding to the strength of the blacks, the poise of Nigger Jim, he reached a few moments of moral radiance. The plight of George Eliot was more severe.

IV The Eighties

Oliver and Fagin

With the opening chapters of *Oliver Twist* Dickens made his way, forever, into world literature. His place in the English tradition was already secure: he had written *The Pickwick Papers*, a work of spectacular comic gifts, marred, it's true, by sentimentalism but lovely as an idyll of gentlemanly Christian innocence. *The Pickwick Papers* seems utterly English, attuned to the idiosyncrasies of its own culture. *Oliver Twist*, however, can attract and hold almost every kind of imagination, since its main figures—the defenseless waif, the devilish fence, the unctuous beadle—speak a language of gesture that quite transcends national cultures. Drawn with those expressionist stabs of language that would become one of Dickens's major resources, *Oliver Twist* anticipates such later, greater novels as *Bleak House* and *Little Dorrit*. True, it lacks the compositional richness and maturity of feeling we find in Dickens's culminating work; but in its opening chapters, where Oliver is coldly brutalized by agents of English society, and in the sequence where Oliver is kidnapped and taken by Bill Sykes on a housebreaking expedition, we can recognize the Dickens who belongs in the company of Gogol, Balzac, and Dostoevsky.

Introduction to *Oliver Twist* (New York: Bantam Books, 1981).

It has been customary to speak of at least two Dickenses, the first an exuberant performer of comedy and the second a mordant social critic increasingly expert in the uses of symbolic grotesquerie. Modern literary criticism has understandably focused on the second, the dark and serious Dickens, but it's only in analysis that the two Dickenses can be separated. In the strongest novels, entertainer and moralist come to seem shadows of one another—finally two voices out of the same mouth.

The entertainer takes over now and again in *Oliver Twist*. He is splendidly busy in the chapter where Bumble courts Mrs. Corney, with one hand round her waist and both eyes on her silver, while expressing— definitively, for all the ages—"the great principle of out-of-door relief," which is "to give the paupers exactly what they don't want, and then they get tired of coming." Entertainer and moralist are not always at ease with one another; they tend at some points to go about their business separately; and that's one reason we find it unprofitable to keep *Oliver Twist* neatly placed in a categorical bin—a crime story, a fairy tale, a novel of education, a social melodrama? The sensible answer is that it is all of these together, mixed up with Dickens's usual disregard for the boundaries of genre.

For all our pleasure in its comic play, *Oliver Twist* finally grips us as a story of moral rage. The opening chapters may seem a little too de-clamatory, even strident—some of Dickens's furious interjections might have been cut. But remember, this is a young man's book, full of anger and mistakes; and one's deepest response to the "overture" of the first few chapters isn't critical at all; it is a blend of astonishment and ad-miration. Oliver begging, "I want more"; the horrible chimney sweep Gamfield explaining that "boys is wery obstinit, and wery lazy, and there's nothingk like a good hot blaze to make 'em come down [from chimneys] with a run"; Bumble growing warm over the ingratitude of the poor ("It's meat," he opines, that has made Oliver so refractory); Dickens sputtering on his own that he wishes he could see "the Phi-losopher" (read, Economist) "making the same sort of meal himself, with the same relish" that Oliver has just made—such bits of incident must survive in collective memory as long as the world knows the taste of the insolence of office.

Some decades ago critics were inclined to "place" *Oliver Twist* his-torically, which often meant to take the sting out of the book. They explained that Dickens had as one of his targets the English Poor Law of 1834, which he regarded as inhumane; that paupers had indeed been treated brutally in England, though not quite so brutally as Dickens imagined; and that the passage of time has improved the conditions of the poor, so that it would be an error to take literally Dickens's version of the poorhouse.* Now all this is true enough, yet by one of those turns of history that makes a joke out of all historical schemas, the social outlook Dickens was attacking has again come to seem familiar. No one talks about "welfare chiselers" in *Oliver Twist*, perhaps because Bumble and Mrs. Corney were born a little too soon; but that apart, we have no difficulty in aligning Dickens's caricature with our own familiar reality.

In these opening chapters, then, the twenty-five-year-old Dickens found his voice and his subject. Through the year 1837 *Oliver Twist* appeared serially in a London magazine, overlapping with *The Pickwick Papers*: it would be hard to imagine a more remarkable literary debut. Many writers take years to find their true voice and inescapable subject; some never do. Perhaps it would be better to say that Dickens's subject found him, laying rough hands on his throat. The remembered humiliations of childhood, when his father had been taken to debtors' prison and he had been sent to labor in a blacking factory, seethed in his imagination from the start of his career to the finish. Whether it is really true, as Graham Greene once said, that all writers form their picture of the world in the years of childhood, I do not know; but it certainly was true for Dickens.

Later on he would often misuse his gifts, sometimes as the result of sheer exuberance, sometimes through a retreat from the fearful conclusions to which his imagination kept driving him—for how could the most popular novelist of Victorian England acknowledge to himself that his strongest books formed a scathing condemnation of early industrial capitalism? Often there is a deep split between what Dickens the writer shows and what his mind imposes on his books in their concluding pages. But finally, his imagination could never really be tamed, it could only be diverted—and even then it would break out again in spontaneous fury. Dickens had a passion for seeing things as they are.

2

A little boy creeps through this book, an orphan, a waif, an outcast. He is a puling, teary little fellow, never rebellious for more than a few minutes, and seldom even angry. He is a perfect little gentleman who has managed somehow to come into the world, and the novel, with a finished code of morality. The wickedness of the world never stains him. Through all his wanderings in "foul and frowzy dens, where vice

---

* Inspired by Malthusian economists who believed there must always be a segment of the population in destitute condition, the Poor Law had as its purpose to prevent or minimize breeding among paupers. The poorhouse was made as repulsive a place as possible; the sexes, including husbands and wives, were separated; the meals were wretched; uniforms were required. Dickens writes in *Oliver Twist* of "three meals of thin gruel a day, with an onion twice a week, and half a roll on Sundays"—a caricature, but not an outrageous or unwarranted one.

is closely packed"—as Dickens put it in his preface to the novel's third edition—Oliver maintains a sublime loyalty to English grammar. Starved, beaten, terrorized, kidnapped, he is nevertheless unwilling to resort to the foul language or gutter slang it may be reasonable to suppose he has heard in the slums of London.

To some readers this represents a strain on their credulity, and so indeed it would be if Oliver were conceived by Dickens as an ordinary realistic figure, just another boy thrust into "the cold, wet, shelterless midnight streets of London." But it would be a mistake to see Oliver in that way. Dickens himself tells us, again in the preface to the third edition, that "I wished to show, in little Oliver, the *principle* of Good surviving through every adverse circumstance and triumphing at last." I stress the word "principle" in order to suggest that more is at stake here than an individual character. For Oliver is one in a series of recurrent figures in the Dickens world, slightly anticipated in *Pickwick* but more fully realized in *Little Dorrit*. Oliver is emblematic of "the principle of Good" sent into the world on a journey of suffering. This journey, which has points of similarity to that of Christian in Bunyan's *Pilgrim's Progress*, Oliver undertakes with no armor other than a blessed helplessness. Oliver is not expected to overcome the evil of the world, nor to struggle vigorously against it, nor even to learn much from his suffering. He is not a figure of strong imposing will—on the contrary, he is usually ready to accept whatever burdens the world imposes. He acts only to refuse evil, never to combat it. Yet, as if by some miracle of grace, this journeyer emerges morally immaculate, quite like the hero of a Western movie who after gunfights doesn't even need to straighten his hat. Everywhere about Oliver evil thrives, but at the end he is as pure as at the start.

This celebration of the passive hero is sometimes related to primitive Christianity, though perhaps what we really mean is that it forms a historical residue of Christianity, clung to by those who can no longer believe God is omnipotent or even attentive, and who must consequently make of passivity a substitute for active moral engagement. The modern sensibility finds this view of things very hard to accept, even though it is a view that keeps recurring, as a benefit of desperation, in modern literature.

Yet in his very powerlessness Oliver reveals an enormous power: the world cannot destroy him. It is as if he had received, from whom we can hardly say, the blessing that mother Rachel schemed so hard to get for her son Jacob. Clearly, no one in this world has blessed Oliver, his blessing must have come from another world; and if so, all it can do for him, through the main stretch of the book, is to protect without rescuing him. It's as if God had given Oliver all that He can—which in the world of Dickens's London is not enough.

Such feelings about "the principle of Good" are by no means unique to Dickens: they are to be found among many sincere Christians. Dostoevsky called Dickens "that great Christian" and saw in Pickwick "a positively good man," perhaps a faint emblem of Christ. The creator of Myshkin would have understood why Dickens located "the principle of Good" in a helpless little boy.

To gather Dickens's intentions regarding Oliver is not, however, to find his treatment entirely satisfying. Most readers learn to brush past Oliver, seeing him as a (slightly inconvenient) convenience of the plot. We care about what happens to him, but hardly suppose anything much is happening within him. Still, it's worth asking why Dickens's effort to realize "the principle of Good"—always very difficult for a novelist— seems shaky in *Oliver Twist* and successful in *Little Dorrit*. A plausible answer might be that Oliver, no matter how extreme his suffering, never gets past the conventions of middle-class behavior. One of his few signs of spontaneous life is the burst of laughter with which he watches Fagin and the boys pantomime the picking of a gentleman's pocket; but whenever Oliver is with Mr. Brownlow, Rose Maylie, and the other paragons of middle-class virtue, he serves mostly as their parrot. Such a goody-goody doesn't make a persuasive agent of "the principle of Good," if only because he seems so inert before the temptations of the Bad. Little Dorrit, by contrast, cares nothing about status or respectability; she neither accepts nor rejects the standards of the world; she is beyond their reach, a selfless creature forever assuaging, healing, and loving those near her. It took Dickens the better part of a lifetime to discover what "the principle of Good" really is.

3

Fleeing poorhouse and apprenticeship, Oliver makes his way to the big city: there is no place else to go. His entry into London, stylishly eased by the Artful Dodger, forms a critical moment in the history of nineteenth-century literature—one of the first encounters with the modern city as physical presence, emblem of excitement, social specter, locus of myth. The early Dickens is still vibrantly responsive to whatever seems fresh in the world, he takes an eager pleasure in the discovery of streets. But London—this note is first struck in *Oliver Twist*—is also pesthole and madhouse, a place of terror from which the child-hero must be rescued periodically through a convalescence in the countryside.

Now it is the mixture of these contradictory feelings about the city that helps give the novel its distinctive tone of diffuse anxiety. The contradictory feelings about the city interweave, clash, and run along uneasy parallels, and from the tension they generate Dickens makes his drama. The darkening vision that will overwhelm Dickens's later novels is already present, shadowlike, in *Oliver Twist*—that vision which will prompt him to write in *Our Mutual Friend* that London is "a hopeless city, with no rent in the leaden canopy of its sky. . . ." Yet in *Oliver Twist* London is also the home of spectacle, lurid and grotesque, and one of Dickens's narrative purposes—slyly helped along by the sequence that starts with the Artful Dodger discovering the hungry Oliver and ends when the boy is brought to Fagin's den—is to involve us in Oliver's excitements of discovery. But more than involve: it is a saving characteristic of this novel that we are never limited to Oliver's milky perceptions.

Fagin's den, one of those spittled gray-and-black hovels in which he hides out, is reached by a labyrinth of stairs, eerie and dark. "The walls and ceilings . . . were perfectly black with age and dirt," but, it's important to note, there is a fire in the den before which "a very old shrivelled Jew, whose villainous-looking and repulsive face was obscured by a quantity of matted red hair," stands roasting some meat. Here Dickens's ambivalence about the city—which finally is to say, about English society—reaches a high point: this London hovel is hell yet also a wretched sort of home; these are thieves and murderers yet also lively figures who have made for themselves a perverse sort of community.

Those of us who have but little taste for a romantic glorification of criminality will resist the temptation to see Dickens as totally caught up with the world of Fagin and Sykes—though the accounts we have of Dickens's public readings from *Oliver Twist*, in which he impersonated its characters with a terrifying vividness, suggest that part of him must have felt a subterranean kinship with these outlaws. (Less, I think, with their criminal deeds than with their experience as outsiders.) We are surely meant by Dickens to deplore the thieves and murderers, to feel disgust and fright before them. Yet their enormous vitality and articulateness of feeling put them in the sharpest contrast to the blandness of the "good" characters. Fagin and his gang talk like recognizable human beings, Mr. Brownlow and the Maylies, as if they had stepped out of a copybook. And when the Artful Dodger, in one of Dickens's most brilliant set pieces, is dragged into court, he sounds like a comic echo of Julien Sorel at the end of *The Red and the Black*. "Gentlemen, I have not the honor to belong to your class," Julien tells his jurors. "This ain't the shop for justice," the Artful Dodger tells his judges.

The living core of the novel is neither the story of Oliver nor the depiction of his protectors; it is primarily those segments of narrative devoted to Fagin and his gang. Just as Dostoevsky often yielded himself to the sinners he was determined finally to make suffer, so Dickens yielded himself to the criminals he knew had to be brought to a relentless punishment. We are talking here not about conscious intent but about those energies of the unconscious which, in every true writer, shape his values.

Fagin is the strongest figure in the book—certainly the most troubling. He is more figure than character, and more force than figure. He barely exists as an individual—barely needs to. We learn nothing about his interior life, we are not invited to see him as "three-dimensional," except, minimally, in the glittering chapter toward the end where he sits in prison waiting to be hanged and suffers that terror of death which finally makes him one of us. Nor is Fagin given the sort of great redeeming speech that Shakespeare gives Shylock. Fagin does cry out before his death, "What right have they to butcher me?" but this has little of the generalizing moral resonance of Shylock's "Hath not a Jew eyes?" Clever and cunning, with a talent for mimicking the moral axioms of the respectable world, Fagin is all of a piece. He is an emanation of historical myth, generic, emblematic, immensely powerful. Having so created him—or, better yet, having so dredged him up out of the folk imagination—Dickens had no need to worry about nuances of depiction.

And Fagin, we cannot forget, is "the Jew." Throughout the novel he is called "the Jew," though in revising for a later edition, especially in the chapter devoted to Fagin's last night, Dickens tried to soften the impact by substituting "Fagin" for "the Jew." It did not help or matter very much: Fagin remains "the Jew" and whoever wants to confront this novel honestly must confront the substratum of feeling that becomes visible through Dickens's obsessive repetition of "the Jew." The film adaptation made several decades ago in England did precisely that. Alec Guinness impersonated Fagin with brilliant, indeed, frightening effect, putting heavy stress on the idea of an archetypal Jewish villain, as well as a secondary stress on the homosexual component of Fagin's gang that Dickens could only hint at.

Most critics have been skittish about Fagin. They have either ignored Dickens's fixed epithet, "the Jew," as if there were nothing problematic or disconcerting about it, or they have tried to blunt the meaning of Dickens's usage by "explaining" Fagin historically. There is, of course, something to explain. Dickens himself, in a letter to a Jewish woman who had protested the stereotypical treatment of Fagin, sought to reduce the problem to one of verisimilitude. "Fagin," he wrote, "is a Jew because it unfortunately was true, of the time to which the story refers, that that class of criminal almost invariably was a Jew." One of these, Ikey Solomons, had been tried and sentenced in a spectacular trial only a few years before Dickens wrote *Oliver Twist*, and it seems likely that Dickens, with his keen reportorial scent, drew upon this case.

I am convinced that, despite some conventionally nasty phrases about Jews in his letters, Dickens was not an anti-Semite—he had neither conscious nor programmatic intent to harm Jews. Indeed, a writer with such intent could probably not have created so "primitive" and haunting a figure as Fagin. For, if the fascination with criminal life that's evident in *Oliver Twist* derives in some twisted way from Dickens's childhood traumas, the representative or mythic strength of Fagin comes, I believe, from somewhere else: it comes from the collective folklore, the sentiments and biases habitual to Western culture, as these have fixed the Jew in the role of villain: thief, fence, corrupter of the young, surrogate of Satan, legatee of Judas. With Fagin, as Edgar Rosenberg says, "we are . . . thrown back to that anonymous crowd of grinning devils who, in the religious drama of the 14th century, danced foully around the Cross and who, in mythology, functioned as bugaboos to frighten little boys . . . [Dickens] has come up with some prehistoric fiend, an aging Lucifer whose depravity explains him wholly."

The spectral image of "the Jew" may indeed be "prehistoric" in the sense that it abides in the timeless space of myth, but it is also very much part of a continuous Western history. The image of the fiendish Jew has survived with remarkable persistence through the Christian centuries. Like Judas, Fagin has red hair, and like Satan, he is compared to a serpent. "As Fagin glided stealthily along, creeping beneath the shelter of the walls and doorways, the hideous old man seemed like some loathsome reptile, engendered in the slime and darkness through which he moved: crawling forth, by night, in search of some rich offal for a meal." Whenever we encounter such overripe language, Fagin expands into a figure other than human: he becomes a monster drawn from the bad dreams of Christianity.

Novels are composed by individual writers, but in some sense they also derive from the cultures in which these writers live. Collective sentiments, collective stories, enter individual fictions. The writer must draw on the substance of his culture, and thereby, so to say, the culture speaks through and past him. All great writers are in part ventriloquists of myth—some inferior writers, nothing else. Fagin the individual figure was conceived by Dickens, but Fagin the archetype comes out of centuries of myth, centuries too of hatred and fear.

The power of Fagin is a collective, an anonymous power. Once we realize this, the question of what "to do" about Fagin comes to seem hopelessly complicated—as if there were something one could "do" to expunge the record of the deepest biases of Western culture! as if one could somehow cancel out the shadowy grotesques of Satan and Judas, Shylock and the Wandering Jew! There is nothing to "do" but confront the historical realities of our culture, and all that it has thrown up from its unsavory depths.

4

Dickens, having launched his child-hero on a terrifying journey through the city, keeps accumulating social difficulties and contradictions that his plot cannot cope with. "Until Oliver wakes up in Mr. Brownlow's house," remarks Arnold Kettle, "he is a poor boy struggling against the inhumanity of the state. After he has slept himself into the Brownlow world he is a young bourgeois who has been done out of his property." Oliver's troubles are miraculously disposed of, through the generosity of Mr. Brownlow—a convenience for the plot and a disaster for the theme. But no serious reader is likely to be satisfied, for the difficulty is not just that the issues cast up by Oliver's story are left hanging in the air; it is that even if we confine ourselves to the narrow boundaries of Dickens's plot, the ending must seem weak and willed. Falling back on Mr. Brownlow, that is, on the individual benevolence of a kindly gentleman, Dickens could not confront the obvious truth that a Mr. Brownlow is utterly unequipped to deal with the problem of Oliver. Nor could Dickens confront the truth already prefigured in Blake's lines:

> Pity would be no more,
> If we did not make somebody Poor:
> And Mercy could no more be,
> If all were as happy as we . . .

Dickens's imagination had led him to a point where his mind could not follow. Endings are always a problem for novelists, and the problem for the young Dickens wasn't simply that he lacked the courage to see his story through to its bitter end; it was that he didn't really know what that bitter end might be. So he wound up, in the person of Mr. Brownlow, with that "Pity" and "Mercy" about which Blake had written so scornfully.

Even writers determined to show things as they really are often have no choice but to leave us anxious and uncertain. Why should we expect "solutions" in their books to problems we cannot manage in our lives? Whatever is vibrant and real in *Oliver Twist*, every reader will recognize; the rest is a sign of the evasions a writer must turn to when his imagination, overextended, is finally balked.

Absalom in Israel

So many secret disappointments and betrayed visions accumulate over the years and bear down upon the consciousness of people who may not even know the source of their dismay. In the culture of Israel, this burden is perhaps the very idea of Israel itself, as if people—at least, some people—were haunted by a vision of what Israel was supposed to be but, in the nature of things, never could become.

This weight of feeling clouds, yet ultimately defines, *Past Continuous*, an Israeli novel of great distinction which was first published in 1977 and has now been put into fluent English. (But with one "concession" to American readers: the occasional paragraphing of what in the Hebrew text is an unbroken flow of language.) I cannot recall, these past several years, having encountered a new work of fiction that has engaged me as strongly as *Past Continuous*, both for its brilliant formal inventiveness and for its relentless truth-seeking scrutiny of the moral life. While a difficult book requiring sharp attentiveness on the part of the reader, it still satisfies traditional expectations that a novel should lure one into an imaginary "world."

Until this book Yaakov Shabtai had been an Israeli literary figure

From *New York Review of Books* 32 (October 10, 1985):5.

of middle stature. A tremendous breakthrough, which can be compared to that of Faulkner when he moved from his early novels to *The Sound and the Fury*, occurred in Shabtai's middle age, the kind of breakthrough that becomes possible when a writer gains possession of his own culture, uncovering its deepest sentiments and secrets. Shabtai died of heart disease in 1981 at the age of forty-seven, leaving behind another unfinished novel.

The opening pages of *Past Continuous* plunge us into a bewildering mixture of fact, memory, reflection. A voice speaks, and it is of an omniscient narrator who seems in complete control. Nothing can be heard or seen except through its mediation. Neither colloquial nor very eloquent, it is self-assured, exhaustive. It records; it quietly corrects both itself and the book's characters; and, although rarely, it keens over their fate. Above all, this voice tries to get things exactly right, as if some higher power had assigned it the obligation of making final judgment.

The opening sentence—"Goldman's father died on the first of April, whereas Goldman himself committed suicide on the first of January"— sets the bounds of time and the tone for all to follow. The present in *Past Continuous* consists of the months between the deaths of father and son, with the speaker, whose identity we don't yet know but whose authority we accept, leading us back, through his own associations of events and impression, to events in the past. As the relatives and friends of Goldman's father, Ephraim, gather after the funeral, there begins an unraveling of shared memories. The local detail is very dense, matted into synoptic vignettes of the characters' lives. There are dozens of characters, though strictly speaking they are glimpsed rather than developed. Shabtai offers only sparse physical descriptions of these people, yet one soon comes to feel that one "knows" a good many of them, for his is an art of the representative, an art of the group. A community is releasing its experience, a generation is sliding toward extinction: the community, the generation of "labor Israel," socialist Zionism, which was central in the creation of the young country but has by now—say, the late 1970s—succumbed to old age and debility. If there can be such a thing as a collective novel, then *Past Continuous* is one.

The book takes off from one of the conventions of Western literature: a myth of historical and moral decline. By no means (and this is worth stressing) should it be taken as a straight account of Israel's recent condition. It offers something more complex and ambiguous: a voice of the culture quarreling with itself, an evocation of buried yearnings and regrets, a social elegy whose tone is somber and unsentimental. Like Faulkner, Shabtai subjects to merciless scrutiny the very myth upon which his book rests and to which he seems residually attached. The griefs weighing upon his characters may thereby, perhaps, be unpacked and allowed to settle in the calm of memory.

In the forefront, though not quite at the center, of *Past Continuous* stand three men in early middle age: Goldman, a reflective and melancholy man, Chekhovian in the way he registers losses, and the book's uncertain center of intelligence; Caesar, whose lechery is almost comic and who registers nothing, but serves, in the novel, as a kind of foil to Goldman; and Israel, a pianist of sensitivity but feeble will, who forms a connecting link with the other characters. These three can be seen as "representing" a generation that has inherited the life of Tel Aviv but not the strength of its founders, a generation, indeed, that in moments of self-pity feels crushed by that strength. As in all myths of decline, the sons have been weakened. Behind this myth there is history, but history bent and misshaped.

Through these younger characters Shabtai reaches toward the older generation, which engages him more keenly. Men and women in their sixties and beyond—one can see them sitting at the beachfront cafés of Tel Aviv, soaking up the sun and reading *Davar*, the labor newspaper—this older generation consists of an elite in an advanced stage of decomposition. Nothing about the manners or appearance of these people would suggest this, and they would hotly deny they ever did form an elite, except perhaps an elite formed to eliminate all elites. Israeli readers would have no more trouble in recognizing these figures—the people of the Histadrut, the cadres of labor Zionism—than southern readers a few decades ago would have had in recognizing the aristocracy of the Sartorises and the Compsons.

Mostly, Shabtai's older characters come from Eastern Europe and have settled, not quite at ease, in Eretz Yisroel with a budget of expectations as wildly improbable as they are (for some of us) affecting: to establish a Jewish nation, to live by an egalitarian ethic, and to create a new kind of Jew, standing erect, doing his own work with his own hands. To put it this way is to yield to abstraction, for what was really involved was a tremendous yearning for social and moral transfiguration, a leap through history, a remaking of souls.

This "design," to lift a phrase from Faulkner's Thomas Sutpen, was partly realized, but for the plebeian veterans of Tel Aviv, stirred in their youth by a whiff of the absolute, the very process of realization brought disappointment. History gave a little but not enough, and now it has left these people—Shabtai's people—with a grief they cannot comprehend or shake off. They seldom talk about it any longer, and some of them have begun to doubt the genuineness of their own feelings, but this hardly matters since those feelings continue to oppress them.

What—as Sutpen asks in *Absalom, Absalom!* about a very different sort of "design"—what went wrong? External circumstances? Strategic blunders? Impossible expectations? Or some deep flaw in the original "design"? Shabtai's older figures have put these questions largely behind them, for it's as if he had deposited them at a point where neither asking nor answering can do much good. Political people stranded in a post-political moment, either they cling to their received values, tightening themselves into righteousness as their world slips away from them, or they slump into an irritable mixture of rectitude and cynicism, a condition Shabtai is very shrewd in depicting, as if it were the atmosphere of his own years.

After Ephraim's funeral the mourners sit in the Goldman apartment, nibbling cakes and chatting emptily. There is little for these people to look forward to, but there is little pleasure in looking back, so they become entangled in foolish quarrels, as blocked in their love as in their enmity. Individually, Shabtai's characters are mostly pitiable, but collectively they bear the stamp of history—history the destroyer—and this lends a certain magnitude to their plight. By its technique, the book creates an enlarged reflection of its theme, with the intricacies of memory cast as emblems of human entanglement. Voice gives way to voice, through the narrator's "overvoice." Goldman's father, Ephraim, a tyrant of idealism who feels "his anger had to be everyone's anger" and believes "in a world order with good and bad and no neutral ground between them," towers over the book, and it's around him that a good many of the other figures turn. The pianist Israel recalls that as a child he had seen Ephraim kill a neighbor's dog because the neighbor, a "dissolute" woman, violated the standards of the "new society." Later, this trivial, chilling incident comes to seem a preparation for a terrible moment illustrating the costs of fanatic purity: Ephraim refuses to meet his brother Lazar, who years earlier, against Ephraim's Zionist advice, had gone off to fight in the Spanish Civil War, ended somehow in Stalin's arctic wastes, and has finally been freed. Ephraim is a man of strong feelings, but they have been corked and soured by the monolith of a redemptive faith.

It is, or was, a faith calling for self-transformation, and the desire for this goal, at once noble and destructive, has many versions, twisted and parodied. Manfred, the old lover of Ephraim's wife, Regina, had begun as a Communist, only to become a student of Christianity "mapping hell as it was described in lay and ecclesiastic literature," and now, stripped of belief, he returns to a love that is nothing but the love of loving "the memory of their love." Shortly after Ephraim's death, Regina acts out a fantasy in reply to the mania for self-transformation: she regresses into the Polish past, calling herself Stefana, "painting her lips in a subtle shade of violet-red," wearing "old silks and velvets," as if to undo all the grim years of Tel Aviv.

Others find different strategies. Erwin, Caesar's father, who had emigrated to Palestine as a pioneer, concludes that there is "always a gap between the world of values and that of action, and that actually everything [is therefore] permitted"—a lesson Caesar takes to heart as he races from woman to woman. Moishe Tzellermaer remakes himself through a religion "which contained neither a belief in God nor reflections on the nature of God," but consists of mere dry rituals dryly observed. Goldman, who has never known the idealistic raptures of the older generation, also turns to religion, dabbling briefly in cabala, "but his religion had nothing to sustain it and died." After this he turns to Taoism and Jungian psychology, which also "die."

The handful of Shabtai's characters who find their way do so by remaining still, accepting the thin margin onto which history has thrust them and trying nonetheless to survive decently. Uncle Lazar, though still acknowledging a "redemptive instinct" in man, concludes "that there [is] no single act in public or private life, however right or revolutionary, which [is] redemptive in the sense that from a certain point onward a new era would commence in which everything would be perfectly good." The thought itself is familiar enough, but the dignity it allows Uncle Lazar is impressive. He forms an alliance with Yehudit Tanfuss, a modest, unassuming woman, and "in the early hours of the evening, they would sit on the balcony talking or reading . . . or [go] for walks arm in arm, which [is] the way they always liked to walk together." And Aunt Zipporah (who made me think of Dilsey) keeps washing clothes and ironing and cooking and helping her sisters and friends through sickness and old age, for she believes in "the dignity of labor" and that "it was forbidden to lose the will to live," and that the difficulties of life "were not accidental but the very stuff of life."

Only the Goldmans, father and son, cannot make their peace with limitation. Pure, sterile, Ephraim resists the trickeries of history until "all of a sudden he turned into an old man . . . and all that was left of him was obduracy and bitter but helpless rage." The aggressions of the father become the self-torments of the son, who before ending his futile life gains a moment of illumination that may be no more—but it is enough—than ordinary sympathy: "Love and hate, together with the force of habit and family ties [reflects Goldman], chained people to each other in a way over which logic and will had no control, and . . . even death could not sever these bonds, except through the stubborn strength of time, which wore everything away, and even then something of the other person remained behind as part of your being forever. . . ." All—rectitude and opportunism, hedonistic frenzy and calm acquiescence—melt into a life that was once to be transfigured but now, simply continuing, must be endured.

About the older generation Shabtai writes with great assurance. About the younger generation, Shabtai's own—Goldman, Israel, Caesar, and the women they pursue and abandon—he is neither judgmental nor very sympathetic, but wary and bemused, as if a writer can understand the chaos of those who came before him but not of his contemporaries. Shabtai describes Caesar's "deepest feeling about life . . . that it was fluid and formless and aimless, and everything was possible in it to an infinite degree, and it could be played backward and forward like a roll of film, just as he wished"—a feeling that's the very opposite of the one held by Goldman's father or Uncle Lazar and Aunt Zipporah.

In certain respects *Past Continuous* seems closer to a chronicle, in which the past is granted a stamp of certainty and contrivances of plot are not allowed to interfere with the passage of events, than to a traditional or even modernist novel, in which events, whether or not ordered by plot, may still be represented as being in flux. But the book's density of texture is closer to the novel than to the chronicle.

Here is a close look at one of the book's most attractive figures, Uncle Lazar, who was caught up in the political struggles of Europe but is now quietly aging in Tel Aviv:

Although the truth is that Uncle Lazar was not a taciturn man by nature, and if he hardly ever spoke it was only because he knew the limitations of human knowledge, the invalidity of human reason, and the restrictions of human possibilities, and everything was so contradictory and ambiguous that doubt seemed the only thing which possessed any reality, and the ability to believe was possessed by only a few, and there was no use hoping for much, and he also knew just how far a person had to deceive himself in order to live through a single day, and how fate could play tricks on people, as it had on him, and that all the words in the world were incapable of moving the world a single centimeter from its course, or bringing back one single day that had passed, or filling in the gaps, or consoling a man whose eyes had been opened, and Uncle Lazar's eyes had been opened, and they remained open, although he was not at all despairing or embittered, but simply very realistic and sober, with all the calm detachment of a man who had experienced much and who saw clearly and for whom life, to which he continued to relate seriously and positively, held no more surprises, because he had already died and risen again. . . .

The Hebrew title, far more evocative than the English one, is *Zikhron Devarim*, signifying a protocol or memorandum, and indeed, the pace and tone of the book are rather like that of a protocol or memorandum: precise, measured, detached. Shabtai's technique is in radical opposition to the prescriptions for the modern novel of Joseph Conrad and Ford Madox Ford: dramatize, dramatize, show rather than tell. There are few large scenes in the book; it consists mostly of compressed biographies, life histories in miniature. The voice of *Past Continuous* tells more than it shows, on the valid premise that, with enough pressure of thought and feeling, the act of telling can become a way of showing.

Chronicling the rise and fall of a generation, almost never stopping for psychological detail or nuance, steadily widening its reach so as to gain the illusion of totality, the voice of *Past Continuous* achieves an authority quite beyond that of the omniscient narrator in the traditional novel. And while its use of associations bears a similarity to "stream of consciousness," especially as practiced by Faulkner, Shabtai's method is finally quite different, since in his book we do not enter the inner life of the characters. Brooking no pretense of relativism, the narrative voice does not hesitate to say with assurance about Ephraim or Lazar or Caesar, "The truth is. . . ." If only as a premise of reading, we come to suppose we are listening to a communal recorder, a choral observer who may just possibly be the consciousness of a city.

The narrator speaks:

> From one day to the next, over the space of a few years, the city was rapidly and relentlessly changing its face, and right in front of [Goldman's] eyes it was engulfing the sand lots and the virgin fields, the vineyards and citrus groves and little woods and Arab villages, and afterward the changes began invading the streets of the older parts of the town, which were dotted here and there with simple one-storied houses surrounded by gardens with a few shrubs and flower beds, and sometimes vegetables and strawberries, and also cypress trees and lemon and orange and mandarin trees, or buildings which attempted to imitate the architectural beauties and splendors of Europe, in the style of Paris or Vienna or Berlin, or even of castles and palaces, but all these buildings no longer had any future because they were old and ill adapted to modern tastes and lifestyles, and especially because the sky-rocketing prices of land and apartments had turned their existence into a terrible waste and enabled their owners to come into fortunes by selling them, and Goldman, who was attached to these streets and houses because they, together with the sand dunes and virgin fields, were the landscape in which he had been born and grown up, knew that this process of destruction was inevitable, and perhaps even necessary, as inevitable as the change in the population of the town, which in the course of a few years had been filled with tens of thousands of new people, who in Goldman's eyes

were invading outsiders who had turned him into a stranger in his own city. . . .

The culminating effect, for this reader at least, is overwhelming. Dispassionate in grief, this narrative voice seldom drops to judgment, though once or twice there is a sentence that can be taken as a judgment of sorts. At the funeral of Goldman's father, a mourner says, "In spite of everything he deserved to be loved." ("Why do you hate the South? . . . *I dont. I dont. I dont hate it. I dont hate it.*")

Kafka once said, "We must have those books that come upon us like ill-fortune, and distress us deeply, like the death of one we love better than ourselves, like suicide. A book must be an ice-ax to break the sea frozen within us." Before he died Yaakov Shabtai wrote such a book.

Why Has Socialism Failed in America?

America never stood still for Marx and Engels. They did not attempt a systematic analysis of the possibilities for socialism in the New World, but if you look into their *Letters to Americans* you will find many interesting aperçus, especially from Engels. Almost all the numerous theories later developed about the fate of American socialism are anticipated in these letters.

As early as 1851, when the socialist Joseph Weydemeyer migrated to the United States, Engels wrote him:

> Your greatest handicap will be that the useful Germans who are worth anything are easily Americanized and abandon all hope of returning home; and then there are the special American conditions: the ease with which the surplus population is drained off to the farms, the necessarily rapid and rapidly growing prosperity of the country, which makes bourgeois conditions look like a beau ideal to them. . . .*

It isn't farfetched to see here a germ of what would later be called American exceptionalism, the idea that historical conditions in the

From *Socialism and America* (New York: Harcourt Brace Jovanovich, 1985).
* August 7, 1851, *Letters to Americans, 1848–1895* (1953), pp. 25–26.

United States differ crucially from those set down in the Marxist model for the development of capitalism, or differ crucially from the way capitalism actually developed in Europe. Consider those remarks of Engels: a recognition of, perhaps irritation with, the sheer attractiveness of America; a casual anticipation of the Turner thesis in the claim that "surplus population is drained off to the farms"; a wry observation about American eagerness to accept the bourgeois style, though this might better have been phrased in the language of American individualism.

At about the same time, Marx was taking a somewhat different approach. "Bourgeois society in the United States," he was writing, "has not yet developed far enough to make the class struggle obvious"*; but he also expected that American industry would grow at so enormous a rate that the United States would be transformed into a major force in the world market, delivering heavy blows against English imperial domination.

Now, if one cares to, it is possible to reconcile Engels's approach with that of Marx. Engels was thinking tactically, about the problems of building a movement, while Marx was thinking historically, about events anticipated but not yet encountered. Marx was asking why the social consequences of the rise of capitalism, such as an intensified class struggle, had not yet appeared in the United States—even though, according to his theory, these consequences were inevitable. He was "testing" a particular historical sequence against his theoretical scheme, and this led him to believe that capitalism would emerge in the United States in its purest and strongest form—purest, because unencumbered by the debris of the precapitalist past, and strongest, because able, both technologically and financially, to leap past the older capitalism of England. Thereby, he concluded, the United States would—or was it, should?—become "the world of the worker, par excellence,"† so that socialist victory might even occur first in the New World. Here Marx was verging on a materialist or "economist" reductionism, and he would repeat this line of reasoning some thirty years later, in 1881, when he wrote that, capitalism in the United States having developed *"more rapidly and more shamelessly* than in any other country,"‡ the upsurge of its working class could be expected to be all the more spectacular.

Engels's observations, because more "local," tend to be more useful. He writes in his 1891 preface to Marx's *The Civil War in France*: "There is no country in which 'politicians' form a more powerful and distinct

---

* March 5, 1852, *Letters to Americans*, pp. 44–45.
† Quoted in R. Laurence Moore, *European Socialists and the American Promised Land* (1970), p. 9.
‡ June 20, 1881, *Letters to Americans*, p. 129.

section of the nation than in North America. There each of the two great parties which alternately succeed each other in power is itself controlled by people who make a business of politics. . . ."*

Had the later American Marxists picked up Engels's tip here, they might have avoided some of their cruder interpretations of the role of the state in this country. More interesting still is Engels's introduction to the 1887 reprint of his book *The Condition of the Working Class in England,* where he acknowledges "the peculiar difficulties for a steady development of a workers party"† in the United States. Engels first makes a bow toward the overarching Marxist model: ". . . there cannot be any doubt that the *ultimate* platform of the American working class must and will be *essentially* the same as that now adopted by the whole militant working class of Europe. . . . [Emphasis added.]" Engels would elsewhere stress the "exceptionalist" aspect, largely tactical, of the American problem. In order to play a role in politics, he says, the American socialists "will have to doff every remnant of foreign garb. They will have to become out and out American. They cannot expect the Americans to come to them; they, the minority and the [German] immigrants [in the Socialist Labor Party] must go to the Americans. . . . And to do that, they must above all else learn English."‡

What may we conclude from all this? That, like other thinkers, Marx and Engels cherished their basic models; that the more closely they examined a particular situation, the more they had to acknowledge "deviations" from their models; that they anticipated, quite intelligently, a good many of the major themes in the discussions about socialist failure in the United States; and that in their efforts to suggest adaptations of the nascent socialist movement, mostly immigrant in composition, to the American setting, they were not very successful. You might suppose, however, that Engels's proposal that the Germans learn English would be regarded, in leftist terminology, as "a minimum demand."

If I have overstressed the differences in approach between Marx and Engels, it is for a reason: to show that both the orthodox view of later socialists, clinging to the authority of the Marxist model, and the heterodox emphasis upon American distinctiveness can legitimately be attributed to the founding fathers of Marxism. An interesting comment on this comes from Theodore Draper in a personal communication: "Whenever the two old boys considered real conditions in real countries, they gave way to the temptation of 'exceptionalism' (I seem to remember

* *The Civil War in France,* 1891 ed. (1934), p. 24.
† *The Condition of the Working Class in England,* 1887 ed.
‡ December 2, 1893, *Letters to Americans,* p. 258.

that it crops up in their writings on India, Italy, Ireland as well). Reality always breaks in as 'exceptions' to the rule."*

2

Werner Sombart's *Why Is There No Socialism in the United States?* first appeared in 1906, and though its thesis has been rendered more sophisticated in numerous later writings, it remains a basic text. I propose here somewhat to minimize—though not to dismiss—Sombart's reasons, which tend mainly to stress objective historical factors standing in the way of socialism in America. But since he saw that some of these factors, like the supply of free land in nineteenth-century America, would not be operative much longer, he concluded—like the Marxists, though not one himself—that in a few decades socialism would thrive in America. In this prediction he was mistaken, and it is important to know why. Here, in schematic form, are some of the Sombartian "objective" factors that account for the failure, or at least difficulties, of American socialism:

1. Since this country had no feudal past, Americans could feel that as free citizens of a "new nation" they were able to express their needs and complaints within the democratic system; in consequence, the sense of class distinctions was much less acute here than in Europe.

2. Material prosperity in the United States, the result of a tremendous economic expansion, undercut the possibilities of socialist growth, since it enabled segments of the working class to gain a measure of

---

* One notable exception, at the opposite extreme from the American, is worth glancing at. Among the Russian radicals of the second half of the nineteenth century there was an intense and significant debate as to the possibility that socialist development in Russia might bypass capitalist and urban industrialization. Must Russia follow the familiar lines of Western development, or can it proceed along its own, "exceptional" path? The concrete issue was the *mir*, or traditional peasant commune. When the Russian Marxist Vera Zasulich wrote Marx in 1881 for his opinion, he devoted himself to this problem with much greater energy than to American problems—it may have seemed more important, or at least closer. After preparing four drafts of a reply, Marx sent the last one to his correspondent, writing that the account in *Capital* of the development of capitalism was *"expressly* limited to the *countries of western Europe"* and therefore provided "no reasons for or against the vitality of the rural community." He added, however, that he had become convinced that "this community is the mainspring of Russia's social regeneration." (Quoted in Russell Jacoby, "Politics of the Crisis Theory," *Telos*, Spring 1975, p. 7.) Later he and Engels wrote that the *mir* could pass on to a higher form of "communal ownership" and avoid the "dissolution which makes up the historical development of the west . . . if the Russian Revolution is the signal of proletarian revolution in the West, so that both complete each other. . . ." (Ibid., p. 8.)

Whether this judgment was correct need hardly concern us here. What matters is Marx's evident readiness to grant that Russia might be an "exception" to the developmental scheme of *Capital*. There is no similar readiness in his writings with regard to the United States, not even to the limited extent one finds it in Engels's letters; and one wonders why. An obvious reason is that Engels lived longer and, as the gray eminence of the movement, had to cope with the hopeless sectarianism of the German exiles who formed the Socialist Labor Party in America during the 1880s. More speculatively, I would say that it was easier for Marx to grant an "exception" to a precapitalist economy mired in absolutism than to an economy becoming quintessentially capitalist, and easier, as well, to acknowledge the political consequences of a "basic" socioeconomic institution like the *mir* in Russia than the political significance of a "superstructural" element like the national culture of America.

satisfaction and imbued others with the hope that America would be their "golden land."

3. The greater opportunities America offered for upward social mobility led most Americans to think in terms of individual improvement rather than collective action—they hoped to rise out of, rather than with, their class.

4. The open frontier, with its possibility of free or cheap land, served as a safety valve for discontent.

5. The American two-party system made it hard for a third party to establish itself and enabled the major parties to appropriate, at their convenience, parts of the programs advanced by reform-oriented third parties.

6. [This comes not from Sombart but from labor historian Selig Perlman:] The massive waves of immigration led to deep ethnic cleavages within the working class, so that earlier, "native" workers rose on the social scale while newer groups of immigrants took the least desirable jobs. It therefore became extremely hard to achieve a unified class consciousness within the American working class.

Neatly bundled together, such "factors" can seem more than sufficient for explaining the distinctive political course of America. But when examined somewhat closely, these factors tend—not, of course, to disappear—but to seem less conclusive: they *are* present, some of them all the time and all of them some of the time, but their bearing upon American socialism remains, I would say, problematic.

A methodological criticism of the Sombartian approach has been made by Aileen Kraditor: that Sombart, like the Marxists, takes for granted a necessary historical course against which American experience is to be found, if not wanting, then deviant, and therefore requiring "special explanation." But it's quite likely, argues Kraditor, that no such over-all historical direction can be located and that what really needs explaining is not why socialism failed in America, but why anyone thought it might succeed. Well, I am prepared to grant the dubiousness of the European model / American deviation approach, but would argue that there is some value in pursuing it tentatively, if only to see *where else* it might lead.

The Sombartian "factors" are too encompassing and thereby virtually ahistorical: they explain too much and thereby too little. They can hardly tell us why the American working class in the 1880s and 1890s engaged in very militant and even violent strikes yet did not "move ahead" to any large-scale socialist beliefs, nor can they tell us why the American socialist movement thrived, more or less, at one moment and collapsed at another. Such large historical "factors" as Sombart invokes may be overdetermining. Insofar as they apply, they leave little room for human agency, diversity, and surprise; they fall too readily into a "vulgar Marxist" assumption that human beings act exclusively or even mainly out of direct economic interest. And as a result, the problem for historians becomes to explain how *any* significant socialist movement ever did appear in this country. Between the Sombartian "factors" and the fate of a particular political movement there is, so to say, too much space; what is missing is the whole range of national culture—how people think, the myths by which they live, the impulsions that move them to action, and, not least of all, the circumstances and approaches of particular socialist movements.*

In any case, let us now glance at some of the Sombartian causes for the failure of American socialism.

Absence of a Feudal Past

This argument has been most skillfully restated by the political theorist Louis Hartz. He isolates

> three factors stemming from the European feudal inheritance, the absence of which in the United States precluded the possibility of a major socialist experience. One is a sense of class which an aristocratic culture communicates to the bourgeoisie and which both communicate to the proletariat. Another is the experience of social revolution implemented by the middle class which the proletariat also inherits. . . . Finally . . . the memory of the medieval corporate spirit which, after liberal assault, the socialist movement seeks to recreate in the form of modern collectivism.†

Behind Hartz's analysis there is a historical truth: that European socialist movements gained part of their following through alliances with bourgeois democratic movements in a common struggle against traditional or "feudal" institutions; and that the socialist movements kept their following by making demands that the plebs be granted political rights, promised but not fully delivered. Hartz makes much of the ab-

---

* "Most of the attempted [Sombartian] answers," writes Daniel Bell, "have discussed not *causes* but *conditions*. . . . An inquiry into the fate of a social movement has to be pinned to the specific questions of time, place, and opportunity. . . ." (*Marxian Socialism in the United States* [1967], p. 5.) Bell's distinction between "condition" and "cause" is suggestive, but hard to maintain. He means, I suppose, that a condition is a relatively stable or latent circumstance that enables or disables a certain course of action—as when we say that the condition of prosperity in the 1920s made the growth of socialism unlikely. A cause is a closely operative, precipitating event—as when we say the Socialist Party's decline during and after World War I was partly caused by governmental repression. Yet I can see the Sombartians replying that if a condition is sufficiently strong and enduring, it may, in its workings, be all but indistinguishable from a cause.

† "Reply," in John H. M. Laslett and Seymour Martin Lipset, eds., *Failure of a Dream? Essays in the History of American Socialism* (1974), p. 421.

sence of this enabling condition in America, and, before him, Lenin had noted that America has one of "the most firmly established democratic systems, which confronts the proletariat with purely socialist tasks."*

In part at least, both Hartz and Lenin are wrong. For just as French socialists in the nineteenth century worked, as the Marxist phrase goes, to "fulfill the bourgeois revolution" by creating social space for the working class, and just as Chartism strove to gain for the English workers political rights within the bourgeois system, so there were in America major "democratic [as distinct from so-called purely socialist] tasks" to be undertaken by socialists and liberals. These concerned large segments of the population: for instance, the struggle for woman suffrage, in which the socialists played an important part, and the struggle for black rights, in which the socialists could have played an important part had it not been for the sectarian Debsian claim that black freedom could be achieved "only" through socialism and consequently required no separate movement or demands. The struggle in Europe to do away with "feudal" or aristocratic hangovers has an equivalent, *mutatis mutandis*, in America as a struggle to live up to the promise of the early republic.

It's interesting that Marx and Engels could not decide whether the distinctiveness of American society was a boon or a burden for American socialism. At one point Engels, quite as if he had just read Hartz, wrote that Americans are "born conservatives—just *because* America is so purely bourgeois, so entirely without a feudal past and therefore proud of its purely bourgeois organization."† At another point, quite as if he had just read Hartz's critics, Engels cited "the more favorable soil of America, where no medieval ruins bar the way. . . ."‡

The argument, then, can cut both ways. Absence of a feudal past has made for greater "civic integration," a feeling among all (except the blacks) that they "belonged." The American working class seems never quite to have regarded itself as the kind of "outsider" or pariah that the working classes of Europe once did. Whatever discontents might develop—numerous and grave in nineteenth-century America, from abolitionism to major strikes—were likely to be acted out within the flexible consensus of American myth, or as a complaint that our values had been betrayed by the plutocrats. Only the Marxists were feckless enough to attempt a head-on collision with the national myth, and what it mostly brought them was a bad headache.

---

* *Letters to Americans*, Appendix, p. 275.

† February 8, 1890, in *Karl Marx and Friedrich Engles: Selected Correspondence, 1846–1895* (1942), p. 467.

‡ *Letters to Americans*, Appendix, p. 287.

But if America, in S. M. Lipset's phrase, was "a new nation" that gave its citizens a strong sense of independence and worth, then precisely this enabled them to fight staunchly for their rights. American labor strikes in the late nineteenth and early twentieth centuries were often more bloody than those in Europe. And it was, I think, two utterly divergent variants of the American myth, two simplified crystallizations at the right and left extremes, that made the class struggle so fierce in America. The capitalists, persuaded that Americans should be able to do as they wished with their property and pay whatever wages they proposed to pay, and the workers, persuaded that Americans (or Americans-in-the-making) should stand up as free men and resist exploitation, appealed to the same deeply embedded myth of the native citizen blessed with freedom by God.

There was a sharp class struggle in America during the decades after the Civil War, even without the questionable benefits of feudal hangovers, and in stressing its presence, as against those who kept talking about "classlessness," the Marxists were right. There was even a kind of class consciousness in the American working class, though this was hard to specify and the Marxists rarely succeeded in doing so, if only because it was a class consciousness that took the form, mostly, of an invocation of early republican values and a moralistic evangelicism. Werner Sombart put the matter well: "There is expressed in the worker, as in all Americans, a boundless optimism, which comes out of a belief in the mission and greatness of his country, a belief that often has a religious tinge."[*] This belief, with its "religious tinge," could be turned toward Social Darwinism or toward unionism, populism, and early socialism.

As for Hartz's third factor—the lack of a remembered "medieval corporate spirit" which might help re-create "modern collectivism"— one may suppose that such a memory did have some influence on European workers in the mid-nineteenth century. (I suspect it has more influence on historians of romanticist inclination.) But it's hard to believe that by the 1920s or 1930s this "memory" played much of a role in the collective expression of, say, the French workers. And if Americans had no such tradition to draw upon, it would be a crude exaggeration to conclude that the only other tradition remaining to us has been an unmodulated "possessive individualism." Herbert Gutman, a historian of the American working class, has nicely distinguished between individualist and independent traditions. There are traditions of independent Americans cooperating for common ends, in everything from frontier

---

[*] *Why Is There No Socialism in the United States?*, C. T. Husbands, ed. (1976), p. 18.

communities to utopian colonies, from abolitionist movements to the early unions; and Gutman has further noted that the agitational literature of American unionism in the late nineteenth century echoed these very themes of the unionism of the 1830s.

It would be wrong simply to dismiss Hartz's analysis, for it speaks to commonly perceived realities and, even with all reasonable qualifications, it has an evident power. But it has to be put forward in more nuanced terms than Hartz has proposed, and this means that his now famous "factors," even if they rendered the rise of socialism in America *difficult*, do not suffice to explain its unhappy fate.

On the Reefs of Roast Beef

America, wrote Sombart, was "the promised land of capitalism," where "on the reefs of roast beef and apple pie socialistic Utopias . . . are sent to their doom."* This pithy sentence appears to carry a self-evident validity, but recent historical and sociological investigations create enough doubts so that, at the very least, we must qualify Sombart's conclusion.

It is an exaggeration to suggest that the American workers, or members of the lower classes, have enjoyed a steady material abundance. Large segments of the population, gasping for breath, have never reached those famous "reefs of roast beef." There is a profound truth in Nathaniel Hawthorne's remark that "in this republican country, amid the fluctuating waves of our social life, somebody is always at the drowning-point."

From the 1870s until the present we have had sharply varying times of well-being and distress, largely in accord with the cyclical character of capitalist boom and crisis; times when the standard of living rose visibly for many workers, as during World War I and the decades between 1940 and 1970; and times when, as in the last third of the nineteenth and first two decades of the twentieth centuries, certain American workers, like the building mechanics, did improve their lot while those working in mills, packing plants, and clothing factories did not. Differentiations of income and material condition among American workers have often been sharper than those in class-ridden Europe. They continue to our present moment, between skilled and / or unionized workers and that segment of the "secondary" work force consisting of ill-paid and largely unorganized blacks, Hispanics, and illegal immigrants in fugitive light industries.

* *Why Is There No Socialism in the United States?*, p. 18.

Still other shadows fall across Sombart's bright picture—for example, the extent to which American workers have been subject to industrial accidents because this country, until recently, refused to pass the kind of social legislation that had long been enacted in Europe. For a good many historians it has nevertheless been the supposed objective advantages of American society when compared with European societies of the late nineteenth and early twentieth centuries—a higher standard of living, a greater degree of social mobility—that largely explain the failures of American socialism. But, as far as I have been able to gather from various historical studies, the evidence regarding standards of living and social mobility remains inconclusive. For one thing, the technical problems in making comparisons on such matters are very severe. It is hard to know exactly how to "measure" standards of living and social mobility, since so many elements of experience, some by no means readily quantifiable, enter into them.

Seymour Martin Lipset, a close observer in this area, writes that "a number of students of social mobility in comparative perspective (Sorokin, Glass, Lipset and Bendix, Miller, Blau and Duncan, and Bourdon) have concluded from an examination of mobility data collected in various countries that the American rate of mass social mobility is not uniquely high, that a number of European countries have had comparable rates. . . ."*

By contrast, Stephan Thernstrom, who has assembled valuable data about working-class mobility in Boston and Newburyport during the nineteenth and first two decades of the twentieth centuries, concludes that mobility was significantly higher in a big city like Boston than in a town like Newburyport, and, indeed, that in Boston "the dream of individual mobility was [not] illusory [during the nineteenth century] and that collective advance was [not] the only realistic hope for the American worker."†

A more recent and notably meticulous study by Peter R. Shergold comparing real wage rates and real family income in Pittsburgh, Pennsylvania, and two English cities, Birmingham and Sheffield, for the years 1899–1913, demonstrates, however, the enormous difficulties of such comparisons. Shergold concludes

> that assertions of relative American affluence must be severely qualified. Unskilled workers experienced similar levels of material welfare in Britain and the United States in the 1900s, and it is quite possible that English laborers actually enjoyed a higher standard of living during the last quarter

* "Comment," in Laslett and Lipset, eds., *Failure of a Dream?*, p. 528.
† "Socialism and Social Mobility," in Laslett and Lipset, eds., *Failure of a Dream?*, p. 519.

of the nineteenth century. The dominant characteristic of the American labor force was not comparative income superiority, but the much greater inequality of wage distribution. The most highly-paid manual employees, primarily skilled workers, earned substantially larger incomes than those in equivalent English occupations, whereas low-paid workers received incomes similar to those in England. In short, the fruits of economic growth, the benefits of emergent corporate capitalism, were far more unevenly distributed among wage earners in the United States than in England.

And again:

It is the comparative inequality of wage rewards in the United States, an income gulf widened by ethnic heterogeneity and racial prejudice, that must provide the socioeconomic context within which to analyze the American labor movement. American workers found it profoundly difficult to perceive their very diverse lifestyles as the product of a common exploitation. It was not a high average standard of living that dictated how they behaved. Rather, in a supreme historical paradox, it was the combination of a uniquely egalitarian ideology—"Americanism"—with extravagant inequality of material circumstances.*

Helpful as Shergold's material is in undermining older assertions about the "objective" reasons for the difficulties of American socialism (and, for that matter, of the American labor movement), the exact pertinence of his work remains debatable. Had he chosen to compare an American industrial city with cities in Eastern or Southern Europe, areas from which so many industrial workers in America emigrated, the economic disparities would probably have been more dramatic—and the statistical difficulties still greater—than in the work he did. In any case, his evidence that skilled workers in an American industrial city were better off than those in a similar English one may help explain the varying fates of socialism in America and England, since skilled workers played an important part in the early socialist movements.

Though the scholarly material on standards of living and social mobility is valuable—indeed, one wishes there were a good deal more—it doesn't by itself sustain Sombartian generalizations about American material conditions as the central cause of the difficulties and failures of American socialism. Even if one believes that Stephan Thernstrom's conclusions about the possibilities of individual improvement in late-nineteenth-century America probably hold for the country as a whole, the evidence is not sufficiently stark or unambiguous to form, or contribute heavily to, a *sufficient* explanation for the sharply different fates of socialism in the United States and Europe.

* *Working-Class Life* (1982), pp. 225, 229.

3

Nor is there any reason to believe, either from experience or research, that affluence necessarily makes for docility among workers. To argue that it does is to succumb to a crude sort of reductive economism, according to which the outlook of the worker is determined by nothing more than his personal circumstances. There has, to the contrary, been a strand of social thought that has seen extreme poverty as a demoralizing condition, likely to inhibit rather than stimulate political activism. S. M. Lipset cites the fact that "strong socialist movements exist in countries with high rates of social mobility," such as Australia and New Zealand, and Michael Harrington that German social democracy's greatest growth occurred at a time of relative prosperity, between the 1870s and World War I. A paper by Philip Dawson and Gilbert Shapiro, following Tocqueville's lead, shows that just before the French Revolution of 1789 those segments of the French bourgeoisie which had significantly improved their position were more vigorous in expressing opposition to the ancien régime than those which had not.

Studies comparing in close detail the conditions of American and European workers tend to be cautious regarding the Sombartian conclusion about "roast beef." A brilliant essay by James Holt comparing trade unions in the British and U.S. steel industries from 1880 to 1914 finds that the main factors thwarting class solidarity among the Americans were the rapidity of technological advance, which reduced the need for skilled workers, who were often the most militant unionists; and the ferocity of American employers, who often used brutal methods to break the unions. "The most striking difference between the two situations [American and British steel industries] concerns the behavior of employers rather than employees. In both countries, the impulse to organize was present among steelworkers but in one [Britain] most employers offered little resistance to union growth while in the other [the United States] they generally fought back vigorously." Holt concludes suggestively:

> The weakness and political conservatism of the American labor movement in the late 19th and early 20th centuries have often been seen primarily as the product of a lack of class consciousness among American workingmen. In the United States, it is suggested, class lines were more fluid and opportunities for advancement more rapid than in European countries. . . . Perhaps so, yet . . . in some ways the American workingman was more rather than less oppressed than his British counterpart. The retreat of so many American union leaders from a youthful socialism to a cautious and conservative "business unionism" may have reflected less a growing enthu-

siasm for the . . . status quo than a resigned acknowledgment that in a land where the propertied middle classes dominated politically and the big corporations ruled supreme in industry, accommodation was more appropriate than confrontation.*

Insofar as the roast-beef argument finds most American workers refusing socialism because they were relatively satisfied with their lot, it would seem to follow that, *for the same reason*, they would also reject militant class action. But many did turn to militant class or labor action. The history of American workers suggests not at all that a surfeit of good things led to passivity and acquiescence; it suggests only—and this is something very different—that the intermittent outbursts of labor militancy did not often end in socialist politics.

The Sombartian argument in its blunt form is not defensible. But to say this isn't to deny that the varying degrees of material comfort among segments of the American working class have probably constituted (to borrow a phrase from Daniel Bell) a limiting condition on the growth of American socialism. This relative or partial material comfort may help explain why American socialism was never likely to become a mass movement encompassing major segments of the working class; but it doesn't suffice for explaining something more interesting: why American socialism has had so uneven a history, with modest peaks and virtual collapse at several points.

What seems crucial is that social mobility in this country has been *perceived* differently from the way it has been perceived in Europe. The myth of opportunity for energetic individuals rests on a measure of historical actuality but also has taken on a power independent of, *even when in conflict with*, the social actuality. This myth has held the imagination of Americans across the decades, including immigrants dreadfully exploited when they came here but who apparently felt that almost anything in the New World, being new, was better than what they had known in the old. Here we enter the realm of national psychology and cultural values, which is indeed what we will increasingly have to do as we approach another of the "objective factors" commonly cited among the reasons for the failure of American socialism.

The Lure of Free Land

As it turns out, escape from onerous work conditions in the East to free land in the West was largely a myth. "In the 1860s, it took $1,000

* "Trade Unionism in the British and U.S. Steel Industries, 1880–1914: A Comparative Study," *Labor History*, 1977, p. 35.

[then a lot of money] to make a go of a farm, and the cost increased later in the century. So for every industrial worker who became a farmer, twenty farmers became city dwellers. And for every free farm acquired by a farmer [under the Homestead Act of 1862], nine were purchased by railroads, speculators, or by the government itself." There follows, however, a crucial proviso: if free land did not actually fulfill its mythic function, many people did not give up the dream that it would.* And perhaps, I'd add, not so much the dream of actually moving to a farm in the West as a shared feeling that the frontier and the wilderness remained powerful symbolic forces enabling Americans to find solace in the thought of escape even when they were not able to act upon it.

But is there not a contradiction between the last two of the Sombartian "objective factors"? If the American worker felt so contented with his life as the roast-beef-and-apple-pie argument suggests, why should he have wanted to escape from it to the rigors of pioneering on the American prairie? This question—the force of which is hardly diminished by the fact that not many workers actually did set out for the West—was asked by the German Social Democratic paper *Vorwärts* when it came to review Sombart's book: ". . . Why under such circumstances [does] the American worker 'escape into freedom' . . . that is, withdraw from the hubbub of capitalism, by settling on hitherto uncultivated land [?] If capitalism is so good to him, he could not help but feel extraordinarily well-off under its sceptre. . . . There is clearly a glaring contradiction here."†

The lure of the frontier, the myth of the West surely held a strong grip on the imaginations of many Americans during the late nineteenth century—and later too. But it soon became an independent power quite apart from any role the West may actually have played as a "safety valve" for urban discontent.

You have surely noticed the direction my argument is taking: away from a stress upon material conditions (even while acknowledging that in the last analysis they may well have constituted a large barrier to socialist growth) and toward a focusing on the immediate problems of American socialists that were or are in part open to solution through an exertion of human intelligence and will. Let me mention two: large-scale immigration, which created ethnic divisions within the working class, and the distinctive political structure of the United States.

---

* Michael Harrington, *Socialism* (1972), p. 116.
† Quoted in Introduction, Sombart, *Why Is There No Socialisms in the United States?*, p. xxiii.

The Immigrant Problem

The rise of American socialism in the late nineteenth and early twentieth centuries coincides with the greatest wave of immigration this country has ever experienced, an immigration drawn largely from Eastern and Southern Europe, with large numbers of Italians, Slavs, Jews, and Poles. When a nonspecialist looks into the historical literature, the main conclusion to be drawn is that it would be foolhardy to draw any large conclusions. Or, if pressed, I would say that the waves of the "new immigrants"—the more poorly educated, largely peasant stock from premodern countries—presented more of a problem to the American *unions* than to the socialists.

Many immigrants in this "second wave" came with a strong desire to work hard, save money, and go back home; they thought of themselves as what we'd call "guest workers," and that is one reason many came without their wives. The rate of return among East Europeans and Italians was very high. Between 1908 and 1910, for South and East Europeans, forty-four out of a hundred who came went back; between 1907 and 1911, for Italians, seventy-three out of a hundred who came went back. Such people were not likely to be attracted to political movements, especially those that might get them in trouble with the authorities or might interfere with their projects for self-exploitation as workers; nor, for the same reasons, were these immigrants often good material for unionization, though a study by Victor Greene has shown that the Slavs in western Pennsylvania, if conditions grew desperate enough, could be recruited as strong supporters of strike actions. As Jerome Karabel has shrewdly remarked: "If . . . a 'safety valve' did indeed exist for the discontented American worker, it was apparently to be found less on the frontier than in tired old Europe."*

Upon arrival, South and East European immigrants often took the worst jobs. Usually without industrial skills, these people were shunted to brute labor, on the railroads and in the steel mills. Their presence enabled the "first wave" of immigrants, from Northern Europe, to rise on the social scale and, above these, the native-born to enter new supervisory posts created by a rapid industrial expansion. The American working class was thereby split into competing ethnic segments—and the contempt native-born and earlier immigrants often showed the newer immigrants did nothing to heal this split. No matter what the Marxist schema might propose, these ethnic divisions were often felt

---

* "The Failure of American Socialism Reconsidered," in Ralph Miliband and John Saville, eds., *The Socialist Register, 1979* (1979), p. 216.

more strongly than any hypothetical class consciousness, except perhaps during strikes, in which a momentary solidarity could be achieved.

Partly in reaction to the ethnic and racial antagonisms they met from other workers, but partly from a natural desire to live with those who spoke the same language, ate the same foods, and shared the same customs, many immigrant workers huddled into ethnic neighborhoods, miniature strongholds in which to beat off the contempt of their "betters." These neighborhoods could often be controlled by shrewd politicians offering practical advice and social help; among the Italians, for instance, by *padroni* doubling as labor contractors in the construction industry. This heavy concentration in ethnic neighborhoods usually made for political conservatism and obviously served to thwart class or political consciousness. Later students would see such neighborhoods as enclaves of parochial narrowness or as communities enabling their members to accumulate strength for a move into the larger American world—obviously they could be both. Recently a more sophisticated analysis, by Ira Katznelson and others, has made much of the split between the immigrant as worker in the plant and as resident in the ethnic community, sometimes able to achieve an intense militancy in bitter economic struggles against employers, yet docile in relation to the conservative leadership of the ethnic neighborhood.

Harsh as the exploitation of immigrant workers often was, many of them retained a stubborn conviction that if they accepted deprivation in the short run, their lot would ultimately be bettered—or at least that of their children would be. Certain immigrant groups, especially the Jews, staked almost everything on the educational opportunities offered by America. Often accompanied by desperate homesickness for the old country and harsh curses for the crudity of life in America, the promise of the New World nevertheless gripped the imagination of the immigrants. American radicals might point to real injustices, but to newcomers who had left behind autocratic and caste-ridden nations, our easy manners and common acceptance of democratic norms could seem wonderfully attractive. And there is a psychological point to be added: it was hard enough to be a Slav in Pittsburgh or a Pole in Chicago without the additional burden of that "anti-Americanism" with which the socialists were often charged.

Much of the "new immigration" consisted of Catholics, people still close to the faith, in whom a suspicion of socialism had been implanted by a strongly conservative clergy. The labor historian Selig Perlman believed that the immigrant character of American labor was a major reason for the difficulties of the socialists: "American labor remains one of the most heterogeneous laboring classes in existence. . . . With a working class of such composition, to make socialism . . . the official 'ism' of the movement, would mean . . . deliberately driving the Catholics . . . out of the labor movement. . . ."*

Now Perlman's point seems beyond dispute if taken simply as an explanation of why socialism could not, or should not, have become the dominant outlook of the American labor movement. But it does not explain very much about socialist fortunes in general—unless, of course, you assume that domination of the American Federation of Labor was the crucial requirement for socialist success in America. That such domination would have helped the socialists is obvious; but it's not at all obvious that, lacking it, they were doomed to extinction or mere sect existence. In truth, the socialists had plenty of possibilities for recruitment within the country at large before they could so much as reach the new immigrants.

Nor should it be supposed that the immigrants formed a solid conservative mass. In the Debsian era, socialist strength was centered in a number of immigrant communities: the Germans, the Jews, and the Finns, all of whom clustered in ethnic neighborhoods that some recent analysts have seen as bulwarks of conservatism. As if to illustrate how the same data can be used for sharply opposing claims, one historian, John H. M. Laslett, has argued that it was the "process of ethnic assimilation" rather than ethnic isolation that hindered the socialists:

> This is perhaps clearest in the case of the Brewery Workers Union, whose socialism may in large part be ascribed to the influences of socialists who came to this country after the abortive German revolution of 1848, and in greater numbers after Bismarck's antisocialist legislation of 1878. The radicalism of the union noticeably declined as these older groups either died off, moved upward into the entrepreneurial or professional middle class, or were replaced by ethnic groups whose commitment to socialism was less intense.†

The immigrants, to be sure, presented practical and moral-political problems for the socialists. Many immigrants, even if friendly to the movement, could not vote, nor did they rush to acquire citizenship. There were segments of the party that harbored disgraceful antiforeign sentiments, and this led to internecine disputes. The plethora of immigrant communities made for difficulties: Morris Hillquit once noted ruefully that the party had to put out propaganda in twenty different

---

* Quoted in Harrington, *Socialism*, p. 131.

† "Socialism and American Trade Unionism," in Laslett and Lipset, eds., *Failure of a Dream?*, p. 214.

languages. For a union trying to organize, say, a steel plant in Pittsburgh, where the work force was split ethnically and linguistically, this could be a devastating problem. For the socialists, however, it would have been crucial only if they had had much of a chance of reaching many of these "new immigrants," or if they had already scored such successes among the indigenous American population that all that remained in their way was the recalcitrance of immigrant workers. Such, obviously, was not the case. No; the argument from the divisive consequences of immigration does not take us very far in explaining the difficulties of American socialism.

It is when we reach the last of our "objective factors," that we come closer to the actual difficulties socialists encountered in America. It was . . .

The American Political System

If the authors of the Constitution had in mind to establish a political system favoring a moderately conservative two-party structure—a kind of "centrism" allowing some flexibility within a stable consensus politics but also putting strong barriers in the way of its principled critics—then they succeeded brilliantly. Our shrewdly designed system combines a great deal of rigidity in its governing structure with a great deal of flexibility in its major parties. Our method of electing presidents requires that the parties be inclusive enough to cement political coalitions before Election Day, and that means bargaining and compromise, which blur political and ideological lines. Our method of governing, however, makes for a continuity of elites, tends to give the political center an overwhelming preponderance, and makes it tremendously difficult for insurgent constituencies to achieve political strength unless they submit to the limits of one of the major parties. In recent years, this peculiar mixture of rigidity and flexibility has, if anything, become more prevalent. The tremendous costliness of running for political office, now that television has largely replaced the public meeting and advertising slogans the political oration, makes it all but impossible for minority parties to compete. It also enables rich men—noble, eccentric, or wicked—to take on an excessive role in political life. Yet the growth of the primary system and the fact that most voters pay even less attention to primaries than to elections means that coherent minorities can often achieve their ends through cleverness and concentration.

There are theorists by the dozen who regard all this as a master stroke in behalf of maintaining democracy. Perhaps they are right. At least, they may be right if the society does not have to confront major crises, as during the immediate pre–Civil War years and the Depression era, when the political system comes under severe strain. But if the system helps maintain democracy, it also seriously disables democratic critics of capitalism.

For the most part, all of this constitutes the common coin of American political science. Let me therefore try to sharpen the focus by discussing the problem from the point of view of the socialist movement as it kept trying to establish itself in the country's political life.

One of my most wearying memories, when I think back to years in various socialist groups, is that of efforts we would make to get on the ballot. Most states had rigid requirements, sometimes mere rigged handicaps, for minor parties. In New York State we had to obtain a certain number of qualified signatures from all the counties, and this would mean sending volunteers to upstate rural communities where signatories ready to help socialists were pretty rare. In Ohio during the 1930s the number of required signatures, as I recall, was outrageously high. Well, we would throw ourselves into the effort of collecting signatures, and then have to face a court challenge from a major party, usually the more liberal one, since it had more to lose from our presence on the ballot than the conservatives. (It's amusing how often Republicans turned out to be staunch "defenders" of minority rights.) If, finally, we did get on the ballot, we were often so exhausted that there was little or no energy, to say nothing of money, left for the actual campaign.

Over and over again the socialists would face this problem: friendly people would come up to our candidates—especially Norman Thomas— and say they agreed with our views but would nevertheless vote for "the lesser evil" because they didn't "want to throw away their vote." We tried to scorn such sentiments, but, given the American political system, especially the zero-sum game for presidential elections, there really was a core of sense in what these people said.

One of the few occasions when the socialist vote was relatively large—in 1912, when the party drew six percent of the vote—is partly explained by the fact that, as Thomas put it, "voters that year were pretty sure that the winner would be either Woodrow Wilson or Theodore Roosevelt, not William H. Taft, and they didn't believe that the difference between these two fairly progressive men was important enough to prevent their voting for their real preference," the socialist Eugene Debs. I'd guess Thomas was right when he added that if America had had "a parliamentary rather than a presidential government, we should have had, under some name or other, a moderately strong socialist party."

The idea of a long-range *political* movement slowly accumulating strength for some ultimate purpose has simply not appealed to the American imagination. Movements outside the political process, yes— from abolitionism to feminism, from municipal reform to civil rights. But let the supporters of these movements enter electoral politics, and the expectation becomes one of quick victory. S. M. Lipset has described this phenomenon:

> . . . Extra-party "movements" arise for moralistic causes, which are initially not electorally palatable. Such movements are not doomed to isolation and inefficacy. If mainstream political leaders recognize that a significant segment of the electorate feels alienated . . . they will readapt one of the major party coalitions. But in so doing, they temper much of the extremist moralistic fervor. . . . The protestors are absorbed into a major party coalition, but, like the abolitionists who joined the Republicans, the Populists who merged with the Democrats, or the radicals who backed the New Deal, they contribute to the policy orientation of the newly formed coalition.*

To which I need only add a clever observation Sombart made in 1906, which is still, I suspect, largely true: "It is an unbearable feeling for an American to belong to a party that always and forever comes out of the election with small figures. . . . A member of a minority party finds himself on election day . . . compelled to stand at one side with martyr-like resignation—something which in no way accords with the American temperament."†

At least a significant number of Americans have never hesitated to "stand at one side with martyr-like resignation" or even with rage in behalf of moral causes. But, curiously, this has not seemed to extend to the electoral system: *there*, they have to strike it rich. That may be one reason they sometimes strike it so poor.

4

The search for answers often leads to nothing more than a redefining of questions. To discount but not dismiss the customary "objective factors" cited as explanations for the failure of American socialism is by no means to reject the idea of "American exceptionalism," namely, that conditions in the United States have differed crucially from the Marxist model for the development of capitalism and / or the way capitalism actually developed in Europe. It is, rather, to transfer our explanatory stress from material conditions to the character of American culture. Exceptionalism among us took primarily an ideological or a mythic form,

---

* "Why No Socialism in the United States?," in Seweryn Bialer, ed., *Sources of Contemporary Radicalism* (1977), p. 128.

† Quoted in Bialer, ed., *Sources of Contemporary Radicalism*, p. 62.

a devotion to the idea that this country could be exempt from the historical burdens that had overwhelmed Europe. It seems obvious that so distinctive a culture, defining itself through an opposition to, even a rejection of, Europe, cannot finally be understood apart from the shaping context of special historical circumstances: it did not arise merely as an idea in someone's head, or an Idea in a Collective Head. Yet I want to stress the independent power, the all-but-autonomous life, of the American myth and its remarkable persistence, despite enormous changes in social conditions. The ideology or myth—call it what you will, as long as you keep your eye fixed on Gatsby's "green light"—seems *almost* impervious to the modifying pressures of circumstance. It isn't, of course; but what strikes one is the extent to which it continues, in good circumstances and bad, to shape our imagination.

What is this myth? It consists in a shared persuasion, often penetrating deeper into our consciousness than mere language can express, that America is the home of a people shaped by or at least sharing in Providence. America is the land of the settler's paradisial wilderness, the setting of the Puritan's New Israel. America is humanity's second chance. Such sentiments rest on a belief that we have already had our revolution and it was led by George Washington, so that appeals for another one are superfluous and malicious, or that, for the millions who came here from Europe in the last one hundred fifty years, the very act of coming constituted a kind of revolution.

That many Americans have found it entirely possible to yield to this myth while simultaneously attacking our socioeconomic institutions, or complaining bitterly that the slaveocracy disgraced us, the plutocrats stole our inheritance, Wall Street fleeced us, the capitalists exploited us, and the military-industrial complex sent our sons to death—all this seems clear. To a simple rationalist or vulgar Marxist, the ability to hold at once to the animating myth behind the founding of America and the most bitter criticism of its violation or abandonment or betrayal may seem a contradiction; but if so, it is precisely from such contradictions that our collective existence has been formed.

The distinctive American ideology takes on a decidedly nonideological mask. I call it, very roughly, Emersonianism, though I know it had its sources in American and indeed European thought long before Emerson. By now, of course, "Emersonianism" has become as elusive and protean a category as Marxism or Freudianism. What I mean to suggest is that Emerson, in a restatement of an old Christian heresy, raised the *I* to semidivine status, thereby providing a religious sanction for the American cult of individualism. Traditional Christianity had seen man as a being like God, but now he was to be seen as one sharing, through osmosis with the oversoul, directly in the substance of divinity. This provided a new vision of man for a culture proposing to define itself as his new home—provided that vision by insisting that man be regarded as a self-creating and self-sufficient being fulfilled through his unmediated relation to nature and God. The traditional European view that human beings are in good measure defined or described through social characteristics and conditions was, at least theoretically, discounted; the new American, singing songs of himself, would create himself through spontaneous assertions, which might at best graze sublimity and at worst drop to egoism. The American, generically considered, could make his fate through will and intuition, a self-induced grace.

Now this vision can be employed in behalf of a wide range of purposes—myth is always promiscuous. It can show forth the Emerson who, in behalf of "a perfect unfolding of individual nature," brilliantly analyzed human alienation in a commercial society, attacking the invasion of "Nature by Trade . . . [as it threatened] to upset the balance of man, and establish a new, universal Monarchy more tyrannical than Babylon or Rome." And it can emerge in the Emerson who told his countrymen that "money . . . is in its effects and laws as beautiful as roses. Property keeps the accounts of the world, and is always moral."

This American vision can be turned toward the authoritarian monomania of Captain Ahab or to the easy fraternity of Ishmael and Queequeg. It can coexist with Daniel Webster and inspire Wendell Phillips. It can be exploited by Social Darwinism and sustain the abolitionists. It can harden into a nasty individualism and yield to the mass conformity Tocqueville dreaded. Arising from the deepest recesses of the American imagination, it resembles Freud's description of dreams as showing "a special tendency to reduce two opposites to a unity or to represent them as one thing." No one has to like this vision, but anyone trying to cope with American experience had better acknowledge its power.

This complex of myth and ideology, sentiment and prejudice, for which I use "Emersonianism" as a convenient label, forms the ground of "American exceptionalism." Politically it has often taken the guise of a querulous antistatism, at times regarded as a native absolute—though that seldom kept many people from aligning it with the demands of big business for government subsidies. It can veer toward an American version of anarchism, suspicious of all laws, forms, and regulations, asserting a fraternity of two, sometimes even one, against all communal structures. Tilt toward the right and you have the worship of "the free market"; tilt toward the left and you have the moralism of American reformers, even the syndicalism of the Industrial Workers of the World.

Snakelike, this "Emersonianism" can also subside into or next to the Lockean moderation of the American Constitution and political arrangement. ("The American Whig leaders" of the postrevolutionary period, Sacvan Bercovitch shrewdly remarks, "brought the violence of revolution under control by making revolution a controlling metaphor of national identity.")

It is notable that most nineteenth-century critics of American society appealed to the standards—violated, they said—of the early republic. They did this not as a tactical device but out of sincere conviction. "We will take up the ball of the Revolution where our fathers dropped it," declared the agrarian radicals of the New York anti-rent movement, "and roll it to the final consummation of freedom and independence of the Masses." The social historian Herbert Gutman finds the same rhetoric in the propaganda of the late-nineteenth-century trade unions. And Sacvan Bercovitch finds it in the declarations of a large number of American radicals throughout that century:

> William Lloyd Garrison organized the American Anti-Slavery Society as "a renewal of the nation's founding principles" and of "the national ideal." Frederick Douglass based his demands for black liberation on America's "destiny" . . . and "the genius of American institutions. . . ." As a leading historian of the period has remarked: ". . . the typical reformer, for all his uncompromising spirit, was no more alienated—no more truly rebellious—than the typical democrat. . . . He might sound radical while nevertheless associating himself with the fundamental principles and underlying tendencies of America."[*]

It's a pity that our indigenous nineteenth-century radicalism had largely exhausted itself by the time small socialist groups, mostly immigrant in composition, began to be organized in the 1880s—or at least could not find a point of significant relation with them. The abolitionist Wendell Phillips began with a pure Emersonian invocation: ". . . We are bullied by institutions. . . . Stand on the pedestal of your own individual independence, summon these institutions about you, and judge them." Once the fight against slavery was won, Phillips moved ahead to other causes, warning against "the incoming flood of the power of incorporated wealth" and calling—in a political style Richard Hofstadter has described as "Yankee homespun" socialism—for an "equalization of property."[†] He became—almost—a bridge between nineteenth-century radicalism and the new American socialism. And like

* "The Rights of Assent: Rhetoric, Ritual and the Ideology of American Consciousness," in Sam B. Girgus, ed., *The American Self: Myth, Ideology and Popular Culture* (1981), p. 21.
† Quoted in Hofstadter, *The American Political Tradition* (1948), pp. 139, 159.

other American dissenters, he held fast to the tradition of invoking the principles of the republic—principles, he said, that had been violated and betrayed.

Recognizing the power of this traditional response is by no means to acquiesce in the delusions that have often been justified in its name. It isn't, for example, to acquiesce in the delusion that America has been or is a "classless" society. Or that there has been any lack among us of bloody battles between capital and labor. Or that there are not today, as in the past, glaring injustices that call for remedy. To recognize the power of the American myth of a covenant blessing the new land is simply to recognize a crucial fact in our history—and one that seems to me at least as decisive for the fate of socialism in this country as the material conditions that are usually cited.

If you go through the writings of American socialists you can find glimmerings and half-recognitions that they have had to function in a culture ill-attuned to their fundamental outlook. The keenest statements on this matter come from an odd pair: an Italian Marxist, Antonio Gramsci, who had no direct contact with America, and an American radical of the 1930s, Leon Samson, remembered only by historians who make the left their specialty. In his *Notebooks* Gramsci writes: "The Anglo-Saxon immigrants are themselves an intellectual, but more especially a moral, elite. . . . They import into America . . . apart from moral energy and energy of will, a certain level of civilization, a certain stage of European historical evolution, which, when transplanted by such men into the virgin soil of America, continues to develop the forces implicit in its nature. . . ."*

In isolation, this passage could almost be taken for a rhapsody celebrating American culture; but Gramsci was a Marxist, and he proceeded to argue that the elements of uniqueness he found in the American past had reached their fulfillment in an apogee of pure capitalism, what he calls "Fordism," an unprecedented rationalization of production setting America apart from the kinds of capitalism known in Europe.

Leon Samson, a maverick socialist of the 1930s, developed a linked notion, that "Americanism" can be seen as a "substitute socialism":

> Like socialism, Americanism is looked upon . . . as a . . . platonic, impersonal attraction toward a system of ideas, a solemn assent to a handful of final notions—democracy, liberty, opportunity, to all of which the American adheres rationalistically much as a socialist adheres to his socialism—because it does him good, because it gives him work, because, so he thinks, it guarantees his happiness. . . . Every concept in socialism has its substitutive

---

* *Selections from the Prison Notebooks* (1971), pp. 21–22.

counter-concept in Americanism, and that is why the socialist argument
falls so fruitlessly on the American ear. . . .*

Both Gramsci and Samson were shrewd enough to locate their "exceptionalism" in the mythic depths of our collective imagination, among
the inner vibrations of our culture. What one may conclude from their
perceptions, as perhaps from my own discussion, is that if socialism is
ever to become a major force in America it must either enter deadly
combat with and destroy the covenant myth or must look for some way
of making its vision of the good society seem a fulfillment of that myth.
Both are difficult propositions, but I need hardly say which is the less
so.

Many socialists have grasped for intuitions along these lines, but
have feared perhaps to articulate them, since they seemed to suggest
that so impalpable a thing as a culture can have a greater power of
influence than industrial structures, levels of production, and standards
of living. And that may explain why many American socialists, including
the intelligent ones, found it safer to retreat into the comforts of the
Marxist system, with its claims to universal applicability and certain
fulfillment.

Would a developed recognition of the problem as I have sketched
it here have brought any large or immediate success to American socialism over the past five or six decades? Probably not. All that such a
recognition might have done—all!—is to endow the American socialists
with a certain independence of mind and a freedom from ideological
rigidity.

So, again, we restate our central question. Not "Why is there no
socialism in America?" There never was a chance for major socialist
victory in this society, this culture. The really interesting question is
"Why could we not build a *significant* socialist movement that would
have a sustained influence?" One answer, of course, is that the kind of
culture I've sketched here makes it almost impossible for a significant
minority party to survive for very long. In America, politics, like everything else, tends to be all or nothing. But whether it might yet be possible
for a significant minority movement to survive—one that would be
political in a broad, educative sense without entangling itself in hopeless
electoral efforts—is another question.

* *Toward a United Front* (1935), pp. 16–17.

Some Inconclusive Conclusions

The analyses and speculations in this article apply mainly to the earlier decades of the century, into the years just before World War II. But the troubles of American—and not only American—socialism in the decades since the thirties must be located in a more terrible—indeed, an apocalyptic—setting. The triumph of Hitlerism called into question a good many traditional assumptions of progress and schemes for human self-determination—called into question the very enterprise of mankind. The rise of Stalinism, a kind of grotesque "double" of the socialist hope, led to the destruction of entire generations, the disillusionment of hundreds of thousands of committed people, the besmirching of the socialist idea itself. As a consequence of the problems thrown up by Hitlerism and Stalinism, there has occurred an inner crisis of belief, a coming-apart of socialist thought. If we consider the crisis of socialism on an international scale within the last fifty years, then clearly these developments count at least as much as, and probably more than, the indigenous American factors discussed here.

There is a school of opinion that holds that American socialism did not fail, but succeeded insofar as it prepared the way, advanced ideas, and trained leaders for mainstream movements of labor, liberalism, and others. This view has an obvious element of truth, perhaps even consolation. Still, no one could be expected to endure the grueling effort to build a socialist movement simply so that it might serve as a "prep school" for other movements. Our final judgment must be more stringent, harder on ourselves: insofar as American socialism proposed ends distinctively its own, it did not succeed.

There is a more sophisticated argument about the fate of American socialism: that finally it did not matter. Europe, with its strong socialist and social-democratic movements, did not achieve democratic socialism; it could reach only the welfare state. The United States, without a major socialist movement, has also reached a welfare state, if at the moment one that is somewhat broken-down. Hence, this argument goes, what does it matter whether or not we have a socialist movement here? I would respond that, largely because of the strength of European socialism, the welfare state in Western Europe has advanced significantly beyond that of the United States, and that there are groups within European socialism, especially in Sweden and France, that now see a need to move "beyond" the welfare state. The presence of these groups has been made possible by the continuing strength of the socialist movement in those countries.

The usual "objective" socioeconomic factors cited as explanations for the difficulties of American socialism are genuine constraints. But I believe that the distinctiveness of American culture has played the more decisive part in thwarting socialist fortunes. And even after both kinds of reasons—the socioeconomic and the cultural—are taken into account, there remains an important margin with regard to intelligence or obtuseness, correct or mistaken strategies, which helped to determine whether American socialism was to be a measurable force or an isolated sect. That the American socialist movement must take upon itself a considerable portion of the responsibility for its failures, I have tried to show elsewhere.

In the United States, socialist movements have usually thrived during times of liberal upswing. They have hastened their own destruction whenever they have pitted themselves head-on against liberalism. If there is any future for socialism in America, it is through declaring itself to be the partial ally of a liberalism with which it shares fundamental democratic values and agrees upon certain immediate objectives; after that, it can be said that socialists propose to extend and thereby fulfill traditional liberal goals by moving toward a democratization of economic and social life. If some liberals express agreement with that perspective, then all the better.

American socialism has suffered from a deep-grained sectarianism, in part a result of the natural inclination of small groups to huddle self-protectively in their loneliness, and in part, especially during the two or three decades after 1917, a result of the baneful influence of Bolshevism. At least as important have been the fundamentalist, evangelical, and deeply antipolitical impulses rooted in our religious and cultural past, impulses that helped to shape the socialist movements in the times of Debs and Thomas far more than their participants recognized. A damaging aspect of this sectarianism was a tendency to settle into postures of righteous moral witness, to the disadvantage of mundane politics.

During its peak moments American socialism tried to combine two roles—that of moral protest and that of political reform—which in America had traditionally been largely separate, and which our political arrangements make it very difficult to unite. In principle, a socialist movement ought to fulfill both of these roles: moral protest largely beyond the political process, and social reform largely within it. A strong argument could be made that the two roles are, or should be, mutually reinforcing, with the one providing moral luster and the other practical effectiveness. But it would take an extraordinary set of circumstances (say, the moment when abolitionism flourished or the moment when the protest against the Vietnam War reached its peak) for a movement in this country to combine the two roles successfully. And what's more, it would take a movement with a degree of sophistication and flexibility that has rarely been available on the left, or anywhere else along the political spectrum.

Still, no socialist movement, if it is to maintain the integrity of its persuasions, can forgo some effort to be both the voice of protest and the agency of reform. It's not a matter of choosing between the roles of moral witness and political actor. It's a matter of finding ways through which to link properly the utopian moralism of the protester with the political realism of the activist; to ensure that the voice of high rectitude will reinforce and give breadth to the daily murmur of the reformer; to adapt to the realities of the American political system without succumbing to a small-souled pragmatism or a hermetic moralism. In some large parties, loosely and democratically structured, this has sometimes been possible, as in the British Labour Party during its best years. In a small party, such as the American Socialist Party even during its best years, this has been almost impossible.

Whether some such alliance of forces or union of impulses might still be created in America is very much a question. I do not know, but think it a project worthy of serious people.

Henry James once said that being an American is a complex fate. We American socialists could add: He didn't know the half of it.

Reaganism: The Spirit of the Times

1986

Franklin Roosevelt's New Deal constituted, let us say, a quarter-revolution. It introduced the rudiments of a welfare state and made "the socialization of concern" into a national value. It signified not a society egalitarian or even just, but at least one that modulated the harshness of "rugged individualism." All later administrations, at least until that of Reagan, more or less accepted the New Deal legacy. Under Reagan, America experienced, let us say, a quarter-counterrevolution.

Segments of the American bourgeoisie had never accepted the general premise or sparse practice of what passed in America for a welfare state; they lived with it faute de mieux, waiting for a chance to shake off trade unions, social measures, and economic regulations. Ideological in a primitive way, they would have stared with incomprehension if you had suggested that their survival as a class might well have been due to the very social measures they despised. And then their moment came—with the inner disintegration of liberalism under Carter that opened the way for Reagan.

From *Dissent* 33 (Fall 1986):4.

The more hard-bitten and fanatic Reaganites brought to office a maximum program: to undo the New Deal, which meant to demolish the fraction of a welfare state we have. When the limits of this perspective became clear to Reagan's managers (most starkly after his administration's defeat in Congress when it tried to tamper with Social Security), the Reaganites fell back, shrewdly enough, on their minimum program. They would weaken, reduce, cripple, starve out the welfare state. And in this they often succeeded. While leaving intact the external structures of certain programs, they proceeded, with firm ideological malice, to cut out and cut down a good many other programs. They brought about a measurable redistribution of income and wealth in behalf of the rich, and they repelled any attempt to pass further social legislation—not that the chickenhearted Democrats made much of an attempt. Perhaps most important, the Reaganites managed to create a political atmosphere in which the social forces favoring the welfare state were forced onto the defensive. The very idea of a national health act, for example, was no longer even mentioned by the few remaining liberals in Congress.

Now there were sectarians—the right is blessed with them as well as the left—who complained that Reagan did not go far enough. David Stockman judged Reagan to be "a consensus politician, not an ideologue." This was a dumb remark, since it has been Reagan's peculiar skill to combine the two roles—consensus politician and ideologue—just as he has put the politics of theater at the service of ideological politics. After all, to be an ideologue doesn't necessarily mean to commit political suicide: as a Washington hand is quoted, "Reagan has never been one to go over a cliff for a cause" (*Newsweek*, April 7, 1986). The shrewder Reaganites understood that if they clung at all costs to their maximum program, they might not even get their minimum. When it comes to political reality, Stockman has nothing to teach Reagan.

But the main achievement of the Reagan administration has not been institutional or programmatic. It has consisted of a spectacular transformation of popular attitudes, values, and styles, though how deep or durable this will prove to be we cannot yet know. In a country where only two decades ago a sizable portion of the population registered distrust of corporate America, the Reaganites have largely succeeded in restoring popular confidence in the virtues of capitalism, the mystical beneficence of "the free market," and the attractiveness of a "minimalist state," even though that state, faithfully attending to corporate needs, has never been close to being minimalist. In the long run, the brilliant manipulation of popular sentiment by Reagan and his men may turn out to be more important than their economic and social enactments.

A certain worldview, not exactly fresh but with some clever decorations, has come to dominate public discourse. Let me try briefly to sift out the main elements of the Reaganite vision.

The primacy of "success," the release of greed. For the segment of Reaganite operatives and backers that came from or represented the new rich of the West and Southwest—real estate developers, oil millionaires, movie magnates, in short, the arriviste bourgeoisie—the policies of the Reagan administration were immediately helpful. Still more important was the largesse with which these policies sanctioned appetites of acquisitiveness and greed that had been present, of course, before Reagan's presidency but not quite so blatantly or unashamedly. It was as if J.R. had found spiritual comrades in the White House, or even an office next door to, say, Michael Deaver. The inner circles of Reaganites and their managerial supporters throughout the country were sublimely untroubled by the cautions of certain skeptics (Felix Rohatyn, for one) in the Eastern financial establishment. Deaver's squalid story—his exploitation of White House connections in behalf of his lobbying firm—was just a minor instance of the by now commonplace shuttling between high governmental posts, especially in the Pentagon, and corporate boardrooms. It will take some years before we know the whole story of this jolly interpenetration between officialdom and corporations, but it takes no gifts of prophecy to foresee that, in its subservience to big money, the Reagan administration is likely to equal or surpass those of Grant and Harding.

The new rich, tasting power and light-headed with a whiff of ideology, could now have it both ways. They could persuade themselves that it was quite legitimate, indeed "the American way," to grab as much as they could, and "Screw you, Jack," if you suffered the consequences; while they were also morally comforted with the fairy tale that the sum of their selfishness would, through a sleight of "the invisible hand," come out as a public good. The corporate buccaneers who now felt free to act out the ethos of Social Darwinism could also preach that "the free market" brought plenty to all (which didn't, however, keep corporate America from pressing for every form of governmental handout that would further its economic interests). After all, few human experiences can be as satisfying as the simultaneous discharge of low desires and high sentiments.

The fever spread. While industrial America was being devastated and thousands of farmers trembled on the edge of bankruptcy, the corporate and financial "community" indulged in a spree of raids and mergers, almost all of them unproductive, sterile, asocial, but decidedly profitable. New terms entered our language: arbitrage, asset-shuffling,

golden parachute, junk bonds, among others. New generations of prof-
iteers, yuppies with clever brains and no minds, flourished in investment
banking. A few may end in jail for "insider" trading. *Newsweek* (May
26, 1986) quotes a disillusioned Wall Streeter: "We have created two
myths in the 1980s. One is that you need to be smart to be an investment
banker. That's wrong. Finance is easy. Myth number two is that investment bankers somehow create value. They don't. They shuffle
around value other people have created. It's a parasitical industry."

Reading about these young Wall Streeters, baby-faced creatures of
the Reagan moment, one feels, almost, a kind of pity for them. Caught
in illegal maneuvers, which in pleading guilty they now say were known
to the top people in their firms, they seem like petty scapegoats, small
fry who had not yet learned what the big fellows know: that you can
evade the law without breaking it or can make yourself a bundle while
remaining just this side of the law since, after all, it's your kind of law.

A psychiatrist, Samuel Klagsbrun, who treats "a lot of lawyers handling mergers and acquisitions," says that for these people "business is
God" (*Wall Street Journal*, June 2, 1986). A young arbitrager reports
that everyone "seems to want to make the quick buck. [They] move
out into the left lane, put it into overdrive and hope the brakes don't
fail when they hit the first curve" (*Newsweek*, May 26, 1986).

And more sedately, Ira Sorkin, the New York director of the Se-
curities and Exchange Commission, says, "Greed knows no bounds.
There's always someone who makes more than you do. Investment
banking is the new gold mine" (*New York Times*, June 2, 1986).

Earning around a million dollars a year, some of these arbitragers
and deal-makers live by a scale of values that can only repel Americans
who still keep a fraction of the republic's animating values. Here is
Hamilton James, thirty-five, of the firm Donaldson Lupkin, who shovels
in over a million a year but says that "if we [his family] want a library
and a room for an *au pair* girl, it could cost a couple million dollars. If
it's anything fancy, four or five million" (*Wall Street Journal*, June 2,
1986). Any bets on what he'll pay the au pair girl?

None of this is new. There were Drew and Fisk, Morgan and Rock-
efeller in the days of and after the robber barons. There were the boys
of Teapot Dome. There was Calvin Coolidge, who declared, "The business of America is business." There was Charlie Wilson, who said,
"What's good for General Motors is good for the United States." Yet
something *is* new, at least for the years since 1933, and that's the social
and moral sanction that Reaganism has given to the ethos of greed. The
Reagan administration did not "cause" the Wall Street shenanigans I've
mentioned; Reagan himself need not say, like Richard Nixon, "I am not

a crook," since no one supposes he is; but the bent of his policy, the tone of his rhetoric, the signals of his response have all enabled, indeed encouraged, the atmosphere of greed.

A few years ago our national heroes were men like Jonas Salk and Martin Luther King and Walter Reuther, but now it's an industrial manager like Lee Iacocca, of Pinto fame, whose book is supposed to show even morons how to become millionaires. Iacocca stars in a television commercial that wonderfully articulates the spirit of the times: he strides through a factory in heroic style, blaring out the virtues of his product, while behind him follows a group of autoworkers, mute and cheerful, happy with the beneficence of Lee the First.

The lure of an earlier America, or the corruptions of nostalgia. Whether intuitively or by calculation, the Reaganites grasped how deeply the collective imagination of this country responded to "pictures" of an earlier, often mythic America—"pictures" of small towns, rugged personal virtues, family stability, and sturdy yeomen cultivating their own farms. The less such "pictures" correspond to social reality, the greater their appeal, for it is obviously more pleasant to reflect upon the America of Franklin and Jefferson than that of Exxon and IBM. And while much of this pastoral nostalgia is manipulated by political hucksters, who have apparently learned something from the commercials of Marlboro cigarettes and Busch beer, there is still, it is important to remember, something authentic being exploited here, a memory prettied up and sweetened but a genuine memory nonetheless.

Badly shaken by Watergate, the Vietnam War, and the countercultural excesses of the late 1960s, many Americans have come to yearn for a return to "traditional values," even if that return was being sponsored politically by a nouveau-riche class which aspired most of all to conspicuous consumption. In any case, we are paying now for the crude anti-Americanism, the feckless nose-thumbing and flag-burning that marked a good part of the counterculture in the late 1960s. We are paying for its insensitivity to native speech and sentiment, an insensitivity that, strangely, is itself part of American tradition. Much of the Reaganite reaction, though eventuating in concrete socioeconomic policies, drew upon feelings of hurt that were held by people not necessarily reactionaries or even conservatives. These feelings were exploited skillfully; many of us on the left quite underestimated the power of vague, incantatory appeals to "tradition"—just as we also warned, to little avail, that the hijinks of "the young" in the late 1960s would be paid for later by the workers, the poor, women, and minorities.

We live in a curiously mixed situation. On the one hand, a managed passivity, submission to television captions, apparent indifference to social suffering, political chicanery, and a blundering president—the expected elements of a "mass society." On the other hand, strong new popular movements that mobilize previously silent segments of the population to struggle over issues like abortion, prayer in the schools, the death penalty, and so on. Such movements are hardly symptoms of a "mass society"; they represent a shrewd appropriation by the right of methods and energies through which labor and liberals helped create a (sort of) welfare state.

Fundamentalism is familiar enough in American history, but the political energies and moral virulence characterizing it today may be rather new. When lined with religious passion and cast as agent of traditional values, right-wing politics takes on a formidable strength.

Pastoral nostalgia, individualist appeals, traditional values, religious fervor—it is the mixture of all these into one stream of collective sentiment that the Reaganites have managed. And up to a point it has worked: many Americans do "feel better about their country," if only because they have a president who says what they wish to hear. One reason this intellectual scam has worked is that so far, with perhaps the exception of Mario Cuomo, no political leader in the opposition has grasped emotionally the power of native speech and symbol. If, as I believe, we are paying for the irresponsibility of the countercultural left, we are also paying for the desiccation of liberalism, which in the figure of Jimmy Carter was reduced to a technological cipher.

It would be foolhardy in a few pages to try to sort out the many strands of American individualism, still one of the strongest components of national myth and belief. The Reaganites do have some claim upon this tradition: there is a clear line of descent from a corrupted late Emersonianism to the "rugged individualism" of Herbert Hoover to the "possessive individualism" of today (to possess: to grab). But the right has no historical ground for the *exclusiveness* of its claim within the American individualist tradition. There is, in reality, no single tradition; there is only an interweaving of many elements in complex, confused, and often contradictory ways. If individualism has often been used to justify economic depredation, it has also provided support to social critics standing alone, and independently, against government and mob, from the Mexican to the Vietnam wars. What is sad is that, through a default of will and imagination, the speech and symbols of individualism have been allowed to fall into the hands of the right.

The power of ideology (or: In America a little goes a long way). Reagan's most effective slogan has been "Get the government off our backs." It appeals to Americans who transfer their frustrations to "the bureaucrats." It appeals to Americans whose small businesses have been squeezed or destroyed by giant competitors. It appeals to Americans bewildered by the merger mania, known in earlier days as the concentration of capital. But above all, it appeals to the executives and managers of Big Business whose institutions were rescued from probable collapse by the welfare state but who never reconciled themselves to the agents of their rescue, and who now feel free to release their yearning for the good old days of "rugged individualism" and union busting.

Sensible people know that the talk about getting the government out of economic life has not led to a significant decline of government intervention in the economy. Indeed, it could not. It has only changed, in a reactionary direction, the social character and goals of government intervention. The policies of the Federal Reserve Board constitute a major intervention into economic life. The readiness of the federal government to bail out Lockheed, Chrysler, and Penn Central is quite as decisive an intervention as a program, if there were one, to help bankrupt farmers and create jobs for the unemployed. As John Kenneth Galbraith tartly observes, "Senator Jesse Helms stands staunchly and rhetorically for the free market and for a uniquely rigorous quota and licensing system for the tobacco producers (or landowners) who help to assure his election" (*New York Review of Books*, June 26, 1986).

About one thing we can be quite certain: the interpenetration of state and society, government and economy is an inescapable fact of modern life. Serious conservatives know this. Deputy Secretary of the Treasury Richard Darman says in a moment of candor: "We've been in the business of economic planning as long as we've been in the business of practical politics" (*New Republic*, May 5, 1986). The only question, but a big one, is whether the government's economic role will be progressive or regressive.

Exposing the cant about "getting the government off our backs," while necessary, is not likely to suffice. For the ideology behind such talk does speak to certain realities: the visible bureaucratization of large institutions, whether private corporations or segments of the state. But this ideology does not speak honestly or realistically to these facts of modern life. Nevertheless, especially when fused with nostalgia for American individualism, this ideological gambit is going to be effective, at least until put to the test of crisis—what can it say to the increasing poverty of even these boom years?—as well as to the test of deceitful practice—what credence does the "free market" rhetoric of a Jesse Helms merit when set against his insistence on government privileges for his tobacco constituency?

The ideology of a reclaimed laissez-faire is having a "run" in some parts of the industrialized world, especially because of social democratic and liberal inadequacies, though only in the United States and Great Britain has it had a modest economic success. The battle between advocates and opponents of the welfare state—which, like it or not, today has greater political urgency than an abstract counterposition between capitalism and socialism—will continue to the end of this century. But meanwhile there are some new ideological wrinkles.

The corporations have discovered the importance of ideas, or at least the manipulation of ideas. Some nine or ten years ago I noticed, in one of those institutional ads that corporations print on the *New York Times* op ed page, a quotation from the literary critic Lionel Trilling. This struck me as a turning point in intellectual life, or at least in our public relations, coming as it did only a few years after some writers had proclaimed "the end of ideology." In the last decade, under the shrewd guardianship of the neoconservative intellectuals—who offer their thoughts to the corporations, though not for free—corporate America has discovered the pragmatic uses of ideology, the importance of entering intellectual debate, and consequently has poured millions into foundations, magazines, conferences. Mobil and Exxon, borrowing apparently from the pages of *Public Interest*, offer solemn essays on political economy; the investment house of Shearson Lehman flashes snappy statements on television about the virtues of capitalism. Credit for enticing the corporations into ideological battle must go in part to Irving Kristol, who has made himself into a sort of back-room broker between the corporations and the Republican Party on one hand and available intellectuals on the other. He has taught American businessmen, at least some of them, the elementary lesson that social struggle takes place, perhaps most of all, in people's heads and that just as dropping some change into the cultural programs of public broadcasting helps create an "aura," so the interests of the business community may be served by subsidizing magazines like *New Criterion* and *Public Interest*, as well as the network of institutes, committees, foundations, and journals in which the neocons flourish.

There are times, however, when our corporate leaders forget all the babble about social responsibility and lapse into mere truth. Here is John Akers, chief executive of IBM, on divesting in South Africa: "If we elect to leave, it will be a business decision. . . . We are not in business to conduct moral activity. We are not in business to conduct socially responsible action. We are in business to conduct business" (*New York Times*, April 23, 1986). One can almost hear Kristol gently remonstrating: Yes, yes, John, but do you have to *say* it?

The war whoop of chauvinism. Shrewdly seizing upon a popular reaction against the often vulgar and mindless anti-Americanism of the

late 1960s, the Reagan administration has succeeded partly in blotting
out memories of the disastrous and destructive American intervention
in Vietnam. A new national mood has been programmed. It's symbol-
ized, half in myth, half in parody, by Rambo. It is released in the un-
sportsmanlike displays at the Los Angeles Olympics. It is embodied,
more fiercely, in the indefensible Reaganite policy of intervening in
Nicaragua. And it is raised to a pitch of madness in the Star Wars program
(which E. P. Thompson has shrewdly described as an instance of American "individualism" gone berserk . . . the lone cowboy now ascending
the heavens to clean up the rustlers). This new national mood draws
upon two contradictory emotions held with about equal intensity: first,
everybody has been kicking poor little America around; and second,
we're the strongest country in the world (as was proved once and for
all in Grenada) and we're going to straighten things out, even if we have
to call in John Wayne to help out Ron.

2

A consequence of these transformations in public discourse has been
a debasement in the social tone of American life, the texture of shared
feelings, the unspoken impulses and biases. About such things one can
only speak impressionistically, but we all recognize them. They strike
upon our nerves. We are living in a moment of moral smallness, a
curdling of generosity, a collapse of idealism. I don't mean to suggest
that most ordinary Americans have become morally bad—of course not;
only that the moral styles, the tones of speech and qualities of symbol
which the Reagan administration and its journalistic and intellectual
allies encourage are pinched and narrow-spirited, sometimes downright
mean.

How else do you explain the readiness of a thirty-five-year-old arbitrager publicly to say that adding "a library and a room for the *au pair*
girl" would come to four or five million dollars—and this at a time when
thousands of New Yorkers had no homes last winter? This chap might
have felt the same way at an earlier moment, but he would have been
too cautious or ashamed to say it. Now, in the Reagan era, it's acceptable.
Or, for that matter, how else do you explain that someone like Ed Koch
can gain favor through a smirking double-talk that shows the folks in
front of the tube how to put down blacks without quite saying so.

To live under an administration that featured such notables as James
Watt and Rita Lavelle; in which the attorney general declares poverty
in America to be merely "anecdotal," and the president himself (ignoring
massive evidence, some of it accumulated by his own administration)
announces that people go hungry in America only if they lack infor-

mation on how to get help; in which the head of the Civil Rights Commission is part Uncle Tom and part, it seems, huckster; in which the president dares to compare the Somocista contras, some of them proven killers, with Washington and Jefferson—is to recall again the force of Brecht's sentence about another (still more) evil time: "He who laughs has not yet heard the terrible tidings."

The favored tone of worldly, or sometimes macho, indifference to the plight of the jobless and the homeless cuts through the whole range of the people in power and their intellectual allies. The sensibilities of the country's elites, all those who make policy and shape opinion, harden. We see it in the systematic refusal of the Reagan administration even to consider programs that would provide jobs for the unemployed; in the steady deterioration of OSHA-determined work safety regulations in factories; in the disdain lining even the surface of official policy toward blacks; in the steady efforts of the civil rights division of the Justice Department to sabotage affirmative action; in the surrender of the Koch administration in New York City to luxury developers; in the admiration shown a gun-toter like Bernhard Goetz; in the mere fact that a rag like the *New York Post* can survive.

3

How deep and durable is this shift in public sentiment? Will the rightward turn continue after Reagan? For that matter, *is* there a turn to the right? A not-very-profound article in the *Atlantic* (May 1986) argues that there has not been one. Its authors, Thomas Ferguson and Joel Rogers, produce an array of poll results showing that majorities of respondents still favor many of the programs associated with liberalism. How then, you may wonder, did Reagan manage to get reelected? Simple, conclude our authors: the economic situation got better and most people vote their pocketbooks.

This would be comforting if true, but at the very least it requires complication. If a majority of Americans favor liberal measures yet a majority of voters chose Reagan, doesn't this suggest that the appeal of the president and his slogans was deeper, more telling than any (perhaps fading or residual or formal) attachment to liberal programs? The polls do not measure *intensity* of commitment, or which of two conflicting sets of opinions held simultaneously may be the stronger. Evidently, for many Americans the appeal of Reagan and at least some of what he represents was stronger than the attachment to welfare-state measures. And that would seem to signify a shift to the right, would it not?

I don't claim to know how strong or lasting this shift will prove to be. One need only look at the dominant style of opinion within the

Democratic Party to see that the rightward shift has all but overcome those who are supposed to resist it. (The code word is "pragmatic.") The very tone of the opposition, such as it is, which the leading Democrats adopt seems clear evidence that the Reaganites have come to set the terms of the debate. Liberal proposals are virtually invisible at the Democratic top. When was the last time that even Senator Ted Kennedy spoke out in favor of his once-featured project of a national health bill? Or that any of the leading Democrats remembered the Humphrey-Hawkins Full Employment Act? Except in their response to Reagan's outrageous feeler about canceling SALT II, the posture of the leading Democrats is defensive—or, worse still, acquiescent, as when Senator Bill Bradley votes for aid to the Nicaraguan contras.

4

Few things about the national condition are more depressing than the collapse of American liberalism. To recall Lionel Trilling's once-famous remark of the 1950s—that in America liberalism is the only viable political tradition—is to thrust oneself back into another world. In the face of the Reaganite victory, the organizational and ideological collapse of American liberalism has been astonishing. Hardly a politician dares acknowledge himself to be a liberal, the very word itself having come to seem a political handicap.

Of the older intellectual spokesmen for liberalism, Arthur Schlesinger, Jr. and John Kenneth Galbraith are still heard from on occasion, but they are understandably intent upon writing their own books and perhaps, again understandably, are weary of polemic. Schlesinger advances a consoling theory—consoling if true—about the periodicity of American politics, according to which the next swing of the pendulum will bring us happily back to liberalism (but why *must* the pendulum keep swinging?). Galbraith aims his neatly ironic shafts against Reaganomics, but with a world-weariness that seems to despair of ever again striking a blow that will tell. As for other social analysts who defend liberal measures and values—writers like Robert Kuttner, Barbara Ehrenreich, Michael Harrington, Robert Reich, Jeff Faux, among others—they are mostly spokesmen for the democratic left who have been forced, in these trying times, to pick up the slack of liberalism. What might be called mainstream liberalism seems quite unable to attract talented new advocates who can speak to audiences beyond the confines of the academy.

Why, one wonders, has American liberalism suffered so severe a decline? That there should have been losses; that the usual crew of opportunists should desert; that veterans would grow tired and step aside—all were to be expected. But so utter a rout? Is it possible, as some writers of the sectarian left have said, that liberalism in America has "exhausted itself"? A full answer to this question will have to wait for others, but here let me note a few possible causes for the unhappy state of American liberalism.

Fundamentally, I'd suggest, we have been witnessing the all-but-inevitable disintegration which affects every party or movement that has held power for a length of time. Success breeds complacency, obtuseness, and corruption, and these in turn make for an incapacity to see, let alone confront, the problems created by success. As long as the American economy was expanding and Keynesian prescriptions were more or less working, New Deal liberalism and its offshoots could retain vitality. But once they had to confront problems no longer soluble through the by now conventional New Deal measures—problems like the Vietnam War, third-world eruptions (Iran), the radical transformation of the world economy, new productive techniques, inflation, and so on—liberalism fell apart. The time had come for policies of a social-democratic slant but these an increasingly insecure liberalism would not approach. The comforts of office, the fears of yesterday's innovators before the risks of tomorrow's innovations—all disabled American liberalism.

Where in the 1930s liberalism was at least in part based on mass movements, notably the trade unions, and could claim a large popular suffrage, by the 1970s it had narrowed into an electoral apparatus or "political class" getting on in years and too much at ease with itself and its received ideas. By contrast, it should in honesty be said, at least some conservatives tried to engage in programmatic thought, speculating in their newly developed think tanks on the problems and contradictions, some contingent but others perhaps fundamental, of the welfare state in a capitalist economy. (That the welfare state might have inherent contradictions was an idea that rarely, if ever, surfaced in liberal thought.) After a time, the once-magical names of Roosevelt and Kennedy lost their glamour; new generations appeared that had little interest in the past and less capacity for memory. Liberalism, once at least occasionally linked with social insurgency, now came to be identified with a troubled status quo: a government that had dragged us into an indefensible war in Vietnam and by the mid-1970s was encountering economic difficulties (stagflation, unemployment) for which it knew no remedies.

The bureaucratization of liberalism, perhaps an unavoidable cost of its success, also meant that it came increasingly to depend on the intervention of the judiciary, especially on such difficult matters as school busing; and this too contributed to the decline of its popular base. As

liberalism lost its charge of innovative energy, the conservative movement appropriated many of the techniques of liberalism's earlier, more
heroic days. For what the conservatives now undertook to do, and in
part succeeded in doing, was to build articulate popular constituencies.

With Jimmy Carter's victory in 1976, the disintegration of American
liberalism quickened. A tradition that in the past had at least partly
drawn upon social idealism and popular commitment now dwindled into
the outlook of an intelligent technocrat. As the political scientists celebrated the ascendency of "pragmatism" (a term that relieves many
people of the need for thinking), another triumph was in preparation,
that of the ideologically aroused Reaganites.

Well, then, is liberalism "exhausted"—not for the moment but historically, finally? Is it being swept off the historical stage, as dogmatists
of right and left gleefully assert? If so, the situation of the American
left, precarious enough already, is far worse than we might suppose, for
every lesson of American history teaches us that the left in America
flourishes mostly during the times when liberalism flourishes. In any
case, it is clearly probable that a collapse of liberalism will benefit the
right far more than the left.

We ought to be skeptical about theories of liberalism's "exhaustion,"
if only because they bear an embarrassing resemblance to earlier, dubious theories about capitalism's "inevitable collapse." American liberalism at its best has a rich tradition: a worldview devoted to political
freedom, pluralist ways of life, and programs for social change. This
liberalism has seen bad times, but found itself again; some of its leading
figures have yielded to shoddy deals, others have stood firm by first
principles. In bad shape right now, it could regain cogency if it were to
confront socioeconomic problems more complex, and requiring more
radical answers, than those of the New Deal era. Neither success nor
failure is ordained: men and women still make their history, at least
some of it.

5

Criticism and more criticism—that's the need of the moment, the
need for tomorrow. Criticism of an administration that exalts greed and
ignores need. Criticism of military chauvinism. Criticism of all those
who, in the name of an abstract equality, would deny blacks a few steps
toward equality through affirmative action. Criticism of every deal or
accord with authoritarian dictatorships. And criticism of "our side" too,
of the sluggishness of portions of the labor movement, of the collapse
of the hopes raised by the French Socialists, of the intellectual drab-
ness of much social democracy.

One needn't be a socialist to engage in such criticism. On some matters, such as the environment, not being a socialist may even render the criticism more effective. But to scan our society from the perspective of democratic socialism offers at least this advantage: it enables a deep-going criticism of the imbalances of wealth and power in our corporate-dominated society, so that we can see those imbalances not as mere blemishes but as injustices built into the very structure of capitalist economy. Perhaps not an advantage in the immediate tactical sense, but very much so for serious intellectual work.

Even if the criticism is not as "fundamental" as we might like, let it be heard. Let people of determination, steady workers with some humor and no fanaticism, keep saying: "This is not what America is supposed to be, this is not how human beings should live."

Writing and the Holocaust

Our subject resists the usual capacities of mind. We may read the Holocaust as the central event of this century; we may register the pain of its unhealed wounds; but finally we must acknowledge that it leaves us intellectually disarmed, staring helplessly at the reality, or, if you prefer, the mystery, of mass extermination. There is little likelihood of finding a rational structure of explanation for the Holocaust: it forms a sequence of events without historical or moral precedent. To think about ways in which the literary imagination might "use" the Holocaust is to entangle ourselves with a multitude of problems for which no aesthetic can prepare us.

The Holocaust is continuous with, indeed forms a sequence of events within, Western history, and at the same time it is a unique historical enterprise. To study its genesis within Western history may help us discover its roots in traditional anti-Semitism, fed in turn by Christian myth, German romanticism, and the breakdown of capitalism in twentieth-century Europe between the wars. But it is a grave error to "elevate" the Holocaust into an occurrence outside of history, a sort of

From *The New Republic* 195 (October 27, 1986):17.

diabolic visitation, for then we tacitly absolve its human agents of responsibility. To do this is a grave error even if, so far and perhaps forever, we lack adequate categories for comprehending how such a sequence of events could occur. The Holocaust was long prepared for in the history of Western civilization, though not all those who engaged in the preparation knew what they were doing or would have welcomed the outcome.

In the concentration camps set up by the Nazis, such as those at Dachau and Buchenwald, there was an endless quantity of sadism, some of it the spontaneous doings of psychopaths and thugs given total command by the Nazi government, and some of it the result of a calculated policy taking into cynical account the consequences of allowing psychopaths and thugs total command. Piles of corpses accumulated in these camps. Yet a thin continuity can be detected between earlier locales of brutality and the "concentrationary universe." In some pitiable sense, the prisoners in these camps still lived—they were starved, broken, tormented, but they still lived. A faint margin of space could sometimes be carved out for the human need to maintain community and personality, even while both were being destroyed. Horrible these camps surely were; but even as they pointed toward, they did not yet constitute the "Final Solution."

The Nazis had an idea. To dehumanize systematically both guards and prisoners, torturers and tortured, meant to create a realm of subjugation no longer responsive to the common norms of human society; and from this process of dehumanization they had themselves set in motion, the Nazis could then "conclude" that, indeed, Jews were not human. This Nazi idea would lead to and draw upon sadism, but at least among the leaders and theoreticians, it was to be distinguished from mere sadism: it was an abstract rage, the most terrible of all rages. This Nazi idea formed a low parody of the messianism that declared that once mankind offered a warrant of faith and conduct, deliverance would come to earth in the shape of a savior bringing the good days—a notion corrupted by false messiahs into a "forcing of days" and by totalitarian movements into the physical elimination of "contaminating" races and classes. There was also in Nazi ideology a low parody of that mania for "completely" remaking societies and cultures that has marked modern political life.

When the Nazis established their realm of subjection in the concentration camps, they brought the impulse to nihilism, so strong in modern culture, to a point of completion no earlier advocate had supposed possible. The Italian-Jewish writer Primo Levi, soon after arriving at Auschwitz, was told by a Nazi guard: *Hier ist kein warum,* here there is no why, here nothing need be explained. This passing observation by a shrewd thug provides as good an insight into the world of the camps as anything found in the entire scholarly literature. What we may still find difficult to grasp is the peculiar blend of ideology and nihilism— the way these two elements of thought, seemingly in friction, were able to join harmoniously, thereby releasing the satanic energies of Nazism.

By now we have an enormous body of memoirs and studies describing the experience of the concentration camps. Inevitably, there are clashes of remembrance and opinion. For the psychoanalyst Bruno Bettelheim, held captive in Dachau and Buchenwald in 1939, it was apparently still possible to cope with life in the camps, if only through inner moral resistance, a struggle to "understand" that might "safeguard [one's ego] in such a way that, if by any good luck he should regain liberty, [the prisoner] would be approximately the same person he was" before being deprived of liberty. Precisely this seemed impossible to Jean Améry, a gifted Austrian-Jewish writer who had been imprisoned in Auschwitz. No survivor, no one who had ever been tortured by the SS, he later wrote, could be "approximately the same person" as before.

Even to hope for survival meant, in Améry's view, to "capitulate unconditionally in the face of reality," and that reality was neither more nor less than the unlimited readiness of the SS to kill. The victim lived under "an absolute sovereign" whose mission—a mission of pleasure— was torture, "in an orgy of unchecked self-expansion." Thereby "the transformation of the person into flesh became complete." As for "the word"—which for Améry signified something akin to what "safeguarding the ego" meant for Bettelheim—it "always dies when the claim of some reality is total." For then no space remains between thought and everything external to thought.

It would be impudent to choose between the testimonies of Bettelheim and Améry. A partial explanation for their differences of memory and understanding may be that Bettelheim was a prisoner in 1939 and Améry in 1943–45. Bettelheim's ordeal predated slightly the "Final Solution," while Améry was held captive in the Auschwitz that Hannah Arendt quite soberly called a "corpse factory." It is also possible that these writers, in reflecting upon more or less similar experiences, were revealing "natural" differences in human response. We cannot be certain.

By the time the Nazis launched their "Final Solution" such differences of testimony had become relatively insignificant. The Holocaust reached its point of culmination as the systematic and impersonal extermination of millions of human beings, denied life, and even death as mankind had traditionally conceived it, simply because they fell under the abstract category of "Jew." It became clear that the sadism before and during the "Final Solution" on the trains that brought the Jews to the camps and in the camps themselves was not just incidental or gratuitous; it was a carefully worked-out preparation for the gas chambers. But for the Nazi leaders, originating theoreticians of death, what mattered most was the *program* of extermination. No personal qualities or accomplishments of the victims, no features of character or appearance, mattered. The abstract perversity of categorization declaring Jews to be *Untermenschen* as determined by allegedly biological traits was unconditional.

No absolute division of kind existed between concentration and death camps, and some, like the grouping of camps at Auschwitz, contained quarters for both slave laborers and gas chambers, with recurrent "selections" from the former feeding the latter. Still, the distinction between the two varieties of camps has some descriptive and analytic value: it enables us to distinguish between what was and was not historically unique about the Holocaust.

Whatever was unique took place in the death camps, forming a sequence of events radically different from all previous butcheries in the history of mankind. Revenge, enslavement, dispersion, large-scale slaughter of enemies, all are a commonplace of the past; but the physical elimination of a categorized segment of mankind was, both as idea and fact, new. "The destruction of Europe's Jews," Claude Lanzmann has written, "cannot be logically deduced from any . . . system of presuppositions. . . . Between the conditions that permitted extermination and the extermination itself—the *fact* of the extermination—there is a break in continuity, a hiatus, an abyss." That abyss forms the essence of the Holocaust.

2

I cannot think of another area of literary discourse in which a single writer has exerted so strong, if diffused, an influence as Theodore Adorno has on discussions of literature and the Holocaust. What Adorno offered in the early 1950s was not a complete text or even a fully developed argument. Yet his few scattered remarks had an immediate impact, evidently because they brought out feelings held by many people.

"After Auschwitz," wrote Adorno, "to write a poem is barbaric." It means to "squeeze aesthetic pleasure out of artistic representation of the naked bodily pain of those who have been knocked down by rifle butts. . . . Through aesthetic principles or stylization . . . the unimaginable ordeal still appears as if it had some ulterior purpose. It is transfigured and stripped of some of its horror, and with this, injustice is already done to the victims."

Adorno was by no means alone in expressing such sentiments, nor in recognizing that his sentiments, no matter how solemnly approved, were not likely to keep anyone from trying to represent through fictions or evoke through poetic symbols the concentration and death camps. A Yiddish poet, Aaron Tsaytlin, wrote in a similar vein after the Holocaust: "Were Jeremiah to sit by the ashes of Israel today, he would not cry out a lamentation. . . . The Almighty Himself would be powerless to open his well of tears. He would maintain a deep silence. For even an outcry is now a lie, even tears are mere literature, even prayers are false."

Tsaytlin's concluding sentence anticipated the frequently asserted but as frequently ignored claim that all responses to the Holocaust are inadequate, including, and perhaps especially, those made with the most exalted sentiments and language. Here, for instance, is Piotr Rawicz, a Jewish writer born in the Ukraine who after his release from the camps wrote in French. In his novel *Blood from the Sky*, Rawicz put down certain precepts that the very existence of his book seems to violate: "The 'literary manner' is an obscenity. . . . Literature [is] the art, occasionally remunerative, of rummaging in vomit. And yet, it would appear, one has to write. So as to trick loneliness, so as to trick other people."

Looking back at such remarks, we may wonder what these writers were struggling to express, what half-formed or hidden feelings prompted their outcries. I will offer a few speculations, confining myself to Adorno.

Adorno was not so naive as to prescribe for writers a line of conduct that would threaten their very future as writers. Through a dramatic outburst he probably meant to focus upon the sheer difficulty—the literary risk, the moral peril—of dealing with the Holocaust in literature. It was as if he were saying: Given the absence of usable norms through which to grasp the meaning (if there is one) of the scientific extermination of millions, given the intolerable gap between the aesthetic conventions and the loathsome realities of the Holocaust, and given the improbability of coming up with images and symbols that might serve as "objective correlatives" for events that the imagination can hardly take in, writers in the post-Holocaust era might be wise to be silent. Silent, at least, about the Holocaust.

This warning, if such it was, had a certain prophetic force. It anticipated, first, the common but mistaken notion that literature somehow has an obligation to encompass all areas of human experience, no matter how extreme or impenetrable they might be; and, second, the corruptions of the mass media that would suppose itself equipped to master upon demand any theme or subject.

Adorno might have been rehearsing a traditional aesthetic idea: that the representation of a horrible event, especially if in drawing upon literary skills it achieves a certain graphic power, could serve to domesticate it, rendering it familiar and in some sense even tolerable, and thereby shearing away part of the horror. The comeliness of even the loosest literary forms is likely to soften the impact of what is being rendered, and in most renderings of imaginary situations we tacitly expect and welcome this. But with a historical event such as the Holocaust—an event regarding which the phrase "such as" cannot really be employed—the chastening aspects of literary mimesis can be felt to be misleading, a questionable way of reconciling us with the irreconcilable or of projecting a symbolic "transcendence" that in actuality is no more than a reflex of our baffled will.

Adorno might have had in mind the possibility of an insidious relation between the represented (or even the merely evoked) Holocaust and the spectator enthralled precisely as, or perhaps even because, he is appalled—a relation carrying a share of voyeuristic sadomasochism. Can we really say that in reading a memoir or novel about the Holocaust, or in seeing a film such as *Shoah*, we gain the pleasure, or catharsis, that is customarily associated with the aesthetic transaction? More disquieting, can we be sure that we do not gain a sort of illicit pleasure from our pained submission to such works? I do not know how to answer these questions, which threaten many of our usual assumptions about what constitutes an aesthetic experience; but I think that even the most disciplined scholar of the Holocaust ought every once in a while to reexamine the nature of his or her responses.

More speculative still is the thought that Adorno, perhaps with only a partial awareness, was turning back to a "primitive" religious feeling—the feeling that there are some things in our experience, or some aspects of the universe, that are too terrible to be looked at directly.

In ancient mythologies and religions there are things and beings that are not to be named. They may be the supremely good or supremely bad, but for mortals they are the unutterable, since there is felt to be a limit to what man may see or dare, certainly to what he may meet. Perseus would turn to stone if he were to look directly at the serpent-headed Medusa, though he would be safe if he looked at her only through a reflection in a mirror or a shield (this latter being, as I shall argue, the very strategy that the cannier writers have adopted in dealing with the Holocaust).

Perhaps dimly, Adorno wished to suggest that the Holocaust might be regarded as a secular equivalent—if there can be such a thing—of that which in the ancient myths could not be gazed at or named directly; that before which men had to avert their eyes; that which in the properly responsive witness would arouse the "holy dread" Freud saw as the essence of taboos. And in such taboos the prohibition was imposed not in order to enforce ignorance but to regulate, or guard against the consequences of, knowledge.

How this taboo might operate without the sanctions and structure of an organized religion and its linked mythology I cannot grasp: it would require a quantity of shared or communal discipline beyond anything we can suppose. Adorno must have known this as well as anyone else. He must have known that in our culture the concept of limit serves mostly as a barrier or hurdle to be overcome, not as a perimeter of respect. Perhaps his remarks are to be taken as a hopeless admonition, a plea for the improvisation of limit that he knew would not and indeed could not be heeded, but which it was necessary to make.

3

Holocaust writings make their primary claim, I would say, through facts recorded or remembered. About this most extreme of human experiences there cannot be too much documentation, and what matters most in such materials is exactitude: the sober number, the somber date. Beyond that, Holocaust writings often reveal the helplessness of the mind before an evil that cannot quite be imagined, or the helplessness of the imagination before an evil that cannot quite be understood. This shared helplessness is the major reason for placing so high a value on the memoir, a kind of writing in which the author has no obligation to do anything but, in accurate and sober terms, tell what he experienced and witnessed.

Can we so readily justify our feelings about the primary worth of reliable testimony? Prudential arguments seem increasingly dubious here, since it should by now be clear that remembering does not necessarily forestall repetition. The instinctive respect we accord honest testimony, regardless of whether it is "well written," may in part be due to a persuasion that the aesthetic is not the primary standard for judgments of human experience, and that there can be, indeed often enough have been, situations in which aesthetic and moral standards come into conflict. Our respect for testimony may also be due in part to an unspoken persuasion that we owe something to the survivors who expose themselves to the trauma of recollection: we feel that we should listen to them apart from whether it "does any good." As for the millions who did not survive, it would be mere indulgence to suppose that any ceremonies of recollection could "make up for" or "transcend" their destruction—all such chatter, too frequent in writings about the Holocaust, is at best a futility of eloquence. Still, there are pieties that civilized people want to confirm even if, sometimes because, these are no more than gestures.

Another piety is to be invoked here. We may feel that heeding the survivors' testimony contributes to the fund of shared consciousness, which also means to our own precarious sense of being, whether individual or collective, and that, somehow, this is good. Henry James speaks somewhere of an ideal observer upon whom nothing is lost, who witnesses the entirety of the human lot, and though James in his concerns is about as far from something like the Holocaust as any writer could be, I think it just to borrow his vision of consciousness for our very different ends. The past summoned by Holocaust memoirs not only tells us something unbearable, and therefore unforgettable, about the life of mankind; it is a crucial part of our own time, if not of our direct experience. To keep the testimony of Holocaust witnesses in the forefront of our consciousness may not make us "better" people, but it may at least bring a touch of accord with our sense of the time we have lived in and where we have come from.

There is still another use of this testimony, and that is to keep the Holocaust firmly within the bounds of history, so that it will not end up as a preface to apocalypse or eschatology, or, worse still, decline into being the legend of a small people. "Nobody," said the historian Ignacy Schipper in Majdanek, "will *want* to believe us, because our disaster is the disaster of the entire civilized world." Schipper's phrasing merits close attention. He does not say that the disaster was experienced by the entire civilized world, which might entail a sentimental "universalizing" of the Holocaust; he says that the disaster of the Jews was (or should have been) shared by the entire civilized world, so that what happened to "us" might form a weight upon the consciousness of that world, even as we may recognize that sooner or later the world will seek to transfer it to some realm "beyond" history, a realm at once more exalted and less accusatory. Yet history is exactly where the Holocaust must remain, and for that, there can never be enough testimony.

Chaim Kaplan's Warsaw diary, covering a bit less than a year from its opening date of September 1, 1938, is a document still recognizably within the main tradition of Western writing: a man observes crucial events and strives to grasp their significance. Kaplan's diary shows the discipline of a trained observer; his prose is lucid and restrained; he records the effort of Warsaw Jewry to keep a fragment of its culture alive even as it stumbles into death; and he reveals a torn soul wondering what premises of faith, or delusion, sustain his "need to record." Barely, precariously, we are still in the world of the human as we have understood it, for nothing can be more human than to keep operating with familiar categories of thought while discovering they will no longer suffice.

Elie Wiesel's first book, *Night*, written simply and without rhetorical indulgence, is a slightly fictionalized record of his sufferings as a boy in Auschwitz and during a forced march together with his father and other prisoners through the frozen countryside to Buchenwald. The father dies of dysentery in Buchenwald, and the boy—or the writer remembering himself as a boy—reveals his guilty relief at feeling that the death of his father has left him "free at last," not as any son might feel but in the sense that now he may be able to save himself without the burden of an ailing father. No sensitive reader will feel an impulse to judgment here. Indeed, that is one of the major effects of honest testimony about the Holocaust—it dissolves any impulse to judge what the victims did or did not do, since there are situations so extreme that it seems immoral to make judgments about those who must endure them. We are transported here into a subworld where freedom and moral sensibility may survive in memory but cannot be exercised in practice. Enforced degradation forms the penultimate step toward the ovens.

The ovens dominate the camps that the Nazis, not inaccurately, called *anus mundi*. Filip Mueller's *Eyewitness Auschwitz* is the artless account of being transported from his native Slovakia in April 1942 to Auschwitz, where he worked for two and a half years as a *Sonderkommando*, or assistant at the gas chambers. Somehow Mueller survived. His narrative is free of verbal embellishment or thematic reflection; he indulges neither in self-apology nor self-attack; he writes neither art nor history. His book is simply the story of a simple man who processed many corpses. Even in this book, terrible beyond any that I have ever read, there are still a few touches recalling what we take to be humanity: efforts at theodicy by men who cannot justify their faith, a recital of the kaddish by doomed prisoners who know that no one else will say it for them. In the world Mueller served, "the transformation of the person into flesh" and of flesh into dust "became complete." It was a world for which, finally, we have no words.

But isn't there, a skeptical voice may interject, a touch of empiricist naiveté in such high claims for Holocaust memoirs? Memory can be treacherous among people who have suffered terribly and must feel a measure of guilt at being alive at all. Nor can we be sure of the truth supplied by damaged and overwrought witnesses, for whatever knowledge we may claim about these matters is likely to come mainly from the very memoirs we find ourselves submitting, however uneasily, to critical judgment.

The skeptical voice is cogent, and I would only say in reply that we are not helpless before the accumulated mass of recollection. Our awe before the suffering and our respect for the sufferers does not disable us from making discriminations of value, tone, authority. There remain the usual historical tests, through both external check and internal comparison; and there is still the reader's ear, bending toward credence or doubt.

The test of the ear is a delicate one, entailing a shift from testimony to witness—a shift that, except perhaps with regard to the scrappiest of chronicles, seems unavoidable. Reading Holocaust memoirs we respond not just to their accounts of what happened; we respond also to qualities of being, tremors of sensibility, as these emerge even from the bloodiest pages. We respond to the modesty or boastfulness, the candor or evasiveness, the self-effacement or self-promotion of the writers. We respond, most of all, to a quality that might be called moral poise, by which I mean a readiness to engage in a complete reckoning with the past, insofar as there can be one—a strength of remembrance that leads the writer into despair and then perhaps a little beyond it, so that he does not flinch from anything, neither shame nor degradation, yet refuses to indulge in those outbursts of self-pity, sometimes sliding into self-aggrandizement, that mar a fair number of Holocaust memoirs.

But is there not something shameful in subjecting the work of survivors to this kind of scrutiny? Perhaps so; yet in choosing to become writers, they have no choice but to accept this burden.

The Holocaust was structured to destroy the very idea of private being. It was a sequence of events entirely "out there," in the objective world, the world of force and power. Yet as we read Holocaust memoirs and reaffirm their value as evidence, we find ourselves veering—less by choice than necessity—from the brute external to the fragile subjective, from matter to voice, from story to storyteller. And this leaves us profoundly uneasy, signifying that our earlier stress upon the value of testimony has now been complicated, perhaps even compromised, by the introduction of aesthetic considerations. We may wish with all our hearts to yield entirely to the demands of memory and evidence, but simply by virtue of reading, we cannot forget that the diarist was a person formed before and the memoirist a person formed after the Holocaust. We are ensnared in the cruelty of remembering, a compounded cruelty, in which our need for truthful testimony lures us into tests of authenticity.

That, in any case, is how we read. I bring as a "negative" witness a memoirist not to be named: he puts his ordeal at the service of a familiar faith or ideology, and it comes to seem sad, for that faith or ideology cannot bear the explanatory and expiatory burdens he would place upon it. Another memoirist, also not to be named: he suborns his grief to public self-aggrandizement, and the grief he declares, surely sincere, is alloyed by streaks of publicity.

But Chaim Kaplan cares for nothing except the impossible effort to comprehend the incomprehensible; Filip Mueller for nothing except to recall happenings even he finds hard to credit; Primo Levi for nothing but to render his days in the camps through a language unadorned and chaste.

We are trapped. Our need for testimony that will forever place the Holocaust squarely within history requires that we respond to voice, nuance, personality. Our desire to see the Holocaust in weightier terms than the merely aesthetic lures us into a shy recognition of the moral reverberations of the aesthetic. This does not make us happy, but the only alternative is the silence we all remember, now and then, to praise.

4

"We became aware," writes Primo Levi, "that our language lacks words to express this offense, the demolition of man." Every serious writer approaching the Holocaust sooner or later says much the same. If there is a way of coping with this difficulty, it lies in a muted tactfulness recognizing that there are some things that can be said and some that cannot.

Let me cite a few sentences from T. S. Eliot: "Great simplicity is only won by an intense moment or by years of intelligent effort, or by both. It represents one of the most arduous conquests of the human spirit: the triumph of feeling and thought over the natural sin of language."

Exactly what Eliot meant by that astonishing phrase, "the natural sin of language," I cannot say with assurance, but that it applies to a fair portion of Holocaust writing, both memoir and fiction, seems to me indisputable. A "natural sin" might here signify the inclination to grow wanton over our deepest griefs, thereby making them the substance of public exploitation. Or a mistaken effort, sincere or grandiose, to whip language into doing more than it can possibly do, more than thought and imagination and prayer can do. Language as it seduces us into the comforting grandiose.

When, by now as a virtual cliché, we say that language cannot deal with the Holocaust, we really have in mind, or perhaps are covering up for, our inadequacies of thought and feeling. We succumb to that "natural sin of language" because anyone who tries seriously to engage with the implications of the Holocaust must come up against a wall of incomprehension: *How could it be?* Not the behavior, admirable or deplorable, of the victims, and not the ideologies the Nazis drew upon form the crux of our bewilderment, but—how could human beings, raised in the center of European civilization, do this? If we then fall back on intellectual shorthand, invoking the problem of radical evil, what are we really doing but expressing our helplessness in another vocabulary? Not only is this an impassable barrier for the thought of moralists and the recall of memoirists; it is, I think, the greatest thematic and psychological difficulty confronting writers of fiction who try to represent or evoke the Holocaust.

For the central question to be asked about these writings, a few of them distinguished and most decent failures, is this: What can the literary imagination, traditionally so proud of its self-generating capacities, add to—how can it go beyond—the intolerable matter cast up by memory? What could be the organizing categories, the implicit premises of perception and comprehension, through which the literary imagination might be able to render intelligible the gassing of twelve thousand people a day at Auschwitz? If, as Sidra DeKoven Ezrahi remarks, literature has traditionally called upon "the timeless archetypes of human experience" to structure and infer significance from its materials, how can this now be done with a sequence of events that radically breaks from those "timeless archetypes"? A novelist can rehearse what we have learned from the documentation of David Rousset and Filip Mueller, from Primo Levi and Eugen Kogon, but apart from some minor smoothing and shaping, what can the novelist *do* with all this? And if, through sheer lack of any other recourse, he does fall back upon the ideological or theological categories of Western thought, he faces the risk of producing a fiction with a severe fissure between rendered event and imposed category—so that even a sympathetic reader may be inclined to judge the work as resembling a failed allegory in which narrative and moral are, at best, chained together by decision.

Let us see all this concretely, as it might affect a novelist's job of work. Yes, the facts are there, fearful and oppressive, piled up endlessly in memoirs and histories. He has studied them, tried to "make sense" of them in his mind, submitted himself to the barrage of horror. But what he needs—and does not have—is something that for most ordinary fictions written about most ordinary themes would come to him spontaneously, without his even being aware that it figures crucially in the act of composition: namely, a structuring set of ethical premises, to which are subordinately linked aesthetic biases, through which he can integrate his materials. These ethical premises and aesthetic biases are likely to obtrude in consciousness only as a felt lack, only when a writer brooding over the endlessness of murder and torment asks how it can be turned or shaped into significant narrative. Nor, if he tries to escape from a confining realism and venture into symbolic or grotesque modes, can he find sufficiently used—you might say, sufficiently "broken in"—myths and metaphors that might serve as workable, publicly recognizable analogues for the Holocaust experience. Before *this* reality, the imagination comes to seem intimidated, helpless. It can rehearse, but neither enlarge nor escape; it can describe happenings, but not endow them with the autonomy and freedom of a complex fiction; it remains—and perhaps this may even figure as a moral obligation—the captive of its raw material.

The Holocaust memoirist, as writer, is in a far less difficult position. True, he needs to order his materials in the rudimentary sense of minimal chronology and reportorial selectivity (though anything he honestly remembers could prove to be significant, even if not part of his own story). Insofar as he remains a memoirist, he is not obliged to interpret what he remembers. But the novelist, even if he supposes he is merely "telling a story," must—precisely in order to tell a story—"make sense" of his materials, either through explicit theory or, what is better, absorbed assumptions. Otherwise, no matter how vivid his style or sincere his feelings, he will finally be at a loss. All he will then be able to do is to present a kind of "fictionalized memoir"—which means not to move very far beyond what the memoirist has already done.

To avoid this difficulty, some novelists have concentrated on those camps that were not just "corpse factories" and that allowed some faint simulacrum of human life; or, like Jorge Semprun in *The Long Voyage,* they have employed flashbacks of life before imprisonment, so as to allow for some of that interplay of character and extension of narrative that is essential to works of imaginative fiction. Once our focus is narrowed, however, to the death camps, the locale of what must be considered the essential Holocaust, the novelist's difficulties come to seem awesome. For then, apart from the lack of cognitive structures, he has to face a number of problems that are specifically, narrowly literary.

The Holocaust is not, essentially, a dramatic subject. Much before, much after, and much surrounding the mass exterminations may be open to dramatic rendering. But the exterminations, in which thousands of dazed and broken people were sent up each day in smoke, hardly knowing and often barely able to respond to their fate, have little of drama in them. Terribleness yes; drama no.

Of those conflicts between wills, those inner clashes of belief and wrenchings of desire, those enactments of passion, all of which make up our sense of the dramatic, there can be little in the course of a fiction focused mainly on the mass exterminations. A heroic figure here, a memorable outcry there—that is possible. But those soon to be dead are already half or almost dead; the gas chambers merely finish the job begun in the ghettos and continued on the trains. The basic minimum of freedom to choose and act that is a central postulate of drama had been taken from the victims.

The extermination process was so "brilliantly" organized that the life, and thereby the moral energy upon which drama ultimately depends, had largely been snuffed out of the victims before they entered the gas chambers. Here, in the death camps, the pitiful margin of space that had been allowed the human enterprise in the concentration camps was negated. Nor was it exactly death that reigned; it was annihilation. What then can the novelist make of this—what great clash or subtle inference—that a Filip Mueller has not already shown?

If the death camps and mass exterminations allow little opening for the dramatic, they also give little space for the tragic in any traditional sense of that term. In classical tragedy man is defeated; in the Holocaust man is destroyed. In tragedy man struggles against forces that overwhelm him, struggles against both the gods and his own nature; and the downfall that follows may have an aspect of grandeur. This struggle allows for the possibility of an enlargement of character through the purgation of suffering, which in turn may bring a measure of understanding and a kind of peace. But except for some religious Jews who were persuaded that the Holocaust was a reenactment of the great tradition of Jewish martyrdom, or for some secular Jews who lived out their ethic by choosing to die in solidarity with their fellows, or for those inmates who undertook doomed rebellions, the Jews destroyed in the camps were not martyrs continuing along the ways of their forefathers. They died, probably most of them, not because they chose at all costs to remain Jews, but because the Nazis chose to believe that being Jewish was an unchangeable, irredeemable condition. They were victims of a destruction that for many of them had little or only a fragmentary meaning— few of the victims, it seems, could even grasp the idea of total annihilation, let alone regard it as an act of high martyrdom. All of this does not make their death less terrible; it makes their death more terrible.

So much so that it becomes an almost irresistible temptation for Holocaust writers, whether discursive or fictional, to search for some redemptive token, some cry of retribution, some balancing of judgment against history's evil, some sign of ultimate spiritual triumph. It is as if, through the retrospect of language, they would lend a tragic aura. . . .

Many of the customary resources and conventions of the novel are unavailable to the writer dealing with the Holocaust. Small shifts in tone due to the surprises of freedom or caprice; the slow, rich development of character through testing and overcoming; the exertion of heroic energies by characters granted unexpectedly large opportunities; the slow emergence of moral flaws through an accumulation of seemingly trivial incidents; the withdrawal of characters into the recesses of their selves; the yielding of characters to large social impulses, movements, energies—these may not be entirely impossible in Holocaust fiction, but all must prove to be painfully limited. Even so apparently simple a matter as how a work of fiction is ended takes on a new and problematic aspect, for while a memoirist can just stop, the novelist must think in terms of resolutions and completions. But what, after having surrendered his characters to their fate, can he suppose those resolutions and completions to be? Finally, all such literary problems come down to the single inclusive problem of freedom. In the past even those writers most inclined to determinism or naturalism have grasped that to animate their narratives they must give at least a touch of freedom to their characters. And that, as his characters inexorably approach the ovens, is precisely what the Holocaust writer cannot do.

5

The Israeli critic Hannah Yaoz, reports Sidra Ezrahi, has "divided Holocaust fiction into historical and transhistorical modes—the first representing a mimetic approach which incorporates the events into the continuum of history and human experience, and the second transfiguring the events into a mythic reality where madness reigns and all historical loci are relinquished." At least with regard to the Holocaust, the notion that there can be a "mythic reality" without "historical loci" seems to me dubious—for where then could the imagination find the materials for its act of "transfiguring"? Still, the division of Holocaust fiction proposed by the Israeli critic has some uses, if only to persuade us that finally both the writers who submit to and those who rebel against the historical mode must face pretty much the same problems.

The "mimetic approach" incorporating "events into the continuum of history" has been most strongly employed by the Polish writer Tadeusz Borowski in his collection of stories *This Way for the Gas, Ladies and Gentlemen*. Himself an Auschwitz survivor, Borowski writes in a cold, harsh, even coarse style, heavy with flaunted cynicism, and offering no reliefs of the heroic. Kapo Tadeusz, the narrator, works not only with but also on behalf of the death system. "Write," he says, "that a portion of the sad fame of Auschwitz belongs to you as well." The wretched truth is that here survival means the complete yielding of self.

Like Filip Mueller in his memoir, Borowski's narrator admits that he lives because there is a steady flow of new "material" from the ghettos to the gas chambers. "It is true, others may be dying, but one is somehow still alive, one has enough food, enough strength to work. . . ." Let the transports stop and Kapo Tadeusz, together with the other members of "Canada" (the labor gang that unloads the transports), will be liquidated.

Kapo Tadeusz lives in a world where mass murder is normal: it is *there*, it works, and it manages very well without moral justifications. The tone of detachment, which in a naturalistic novel would signal moral revulsion from represented ugliness, has here become a condition of survival. To lapse into what we might regard as human feeling—and sometimes Kapo Tadeusz and his fellow-prisoners do that—is to risk not only the ordeal of memory but the loss of life: a pointless loss, without record or rebellion.

Borowski's style conveys the rhythm of a hammering factuality, and in a way almost too complex to describe, one appreciates his absolute refusal to strike any note of redemptive nobility. Truthful and powerful as they are, Borowski's stories seem very close to those relentless Holocaust memoirs that show that there need be no limit to dehumanization. And that is just the point: for truthful and powerful as they are, Borowski's stories "work" mainly as testimony. Their authenticity makes us, I would say, all but indifferent to their status as art. We do not, perhaps cannot, read these stories as mediated fictions, imaginative versions of a human milieu in which men and women enter the usual range of relations. In Kapo Tadeusz's barrack there is simply no space for that complex interplay of action, emotion, dream, ambivalence, generosity, envy, and love that forms the basis of Western literature. The usual norms of human conduct—except for flashes of memory threatening survival—do not operate here. "We are not evoking evil irresponsibly," writes Borowski, "for we have now become part of it." Nor does it really matter whether Borowski was drawing upon personal memories or "making up" some of his stories. Composed in the fumes of destruction, even the stories he might have "made up" are not actually "made up": they are the substance of collective memory. *Hier ist kein warum.*

Inevitably, some Holocaust writers would try to escape from the vise of historical realism, and one of the most talented of these was the Ukrainian Jew Piotr Rawicz. Resting on a very thin narrative base, Rawicz's novel *Blood from the Sky* is a sustained, almost heroic rebellion against the demands of narrative—though in the end those demands reassert themselves, even providing the strongest parts of this wantonly brilliant book. What starts out as a traditional story soon turns into expressionist phantasmagoria seeking to project imagistic tokens for the Holocaust, or at least for the hallucinations it induces in the minds of witnesses. The story, often pressed far into the background, centers on a rich, highly educated, aristocratic Jew named Boris who saves himself from the Nazis through his expert command of German and Ukrainian— also through a disinclination to indulge in noble gestures. Upon this fragile strand of narrative Rawicz hangs a series of vignettes, excoriations, prose and verse poems, and mordant reflections of varying quality. The most effective are the ones visibly tied to some historical event, as in a brief sketch of a Nazi commander who orders the transport from Boris's town of all women named Goldberg because a woman of that name has infected him with a venereal disease. Symbolically freighted passages achieve their greatest force when they are also renderings of social reality, as in this description of a work party of prisoners sent by the Nazis to tear apart a Jewish cemetery:

> The party was demolishing some old tombstones. The blind, deafening hammer blows were scattering the sacred characters from inscriptions half a millennium old, and composed in praise of some holy man. . . . An *aleph* would go flying off to the left, while a *he* carved on another piece of stone dropped to the right. A *gimel* would bite the dust and a *nun* follow in its wake. . . . Several examples of *shin*, a letter symbolizing the miraculous intervention of God, had just been smashed and trampled on by the hammers and feet of these moribund workmen.

And then, several sentences later: "Death—that of their fellow men, of the stones, of their own—had become unimportant to them; but hunger hadn't."

The strength of this passage rests upon a fusion of event described and symbol evoked, but that fusion is successfully achieved because the realistic description is immediately persuasive in its own right. Mimesis remains the foundation. When Rawicz, however, abandons story and character in his straining after constructs of language that will in some sense "parallel" the Holocaust theme, the prose cracks under an intolerable pressure. We become aware of an excess of tension between the narrative (pushed into the background but through its sheer horror still dominant) and the virtuosity of language (too often willed and literary). Rawicz's outcroppings of expressionist rage and grief, no matter how graphic in their own right, can only seem puny when set against the events looming across the book.

Still, there are passages in which Rawicz succeeds in endowing his language with a kind of hallucinatory fury, and then it lures us into an autonomous realm of the horrifying and the absurd. But when that happens, virtuosity takes command, coming to seem self-sufficient, without fixed points of reference, as if floating off on its own. Losing the causal tie with the Holocaust that the writer evidently hopes to maintain, the language overflows as if a discharge of sheer nausea. At least with regard to Holocaust fiction, I would say that efforts to employ "transhistorical modes" or "mythic reality" are likely to collapse into the very "continuum of history" they seek to escape—or else to come loose from the grounds of their creation.

6

M 'ken nisht, literally, Yiddish for "one cannot"—so the Israeli writer Aharon Applefeld once explained why in his fictions about the Holocaust he did not try to represent it directly, always ending before or starting after the exterminations. He spoke with the intuitive shrewdness of the writer who knows when to stop—a precious gift. But his remark also conveyed a certain ambiguity, as if *m 'ken nisht* had a way of becoming *m 'tur nisht*, "one must not," so that an acknowledgment of limit might serve as a warning of the forbidden.

In approaching the Holocaust, the canniest writers keep a distance. They know or sense that their subject cannot be met full-face. It must be taken on a tangent, with extreme wariness, through strategies of indirection and circuitous narratives that leave untouched the central horror—leave it untouched but always invoke or evoke it as hovering shadow. And this brings us to another of the ironies that recur in discussing this subject. We may begin with a suspicion that it is morally unseemly to submit Holocaust writings to fine critical discriminations, yet once we speak, as we must, about ways of approaching or apprehending this subject, we find ourselves going back to a fundamental concern of literary criticism, namely, how a writer validates his material.

Before. Aharon Applefeld's *Badenheim 1939* is a novella that at first glance contains little more than a series of banal incidents in a Jewish resort near Vienna at the start of World War II. Each trivial event brings with it a drift of anxiety. A character feels "haunted by a hidden fear, not her own." Posters go up in the town: "The Air Is Fresher in Poland." Guests in the hotel fear that "some alien spirit [has] descended." A musician explains deportations of Jews as if he were the very spirit of the century: it is "Historical Necessity." Applefeld keeps accumulating nervous detail; the writing flows seamlessly, enticingly, until one notices that the logic of this quiet narrative is a logic of hallucination and its quietness mounts into a thick cloud of foreboding. At the end, the guests are being packed into "four filthy freight cars"—but here Applefeld abruptly stops, as if recognizing a limit to the sovereignty of words. Nothing is said or shown of what is to follow: the narrative is as furtive as the history it evokes; the unspeakable is not to be named.

During. Pierre Gascar, a Frenchman, not Jewish, who was a POW during World War II, has written in his long story "The Seasons of the Dead" one of the very few masterpieces of Holocaust fiction. Again, no accounts of torture or portrayal of concentration camps or imaginings of the gas chambers. All is evoked obliquely, through a haze of fearfulness and disbelief. The narrator makes no effort to hide his Parisian sophistication, but what he sees as a prisoner sent to a remote camp in Poland breaks down his categories of thought and leaves him almost beyond speech.

Gascar's narrator is assigned to a detail that takes care of a little cemetery molded with pick and shovel for French soldiers who have died: "We were a team of ghosts returning every morning to a green peaceful place, we were workers in death's garden." In a small way "death's garden" is also life's, for with solemn attentiveness the men who work there preserve the civilizing rituals of burial through which mankind has traditionally tried to give some dignity to death. Gradually signs of another kind of death assault these men, death cut off from either natural process or social ritual. The French prisoners working in their little graveyard cannot help seeing imprisoned Jews of a nearby village go about their wretched tasks. One morning they find "a man lying dead by the roadside on the way to the graveyard" who has "no distinguishing mark, save the armlet with the star of David"; and as they dig new graves for their French comrades, they discover "the arm of [a] corpse . . . pink . . . like certain roots." Their cemetery, with its carefully "idealized dead," is actually in "the middle of a charnel, a heap of corpses lying side by side. . . ." And then the trains come, with their stifled cries, "the human voice, hovering over the infinite expanse of suffering like a bird over the infinite sea." As in Claude Lanzmann's great film *Shoah*, the trains go back and forth, endlessly, in one direction filled with broken human creatures, and in the other empty. Death without coffins, without reasons, without rituals, without witnesses: the realization floods into the consciousness of the narrator and a few other prisoners. "Death can never appease this pain; this stream of black grief will flow forever"—so the narrator tells himself. No explanation follows, no consolation. There is only the enlarging grief of discovery, with the concluding sentence: "I went back to my dead"—both kinds, surely. And nothing else.

After. In a long story, "A Plaque on Via Mazzini," the Italian-Jewish writer Giorgio Bassani adopts as his narrative voice the amiable coarseness of a commonplace citizen of Ferrara, the north Italian town that before the war had four hundred Jews, one hundred eighty-three of whom were deported. One of them comes back, in August 1945: Geo Josz, bloated with the fat of endema starvation, with hands "callused beyond all belief, but with white backs where a registration number, tattooed a bit over the right wrist . . . could be read distinctly, all five numbers, preceded by the letter J." Not unsympathetic but intent upon going about their business, the citizens of Ferrara speak through the narrator: "What did he want, now?" Ferrara does not know what to make of this survivor, unnerving in his initial quiet, with his "obsessive, ill-omened face" and his bursts of sarcasm. In his attic room Josz papers all four walls with pictures of his family, destroyed in Buchenwald. When he meets an uncle who had fawned upon the fascists, he lets out "a shrill cry, ridiculously, hysterically passionate, almost savage." Encountering a broken-down old count who had spied for the fascist police, he slaps him twice—it's not so much his presence that Josz finds unbearable as his whistling "Lili Marlene."

As if intent upon making everyone uncomfortable, Josz resumes "wearing the same clothes he had been wearing when he came back from Germany . . . fur hat and leather jerkin included." Even the warm-hearted conclude: "It was impossible . . . to converse with a man in costume! And on the other hand, if they let him do the talking, he immediately started telling about . . . the end of all his relatives; and he went on like that for whole hours, until you didn't know how to get away from him."

A few years later Josz disappears, forever, "leaving not the slightest trace after him." The Ferrarese, remembering him for a little while, "would shake their heads good-naturedly," saying, "If he had only been a bit more patient." What Geo Josz thinks or feels, what he remembers or wants, what boils up within him after returning to his town, Bassani never tells. There is no need to. Bassani sees this bit of human wreckage from a cool distance, charting the gap between Josz and those who encounter him on the street or at a café, no doubt wishing him well, but naturally, in their self-preoccupation, unable to enter his memories or obsessions. His very presence is a reproach, and what, if anything, they can do to reply or assuage they do not know. For they are ordinary people and he . . . The rest seeps up between the words.

Aftermath. On the face of it, "My Quarrel with Hersh Rasseyner," by the Yiddish writer Chaim Grade, is an ideological dialogue between a badly shaken skeptic, evidently the writer himself, and a zealous believer, Hersh Rasseyner, who belongs to the Mussarist sect, "a movement that gives special importance to ethical and ascetic elements in

Judaism." But the voices of the two speakers—as they meet across a span of years from 1937 to 1948—are so charged with passion and sincerity that we come to feel close to both of them.

Like Grade himself, the narrator had been a Mussarist in his youth, only to abandon the Yeshiva for a career as a secular writer. Yet something of the Yeshiva's training in dialectic has stuck to the narrator, though Grade is shrewd enough to give the stronger voice to Hersh Rasseyner, his orthodox antagonist. What they are arguing about, presumably, are eternal questions of faith and skepticism—the possibility of divine benevolence amid the evil of His creation, the value of clinging to faith after a Holocaust that His hand did not stop. In another setting all this might seem an intellectual exercise, but here, as these two men confront one another, their dispute signifies nothing less than the terms upon which they might justify their lives. For Hersh Rasseyner the gas chambers are the inevitable outcome of a trivialized worldliness and an enfeebled morality that lacks the foundation of faith. For the narrator, the gas chambers provoke unanswerable questions about a God who has remained silent. Back and forth the argument rocks, with Hersh Rasseyner usually on the attack, for he is untroubled by doubt, while the narrator can only say: "You have a ready answer, while we have not silenced our doubts, and perhaps we will never be able to silence them." With "a cry of impotent anger against heaven"—a heaven in which he does not believe but to which he continues to speak—the narrator finally offers his hand to Hersh Rasseyner in a gesture of forlorn comradeship: "We are the remnant. . . ."

In its oppressive intensity and refusal to rest with any fixed "position," Grade's story makes us realize that even the most dreadful event in history has brought little change in the thought of mankind. History may spring endless surprises, but our responses are very limited. In the years after the Holocaust there was a certain amount of speculation that human consciousness could no longer be what it had previously been. Exactly what it might mean to say that after the Holocaust consciousness has been transformed is very hard to determine. Neither of Grade's figures—nor, to be honest, the rest of us—shows any significant sign of such a transformation. For good and bad, we remain the commonplace human stock, and whatever it is that we may do about the Holocaust we shall have to do with the worn historical consciousness received from mankind's past. In Grade's story, as in other serious fictions touching upon the Holocaust, there is neither throb of consolation nor peal of redemption, nothing but an anxious turning toward and away from what our century has left us.

7

The mind rebels against such conclusions. It yearns for compensations it knows cannot be found; it yearns for tokens of transcendence in the midst of torment. To suppose that some redemptive salvage can be eked out of the Holocaust is, as we like to say, only human. And that is one source of the falsity that seeps through a good many accounts of the Holocaust, whether fiction or memoir—as it seeps through the language of many high-minded commentators. "To talk of despair," writes Albert Camus, "is to conquer it." Is it now? "The destiny of the Jewish people, whom no earthly power has ever been able to defeat"— so speaks a character in Jean-François Steiner's novel about a revolt in Treblinka. Perhaps appropriate for someone urging fellow-prisoners into a doomed action, such sentiments, if allowed to determine the moral scheme of Holocaust writing, lead to self-delusion. The plain and bitter truth is that while Hitler did not manage to complete the "Final Solution," he did manage to destroy an entire Jewish world.

"It is foolish," writes Primo Levi, "to think that human justice can eradicate" the crimes of Auschwitz. Or that the human imagination can encompass and transfigure them. Some losses cannot be made up, neither in time nor in eternity. They can only be mourned. In a poem entitled "Written in Pencil in the Sealed Freight Car," the Israeli poet Don Pagis writes:

> Here in this transport
> I Eve
> and Abel my son
> if you should see my older son
> Cain son of man
> tell him that I

Cry to heaven or cry to earth: that sentence will never be completed.

Justice for Leskov

A storyteller is very different from someone who writes a lot of stories. A storyteller celebrates that "gusto in art" which, according to Hazlitt, is "the power or passion to define an object"—that active pleasure in composition, a kind of conquering, which the story conveys and the audience is trained to share.

Consider as an example "The Amazon," a long story by the Russian writer Nikolai Leskov (1831–1895) about a procuress who deceives everyone near her without the faintest compunction, yet in her "fat little heart" finds it impossible to think anything but well of herself. At no point does Leskov excuse or grow sentimental over her vice, yet she emerges—in a sublime accumulation of hypocrisy—as the agent of an indiscriminate life force, and we end up accepting, even relishing, her as an implacable reality. Moral judgment shrinks to the imperiled or even irrelevant; narrative crushes scruple.

This is not the kind of writing that easily charms modern readers. We are, with reason, suspicious of claims to abounding zest. It can mask coarseness of mind or metaphysical incapacity, perhaps also a refusal to listen to the bad news of our time. This cultural position may be one

From *New York Review of Books* 34 (April 23, 1987):7.

reason why the splendid Nikolai Leskov—author of stories and novels, but at his best in the long story—has never caught on outside Russia. In principle, we ought to be able to respond strongly to both Leskov and Beckett, but it takes some stretching, a deliberate effort to employ conflicting portions of one's sensibility. It also requires what is quite as difficult, to find ways of slipping past the imperialism of current taste.

There is another reason why cultivated Western readers are likely to be only slightly familiar with Leskov. "The Anglo-Saxon public," wrote the literary historian D. S. Mirsky some years ago, "have made up their mind as to what they want from a Russian writer, and Leskov does not fit in with this idea." It's a hard fate for a writer like Leskov— to be one of the most "Russian" of Russian writers, with a deeply intuitive grasp of the customs of his country, yet to fail to satisfy those expectations of spirituality we in the West have come to impose on Russian literature.

Some attempts to promote Leskov have been made: essays by Walter Benjamin and V. S. Pritchett, volumes of his selected writings, more or less adequately translated and annotated; but if you really want to get an idea of his range and quality, you have to hunt around in obscure and out-of-print books, none altogether satisfactory.

Does it matter? I think so. Leskov is a writer who yields enormous pleasure, breaking past sectarian literary and ideological premises. But more, we live in a moment of lowered cultural and emotional expectations, after the fall of modernism but without anything very strong to replace it. To go back to certain earlier writers is to regain a sense of human possibility. To go back to Leskov is to regain a sense of the passion, sometimes the joy, that can be part of the human enterprise.

In Leskov's stories you will find very little probing into motives, or shadings of character, or penetration into the inner self, or yearnings for religious transcendence; nor is there authorial play with time sequences and points of view. What then remains? A very great deal, most of all the art of telling stories and the vision of life which enables that art. Nor does this art rely on an outmoded or contrived simplicity: it draws upon both a demanding aesthetic and a "philosophy" of life. The aesthetic makes narrative the dominant element of fiction, overwhelming and sometimes even suppressing character, thematic comment, and stylistic texture. Narrative becomes, if not quite an end in itself, then an autonomous source of pleasure, somewhat in the way Pope's rhymes can be. But for all his virtuoso's craftiness—which, rather curiously, can approach an "art for art's sake" aesthetic, that is, storytelling without any exterior rationale—the storyteller usually works out of, or edges back into, a belief in a solid, this-worldly reality. Bringing a sense of renewal to his audience, he turns to the world for his own renewal, and then, by virtue of having acknowledged the world's claims upon him, he finds that moral judgments creep into his storytelling.

But not without difficulty and internal conflicts. In a number of Leskov's stories there is a clash between narrative momentum and moral intent, and this often creates a sense of unbalance. The one story of his that the English-reading public is likely to know, "Lady Macbeth of the Mtsensk District"—a fierce, even horrifying account of lust, murder, and betrayal—has such a strong narrative drive that it becomes hard to find a moral theme in the story. More to the point, as one gets caught up with its rush of events, one loses interest in trying to find a moral theme. For a Tolstoyan dubious about the value of art, "Lady Macbeth of the Mtsensk District" could serve as a prime instance of art's amoral power to inflame readers into complicity with frightful desires and acts. Leskov himself wrote that in composing this grim story he often felt himself to be in a state of terror, and one can understand why. He had come up against the terror of art—its capacity, like that of physical beauty, to make everything but itself seem inconsequential.

Leskov never wrote anything again like "Lady Macbeth of the Mtsensk District," but he had plenty of other stories to tell and plenty of figures to impersonate in the telling. The world for Leskov was inexhaustible—that's the storyteller's signature. He has no interest in the maneuvers of the self, he enjoys imagining *other* people. Some of Leskov's best pieces deal with Russian religious life, a subject about which he knows more than his religiously exalted contemporaries; but church, priest, icon, and chant all figure for him as aspects of Russian daily life. Upon becoming in his later years a convert or semiconvert to Tolstoyism, he produced a group of sketches of "righteous men." What is remarkable about those I've read in English versions is their rootedness in ordinary life without any touch, or taint, of the angelic. Exuberance Leskov has abundantly, spiritual exaltation rarely.

It would be a mistake to think of Leskov as a realist of any conventional sort. He adores high colorings, fine gestures, narratives of suspense, surprise, and (his own words) "gay confusion." D. S. Mirsky offers a nice comparison: "If Turgenev's or Chekhov's world may be compared to a landscape by Corot, Leskov's is a picture by Breughel the Elder, full of gay and bright colors and grotesque forms." And if Leskov never reaches the illuminations of Dostoevsky or Tolstoy, it is quite enough that, like the shrewd Russian craftsmen he admired, he should be in command of the mundane.

2

In the opening lines of Professor Hugh McLean's magisterial biography of Leskov we encounter such words as "embittered," "irritably," "resentment," and "self-pity."* That these words are appropriate both Leskov's friends and his enemies confirm, yet so far as I can see there is very little reason to apply them to his fiction. The irritability for which he became notorious during his lifetime can readily be separated from the good-natured and often high-spirited tone of his writing. How to explain this split I do not know.

Unlike so many other Russian writers of his time, Leskov was not born into the landowning gentry. While some of his stories examine relations between landowners and serfs in a humane spirit, these relations are not a central theme of his fiction. Born in south central Russia and raised in the town of Oryol, Leskov writes mainly with the voice of a townsman, shrewd but not conspicuously sophisticated, and apparently indifferent to the dream of a pastoral idyll that pervaded a good part of Russian literature in the nineteenth century, from the elder Aksakov to, recurrently, Turgenev and Tolstoy.

Two religious traditions compete within Leskov, and neither dominates. His father descended from generations of Orthodox priests, but had himself settled into the routine of a civil servant, professing a rather dry rationalist version of the faith; the mother, from merchant stock, was piously Orthodox. Both strains figure in Leskov's stories, though never in a fanatical spirit; they become secularized as elements of national culture.

Leskov followed roughly the typical progress of the bright provincial boy, step by step to the capital. He dropped out of school in his mid-teens, finding employment in the law courts; at the age of seventeen or eighteen he got himself transferred to Kiev, where he learned Polish and came to know Ukrainian nationalists—an experience that would temper, if not entirely quench, his Russian nationalism. In Kiev he also began to develop what would be a lifelong interest in local customs and speech; many of his stories are enlivened with bits of colloquial Ukrainian (something, of course, that cannot come through in translation).

In 1857 Leskov went to work as a traveling agent for his uncle, a Russified Scotsman named Alexander Scott, whose firm managed the estates of noblemen. Scott, who tried with varying results to introduce modern business methods in the Russian countryside, would later become a model for a number of Leskov's characters, strong-willed, en-

---

*Hugh McLean, *Nikolai Leskov* (Harvard University Press, 1977). Indispensable for its scholarship, stimulating for its criticism. I am greatly indebted to this work.

ergetic fellows set up in opposition to the "superfluous man" who figures so importantly in Russian literature. (In one of his finest stories, "The Musk-Ox," Leskov offers a deeply sympathetic portrait of a "superfluous man," drawn more in ethical and religious than in political terms, as if to show that he can write—as all great writers must—in opposition to his own preconceptions.) Traveling for several years throughout Russia on behalf of Scott's firm, Leskov acquired a wide knowledge of provincial life, of the Russia beyond the two major cities; and in his writings he would draw upon this accumulated store of impression, memory, legend, and anecdote—especially anecdote, a main source of his fiction.

In 1860, still not yet thirty, Leskov moved to St. Petersburg to become a full-time journalist. His deepest inclination was to join the movement toward a moderate progressivism that began with Alexander II's coming to the throne. This meant that sooner or later he would clash with the literary radicals who, for a brief time, seemed his natural allies. When the break came in the spring of 1861, it took on an especially venomous character.

St. Petersburg had been beset by mysterious fires, which, according to rumors spreading through the city, had been started by student radicals; these rumors gained credence when a proclamation breathing fire and violence was issued by an anonymous group calling itself Young Russia. In good faith Leskov wrote an article defending the students and challenging the police to produce evidence that arson had been committed. Whereupon the literary left called him a provocateur, for wasn't he really hinting that the fires might indeed have been set by some of the student radicals? To the leftist intelligentsia, or at least that part intransigently opposed to the government, Leskov now became anathema. Not being the sort of man who turns the other cheek, he retaliated with fierce polemics and a roman à clef, No Way Out, that further enraged the radicals.

From then on, it was open war. The leftist critic Pisarev called for a boycott of Leskov's work; magazines closed their pages to him; for some years he could appear only in conservative journals with which he was not fully in sympathy. One of these, the Russian Messenger, printed two of his best works, the novel The Cathedral Folk and the long story "The Sealed Angel."

The contentious Leskov could not long be comfortable with the conservatives, and by 1874 he had broken with them too. His standing with the Russian reading public remained secure, but a good part of the intelligentsia, to whom his buoyant stories seemed deficient in "higher" values, chose to disparage him: he offered no answer to the heartbreak of Russia.

Leskov's position in the literary life of his country would always be somewhat anomalous: simultaneously at home and estranged. He knew the folk culture of Russia intimately, yet there is a streak of displacement, perhaps even of deracination, in his personality. He knew the countryside at first hand, yet he was not fully at ease with any of the fixed social classes in czarist Russia. For a writer this can be a real advantage: it enabled Leskov to portray colorful segments of Russian life, such as that of the Old Believers, which his great contemporaries knew little about, and it kept him at a sensible distance from extremist intellectual tendencies such as the Slavophiles and the nihilists. But Leskov the man seems to have been always at odds. Prey to the embarrassments of the autodidact, he became an easy target for anyone who cared to taunt him about his lack of formal education.

He was something of a "musk ox" himself, and he went his own way. By the 1870s he was moving toward a modified Tolstoyism. He praised Tolstoy as the greatest man of his age but made sharp criticisms of the ascetic and fanatical aspects of the Tolstoyan movement. What appealed to Leskov in Tolstoy's prophetic position was its "Protestantism," the strong emphasis on individual moral judgment and responsibility. From his own version of the Tolstoyan outlook, Leskov worked up a series of biting satirical sketches about religious obscurantism and state bureaucratism, sketches written in behalf of a practical morality, a Christianity of conduct rather than spirit. These pieces, while lively enough, do not strike me as among Leskov's best. The great Leskov— a magician of anecdote—writes not out of polemical intent but out of a loving engagement with the habits of the Russians.

One of these satirical stories, "The March Hare," written a year before Leskov's death, is, however, a major success: a spoof on the hunt for subversives in which a featherbrained provincial official, Onopry Opanassovich, whose true vocation is for taking a snooze, must keep on the lookout for men who "go about wearing long hair . . . and women [who] cut their hair short and walk about in dark eye-glasses and they all call themselves Socialists, or which is the same thing, underminers of foundations." Helped by his accommodating young coachman, Onopry Opanassovich gets into one ridiculous muddle after another, until he discovers that the author of the subversive leaflets that have been alarming his superiors is that very coachman. Upon learning this, the poor official loses his wits and ends up amiably babbling in an asylum, where the narrator of the story extracts from him an account of his adventures. Even while making its serious point about the absurdity of witch hunts, "The March Hare" slides deeply into farce: it's as if the Three Stooges had declared a passion for politics.

Every editor to whom Leskov sent the story turned it down, fearing it would make trouble with the censors (as indeed it would have). Not until 1917, after the fall of the czar, did "The March Hare" see print. About this work Leskov wrote: "I am trying to show that ideas can be fought only with ideas and that the measures for the violent suppression of ideas are likely to produce the most unexpected results." The story itself is much wilder than Leskov's remark suggests, but his sentiment remains valuable—especially when one remembers that it came from a writer whose opinions may have been moderate but whose temperament was not.

3

"Lady Macbeth of the Mtsensk District," an early work, is perhaps the most spectacular story Leskov ever wrote, though it is not really typical of his narrative approach. The story is told in the traditional omniscient voice and portrays, with a ruthlessness matched only in Verga's short story "The Wolf," a deliberate and untroubled abandonment to the chaos of passion.

Katerina, the bored young wife of a wealthy merchant, becomes sexually entangled with Sergei, an employee of her husband. The two young lovers yield themselves completely to their lust, and do not hesitate to kill her husband and her father-in-law in its behalf. Caught by the authorities, they are transported to Siberia, where Sergei, slipping into a weakness merely human, drops Katerina for another woman. The unrelenting Katerina, "without removing her gaze from the dark waters bent forward and seizing [her rival] Sonnetka by the legs, with one lunge pulled her overboard" to an icy grave. The appalling Katerina does not hesitate for a moment: there is no remorse, no guilt. Leskov, as the recorder of terrible events, neither celebrates nor condemns; there is not a shred of the redemptive in the story.

Katerina utters her last words not as a prayer but as an unrepentant *Liebestod*: "How you and I loved each other; sat long autumn nights together; sent people from the light of day by violent deaths." In any usual sense Katerina is hardly a character, she figures as a tremor or upheaval of nature. And the contrast Leskov would invoke through his title is at best a partial one. Shakespeare's Lady Macbeth uses her sexuality as a means to gain political power; Leskov's Katerina—in Leskov's conception at least, more impressive—submits unconditionally to sexuality with no other object in mind, at least until it becomes entwined for her with the thrill of murder.

Twice Leskov breaks the relentless narrative with bits of symbolic action: the first is a Hardyesque moment, when Katerina is weighed by her husband's workers on the scale they use for animals (she weighs three poods), and the second when, in an erotic daydream, she imagines a cat is snuggling into her bed: "He stretched out his head to her, thrust his blunt nose coaxingly against her firm breasts and began to sing a soft song." Rarely, if at all, is the narrative, in its steadily quickening pace, interrupted by any nuance of thought, or by a sense of prudential uneasiness.

The opera Dmitri Shostakovich based on Leskov's story, *Katerina Ismailova*, while a powerful work, uses a libretto which significantly weakens Leskov's story. Shostakovich "humanizes" Katerina, treating her as a social victim. In the last act, he introduces a chorus of prisoners in Siberia who sing about their plight; the song is beautiful, but in spirit far from Leskov. On the other hand, the orchestral music is stark and brutal, so that one might say that in the medium most his own Shostakovich grasped entirely Leskov's intention.

The Leskov who wrote "Lady Macbeth of the Mtsensk District" was surely a remarkable writer, but he was not a storyteller. This is the kind of fiction a writer may, if he is lucky and has some genius, bring off once or twice, a piece that radiates enormous narrative authority by sacrificing almost everything else. I suspect that Leskov's moral sense was taken aback by what he had done here and this prompted him shrewdly to retreat a little. Leskov the writer is, for the most part, a virtuoso of good nature, the ethnologist of his tribe, not the witness to lust and murder. For what appealed most pleasingly to his imagination he had to turn to other subjects, other techniques.

4

Far more typical of Leskov's work is the narrative stratagem the Russians call *skaz*, defined by Victor Erlich as "the mimicry of intonational, lexical, and phraseological mannerisms of a lowbrow narrator . . . which enacts and parodies the pattern of a bumbling, chatty narration." The technique, if not the name, is familiar enough: Ring Lardner used it well, Sholom Aleichem better. But Leskov, no doubt with the example of Gogol behind him, makes something quite extraordinary out of *skaz*.

Leskov's simulated oral narrative, "bumbling" and "chatty," usually enforces a meandering pace, with amusing remarks and digressions, but in his longer stories the effect is often of an unusual combination of speeds, adagio and allegro together. The narrator ambles, his narratives race. We seem—is this just an illusion?—to be moving along two planes of velocity, with the narrator chattering away in customary *skaz* fashion while the internal stories and anecdotes move with a masterful briskness.

The effect can be dazzling, as if a juggler were twirling two sets of balls at different rates of speed.

In Leskov's masterpiece, the short novel or long story called *The Enchanted Wanderer*, he piles an astonishing number of disasters onto the back of a gentle-souled giant in whom touches of the simpleton appear side by side with a suggestion of the saint. This sort of character is ideally suited to a picaresque tale: he can endure numerous ordeals, he is too innocent to rebel, he lives forever in hope of redemption or at least recovery, and he likes to tell people about his experiences.

Born a serf, the giant Ivan Severyanovich Flyagin as a boy accidentally kills someone, and then in a dream meets a fearful vision of his fate. He will have to wander about, suffering endlessly but unable to die. (Leskov is canny enough not to stress the legendary sources of this story.) Ivan has an early brush with Gypsies (a nearly obligatory convention of picaresque narratives). He becomes a nursemaid for a kidnapped child. He witnesses a barbaric contest between two Tartars, who whip each other into insensibility over the privilege of buying a magnificent horse each one wants:

> The dignified Tartar told [the two contestants] to wait, handed them the whips in due order and gently clapped his hands: once, twice, thrice. . . . Bakchey instantly lashed Chepkun over his shoulder across his bare back; Chepkun countered with the same and they began to entertain each other in this fashion. They stared into each other's eyes, butted their soles together and each hung on to the other's left hand, while they flogged each other with their right ones. . . . Oh, they did it grandly! If one gave a good cut, the other answered him with a better one!

The Tartars keep Ivan captive for several years and to prevent his escape slit the soles of his feet and fill them with horsehairs. After his escape, he declines into a drunken valet to a disreputable army officer, through whom, however, he meets a ravishing Gypsy girl. He loves the girl dearly: " 'This,' I thought, 'this here is the true beauty that they call the perfection of nature.' " The love affair ends badly, as by the strict rules of such narratives it must, and Ivan retires to a monastery. Even there he makes trouble, experiencing revelations of the Apocalypse. A doctor interviews Ivan:

> "What a drum you are, brother," [the doctor] said, "no amount of beating seems to settle your business."
> "What's to be done," I said, "possibly it must be so."

In its external rhythm of event *The Enchanted Wanderer* may seem akin to picaresque narratives by Smollett, but Leskov's story is very different in tone. Leskov is less brutal than Smollett, less concerned with an accumulation of violence and pratfalls. In his hands picaresque comes to be not just a vehicle for energy, but also a medium of values; he creates in Ivan a figure all but impervious to the world's hardness of spirit and thereby peculiarly endearing.

Inevitably critics have seen *The Enchanted Wanderer* as, in McLean's words, a "disquisition on the Russian national character," stressing meek endurance and gaiety. Maxim Gorky, a great admirer of Leskov, wrote: "His heroes do not abandon the world for Theban deserts, virgin forests, caves and hermitages in which, alone with God, they implore him to grant them a pure and beatific life in paradise. They foolishly thrust themselves into the thickest mire of life on earth, where man has sunk deep, smothered in blood." Such Russian wanderers, Gorky explains, "are men of inexhaustible, fantastic energy which they could find no usual manner of applying. Deprived of the possibility of making history, they created anecdotes." Such readings are plausible, and Gorky's fine last sentence echoes an entire tradition of Russian criticism. Yet they seem to me to miss an essential quality of Leskov's story. What he has achieved here no doubt has its distinctive national significance, but to a non-Russian the story asks to be read as an evocation, both cheering and saddening, of the necessary absurdity of human effort. The piling up of disasters, as in Faulkner's *As I Lay Dying*, forms the basis for irresistible comedy: after a while there is nothing you can do but laugh. Leskov's giant thinks he has been enchanted by an agency of misfortune, but what has really enchanted him is life itself.

5

Another version of the saintly simpleton appears in Leskov's novel *The Cathedral Folk*, this time as Deacon Akhilla, who lives with a group of priests in Stargorod. This character type seems especially attractive to writers who have abandoned the church but retain feelings of reverence for the moral norms of early Christianity.

The Cathedral Folk, though a less accomplished work than *The Enchanted Wanderer*, is still very much alive as an attack upon the sloth of the Orthodox Church and as a portrayal of the daily routine of its priests. There are fine sections dealing with one of Leskov's "just men," Father Tuberózov, who resists the demands of the ecclesiastic bureaucracy that he harass the Old Believers. Once, however, Leskov approaches matters of belief—theism, atheism—he is out of his depth.

Such flaws hardly matter once the mischievous figure of Deacon

Akhilla strides into sight. Akhilla may be drawn, roughly, from the same general conception as Flyagin in *The Enchanted Wanderer*, but the two characters are treated in quite different ways, largely because of the different requirements of a full-scale novel and a longish picaresque tale. Flyagin is essentially a solitary figure shuffled from one setting to another, whereas Akhilla can be shown in complicating relations with other characters. The tense but charming friendship between Akhilla and Father Tuberózov reminds one, a little, of the pairing of Sancho Panza and Don Quixote—except that here it's the serious-minded Father Tuberózov who serves as a foil for the mischievous Akhilla, a character who "exists" in memory despite all the recent warnings by critics that fictional characters cannot escape the pages in which they appear.

Akhilla serves as Leskov's testimony to the life force, by which we mean, I suppose, that charge or flow of energy which courses through (sometimes past) individuals. The idea of the life force, sometimes sweeping past moral norms and constraints, is embedded in romanticism, but only occasionally does Leskov project it through romantic images. The natural world, either as presence or symbol, does not figure strongly in Leskov's imagination. He admires the rational exercise of will, he loves energy as a token of sociability, and these matter for him within the movement of the material world.

Finally it is not even society as such that commands Leskov's main attention; it's the culture of old Russia and the behavior of its people that offer traditional delights even to a progressive who knows that it is necessary to enter the modern world. No other nineteenth-century writer, to my knowledge, provides so intimate a portrait of the inner recesses of Russian life, its customs, mores, and folk culture. Leskov's story "A Robbery," for instance, is a genial comedy about a quick-tempered merchant who arrives in town seeking new singers for his village church. His religion may be tepid, but he cares about the quality, or perhaps only the volume, of the singers' voices: " 'I'll have to explain to them [says the merchant] all the sorts of singing we in Eletz admire most. We'll listen to how they tune up and how they manage with all the different types—if they can get a really low growl when they sing the "Vestment" . . . if they put in the right wail doing "In her Blessed Assumption," and do the memorial howl. It won't take long.' " Nothing in Leskov takes very long: after some farcical maneuvers (you might suppose Leskov had watched silent movies), the story reaches a happy climax with two stentorian deacons booming away.

More complex is "The Sealed Angel," a long story in which Leskov displays his knowledge of Russian icon painting (such as the difference between the Novgorod and Stroganov schools). The story is a triumph of *skaz*; its witty and talkative narrator is a spokesman for a company of Old Believers, skilled construction workers who carry their culture and their icons with them as they take on a project "on the river Dnieper." When their most cherished icon is filched from them, they realize that guile will be their only recourse, and they send the narrator to a distant town in order to find the one painter who can still make a good facsimile of their precious icon. With this fake, they can then contrive to get back their original—a scheme Leskov adorns with some tension-making farcical business. All ends well, perhaps a bit too well. The Orthodox bishop who had appropriated the icon is deceived with the counterfeit; the Old Believers are so overjoyed that they show their respect for the bishop by returning to Orthodoxy—a dubious ending Leskov later said was tacked on to please a conservative editor.

This flaw does not prevent "The Sealed Angel" from being one of Leskov's richest and funniest portraits of Russian life, with even an unobtrusive "class" angle (the Old Believers are honest workmen; their enemies, bureaucrats, church functionaries, meddling ladies). All moves easily, smoothly, in this joyous celebration of the way simple people manage their lives, honestly by preference and through guile when necessary. It is a story, I imagine, that Russians have always cherished.

6

Leskov writes out of what seems a relaxed closeness to folk sources— a closeness, as well, to readers who are not of course the folk but may be supposed to share with him folk memories or at least sentiments regarding the folk. What matters is that, in the bond between writer and reader, the folk should still be felt as near.*

It may even seem at times that as a narrative strategy Leskov treats his readers as if they *were* the folk, though with an occasional wink to indicate they are nothing of the sort. Leskov's readers are thereby lured into a pleasant compact which enables him to assume that air of easy self-assurance that is the storyteller's privilege and thereby to speed along without having to burden himself with moral dilemmas, psychological enigmas, troubling ideas, and other impedimenta.

In his various narrative modes, Leskov almost always depends on a

---

* This can lead to amusing mix-ups. The Leskov story most popular in Russia, "The Lefthander," was prefaced in its first printing with a Defoe-ish note saying, "I have transcribed this legend." So utterly folklike did this story seem—a comic account of how Russian craftsmen, in behalf of national honor, go English craftsmen one better in the art of molding a steel flea—that some contemporary reviewers took Leskov at his word. One of them, Professor McLean reports, concluded that "Mr. Leskov's authorial participation . . . in the narrative is limited to simple stenography. And one should do Mr. Leskov justice: he is a superb stenographer." Bristling at this slight to his originality, Leskov wrote a letter insisting that he had made up the entire story himself. Stenography indeed!

principle of stringent exclusion. Walter Benjamin, in a brilliant essay on Leskov, writes: "There is nothing that commands a story to memory more effectively than the chaste compactness which precludes psychological analysis." The phrase "chaste compactness" suggests that the drive and economy of a narrative unperturbed by psychological analysis are gained at the price of a willed, perhaps assumed innocence. "Chaste compactness"—which in Leskov can coexist with a rambling manner simulating oral storytelling—also means that the kind of reflection we may value in Proust or Mann is excluded. A free flow of narrative is gained through the complicity of author and reader sharing a world view; not too much need be said, and less explained, so that the narrative can brush everything else aside, arrogant in self-sufficiency.

Modern writers strain for insight, but a writer like Leskov is content to float along on his little tributary to the river of received wisdom. So long as the writer remains firmly in touch with his culture, he can indeed become a channel of sorts for the wisdom of the past. Once there's something to explain, the best such a writer can hope for is to become a novelist.

The Fate of Solzhenitsyn

What has happened to Aleksandr Solzhenitsyn? The novelist, now living in the United States, who sketched the gulag with such crisp exactitude in *One Day in the Life of Ivan Denisovich*, who grazed moral sublimity in his beautiful story "Matryona's House," and who created a vibrant exchange of Russian intellectual opinion in *The First Circle* has all but vanished. Replacing him is a shrill and splenetic polemicist who shatters his fictions in behalf of questionable theories, showers adversaries with sarcastic contempt, and employs his talents to cudgel readers into submitting to his increasingly authoritarian views.

For at least twenty years Solzhenitsyn has been working on a vast cycle of novels called "The Red Wheel," which he envisages as a panorama of modern Russia, but still more as a corrective to what he regards as the distortions of Russian history by writers contaminated with liberal and radical ideas. *August 1914* appeared in an earlier version in 1972; now completely retranslated into serviceable English by H. T. Willetts, it is some three hundred pages longer than the first version. The book forms the opening volume of "The Red Wheel," which is structured as a series of what the author calls "knots," or renderings of crucial his-

From *The New York Times Book Review* 138 (July 2, 1989), as "The Great War and Russian Memory."

torical moments that have determined the course of Russian, perhaps all of modern, history.

This is a swollen and misshapen book, a good many of its pages laden with obscure historical detail in small print that, I can testify, causes strain on both eyes and nerves. Solzhenitsyn writes with the single-mindedness of a man possessed—prophecy being not the least risk of aging. He writes out of the conviction that he has the correct view—the only correct view?—of his country's tragic experience, and it becomes very hard, indeed impossible, to respond to *August 1914* in strictly literary terms. Solzhenitsyn himself would probably not want that; he is after "bigger" game.

Despite an occasional borrowing from modern literature, such as his use of the "newsreel" device in John Dos Passos's *U.S.A.*, Solzhenitsyn's novel begins in the customary manner of multilayered nineteenth-century fiction, with several vignettes of Russian figures and families shortly before World War I. We meet a wealthy merchant, Tomchak, and his daughter Ksenia. We meet an idealistic student, Sanya, who has a brief talk with the venerable Leo Tolstoy (a piquant incident that was, I think, richer in the 1972 version, which contained some Tolstoyan reflections on poetry that Solzhenitsyn has now cut).

Several strands of action are thus initiated, and readers familiar with the schema of the traditional novel will await the reappearance of these characters, juxtaposed in both amity and conflict. But that seldom happens in these eight hundred fifty-four pages, and only at very long intervals. The characters glimpsed at the outset are suspended in limbo while Solzhenitsyn turns to what really concerns him: an exhaustive account of Russia's military disasters in 1914. By the time he troubles to get back to his fictional characters, mostly at the very end of this very long book, it has become hard even to recall who the characters are or why we should care about them—since Solzhenitsyn himself doesn't invest much emotional energy in them. The fictional portion of *August 1914* soon comes to seem merely dutiful, and largely without that desire to imagine other people that is the mark of the true novelist.

Solzhenitsyn has made a close study of czarism's military fiasco, for which he offers two plausible explanations: that Russia's haste in trying to help a beleaguered ally, France, led to throwing hundreds of thousands of ill-trained and poorly armed troops into battle, and that incompetence was rife among the higher officers of the Russian army. Mediocrities favored by the byzantine court, the Russian generals proved "incapable of coordinating the movements of large bodies of men." One General Artamonov, for instance, might have made "a pretty good deacon," or "an excellent private soldier provided he had a strict NCO over him," but as a commander he is a total disaster.

All is muddle, sloth, backwardness, sly falsification. It is as if Solzhenitsyn were intent, though he probably is not, upon confirming the usual view of czarism's essential rottenness, or as if he were deliberately following the judgments of Stendhal and Tolstoy that warfare is inherently chaotic—though without the former's brilliance or the latter's penetration.

There are some good pages in the hundreds that sag under endless battle detail. Especially so are those about the historical General Samsonov, whom Solzhenitsyn models in part on Tolstoy's Kutuzov in *War and Peace*, but without Kutuzov's intuitive strategic grasp or mysterious good fortune. Also strong are some pages devoted to the fictional Colonel Vorotyntsev, an officer who travels from corps to corps as the witness of defeat and who comes, meanwhile, to serve as Solzhenitsyn's center of intelligence. Samsonov speaks for traditional patriarchal Russia, blunt and honest but quite lost in modern warfare (as Tolstoy's Kutuzov might also have been), while the nervously intelligent Vorotyntsev speaks as the modernizing voice that Solzhenitsyn apparently wishes had been commanding in 1914, loyal to czarism but impatient with the feeble czar and his scraping court.

The pages devoted to battle on the eastern front—pages crammed with dull generals, obscure place names, confusing divisional maneuvers—soon become wearying. It is possible that some Russian readers, at least those leaning, in the days of glasnost, toward a chauvinist nostalgia, may be roused to excitement by the doings of Generals Zhilinsky and Martos, but it is hard to suppose anyone else will. Some fatal lack of proportion is at work here, an indulgence of authorial vanity and ideological obsession.

It will no doubt be said that in *War and Peace* Tolstoy also devoted many pages to battle. Yes, but Tolstoy was Tolstoy, the greatest master of prose narrative we have ever had. Tolstoy was also generous enough to provision his novel with a rich and varied cast, taking the precaution to make most vivid precisely those characters with whose opinions he disagreed. By now Solzhenitsyn has become too impatient, too irritable for the novelist's job, and one readily surmises the reason: for a writer pulsing with prophetic urgency, mere literature dwindles in importance.

The new material in *August 1914* centers on historical events that took place several years before the war. Pyotr Arkadievich Stolypin, a shrewd politician, was prime minister of Russia from 1906 to 1911, when he was assassinated by Dmitri Bogrov, a shady figure who had successively been linked to revolutionary terrorists and the czarist secret police and who had perhaps become a double agent betraying both sides. In fairness, it should be said that Solzhenitsyn does try to get inside Bogrov to scrutinize his motives, but not with much success; for he cannot control his anger and disgust, and too often he descends to sarcasm, the lowest of rhetorical devices.

It is Solzhenitsyn's thesis that if Stolypin had been able to complete the reforms he had begun, Russia might have been spared the traumas of Bolshevism, but that a tacit alliance of reactionary officials and revolutionary insurgents thwarted Stolypin's plans. He had proposed to grant the recently emancipated peasants legal right to small allotments of land and thereby to free them from their dependence on the *mir*, or agricultural commune. Had this happened, Solzhenitsyn argues, Russia might have become a modern society resting on an independent agrarian class.

Contemporary readers, especially non-Russians, need not hurry to form a judgment of this political speculation, though a touch of skepticism may be in order. A more balanced view of Stolypin—in seven, not seventy, pages—appears in a book by the distinguished historian Leonard Schapiro, *Russian Studies*. Stolypin, Schapiro writes, was "a man who was both a repressive upholder of order and one who achieved reform by defiance of the constitution" granted by Czar Nicholas II in 1906. What seems decisive here is that after Stolypin's murder there was no significant leader or group of leaders in official Russia prepared to continue his work—the mental obscurantism of czarism was simply too thick.

Only when writing about Stolypin ("a figure of epic presence") does Solzhenitsyn relax into ease or rise to something like lyricism. This idealization of a bureaucrat who was hated by Russian democrats and leftists for his severe repressions after the 1905 revolution is not just a whim; it is the thought-out conclusion of the political outlook Solzhenitsyn has adopted in recent years, one that might be described as modernizing authoritarianism. "The secret ballot," he scoffs, "suited the Russian peasant as a saddle suits a cow"—and since peasants formed the bulk of the Russian population, democracy could have played little or no role. As for the rationale he offers, it is all too familiar: right and left authoritarians proclaim it everywhere, with the same haughty certitude.

Somewhat sprightlier than the long chapter on Stolypin is his eighty-page historical excursus about Nicholas II, the last of Russia's hereditary autocrats. Though caustic at times about this royal dunce—some passages here recall Trotsky's more concise and elegant excoriation in his

History of the Russian Revolution—Solzhenitsyn seems finally unable to come to a clear judgment about the czar. At one point he writes that the czar was a "weak but virtuous man," yet the overwhelming thrust of his own depiction is to show Nicholas as petty, selfish, mindless. When Stolypin lay dying in a hospital, the czar did not even bother to visit his minister, apparently suspecting him of "liberalism." That hardly seems evidence of virtue, either weak or strong.

Solzhenitsyn winds up *August 1914* with one of his better scenes, in which Colonel Vorotyntsev reports to the grand duke, supreme commander of Russia's armies. The colonel's few honest words acknowledging defeat are scorned, the general staff clings to its deceptions, Russia is doomed.

What, I asked at the outset, has happened to Solzhenitsyn? The answer is that his zealotry has brought about a hardening of spirit, a loss in those humane feelings and imaginative outreachings that make us value a work of literature, regardless of the writer's political opinions. In *August 1914* Russian radicals are portrayed as rapists, murderers, "mad dogs"; and while, as polemicist, Solzhenitsyn has every right to attack them, as novelist he has a primary obligation to make them seem plausible versions of men and women. The Russian middle class, sneeringly referred to as "society," is shown to be preparing the way for Lenin by joining in irresponsible attacks on czarism.

A still deeper revelation of Solzhenitsyn's current state of mind is to be found in this sentence: "An aversion to Russia and the Russian people, and a belief that everyone in Russia was oppressed and that there was no freedom there, had been created by relentless Jewish propaganda" in America.

This is ugly stuff. Could Solzhenitsyn not have found it in his heart—it would have taken just two more lines—to mention that this "Jewish propaganda" was in response to the Kishinev pogrom of 1903 and a succession of pogroms two years later, during which czarist authorities either gave the killers a free hand or looked the other way? These pogroms "cost the Russian Jews about 1,000 dead [and] 7,000–8,000 wounded," we read in *The Russian Jew Under Tsars and Soviets* by Salo Baron (a scholarly work that, in view of Solzhenitsyn's declared interest in history, he might do well to consult).

It is all very sad, this self-immolation of a once major writer who a quarter of a century ago, in *The First Circle* and *Cancer Ward*, won our admiration for his loveliness of feeling. The Russian critic M. M. Bakhtin once remarked that "for the prose artist the world is full of the words of other people." By now, for the prose artist Aleksandr Solzhenitsyn the world resounds with the words of only one person.

Thinking about Socialism

1985

Christianity did not "die" in the nineteenth century. Millions held fast to the faith; churches survived; theological controversies flourished. Yet we can now see that in the decades after the Enlightenment, Christianity suffered deep wounds, which could not be healed—sometimes were even made worse—by the sincere efforts of various thinkers to refine and revise the faith. Gradually Christianity lost its claim to speak for the whole of Western culture; gradually it lost the ability to hold the imagination of serious young people. Some of them it could still attract, but not with the assurance of the past.

Has something like this been happening to socialism these past several decades? Powerful parties in Europe still employ the socialist vocabulary, and millions of people still accept the socialist label, yet some deep inner crisis of belief, to say nothing of public failures and defeats, has beset socialism. The soaring passions of the early movement are gone, and those of us who strive for socialist renewal cannot help wondering whether we are caught in a drift of historical decline, perhaps

From *Socialism and America* (New York: Harcourt Brace Jovanovich, 1985).

beyond reversing, perhaps to yield at some future moment to a new radical humanism. And perhaps too it does not really matter: each generation must do what it can.

"To the question of the elements of social restructure [i.e., socialism] Marx and Engels never gave a positive answer, because they had no inner relation to the idea. Marx might occasionally allude to 'the elements of the new society' . . . but the political act of revolution remained the one thing worth striving for."*

This observation by Martin Buber, while slightly overstated, embodies an essential truth. Marx and Engels praised the early-nineteenth-century "utopian socialists" for their boldness in projecting visions of a new Golden Age, but they were also contemptuous of the utopians' habit of indulging in detailed "future-painting." Where the utopians, wrote Marx, pictured a socialist society as "an ideal to which reality will have to adjust itself,"† he saw the movement toward socialism as a necessary outcome of concrete social conflicts. He wanted to place the socialist project within the course of historical development, and this he did by specifying two driving forces: first, the evolution of economic techniques and structures, leading to a concentration of ownership and wealth, a recurrence of social crisis, and a sharpening of class conflict; and second, the gathering strength and rising consciousness of the working class, derived from or enabled by its crucial position within capitalist economy. By now it seems clear that Marx was keener in analyzing the "driving forces" of the economy than in allocating the "tasks" of the proletariat, a class that has shown itself capable of intermittent rebellion but not, at least thus far, of serving as the pivot of socialist transformation.

To read the passages in Marx's writings that deal with the socialist future—they are scattered, infrequent, and fragmentary—is to recognize how valid is the charge that he slips into a vague and static perfectionism. What we get from his remarks is a vision of a world marvelously free of social—and, indeed, nonsocial—conflict: no longer in thrall to alienation, exploitation, and social fetishism, humanity reaches, for the first time, a high plateau of the human. In the Marxist anticipation of the good society there is little recognition of the sheer recalcitrance of all social arrangements, the limitations that characterize the human species, the likely persistence into the future of error, stupidity, and ill will. Even convinced socialists must by now feel some skepticism about this version of utopia.

* Martin Buber, *Paths in Utopia* (1949), p. 96.
† Karl Marx and Friedrich Engels, *The German Ideology* (1942), p. 26.

Marxists would reply, with some irritation, that their vision of ultimate social harmony depends on the unfolding of a lengthy historical sequence during which not just new values and habits but a new humanity would emerge. Perhaps so. There is no way to disprove such expectations, any more than to dispel the skepticism they arouse. Far more troubling, at least for a socialist living toward the end of the twentieth century, is the fact that this vision of a society in which "the state withers away" and "the antithesis between physical and mental labor vanishes" does very little to help us achieve a qualitatively better, if still imperfect, society—the kind that some of us call socialism.

Yet it's only fair to add that Marx's failure to engage critically with the problem of the envisaged socialist society did have some positive aspects. If the society of the future is to be entrusted to its living actors, then Marx was right, perhaps, in thinking it imprudent to detail its features in advance. History must be left to those who will make it.

But there is another, less attractive, reason for Marx's failure to draw "the face" of a socialist society. Marxism offers a strong theory of social change but has little to say about political arrangements—structures of government, balances of power, agencies of representation. Marxism has usually failed to consider with sufficient attention what we might call the trans- or supraclass elements of politics—those elements likely to be present (and perplexing) in any society. Except for some brilliant remarks in *The Eighteenth Brumaire of Louis Bonaparte*, Marx gave little weight to politics as an autonomous activity, politics as more than epiphenomenon, politics as a realm with its own powers, procedures, and norms. As Paul Ricoeur has written, "Politics embodies a human relationship which is not reducible to class conflict or socioeconomic tensions. . . . Even the state most in subjection to a dominant class is also a state precisely to the extent that it expresses the fundamental will of the nation as a whole. . . . On the other hand, politics develops evils of its own—evils specific to the exercise of power."*

From such perceptions there follows a problematic view of the entire process of change that is supposed to lead to socialism. But if sophisticated Marxists have recently begun to recognize the autonomy of politics, it must in honesty be added that this was by no means the prevalent view of the socialist movement during its formative, most powerful years. During the three or four decades after Marx's death, the movement as an institution grew stronger, but its vision of the goal for which it was striving declined into a slackness of perfection, only tenuously, through a papery chain of rhetoric, related to the issues and

* "Power and the State," in Irving Howe, ed., *Essential Works of Socialism* (1976), p. 736.

struggles of the moment. Socialism came gradually to be "defined" as a condition of classlessness, the possibility and nature of which were seen more as premise than problem; and since the inclination of Marxists was to think about conflicts and evils as the consequence of class domination, it followed—did it not?—that the eradication of classes must sooner or later mean the disappearance of these afflictions. I exaggerate a little, but not, I fear, by very much. Among social democrats this habit of thought encouraged an easy confidence in the benefits of historical evolution; among revolutionary Marxists, a faith in the self-elected vanguard party that would satisfy the ends of history.

Until about World War I, this genial mythicizing of an assured future may not have done too much damage, for in those early years the main work of the left was to rouse the previously mute lower classes to the need for historical action. Indeed, the visionary tone of early Marxism helped give the workers a quasireligious confidence in their own powers. Had the movement achieved nothing else, this arousal of the plebs would still be to its credit. In fact, it also helped bring about valuable social changes, a sequence of reforms eventuating in the welfare state.

The problem of socialism would become acute when a socialist movement approached power, or in quite different circumstances, when it was weak and under sharp intellectual attack. In both of these extreme circumstances, the poverty of Marxist (not all socialist) thought regarding the "face of socialism" becomes very serious. Between immediate struggles for specific reforms and rosy invocations of the cooperative commonwealth still to come, *a whole space is missing*—the space of social reconstruction. In the writings of the English guild socialists we find some hints on these matters, but not enough. Only in the last fifteen or twenty years, under the impact of crisis and defeat, has some of that "missing space" been occupied through the writings of a number of serious thinkers—I shall be discussing them later—who have tried to offer some guidelines (not blueprints) for a socialist society. The work is just beginning. Can it still be in time? I do not know.

2

Why has European social democracy been unable to advance further than the welfare state of Scandinavia? I list some of the possible answers: Social-democratic parties often came to office without parliamentary majorities, which meant they had to enter coalitions that imposed severe constraints. Social-democratic parties were often voted into office at moments when capitalist economies were suffering breakdowns, which meant that precisely the condition prompting their victories also limited their capacity for taking radical measures. Social-democratic parties in office frequently had to face flights of capital, a problem that, within the limits of the nation-state, proved very difficult to cope with. And social-democratic parties, settling into the routines of institutional life, began to lose their radical edge.

I want, however, to stress another reason for the difficulties of social-democratic parties. They often had no clear idea, no worked-out vision, of what a socialist transformation might entail. Given their commitment to democracy, their justified distaste for Bolshevik dictatorship, and the recognition that a good part of their electorate cared more about par-ticular measures than about a new society, they began to find the idea of socialism increasingly slippery, evanescent, insubstantial. No doubt, in some instances there were also the betrayals of principle that the far left charged against social democracy, but most of the time, I think, it was victimized by its own intellectual slackness. The social democrats thought they knew what had to be done the next day, but when it came to their sacred "historic mission" they often grew uncertain and timid. And sometimes they were struck dumb.

Not so the Bolsheviks. *They knew.* Their aura of certainty, their persuasion that history lay snugly in the party's fist, helped the Com-munists win the support of many European workers and intellectuals during the years between world wars. Yet even a glance at the Bolshevik record after the November 1917 revolution will show that Lenin and his comrades had only the most sketchy and confused ideas about the socioeconomic policies that might enable a socialist transformation. The seizure of power—about *that* they could speak with authority.

Shortly before the Russian Revolution, Lenin had written that if the Bolsheviks came to power in backward, war-devastated Russia, they would establish "workers' control" over industry; but he did not propose large-scale nationalizations. From November 1917 to the summer of 1918, the Bolsheviks favored what we'd now call a mixed economy, in which, for a time at least, large areas of private ownership of industry would continue, but production and investment decisions would be controlled by the leftist state together, presumably, with working-class institutions. This view was in accord with Lenin's realistic understanding that socialism—seen traditionally by Marxists as a society presupposing economic abundance and a high level of culture—could not be achieved in a country like Russia, certainly not without substantial aid from the industrial West.

Once in power, the Bolsheviks veered wildly in their economic policies. At the start of the civil war they abandoned their initial mod-eration and introduced the draconian measures of war communism: virtually complete nationalization of enterprises, the requisitioning of agricultural products, and a highly centralized political-economic command. Many Bolsheviks came to regard all this as the appropriate road to socialism, though in later years some of them would admit that grave errors had been made, with the necessities of an extreme situation being mistakenly elevated into general principles.

War communism intensified the economic disaster that was already well advanced as a result of Russian defeat in the war. There now followed a sharp drop in production; further depletion of industrial plant; a radical cut in the size of the working class; a decline in labor productivity, etc. Some of these setbacks were a result of difficulties created by the civil war; some due to a mixture of Bolshevik arrogance and inexperience; but some the fruit of a by now habitual refusal on the left to think concretely, problematically, about the social transformation that might follow the assumption of political power.

Between 1917 and 1923, Bolshevik oscillations on economic policy found a vivid reflection in Trotsky's writings. At one point he proposed the creation of labor armies, a kind of militarized garrison economy; this ghastly idea, meeting with bitter resistance from Bolshevik and other trade unionists, was rejected. At another point, veering sharply, Trotsky proposed an economic course anticipating the New Economic Policy that would in fact be introduced in 1921: a considerable loosening of state controls, a return to a partly free market, something like a mixed economy. This proposal was at first rejected by the Bolsheviks, but under the pressures of reality they finally introduced the NEP. What we can see here is a deep incoherence, a floundering by gifted ideologues who had not anticipated, while still out of power and in a position to think theoretically, that the taking of power would by no means exempt them from the difficulties faced by their adversaries.

In his biography of the "right" Bolshevik leader Bukharin, Stephen F. Cohen remarks that Lenin took a "censorious attitude toward discussing future problems. He preferred Napoleon's advice, 'On s'engage et puis . . . on voit.' "* "One engages, and then one sees." Alas, we have seen.

3

Were I writing a comprehensive study of modern socialism, a central emphasis would have to be put on the enormous damage wrought by Stalinism once it grew powerful in the 1930s. Insofar as right- and left-wing dogmatists found it convenient to identify the Russian dictatorship with socialism, they joined to discredit the entire socialist idea. And

---

* *Bukharin and the Bolshevik Revolution* (1975), p. 54.

insofar as that identification grew popular, so too did the discrediting.

One result was that the already festering crisis of socialist thought became more severe. For the past several decades the socialist experience has involved a dislodgment of received persuasions, a melting-down of ideological structures, and a search for new—or for cleansed and reaffirmed old—values. For the socialists themselves this has often been a clarifying and chastening experience; but for their movement it brought grave difficulties. Introspection rarely makes for public effectiveness.

Many socialists of my generation would customarily defend their beliefs through what I'd call a hygienic negative: "We entirely reject any sort of party-state dictatorship. Nor do we want a complete nationalization of industry. . . . Less and less does that seem an avenue to the cooperative commonwealth."

After a time such responses came close to being instinctive. Serious socialists would now describe the desired society by invoking desired *qualities*, with a stress on sentiments of freedom, attitudes of fraternity, and, sometimes, priorities of social allocation. They proposed, first of all, to secure the socialist idea in the realm of values, whereas, to simplify a little, the tradition in which some of us had been raised was one that focused on institutional changes. In making this shift, these socialists were doing something morally and politically necessary, but also tactically disabling. For unless plausible social structures and agencies could be located for realizing the values that were now being placed at the center of socialist thought, we were finally left with little more than our good will.

Nevertheless, the clarification of socialist values was the essential task during, say, the past half-century: little of importance could be accomplished on the left until that was done. And if these values are now accepted as truisms, it is because a bitter struggle had to be conducted in their behalf. It is useful to restate a few:

• There is no necessary historical sequence from capitalism to socialism, or any irrefutable reason for supposing history moves along a steadily upward curve. Unforeseen societies—mixed, retrogressive, opaque—can persist for long periods of time.

• The abolition of capitalism is not necessarily a step toward human liberation; it can lead, and has led, to societies far more repressive than capitalism at its worst.

• Socialism is not to be "defined" as a society in which private property has been abolished; what is decisive is the political character of the regime exercising control over a postcapitalist or mixed economy.

• A "complete" transformation of humanity is a corrupt fantasy that can lead to a mixture of terror and apathy.

• Socialism should be envisaged as a society in which the means of production, to an extent that need not be rigidly determined in advance, are collectively or socially owned—which means democratically controlled. An absolute prerequisite is the preservation and growth of democracy.

One result of this reshaping, or cleansed reassertion, of the socialist idea was that in the very course of acquiring an increasingly humane and democratic character, it also came to suffer from greater uncertainty with regard to social arrangements and institutional mechanisms. The reassertion of values led to skepticism about certain elements of traditional Marxist thought. Three instances:

• *The assumption that the proletariat would serve as the leading agency of social transformation.*

History has vetoed this idea. The working class has not been able to "transcend" its role within capitalist society, except perhaps during brief outbursts of rebellion; and now, as a result of technological innovations, its specific gravity as social class and political actor seems to be in decline. As if in response to this development, there has appeared a tendency to regard socialism as a goal transcending the interests of one or another class. There is something attractive about this, but also something that betrays political uncertainty. For to say that a social vision is the province of all, risks making it the passion of none.

• *The assumption that the nationalization of industry would, if accompanied by a socialist winning of office, smooth the way for the new society.*

Significant socialist texts can readily be cited that make it clear that nationalization is not necessarily to be taken as an equivalent or even a precondition of socialism.* Yet it would be misleading to lean too heavily on these texts, since I am certain that an appeal to older socialists would

---

* As far back as 1892, Karl Kautsky, an accredited legatee of Marx, wrote: "It does not follow that every nationalization of an economic function or an industry is a step toward the cooperative commonwealth. . . . If the modern state nationalizes certain industries, it does not do so for the purpose of restricting capitalist exploitation, but for the purpose of protecting the capitalist system. . . . As an exploiter of labor, the state is superior to any private capitalist." ("The Commonwealth of the Future," in Howe, ed., *Essential Works*, p. 169.)

And Morris Hillquit, the American socialist leader: "Socialists entertain no illusions as to the benefits of governmentally-owned industries under the present regime. . . . Its effect may be decidedly reactionary. . . . The demand for national or municipal ownership of industries is always qualified [by socialists] with a provision for the democratic administration of such industries. . . ." (Quoted in William English Walling, *Progressivism and After* (1914), pp. 169–70.)

I cite these two influential figures to show that such ideas do go back to earlier generations of socialist thinkers.

yield the recollection that in the movement there has been a strong habitual tendency to put great faith in the value of nationalization.

In the Communist dictatorships the mere takeover of industry made for a frightful concentration (and fusion) of political and economic power. In some capitalist countries, portions of the economy have been nationalized, sometimes because socialist governments wished to make at least a dent in bourgeois ownership, sometimes because governments, bourgeois or socialist, came to the rescue of enterprises on the rim of bankruptcy. The results have not been very inspiring, especially when no efforts were made to introduce democratic participation by workers in the management of the newly nationalized industries.

Serious problems have arisen in the operation of such industries, some of them due to the inherent difficulties of functioning by a calculus of profit while trying, within an economy still largely capitalist, to satisfy social goals. What should be the criteria for measuring efficiency in nationalized enterprises? If they are taken over because they have failed in private hands, what order of losses should society be prepared to accept? How are decisions to be made regarding capital investment? Such questions can be answered; and in part the answers are similar to those that might be provided with regard to private enterprise (since the criterion of profitability cannot simply be dismissed); but the answers should also be different from those prevailing under private enterprise (since such factors as "externalities" are now to be taken into systematic account).

Nationalization of industry has been part of a worldwide drift toward the interpenetration of state and society. It can be a device for trying to solve a crisis of capitalist economy; it can perhaps help to create a modern infrastructure in third-world economies; it can form part of the breakdown of "civil society" that enables the rise of totalitarianism; and it can be initiated by a socialist government intent upon deepening democratic practices in all areas of social life. Nationalization seems, in short, to be a somewhat neutral device, available to just about every kind of government: but whatever else, it is surely not a sufficient condition for a socialist transformation.

• *The assumption that economic planning is a unique aspect or virtue of socialist society, ensuring both justice and orderliness in economic affairs, such as unplanned economies are not likely to match.*

By now we have learned otherwise. Planning does not necessarily offer an encompassing method for the solution of socioeconomic problems. As earlier Marxists like Kautsky and Bukharin glimpsed, planning does not have to wait for the happy arrival of socialism, but is at least partly to be found in "late"—that is, monopoly or cartel—versions of capitalism. Like any other human enterprise, planning is subject to error, manipulation, bureaucratic sluggishness, and sheer ill will, so that it must always be tentative, proximate, and fallible. "Total" planning—that is, a command economy—entails authoritarian political structures. Democratic planning, upon which some socialists place great hopes, is at once attractive, complex, and problematic. There are ways in which planning must always be somewhat at odds with democratic procedures, if only because it often depends, in modern societies, on skilled professionals likely to develop their own caste or bureaucratic interests. On the other hand, "popular participation [can] inform the planner about the social terrain he is trying to map; the planner [can] facilitate the democratic process by presenting to the people intelligent alternatives for their choice."* No assertion of general principles or intent can remove the constant need for a nuanced and vigilant mediation between agencies of planning and a political democracy.

If, then, one considers the revisions in socialist thinking that we have had to make in recent decades, it becomes clear that we find ourselves in an uncomfortable but, I would contend, worthwhile difficulty—refining our values, growing somewhat uncertain about our means, sloughing off old ideological baggage. Leszek Kolakowski has put this matter well:

> Where are we now? What we lack in our thinking about society in socialist terms is not general values . . . but rather knowledge about how these values can be prevented from clashing with each other when put into practice. . . .
>
> Are we [then] fools to keep thinking in socialist terms? I do not think so. Whatever has been done in Western Europe to bring about more justice, more security, more educational opportunities, more welfare . . . could never have been achieved without the pressures of socialist ideologies and movements, for all their naivetés and illusions.†

During the last fifteen or twenty years, then, we have seen a significant shift in the nature and direction of socialist thought. The clarification of values toward which some of us had to devote major energies has now been achieved, at least in part, and as a result socialist thinkers have been able to turn to a study of those institutions and mechanisms through which these values might be realized in actuality.

4

A number of writers have tackled the problems that seem likely to appear during a "transition period" between capitalism and socialism.

* Harold Orlans, "Democracy and Social Planning," *Dissent*, Spring 1954, p. 194.
† "Introduction," in Kolakowski and Hampshire, eds., *The Socialist Idea*, p. 15.

Writers like Alec Nove, Michael Harrington, and Radoslav Selucky have
offered proposals for the kind of immediate reforms (civil rights, wom-
en's rights, racial equality) that are not uniquely socialist in character
but upon which liberals and socialists can happily agree. Next would
come "structural reforms," such as tax proposals aiming at a gradual
redistribution of income and wealth, and efforts to achieve full employment, which would surely entail some over-all economic planning.
These latter "structural reforms" might be described as extending and
deepening the welfare state. Beyond this second group of proposals lies
a third—those that would begin to change the fundamental relationships
of power and property, such as a "challenge to corporate control of the
investment process by insisting that public policy concern itself with
what is produced . . . [to] include public controls over private investment
decisions, such as specifying the conditions under which corporations
can leave a locality or oligopolies can raise prices. . . ."* Steps might
also be taken toward creating "social property," pilot projects of enterprises democratically owned and controlled by employees, with the government encouraging, through generous credit and other provisions, the
establishment of producer and consumer cooperatives, "small-scale, de-
alienating, good for training workers in running their own affairs."†

Such a bundle of reforms, graduated in their social penetration,
would signify a radical series of changes, even if not yet reaching a
socialist society. One lesson to be learned from past efforts of socialist
governments is that much depends on pacing. Too slow a rate of change
disappoints enthusiastic followers; too rapid can lead to the loss of
middle-class support, excessive inflation (there is bound to be some),
and serious disturbances. Choices would have to be made, so that fundamental socioeconomic measures would not be jeopardized by divisions over secondary or symbolic issues. And a socialist government, it
should be remembered, would also have a stake in maintaining a good
measure of national cohesion and civility, even if its legislation antag-
onized large property owners and small ideologues.

Such transitional measures, whatever their ultimate benefits, are certain to create immediate difficulties. Substantial benefits for the poorest
segments of the population—absolutely; but if on too lavish a scale,
these can result in an inflation threatening both the economic program
and the political stability of the government. Sweeping tax reforms—
desirable; but if too sweeping, they can alienate segments of the middle
class whose support a socialist government needs. A wealth tax—

---

* Michael Harrington, "What Socialists Would Do in America—If They Could," in Irving
Howe, ed., *Twenty-five Years of Dissent: An American Tradition* (1979), p. 23.
† Alec Nove, *The Economics of Feasible Socialism* (1983), p. 174.

attractive; but it can lead to capital flight. Economic controls—probably unavoidable; but they entail the likelihood of shortages, black markets, misallocation of resources, economic imbalances.

One suggested way of alleviating these difficulties would be to stress the need for higher productivity, "a larger pie," so that most segments of the population would be satisfied with immediate benefits. But it's by no means certain that in a transitional period this could be achieved. And such proposals for economic growth would encounter a bumpy course: they would be opposed by people who feared the ecological consequences and thought "consumerism" at variance with the socialist ethos, as well as by entrepreneurs and managers reluctant to help raise productivity at the very moment their "prerogatives" were being curbed. At least with regard to the managers, however, an imaginative government would work very hard to gain their cooperation, arguing that many of them, especially at middle levels, had no unalterable stake in perpetuating corporate control of economic life or in vast social inequities.

A democratic commitment—unconditional as it is and must be—may well constrain, delay, and even thwart socialist programs. Socialist governments do not rest on undifferentiated popular support, and many of their voters might not wish them to go beyond limited reforms. Socialist governments must put into office people who lack experience and often, in consequence, make mistakes or slip into caution, even confusion. Socialist governments need to find channels to capital growth, but the tensions created by the changes they initiate can lead to panic and "sabotage" in capital markets. And even the best-conceived program of transition is likely to be hostage to the business cycle, as well as to imbalances of wealth and power among the nations.

There is no undemocratic road to socialism; there are only undemocratic roads that can bring, and have brought, nations to barbaric mockeries of the socialist idea. If we were forced to conclude that there cannot be a democratic road to socialism, then we would also have to conclude that the entire socialist enterprise is illusory.

We understand now—experience must teach us *something*—that the transition from capitalism to socialism is likely to be a lengthy process, interrupted by setbacks, and fraught with tensions, conflicts, difficulties, and errors. But if it is to be a socialism of free men and women, there can be no other way.

5

Between the period of "transition" and a "full" or achieved socialism there is no thick or impenetrable wall. The distinction is mostly an analytical convenience. A healthy society must always be in transition; a dynamic socialism can never be "full."

What, then, would the social structure of a democratic-socialist society look like? Mulling over this question, I find myself in some sympathy with the traditional leftist reluctance to indulge in "future-painting." Certainly there can be no call, at this point in history, for either prediction or prescription. But, also, it is too late to trust simply to the workings of history; tokens must be offered of the *direction* in which we hope to move, even if, and perhaps especially if, there is no immediate possibility of reaching the desired goal.

But must not any discussion of a socialist society now seem remote, unrelated to current needs and concerns? It all depends on the spirit and terms in which we approach the matter. Everyone knows that today in the United States socialism is not on the political agenda; but can anyone be certain that there will not be new or recurrent social crises that will give an unexpected relevance to at least some of the basic socialist proposals? Within or close to a number of European socialist parties there are significant groups of political people that are seriously trying to sketch out "the face of socialism." Though involved in powerful parties, these people also know that a socialist transformation is not on the immediate agenda in Europe. But they understand that, in view of the volatility of modern history and the appearance of unexpected possibilities, it is necessary to think now with regard to what may be done the day after tomorrow. (And perhaps the day after tomorrow will come—tomorrow.) There is, furthermore, one great advantage in being powerless, and that is that it enables, sometimes stimulates, serious thought. Reestablishing socialism as an idea is not a sufficient, but it is surely a necessary, condition for reestablishing it as a dynamic politics. So, with all the necessary qualifications as to tentativeness and speculativeness, I proceed to offer a sketch of a sketch, cheerfully pilfered from the work of several recent writers. Among them are Oscar Lange, Abram Bergson, George Lichtheim, Radoslav Selucky, Henry Pachter, Wlodzimierz Brus, Michael Harrington, and Alec Nove.

Let us focus on two models for a democratic socialism offered by Radoslav Selucky, a Czech exile now living in the West, and Alec Nove, an economist living in Scotland. As a matter of strict principle, both agree on the need for multiparty democracy. Anything remotely like the centralized "command economies" of Eastern Europe must be entirely avoided, since these are economically inept, politically repressive, and intellectually intolerable. Both writers agree also on the need for a market economy, subject to controls by a democratic polity. Laissez-faire would be quite as inoperative under advanced socialism as it has turned out to be under advanced capitalism. Where they differ significantly is with regard to structures of property and productive relations in a "market socialism." Selucky strongly favors social controls from below, whereas Nove would encourage a greater variety in the modes of ownership. I suppose that Selucky's views on this matter are more attractive and Nove's more realistic.

Selucky lists a number of concise premises for his model, the essential ones of which I quote:

> The means of production are owned socially and managed by those who make use of them.
>
> Social ownership of the means of production is separated from the state.
>
> Producing and trading enterprises are autonomous from the state and independent of each other. They operate within the framework of the market which is regulated by a central indicative plan.
>
> The institutions which provide health, education and welfare services are wholly exempt from the market.
>
> The right to participate in direct management of the work units *operating in the market* is derived from labor.
>
> The right to participate in direct management of the work units *exempt wholly or partly from the market* is derived proportionally from labor, ownership, and consumption of the provided services and utilities.
>
> The right to participate in indirect political control over, and regulation of, the socially owned means of production is derived from one's position as a citizen.
>
> Health and education services and social benefits for the disabled are distributed according to one's needs.
>
> Economic equality consists of each individual's equal access to the means of production, health and education services, social benefits and self-management [in economic enterprises]. Since it does not include egalitarian distribution of income, individuals—while equal in essence—are unequal in their existence.
>
> The principle of self-management is limited to microeconomic units only.*

This model seems attractive in several respects. It stresses—as, after the experiences of our century, socialists must stress—the separation of political and economic power. It proposes a dispersal of economic power in horizontal enterprises, each largely self-sustaining and freely administered, though subject to both market signals and social regulation. It provides consumers with freedom of choice, and citizens with free occupational and educational choices. It favors a market mechanism that would be interdependent with "indicative" planning—that is, planning not merely imposed from above but with institutional mechanisms for

---

* *Marxism, Socialism and Freedom* (1979), pp. 179–80.

democratic decision-making and checks from below. And it rests on direct democracy within the workplace insofar as that is possible, and on representative democracy in the society as a whole.

This model presupposes the flourishing of "civil society" and its autonomous "secondary institutions" (trade unions, political groups, fraternal societies, and so on) apart from and, when necessary, in opposition to the state. The intent is clearly to make possible a pluralist flexibility that is present in, though often only claimed for, capitalist democracy, while at the same time eliminating many of its socially retrogressive features.

In such a socialist society, wage levels would be subject to the law of supply and demand, shaped in part through collective bargaining undertaken by free trade unions, though also (as is sometimes now true in industrial nations) bounded by social regulations such as "incomes policies." Wage differentials would remain, in accordance with pressures of scarcity and skill, though again subject to social boundaries. The market would provide goods and services; it would regulate prices, except for those controlled as part of public policy and those products the society might decide to provide without cost. And while in its initial phases a democratic-socialist society would have to strive for increases in production and higher productivity, it might after a time, through modest increments, supersede the efficiency principle in behalf of more attractive social ends.

Alec Nove's model for democratic socialism differs from Selucky's in one crucial respect. Selucky, writes Nove,

> appears to envisage an evolution toward one type of producing unit. In my view it is possible and desirable to have several. . . . The citizens can choose, for example, what sorts of private initiative to encourage or to tolerate, the desirable forms of cooperatives, the extent of workers' participation in management, and much else besides. They can experiment, learn from experience, commit and correct errors. . . . Suppose that we have a legal structure which permits the following species:
>   1. State enterprises, centrally controlled and administered, hereinafter [called] *centralized state corporations.*
>   2. State-owned (or socially-owned) enterprises with full autonomy and a management responsible to the workforce, hereinafter [called] *socialized enterprises.*
>   3. *Cooperative enterprises.*
>   4. *Small-scale private enterprise,* subject to clearly defined limits.
>   5. *Individuals* (e.g., freelance journalists, plumbers, artists).*

* *Economics,* p. 200.

The idea of a greater diversity of production units is in principle appealing, since the aim of a socialist society ought to be the maximizing of opportunity, choice, and freedom as long as these remain within democratically agreed-upon bounds. The "centralized state corporations" would include, besides banks, enterprises that are necessarily very large or occupy a monopoly position, or both—where significant economies of scale can be realized. Among examples of such "state corporations" are power stations, and oil and petrochemical complexes. But the criterion here ought to be technological, not the corporate structure that prevails today, since some present-day corporations are large because of the power it gives them over the market, rather than because of any criteria of efficiency. A danger might arise that some of these giant enterprises would assume a monopoly posture under socialism as disadvantageous to consumers and workers as under capitalism. To rein in such enterprises, both of our models envisage "tripartite management" (government, consumers, workers).

In the socialized and cooperative enterprises, according to the Nove model, managers would be appointed by an elected committee representing the employees and would be responsible to that committee for basic policy. One main difference between socialized and cooperative enterprises is that in the former the state would have "a residual responsibility for their use or misuse, or for debts incurred," whereas a cooperative could freely dispose of its property or decide to go out of business (again, no doubt, within the bounds of social regulations). As for small-scale private enterprise:

> Presumably even the fanatical dogmatist would accept the existence of freelance writers, painters and dressmakers. My own list would be longer. Indeed, there should be no list. If any activity (not actually a "social bad" in itself) can be fruitfully and profitably undertaken by any individual, this sets up the presumption of its legitimacy. . . . So long as it is one individual, there would probably be no objection. . . . But there would be also the possibility of a private entrepreneur actually employing a few people, which makes him an "exploiter" insofar as he makes a profit out of their work. . . .
> Subject to limits, this should be allowed.
> Subject to what limits? This could be decided democratically in the light of circumstances and experience. The limit could be on numbers employed, or on the value of capital assets, and could be varied by sector. One possible rule might be that above this limit there be a choice, either to convert into a cooperative or to become a socialized enterprise, with proper compensation for the original entrepreneur. . . . Be it noted that there is no provision for any class of capitalists; our small private entrepreneur *works*, even when

employing a few others. There is then no *unearned* income, arising simply from *ownership* of capital or land.*

Scale as well as structure is important. The larger the enterprise, the more difficult self-management becomes and the more likely its bureaucratic deformation. But I do not see why even in subdivisions of Nove's "centralized state enterprises" there could not be nurtured at least a measure of workers' control regarding such matters as relations to and pace of work, even if it is granted that on large over-all decisions (how much oil Britain should extract from the North Sea) there would have to be vertical decision-making subject to the check of the democratic polity.

In Nove's model the extent of central planning is, then, greater than in Selucky's. Making major investment decisions; monitoring decentralized investments; administering such "naturally" central productive activities as electricity, oil, railways (today "public," actually private, utilities); setting ground rules for the autonomous economic sectors, "with reserve powers of intervention when things got out of balance" (today bailing out Chrysler, Penn Central); drafting long-term plans—all these, subject to decision and check by parliament or congress, would be the responsibility of central planning, thus entailing a greater concentration of economic power than many socialists, myself included, would prefer. But who can say with assurance? One encounters here a deep tension between the technological-economic realm and the democratic-social arrangements of a socialist (perhaps any modern) society. Mediating between these forces would become a major responsibility for both state and society, government and the people, in a free socialist order.

In all such projected arrangements a crucial factor must surely be the morale and consciousness of the people. It isn't necessary, or desirable, to envisage a constant state of intense participation in public affairs, a noisy turmoil of activists, in order to recognize that the felt quality—as distinct from the mere economic workability—of such a society would depend on the fundamental concern of a sizable portion of the population. "No social system," Joseph Schumpeter has remarked, "can work that is based exclusively upon a network of free contracts . . . and in which everyone is supposed to be guided by nothing except his own (short-run) utilitarian ends."† True for any democratic society, this would be all the more true for one aspiring to realize socialist ideals.

---

* Nove, *Economics*, p. 207.
† Quoted in Nove, *Economics*, p. 204.

If put to the test of reality, such projections would surely require many changes. But the purpose of this sort of model is not to "appropriate" the future; it is to indicate the nature of thought in the present. Nor need it be denied that such models contain within themselves a good many unresolved problems, tensions, perhaps even contradictions. They *should* contain them, for that is what lends a savor of reality. Let me now, in no particular order, consider a few of these problems:

• The Selucky and Nove models of ownership suffer from opposite difficulties. Selucky's lacks variety and flexibility in its proposals: why should there not be a range of democratic structures in economic life just as there is in political life? Nove's model, by contrast, gives an uncomfortably strong place to "centralized state corporations." The ogre of bureaucratism rises with regard to both—in opposite ways, the one through rigidity and the other through concentration. In principle one would like to combine Selucky's stress upon worker self-management with Nove's stress upon varieties of property, but that may be asking for the best of all possible worlds, something actuality is chary of providing.

• Neither of our model-makers discusses sufficiently one major problem: the place of unions in a democratic-socialist society. If the workers own an enterprise cooperatively or if they manage one democratically, is there still a need for unions? I would say yes, unambiguously. Insofar as we think of a socialist society as one with autonomous institutions and enterprises, this entails the likelihood and even desirability of democratically contained conflict; and insofar as there is conflict, the weaker segments of the population should be able to protect themselves through organization. It's possible to foresee a situation in which a minority of workers in a self-managed enterprise believes it is being mistreated by the majority; that minority thereupon organizes itself into something very much like a union. In the "centralized state corporations" that Nove proposes as one mode of socialist ownership, there would surely be a need for strong unions to resist bureaucratic dictate. As for cooperatives, take the example of the Israeli kibbutzim. They function pretty much like cooperatives, but also hire outside labor at wage rates; the people so hired may well feel they need a union to protect themselves against the benign or not-so-benign edicts of the cooperatives. So it could be in many areas of a socialist society. A pluralism of institutions signifies a plurality of interests, and these must express themselves openly through modulated conflict-and-cooperation.

• It would be hard, according to the economist Abram Bergson, to work out satisfactory criteria of success and reward for managers of the autonomous productive units in a socialist society. Pressed by the often clashing interests of the worker-employers and the central planning agencies of the state, managers might hesitate to take risks or use their initiative. They would need, also, to adjudicate between local interests and larger, more distant social goals, which might put them in a crossfire and cause them to yield to whichever side was the strongest. Incentives would have to be attached to their jobs, allowing them sufficient authority to display leadership while still subjecting them to the democratic check of worker-employers. In cases of major disputes, decisions would have to be referred to the next-highest level of authority, perhaps an industrywide council.

• Nor is it difficult to foresee conflicts among autonomous enterprises as they compete for the credits, subsidies, tax breaks, and contracts that are to be had from the state. Just as, under capitalism, competition tends to destroy competition, so it is by no means excluded that self-managed enterprises can form rings or cartels. This would have to be resisted except perhaps in circumstances where economies of scale are *very* substantial. It might even be necessary to introduce a species of "socialist antitrust" legislation. For until the society reached an unforeseeable state of material abundance, a major source of conflict could well be that between general and partial interests, society as a whole and its regions, social groups and industrial units.

As Selucky says very sensibly, "Since no [complete] harmony of interests is possible at every level of society," there would have to be mediators to control the conflicting interests. "To regulate the conflicts, two mediators are necessary: the market mechanism for economics and the multi-party system for politics."*

• Employment and income policies could also bring serious difficulties—for instance, coping with tendencies toward local monopolizing of jobs where enterprise profits are high; working out income policies that might arouse opposition from unions but could be seen as justifiable for the common good; finding ways to help workers whom technological changes in a given industry or enterprise have rendered superfluous; deciding upon—or establishing criteria for deciding upon—appropriate surpluses for capital investments and new technologies as against the "natural" inclination of self-managed communities to reap immediate rewards, and so on. For that matter, it is foolhardy to suppose that unemployment might not be a problem in a democratic-socialist society: all one can reasonably expect is a readiness to deal with it fairly.

• Another complex of problems worth at least pointing to concerns how, when, and whether the state should intervene if a self-managed

---

* Selucky, *Marxism*, p. 185.

enterprise is failing. For some would fail, the operation of even a regulated market under socialism having some parallels to its operation under capitalism.

• Many such problems constitute disadvantages probably inseparable from the advantages of a regulated market, and they seem to reinforce the traditional critiques, both Marxist and romantic, of the market. That the market subjects the human encounter to the fetishism of commodities, signifying that men are not entirely free from the rule of impersonal exchange and wage labor, is true. But unless we can suppose an implausible cornucopia of goods and services, we had better accept the idea of a regulated market as necessary under a feasible democratic socialism.

A socially controlled market would also have some attractive features. The argument against capitalism first made by R. H. Tawney still holds—not that it's bad if people take some risks but that in a society where a few have much and most have little or nothing, the majority doesn't enjoy the privilege of taking risks. Risk, thought Tawney, is "bracing if it is voluntarily undertaken," and in a cooperative commonwealth, self-managed enterprises and producers' cooperatives could take socially useful risks that would bring into play their energies and minds.

Still, the market has the drawbacks traditionally noted by the left, and one possible way of getting past some of these, as also perhaps moving a bit closer to Marx's vision of "free associated producers," is a modest increase in society's provision of free goods. Some commodities could be produced in such abundance and at so small a cost, it would be economical to dispose of them at zero price rather than incur the overhead costs of charging for them. Even today, some health and many educational services are free, which in actuality means they are carried as a shared or social cost. In a cooperative commonwealth, such provision might be extended to milk, perhaps even bread. Would people take more than they need, would there be waste at first? Probably; yet that might not be so wasteful as many of the practices we simply take for granted in a capitalist society. And as free access to a modest number of basic goods became customary, misuse of the privilege would probably decrease. Nevertheless, in a market socialism such free provision could only be marginal.

• All of these problems are instances of a larger problem often cited by conservatives, for whom socialism is anathema, as the market is for doctrinal Marxists. It is possible that the autonomous enterprises might repeat some of the socially undesirable behavior with which we are familiar in corporate capitalism, functioning as "socialist corporate" units in quite as selfish a spirit as present-day corporations are known to do. When doctrinaire leftists (or rightists, for that matter) point to possible abuses in a market socialism, they are almost always pointing to risks present in any democratic society. Mistakes and abuses are always with us; this is a condition of freedom and can be eliminated only by eliminating freedom itself.

What would be needed in a democratic-socialist society (as today in a democratic-capitalist society) is some version of the welfare state. Through electoral decisions, compromises, and bargaining, it could adjudicate among conflicting parts of the population, setting rules for the operation of the market while protecting both the norms of the society and the rights of its citizens.

6

Finally, the socialist aspiration has less to do with modes of property ownership than with qualities of social life. That is why the case for socialism rests not just on its proposed reduction of inequities in wealth and power, but on its wish to democratize economic practice. The two values—equality and freedom—are sometimes, of course, in tension, but when regarded in a spirit of generosity and humaneness, they flourish together, as they seem to have flourished during the early days of the American republic.

The egalitarian ideal has been very strong in socialist thought and tradition. It should be. There is something morally repulsive in the maldistribution of wealth and income in a country like the United States. And this state of affairs is not only morally repulsive but also socially unjust, a major barrier to the genuine realization of the democratic idea. Now any proposal can be pushed too far, turning into a parody of itself. An egalitarianism enforced by authoritarian decree—what's called in Eastern Europe "barracks egalitarianism"—is something utterly alien to the socialist idea. Our vision of egalitarianism implies a steady and gradual rectification of inequities through education, legislation, and popular assent; it aims not for some absurd version of total equality (whatever that might mean) but, rather, for progress toward the fair sharing of socioeconomic goods and political power, which would allow each person to fulfill his or her potentialities.

One precondition is both political and economic democracy, with the latter signifying the replacement, insofar as possible, of "vertical," hierarchical structures by "horizontal," egalitarian ones. Workers' control, self-management by those who work in an enterprise—some such concept is crucial to the socialist hope. One needn't be a fanatic and set up standards so impossibly high that they will fall of their own weight. But in the end socialists have no choice but to accept the wager—either a genuine, if imperfect, economic democracy is realizable or the entire socialist enterprise must be relegated to historical fantasy.

No longer tolerating their reduction to mere factors of production, workers would learn through experience to demand their rights as free, autonomous men and women. They would form cooperatives. They would acquire some of the skills of management (those arcane mysteries, it's sometimes said, which must forever remain beyond the reach of the lowly). And in time there could be a trade-off between some of the efficiencies brought about (allegedly) by authoritarian forms of organization and the growing creativity of cooperative production.

Too often in recent socialist literature the idea, sometimes merely the slogan, of workers' control has remained gloriously vague. What does it mean precisely? That decisions regarding production, prices, wages, and investment in a giant enterprise like a "socialist GM" would be made by the assembled workers or even their representatives? And if so, how would it be possible to avoid the linked plagues of bureaucratism, demagogic manipulation, clique maneuverings, endless filibustering, ignorant narrowness, cronyism in elections, and a selfish resistance to the larger needs of society?

One frequent argument against self-management proposals is that their advocates tend to minimize the sheer complexity of modern enterprise. Laymen (workers) would have difficulty in securing relevant information from managers; they would often be unable to grasp the technical aspects of the information they got; and they would lack the time needed to reflect upon what they did grasp in order to arrive at coherent plans. There is of course some truth to this argument, though it largely proceeds on the assumption that workers in a better society will remain quite as workers are today. But there is reason to expect that with higher levels of education and a greater provision for time, leisure, and training within the organized work community, some of these problems could be overcome. Lethargy isn't a universal constant; it is a socially conditioned phenomenon open to change. "Full" participation in managerial activities might, in some situations, turn out to be a chimera; but there surely could be a large measure of selective control by workers, even in giant enterprises, with technicalities left to managers and large policy issues decided through democratic mechanisms.

A somewhat different problem is raised in a recent study by Allen Graubard, who sees workers' control, narrowly conceived, as clashing with public rights. A large corporation "is a national resource. . . . The same argument against private control of the founder-owner or by the current corporate owner works . . . against private control by the community of employees. The authority for major decisions of the enterprise should rest in the larger public, the democratic polity."*

This criticism can best be regarded as a warning against *exclusive* control of major enterprises by the workers within them—though even that should not preclude a good measure of self-management with regard to intraplant arrangements. About such matters it would be foolish to be dogmatic; far better to recognize a multiplicity of interests and outlooks, with the certainty that, if ventures in self-management are undertaken, they will be subject to many difficulties.

The practical impediments to workers' self-management that both sophisticated organization theorists and "the man in the street" detect are often real enough—but are the consequent objections very much more cogent than similar arguments once used against the feasibility of political democracy?

The excrescence of bureaucratism might indeed flourish on the structure of self-management. Who in the twentieth century can deny that possibility (or *any* possibility)? Here everything depends on conscious effort, that vigilance which had better be eternal—quite as with regard to political democracy. And there is much cogency in an argument advanced by George Lichtheim:

> A future advance will probably have to start from a concept of technical education which envisages it not simply as a means of improving efficiency, but as a link between the worker and the planner. . . . For the worker technology holds the most direct access to science and everything that lies beyond it. But technical education without responsible participation soon loses its spur. . . . For [socialists], its significance . . . lies in the fact that it arises spontaneously out of the modern process of work, while at the same time it enables the worker to develop his individuality.†

In practice, self-management would sometimes thrive, sometimes stumble, but always be marked, like all human enterprises, by imperfections. There is one argument, however, against self-management that seems to me peculiarly insidious: it is offered, as you might expect, by ex-radicals, and its main thrust is that workers "show little interest" in the idea.

In certain empirical respects, this is not even true. Through their unions, workers have often fought very hard for such noneconomic rights as grievance mechanisms and proper work atmospheres. These inroads on traditional "management prerogatives" often constitute mod-

---

* "Ideas of Economic Democracy," *Dissent*, Fall 1984, p. 421.
† "Collectivism Reconsidered," in Howe, ed., *Essential Works*, p. 757.

est beginnings of economic democracy, whether or not those who make the inroads so conceptualize them. Still, for the sake of the argument, let us grant the conservative claim that workers today "show little interest" in self-management proposals. To stop there would be supinely to acquiesce in "the given." For this argument against self-management is essentially an extension of a larger skepticism about democratic politics. How often have we not heard that most people care more about their bellies than their freedoms? Or that in the United States millions of citizens don't even bother to vote? Notions of self-management, our conservatives tell us, are mere futile efforts by small groups of intellectuals to "impose their fantasies" upon ordinary people who seem quite content to allow the corporations to determine their work lives.

Few of us are born passionate democrats. The values of freedom have to be learned. Centuries passed before masses of men came to feel that democracy is a necessity of life. All the while it was a not very large company of intellectuals who sought to "impose their fantasies" about democracy upon ordinary people. Even today, who can say that this persuasion has taken deep enough root?

It may be a long time before the value of democratic norms is secured in socioeconomic life. An independent Yugoslav writer, Branko Horvat, reports that in his country "inherited authoritarian attitudes are so deeply ingrained that they are unconsciously carried into self-management."* Could it be otherwise, especially in a country with little experience in political democracy, before or after Tito?

Nothing is ordained. Socialism, self-management, economic democracy are options, sometimes brighter, sometimes dimmer. The realization of the socialist hope depends on the growth of consciousness, a finer grasp of the possibilities of citizenship and comradeship than now prevails. Times change. We will emerge from our present slough of small-spirited conservative acquiescence and live again by more generous aspirations. The idea of self-management could then take a somewhat more prominent place on the agenda of public discourse—kept alive by "unrealistic intellectuals," "visionary socialists."

7

Amid such turnings and reassessment of political thought, a harsh question intrudes itself: Does the socialist idea, even if rendered more sophisticated than it was in the past, still survive as a significant option? Has it outlived its historical moment?

Socialist movements have great achievements to their credit, yet

* *The Political Economy of Socialism* (1983), p. 255.

nowhere on the globe can one point to a free, developed socialist society. Socialism has been shaken by failures, torn by doubts. Its language and symbols have been appropriated by parodic totalitarianism, and from this trauma we have still to recover.

Historical energy and idealism cannot be supplied on demand. Once an idea becomes contaminated or a generation exhausted, it is a long time before new energies can be summoned, if summoned at all. Whether socialism can be revived as a living idea—which is something different from the mere survival of European social-democratic parties as established institutions—is by now very much a question. So too is the possibility, or hope, that socialism may serve as a bridge toward a radical new humanism. In any case, socialists remain. They engage themselves with the needs of the moment, struggling for betterment in matters large and small, reforms major and modest: they do not sit and wait for the millennium. And they continue also to grapple with fragments of a tradition.

This intellectual effort, it must be admitted, can handicap them politically. Not many people became socialists because they were persuaded of the correctness of Marxist economics or supposed the movement served their "class interests." They became socialists because they were moved to fervor by the call to brotherhood and sisterhood; because the world seemed aglow with the vision of a time in which humanity might live in justice and peace. Whatever we may now claim for a refurbished socialism, we can hardly claim that it satisfies the emotions as once the early movement did.

If it is true that utopian-apocalyptic expectations are indispensable to a movement advocating major social change, then democratic socialists are in deeper trouble than even they recognize. For in politics, as elsewhere, choices must be made. You cannot opt for the rhythms of a democratic politics and still expect it to yield the pathos and excitement of revolutionary movements. Our hope must be that there are other kinds of fervor—quieter, less melodramatic, morally stronger—which a democratic reformist politics can evoke.

Modern postindustrial society, with its relatively high levels of culture and education, may enable a politics offering proposals for major social change while also avoiding the delusions of "total" transformation. A liberal socialism, at once pragmatic and idealistic, may yet be able to win the loyalties of a new public, cutting across class lines and appealing to the best in humanity.

Our problem may be restated as that of utopianism: Does the utopian vision still have value for us?

The "utopia" imposed through force and terror by a self-chosen vanguard is hell. The utopia of a "withering away of the state" is a fantasy gone stale. But there remains a utopian outlook that relates immediate objectives to ultimate goals, and it is to this that socialists cling. As Leszek Kolakowski has written: ". . . goals now unattainable will never be reached unless they are articulated when they are still unattainable. . . . The existence of a utopia as a utopia is the necessary prerequisite for its eventually ceasing to be a utopia."*

"Very nice," a friendly voice interjects, "but socialism—has not that name been soiled in the pillagings of our century? Might it not be better for a movement to shake itself clear of all the old confusions, defeats, betrayals?"

At least with regard to America, we continue to speak of small groups trying to keep alive a tradition. Suppose, indeed, we were to conclude that the socialist label creates more trouble than it's worth: we would then have to cast about for a new vocabulary, something not to be won through fiat. How much would actually change if our words were to change? If, say, we ceased calling ourselves socialists and instead announced that henceforth we are to be known as—what? "Economic democrats" or "democratic radicals"? The substance of our problems would remain, the weight of this century's burdens still press upon us. We would still regard capitalist society as an unjust society, still find intolerable its inequities, still be repelled by its ethic of greed, and still be trying to sketch the outlines of a better society.

Isaiah Berlin has written that liberalism is "a notoriously exposed, dangerous, and ungrateful position." I would borrow his words for democratic socialism, which is not quite the same as, but, in my sense of things, has a kinship with his liberalism.

For those socialists who have experienced in their bones the meaning of our century, the time has not yet come, I believe, to cast off its burdens. Such a time may come. Meanwhile, we hope to serve as a link to those friends of tomorrow who will have so completely absorbed the lessons of our age that they will not need to rehearse them. Whatever the fate of socialism, the yearning for a better mode of life which found expression in its thought and its struggle will reappear. Of that I am absolutely certain.

---

* "The Concept of the Left," in Howe, ed., *Essential Works*, p. 686.

1990

This essay was written a few years before the great democratic upheavals in Eastern Europe during 1989, upheavals which deposed the
Communist dictatorships. The crack-up of the Communist regimes, in
my judgment, vindicated the sustained and principled criticisms which
democratic socialists have made for some decades of both the political
tyranny and the overly centralized "command" economies of Communism. Still—I regard this as a moral and historical tragedy—in popular
discourse and with the shared agreement of both the ideological right
and the authoritarian left, it became popular to describe the collapse of
the Communist dictatorships as a "defeat for socialism." I would say:
Quite the contrary, it is a defeat only if you acquiesce in the false
identification of these dictatorships with socialism. In actuality, for democratic socialists throughout the world, these dictatorships were the very
opposite, they were enemies of our desire and our vision. Yet, there is
the fact of this popular misidentification—not the least of the costs we
must pay for the curse of Stalinism!

Whatever direction the post-Communist societies of Eastern Europe
may take, they will surely need a strong measure of social democratic
legislation, improvising a kind of welfare state to protect the poor and
defenseless. Later, once the shadow of Stalinism recedes, it will be
possible, I believe, for the issues raised in this essay to come to the fore
once again.